A STORM OF SWORDS
ONE: STEEL AND SNOW

George R. R. Martin is the author of nine novels, several collections of short stories and numerous screenplays for television dramas and feature films. He lives in Santa Fe, New Mexico.

Praise for *A Song of Ice and Fire*:

'This is one of those rare and effortless reads'
ROBIN HOBB

'George R. R. Martin is one of our very best writers, and this is one of his very best books.' RAYMOND E. FEIST

'Such a splendid tale. I read my eyes out – I couldn't stop till I'd finished and it was dawn.' ANNE MCCAFFREY

'George Martin is assuredly a new mastger craftsman in the guild of heroic fantasy.' KATHARINE KERR

'Few created worlds are as imaginative and diverse'
JANNY WURTS

By George R. R. Martin

A SONG OF ICE AND FIRE:
Book One: *A Game of Thrones*
Book Two: *A Clash of Kings*
Book Three, part one: *A Storm of Swords: Steel and Snow*
Book Three, part two: *A Storm of Swords: Blood and Gold*
Book Four: *A Feast for Crows*

Fevre Dream
The Armageddon Rag
Tuf Voyaging
Dying of the Light
Sandkings
Portraits of His Children
A Song for Lya
Songs of Stars and Shadows
Windhaven (with Lisa Tuttle)
Nightflyers

Voyager

A STORM OF SWORDS

ONE: STEEL AND SNOW

BOOK THREE OF
A SONG OF ICE AND FIRE

George R. R. Martin

HarperCollins*Publishers*

Voyager
An Imprint of HarperCollins*Publishers*
77–85 Fulham Palace Road,
Hammersmith, London W6 8JB

www.voyager-books.co.uk

This paperback edition 2003
17

Previously published in paperback by *Voyager* 2001

First published in Great Britain by *Voyager* 2000

ISBN-13 978-0-00-647990-1
ISBN-10 0-00-647990-1

Set in Trump Medieval
Typeset by Rowland Phototypesetting Ltd
Bury St Edmunds, Suffolk

Printed and bound in Great Britain by
Clays Ltd, St Ives plc

A NOTE ON CHRONOLOGY

A Song of Ice and Fire is told through the eyes of characters who are sometimes hundreds or even thousands of miles apart from one another. Some chapters cover a day, some only an hour; others might span a fortnight, a month, half a year. With such a structure, the narrative cannot be strictly sequential; sometimes important things are happening simultaneously, a thousand leagues apart.

In the case of the volume now in hand, the reader should realize that the opening chapters of *A Storm of Swords* do not follow the closing chapters of *A Clash of Kings* so much as overlap them. I open with a look at some of the things that were happening on the Fist of the First Men, at Riverrun, Harrenhal, and on the Trident while the Battle of the Blackwater was being fought at King's Landing, and during its aftermath . . .

George R. R. Martin

for Phyllis
who made me put the dragons in

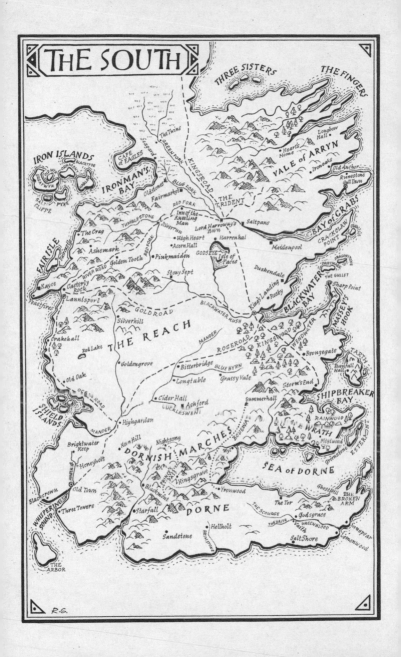

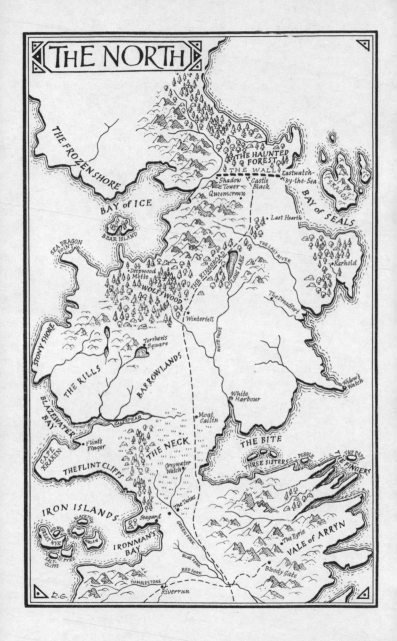

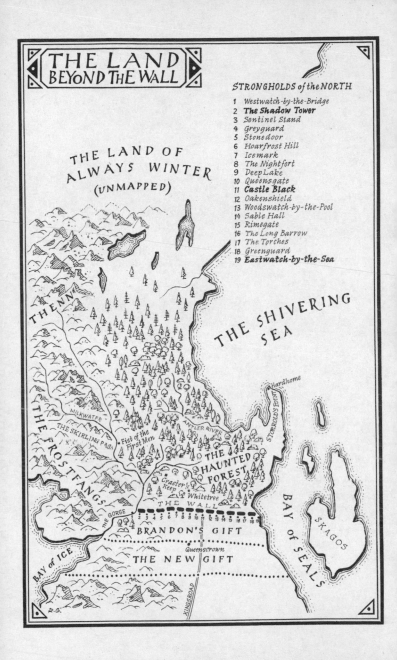

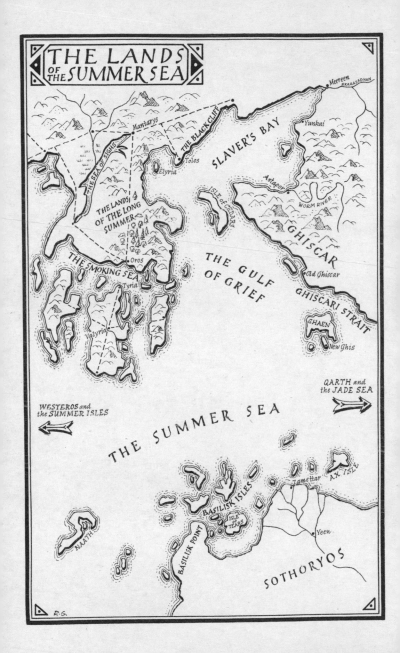

PROLOGUE

The day was grey and bitter cold, and the dogs would not take the scent.

The big black bitch had taken one sniff at the bear tracks, backed off, and skulked back to the pack with her tail between her legs. The dogs huddled together miserably on the riverbank as the wind snapped at them. Chett felt it too, biting through his layers of black wool and boiled leather. It was too bloody cold for man or beast, but here they were. His mouth twisted, and he could almost feel the boils that covered his cheeks and neck growing red and angry. *I should be safe back at the Wall, tending the bloody ravens and making fires for old Maester Aemon.* It was the bastard Jon Snow who had taken that from him, him and his fat friend Sam Tarly. It was their fault he was here, freezing his bloody balls off with a pack of hounds deep in the haunted forest.

"Seven hells." He gave the leashes a hard yank to get the dogs' attention. "*Track*, you bastards. That's a bear print. You want some meat or no? *Find!*" But the hounds only huddled closer, whining. Chett snapped his short lash above their heads, and the black bitch snarled at him. "Dog meat would taste as good as bear," he warned her, his breath frosting with every word.

Lark the Sisterman stood with his arms crossed over his chest and his hands tucked up into his armpits. He wore black wool gloves, but he was always complaining how his fingers were frozen. "It's too bloody cold to hunt," he said. "Bugger this bear, he's not worth freezing over."

"We can't go back emptyhanded, Lark," rumbled Small Paul through the brown whiskers that covered most of his face. "The Lord Commander wouldn't like that." There was ice under the big man's squashed pug nose, where his snot had frozen. A huge hand in a thick fur glove clenched tight around the shaft of a spear.

"Bugger that Old Bear too," said the Sisterman, a thin man with sharp features and nervous eyes. "Mormont will be dead before daybreak, remember? Who cares what he likes?"

Small Paul blinked his black little eyes. Maybe he *had* forgotten, Chett thought; he was stupid enough to forget most anything. "Why do we have to kill the Old Bear? Why don't we just go off and let him be?"

"You think he'll let *us* be?" said Lark. "He'll hunt us down. You want to be hunted, you great muttonhead?"

"No," said Small Paul. "I don't want that. I don't."

"So you'll kill him?" said Lark.

"Yes." The huge man stamped the butt of his spear on the frozen riverbank. "I will. He shouldn't hunt us."

The Sisterman took his hands from his armpits and turned to Chett. "We need to kill *all* the officers, I say."

Chett was sick of hearing it. "We been over this. The Old Bear dies, and Blane from the Shadow Tower. Grubbs and Aethan as well, their ill luck for drawing the watch, Dywen and Bannen for their tracking, and Ser Piggy for the ravens. That's *all*. We kill them quiet, while they sleep. One scream and we're wormfood, every one of us." His boils were red with rage. "Just do your bit and see that your cousins do theirs. And Paul, try and remember, it's *third* watch, not second."

"Third watch," the big man said, through hair and frozen snot. "Me and Softfoot. I remember, Chett."

The moon would be black tonight, and they had jiggered the watches so as to have eight of their own standing sentry, with two more guarding the horses. It wasn't going to get much riper than that. Besides, the wildlings could be upon them any day now. Chett meant to be well away from here before that happened. He meant to live.

Three hundred sworn brothers of the Night's Watch had ridden north, two hundred from Castle Black and another hundred from the Shadow Tower. It was the biggest ranging in living memory, near a third of the Watch's strength. They meant to find Ben Stark, Ser Waymar Royce, and the other rangers who'd gone missing, and discover why the wildlings were leaving their villages. Well, they were no closer to Stark and Royce than when they'd left the Wall, but they'd learned where all the wildlings had gone – up into the icy heights of the godsforsaken Frostfangs. They could squat up there till the end of time and it wouldn't prick Chett's boils none.

But no. They were coming down. Down the Milkwater.

Chett raised his eyes and there it was. The river's stony banks were bearded by ice, its pale milky waters flowing endlessly down out of the Frostfangs. And now Mance Rayder and his wildlings were flowing down the same way. Thoren Smallwood had returned in a lather three days past. While he was telling the Old Bear what his scouts had seen, his man Kedge Whiteye told the rest of them. "They're still well up the foothills, but they're coming," Kedge said, warming his hands over the fire. "Harma the Dogshead has the van, the poxy bitch. Goady crept up on her camp and saw her plain by the fire. That fool Tumberjon wanted to pick her off with an arrow, but Smallwood had better sense."

Chett spat. "How many were there, could you tell?"

"Many and more. Twenty, thirty thousand, we didn't stay to count. Harma had five hundred in the van, every one ahorse."

The men around the fire exchanged uneasy looks. It was a rare thing to find even a dozen mounted wildlings, and *five hundred* . . .

"Smallwood sent Bannen and me wide around the van to catch a peek at the main body," Kedge went on. "There was no end of them. They're moving slow as a frozen river, four, five miles a day, but they don't look like they mean to go back to their villages neither. More'n half were women and children, and they were driving their animals before them, goats, sheep, even aurochs dragging sledges. They'd loaded up with bales of fur and sides of meat, cages of chickens, butter churns and spinning wheels, every damn thing they own. The mules and garrons was so heavy laden you'd think their backs would break. The women as well."

"And they follow the Milkwater?" Lark the Sisterman asked.

"I said so, didn't I?"

The Milkwater would take them past the Fist of the First Men, the ancient ringfort where the Night's Watch had made its camp. Any man with a thimble of sense could see that it was time to pull up stakes and fall back on the Wall. The Old Bear had strengthened the Fist with spikes and pits and caltrops, but against such a host all that was pointless. If they stayed here, they would be engulfed and overwhelmed.

And Thoren Smallwood wanted to *attack*. Sweet Donnel Hill was squire to Ser Mallador Locke, and the night before last Smallwood had come to Locke's tent. Ser Mallador had been of the same mind as old Ser Ottyn Wythers, urging a retreat on the Wall, but Smallwood wanted to convince him otherwise. "This King-beyond-the-Wall will never look for us so far north," Sweet Donnel reported him saying. "And this great host of his is a shambling horde, full of useless mouths who won't know what end of a sword to hold. One blow will take all the fight out of them and send them howling back to their hovels for another fifty years."

Three hundred against thirty thousand. Chett called that rank madness, and what was madder still was that Ser Mallador had been persuaded, and the two of them together were on the point of persuading the Old Bear. "If we wait too long, this chance may be lost, never to come again," Smallwood was saying to anyone who would listen. Against that, Ser Ottyn Wythers said, "We are the shield that guards the realms of men. You do not throw away your shield for no good purpose," but to that Thoren Smallwood said, "In a swordfight, a man's surest defense is the swift stroke that slays his foe, not cringing behind a shield."

Neither Smallwood nor Wythers had the command, though. Lord Mormont did, and Mormont was waiting for his other scouts, for Jarman Buckwell and the men who'd climbed the Giant's Stair, and for Qhorin Halfhand and Jon Snow, who'd gone to probe the Skirling Pass. Buckwell and the Halfhand were late in returning, though. *Dead, most like.* Chett pictured Jon Snow lying blue and frozen on some bleak mountaintop with a wildling spear up his bastard's arse. The thought made him smile. *I hope they killed his bloody wolf as well.*

"There's no bear here," he decided abruptly. "Just an old print, that's all. Back to the Fist." The dogs almost yanked him off his feet, as eager to get back as he was. Maybe they thought they were going to get fed. Chett had to laugh. He hadn't fed them for three days now, to turn them mean and hungry. Tonight, before slipping off into the dark, he'd turn them loose among the horse lines, after Sweet Donnel Hill and Clubfoot Karl cut the tethers. *They'll have snarling hounds and panicked horses all over the Fist, running through fires, jumping the ringwall, and trampling down tents.* With all the confusion, it might be hours before anyone noticed that fourteen brothers were missing.

Lark had wanted to bring in twice that number, but what could you expect from some stupid fishbreath Sisterman? Whisper a word in the wrong ear and before you knew it you'd be short a head. No, fourteen was a good number, enough to do what needed doing but not so many that they couldn't keep the secret. Chett had recruited most of them himself. Small Paul was one of his; the strongest man on the Wall, even if he was slower than a dead snail. He'd once broken a wildling's back with a hug. They had Dirk as well, named for his favorite weapon, and the little grey man the brothers called Softfoot, who'd raped a hundred women in his youth, and liked to boast how none had ever seen nor heard him until he shoved it up inside them.

The plan was Chett's. He was the clever one; he'd been

steward to old Maester Aemon for four good years before
that bastard Jon Snow had done him out so his job could
be handed to his fat pig of a friend. When he killed Sam
Tarly tonight, he planned to whisper, "Give my love to
Lord Snow," right in his ear before he sliced Ser Piggy's
throat open to let the blood come bubbling out through
all those layers of suet. Chett knew the ravens, so he
wouldn't have no trouble there, no more than he would
with Tarly. One touch of the knife and that craven would
piss his pants and start blubbering for his life. *Let him
beg, it won't do him no good*. After he opened his throat,
he'd open the cages and shoo the birds away, so no messages reached the Wall. Softfoot and Small Paul would kill
the Old Bear, Dirk would do Blane, and Lark and his
cousins would silence Bannen and old Dywen, to keep
them from sniffing after their trail. They'd been caching
food for a fortnight, and Sweet Donnel and Clubfoot Karl
would have the horses ready. With Mormont dead, command would pass to Ser Ottyn Wythers, an old done man,
and failing. *He'll be running for the Wall before sundown,
and he won't waste no men sending them after us neither*.

The dogs pulled at him as they made their way through
the trees. Chett could see the Fist punching its way up
through the green. The day was so dark that the Old Bear
had the torches lit, a great circle of them burning all along
the ringwall that crowned the top of the steep stony hill.
The three of them waded across a brook. The water was
icy cold, and patches of ice were spreading across its surface. "I'm going to make for the coast," Lark the Sisterman
confided. "Me and my cousins. We'll build us a boat, sail
back home to the Sisters."

*And at home they'll know you for deserters and lop
off your fool heads*, thought Chett. There was no leaving
the Night's Watch, once you said your words. Anywhere
in the Seven Kingdoms, they'd take you and kill you.

Ollo Lophand now, he was talking about sailing back
to Tyrosh, where he claimed men didn't lose their hands
for a bit of honest thievery, nor get sent off to freeze their
life away for being found in bed with some knight's wife.
Chett had weighed going with him, but he didn't speak

their wet girly tongue. And what could he do in Tyrosh? He had no trade to speak of, growing up in Hag's Mire. His father had spent his life grubbing in other men's fields and collecting leeches. He'd strip down bare but for a thick leather clout, and go wading in the murky waters. When he climbed out he'd be covered from nipple to ankle. Sometimes he made Chett help pull the leeches off. One had attached itself to his palm once, and he'd smashed it against a wall in revulsion. His father beat him bloody for that. The maesters bought the leeches at twelve-for-a-penny.

Lark could go home if he liked, and the damn Tyroshi too, but not Chett. If he never saw Hag's Mire again, it would be too bloody soon. He had liked the look of Craster's Keep, himself. Craster lived high as a lord there, so why shouldn't he do the same? That would be a laugh. Chett the leechman's son, a lord with a keep. His banner could be a dozen leeches on a field of pink. But why stop at lord? Maybe he should be a king. *Mance Rayder started out a crow. I could be a king same as him, and have me some wives.* Craster had nineteen, not even counting the young ones, the daughters he hadn't gotten around to bedding yet. Half them wives were as old and ugly as Craster, but that didn't matter. The old ones Chett could put to work cooking and cleaning for him, pulling carrots and slopping pigs, while the young ones warmed his bed and bore his children. Craster wouldn't object, not once Small Paul gave him a hug.

The only women Chett had ever known were the whores he'd bought in Mole's Town. When he'd been younger, the village girls took one look at his face, with its boils and its wen, and turned away sickened. The worst was that slattern Bessa. She'd spread her legs for every boy in Hag's Mire so he'd figured why not him too? He even spent a morning picking wildflowers when he heard she liked them, but she'd just laughed in his face and told him she'd crawl in a bed with his father's leeches before she'd crawl in one with him. She stopped laughing when he put his knife in her. That was sweet, the look on her face, so he pulled the knife out and put it in her again. When they caught him down near Sevenstreams, old Lord Walder Frey hadn't even bothered to come himself to do the judging. He'd sent one of his *bastards*, that Walder Rivers, and the next thing Chett had known he was walking to the Wall with that foul-smelling black devil Yoren. To pay for his one sweet moment, they took his whole life.

But now he meant to take it back, and Craster's women too. *That twisted old wildling has the right of it. If you want a woman to wife you take her, and none of this giving her flowers so that maybe she don't notice your bloody boils.* Chett didn't mean to make *that* mistake again.

It would work, he promised himself for the hundredth time. *So long as we get away clean.* Ser Ottyn would strike south for the Shadow Tower, the shortest way to the Wall. *He won't bother with us, not Wythers, all he'll want is to get back whole.* Thoren Smallwood now, he'd want to press on with the attack, but Ser Ottyn's caution ran too deep, and he was senior. *It won't matter anyhow. Once we're gone, Smallwood can attack anyone he likes. What do we care? If none of them ever returns to the Wall, no one will ever come looking for us, they'll think we died with the rest.* That was a new thought, and for a moment it tempted him. But they would need to kill Ser Ottyn and Ser Mallador Locke as well to give Smallwood the command, and both of them were well-attended day and night . . . no, the risk was too great.

"Chett," said Small Paul as they trudged along a stony game trail through sentinels and soldier pines, "what about the bird?"

"What bloody bird?" The last thing he needed now was some muttonhead going on about a bird.

"The Old Bear's raven," Small Paul said. "If we kill him, who's going to feed his bird?"

"Who bloody well cares? Kill the bird too if you like."

"I don't want to hurt no bird," the big man said. "But that's a talking bird. What if it tells what we did?"

Lark the Sisterman laughed. "Small Paul, thick as a castle wall," he mocked.

"You shut up with that," said Small Paul dangerously.

"Paul," said Chett, before the big man got too angry, "when they find the old man lying in a pool of blood with his throat slit, they won't need no bird to tell them someone killed him."

Small Paul chewed on that a moment. "That's true," he allowed. "Can I keep the bird, then? I like that bird."

"He's yours," said Chett, just to shut him up.

"We can always eat him if we get hungry," offered Lark.

Small Paul clouded up again. "Best not try and eat *my* bird, Lark. Best not."

Chett could hear voices drifting through the trees. "Close your bloody mouths, both of you. We're almost to the Fist."

They emerged near the west face of the hill, and walked around south where the slope was gentler. Near the edge of the forest a dozen men were taking archery practice. They had carved outlines on the trunks of trees, and were loosing shafts at them. "Look," said Lark. "A pig with a bow."

Sure enough, the nearest bowman was Ser Piggy himself, the fat boy who had stolen his place with Maester Aemon. Just the sight of Samwell Tarly filled him with anger. Stewarding for Maester Aemon had been as good a life as he'd ever known. The old blind man was undemanding, and Clydas had taken care of most of his wants anyway. Chett's duties were easy: cleaning the rookery, a few fires to build, a few meals to fetch . . . and Aemon never once hit him. *Thinks he can just walk in and shove me out, on account of being highborn and knowing how to read. Might be I'll ask him to read my knife before I open his throat with it.* "You go on," he told the others, "I want to watch this." The dogs were pulling, anxious to go with them, to the food they thought would be waiting at the top. Chett kicked the bitch with the toe of his boot, and that settled them down some.

He watched from the trees as the fat boy wrestled with a longbow as tall as he was, his red moon face screwed up with concentration. Three arrows stood in the ground before him. Tarly nocked and drew, held the draw a long moment as he tried to aim, and let fly. The shaft vanished into the greenery. Chett laughed loudly, a snort of sweet disgust.

"We'll never find that one, and I'll be blamed," announced Edd Tollett, the dour grey-haired squire everyone called Dolorous Edd. "Nothing ever goes missing that they don't look at me, ever since that time I lost my horse. As if that could be helped. He was white and it was snowing, what did they expect?"

"The wind took that one," said Grenn, another friend of Lord Snow's. "Try to hold the bow steady, Sam."

"It's heavy," the fat boy complained, but he pulled the second arrow all the same. This one went high, sailing through the branches ten feet above the target.

"I believe you knocked a leaf off that tree," said Dolorous Edd. "Fall is falling fast enough, there's no need to help it." He sighed. "And we all know what follows fall. Gods, but I am cold. Shoot the last arrow, Samwell, I believe my tongue is freezing to the roof of my mouth."

Ser Piggy lowered the bow, and Chett thought he was going to start bawling. "It's too hard."

"Notch, draw, and loose," said Grenn. "Go on."

Dutifully, the fat boy plucked his final arrow from the earth, notched it to his longbow, drew, and released. He did it quickly, without squinting along the shaft painstakingly as he had the first two times. The arrow struck the charcoal outline low in the chest and hung quivering. "I *hit* him." Ser Piggy sounded shocked. "Grenn, did you see? Edd, look, I hit him!"

"Put it between his ribs, I'd say," said Grenn.

"Did I kill him?" the fat boy wanted to know.

Tollett shrugged. "Might have punctured a lung, if he had a lung. Most trees don't, as a rule." He took the bow from Sam's hand. "I've seen worse shots, though. Aye, and made a few."

Ser Piggy was beaming. To look at him you'd think he'd actually *done* something. But when he saw Chett and the dogs, his smile curled up and died squeaking.

"You hit a tree," Chett said. "Let's see how you shoot when it's Mance Rayder's lads. They won't stand there with their arms out and their leaves rustling, oh no.

They'll come right at you, screaming in your face, and I bet you'll piss those breeches. One o' them will plant his axe right between those little pig eyes. The last thing you'll hear will be the *thunk* it makes when it bites into your skull."

The fat boy was shaking. Dolorous Edd put a hand on his shoulder. "Brother," he said solemnly, "just because it happened that way for you doesn't mean Samwell will suffer the same."

"What are you talking about, Tollett?"

"The axe that split your skull. Is it true that half your wits leaked out on the ground and your dogs ate them?"

The big lout Grenn laughed, and even Samwell Tarly managed a weak little smile. Chett kicked the nearest dog, yanked on their leashes, and started up the hill. *Smile all you want, Ser Piggy. We'll see who laughs tonight.* He only wished he had time to kill Tollett as well. *Gloomy horsefaced fool, that's what he is.*

The climb was steep, even on this side of the Fist, which had the gentlest slope. Partway up the dogs started barking and pulling at him, figuring that they'd get fed soon. He gave them a taste of his boot instead, and a crack of the whip for the big ugly one that snapped at him. Once they were tied up, he went to report. "The prints were there like Giant said, but the dogs wouldn't track," he told Mormont in front of his big black tent. "Down by the river like that, could be old prints."

"A pity." Lord Commander Mormont had a bald head and a great shaggy grey beard, and sounded as tired as he looked. "We might all have been better for a bit of fresh meat." The raven on his shoulder bobbed its head and echoed, "*Meat. Meat. Meat.*"

We could cook the bloody dogs, Chett thought, but he kept his mouth shut until the Old Bear sent him on his way. *And that's the last time I'll need to bow my head to that one,* he thought to himself with satisfaction. It seemed to him that it was growing even colder, which he would have sworn wasn't possible. The dogs huddled together miserably in the hard frozen mud, and Chett was half tempted to crawl in with them. Instead he wrapped a black wool scarf round the lower part of his face, leaving a slit for his mouth between the winds. It was warmer if he kept moving, he found, so he made a slow circuit of the perimeter with a wad of sourleaf, sharing a chew or two with the black brothers on guard and hearing what they had to say. None of the men on the day watch was part of his scheme; even so, he figured it was good to have some sense of what they were thinking.

Mostly what they were thinking was that it was bloody cold.

The wind was rising as the shadows lengthened. It made a high thin sound as it shivered through the stones of the ringwall. "I hate that sound," little Giant said. "It sounds like a babe in the brush, wailing away for milk."

When he finished the circuit and returned to the dogs, he found Lark waiting for him. "The officers are in the Old Bear's tent again, talking something fierce."

"That's what they do," said Chett. "They're highborn, all but Blane, they get drunk on words instead of wine."

Lark sidled closer. "Cheese-for-wits keeps going on about the bird," he warned, glancing about to make certain no one was close. "Now he's asking if we cached any seed for the damn thing."

"It's a raven," said Chett. "It eats corpses."

Lark grinned. "His, might be?"

Or yours. It seemed to Chett that they needed the big man more than they needed Lark. "Stop fretting about Small Paul. You do your part, he'll do his."

Twilight was creeping through the woods by the time he rid himself of the Sisterman and sat down to edge his sword. It was bloody hard work with his gloves on, but he wasn't about to take them off. Cold as it was, any fool that touched steel with a bare hand was going to lose a patch of skin.

The dogs whimpered when the sun went down. He gave them water and curses. "Half a night more, and you can find your own feast." By then he could smell supper.

Dywen was holding forth at the cookfire as Chett got his heel of hardbread and a bowl of bean and bacon soup from Hake the cook. "The wood's too silent," the old forester was saying. "No frogs near that river, no owls in the dark. I never heard no deader wood than this."

"Them teeth of yours sound pretty dead," said Hake.

Dywen clacked his wooden teeth. "No wolves neither. There was, before, but no more. Where'd they go, you figure?"

"Someplace warm," said Chett.

Of the dozen odd brothers who sat by the fire, four were his. He gave each one a hard squinty look as he ate, to see if any showed signs of breaking. Dirk seemed calm enough, sitting silent and sharpening his blade, the way he did every night. And Sweet Donnel Hill was all easy japes. He had white teeth and fat red lips and yellow locks that he wore in an artful tumble about his shoulders, and he claimed to be the bastard of some Lannister. Maybe he was at that. Chett had no use for pretty boys, nor for bastards neither, but Sweet Donnel seemed like to hold his own.

He was less certain about the forester the brothers called Sawwood, more for his snoring than for anything to do with trees. Just now he looked so restless he might never snore again. And Maslyn was worse. Chett could see sweat trickling down his face, despite the frigid wind. The beads of moisture sparkled in the firelight, like so many little wet jewels. Maslyn wasn't eating neither, only staring at his soup as if the smell of it was about to make him sick. *I'll need to watch that one*, Chett thought.

"Assemble!" The shout came suddenly, from a dozen throats, and quickly spread to every part of the hilltop camp. "Men of the Night's Watch! Assemble at the central fire!"

Frowning, Chett finished his soup and followed the rest.

The Old Bear stood before the fire with Smallwood, Locke, Wythers, and Blane ranged behind him in a row. Mormont wore a cloak of thick black fur, and his raven perched upon his shoulder, preening its black feathers. *This can't be good.* Chett squeezed between Brown Bernarr and some Shadow Tower men. When everyone was gathered, save for the watchers in the woods and the guards on the ringwall, Mormont cleared his throat and spat. The spittle was frozen before it hit the ground. "Brothers," he said, "men of the Night's Watch."

"*Men!*" his raven screamed. "*Men! Men!*"

"The wildlings are on the march, following the course of the Milkwater down out of the mountains. Thoren believes their van will be upon us ten days hence. Their most seasoned raiders will be with Harma Dogshead in that van. The rest will likely form a rearguard, or ride in close company with Mance Rayder himself. Elsewhere their fighters will be spread thin along the line of march. They have oxen, mules, horses . . . but few enough. Most will be afoot, and ill-armed and untrained. Such weapons as they carry are more like to be stone and bone than steel. They are burdened with women, children, herds of sheep and goats, and all their worldly goods besides. In short, though they are numerous, they are vulnerable . . . and *they do not know that we are here.* Or so we must pray."

They know, thought Chett. *You bloody old pus bag, they know, certain as sunrise. Qhorin Halfhand hasn't come back, has he? Nor Jarman Buckwell. If any of them got caught, you know damned well the wildlings will have wrung a song or two out of them by now.*

Smallwood stepped forward. "Mance Rayder means to break the Wall and bring red war to the Seven Kingdoms. Well, that's a game two can play. On the morrow we'll bring the war to him."

"We ride at dawn with all our strength," the Old Bear said as a murmur went through the assembly. "We will ride north, and loop around to the west. Harma's van will be well past the Fist by the time we turn. The foothills of the Frostfangs are full of narrow winding valleys made for ambush. Their line of march will stretch for many miles. We shall fall on them in several places at once, and make them swear we were three thousand, not three hundred."

"We'll hit hard and be away before their horsemen can form up to face us," Thoren Smallwood said. "If they pursue, we'll lead them a merry chase, then wheel and hit again farther down the column. We'll burn their wagons, scatter their herds, and slay as many as we can. Mance

Rayder himself, if we find him. If they break and return to their hovels, we've won. If not, we'll harry them all the way to the Wall, and see to it that they leave a trail of corpses to mark their progress."

"*There are thousands*," someone called from behind Chett.

"*We'll die*." That was Maslyn's voice, green with fear.

"*Die*," screamed Mormont's raven, flapping its black wings. "*Die, die, die*."

"Many of us," the Old Bear said. "Mayhaps even all of us. But as another Lord Commander said a thousand years ago, that is why they dress us in black. Remember your words, brothers. For we are the swords in the darkness, the watchers on the walls . . ."

"The fire that burns against the cold." Ser Mallador Locke drew his longsword.

"The light that brings the dawn," others answered, and more swords were pulled from scabbards.

Then all of them were drawing, and it was near three hundred upraised swords and as many voices crying, "*The horn that wakes the sleepers! The shield that guards the realms of men!*" Chett had no choice but to join his voice to the others. The air was misty with their breath, and firelight glinted off the steel. He was pleased to see Lark and Softfoot and Sweet Donnel Hill joining in, as if they were as big fools as the rest. That was good. No sense to draw attention, when their hour was so close.

When the shouting died away, once more he heard the sound of the wind picking at the ringwall. The flames swirled and shivered, as if they too were cold, and in the sudden quiet the Old Bear's raven cawed loudly and once again said, "*Die*."

Clever bird, thought Chett as the officers dismissed them, warning everyone to get a good meal and a long rest tonight. Chett crawled under his furs near the dogs, his head full of things that could go wrong. What if that bloody oath gave one of his a change of heart? Or Small Paul forgot and tried to kill Mormont during the second watch in place of the third? Or Maslyn lost his courage, or someone turned informer, or . . .

He found himself listening to the night. The wind did sound like a wailing child, and from time to time he could hear men's voices, a horse's whinny, a log spitting in the fire. But nothing else. *So quiet.*

He could see Bessa's face floating before him. *It wasn't the knife I wanted to put in you,* he wanted to tell her. *I picked you flowers, wild roses and tansy and goldencups, it took me all morning.* His heart was thumping like a drum, so loud he feared it might wake the camp. Ice caked his beard all around his mouth. *Where did that come from, with Bessa?* Whenever he'd thought of her before, it had only been to remember the way she'd looked, dying. What was wrong with him? He could hardly breathe. Had he gone to sleep? He got to his knees, and something wet and cold touched his nose. Chett looked up.

Snow was falling.

He could feel tears freezing to his cheeks. *It isn't fair,* he wanted to scream. Snow would ruin everything he'd worked for, all his careful plans. It was a heavy fall, thick white flakes coming down all about him. How would they find their food caches in the snow, or the game trail they meant to follow east? *They won't need Dywen nor Bannen to hunt us down neither, not if we're tracking through fresh snow.* And snow hid the shape of the ground, especially by night. A horse could stumble over a root, break a leg on a stone. *We're done,* he realized. *Done before we began. We're lost.* There'd be no lord's life for the leechman's son, no keep to call his own, no wives nor crowns. Only a wildling's sword in his belly, and then an unmarked grave. *The snow's taken it all from me . . . the bloody snow . . .*

Snow had ruined him once before. Snow and his pet pig.

Chett got to his feet. His legs were stiff, and the falling snowflakes turned the distant torches to vague orange glows. He felt as though he were being attacked by a cloud of pale cold bugs. They settled on his shoulders, on his head, they flew at his nose and his eyes. Cursing, he brushed them off. *Samwell Tarly,* he remembered. *I can still deal with Ser Piggy.* He wrapped his scarf around his face, pulled up his hood, and went striding through the camp to where the coward slept.

The snow was falling so heavily that he got lost among the tents, but finally he spotted the snug little windbreak the fat boy had made for himself between a rock and the raven cages. Tarly was buried beneath a mound of black wool blankets and shaggy furs. The snow was drifting in to cover him. He looked like some kind of soft round mountain. Steel whispered on leather faint as hope as Chett eased his dagger from its sheath. One of the ravens *quork*ed. "Snow," another muttered, peering through the bars with black eyes. The first added a "Snow" of its own. He edged past them, placing each foot carefully. He would clap his left hand down over the fat boy's mouth to muffle his cries, and then . . .

Uuuuuuuhoooooooooo.

He stopped midstep, swallowing his curse as the sound of the horn shuddered through the camp, faint and far, yet unmistakable. *Not now. Gods be damned, not NOW!* The Old Bear had hidden far-eyes in a ring of trees around the Fist, to give warning of any approach. *Jarman Buckwell's back from the Giant's Stair*, Chett figured, *or Qhorin Half-hand from the Skirling Pass.* A single blast of the horn meant brothers returning. If it was the Halfhand, Jon Snow might be with him, alive.

Sam Tarly sat up puffy-eyed and stared at the snow in confusion. The ravens were cawing noisily, and Chett could hear his dogs baying. *Half the bloody camp's awake.* His gloved fingers clenched around the dagger's hilt as he waited for the sound to die away. But no sooner had it gone than it came again, louder and longer.

Uuuuuuuuuuuuuhooooooooooooooooo.

"Gods," he heard Sam Tarly whimper. The fat boy lurched to his knees, his feet tangled in his cloak and blankets. He kicked them away and reached for a chain-mail hauberk he'd hung on the rock nearby. As he slipped the huge tent of a garment down over his head and wriggled into it, he spied Chett standing there. "Was it two?" he asked. "I dreamed I heard two blasts . . ."

"No dream," said Chett. "Two blasts to call the Watch

to arms. Two blasts for foes approaching. There's an axe out there with *Piggy* writ on it, fat boy. Two blasts means *wildlings*." The fear on that big moon face made him want to laugh. "Bugger them all to seven hells. Bloody Harma. Bloody Mance Rayder. Bloody Smallwood, he said they wouldn't be on us for another – "

Uuuuuuuuuuuuuuuuhoooooooooooooooooooooooooooooo.

The sound went on and on and on, until it seemed it would never die. The ravens were flapping and screaming, flying about their cages and banging off the bars, and all about the camp the brothers of the Night's Watch were rising, donning their armor, buckling on swordbelts, reaching for battleaxes and bows. Samwell Tarly stood shaking, his face the same color as the snow that swirled down all around them. "Three," he squeaked to Chett, "that was three, I heard three. They never blow three. Not for hundreds and thousands of years. Three means – "

" – *Others*." Chett made a sound that was half a laugh and half a sob, and suddenly his smallclothes were wet, and he could feel the piss running down his leg, see steam rising off the front of his breeches.

JAIME

An east wind blew through his tangled hair, as soft and fragrant as Cersei's fingers. He could hear birds singing, and feel the river moving beneath the boat as the sweep of the oars sent them toward the pale pink dawn. After so long in darkness, the world was so sweet that Jaime Lannister felt dizzy. *I am alive, and drunk on sunlight.* A laugh burst from his lips, sudden as a quail flushed from cover.

"Quiet," the wench grumbled, scowling. Scowls suited her broad homely face better than a smile. Not that Jaime had ever seen her smiling. He amused himself by picturing her in one of Cersei's silken gowns in place of her studded leather jerkin. *As well dress a cow in silk as this one.*

But the cow could row. Beneath her roughspun brown breeches were calves like cords of wood, and the long muscles of her arms stretched and tightened with each stroke of the oars. Even after rowing half the night, she showed no signs of tiring, which was more than could be said for his cousin Ser Cleos, laboring on the other oar. *A big strong peasant wench to look at her, yet she speaks like one highborn and wears longsword and dagger. Ah, but can she use them?* Jaime meant to find out, as soon as he rid himself of these fetters.

He wore iron manacles on his wrists and a matching pair about his ankles, joined by a length of heavy chain no more than a foot long. "You'd think my word as a Lannister was not good enough," he'd japed as they bound him. He'd been very drunk by then, thanks to Catelyn Stark. Of their escape from Riverrun, he recalled only bits and pieces. There had been some trouble with the gaoler, but the big wench had overcome him. After that they had climbed an endless stair, around and around. His legs were weak as grass, and he'd stumbled twice or thrice, until the wench lent him an arm to lean on. At some point he was bundled into a traveler's cloak and shoved into the bottom of a skiff. He remembered listening to Lady Catelyn command someone to raise the portcullis on the Water Gate. She was sending Ser Cleos Frey back to King's Landing with new terms for the queen, she'd declared in a tone that brooked no argument.

He must have drifted off then. The wine had made him sleepy, and it felt good to stretch, a luxury his chains had not permitted him in the cell. Jaime had long ago learned to snatch sleep in the saddle during a march. This was no harder. *Tyrion is going to laugh himself sick when he hears how I slept through my own escape.* He was awake now, though, and the fetters were irksome. "My lady," he called out, "if you'll strike off these chains, I'll spell you at those oars."

She scowled again, her face all horse teeth and glowering suspicion. "You'll wear your chains, Kingslayer."

"You figure to row all the way to King's Landing, wench?"

"You will call me Brienne. Not *wench.*"

"My name is Ser Jaime. Not Kingslayer."

"Do you deny that you slew a king?"

"No. Do you deny your sex? If so, unlace those breeches and show me." He gave her an innocent smile. "I'd ask you to open your bodice, but from the look of you that wouldn't prove much."

Ser Cleos fretted. "Cousin, remember your courtesies."

The Lannister blood runs thin in this one. Cleos was his Aunt Genna's son by that dullard Emmon Frey, who had lived in terror of Lord Tywin Lannister since the day he wed his sister. When Lord Walder Frey had brought the

Twins into the war on the side of Riverrun, Ser Emmon had chosen his wife's allegiance over his father's. *Casterly Rock got the worst of that bargain*, Jaime reflected. Ser Cleos looked like a weasel, fought like a goose, and had the courage of an especially brave ewe. Lady Stark had promised him release if he delivered her message to Tyrion, and Ser Cleos had solemnly vowed to do so.

They'd all done a deal of vowing back in that cell, Jaime most of all. That was Lady Catelyn's price for loosing him. She had laid the point of the big wench's sword against his heart and said, "Swear that you will never again take up arms against Stark nor Tully. Swear that you will compel your brother to honor his pledge to return my daughters safe and unharmed. Swear on your honor as a knight, on your honor as a Lannister, on your honor as a Sworn Brother of the Kingsguard. Swear it by your sister's life, and your father's, and your son's, by the old gods and the new, and I'll send you back to your sister. Refuse, and I will have your blood." He remembered the prick of the steel through his rags as she twisted the point of the sword.

I wonder what the High Septon would have to say about the sanctity of oaths sworn while dead drunk, chained to a wall, with a sword pressed to your chest? Not that Jaime was truly concerned about that fat fraud, or the gods he claimed to serve. He remembered the pail Lady Catelyn had kicked over in his cell. A strange woman, to trust her girls to a man with shit for honor. Though she was trusting him as little as she dared. *She is putting her hope in Tyrion, not in me.* "Perhaps she is not so stupid after all," he said aloud.

His captor took it wrong. "I am not stupid. Nor deaf."

He was gentle with her; mocking this one would be so easy there would be no sport to it. "I was speaking to myself, and not of you. It's an easy habit to slip into in a cell."

She frowned at him, pushing the oars forward, pulling them back, pushing them forward, saying nothing.

As glib of tongue as she is fair of face. "By your speech, I'd judge you nobly born."

"My father is Selwyn of Tarth, by the grace of the gods Lord of Evenfall." Even that was given grudgingly.

"Tarth," Jaime said. "A ghastly large rock in the narrow sea, as I recall. And Evenfall is sworn to Storm's End. How is it that you serve Robb of Winterfell?"

"It is Lady Catelyn I serve. And she commanded me to deliver you safe to your brother Tyrion at King's Landing, not to bandy words with you. Be silent."

"I've had a bellyful of silence, woman."

"Talk with Ser Cleos then. I have no words for monsters."

Jaime hooted. "Are there monsters hereabouts? Hiding beneath the water, perhaps? In that thick of willows? And me without my sword!"

"A man who would violate his own sister, murder his king, and fling an innocent child to his death deserves no other name."

Innocent! The wretched boy was spying on us. All Jaime had wanted was an hour alone with Cersei. Their journey north had been one long torment; seeing her every day, unable to touch her, knowing that Robert stumbled drunkenly into her bed every night in that great creaking wheelhouse. Tyrion had done his best to keep him in a good humor, but it had not been enough. "You will be courteous as concerns Cersei, wench," he warned her.

"My name is Brienne, not *wench*."

"What do you care what a monster calls you?"

"My name is Brienne," she repeated, dogged as a hound.

"Lady Brienne?" She looked so uncomfortable that Jaime sensed a weakness. "Or would *Ser* Brienne be more to your taste?" He laughed. "No, I fear not. You can trick out a milk cow in crupper, crinet, and chamfron, and bard her all in silk, but that doesn't mean you can ride her into battle."

"Cousin Jaime, please, you ought not speak so roughly." Under his cloak, Ser Cleos wore a surcoat quartered with the twin towers of House Frey and the golden lion of Lannister. "We have far to go, we should not quarrel amongst ourselves."

"When I quarrel I do it with a sword, coz. I was speaking to the lady. Tell me, wench, are all the women on Tarth as homely as you? I pity the men, if so. Perhaps they do not know what real women look like, living on a dreary mountain in the sea."

"Tarth is beautiful," the wench grunted between strokes. "The Sapphire Isle, it's called. Be quiet, monster, unless you mean to make me gag you."

"She's rude as well, isn't she, coz?" Jaime asked Ser Cleos. "Though she has steel in her spine, I'll grant you. Not many men dare name me monster to my face." *Though behind my back they speak freely enough, I have no doubt.*

Ser Cleos coughed nervously. "Lady Brienne had those lies from Catelyn Stark, no doubt. The Starks cannot hope to defeat you with swords, ser, so now they make war with poisoned words."

They did defeat me with swords, you chinless cretin. Jaime smiled knowingly. Men will read all sorts of things into a knowing smile, if you let them. *Has cousin Cleos truly swallowed this kettle of dung, or is he striving to ingratiate himself? What do we have here, an honest mutton-head or a lickspittle?*

Ser Cleos prattled blithely on. "Any man who'd believe that a Sworn Brother of the Kingsguard would harm a child does not know the meaning of honor."

Lickspittle. If truth be told, Jaime had come to rue heaving Brandon Stark out that window. Cersei had given him no end of grief afterward, when the boy refused to die. "He was seven, Jaime," she'd berated him. "Even if he understood what he saw, we should have been able to frighten him into silence."

"I didn't think you'd want –"

"You *never* think. If the boy should wake and tell his father what he saw –"

"If if if." He had pulled her into his lap. "If he wakes we'll say he was dreaming, we'll call him a liar, and should worse come to worst I'll kill Ned Stark."

"And then what do you imagine *Robert* will do?"

"Let Robert do as he pleases. I'll go to war with him if

I must. The War for Cersei's Cunt, the singers will call it."

"Jaime, let go of me!" she raged, struggling to rise.

Instead he had kissed her. For a moment she resisted, but then her mouth opened under his. He remembered the taste of wine and cloves on her tongue. She gave a shudder. His hand went to her bodice and yanked, tearing the silk so her breasts spilled free, and for a time the Stark boy had been forgotten.

Had Cersei remembered him afterward and hired this man Lady Catelyn spoke of, to make sure the boy never woke? *If she wanted him dead she would have sent me. And it is not like her to chose a catspaw who would make such a royal botch of the killing.*

Downriver, the rising sun shimmered against the wind-whipped surface of the river. The south shore was red clay, smooth as any road. Smaller streams fed into the greater, and the rotting trunks of drowned trees clung to the banks. The north shore was wilder. High rocky bluffs rose twenty feet above them, crowned by stands of beech, oak, and chestnut. Jaime spied a watchtower on the heights ahead, growing taller with every stroke of the oars. Long before they were upon it, he knew that it stood abandoned, its weathered stones overgrown with climbing roses.

When the wind shifted, Ser Cleos helped the big wench run up the sail, a stiff triangle of striped red-and-blue canvas. Tully colors, sure to cause them grief if they encountered any Lannister forces on the river, but it was the only sail they had. Brienne took the rudder. Jaime threw out the leeboard, his chains rattling as he moved. After that, they made better speed, with wind and current both favoring their flight. "We could save a deal of traveling if you delivered me to my father instead of my brother," he pointed out.

"Lady Catelyn's daughters are in King's Landing. I will return with the girls or not at all."

Jaime turned to Ser Cleos. "Cousin, lend me your knife."

"No." The woman tensed. "I will not have you armed." Her voice was as unyielding as stone.

She fears me, even in irons. "Cleos, it seems I must ask you to shave me. Leave the beard, but take the hair off my head."

"You'd be shaved bald?" asked Cleos Frey.

"The realm knows Jaime Lannister as a beardless knight with long golden hair. A bald man with a filthy yellow beard may pass unnoticed. I'd sooner not be recognized while I'm in irons."

The dagger was not as sharp as it might have been. Cleos hacked away manfully, sawing and ripping his way through the mats and tossing the hair over the side. The golden curls floated on the surface of the water, gradually falling astern. As the tangles vanished, a louse went crawling down his neck. Jaime caught it and crushed it against his thumbnail. Ser Cleos picked others from his scalp and flicked them into the water. Jaime doused his head and made Ser Cleos whet the blade before he let him scrape away the last inch of yellow stubble. When that was done, they trimmed back his beard as well.

The reflection in the water was a man he did not know. Not only was he bald, but he looked as though he had aged five years in that dungeon; his face was thinner, with hollows under his eyes and lines he did not remember. *I don't look as much like Cersei this way. She'll hate that.*

By midday, Ser Cleos had fallen asleep. His snores sounded like ducks mating. Jaime stretched out to watch the world flow past; after the dark cell, every rock and tree was a wonder.

A few one-room shacks came and went, perched on tall poles that made them look like cranes. Of the folk who lived there they saw no sign. Birds flew overhead, or cried out from the trees along the shore, and Jaime glimpsed silvery fish knifing through the water. *Tully trout, there's a bad omen*, he thought, until he saw a worse – one of the floating logs they passed turned out to be a dead man, bloodless and swollen. His cloak was tangled in the roots of a fallen tree, its color unmistakably Lannister crimson. He wondered if the corpse had been someone he knew.

The forks of the Trident were the easiest way to move goods or men across the riverlands. In times of peace, they would have encountered fisherfolk in their skiffs, grain barges being poled downstream, merchants selling needles and bolts of cloth from floating shops, perhaps even a gaily painted mummer's boat with quilted sails of half a hundred colors, making its way upriver from village to village and castle to castle.

But the war had taken its toll. They sailed past villages, but saw no villagers. An empty net, slashed and torn and hanging from some trees, was the only sign of fisherfolk. A young girl watering her horse rode off as soon as she glimpsed their sail. Later they passed a dozen peasants digging in a field beneath the shell of a burnt towerhouse. The men gazed at them with dull eyes, and went back to their labors once they decided the skiff was no threat.

The Red Fork was wide and slow, a meandering river of loops and bends dotted with tiny wooded islets and frequently choked by sandbars and snags that lurked just below the water's surface. Brienne seemed to have a keen eye for the dangers, though, and always seemed to find the channel. When Jaime complimented her on her knowledge of the river, she looked at him suspiciously and said, "I do not know the river. Tarth is an island. I learned to manage oars and sail before I ever sat a horse."

Ser Cleos sat up and rubbed at his eyes. "Gods, my arms are sore. I hope the wind lasts." He sniffed at it. "I smell rain."

Jaime would welcome a good rain. The dungeons of Riverrun were not the cleanest place in the Seven Kingdoms. By now he must smell like an overripe cheese.

Cleos squinted downriver. "Smoke."

A thin grey finger crooked them on. It was rising from the south bank several miles on, twisting and curling. Below, Jaime made out the smouldering remains of a large building, and a live oak full of dead women.

The crows had scarcely started on their corpses. The thin ropes cut deeply into the soft flesh of their throats, and when the wind blew they twisted and swayed. "This was not chivalrously done," said Brienne when they were close enough to see it clearly. "No true knight would condone such wanton butchery."

"True knights see worse every time they ride to war, wench," said Jaime. "And *do* worse, yes."

Brienne turned the rudder toward the shore. "I'll leave no innocents to be food for crows."

"A heartless wench. Crows need to eat as well. Stay to the river and leave the dead alone, woman."

They landed upstream of where the great oak leaned out over the water. As Brienne lowered the sail, Jaime climbed out, clumsy in his chains. The Red Fork filled his boots and soaked through the ragged breeches. Laughing, he dropped to his knees, plunged his head under the water, and came up drenched and dripping. His hands were caked with dirt, and when he rubbed them clean in the current they seemed thinner and paler than he remembered. His legs were stiff as well, and unsteady when he put his weight upon them. *I was too bloody long in Hoster Tully's dungeon.*

Brienne and Cleos dragged the skiff onto the bank. The corpses hung above their heads, ripening in death like foul fruit. "One of us will need to cut them down," the wench said.

"I'll climb." Jaime waded ashore, clanking. "Just get these chains off."

The wench was staring up at one of the dead women. Jaime shuffled closer with small stutter steps, the only kind the foot-long chain permitted. When he saw the crude sign hung about the neck of the highest corpse, he smiled. "*They Lay With Lions,*" he read. "Oh, yes, woman, this was most *unchivalrously* done . . . but by your side, not mine. I wonder who they were, these women?"

"Tavern wenches," said Ser Cleos Frey. "This was an inn, I remember it now. Some men of my escort spent the night here when we last returned to Riverrun." Nothing remained of the building but the stone foundation and a tangle of collapsed beams, charred black. Smoke still rose from the ashes.

Jaime left brothels and whores to his brother Tyrion; Cersei was the only woman he had ever wanted. "The girls pleasured some of my lord father's soldiers, it would seem. Perhaps served them food and drink. That's how they earned their traitors' collars, with a kiss and a cup of ale." He glanced up and down the river, to make certain they were quite alone. "This is Bracken land. Lord Jonos might have ordered them killed. My father burned his castle, I fear he loves us not."

"It might be Marq Piper's work," said Ser Cleos. "Or that wisp o' the wood Beric Dondarrion, though I'd heard he kills only soldiers. Perhaps a band of Roose Bolton's northmen?"

"Bolton was defeated by my father on the Green Fork."

"But not broken," said Ser Cleos. "He came south again when Lord Tywin marched against the fords. The word at Riverrun was that he'd taken Harrenhal from Ser Amory Lorch."

Jaime liked the sound of that not at all. "Brienne," he said, granting her the courtesy of the name in the hopes that she might listen, "if Lord Bolton holds Harrenhal, both the Trident and the kingsroad are likely watched."

He thought he saw a touch of uncertainty in her big blue eyes. "You are under my protection. They'd need to kill me."

"I shouldn't think that would trouble them."

"I am as good a fighter as you," she said defensively. "I was one of King Renly's chosen seven. With his own hands, he cloaked me with the striped silk of the Rainbow Guard."

"The *Rainbow* Guard? You and six other girls, was it? A singer once said that all maids are fair in silk ... but he never met you, did he?"

The woman turned red. "We have graves to dig." She went to climb the tree.

The lower limbs of the oak were big enough for her to stand upon once she'd gotten up the trunk. She walked amongst the leaves, dagger in hand, cutting down the corpses. Flies swarmed around the bodies as they fell, and the stench grew worse with each one she dropped. "This is a deal of trouble to take for whores," Ser Cleos complained. "What are we supposed to dig with? We have no spades, and I will not use my sword, I –"

Brienne gave a shout. She jumped down rather than climbing. "To the boat. Be quick. There's a sail."

They made what haste they could, though Jaime could hardly run, and had to be pulled back up into the skiff by his cousin. Brienne shoved off with an oar and raised sail hurriedly. "Ser Cleos, I'll need you to row as well."

He did as she bid. The skiff began to cut the water a bit faster; current, wind, and oars all worked for them. Jaime sat chained, peering upriver. Only the top of the other sail was visible. With the way the Red Fork looped, it looked to be across the fields, moving north behind a screen of trees while they moved south, but he knew that was deceptive. He lifted both hands to shade his eyes. "Mud red and watery blue," he announced.

Brienne's big mouth worked soundlessly, giving her the look of a cow chewing its cud. "Faster, ser."

The inn soon vanished behind them, and they lost sight of the top of the sail as well, but that meant nothing. Once the pursuers swung around the loop they would become visible again. "We can hope the noble Tullys will stop to bury the dead whores, I suppose." The prospect of returning to his cell did not appeal to Jaime. *Tyrion could think of something clever now, but all that occurs to me is to go at them with a sword.*

For the good part of an hour they played peek-and-seek with the pursuers, sweeping around bends and between small wooded isles. Just when they were starting to hope that somehow they might have left behind the pursuit, the distant sail became visible again. Ser Cleos paused in his stroke. "The Others take them." He wiped sweat from his brow.

"*Row!*" Brienne said.

"That is a river galley coming after us," Jaime announced after he'd watched for a while. With every stroke, it seemed to grow a little larger. "Nine oars on each side, which means eighteen men. More, if they crowded on fighters as well as rowers. And larger sails than ours. We cannot outrun her."

Ser Cleos froze at his oars. "Eighteen, you said?"

"Six for each of us. I'd want eight, but these bracelets hinder me somewhat." Jaime held up his wrists. "Unless the Lady Brienne would be so kind as to unshackle me?"

She ignored him, putting all her effort into her stroke.

"We had half a night's start on them," Jaime said. "They've been rowing since dawn, resting two oars at a time. They'll be exhausted. Just now the sight of our sail has given them a burst of strength, but that will not last. We ought to be able to kill a good many of them."

Ser Cleos gaped. "But . . . there are *eighteen*."

"At the least. More likely twenty or twenty-five."

His cousin groaned. "We can't hope to defeat eighteen."

"Did I say we could? The best we can hope for is to die with swords in our hands." He was perfectly sincere. Jaime Lannister had never been afraid of death.

Brienne broke off rowing. Sweat had stuck strands of her flax-colored hair to her forehead, and her grimace made her look homelier than ever. "You are under my protection," she said, her voice so thick with anger that it was almost a growl.

He had to laugh at such fierceness. *She's the Hound with teats*, he thought. *Or would be, if she had any teats to speak of.* "Then protect me, wench. Or free me to protect myself."

The galley was skimming downriver, a great wooden dragonfly. The water around her was churned white by the furious action of her oars. She was gaining visibly, the men on her deck crowding forward as she came on. Metal glinted in their hands, and Jaime could see bows as well. *Archers*. He hated archers.

At the prow of the onrushing galley stood a stocky man with a bald head, bushy grey eyebrows, and brawny arms. Over his mail he wore a soiled white surcoat with a weeping willow embroidered in pale green, but his cloak was fastened with a silver trout. *Riverrun's captain of guards.* In his day Ser Robin Ryger had been a notably tenacious fighter, but his day was done; he was of an age with Hoster Tully, and had grown old with his lord.

When the boats were fifty yards apart, Jaime cupped his hands around his mouth and shouted back over the water. *"Come to wish me godspeed, Ser Robin?"*

"Come to take you back, Kingslayer," Ser Robin Ryger bellowed. *"How is it that you've lost your golden hair?"*

"*I hope to blind my enemies with the sheen off my head. It's worked well enough for you.*"

Ser Robin was unamused. The distance between skiff and galley had shrunk to forty yards. "*Throw your oars and your weapons into the river, and no one need be harmed.*"

Ser Cleos twisted around. "Jaime, tell him we were freed by Lady Catelyn ... an exchange of captives, lawful ..."

Jaime told him, for all the good it did. "*Catelyn Stark does not rule in Riverrun,*" Ser Robin shouted back. Four archers crowded into position on either side of him, two standing and two kneeling. "*Cast your swords into the water.*"

"*I have no sword,*" he returned, "*but if I did, I'd stick it through your belly and hack the balls off those four cravens.*"

A flight of arrows answered him. One thudded into the mast, two pierced the sail, and the fourth missed Jaime by a foot.

Another of the Red Fork's broad loops loomed before them. Brienne angled the skiff across the bend. The yard swung as they turned, their sail cracking as it filled with wind. Ahead a large island sat in midstream. The main channel flowed right. To the left a cutoff ran between the island and the high bluffs of the north shore. Brienne moved the tiller and the skiff sheared left, sail rippling. Jaime watched her eyes. *Pretty eyes*, he thought, *and calm*. He knew how to read a man's eyes. He knew what fear looked like. *She is determined, not desperate.*

Thirty yards behind, the galley was entering the bend. "Ser Cleos, take the tiller," the wench commanded. "Kingslayer, take an oar and keep us off the rocks."

"As my lady commands." An oar was not a sword, but the blade could break a man's face if well swung, and the shaft could be used to parry.

Ser Cleos shoved the oar into Jaime's hand and scrambled aft. They crossed the head of the island and turned sharply down the cutoff, sending a wash of water against the face of the bluff as the boat tilted. The island was densely wooded, a tangle of willows, oaks, and tall pines that cast deep shadows across the rushing water, hiding snags and the rotted trunks of drowned trees. To their left the bluff rose sheer and rocky, and at its foot the river foamed whitely around broken boulders and tumbles of rock fallen from the cliff face.

They passed from sunlight into shadow, hidden from the galley's view between the green wall of the trees and the stony grey-brown bluff. *A few moments' respite from the arrows*, Jaime thought, pushing them off a half-submerged boulder.

The skiff rocked. He heard a soft splash, and when he glanced around, Brienne was gone. A moment later he spied her again, pulling herself from the water at the base of the bluff. She waded through a shallow pool, scrambled over some rocks, and began to climb. Ser Cleos goggled, mouth open. *Fool*, thought Jaime. "Ignore the wench," he snapped at his cousin. "Steer."

They could see the sail moving behind the trees. The river galley came into full view at the top of the cutoff, twenty-five yards behind. Her bow swung hard as she came around, and a half-dozen arrows took flight, but all went well wide. The motion of the two boats was giving the archers difficulty, but Jaime knew they'd soon enough learn to compensate. Brienne was halfway up the cliff face, pulling herself from handhold to handhold. *Ryger's sure to see her, and once he does he'll have those bowmen bring her down.* Jaime decided to see if the old man's pride would make him stupid. "*Ser Robin,*" he shouted, "*hear me for a moment.*"

Ser Robin raised a hand, and his archers lowered their bows. "*Say what you will, Kingslayer, but say it quickly.*"

The skiff swung through a litter of broken stones as Jaime called out, "*I know a better way to settle this – single combat. You and I.*"

"*I was not born this morning, Lannister.*"

"*No, but you're like to die this afternoon.*" Jaime raised his hands so the other could see the manacles. "*I'll fight you in chains. What could you fear?*"

"*Not you, ser. If the choice were mine, I'd like nothing*

better, but I am commanded to bring you back alive if possible. Bowmen." He signaled them on. *"Notch. Draw. Loo –"*

The range was less than twenty yards. The archers could scarcely have missed, but as they pulled on their longbows a rain of pebbles cascaded down around them. Small stones rattled on their deck, bounced off their helms, and made splashes on both sides of the bow. Those who had wits enough to understand raised their eyes just as a boulder the size of a cow detached itself from the top of the bluff. Ser Robin shouted in dismay. The stone tumbled through the air, struck the face of the cliff, cracked in two, and smashed down on them. The larger piece snapped the mast, tore through the sail, sent two of the archers flying into the river, and crushed the leg of a rower as he bent over his oar. The rapidity with which the galley began to fill with water suggested that the smaller fragment had punched right through her hull. The oarsman's screams echoed off the bluff while the archers flailed wildly in the current. From the way they were splashing, neither man could swim. Jaime laughed.

By the time they emerged from the cutoff, the galley was foundering amongst pools, eddies, and snags, and Jaime Lannister had decided that the gods were good. Ser Robin and his thrice-damned archers would have a long wet walk back to Riverrun, and he was rid of the big homely wench as well. *I could not have planned it better myself. Once I'm free of these irons . . .*

Ser Cleos raised a shout. When Jaime looked up, Brienne was lumbering along the clifftop well ahead of them, having cut across a finger of land while they were following the bend in the river. She threw herself off the rock, and looked almost graceful as she folded into a dive. It would have been ungracious to hope that she would smash her head on a stone. Ser Cleos turned the skiff toward her. Thankfully, Jaime still had his oar. *One good swing when she comes paddling up and I'll be free of her.*

Instead he found himself stretching the oar out over the water. Brienne grabbed hold, and Jaime pulled her in. As he helped her into the skiff, water ran from her hair and dripped from her sodden clothing to pool on the deck. *She's even uglier wet. Who would have thought it possible?* "You're a bloody stupid wench," he told her. "We could have sailed on without you. I suppose you expect me to thank you?"

"I want none of your thanks, Kingslayer. I swore an oath to bring you safe to King's Landing."

"And you actually mean to keep it?" Jaime gave her his brightest smile. "Now there's a wonder."

CATELYN

Ser Desmond Grell had served House Tully all his life. He had been a squire when Catelyn was born, a knight when she learned to walk and ride and swim, master-at-arms by the day that she was wed. He had seen Lord Hoster's little Cat become a young woman, a great lord's lady, mother to a king. *And now he has seen me become a traitor as well.*

Her brother Edmure had named Ser Desmond castellan of Riverrun when he rode off to battle, so it fell to him to deal with her crime. To ease his discomfort he brought her father's steward with him, dour Utherydes Wayn. The two men stood and looked at her; Ser Desmond stout, red-faced, embarrassed, Utherydes grave, gaunt, melancholy. Each waited for the other to speak. *They have given their lives to my father's service, and I have repaid them with disgrace,* Catelyn thought wearily.

"Your sons," Ser Desmond said at last. "Maester Vyman told us. The poor lads. Terrible. Terrible. But . . ."

"We share your grief, my lady," said Utherydes Wayn. "All Riverrun mourns with you, but . . ."

"The news must have driven you mad," Ser Desmond broke in, "a madness of grief, a *mother's* madness, men will understand. You did not know . . ."

"I did," Catelyn said firmly. "I understood what I was doing and knew it was treasonous. If you fail to punish me, men will believe that we connived together to free Jaime Lannister. It was mine own act and mine alone, and I alone must answer for it. Put me in the Kingslayer's empty irons, and I will wear them proudly, if that is how it must be."

"Fetters?" The very word seemed to shock poor Ser Desmond. "For the king's mother, my lord's own daughter? Impossible."

"Mayhaps," said the steward Utherydes Wayn, "my lady would consent to be confined to her chambers until Ser Edmure returns. A time alone, to pray for her murdered sons?"

"Confined, aye," Ser Desmond said. "Confined to a tower cell, that would serve."

"If I am to be confined, let it be in my father's chambers, so I might comfort him in his last days."

Ser Desmond considered a moment. "Very well. You shall lack no comfort nor courtesy, but freedom of the castle is denied you. Visit the sept as you need, but elsewise remain in Lord Hoster's chambers until Lord Edmure returns."

"As you wish." Her brother was no lord while their father lived, but Catelyn did not correct him. "Set a guard on me if you must, but I give you my pledge that I shall attempt no escape."

Ser Desmond nodded, plainly glad to be done with his distasteful task, but sad-eyed Utherydes Wayn lingered a moment after the castellan took his leave. "It was a grave thing you did, my lady, but for naught. Ser Desmond has sent Ser Robin Ryger after them, to bring back the Kingslayer . . . or failing that, his head."

Catelyn had expected no less. *May the Warrior give strength to your sword arm, Brienne,* she prayed. She had done all she could; nothing remained but to hope.

Her things were moved into her father's bedchamber, dominated by the great canopied bed she had been born in, its pillars carved in the shapes of leaping trout. Her father himself had been moved half a turn down the stair, his sickbed placed to face the triangular balcony that opened off his solar, from whence he could see the rivers that he had always loved so well.

Lord Hoster was sleeping when Catelyn entered. She went out to the balcony and stood with one hand on the rough stone balustrade. Beyond the point of the castle the swift Tumblestone joined the placid Red Fork, and she could see a long way downriver. *If a striped sail comes from the east, it will be Ser Robin returning.* For the moment the surface of the waters was empty. She thanked the gods for that, and went back inside to sit with her father.

Catelyn could not say if Lord Hoster knew that she was there, or if her presence brought him any comfort, but it gave her solace to be with him. *What would you say if you knew my crime, Father?* she wondered. *Would you have done as I did, if it were Lysa and me in the hands of our enemies? Or would you condemn me too, and call it mother's madness?*

There was a smell of death about that room; a heavy smell, sweet and foul, clinging. It reminded her of the sons that she had lost, her sweet Bran and her little Rickon, slain at the hand of Theon Greyjoy, who had been Ned's ward. She still grieved for Ned, she would always grieve for Ned, but to have her babies taken as well . . . "It is a monstrous cruel thing to lose a child," she whispered softly, more to herself than to her father.

Lord Hoster's eyes opened. "*Tansy,*" he husked in a voice thick with pain.

He does not know me. Catelyn had grown accustomed to him taking her for her mother or her sister Lysa, but Tansy was a name strange to her. "It's Catelyn," she said. "It's Cat, Father."

"Forgive me . . . the blood . . . oh, please . . . Tansy . . ."

Could there have been another woman in her father's life? Some village maiden he had wronged when he was young, perhaps? *Could he have found comfort in some serving wench's arms after Mother died?* It was a queer thought, unsettling. Suddenly she felt as though she had not known her father at all. "Who is Tansy, my lord? Do you want me to send for her, Father? Where would I find the woman? Does she still live?"

Lord Hoster groaned. "*Dead.*" His hand groped for hers. "You'll have others . . . sweet babes, and trueborn."

Others? Catelyn thought. *Has he forgotten that Ned is gone? Is he still talking to Tansy, or is it me now, or Lysa, or Mother?*

When he coughed, the sputum came up bloody. He clutched her fingers. "... be a good wife and the gods will bless you ... sons ... trueborn sons ... *aaahhh.*" The sudden spasm of pain made Lord Hoster's hand tighten. His nails dug into her hand, and he gave a muffled scream.

Maester Vyman came quickly, to mix another dose of milk of the poppy and help his lord swallow it down. Soon enough, Lord Hoster Tully had fallen back into a heavy sleep.

"He was asking after a woman," said Cat. "Tansy."

"Tansy?" The maester looked at her blankly.

"You know no one by that name? A serving girl, a woman from some nearby village? Perhaps someone from years past?" Catelyn had been gone from Riverrun for a very long time.

"No, my lady. I can make inquiries, if you like. Utherydes Wayn would surely know if any such person ever served at Riverrun. Tansy, did you say? The smallfolk often name their daughters after flowers and herbs." The maester looked thoughtful. "There was a widow, I recall, she used to come to the castle looking for old shoes in need of new soles. Her name was Tansy, now that I think on it. Or was it Pansy? Some such. But she has not come for many years ..."

"Her name was Violet," said Catelyn, who remembered the old woman very well.

"Was it?" The maester looked apologetic. "My pardons, Lady Catelyn, but I may not stay. Ser Desmond has decreed that we are to speak to you only so far as our duties require."

"Then you must do as he commands." Catelyn could not blame Ser Desmond; she had given him small reason to trust her, and no doubt he feared that she might use the loyalty that many of the folk of Riverrun would still feel toward their lord's daughter to work some further mischief. *I am free of the war, at least,* she told herself, *if only for a little while.*

After the maester had gone, she donned a woolen cloak and stepped out onto the balcony once more. Sunlight shimmered on the rivers, gilding the surface of the waters as they rolled past the castle. Catelyn shaded her eyes against the glare, searching for a distant sail, dreading the sight of one. But there was nothing, and nothing meant that her hopes were still alive.

All that day she watched, and well into the night, until her legs ached from the standing. A raven came to the castle in late afternoon, flapping down on great black wings to the rookery. *Dark wings, dark words,* she thought, remembering the last bird that had come and the horror it had brought.

Maester Vyman returned at evenfall to minister to Lord Tully and bring Catelyn a modest supper of bread, cheese, and boiled beef with horseradish. "I spoke to Utherydes Wayn, my lady. He is quite certain that no woman by the name of Tansy has ever been at Riverrun during his service."

"There was a raven today, I saw. Has Jaime been taken again?" *Or slain, gods forbid?*

"No, my lady, we've had no word of the Kingslayer."

"Is it another battle, then? Is Edmure in difficulty? Or Robb? Please, be kind, put my fears at rest."

"My lady, I should not . . ." Vyman glanced about, as if to make certain no one else was in the room. "Lord Tywin has left the riverlands. All's quiet on the fords."

"Whence came the raven, then?"

"From the west," he answered, busying himself with Lord Hoster's bedclothes and avoiding her eyes.

"Was it news of Robb?"

He hesitated. "Yes, my lady."

"Something is wrong." She knew it from his manner. He was hiding something from her. "Tell me. Is it Robb? Is he hurt?" *Not dead, gods be good, please do not tell me that he is dead.*

"His Grace took a wound storming the Crag," Maester Vyman said, still evasive, "but writes that it is no cause for concern, and that he hopes to return soon."

"A wound? What sort of wound? How serious?"

"No cause for concern, he writes."

"All wounds concern me. Is he being cared for?"

"I am certain of it. The maester at the Crag will tend to him, I have no doubt."

"Where was he wounded?"

"My lady, I am commanded not to speak with you. I am sorry." Gathering up his potions, Vyman made a hurried exit, and once again Catelyn was left alone with her father. The milk of the poppy had done its work, and Lord Hoster was sunk in heavy sleep. A thin line of spittle ran down from one corner of his open mouth to dampen his pillow. Catelyn took a square of linen and wiped it away gently. When she touched him, Lord Hoster moaned. "Forgive me," he said, so softly she could scarcely hear the words. "Tansy . . . blood . . . the blood . . . gods be kind . . ."

His words disturbed her more than she could say, though she could make no sense of them. *Blood*, she thought. *Must it all come back to blood? Father, who was this woman, and what did you do to her that needs so much forgiveness?*

That night Catelyn slept fitfully, haunted by formless dreams of her children, the lost and the dead. Well before the break of day, she woke with her father's words echoing in her ears. *Sweet babes, and trueborn . . . why would he say that, unless . . . could he have fathered a bastard on this woman Tansy?* She could not believe it. Her brother Edmure, yes; it would not have surprised her to learn that Edmure had a dozen natural children. But not her father, not Lord Hoster Tully, never.

Could Tansy be some pet name he called Lysa, the way he called me Cat? Lord Hoster had mistaken her for her sister before. *You'll have others,* he said. *Sweet babes, and trueborn.* Lysa had miscarried five times, twice in the Eyrie, thrice at King's Landing . . . but never at Riverrun, where Lord Hoster would have been at hand to comfort her. *Never, unless . . . unless she was with child, that first time . . .*

She and her sister had been married on the same day, and left in their father's care when their new husbands had ridden off to rejoin Robert's rebellion. Afterward, when their moon blood did not come at the accustomed time, Lysa had gushed happily of the sons she was certain they carried. "Your son will be heir to Winterfell and mine to the Eyrie. Oh, they'll be the best of friends, like your Ned and Lord Robert. They'll be more brothers than cousins, truly, I just know it." *She was so happy.*

But Lysa's blood had come not long after, and all the joy had gone out of her. Catelyn had always thought that Lysa had simply been a little late, but if she *had* been with child . . .

She remembered the first time she gave her sister Robb to hold; small, red-faced, and squalling, but strong even then, full of life. No sooner had Catelyn placed the babe in her sister's arms than Lysa's face dissolved into tears. Hurriedly she had thrust the baby back at Catelyn and fled.

If she had lost a child before, that might explain Father's words, and much else besides . . . Lysa's match with Lord Arryn had been hastily arranged, and Jon was an old man even then, older than their father. *An old man without an heir.* His first two wives had left him childless, his brother's son had been murdered with Brandon Stark in King's Landing, his gallant cousin had died in the Battle of the Bells. He needed a young wife if House Arryn was to continue . . . *a young wife known to be fertile.*

Catelyn rose, threw on a robe, and descended the steps to the darkened solar to stand over her father. A sense of helpless dread filled her. "Father," she said, "Father, I know what you did." She was no longer an innocent bride with a head full of dreams. She was a widow, a traitor, a grieving mother, and wise, wise in the ways of the world. "You made him take her," she whispered. "Lysa was the price Jon Arryn had to pay for the swords and spears of House Tully."

Small wonder her sister's marriage had been so loveless. The Arryns were proud, and prickly of their honor. Lord Jon might wed Lysa to bind the Tullys to the cause of the rebellion, and in hopes of a son, but it would have been hard for him to love a woman who came to his bed soiled and unwilling. He would have been kind, no doubt; dutiful, yes; but Lysa needed warmth.

The next day, as she broke her fast, Catelyn asked for quill and paper and began a letter to her sister in the Vale of Arryn. She told Lysa of Bran and Rickon, struggling with the words, but mostly she wrote of their father. *His thoughts are all of the wrong he did you, now that his time grows short. Maester Vyman says he dare not make the milk of the poppy any stronger. It is time for Father to lay down his sword and shield. It is time for him to rest. Yet he fights on grimly, will not yield. It is for your sake, I think. He needs your forgiveness. The war has made the road from the Eyrie to Riverrun dangerous to travel, I know, but surely a strong force of knights could see you safely through the Mountains of the Moon? A hundred men, or a thousand? And if you cannot come, will you not write him at least? A few words of love, so he might die in peace? Write what you will, and I shall read it to him, and ease his way.*

Even as she set the quill aside and asked for sealing wax, Catelyn sensed that the letter was like to be too little and too late. Maester Vyman did not believe Lord Hoster would linger long enough for a raven to reach the Eyrie and return. *Though he has said much the same before* . . . Tully men did not surrender easily, no matter the odds. After she entrusted the parchment to the maester's care, Catelyn went to the sept and lit a candle to the Father Above for her own father's sake, a second to the Crone, who had let the first raven into the world when she peered through the door of death, and a third to the Mother, for Lysa and all the children they had both lost.

Later that day, as she sat at Lord Hoster's bedside with a book, reading the same passage over and over, she heard the sound of loud voices and a trumpet's blare. *Ser Robin*, she thought at once, flinching. She went to the balcony, but there was nothing to be seen out on the rivers, but she could hear the voices more clearly from outside, the sound of many horses, the clink of armor, and here and there a cheer. Catelyn made her way up the winding stairs to the roof of the keep. *Ser Desmond did not forbid me the roof*, she told herself as she climbed.

The sounds were coming from the far side of the castle, by the main gate. A knot of men stood before the portcullis as it rose in jerks and starts, and in the fields beyond, outside the castle, were several hundred riders. When the wind blew, it lifted their banners, and she trembled in relief at the sight of the leaping trout of Riverrun. *Edmure.*

It was two hours before he saw fit to come to her. By then the castle rang to the sound of noisy reunions as men embraced the women and children they had left behind. Three ravens had risen from the rookery, black wings beating at the air as they took flight. Catelyn watched them from her father's balcony. She had washed her hair, changed her clothing, and prepared herself for her brother's reproaches . . . but even so, the waiting was hard.

When at last she heard sounds outside her door, she sat and folded her hands in her lap. Dried red mud spattered Edmure's boots, greaves, and surcoat. To look at him, you would never know he had won his battle. He was thin and drawn, with pale cheeks, unkempt beard, and too-bright eyes.

"Edmure," Catelyn said, worried, "you look unwell. Has something happened? Have the Lannisters crossed the river?"

"I threw them back. Lord Tywin, Gregor Clegane, Addam Marbrand, I turned them away. Stannis, though . . ." He grimaced.

"Stannis? What of Stannis?"

"He lost the battle at King's Landing," Edmure said unhappily. "His fleet was burned, his army routed."

A Lannister victory was ill tidings, but Catelyn could not share her brother's obvious dismay. She still had nightmares about the shadow she had seen slide across Renly's tent and the way the blood had come flowing out through the steel of his gorget. "Stannis was no more a friend than Lord Tywin."

"You do not understand. Highgarden has declared

for Joffrey. Dorne as well. All the south." His mouth tightened. "And *you* see fit to loose the Kingslayer. You had no right."

"I had a mother's right." Her voice was calm, though the news about Highgarden was a savage blow to Robb's hopes. She could not think about that now, though.

"No right," Edmure repeated. "He was Robb's captive, your *king's* captive, and Robb charged me to keep him safe."

"Brienne will keep him safe. She swore it on her sword."

"That *woman?"*

"She will deliver Jaime to King's Landing, and bring Arya and Sansa back to us safely."

"Cersei will never give them up."

"Not Cersei. Tyrion. He swore it, in open court. And the Kingslayer swore it as well."

"Jaime's word is worthless. As for the Imp, it's said he took an axe in the head during the battle. He'll be dead before your Brienne reaches King's Landing, if she ever does."

"Dead?" *Could the gods truly be so merciless!* She had made Jaime swear a hundred oaths, but it was his brother's promise she had pinned her hopes on.

Edmure was blind to her distress. "Jaime was *my* charge, and I mean to have him back. I've sent ravens –"

"Ravens to whom? How many?"

"Three," he said, "so the message will be certain to reach Lord Bolton. By river or road, the way from Riverrun to King's Landing must needs take them close by Harrenhal."

"Harrenhal." The very word seemed to darken the room. Horror thickened her voice as she said, "Edmure, do you know what you have done?"

"Have no fear, I left your part out. I wrote that Jaime had escaped, and offered a thousand dragons for his recapture."

Worse and worse, Catelyn thought in despair. *My brother is a fool.* Unbidden, unwanted, tears filled her eyes. "If this was an escape," she said softly, "and not an exchange of hostages, why should the Lannisters give my daughters to Brienne?"

"It will never come to that. The Kingslayer will be returned to us, I have made certain of it."

"All you have made certain is that I shall never see my daughters again. Brienne might have gotten him to King's Landing safely . . . *so long as no one was hunting for them.* But now . . ." Catelyn could not go on. "Leave me, Edmure." She had no right to command him, here in the castle that would soon be his, yet her tone would brook no argument "Leave me to Father and my grief, I have no more to say to you. Go. *Go.*" All she wanted was to lie down, to close her eyes and sleep, and pray no dreams would come.

ARYA

The sky was as black as the walls of Harrenhal behind them, and the rain fell soft and steady, muffling the sound of their horses' hooves and running down their faces.

They rode north, away from the lake, following a rutted farm road across the torn fields and into the woods and streams. Arya took the lead, kicking her stolen horse to a brisk heedless trot until the trees closed in around her. Hot Pie and Gendry followed as best they could. Wolves howled off in the distance, and she could hear Hot Pie's heavy breathing. No one spoke. From time to time Arya glanced over her shoulder, to make sure the two boys had not fallen too far behind, and to see if they were being pursued.

They would be, she knew. She had stolen three horses from the stables and a map and a dagger from Roose Bolton's own solar, and killed a guard on the postern gate, slitting his throat when he knelt to pick up the worn iron coin that Jaqen H'ghar had given her. Someone would find him lying dead in his own blood, and then the hue and cry would go up. They would wake Lord Bolton and search Harrenhal from crenel to cellar, and when they did they would find the map and the dagger missing, along with some swords from the armory, bread and cheese from the kitchens, a baker boy, a 'prentice smith, and a cupbearer called Nan . . . or Weasel, or Arry, depending on who you asked.

The Lord of the Dreadfort would not come after them himself. Roose Bolton would stay abed, his pasty flesh dotted with leeches, giving commands in his whispery soft voice. His man Walton might lead the hunt, the one they called Steelshanks for the greaves he always wore on his long legs. Or perhaps it would be slobbery Vargo Hoat and his sellswords, who named themselves the Brave Companions. Others called them Bloody Mummers (though never to their faces), and sometimes the Footmen, for Lord Vargo's habit of cutting off the hands and feet of men who displeased him.

If they catch us, he'll cut off our hands and feet, Arya thought, *and then Roose Bolton will peel the skin off us.* She was still dressed in her page's garb, and on the breast over her heart was sewn Lord Bolton's sigil, the flayed man of the Dreadfort.

Every time she looked back, she half expected to see a blaze of torches pouring out the distant gates of Harrenhal or rushing along the tops of its huge high walls, but there was nothing. Harrenhal slept on, until it was lost in darkness and hidden behind the trees.

When they crossed the first stream, Arya turned her horse aside and led them off the road, following the twisting course of the water for a quarter-mile before finally scrambling out and up a stony bank. If the hunters brought dogs, that might throw them off the scent, she hoped. They could not stay on the road. *There is death on the road,* she told herself, *death on all the roads.*

Gendry and Hot Pie did not question her choice. She had the map, after all, and Hot Pie seemed almost as terrified of her as of the men who might be coming after them. He had seen the guard she'd killed. *It's better if he's scared of me,* she told herself. *That way he'll do like I say, instead of something stupid.*

She should be more frightened herself, she knew. She was only ten, a skinny girl on a stolen horse with a dark forest ahead of her and men behind who would gladly cut off her feet. Yet somehow she felt calmer than she ever had in Harrenhal. The rain had washed the guard's blood off her fingers, she wore a sword across her back, wolves were prowling through the dark like lean grey shadows, and Arya Stark was unafraid. *Fear cuts deeper than swords*, she whispered under her breath, the words that Syrio Forel had taught her, and Jaqen's words too, *valar morghulis*.

The rain stopped and started again and stopped once more and started, but they had good cloaks to keep the water off. Arya kept them moving at a slow steady pace. It was too black beneath the trees to ride any faster; the boys were no horsemen, neither one, and the soft broken ground was treacherous with half-buried roots and hidden stones. They crossed another road, its deep ruts filled with runoff, but Arya shunned it. Up and down the rolling hills she took them, through brambles and briars and tangles of underbrush, along the bottoms of narrow gullies where branches heavy with wet leaves slapped at their faces as they passed.

Gendry's mare lost her footing in the mud once, going down hard on her hindquarters and spilling him from the saddle, but neither horse nor rider was hurt, and Gendry got that stubborn look on his face and mounted right up again. Not long after, they came upon three wolves devouring the corpse of a fawn. When Hot Pie's horse caught the scent, he shied and bolted. Two of the wolves fled as well, but the third raised his head and bared his teeth, prepared to defend his kill. "Back off," Arya told Gendry. "Slow, so you don't spook him." They edged their mounts away, until the wolf and his feast were no longer in sight. Only then did she swing about to ride after Hot Pie, who was clinging desperately to the saddle as he crashed through the trees.

Later they passed through a burned village, threading their way carefully between the shells of blackened hovels and past the bones of a dozen dead men hanging from a row of apple trees. When Hot Pie saw them he began to pray, a thin whispered plea for the Mother's mercy, repeated over and over. Arya looked up at the fleshless dead in their wet rotting clothes and said her own prayer.

Ser Gregor, it went, *Dunsen, Polliver, Raff the Sweetling. The Tickler and the Hound. Ser Ilyn, Ser Meryn, King Joffrey, Queen Cersei.* She ended it with *valar morghulis*, touched Jaqen's coin where it nestled under her belt, and then reached up and plucked an apple from among the dead men as she rode beneath them. It was mushy and overripe, but she ate it, worms and all.

That was the day without a dawn. Slowly the sky lightened around them, but they never saw the sun. Black turned to grey, and colors crept timidly back into the world. The soldier pines were dressed in somber greens, the broadleafs in russets and faded golds already beginning to brown. They stopped long enough to water the horses and eat a cold, quick breakfast, ripping apart a loaf of the bread that Hot Pie had stolen from the kitchens and passing chunks of hard yellow cheese from hand to hand.

"Do you know where we're going?" Gendry asked her.

"North," said Arya.

Hot Pie peered around uncertainly. "Which way is north?"

She used her cheese to point. "That way."

"But there's no sun. How do you know?"

"From the moss. See how it grows mostly on one side of the trees? That's south."

"What do we want with the north?" Gendry wanted to know.

"The Trident." Arya unrolled the stolen map to show them. "See? Once we reach the Trident, all we need to do is follow it upstream till we come to Riverrun, here." Her finger traced the path. "It's a long way, but we can't get lost so long as we keep to the river."

Hot Pie blinked at the map. "Which one is Riverrun?"

Riverrun was painted as a castle tower, in the fork between the flowing blue lines of two rivers, the Tumblestone and the Red Fork. "There." She touched it. "*Riverrun*, it reads."

"You can read writing?" he said to her, wonderingly, as if she'd said she could walk on water.

She nodded. "We'll be safe once we reach Riverrun."

"We will? Why?"

Because Riverrun is my grandfather's castle, and my brother Robb will be there, she wanted to say. She bit her lip and rolled up the map. "We just will. But only if we get there." She was the first one back in the saddle. It made her feel bad to hide the truth from Hot Pie, but she did not trust him with her secret. Gendry knew, but that was different. Gendry had his own secret, though even he didn't seem to know what it was.

That day Arya quickened their pace, keeping the horses to a trot as long as she dared, and sometimes spurring to a gallop when she spied a flat stretch of field before them. That was seldom enough, though; the ground was growing hillier as they went. The hills were not high, nor especially steep, but there seemed to be no end of them, and they soon grew tired of climbing up one and down the other, and found themselves following the lay of the land, along streambeds and through a maze of shallow wooded valleys where the trees made a solid canopy overhead.

From time to time she sent Hot Pie and Gendry on while she doubled back to try to confuse their trail, listening all the while for the first sign of pursuit. *Too slow*, she thought to herself, chewing her lip, *we're going too slow, they'll catch us for certain*. Once, from the crest of a ridge, she spied dark shapes crossing a stream in the valley behind them, and for half a heartbeat she feared that Roose Bolton's riders were on them, but when she looked again she realized they were only a pack of wolves. She cupped her hands around her mouth and howled down at them, "*Ahooooooooo, ahooooooooo*." When the largest of the wolves lifted its head and howled back, the sound made Arya shiver.

By midday Hot Pie had begun to complain. His arse was sore, he told them, and the saddle was rubbing him raw inside his legs, and besides he had to get some sleep. "I'm so tired I'm going to fall off the horse."

Arya looked at Gendry. "If he falls off, who do you think will find him first, the wolves or the Mummers?"

"The wolves," said Gendry. "Better noses."

Hot Pie opened his mouth and closed it. He did not fall off his horse. The rain began again a short time later. They still had not seen so much as a glimpse of the sun. It was growing colder, and pale white mists were threading between the pines and blowing across the bare burned fields.

Gendry was having almost as bad a time of it as Hot Pie, though he was too stubborn to complain. He sat awkwardly in the saddle, a determined look on his face beneath his shaggy black hair, but Arya could tell he was no horseman. *I should have remembered*, she thought to herself. She had been riding as long as she could remember, ponies when she was little and later horses, but Gendry and Hot Pie were city-born, and in the city smallfolk walked. Yoren had given them mounts when he took them from King's Landing, but sitting on a donkey and plodding up the kingsroad behind a wagon was one thing. Guiding a hunting horse through wild woods and burned fields was something else.

She would make much better time on her own, Arya knew, but she could not leave them. They were her pack, her friends, the only living friends that remained to her, and if not for her they would still be safe at Harrenhal, Gendry sweating at his forge and Hot Pie in the kitchens. *If the Mummers catch us, I'll tell them that I'm Ned Stark's daughter and sister to the King in the North. I'll command them to take me to my brother, and to do no harm to Hot Pie and Gendry.* They might not believe her, though, and even if they did . . . Lord Bolton was her brother's bannerman, but he frightened her all the same. *I won't let them take us*, she vowed silently, reaching back over her shoulder to touch the hilt of the sword that Gendry had stolen for her. *I won't.*

Late that afternoon, they emerged from beneath the trees and found themselves on the banks of a river. Hot Pie gave a whoop of delight. "The *Trident*! Now all we have to do is go upstream, like you said. We're almost there!"

Arya chewed her lip. "I don't think this is the Trident." The river was swollen by the rain, but even so it couldn't be much more than thirty feet across. She remembered the Trident as being much wider. "It's too little to be the

Trident," she told them, "and we didn't come far enough."

"Yes we did," Hot Pie insisted. "We rode all day, and hardly stopped at all. We must have come a long way."

"Let's have a look at that map again," said Gendry.

Arya dismounted, took out the map, unrolled it. The rain pattered against the sheepskin and ran off in rivulets. "We're someplace here, I think," she said, pointing, as the boys peered over her shoulders.

"But," said Hot Pie, "that's hardly any ways at all. See, Harrenhal's there by your finger, you're almost *touching* it. And we rode all day!"

"There's miles and miles before we reach the Trident," she said. "We won't be there for *days*. This must be some different river, one of these, see." She showed him some of the thinner blue lines the mapmaker had painted in, each with a name painted in fine script beneath it. "The Darry, the Greenapple, the Maiden . . . here, this one, the Little Willow, it might be that."

Hot Pie looked from the line to the river. "It doesn't look so little to me."

Gendry was frowning as well. "The one you're pointing at runs into that other one, see."

"The Big Willow," she read.

"The Big Willow, then. See, and the Big Willow runs into the Trident, so we could follow the one to the other, but we'd need to go downstream, not up. Only if this river *isn't* the Little Willow, if it's this other one here . . ."

"Rippledown Rill," Arya read.

"See, it loops around and flows down toward the lake, back to Harrenhal." He traced the line with a finger.

Hot Pie's eyes grew wide. "*No!* They'll kill us for sure."

"We have to know which river this is," declared Gendry, in his stubbornest voice. "We have to know."

"Well, we *don't*." The map might have names written beside the blue lines, but no one had written a name on the riverbank. "We won't go up- *or* downstream," she decided, rolling up the map. "We'll cross and keep going north, like we were."

"Can horses swim?" asked Hot Pie. "It looks *deep*, Arry. What if there are snakes?"

"Are you sure we're going north?" asked Gendry. "All these hills . . . if we got turned around . . ."

"The moss on the trees –"

He pointed to a nearby tree. "That tree's got moss on three sides, and that next one has no moss at all. We could be lost, just riding around in a circle."

"We could be," said Arya, "but I'm going to cross the river anyway. You can come or you can stay here." She climbed back into the saddle, ignoring the both of them. If they didn't want to follow, they could find Riverrun on their own, though more likely the Mummers would just find them.

She had to ride a good half mile along the bank before she finally found a place where it looked as though it might be safe to cross, and even then her mare was reluctant to enter the water. The river, whatever its name, was running brown and fast, and the deep part in the middle came up past the horse's belly. Water filled her boots, but she pressed in her heels all the same and climbed out on the far bank. From behind she heard splashing, and a mare's nervous whinny. *They followed, then. Good.* She turned to watch as the boys struggled across and emerged dripping beside her. "It wasn't the Trident," she told them. "It *wasn't*."

The next river was shallower and easier to ford. That one wasn't the Trident either, and no one argued with her when she told them they would cross it.

Dusk was settling as they stopped to rest the horses once more and share another meal of bread and cheese. "I'm cold and wet," Hot Pie complained. "We're a long way from Harrenhal now, for sure. We could have us a fire –"

"*NO!*" Arya and Gendry both said, at the exact same instant. Hot Pie quailed a little. Arya gave Gendry a sideways look. *He said it with me, like Jon used to do, back in Winterfell.* She missed Jon Snow the most of all her brothers.

"Could we sleep at least?" Hot Pie asked. "I'm so tired, Arry, and my arse is sore. I think I've got blisters."

"You'll have more than that if you're caught," she said. "We've got to keep going. We've *got* to."

"But it's almost dark, and you can't even see the moon."

"Get back on your horse."

Plodding along at a slow walking pace as the light faded around them, Arya found her own exhaustion weighing heavy on her. She needed sleep as much as Hot Pie, but they dare not. If they slept, they might open their eyes to find Vargo Hoat standing over them with Shagwell the Fool and Faithful Urswyck and Rorge and Biter and Septon Utt and all his other monsters.

Yet after a while the motion of her horse became as soothing as the rocking of a cradle, and Arya found her eyes growing heavy. She let them close, just for an instant, then snapped them wide again. *I can't go to sleep,* she screamed at herself silently, *I can't, I can't.* She knuckled at her eye and rubbed it hard to keep it open, clutching the reins tightly and kicking her mount to a canter. But neither she nor the horse could sustain the pace, and it was only a few moments before they fell back to a walk again, and a few more until her eyes closed a second time. This time they did not open quite so quickly.

When they did, she found that her horse had come to a stop and was nibbling at a tuft of grass, while Gendry was shaking her arm. "You fell asleep," he told her.

"I was just resting my eyes."

"You were resting them a long while, then. Your horse was wandering in a circle, but it wasn't till she stopped that I realized you were sleeping. Hot Pie's just as bad, he rode into a tree limb and got knocked off, you should have heard him yell. Even *that* didn't wake you up. You need to stop and sleep."

"I can keep going as long as you can." She yawned.

"Liar," he said. "You keep going if you want to be stupid, but I'm stopping. I'll take the first watch. You sleep."

"What about Hot Pie?"

Gendry pointed. Hot Pie was already on the ground, curled up beneath his cloak on a bed of damp leaves and snoring softly. He had a big wedge of cheese in one fist, but it looked as though he had fallen asleep between bites.

It was no good arguing, Arya realized; Gendry had the right of it. *The Mummers will need to sleep too*, she told herself, hoping it was true. She was so weary it was a struggle even to get down from the saddle, but she remembered to hobble her horse before finding a place beneath a beech tree. The ground was hard and damp. She wondered how long it would be before she slept in a bed again, with hot food and a fire to warm her. The last thing she did before closing her eyes was unsheathe her sword and lay it down beside her. "Ser Gregor," she whispered, yawning. "Dunsen, Polliver, Raff the Sweetling. The Tickler and . . . the Tickler . . . the Hound . . ."

Her dreams were red and savage. The Mummers were in them, four at least, a pale Lyseni and a dark brutal axeman from Ib, the scarred Dothraki horse lord called Iggo and a Dornishman whose name she never knew. On and on they came, riding through the rain in rusting mail and wet leather, swords and axe clanking against their saddles. They thought they were hunting her, she knew with all the strange sharp certainty of dreams, but they were wrong. She was hunting them.

She was no little girl in the dream; she was a wolf, huge and powerful, and when she emerged from beneath the trees in front of them and bared her teeth in a low rumbling growl, she could smell the rank stench of fear from horse and man alike. The Lyseni's mount reared and screamed in terror, and the others shouted at one another in mantalk, but before they could act the other wolves came hurtling from the darkness and the rain, a great pack of them, gaunt and wet and silent.

The fight was short but bloody. The hairy man went down as he unslung his axe, the dark one died stringing an arrow, and the pale man from Lys tried to bolt. Her brothers and sisters ran him down, turning him again and again, coming at him from all sides, snapping at the legs of his horse and tearing the throat from the rider when he came crashing to the earth.

Only the belled man stood his ground. His horse kicked

in the head of one of her sisters, and he cut another almost in half with his curved silvery claw as his hair tinkled softly.

Filled with rage, she leapt onto his back, knocking him head-first from his saddle. Her jaws locked on his arm as they fell, her teeth sinking through the leather and wool and soft flesh. When they landed she gave a savage jerk with her head and ripped the limb loose from his shoulder. Exulting, she shook it back and forth in her mouth, scattering the warm red droplets amidst the cold black rain.

TYRION

He woke to the creak of old iron hinges.

"Who?" he croaked. At least he had his voice back, raw and hoarse though it was. The fever was still on him, and Tyrion had no notion of the hour. How long had he slept this time? He was so weak, so damnably weak. "Who?" he called again, more loudly. Torchlight spilled through the open door, but within the chamber the only light came from the stub of a candle beside his bed.

When he saw a shape moving toward him, Tyrion shivered. Here in Maegor's Holdfast, every servant was in the queen's pay, so any visitor might be another of Cersei's catspaws, sent to finish the work Ser Mandon had begun.

Then the man stepped into the candlelight, got a good look at the dwarf's pale face, and chortled. "Cut yourself shaving, did you?"

Tyrion's fingers went to the great gash that ran from above one eye down to his jaw, across what remained of his nose. The proud flesh was still raw and warm to the touch. "With a fearful big razor, yes."

Bronn's coal-black hair was freshly washed and brushed straight back from the hard lines of his face, and he was dressed in high boots of soft, tooled leather, a wide belt studded with nuggets of silver, and a cloak of pale green silk. Across the dark grey wool of his doublet, a burning chain was embroidered diagonally in bright green thread.

"Where have you been?" Tyrion demanded of him. "I sent for you . . . it must have been a fortnight ago."

"Four days ago, more like," the sellsword said, "and I've been here twice, and found you dead to the world."

"Not dead. Though my sweet sister did try." Perhaps he should not have said that aloud, but Tyrion was past caring. Cersei was behind Ser Mandon's attempt to kill him, he knew that in his gut. "What's that ugly thing on your chest?"

Bronn grinned. "My knightly sigil. A flaming chain, green, on a smoke-grey field. By your lord father's command, I'm Ser Bronn of the Blackwater now, Imp. See you don't forget it."

Tyrion put his hands on the featherbed and squirmed back a few inches, against the pillows. "I was the one who promised you knighthood, remember?" He had liked that *"by your lord father's command"* not at all. Lord Tywin had wasted little time. Moving his son from the Tower of the Hand to claim it for himself was a message anyone could read, and this was another. "I lose half my nose and you gain a knighthood. The gods have a deal to answer for." His voice was sour. "Did my father dub you himself?"

"No. Them of us as survived the fight at the winch towers got ourselves dabbed by the High Septon and dubbed by the Kingsguard. Took half the bloody day, with only three of the White Swords left to do the honors."

"I knew Ser Mandon died in the battle." *Shoved into the river by Pod, half a heartbeat before the treacherous bastard could drive his sword through my heart.* "Who else was lost?"

"The Hound," said Bronn. "Not dead, only gone. The gold cloaks say he turned craven and you led a sortie in his place."

Not one of my better notions. Tyrion could feel the scar tissue pull tight when he frowned. He waved Bronn toward a chair. "My sister has mistaken me for a mushroom. She keeps me in the dark and feeds me shit. Pod's a good lad, but the knot in his tongue is the size of Casterly

Rock, and I don't trust half of what he tells me. I sent him to bring Ser Jacelyn and he came back and told me he's dead."

"Him, and thousands more." Bronn sat.

"How?" Tyrion demanded, feeling that much sicker.

"During the battle. Your sister sent the Kettleblacks to fetch the king back to the Red Keep, the way I hear it. When the gold cloaks saw him leaving, half of them decided they'd leave with him. Ironhand put himself in their path and tried to order them back to the walls. They say Bywater was blistering them good and almost had 'em ready to turn when someone put an arrow through his neck. He didn't seem so fearsome then, so they dragged him off his horse and killed him."

Another debt to lay at Cersei's door. "My nephew," he said, "Joffrey. Was he in any danger?"

"No more'n some, and less than most."

"Had he suffered any harm? Taken a wound? Mussed his hair, stubbed his toe, cracked a nail?"

"Not as I heard."

"I warned Cersei what would happen. Who commands the gold cloaks now?"

"Your lord father's given them to one of his westermen, some knight named Addam Marbrand."

In most cases the gold cloaks would have resented having an outsider placed over them, but Ser Addam Marbrand was a shrewd choice. Like Jaime, he was the sort of man other men liked to follow. *I have lost the City Watch.* "I sent Pod looking for Shagga, but he's had no luck."

"The Stone Crows are still in the kingswood. Shagga seems to have taken a fancy to the place. Timett led the Burned Men home, with all the plunder they took from Stannis's camp after the fighting. Chella turned up with a dozen Black Ears at the River Gate one morning, but your father's red cloaks chased them off while the Kingslanders threw dung and cheered."

Ingrates. The Black Ears died for them. Whilst Tyrion lay drugged and dreaming, his own blood had pulled his claws out, one by one. "I want you to go to my sister. Her precious son made it through the battle unscathed,

so Cersei has no more need of a hostage. She swore to free
Alayaya once – "

"She did. Eight, nine days ago, after the whipping."

Tyrion shoved himself up higher, ignoring the sudden
stab of pain through his shoulder. *"Whipping?"*

"They tied her to a post in the yard and scourged her,
then shoved her out the gate naked and bloody."

She was learning to read, Tyrion thought, absurdly.
Across his face the scar stretched tight, and for a moment
it felt as though his head would burst with rage. Alayaya
was a whore, true enough, but a sweeter, braver, more
innocent girl he had seldom met. Tyrion had never
touched her; she had been no more than a veil, to hide
Shae. In his carelessness, he had never thought what the
role might cost her. "I promised my sister I would treat
Tommen as she treated Alayaya," he remembered aloud.
He felt as though he might retch. "How can I scourge an
eight-year-old boy?" *But if I don't, Cersei wins.*

"You don't have Tommen," Bronn said bluntly. "Once
she learned that Ironhand was dead, the queen sent the
Kettleblacks after him, and no one at Rosby had the balls
to say them nay."

Another blow; yet a relief as well, he must admit it. He
was fond of Tommen. "The Kettleblacks were supposed to
be ours," he reminded Bronn with more than a touch of
irritation.

"They were, so long as I could give them two of your
pennies for every one they had from the queen, but now
she's raised the stakes. Osney and Osfryd were made
knights after the battle, same as me. Gods know what for,
no one saw them do any fighting."

*My hirelings betray me, my friends are scourged and
shamed, and I lie here rotting*, Tyrion thought. *I thought
I won the bloody battle. Is this what triumph tastes like?*
"Is it true that Stannis was put to rout by Renly's ghost?"

Bronn smiled thinly. "From the winch towers, all we
saw was banners in the mud and men throwing down their
spears to run, but there's hundreds in the pot shops and
brothels who'll tell you how they saw Lord Renly kill this
one or that one. Most of Stannis's host had been Renly's

to start, and they went right back over at the sight of him in that shiny green armor."

After all his planning, after the sortie and the bridge of ships, after getting his face slashed in two, Tyrion had been eclipsed by a dead man. *If indeed Renly is dead.* Something else he would need to look into. "How did Stannis escape?"

"His Lyseni kept their galleys out in the bay, beyond your chain. When the battle turned bad, they put in along the bay shore and took off as many as they could. Men were killing each other to get aboard, toward the end."

"What of Robb Stark, what has he been doing?"

"There's some of his wolves burning their way down toward Duskendale. Your father's sending this Lord Tarly to sort them out. I'd half a mind to join him. It's said he's a good soldier, and openhanded with the plunder."

The thought of losing Bronn was the final straw. "No. Your place is here. You're the captain of the Hand's guard."

"You're not the Hand," Bronn reminded him sharply. "Your father is, and he's got his own bloody guard."

"What happened to all the men you hired for me?"

"Some died at the winch towers. That uncle of yours, Ser Kevan, he paid the rest of us and tossed us out."

"How good of him," Tyrion said acidly. "Does that mean you've lost your taste for gold?"

"Not bloody likely."

"Good," said Tyrion, "because as it happens, I still have need of you. What do you know of Ser Mandon Moore?"

Bronn laughed. "I know he's bloody well drowned."

"I owe him a great debt, but how to pay it?" He touched his face, feeling the scar. "I know precious little of the man, if truth be told."

"He had eyes like a fish and he wore a white cloak. What else do you need to know?"

"Everything," said Tyrion, "for a start." What he wanted was proof that Ser Mandon had been Cersei's, but he dare not say so aloud. In the Red Keep a man did best to hold his tongue. There were rats in the walls, and little birds who talked too much, and spiders. "Help me up," he said, struggling with the bedclothes. "It's time I paid a call on my father, and past time I let myself be seen again."

"Such a pretty sight," mocked Bronn.

"What's half a nose, on a face like mine? But speaking of pretty, is Margaery Tyrell in King's Landing yet?"

"No. She's coming, though, and the city's mad with love for her. The Tyrells have been carting food up from Highgarden and giving it away in her name. Hundreds of wayns each day. There's thousands of Tyrell men swaggering about with little golden roses sewn on their doublets, and not a one is buying his own wine. Wife, widow, or whore, the women are all giving up their virtue to every peach-fuzz boy with a gold rose on his teat."

They spit on me, and buy drinks for the Tyrells. Tyrion slid from the bed to the floor. His legs turned wobbly beneath him, the room spun, and he had to grasp Bronn's arm to keep from pitching headlong into the rushes. "*Pod!*" he shouted. "Podrick Payne! Where in the seven hells are you?" Pain gnawed at him like a toothless dog. Tyrion hated weakness, especially his own. It shamed him, and shame made him angry. "Pod, *get in here!*"

The boy came running. When he saw Tyrion standing and clutching Bronn's arm, he gaped at them. "My lord. You stood. Is that ... do you ... do you need wine? Dreamwine? Should I get the maester? He said you must stay. Abed, I mean."

"I have stayed abed too long. Bring me some clean garb."

"Garb?"

How the boy could be so clearheaded and resourceful in battle and so confused at all other times Tyrion could never comprehend. "Clothing," he repeated. "Tunic, doublet, breeches, hose. For me. To dress in. So I can leave this bloody cell."

It took all three of them to clothe him. Hideous though his face might be, the worst of his wounds was the one at the juncture of shoulder and arm, where his own mail had been driven back into his armpit by an arrow. Pus and blood still seeped from the discolored flesh whenever Maester Frenken changed his dressing, and any movement sent a stab of agony through him.

In the end, Tyrion settled for a pair of breeches and an oversized bed robe that hung loosely about his shoulders. Bronn yanked his boots onto his feet while Pod went in search of a stick for him to lean on. He drank a cup of dreamwine to fortify himself. The wine was sweetened with honey, with just enough of the poppy to make his wounds bearable for a time.

Even so, he was dizzy by the time he turned the latch, and the descent down the twisting stone steps made his legs tremble. He walked with the stick in one hand and the other on Pod's shoulder. A serving girl was coming up as they were going down. She stared at them with wide white eyes, as if she were looking at a ghost. *The dwarf has risen from the dead,* Tyrion thought. *And look, he's uglier than ever, run tell your friends.*

Maegor's Holdfast was the strongest place in the Red Keep, a castle within the castle, surrounded by a deep dry moat lined with spikes. The drawbridge was up for the night when they reached the door. Ser Meryn Trant stood before it in his pale armor and white cloak. "Lower the bridge," Tyrion commanded him.

"The queen's orders are to raise the bridge at night." Ser Meryn had always been Cersei's creature.

"The queen's asleep, and I have business with my father."

There was magic in the name of Lord Tywin Lannister. Grumbling, Ser Meryn Trant gave the command, and the drawbridge was lowered. A second Kingsguard knight stood sentry across the moat. Ser Osmund Kettleblack managed a smile when he saw Tyrion waddling toward him. "Feeling stronger, m'lord?"

"Much. When's the next battle? I can scarcely wait."

When Pod and he reached the serpentine steps, however, Tyrion could only gape at them in dismay. *I will never climb those by myself,* he confessed to himself. Swallowing his dignity, he asked Bronn to carry him, hoping against hope that at this hour there would be no one to see and smile, no one to tell the tale of the dwarf being carried up the steps like a babe in arms.

The outer ward was crowded with tents and pavilions,

dozens of them. "Tyrell men," Podrick Payne explained as they threaded their way through a maze of silk and canvas. "Lord Rowan's too, and Lord Redwyne's. There wasn't room enough for all. In the castle, I mean. Some took rooms. Rooms in the city. In inns and all. They're here for the wedding. The king's wedding, King Joffrey's. Will you be strong enough to attend, my lord?"

"Ravening weasels could not keep me away." There was this to be said for weddings over battles, at least; it was less likely that someone would cut off your nose.

Lights still burned dimly behind shuttered windows in the Tower of the Hand. The men on the door wore the crimson cloaks and lion-crested helms of his father's household guard. Tyrion knew them both, and they admitted him on sight . . . though neither could bear to look long at his face, he noted.

Within, they came upon Ser Addam Marbrand, descending the turnpike stair in the ornate black breast-plate and cloth-of-gold cloak of an officer in the City Watch. "My lord," he said, "how good to see you on your feet. I'd heard –"

" – rumors of a small grave being dug? Me too. Under the circumstances it seemed best to get up. I hear you're commander of the City Watch. Shall I offer congratulations or condolences?"

"Both, I fear." Ser Addam smiled. "Death and desertion have left me with some forty-four hundred. Only the gods and Littlefinger know how we are to go on paying wages for so many, but your sister forbids me to dismiss any."

Still anxious, Cersei? The battle's done, the gold cloaks won't help you now. "Do you come from my father?" he asked.

"Aye. I fear I did not leave him in the best of moods. Lord Tywin feels forty-four hundred guardsmen more than sufficient to find one lost squire, but your cousin Tyrek remains missing."

Tyrek was the son of his late Uncle Tygett, a boy of thirteen. He had vanished in the riot, not long after wedding the Lady Ermesande, a suckling babe who happened to be the last surviving heir of House Hayford. *And likely the first bride in the history of the Seven Kingdoms to be widowed before she was weaned.* "I couldn't find him either," confessed Tyrion.

"He's feeding worms," said Bronn with his usual tact. "Ironhand looked for him, and the eunuch rattled a nice fat purse. They had no more luck than we did. Give it up, ser."

Ser Addam gazed at the sellsword with distaste. "Lord Tywin is stubborn where his blood is concerned. He will have the lad, alive or dead, and I mean to oblige him." He looked back to Tyrion. "You will find your father in his solar."

My solar, thought Tyrion. "I believe I know the way."

The way was up more steps, but this time he climbed under his own power, with one hand on Pod's shoulder. Bronn opened the door for him. Lord Tywin Lannister was seated beneath the window, writing by the glow of an oil lamp. He raised his eyes at the sound of the latch. "Tyrion." Calmly, he laid his quill aside.

"I'm pleased you remember me, my lord." Tyrion released his grip on Pod, leaned his weight on the stick, and waddled closer. *Something is wrong,* he knew at once.

"Ser Bronn," Lord Tywin said, "Podrick. Perhaps you had best wait without until we are done."

The look Bronn gave the Hand was little less than insolent; nonetheless, he bowed and withdrew, with Pod on his heels. The heavy door swung shut behind them, and Tyrion Lannister was alone with his father. Even with the windows of the solar shuttered against the night, the chill in the room was palpable. *What sort of lies has Cersei been telling him?*

The Lord of Casterly Rock was as lean as a man twenty years younger, even handsome in his austere way. Stiff blond whiskers covered his cheeks, framing a stern face, a bald head, a hard mouth. About his throat he wore a chain of golden hands, the fingers of each clasping the wrist of the next. "That's a handsome chain," Tyrion said. *Though it looked better on me.*

Lord Tywin ignored the sally. "You had best be seated. Is it wise for you to be out of your sickbed?"

"I am sick of my sickbed." Tyrion knew how much his

father despised weakness. He claimed the nearest chair. "Such pleasant chambers you have. Would you believe it, while I was dying, someone moved me to a dark little cell in Maegor's?"

"The Red Keep is overcrowded with wedding guests. Once they depart, we will find you more suitable accommodations."

"I rather liked *these* accommodations. Have you set a date for this great wedding?"

"Joffrey and Margaery shall marry on the first day of the new year, which as it happens is also the first day of the new century. The ceremony will herald the dawn of a new era."

A new Lannister era, thought Tyrion. "Oh, bother, I fear I've made other plans for that day."

"Did you come here just to complain of your bedchamber and make your lame japes? I have important letters to finish."

"Important letters. To be sure."

"Some battles are won with swords and spears, others with quills and ravens. Spare me these coy reproaches, Tyrion. I visited your sickbed as often as Maester Ballabar would allow it, when you seemed like to die." He steepled his fingers under his chin. "Why did you dismiss Ballabar?"

Tyrion shrugged. "Maester Frenken is not so determined to keep me insensate."

"Ballabar came to the city in Lord Redwyne's retinue. A gifted healer, it's said. It was kind of Cersei to ask him to look after you. She feared for your life."

Feared that I might keep it, you mean. "Doubtless that's why she's never once left my bedside."

"Don't be impertinent. Cersei has a royal wedding to plan, I am waging a war, and you have been out of danger for at least a fortnight." Lord Tywin studied his son's disfigured face, his pale green eyes unflinching. "Though the wound is ghastly enough, I'll grant you. What madness possessed you?"

"The foe was at the gates with a battering ram. If Jaime had led the sortie, you'd call it valor."

"Jaime would never be so foolish as to remove his helm in battle. I trust you killed the man who cut you?"

"Oh, the wretch is dead enough." Though it had been Podrick Payne who'd killed Ser Mandon, shoving him into the river to drown beneath the weight of his armor. "A dead enemy is a joy forever," Tyrion said blithely, though Ser Mandon was not his true enemy. The man had no reason to want him dead. *He was only a catspaw, and I believe I know the cat. She told him to make certain I did not survive the battle.* But without proof Lord Tywin would never listen to such a charge. "Why are you here in the city, Father?" he asked. "Shouldn't you be off fighting Lord Stannis or Robb Stark or someone?" *And the sooner the better.*

"Until Lord Redwyne brings his fleet up, we lack the ships to assail Dragonstone. It makes no matter. Stannis Baratheon's sun set on the Blackwater. As for Stark, the boy is still in the west, but a large force of northmen under Helman Tallhart and Robett Glover are descending toward Duskendale. I've sent Lord Tarly to meet them, while Ser Gregor drives up the kingsroad to cut off their retreat. Tallhart and Glover will be caught between them, with a third of Stark's strength."

"Duskendale?" There was nothing at Duskendale worth such a risk. Had the Young Wolf finally blundered?

"It's nothing you need trouble yourself with. Your face is pale as death, and there's blood seeping through your dressings. Say what you want and take yourself back to bed."

"What I want . . ." His throat felt raw and tight. What *did* he want? *More than you can ever give me, Father.* "Pod tells me that Littlefinger's been made Lord of Harrenhal."

"An empty title, so long as Roose Bolton holds the castle for Robb Stark, yet Lord Baelish was desirous of the honor. He did us good service in the matter of the Tyrell marriage. A Lannister pays his debts."

The Tyrell marriage had been Tyrion's notion, in point of fact, but it would seem churlish to try to claim that now. "That title may not be as empty as you think," he warned. "Littlefinger does nothing without good reason. But be that as it may. You said something about paying debts, I believe?"

"And you want your own reward, is that it? Very well. What is it you would have of me? Lands, castle, some office?"

"A little bloody gratitude would make a nice start."

Lord Tywin stared at him, unblinking. "Mummers and monkeys require applause. So did Aerys, for that matter. You did as you were commanded, and I am sure it was to the best of your ability. No one denies the part you played."

"The *part* I played?" What nostrils Tyrion had left must surely have flared. "I saved your bloody city, it seems to me."

"Most people seem to feel that it was my attack on Lord Stannis's flank that turned the tide of battle. Lords Tyrell, Rowan, Redwyne, and Tarly fought nobly as well, and I'm told it was your sister Cersei who set the pyromancers to making the wildfire that destroyed the Baratheon fleet."

"While all I did was get my nosehairs trimmed, is that it?" Tyrion could not keep the bitterness out of his voice.

"Your chain was a clever stroke, and crucial to our victory. Is that what you wanted to hear? I am told we have you to thank for our Dornish alliance as well. You may be pleased to learn that Myrcella has arrived safely at Sunspear. Ser Arys Oakheart writes that she has taken a great liking to Princess Arianne, and that Prince Trystane is enchanted with her. I mislike giving House Martell a hostage, but I suppose that could not be helped."

"We'll have our own hostage," Tyrion said. "A council seat was also part of the bargain. Unless Prince Doran brings an army when he comes to claim it, he'll be putting himself in our power."

"Would that a council seat were all Martell came to claim," Lord Tywin said. "You promised him vengeance as well."

"I promised him justice."

"Call it what you will. It still comes down to blood."

"Not an item in short supply, surely? I splashed through lakes of it during the battle." Tyrion saw no reason not to cut to the heart of the matter. "Or have you grown so fond of Gregor Clegane that you cannot bear to part with him?"

"Ser Gregor has his uses, as did his brother. Every lord has need of a beast from time to time . . . a lesson you seem to have learned, judging from Ser Bronn and those clansmen of yours."

Tyrion thought of Timett's burned eye, Shagga with his axe, Chella in her necklace of dried ears. And Bronn. Bronn most of all. "The woods are full of beasts," he reminded his father. "The alleyways as well."

"True. Perhaps other dogs would hunt as well. I shall think on it. If there is nothing else . . ."

"You have important letters, yes." Tyrion rose on unsteady legs, closed his eyes for an instant as a wave of dizziness washed over him, and took a shaky step toward the door. Later, he would reflect that he should have taken a second, and then a third. Instead he turned. "What do I want, you ask? I'll tell you what I want. I want what is mine by rights. I want Casterly Rock."

His father's mouth grew hard. "Your brother's birthright?"

"The knights of the Kingsguard are forbidden to marry, to father children, and to hold land, you know that as well as I. The day Jaime put on that white cloak, he gave up his claim to Casterly Rock, but never once have you acknowledged it. It's past time. I want you to stand up before the realm and proclaim that I am your son and your lawful heir."

Lord Tywin's eyes were a pale green flecked with gold, as luminous as they were merciless. "Casterly Rock," he declared in a flat cold dead tone. And then, "Never."

The word hung between them, huge, sharp, poisoned.

I knew the answer before I asked, Tyrion thought. *Eighteen years since Jaime joined the Kingsguard, and I never once raised the issue. I must have known. I must always have known.* "Why?" he made himself ask, though he knew he would rue the question.

"You ask that? You, who killed your mother to come into the world? You are an ill-made, devious, disobedient, spiteful little creature full of envy, lust, and low cunning. Men's laws give you the right to bear my name and display my colors, since I cannot prove that you are not mine. To teach me humility, the gods have condemned me to watch you waddle about wearing that proud lion that was my father's sigil and his father's before him. But neither gods nor men shall ever compel me to let you turn Casterly Rock into your whorehouse."

"My *whorehouse?*" The dawn broke; Tyrion understood all at once where this bile had come from. He ground his teeth together and said, "Cersei told you about Alayaya."

"Is that her name? I confess, I cannot remember the names of all your whores. Who was the one you married as a boy?"

"Tysha." He spat out the answer, defiant.

"And that camp follower on the Green Fork?"

"Why do you care?" he asked, unwilling even to speak Shae's name in his presence.

"I don't. No more than I care if they live or die."

"It was *you* who had Yaya whipped." It was not a question.

"Your sister told me of your threats against my grandsons." Lord Tywin's voice was colder than ice. "Did she lie?"

Tyrion would not deny it. "I made threats, yes. To keep Alayaya safe. So the Kettleblacks would not misuse her."

"To save a whore's virtue, you threatened your own House, your own kin? Is that the way of it?"

"You were the one who taught me that a good threat is often more telling than a blow. Not that Joffrey hasn't tempted me sore a few hundred times. If you're so anxious to whip people, start with him. But Tommen . . . why would I harm Tommen? He's a good lad, and mine own blood."

"As was your mother." Lord Tywin rose abruptly, to tower over his dwarf son. "Go back to your bed, Tyrion, and speak to me no more of *your rights* to Casterly Rock.

You shall have your reward, but it shall be one I deem appropriate to your service and station. And make no mistake – this was the last time I will suffer you to bring shame onto House Lannister. You are *done* with whores. The next one I find in your bed, I'll hang."

DAVOS

He watched the sail grow for a long time, trying to decide whether he would sooner live or die.

Dying would be easier, he knew. All he had to do was crawl inside his cave and let the ship pass by, and death would find him. For days now the fever had been burning through him, turning his bowels to brown water and making him shiver in his restless sleep. Each morning found him weaker. *It will not be much longer*, he had taken to telling himself.

If the fever did not kill him, thirst surely would. He had no fresh water here, but for the occasional rainfall that pooled in hollows on the rock. Only three days past (or had it been four? On his rock, it was hard to tell the days apart) his pools had been dry as old bone, and the sight of the bay rippling green and grey all around him had been almost more than he could bear. Once he began to drink seawater the end would come swiftly, he knew, but all the same he had almost taken that first swallow, so parched was his throat. A sudden squall had saved him. He had grown so feeble by then that it was all he could do to lie in the rain with his eyes closed and his mouth open, and let the water splash down on his cracked lips and swollen tongue. But afterward he felt a little stronger, and the island's pools and cracks and crevices once more had brimmed with life.

But that had been three days ago (or maybe four), and most of the water was gone now. Some had evaporated, and he had sucked up the rest. By the morrow he would be tasting the mud again, and licking the damp cold stones at the bottom of the depressions.

And if not thirst or fever, starvation would kill him. His island was no more than a barren spire jutting up out of the immensity of Blackwater Bay. When the tide was low, he could sometimes find tiny crabs along the stony strand where he had washed ashore after the battle. They nipped his fingers painfully before he smashed them apart on the rocks to suck the meat from their claws and the guts from their shells.

But the strand vanished whenever the tide came rushing in, and Davos had to scramble up the rock to keep from being swept out into the bay once more. The point of the spire was fifteen feet above the water at high tide, but when the bay grew rough the spray went even higher, so there was no way to keep dry, even in his cave (which was really no more than a hollow in the rock beneath an overhang). Nothing grew on the rock but lichen, and even the seabirds shunned the place. Now and again some gulls would land atop the spire and Davos would try to catch one, but they were too quick for him to get close. He took to flinging stones at them, but he was too weak to throw with much force, so even when his stones hit the gulls would only scream at him in annoyance and then take to the air.

There were other rocks visible from his refuge, distant stony spires taller than his own. The nearest stood a good forty feet above the water, he guessed, though it was hard to be sure at this distance. A cloud of gulls swirled about it constantly, and often Davos thought of crossing over to raid their nests. But the water was cold here, the currents strong and treacherous, and he knew he did not have the strength for such a swim. That would kill him as sure as drinking seawater.

Autumn in the narrow sea could often be wet and rainy, he remembered from years past. The days were not bad so long as the sun was shining, but the nights were growing colder and sometimes the wind would come gusting across the bay, driving a line of whitecaps before it, and before long Davos would be soaked and shivering. Fever and chills assaulted him in turn, and of late he had developed a persistent racking cough.

His cave was all the shelter he had, and that was little enough. Driftwood and bits of charred debris would wash up on the strand during low tide, but he had no way to strike a spark or start a fire. Once, in desperation, he had tried rubbing two pieces of driftwood against each other, but the wood was rotted, and his efforts earned him only blisters. His clothes were sodden as well, and he had lost one of his boots somewhere in the bay before he washed up here.

Thirst; hunger; exposure. They were his companions, with him every hour of every day, and in time he had come to think of them as his friends. Soon enough, one or the other of his friends would take pity on him and free him from this endless misery. Or perhaps he would simply walk into the water one day, and strike out for the shore that he knew lay somewhere to the north, beyond his sight. It was too far to swim, as weak as he was, but that did not matter. Davos had always been a sailor; he was meant to die at sea. *The gods beneath the waters have been waiting for me*, he told himself. *It's past time I went to them.*

But now there was a sail; only a speck on the horizon, but growing larger. *A ship where no ship should be.* He knew where his rock lay, more or less; it was one of a series of sea monts that rose from the floor of Blackwater Bay. The tallest of them jutted a hundred feet above the tide, and a dozen lesser monts stood thirty to sixty feet high. Sailors called them *spears of the merling king*, and knew that for every one that broke the surface, a dozen lurked treacherously just below it. Any captain with sense kept his course well away from them.

Davos watched the sail swell through pale red-rimmed eyes, and tried to hear the sound of the wind caught in the canvas. *She is coming this way.* Unless she changed course soon, she would pass within hailing distance of his meager refuge. It might mean life. If he wanted it. He was not sure he did.

Why should I live? he thought as tears blurred his vision. *Gods be good, why? My sons are dead, Dale and Allard, Maric and Matthos, perhaps Devan as well. How can a father outlive so many strong young sons? How would I go on? I am a hollow shell, the crab's died, there's nothing left inside. Don't they know that?*

They had sailed up the Blackwater Rush flying the fiery heart of the Lord of Light. Davos and *Black Betha* had been in the second line of battle, between Dale's *Wraith* and Allard on *Lady Marya*. Maric his third-born was oarmaster on *Fury*, at the center of the first line, while Matthos served as his father's second. Beneath the walls of the Red Keep Stannis Baratheon's galleys had joined in battle with the boy king Joffrey's smaller fleet, and for a few moments the river had rung to the thrum of bowstrings and the crash of iron rams shattering oars and hulls alike.

And then some vast beast had let out a roar, and green flames were all around them: wildfire, pyromancer's piss, the jade demon. Matthos had been standing at his elbow on the deck of *Black Betha* when the ship seemed to lift from the water. Davos found himself in the river, flailing as the current took him and spun him around and around. Upstream, the flames had ripped at the sky, fifty feet high. He had seen *Black Betha* afire, and *Fury*, and a dozen other ships, had seen burning men leaping into the water to drown. *Wraith* and *Lady Marya* were gone, sunk or shattered or vanished behind a veil of wildfire, and there was no time to look for them, because the mouth of the river was almost upon him, and across the mouth of the river the Lannisters had raised a great iron chain. From bank to bank there was nothing but burning ships and wildfire. The sight of it seemed to stop his heart for a moment, and he could still remember the sound of it, the crackle of flames, the hiss of steam, the shrieks of dying men, and the beat of that terrible heat against his face as the current swept him down toward hell.

All he needed to do was nothing. A few moments more, and he would be with his sons now, resting in the cool green mud on the bottom of the bay, with fish nibbling at his face.

Instead he sucked in a great gulp of air and dove, kicking for the bottom of the river. His only hope was to pass under the chain and the burning ships and the wildfire that floated on the surface of the water, to swim hard for the safety of the bay beyond. Davos had always been a strong swimmer, and he'd worn no steel that day, but for the helm he'd lost when he'd lost *Black Betha*. As he knifed through the green murk, he saw other men struggling beneath the water, pulled down to drown beneath the weight of plate and mail. Davos swam past them, kicking with all the strength left in his legs, giving himself up to the current, the water filling his eyes. Deeper he went, and deeper, and deeper still. With every stroke it grew harder to hold his breath. He remembered seeing the bottom, soft and dim, as a stream of bubbles burst from his lips. Something touched his leg . . . a snag or a fish or a drowning man, he could not tell.

He needed air by then, but he was afraid. Was he past the chain yet, was he out in the bay? If he came up under a ship he would drown, and if he surfaced amidst the floating patches of wildfire his first breath would sear his lungs to ash. He twisted in the water to look up, but there was nothing to see but green darkness and then he spun too far and suddenly he could no longer tell up from down. Panic took hold of him. His hands flailed against the bottom of the river and sent up a cloud of mud that blinded him. His chest was growing tighter by the instant. He clawed at the water, kicking, pushing himself, turning, his lungs screaming for air, kicking, kicking, lost now in the river murk, kicking, kicking, kicking until he could kick no longer. When he opened his mouth to scream, the water came rushing in, tasting of salt, and Davos Seaworth knew that he was drowning.

The next he knew the sun was up, and he lay upon a stony strand beneath a spire of naked stone, with the empty bay all around and a broken mast, a burned sail, and a swollen corpse beside him. The mast, the sail, and the dead man vanished with the next high tide, leaving

Davos alone on his rock amidst the spears of the merling king.

His long years as a smuggler had made the waters around King's Landing more familiar to him than any home he'd ever had, and he knew his refuge was no more than a speck on the charts, in a place that honest sailors steered away from, not toward . . . though Davos himself had come by it once or twice in his smuggling days, the better to stay unseen. *When they find me dead here, if ever they do, perhaps they will name the rock for me,* he thought. *Onion Rock, they'll call it; it will be my tombstone and my legacy.* He deserved no more. *The Father protects his children,* the septons taught, but Davos had led his boys into the fire. Dale would never give his wife the child they had prayed for, and Allard, with his girl in Oldtown and his girl in King's Landing and his girl in Braavos, they would all be weeping soon. Matthos would never captain his own ship, as he'd dreamed. Maric would never have his knighthood.

How can I live when they are dead? So many brave knights and mighty lords have died, better men than me, and highborn. Crawl inside your cave, Davos. Crawl inside and shrink up small and the ship will go away, and no one will trouble you ever again. Sleep on your stone pillow, and let the gulls peck out your eyes while the crabs feast on your flesh. You've feasted on enough of them, you owe them. Hide, smuggler. Hide, and be quiet, and die.

The sail was almost on him. A few moments more, and the ship would be safely past, and he could die in peace.

His hand reached for his throat, fumbling for the small leather pouch he always wore about his neck. Inside he kept the bones of the four fingers his king had shortened for him, on the day he made Davos a knight. *My luck.* His shortened fingers patted at his chest, groping, finding nothing. The pouch was gone, and the fingerbones with them. Stannis could never understand why he'd kept the bones. "To remind me of my king's justice," he whispered through cracked lips. But now they were gone. *The fire took my luck as well as my sons.* In his dreams the river was still aflame and demons danced upon the waters with fiery whips in their hands, while men blackened and burned beneath the lash. "Mother, have mercy," Davos prayed. "Save me, gentle Mother, save us all. My luck is gone, and my sons." He was weeping freely now, salt tears streaming down his cheeks. "The fire took it all . . . the fire . . ."

Perhaps it was only wind blowing against the rock, or the sound of the sea on the shore, but for an instant Davos Seaworth heard her answer. "You called the fire," she whispered, her voice as faint as the sound of waves in a seashell, sad and soft. "You burned us . . . burned us . . . burrrrned usssssss."

"It was *her!*" Davos cried. "Mother, don't forsake us. It was her who burned you, the red woman, Melisandre, *her!*" He could see her; the heart-shaped face, the red eyes, the long coppery hair, her red gowns moving like flames as she walked, a swirl of silk and satin. She had come from Asshai in the east, she had come to Dragonstone and won Selsye and her queen's men for her alien god, and then the king, Stannis Baratheon himself. He had gone so far as to put the fiery heart on his banners, the fiery heart of R'hllor, Lord of Light and God of Flame and Shadow. At Melisandre's urging, he had dragged the Seven from their sept at Dragonstone and burned them before the castle gates, and later he had burned the godswood at Storm's End as well, even the heart tree, a huge white weirwood with a solemn face.

"It was her work," Davos said again, more weakly. *Her work, and yours, onion knight. You rowed her into Storm's End in the black of night, so she might loose her shadow child. You are not guiltless, no. You rode beneath her banner and flew it from your mast. You watched the Seven burn at Dragonstone, and did nothing. She gave the Father's justice to the fire, and the Mother's mercy, and the wisdom of the Crone. Smith and Stranger, Maid and Warrior, she burnt them all to the glory of her cruel god, and you stood and held your tongue. Even when she killed old Maester Cressen, even then, you did nothing.*

The sail was a hundred yards away and moving fast

across the bay. In a few more moments it would be past him, and dwindling.

Ser Davos Seaworth began to climb his rock.

He pulled himself up with trembling hands, his head swimming with fever. Twice his maimed fingers slipped on the damp stone and he almost fell, but somehow he managed to cling to his perch. If he fell he was dead, and he had to live. For a little while more, at least. There was something he had to do.

The top of the rock was too small to stand on safely, as weak as he was, so he crouched and waved his fleshless arms. *"Ship,"* he screamed into the wind. "Ship, here, *here!"* From up here, he could see her more clearly; the lean striped hull, the bronze figurehead, the billowing sail. There was a name painted on her hull, but Davos had never learned to read. *"Ship,"* he called again, *"help me, HELP ME!"*

A crewman on her forecastle saw him and pointed. He watched as other sailors moved to the gunwale to gape at him. A short while later the galley's sail came down, her oars slid out, and she swept around toward his refuge. She was too big to approach the rock closely, but thirty yards away she launched a small boat. Davos clung to his rock and watched it creep toward him. Four men were rowing, while a fifth sat in the prow. "You," the fifth man called out when they were only a few feet from his island, "you up on the rock. Who are you?"

A smuggler who rose above himself, thought Davos, *a fool who loved his king too much, and forgot his gods.* "I . . ." His throat was parched, and he had forgotten how to talk. The words felt strange on his tongue and sounded stranger in his ears. "I was in the battle. I was . . . a captain, a . . . a knight, I was a knight."

"Aye, ser," the man said, "and serving which king?"

The galley might be Joffrey's, he realized suddenly. If he spoke the wrong name now, she would abandon him to his fate. But no, her hull was striped. She was Lysene, she was Salladhor Saan's. The Mother sent her here, the Mother in her mercy. She had a task for him. *Stannis lives,* he knew then. *I have a king still. And sons, I have other sons, and a wife loyal and loving.* How could he have forgotten? The Mother was merciful indeed.

"Stannis," he shouted back at the Lyseni. "Gods be good, I serve King Stannis."

"Aye," said the man in the boat, "and so do we."

SANSA

The invitation seemed innocent enough, but every time Sansa read it her tummy tightened into a knot. *She's to be queen now, she's beautiful and rich and everyone loves her, why would she want to sup with a traitor's daughter?* It could be curiosity, she supposed; perhaps Margaery Tyrell wanted to get the measure of the rival she'd displaced. *Does she resent me, I wonder? Does she think I bear her ill will . . . ?*

Sansa had watched from the castle walls as Margaery Tyrell and her escort made their way up Aegon's High Hill. Joffrey had met his new bride-to-be at the King's Gate to welcome her to the city, and they rode side by side through cheering crowds, Joff glittering in gilded armor and the Tyrell girl splendid in green with a cloak of autumn flowers blowing from her shoulders. She was sixteen, brown-haired and brown-eyed, slender and beautiful. The people called out her name as she passed, held up their children for her blessing, and scattered flowers under the hooves of her horse. Her mother and grandmother followed close behind, riding in a tall wheelhouse whose sides were carved into the shape of a hundred twining roses, every one gilded and shining. The smallfolk cheered them as well.

The same smallfolk who pulled me from my horse and would have killed me, if not for the Hound. Sansa had done nothing to make the commons hate her, no more than Margaery Tyrell had done to win their love. *Does she want me to love her too?* She studied the invitation, which looked to be written in Margaery's own hand. *Does she want my blessing?* Sansa wondered if Joffrey knew of this supper. For all she knew, it might be his doing. That thought made her fearful. If Joff was behind the invitation, he would have some cruel jape planned to shame her in the older girl's eyes. Would he command his Kingsguard to strip her naked once again? The last time he had done that his uncle Tyrion had stopped him, but the Imp could not save her now.

No one can save me but my Florian. Ser Dontos had promised he would help her escape, but not until the night of Joffrey's wedding. The plans had been well laid, her dear devoted knight-turned-fool assured her; there was nothing to do until then but endure, and count the days.

And sup with my replacement...

Perhaps she was doing Margaery Tyrell an injustice. Perhaps the invitation was no more than a simple kindness, an act of courtesy. *It might be just a supper.* But this was the Red Keep, this was King's Landing, this was the court of King Joffrey Baratheon, the First of His Name, and if there was one thing that Sansa Stark had learned here, it was mistrust.

Even so, she must accept. She was nothing now, the discarded daughter of a traitor and disgraced sister of a rebel lord. She could scarcely refuse Joffrey's queen to-be.

I wish the Hound were here. The night of the battle, Sandor Clegane had come to her chambers to take her from the city, but Sansa had refused. Sometimes she lay awake at night, wondering if she'd been wise. She had his stained white cloak hidden in a cedar chest beneath her summer silks. She could not say why she'd kept it. The Hound had turned craven, she heard it said; at the height of the battle, he got so drunk the Imp had to take his men. But Sansa understood. She knew the secret of his burned face. *It was only the fire he feared.* That night, the wildfire had set the river itself ablaze, and filled the very air with green flame. Even in the castle, Sansa had been afraid. Outside . . . she could scarcely imagine it.

Sighing, she got out quill and ink, and wrote Margaery Tyrell a gracious note of acceptance.

When the appointed night arrived, another of the Kingsguard came for her, a man as different from Sandor Clegane as . . . *well, as a flower from a dog.* The sight of Ser Loras Tyrell standing on her threshold made Sansa's heart beat a little faster. This was the first time she had been so close to him since he had returned to King's Landing, leading the vanguard of his father's host. For a moment she did not know what to say. "Ser Loras," she finally managed, "you . . . you look so lovely."

He gave her a puzzled smile. "My lady is too kind. And beautiful besides. My sister awaits you eagerly."

"I have so looked forward to our supper."

"As has Margaery, and my lady grandmother as well." He took her arm and led her toward the steps.

"Your grandmother?" Sansa was finding it hard to walk and talk and think all at the same time, with Ser Loras touching her arm. She could feel the warmth of his hand through the silk.

"Lady Olenna. She is to sup with you as well."

"Oh," said Sansa. *I am talking to him, and he's touching me, he's holding my arm and touching me.* "The Queen of Thorns, she's called. Isn't that right?"

"It is." Ser Loras laughed. *He has the warmest laugh,* she thought as he went on, "You'd best not use that name in her presence, though, or you're like to get pricked."

Sansa reddened. Any fool would have realized that no woman would be happy about being called "the Queen of Thorns." *Maybe I truly am as stupid as Cersei Lannister says.* Desperately she tried to think of something clever and charming to say to him, but her wits had deserted her. She almost told him how beautiful he was, until she remembered that she'd already done that.

He *was* beautiful, though. He seemed taller than he'd been when she'd first met him, but still so lithe and graceful, and Sansa had never seen another boy with such wonderful eyes. *He's no boy, though, he's a man grown, a knight of the Kingsguard.* She thought he looked even finer in white than in the greens and golds of House Tyrell. The only spot of color on him now was the brooch that clasped his cloak; the rose of Highgarden wrought in soft yellow gold, nestled in a bed of delicate green jade leaves.

Ser Balon Swann held the door of Maegor's for them to pass. He was all in white as well, though he did not wear it half so well as Ser Loras. Beyond the spiked moat, two dozen men were taking their practice with sword and shield. With the castle so crowded, the outer ward had been given over to guests to raise their tents and pavilions, leaving only the smaller inner yards for training. One of the Redwyne twins was being driven backward by Ser Tallad, with the eyes on his shield. Chunky Ser Kennos of Kayce, who chuffed and puffed every time he raised his longsword, seemed to be holding his own against Osney Kettleblack, but Osney's brother Ser Osfryd was savagely punishing the frog-faced squire Morros Slynt. Blunted swords or no, Slynt would have a rich crop of bruises by the morrow. It made Sansa wince just to watch. *They have scarcely finished burying the dead from the last battle, and already they are practicing for the next one.*

On the edge of the yard, a lone knight with a pair of golden roses on his shield was holding off three foes. Even as they watched, he caught one of them alongside the head, knocking him senseless. "Is that your brother?" Sansa asked.

"It is, my lady," said Ser Loras. "Garlan often trains against three men, or even four. In battle it is seldom one against one, he says, so he likes to be prepared."

"He must be very brave."

"He is a great knight," Ser Loras replied. "A better sword than me, in truth, though I'm the better lance."

"I remember," said Sansa. "You ride wonderfully, ser."

"My lady is gracious to say so. When has she seen me ride?"

"At the Hand's tourney, don't you remember? You rode a white courser, and your armor was a hundred different kinds of flowers. You gave me a rose. A *red* rose. You threw white roses to the other girls that day." It made her flush to speak of it. "You said no victory was half as beautiful as me."

Ser Loras gave her a modest smile. "I spoke only a simple truth, that any man with eyes could see."

He doesn't remember, Sansa realized, startled. *He is only being kind to me, he doesn't remember me or the rose or any of it.* She had been so certain that it meant something, that it meant *everything.* A *red* rose, not a white. "It was after you unhorsed Ser Robar Royce," she said, desperately.

He took his hand from her arm. "I slew Robar at Storm's End, my lady." It was not a boast; he sounded sad.

Him, and another of King Renly's Rainbow Guard as well, yes. Sansa had heard the women talking of it round the well, but for a moment she'd forgotten. "That was when Lord Renly was killed, wasn't it? How terrible for your poor sister."

"For Margaery?" His voice was tight. "To be sure. She was at Bitterbridge, though. She did not see."

"Even so, when she heard . . ."

Ser Loras brushed the hilt of his sword lightly with his hand. Its grip was white leather, its pommel a rose in alabaster. "Renly is dead. Robar as well. What use to speak of them?"

The sharpness in his tone took her aback. "I . . . my lord, I . . . I did not mean to give offense, ser."

"Nor could you, Lady Sansa," Ser Loras replied, but all the warmth had gone from his voice. Nor did he take her arm again.

They ascended the serpentine steps in a deepening silence.

Oh, why did I have to mention Ser Robar? Sansa thought. *I've ruined everything. He is angry with me now.* She tried to think of something she might say to make amends, but all the words that came to her were lame and weak. *Be quiet, or you will only make it worse,* she told herself.

Lord Mace Tyrell and his entourage had been housed behind the royal sept, in the long slate-roofed keep that had been called the Maidenvault since King Baelor the

Blessed had confined his sisters therein, so the sight of them might not tempt him into carnal thoughts. Outside its tall carved doors stood two guards in gilded halfhelms and green cloaks edged in gold satin, the golden rose of Highgarden sewn on their breasts. Both were seven-footers, wide of shoulder and narrow of waist, magnificently muscled. When Sansa got close enough to see their faces, she could not tell one from the other. They had the same strong jaws, the same deep blue eyes, the same thick red mustaches. "Who are they?" she asked Ser Loras, her discomfit forgotten for a moment.

"My grandmother's personal guard," he told her. "Their mother named them Erryk and Arryk, but Grandmother can't tell them apart, so she calls them Left and Right."

Left and Right opened the doors, and Margaery Tyrell herself emerged and swept down the short flight of steps to greet them. "Lady Sansa," she called, "I'm so pleased you came. Be welcome."

Sansa knelt at the feet of her future queen. "You do me great honor, Your Grace."

"Won't you call me Margaery? Please, rise. Loras, help the Lady Sansa to her feet. Might I call you Sansa?"

"If it please you." Ser Loras helped her up.

Margaery dismissed him with a sisterly kiss, and took Sansa by the hand. "Come, my grandmother awaits, and she is not the most patient of ladies."

A fire was crackling in the hearth, and sweet-swelling rushes had been scattered on the floor. Around the long trestle table a dozen women were seated.

Sansa recognized only Lord Tyrell's tall, dignified wife, Lady Alerie, whose long silvery braid was bound with jeweled rings. Margaery performed the other introductions. There were three Tyrell cousins, Megga and Alla and Elinor, all close to Sansa's age. Buxom Lady Janna was Lord Tyrell's sister, and wed to one of the green-apple Fossoways; dainty, bright-eyed Lady Leonette was a Fossoway as well, and wed to Ser Garlan. Septa Nysterica had a homely pox-scarred face but seemed jolly. Pale, elegant Lady Graceford was with child, and Lady Bulwer *was* a child, no more than eight. And "Merry" was what she was to call boisterous plump Meredyth Crane, but most definitely *not* Lady Merryweather, a sultry black-eyed Myrish beauty.

Last of all, Margaery brought her before the wizened white-haired doll of a woman at the head of the table. "I am honored to present my grandmother the Lady Olenna, widow to the late Luthor Tyrell, Lord of Highgarden, whose memory is a comfort to us all."

The old woman smelled of rosewater. *Why, she's just the littlest bit of a thing.* There was nothing the least bit thorny about her. "Kiss me, child," Lady Olenna said, tugging at Sansa's wrist with a soft spotted hand. "It is so kind of you to sup with me and my foolish flock of hens."

Dutifully, Sansa kissed the old woman on the cheek. "It is kind of you to have me, my lady."

"I knew your grandfather, Lord Rickard, though not well."

"He died before I was born."

"I am aware of that, child. It's said that your Tully grandfather is dying too. Lord Hoster, surely they told you? An old man, though not so old as me. Still, night falls for all of us in the end, and too soon for some. You would know that more than most, poor child. You've had your share of grief, I know. We are sorry for your losses."

Sansa glanced at Margaery. "I was saddened when I heard of Lord Renly's death, Your Grace. He was very gallant."

"You are kind to say so," answered Margaery.

Her grandmother snorted. "Gallant, yes, and charming, and very clean. He knew how to dress and he knew how to smile and he knew how to bathe, and somehow he got the notion that this made him fit to be king. The Baratheons have always had some queer notions, to be sure. It comes from their Targaryen blood, I should think." She sniffed. "They tried to marry me to a Targaryen once, but I soon put an end to that."

"Renly was brave and gentle, Grandmother," said Margaery. "Father liked him as well, and so did Loras."

"Loras is young," Lady Olenna said crisply, "and very good at knocking men off horses with a stick. That does not make him wise. As to your father, would that I'd been born a peasant woman with a big wooden spoon, I might have been able to beat some sense into his fat head."

"*Mother*," Lady Alerie scolded.

"Hush, Alerie, don't take that tone with me. And don't call me Mother. If I'd given birth to you, I'm sure I'd remember. I'm only to blame for your husband, the lord oaf of Highgarden."

"Grandmother," Margaery said, "mind your words, or what will Sansa think of us?"

"She might think we have some wits about us. One of us, at any rate." The old woman turned back to Sansa. "It's treason, I warned them, Robert has two sons, and Renly has an older brother, how can he *possibly* have any claim to that ugly iron chair? Tut-tut, says my son, don't you want your sweetling to be queen? You Starks were kings once, the Arryns and the Lannisters as well, and even the Baratheons through the female line, but the Tyrells were no more than stewards until Aegon the Dragon came along and cooked the rightful King of the Reach on the Field of Fire. If truth be told, even our claim to Highgarden is a bit dodgy, just as those dreadful Florents are always whining. 'What does it matter?' you ask, and of course it doesn't, except to oafs like my son. The thought that one day he may see his grandson with his arse on the Iron Throne makes Mace puff up like . . . now, what do you call it? Margaery, you're clever, be a dear and tell your poor old half-daft grandmother the name of that queer fish from the Summer Isles that puffs up to ten times its own size when you poke it."

"They call them puff fish, Grandmother."

"Of course they do. Summer Islanders have no imagination. My son ought to take the puff fish for his sigil, if truth be told. He could put a crown on it, the way the Baratheons do their stag, mayhap that would make him happy. We should have stayed well out of all this bloody foolishness if you ask me, but once the cow's been milked there's no squirting the cream back up her udder. After Lord Puff Fish put that crown on Renly's head, we were into the pudding up to our knees, so here we are to see things through. And what do you say to that, Sansa?"

Sansa's mouth opened and closed. She felt very like a puff fish herself. "The Tyrells can trace their descent back to Garth Greenhand," was the best she could manage at short notice.

The Queen of Thorns snorted. "So can the Florents, the Rowans, the Oakhearts, and half the other noble houses of the south. Garth liked to plant his seed in fertile ground, they say. I shouldn't wonder that more than his hands were green."

"*Sansa*," Lady Alerie broke in, "you must be very hungry. Shall we have a bite of boar together, and some lemon cakes?"

"Lemon cakes are my favorite," Sansa admitted.

"So we have been told," declared Lady Olenna, who obviously had no intention of being hushed. "That Varys creature seemed to think we should be grateful for the information. I've never been quite sure what the *point* of a eunuch is, if truth be told. It seems to me they're only men with the useful bits cut off. Alerie, will you have them bring the food, or do you mean to starve me to death? Here, Sansa, sit here next to me, I'm much less boring than these others. I hope that you're fond of fools."

Sansa smoothed down her skirts and sat. "I think . . . fools, my lady? You mean . . . the sort in motley?"

"Feathers, in this case. What did you imagine I was speaking of? My son? Or these lovely ladies? No, don't blush, with your hair it makes you look like a pomegranate. All men are fools, if truth be told, but the ones in motley are more amusing than ones with crowns. Margaery, child, summon Butterbumps, let us see if we can't make Lady Sansa smile. The rest of you be seated, do I have to tell you everything? Sansa must think that my granddaughter is attended by a flock of sheep."

Butterbumps arrived before the food, dressed in a jester's suit of green and yellow feathers with a floppy coxcomb. An immense round fat man, as big as three Moon Boys, he came cartwheeling into the hall, vaulted onto the table, and laid a gigantic egg right in front of Sansa. "Break it, my lady," he commanded. When she did, a dozen yellow chicks escaped and began running in all directions. *"Catch them!"* Butterbumps exclaimed. Little Lady Bulwer snagged one and handed it to him, whereby he tilted back his head, popped it into his huge rubbery mouth, and seemed to swallow it whole. When he belched, tiny yellow feathers flew out his nose. Lady Bulwer began to wail in distress, but her tears turned into a sudden squeal of delight when the chick came squirming out of the sleeve of her gown and ran down her arm.

As the servants brought out a broth of leeks and mushrooms, Butterbumps began to juggle and Lady Olenna pushed herself forward to rest her elbows on the table. "Do you know my son, Sansa? Lord Puff Fish of Highgarden?"

"A great lord," Sansa answered politely.

"A great oaf," said the Queen of Thorns. "His father was an oaf as well. My husband, the late Lord Luthor. Oh, I loved him well enough, don't mistake me. A kind man, and not unskilled in the bedchamber, but an appalling oaf all the same. He managed to ride off a cliff whilst hawking. They say he was looking up at the sky and paying no mind to where his horse was taking him.

"And now my oaf son is doing the same, only he's riding a lion instead of a palfrey. It is easy to mount a lion and not so easy to get off, I warned him, but he only chuckles. Should you ever have a son, Sansa, beat him frequently so he learns to mind you. I only had the one boy and I hardly beat him at all, so now he pays more heed to Butterbumps than he does to me. A lion is not a lap cat, I told him, and he gives me a 'tut-tut-Mother.' There is entirely too much tut-tutting in this realm, if you ask me. All these kings would do a deal better if they would put down their swords and listen to their mothers."

Sansa realized that her mouth was open again. She filled it with a spoon of broth while Lady Alerie and the other women were giggling at the spectacle of Butterbumps bouncing oranges off his head, his elbows, and his ample rump.

"I want you to tell me the truth about this royal boy," said Lady Olenna abruptly. "This Joffrey."

Sansa's fingers tightened round her spoon. *The truth? I can't. Don't ask it, please, I can't.* "I . . . I . . . I . . ."

"You, yes. Who would know better? The lad seems kingly enough, I'll grant you. A bit full of himself, but that would be his Lannister blood. We have heard some troubling tales, however. Is there any truth to them? Has this boy mistreated you?"

Sansa glanced about nervously. Butterbumps popped a whole orange into his mouth, chewed and swallowed, slapped his cheek, and blew seeds out of his nose. The women giggled and laughed. Servants were coming and going, and the Maidenvault echoed to the clatter of spoons and plates. One of the chicks hopped back onto the table and ran through Lady Graceford's broth. No one seemed to be paying them any mind, but even so, she was frightened.

Lady Olenna was growing impatient. "Why are you gaping at Butterbumps? I asked a question, I expect an answer. Have the Lannisters stolen your tongue, child?"

Ser Dontos had warned her to speak freely only in the godswood. "Joff . . . King Joffrey, he's . . . His Grace is very fair and handsome, and . . . and as brave as a lion."

"Yes, all the Lannisters are lions, and when a Tyrell breaks wind it smells just like a rose," the old woman snapped. "But how *kind* is he? How clever? Has he a good heart, a gentle hand? Is he chivalrous as befits a king? Will he cherish Margaery and treat her tenderly, protect her honor as he would his own?"

"He will," Sansa lied. "He is very . . . very comely."

"You said that. You know, child, some say that you are as big a fool as Butterbumps here, and I am starting to believe them. *Comely?* I have taught my Margaery what comely is worth, I hope. Somewhat less than a mummer's fart. Aerion Brightfire was comely enough, but a monster all the same. The question is, what is Joffrey?" She reached to snag a passing servant. "I am not fond of leeks. Take this broth away, and bring me some cheese."

"The cheese will be served after the cakes, my lady."

"The cheese will be served when I want it served, and I want it served now." The old woman turned back to Sansa. "Are you frightened, child? No need for that, we're only women here. Tell me the truth, no harm will come to you."

"My father always told the truth." Sansa spoke quietly, but even so, it was hard to get the words out.

"Lord Eddard, yes, he had that reputation, but they named him traitor and took his head off even so." The old woman's eyes bore into her, sharp and bright as the points of swords.

"Joffrey," Sansa said. "Joffrey did that. He promised me he would be merciful, and cut my father's head off. He said *that* was mercy, and he took me up on the walls and made me look at it. The head. He wanted me to weep, but . . ." She stopped abruptly, and covered her mouth. *I've said too much, oh gods be good, they'll know, they'll hear, someone will tell on me.*

"Go on." It was Margaery who urged. Joffrey's own queen-to-be. Sansa did not know how much she had heard.

"I can't." *What if she tells him, what if she tells? He'll kill me for certain then, or give me to Ser Ilyn.* "I never meant . . . my father was a traitor, my brother as well, I have the traitor's blood, please, don't make me say more."

"Calm yourself, child," the Queen of Thorns commanded.

"She's terrified, Grandmother, just look at her."

The old woman called to Butterbumps. "*Fool!* Give us a song. A long one, I should think. 'The Bear and the Maiden Fair' will do nicely."

"It will!" the huge jester replied. "It will do nicely indeed! Shall I sing it standing on my head, my lady?"

"Will that make it sound better?"

"No."

"Stand on your feet, then. We wouldn't want your hat to fall off. As I recall, you never wash your hair."

"As my lady commands." Butterbumps bowed low, let loose an enormous belch, then straightened, threw out his belly, and bellowed. *"A bear there was, a bear, a BEAR! All black and brown, and covered with hair . . ."*

Lady Olenna squirmed forward. "Even when I was a girl younger than you, it was well known that in the Red Keep the very walls have ears. Well, they will be the better for a song, and meanwhile we girls shall speak freely."

"But," Sansa said, "Varys . . . he *knows*, he always . . ."

"*Sing louder!*" the Queen of Thorns shouted at Butterbumps. "These old ears are almost deaf, you know. Are you whispering at me, you fat fool? I don't pay you for whispers. *Sing!*"

"*. . . THE BEAR!*" thundered Butterbumps, his great deep voice echoing off the rafters. "*OH, COME, THEY SAID, OH COME TO THE FAIR! THE FAIR? SAID HE, BUT I'M A BEAR! ALL BLACK AND BROWN, AND COVERED WITH HAIR!*"

The wrinkled old lady smiled. "At Highgarden we have many spiders amongst the flowers. So long as they keep to themselves we let them spin their little webs, but if they get underfoot we step on them." She patted Sansa on the back of the hand. "Now, child, the truth. What sort of man is this Joffrey, who calls himself Baratheon but looks so very Lannister?"

"*AND DOWN THE ROAD FROM HERE TO THERE. FROM HERE! TO THERE! THREE BOYS, A GOAT, AND A DANCING BEAR!*"

Sansa felt as though her heart had lodged in her throat. The Queen of Thorns was so close she could smell the old woman's sour breath. Her gaunt thin fingers were pinching her wrist. To her other side, Margaery was listening as well. A shiver went through her. "A monster," she whispered, so tremulously she could scarcely hear her own voice. "Joffrey is a monster. He lied about the butcher's boy and made Father kill my wolf. When I displease him, he has the Kingsguard beat me. He's evil and cruel, my lady, it's so. And the queen as well."

Lady Olenna Tyrell and her granddaughter exchanged a look. "Ah," said the old woman, "that's a pity."

Oh, gods, thought Sansa, horrified. *If Margaery won't marry him, Joff will know that I'm to blame.* "Please," she blurted, "don't stop the wedding . . ."

"Have no fear, Lord Puff Fish is determined that Margaery shall be queen. And the word of a Tyrell is worth more than all the gold in Casterly Rock. At least it was in my day. Even so, we thank you for the truth, child."

"*. . . DANCED AND SPUN, ALL THE WAY TO THE FAIR! THE FAIR! THE FAIR!*" Butterbumps hopped and roared and stomped his feet.

"Sansa, would you like to visit Highgarden?" When Margaery Tyrell smiled, she looked very like her brother Loras. "All the autumn flowers are in bloom just now, and there are groves and fountains, shady courtyards, marble colonnades. My lord father always keeps singers at court, sweeter ones than Butters here, and pipers and fiddlers and harpers as well. We have the best horses, and pleasure boats to sail along the Mander. Do you hawk, Sansa?"

"A little," she admitted.

"*OH, SWEET SHE WAS, AND PURE, AND FAIR! THE MAID WITH HONEY IN HER HAIR!*"

"You will love Highgarden as I do, I know it." Margaery brushed back a loose strand of Sansa's hair. "Once you see it, you'll never want to leave. And perhaps you won't have to."

"*HER HAIR! HER HAIR! THE MAID WITH HONEY IN HER HAIR!*"

"Shush, child," the Queen of Thorns said sharply. "Sansa hasn't even told us that she would like to come for a visit."

"Oh, but I would," Sansa said. Highgarden sounded like the place she had always dreamed of, like the beautiful magical court she had once hoped to find at King's Landing.

"*. . . SMELLED THE SCENT ON THE SUMMER AIR. THE BEAR! THE BEAR! ALL BLACK AND BROWN AND COVERED WITH HAIR.*"

"But the queen," Sansa went on, "she won't let me go . . ."

"She will. Without Highgarden, the Lannisters have no hope of keeping Joffrey on his throne. If my son the lord oaf asks, she will have no choice but to grant his request."

"Will he?" asked Sansa. "Will he ask?"

Lady Olenna frowned. "I see no need to give him a choice. Of course, he has no hint of our true purpose."

"*HE SMELLED THE SCENT ON THE SUMMER AIR!*"

Sansa wrinkled her brow. "Our true purpose, my lady?"

"HE SNIFFED AND ROARED AND SMELLED IT THERE! HONEY ON THE SUMMER AIR!"

"To see you safely wed, child," the old woman said, as Butterbumps bellowed out the old, old song, "to my grandson."

Wed to Ser Loras, oh . . . Sansa's breath caught in her throat. She remembered Ser Loras in his sparkling sapphire armor, tossing her a rose. Ser Loras in white silk, so pure, innocent, beautiful. The dimples at the corner of his mouth when he smiled. The sweetness of his laugh, the warmth of his hand. She could only imagine what it would be like to pull up his tunic and caress the smooth skin underneath, to stand on her toes and kiss him, to run her fingers through those thick brown curls and drown in his deep brown eyes. A flush crept up her neck.

"OH, I'M A MAID, AND I'M PURE AND FAIR! I'LL NEVER DANCE WITH A HAIRY BEAR! A BEAR! A BEAR! I'LL NEVER DANCE WITH A HAIRY BEAR!"

"Would you like that, Sansa?" asked Margaery. "I've never had a sister, only brothers. Oh, please say yes, please say that you will consent to marry my brother."

The words came tumbling out of her. "Yes. I will. I would like that more than anything. To wed Ser Loras, to love him . . ."

"Loras?" Lady Olenna sounded annoyed. "Don't be foolish, child. Kingsguard never wed. Didn't they teach you anything in Winterfell? We were speaking of my grandson Willas. He is a bit old for you, to be sure, but a dear boy for all that. Not the least bit oafish, and heir to Highgarden besides."

Sansa felt dizzy; one instant her head was full of dreams of Loras, and the next they had all been snatched away. *Willas? Willas?* "I," she said stupidly. *Courtesy is a lady's armor. You must not offend them, be careful what you say.* "I do not know Ser Willas. I have never had the pleasure, my lady. Is he . . . is he as great a knight as his brothers?"

". . . LIFTED HER HIGH INTO THE AIR! THE BEAR! THE BEAR!"

"No," Margaery said. "He has never taken vows."

Her grandmother frowned. "Tell the girl the truth. The poor lad is crippled, and that's the way of it."

"He was hurt as a squire, riding in his first tourney," Margaery confided. "His horse fell and crushed his leg."

"That snake of a Dornishman was to blame, that Oberyn Martell. And his maester as well."

"I CALLED FOR A KNIGHT, BUT YOU'RE A BEAR! A BEAR! A BEAR! ALL BLACK AND BROWN AND COVERED WITH HAIR!"

"Willas has a bad leg but a good heart," said Margaery. "He used to read to me when I was a little girl, and draw me pictures of the stars. You will love him as much as we do, Sansa."

"SHE KICKED AND WAILED, THE MAID SO FAIR, BUT HE LICKED THE HONEY FROM HER HAIR. HER HAIR! HER HAIR! HE LICKED THE HONEY FROM HER HAIR!"

"When might I meet him?" asked Sansa, hesitantly.

"Soon," promised Margaery. "When you come to High-garden, after Joffrey and I are wed. My grandmother will take you."

"I will," said the old woman, patting Sansa's hand and smiling a soft wrinkly smile. "I will indeed."

"THEN SHE SIGHED AND SQUEALED AND KICKED THE AIR! MY BEAR! SHE SANG. MY BEAR SO FAIR! AND OFF THEY WENT, FROM HERE TO THERE, THE BEAR, THE BEAR, AND THE MAIDEN FAIR." Butterbumps roared the last line, leapt into the air, and came down on both feet with a crash that shook the wine cups on the table. The women laughed and clapped.

"I thought that dreadful song would never end," said the Queen of Thorns. "But look, here comes my cheese."

JON

The world was grey darkness, smelling of pine and moss and cold. Pale mists rose from the black earth as the riders threaded their way through the scatter of stones and scraggly trees, down toward the welcoming fires strewn like jewels across the floor of the river valley below. There were more fires than Jon Snow could count, hundreds of fires, thousands, a second river of flickery lights along the banks of the icy white Milkwater. The fingers of his sword hand opened and closed.

They descended the ridge without banners or trumpets, the quiet broken only by the distant murmur of the river, the clop of hooves, and the clacking of Rattleshirt's bone armor. Somewhere above an eagle soared on great blue-grey wings, while below came men and dogs and horses and one white direwolf.

A stone bounced down the slope, disturbed by a passing hoof, and Jon saw Ghost turn his head at the sudden sound. He had followed the riders at a distance all day, as was his custom, but when the moon rose over the soldier pines he'd come bounding up, red eyes aglow. Rattleshirt's dogs greeted him with a chorus of snarls and growls and wild barking, as ever, but the direwolf paid them no mind. Six days ago, the largest hound had attacked him from behind as the wildlings camped for the night, but Ghost had turned and lunged, sending the dog fleeing with a bloody haunch. The rest of the pack maintained a healthy distance after that.

Jon Snow's garron whickered softly, but a touch and a soft word soon quieted the animal. Would that his own fears could be calmed so easily. He was all in black, the black of the Night's Watch, but the enemy rode before and behind. *Wildlings, and I am with them.* Ygritte wore the cloak of Qhorin Halfhand. Lenyl had his hauberk, the big spearwife Ragwyle his gloves, one of the bowmen his boots. Qhorin's helm had been won by the short homely man called Longspear Ryk, but it fit poorly on his narrow head, so he'd given that to Ygritte as well. And Rattleshirt had Qhorin's bones in his bag, along with the bloody head of Ebben, who set out with Jon to scout the Skirling Pass. *Dead, all dead but me, and I am dead to the world.*

Ygritte rode just behind him. In front was Longspear Ryk. The Lord of Bones had made the two of them his guards. "If the crow flies, I'll boil your bones as well," he warned them when they had set out, smiling through the crooked teeth of the giant's skull he wore for a helm.

Ygritte hooted at him. "*You* want to guard him? If you want us to do it, leave us be and we'll do it."

These are a free folk indeed, Jon saw. Rattleshirt might lead them, but none of them was shy in talking back to him.

The wildling leader fixed him with an unfriendly stare. "Might be you fooled these others, crow, but don't think you'll be fooling Mance. He'll take one look a' you and know you're false. And when he does, I'll make a cloak o' your wolf there, and open your soft boy's belly and sew a weasel up inside."

Jon's sword hand opened and closed, flexing the burned fingers beneath the glove, but Longspear Ryk only laughed. "And where would you find a weasel in the snow?"

That first night, after a long day ahorse, they made camp in a shallow stone bowl atop a nameless mountain, huddling close to the fire while the snow began to fall. Jon watched the flakes melt as they drifted over the flames. Despite his layers of wool and fur and leather, he'd felt cold to the bone. Ygritte sat beside him after she had eaten, her hood pulled up and her hands tucked into her sleeves for warmth. "When Mance hears how you did for Half-hand, he'll take you quick enough," she told him.

"Take me for what?"

The girl laughed scornfully. "For one o' us. D'ya think you're the first crow ever flew down off the Wall? In your hearts you all want to fly free."

"And when I'm free," he said slowly, "will I be free to go?"

"Sure you will." She had a warm smile, despite her crooked teeth. "And we'll be free to kill you. It's *dangerous* being free, but most come to like the taste o' it." She put her gloved hand on his leg, just above the knee. "You'll see."

I will, thought Jon. *I will see, and hear, and learn, and when I have I will carry the word back to the Wall.* The wildlings had taken him for an oathbreaker, but in his heart he was still a man of the Night's Watch, doing the last duty that Qhorin Halfhand had laid on him. *Before I killed him.*

At the bottom of the slope they came upon a little stream flowing down from the foothills to join the Milk-water. It looked all stones and glass, though they could hear the sound of water running beneath the frozen surface. Rattleshirt led them across, shattering the thin crust of ice.

Mance Rayder's outriders closed in as they emerged. Jon took their measure with a glance: eight riders, men and women both, clad in fur and boiled leather, with here and there a helm or bit of mail. They were armed with spears and fire-hardened lances, all but their leader, a fleshy blond man with watery eyes who bore a great curved scythe of sharpened steel. *The Weeper*, he knew at once. The black brothers told tales of this one. Like Rattleshirt and Harma Dogshead and Alfyn Crowkiller, he was a known raider.

"The Lord o' Bones," the Weeper said when he saw them. He eyed Jon and his wolf. "Who's this, then?"

"A crow come over," said Rattleshirt, who preferred to be called the Lord of Bones, for the clattering armor he wore. "He was afraid I'd take his bones as well as Half-hand's." He shook his sack of trophies at the other wildlings.

"He slew Qhorin Halfhand," said Longspear Ryk. "Him and that wolf o' his."

"And did for Orell too," said Rattleshirt.

"The lad's a warg, or close enough," put in Ragwyle, the big spearwife. "His wolf took a piece o' Halfhand's leg."

The Weeper's red rheumy eyes gave Jon another look. "Aye? Well, he has a wolfish cast to him, now as I look close. Bring him to Mance, might be he'll keep him." He wheeled his horse around and galloped off, his riders hard behind him.

The wind was blowing wet and heavy as they crossed the valley of the Milkwater and rode singlefile through the river camp. Ghost kept close to Jon, but the scent of him went before them like a herald, and soon there were wildling dogs all around them, growling and barking. Lenyl screamed at them to be quiet, but they paid him no heed. "They don't much care for that beast o' yours," Longspear Ryk said to Jon.

"They're dogs and he's a wolf," said Jon. "They know he's not their kind." *No more than I am yours.* But he had his duty to be mindful of, the task Qhorin Halfhand had laid upon him as they shared that final fire – to play the part of turncloak, and find whatever it was that the wildlings had been seeking in the bleak cold wilderness of the Frostfangs. "Some *power*," Qhorin had named it to the Old Bear, but he had died before learning what it was, or whether Mance Rayder had found it with his digging.

There were cookfires all along the river, amongst wayns and carts and sleds. Many of the wildlings had thrown up tents, of hide and skin and felted wool. Others sheltered behind rocks in crude lean-tos, or slept beneath their wagons. At one fire Jon saw a man hardening the points of long wooden spears and tossing them in a pile. Else-where two bearded youths in boiled leather were sparring with staffs, leaping at each other over the flames, grunting each time one landed a blow. A dozen women sat nearby in a circle, fletching arrows.

Arrows for my brothers, Jon thought. *Arrows for my father's folk, for the people of Winterfell and Deepwood Motte and the Last Hearth. Arrows for the north.*

But not all he saw was warlike. He saw women dancing as well, and heard a baby crying, and a little boy ran in front of his garron, all bundled up in fur and breathless from play. Sheep and goats wandered freely, while oxen plodded along the riverbank in search of grass. The smell of roast mutton drifted from one cookfire, and at another he saw a boar turning on a wooden spit.

In an open space surrounded by tall green soldier pines, Rattleshirt dismounted. "We'll make camp here," he told Lenyl and Ragwyle and the others. "Feed the horses, then the dogs, then yourself. Ygritte, Longspear, bring the crow so Mance can have his look. We'll gut him after."

They walked the rest of the way, past more cookfires and more tents, with Ghost following at their heels. Jon had never seen so many wildlings. He wondered if anyone ever had. *The camp goes on forever,* he reflected, *but it's more a hundred camps than one, and each more vulnerable than the last.* Stretched out over long leagues, the wildlings had no defenses to speak of, no pits nor sharpened stakes, only small groups of outriders patrolling their perimeters. Each group or clan or village had simply stopped where they wanted, as soon as they saw others stopping or found a likely spot. *The free folk.* If his brothers were to catch them in such disarray, many of them would pay for that freedom with their life's blood. They had numbers, but the Night's Watch had discipline, and in battle discipline beats numbers nine times of every ten, his father had once told him.

There was no doubting which tent was the king's. It was thrice the size of the next largest he'd seen, and he could hear music drifting from within. Like many of the lesser tents it was made of sewn hides with the fur still on, but Mance Rayder's hides were the shaggy white pelts of snow bears. The peaked roof was crowned with a huge set of antlers from one of the giant elks that had once roamed freely throughout the Seven Kingdoms, in the times of the First Men.

Here at least they found defenders; two guards at the flap of the tent, leaning on tall spears with round leather shields strapped to their arms. When they caught sight of Ghost, one of them lowered his spearpoint and said, "That beast stays here."

"Ghost, stay," Jon commanded. The direwolf sat.

"Longspear, watch the beast." Rattleshirt yanked open the tent and gestured Jon and Ygritte inside.

The tent was hot and smoky. Baskets of burning peat stood in all four corners, filling the air with a dim reddish light. More skins carpeted the ground. Jon felt utterly alone as he stood there in his blacks, awaiting the pleasure of the turncloak who called himself King-beyond-the-Wall. When his eyes had adjusted to the smoky red gloom, he saw six people, none of whom paid him any mind. A dark young man and a pretty blonde woman were sharing a horn of mead. A pregnant woman stood over a brazier cooking a brace of hens, while a grey-haired man in a tattered cloak of black and red sat crosslegged on a pillow, playing a lute and singing:

> *The Dornishman's wife was as fair as the sun,*
> *and her kisses were warmer than spring.*
> *But the Dornishman's blade was made of black steel,*
> *and its kiss was a terrible thing.*

Jon knew the song, though it was strange to hear it here, in a shaggy hide tent beyond the Wall, ten thousand leagues from the red mountains and warm winds of Dorne.

Rattleshirt took off his yellowed helm as he waited for the song to end. Beneath his bone-and-leather armor he was a small man, and the face under the giant's skull was ordinary, with a knobby chin, thin mustache, and sallow, pinched cheeks. His eyes were close-set, one eyebrow creeping all the way across his forehead, dark hair thinning back from a sharp widow's peak.

The Dornishman's wife would sing as she bathed,
in a voice that was sweet as a peach,
But the Dornishman's blade had a song of its own,
and a bite sharp and cold as a leech.

Beside the brazier, a short but immensely broad man sat on a stool, eating a hen off a skewer. Hot grease was running down his chin and into his snow-white beard, but he smiled happily all the same. Thick gold bands graven with runes bound his massive arms, and he wore a heavy shirt of black ringmail that could only have come from a dead ranger. A few feet away, a taller, leaner man in a leather shirt sewn with bronze scales stood frowning over a map, a two-handed greatsword slung across his back in a leather sheath. He was straight as a spear, all long wiry muscle, clean-shaved, bald, with a strong straight nose and deepset grey eyes. He might even have been comely if he'd had ears, but he had lost both along the way, whether to frostbite or some enemy's knife Jon could not tell. Their lack made the man's head seem narrow and pointed.

Both the white-bearded man and the bald one were warriors, that was plain to Jon at a glance. *These two are more dangerous than Rattleshirt by far.* He wondered which was Mance Rayder.

As he lay on the ground with the darkness around,
and the taste of his blood on his tongue,
His brothers knelt by him and prayed him a prayer,
and he smiled and he laughed and he sung,
"Brothers, oh brothers, my days here are done,
the Dornishman's taken my life,
But what does it matter, for all men must die,
and I've tasted the Dornishman's wife!"

As the last strains of "The Dornishman's Wife" faded, the bald earless man glanced up from his map and scowled ferociously at Rattleshirt and Ygritte, with Jon between them. "What's this?" he said. "A crow?"

"The black bastard what gutted Orell," said Rattleshirt, "and a bloody warg as well."

"You were to kill them all."

"This one come over," explained Ygritte. "He slew Qhorin Halfhand with his own hand."

"This *boy?*" The earless man was angered by the news. "The Halfhand should have been mine. Do you have a name, crow?"

"Jon Snow, Your Grace." He wondered whether he was expected to bend the knee as well.

"Your Grace?" The earless man looked at the big white-bearded one. "You see. He takes me for a king."

The bearded man laughed so hard he sprayed bits of chicken everywhere. He rubbed the grease from his mouth with the back of a huge hand. "A blind boy, must be. Who ever heard of a king without ears? Why, his crown would fall straight down to his neck! Har!" He grinned at Jon, wiping his fingers clean on his breeches. "Close your beak, crow. Spin yourself around, might be you'd find who you're looking for."

Jon turned.

The singer rose to his feet. "I'm Mance Rayder," he said as he put aside the lute. "And you are Ned Stark's bastard, the Snow of Winterfell."

Stunned, Jon stood speechless for a moment, before he recovered enough to say, "How ... how could you know ..."

"That's a tale for later," said Mance Rayder. "How did you like the song, lad?"

"Well enough. I'd heard it before."

"But what does it matter, for all men must die," the King-beyond-the-Wall said lightly, *"and I've tasted the Dornishman's wife.* Tell me, does my Lord of Bones speak truly? Did you slay my old friend the Halfhand?"

"I did." *Though it was his doing more than mine.*

"The Shadow Tower will never again seem as fearsome," the king said with sadness in his voice. "Qhorin was my enemy. But also my brother, once. So ... shall I thank you for killing him, Jon Snow? Or curse you?" He gave Jon a mocking smile.

The King-beyond-the-Wall looked nothing like a king, nor even much a wildling. He was of middling height, slender, sharp-faced, with shrewd brown eyes and long brown hair that had gone mostly to grey. There was no crown on his head, no gold rings on his arms, no jewels at his throat, not even a gleam of silver. He wore wool and leather, and his only garment of note was his ragged black wool cloak, its long tears patched with faded red silk.

"You ought to thank me for killing your enemy," Jon said finally, "and curse me for killing your friend."

"*Har!*" boomed the white-bearded man. "Well answered!"

"Agreed." Mance Rayder beckoned Jon closer. "If you would join us, you'd best know us. The man you took for me is Styr, Magnar of Thenn. *Magnar* means 'lord' in the Old Tongue." The earless man stared at Jon coldly as Mance turned to the white-bearded one. "Our ferocious chicken-eater here is my loyal Tormund. The woman – "

Tormund rose to his feet. "Hold. You gave Styr his style, give me mine."

Mance Rayder laughed. "As you wish. Jon Snow, before you stands Tormund Giantsbane, Tall-talker, Hornblower, and Breaker of Ice. And here also Tormund Thunderfist, Husband to Bears, the Mead-king of Ruddy Hall, Speaker to Gods and Father of Hosts."

"That sounds more like me," said Tormund. "Well met, Jon Snow. I am fond o' wargs, as it happens, though not o' Starks."

"The good woman at the brazier," Mance Rayder went on, "is Dalla." The pregnant woman smiled shyly. "Treat her like you would any queen, she is carrying my child." He turned to the last two. "This beauty is her sister Val. Young Jarl beside her is her latest pet."

"I am no man's pet," said Jarl, dark and fierce.

"And Val's no man," white-bearded Tormund snorted. "You ought to have noticed that by now, lad."

"So there you have us, Jon Snow," said Mance Rayder. "The King-beyond-the-Wall and his court, such as it is. And now some words from you, I think. Where did you come from?"

"Winterfell," he said, "by way of Castle Black."

"And what brings you up the Milkwater, so far from the fires of home?" He did not wait for Jon's answer, but looked at once to Rattleshirt. "How many were they?"

"Five. Three's dead and the boy's here. T'other went up a mountainside where no horse could follow."

Rayder's eyes met Jon's again. "Was it only the five of you? Or are more of your brothers skulking about?"

"We were four and the Halfhand. Qhorin was worth twenty common men."

The King-beyond-the-Wall smiled at that. "Some thought so. Still . . . a boy from Castle Black with rangers from the Shadow Tower? How did that come to be?"

Jon had his lie all ready. "The Lord Commander sent me to the Halfhand for seasoning, so he took me on his ranging."

Styr the Magnar frowned at that. "Ranging, you call it . . . why would crows come ranging up the Skirling Pass?"

"The villages were deserted," Jon said, truthfully. "It was as if all the free folk had vanished."

"Vanished, aye," said Mance Rayder. "And not just the free folk. Who told you where we were, Jon Snow?"

Tormund snorted. "It were Craster, or I'm a blushing maid. I told you, Mance, that creature needs to be shorter by a head."

The king gave the older man an irritated look. "Tormund, some day try thinking before you speak. I know it was Craster. I asked Jon to see if he would tell it true."

"Har." Tormund spat. "Well, I stepped in that!" He grinned at Jon. "See, lad, that's why he's king and I'm not. I can outdrink, outfight, and outsing him, and my member's thrice the size o' his, but Mance has cunning. He was raised a crow, you know, and the crow's a tricksy bird."

"I would speak with the lad alone, my Lord of Bones," Mance Rayder said to Rattleshirt. "Leave us, all of you."

"What, me as well?" said Tormund.

"No, you especially," said Mance.

"I eat in no hall where I'm not welcome." Tormund got to his feet. "Me and the hens are leaving." He snatched another chicken off the brazier, shoved it into a pocket sewn in the lining of his cloak, said "Har," and left licking his fingers. The others followed him out, all but the woman Dalla.

"Sit, if you like," Rayder said when they were gone. "Are you hungry? Tormund left us two birds at least."

"I would be pleased to eat, Your Grace. And thank you."

"Your Grace?" The king smiled. "That's not a style one often hears from the lips of free folk. I'm Mance to most, *the* Mance to some. Will you take a horn of mead?"

"Gladly," said Jon.

The king poured himself as Dalla cut the well-crisped hens apart and brought them each a half. Jon peeled off his gloves and ate with his fingers, sucking every morsel of meat off the bones.

"Tormund spoke truly," said Mance Rayder as he ripped apart a loaf of bread. "The black crow is a tricksy bird, that's so ... but I was a crow when you were no bigger than the babe in Dalla's belly, Jon Snow. So take care not to play tricksy with me."

"As you say, Your – Mance."

The king laughed. "Your Mance! Why not? I promised you a tale before, of how I knew you. Have you puzzled it out yet?"

Jon shook his head. "Did Rattleshirt send word ahead?"

"By wing? We have no trained ravens. No, I knew your face. I've seen it before. Twice."

It made no sense at first, but as Jon turned it over in his mind, dawn broke. "When you were a brother of the Watch ..."

"Very good! Yes, that was the first time. You were just a boy, and I was all in black, one of a dozen riding escort to old Lord Commander Qorgyle when he came down to see your father at Winterfell. I was walking the wall around the yard when I came on you and your brother Robb. It had snowed the night before, and the two of you had built a great mountain above the gate and were waiting for someone likely to pass underneath."

"I remember," said Jon with a startled laugh. A young

black brother on the wallwalk, yes . . . "You swore not to tell."

"And kept my vow. That one, at least."

"We dumped the snow on Fat Tom. He was Father's slowest guardsman." Tom had chased them around the yard afterward, until all three were red as autumn apples. "But you said you saw me twice. When was the other time?"

"When King Robert came to Winterfell to make your father Hand," the King-beyond-the-Wall said lightly.

Jon's eyes widened in disbelief. "That can't be so."

"It was. When your father learned the king was coming, he sent word to his brother Benjen on the Wall, so he might come down for the feast. There is more commerce between the black brothers and the free folk than you know, and soon enough word came to my ears as well. It was too choice a chance to resist. Your uncle did not know me by sight, so I had no fear from that quarter, and I did not think your father was like to remember a young crow he'd met briefly years before. I wanted to see this Robert with my own eyes, king to king, and get the measure of your uncle Benjen as well. He was First Ranger by then, and the bane of all my people. So I saddled my fleetest horse, and rode."

"But," Jon objected, "the Wall . . ."

"The Wall can stop an army, but not a man alone. I took a lute and a bag of silver, scaled the ice near Long Barrow, walked a few leagues south of the New Gift, and bought a horse. All in all I made much better time than Robert, who was traveling with a ponderous great wheelhouse to keep his queen in comfort. A day south of Winterfell I came up on him and fell in with his company. Freeriders and hedge knights are always attaching themselves to royal processions, in hopes of finding service with the king, and my lute gained me easy acceptance." He laughed. "I know every bawdy song that's ever been made, north or south of the Wall. So there you are. The night your father feasted Robert, I sat in the back of his hall on a bench with the other freeriders, listening to Orland of Oldtown play the high harp and sing of dead kings beneath the sea. I betook of your lord father's meat and mead, had a look at Kingslayer and Imp . . . and made passing note of Lord Eddard's children and the wolf pups that ran at their heels."

"Bael the Bard," said Jon, remembering the tale that Ygritte had told him in the Frostfangs, the night he'd almost killed her.

"Would that I were. I will not deny that Bael's exploit inspired mine own . . . but I did not steal either of your sisters that I recall. Bael wrote his own songs, and lived them. I only sing the songs that better men have made. More mead?"

"No," said Jon. "If you had been discovered . . . taken . . ."

"Your father would have had my head off." The king gave a shrug. "Though once I had eaten at his board I was protected by guest right. The laws of hospitality are as old as the First Men, and sacred as a heart tree." He gestured at the board between them, the broken bread and chicken bones. "Here you are the guest, and safe from harm at my hands . . . this night, at least. So tell me truly, Jon Snow. Are you a craven who turned your cloak from fear, or is there another reason that brings you to my tent?"

Guest right or no, Jon Snow knew he walked on rotten ice here. One false step and he might plunge through, into water cold enough to stop his heart. *Weigh every word before you speak it*, he told himself. He took a long draught of mead to buy time for his answer. When he set the horn aside he said, "Tell me why you turned your cloak, and I'll tell you why I turned mine."

Mance Rayder smiled, as Jon had hoped he would. The king was plainly a man who liked the sound of his own voice. "You will have heard stories of my desertion, I have no doubt."

"Some say it was for a crown. Some say for a woman. Others that you had the wildling blood."

"The wildling blood is the blood of the First Men, the same blood that flows in the veins of the Starks. As to a crown, do you see one?"

"I see a woman." He glanced at Dalla.

Mance took her by the hand and pulled her close. "My lady is blameless. I met her on my return from your father's castle. The Halfhand was carved of old oak, but I am made of flesh, and I have a great fondness for the charms of women . . . which makes me no different from three-quarters of the Watch. There are men still wearing black who have had ten times as many women as this poor king. You must guess again, Jon Snow."

Jon considered a moment. "The Halfhand said you had a passion for wildling music."

"I did. I do. That's closer to the mark, yes. But not a hit." Mance Rayder rose, unfastened the clasp that held his cloak, and swept it over the bench. "It was for this."

"A cloak?"

"The black wool cloak of a Sworn Brother of the Night's Watch," said the King-beyond-the-Wall. "One day on a ranging we brought down a fine big elk. We were skinning it when the smell of blood drew a shadowcat out of its lair. I drove it off, but not before it shredded my cloak to ribbons. Do you see? Here, here, and here?" He chuckled. "It shredded my arm and back as well, and I bled worse than the elk. My brothers feared I might die before they got me back to Maester Mullin at the Shadow Tower, so they carried me to a wildling village where we knew an old wisewoman did some healing. She was dead, as it happened, but her daughter saw to me. Cleaned my wounds, sewed me up, and fed me porridge and potions until I was strong enough to ride again. And she sewed up the rents in my cloak as well, with some scarlet silk from Asshai that her grandmother had pulled from the wreck of a cog washed up on the Frozen Shore. It was the greatest treasure she had, and her gift to me." He swept the cloak back over his shoulders. "But at the Shadow Tower, I was given a new wool cloak from stores, black and black, and trimmed with black, to go with my black breeches and black boots, my black doublet and black mail. The new cloak had no frays nor rips nor tears . . . and most of all, no red. The men of the Night's Watch dressed in *black*, Ser Denys Mallister reminded me sternly, as if I had forgotten. My old cloak was fit for burning now, he said.

"I left the next morning . . . for a place where a kiss was not a crime, and a man could wear any cloak he chose." He closed the clasp and sat back down again. "And you, Jon Snow?"

Jon took another swallow of mead. *There is only one tale that he might believe.* "You say you were at Winterfell, the night my father feasted King Robert."

"I did say it, for I was."

"Then you saw us all. Prince Joffrey and Prince Tommen, Princess Myrcella, my brothers Robb and Bran and Rickon, my sisters Arya and Sansa. You saw them walk the center aisle with every eye upon them and take their seats at the table just below the dais where the king and queen were seated."

"I remember."

"And did you see where I was seated, Mance?" He leaned forward. "Did you see where they put the bastard?"

Mance Rayder looked at Jon's face for a long moment. "I think we had best find you a new cloak," the king said, holding out his hand.

DAENERYS

Across the still blue water came the slow steady beat of drums and the soft swish of oars from the galleys. The great cog groaned in their wake, the heavy lines stretched taut between. *Balerion*'s sails hung limp, drooping forlorn from the masts. Yet even so, as she stood upon the forecastle watching her dragons chase each other across a cloudless blue sky, Daenerys Targaryen was as happy as she could ever remember being.

Her Dothraki called the sea *the poison water*, distrusting any liquid that their horses could not drink. On the day the three ships had lifted anchor at Qarth, you would have thought they were sailing to hell instead of Pentos. Her brave young bloodriders had stared off at the dwindling coastline with huge white eyes, each of the three determined to show no fear before the other two, while her handmaids Irri and Jhiqui clutched the rail desperately and retched over the side at every little swell. The rest of Dany's tiny *khalasar* remained below decks, preferring the company of their nervous horses to the terrifying landless world about the ships. When a sudden squall had enveloped them six days into the voyage, she heard them through the hatches; the horses kicking and screaming, the riders praying in thin quavery voices each time *Balerion* heaved or swayed.

No squall could frighten Dany, though. *Daenerys*

Stormborn, she was called, for she had come howling into the world on distant Dragonstone as the greatest storm in the memory of Westeros howled outside, a storm so fierce that it ripped gargoyles from the castle walls and smashed her father's fleet to kindling.

The narrow sea was often stormy, and Dany had crossed it half a hundred times as a girl, running from one Free City to the next half a step ahead of the Usurper's hired knives. She loved the sea. She liked the sharp salty smell of the air, and the vastness of horizons bounded only by a vault of azure sky above. It made her feel small, but free as well. She liked the dolphins that sometimes swam along beside *Balerion*, slicing through the waves like silvery spears, and the flying fish they glimpsed now and again. She even liked the sailors, with all their songs and stories. Once on a voyage to Braavos, as she'd watched the crew wrestle down a great green sail in a rising gale, she had even thought how fine it would be to be a sailor. But when she told her brother, Viserys had twisted her hair until she cried. "You are blood of the dragon," he had screamed at her. "A *dragon*, not some smelly fish."

He was a fool about that, and so much else, Dany thought. *If he had been wiser and more patient, it would be him sailing west to take the throne that was his by rights*. Viserys had been stupid and vicious, she had come to realize, yet sometimes she missed him all the same. Not the cruel weak man he had become by the end, but the brother who had sometimes let her creep into his bed, the boy who told her tales of the Seven Kingdoms, and talked of how much better their lives would be once he claimed his crown.

The captain appeared at her elbow. "Would that this *Balerion* could soar as her namesake did, Your Grace," he said in bastard Valyrian heavily flavored with accents of Pentos. "Then we should not need to row, nor tow, nor pray for wind."

"Just so, Captain," she answered with a smile, pleased to have won the man over. Captain Groleo was an old Pentoshi like his master, Illyrio Mopatis, and he had been nervous as a maiden about carrying three dragons on his ship. Half a hundred buckets of seawater still hung from the gunwales, in case of fires. At first Groleo had wanted the dragons caged and Dany had consented to put his fears at ease, but their misery was so palpable that she soon changed her mind and insisted they be freed.

Even Captain Groleo was glad of that, now. There had been one small fire, easily extinguished; against that, *Balerion* suddenly seemed to have far fewer rats than she'd had before, when she sailed under the name *Saduleon*. And her crew, once as fearful as they were curious, had begun to take a queer fierce pride in "their" dragons. Every man of them, from captain to cook's boy, loved to watch the three fly . . . though none so much as Dany.

They are my children, she told herself, *and if the* maegi *spoke truly, they are the only children I am ever like to have.*

Viserion's scales were the color of fresh cream, his horns, wing bones, and spinal crest a dark gold that flashed bright as metal in the sun. Rhaegal was made of the green of summer and the bronze of fall. They soared above the ships in wide circles, higher and higher, each trying to climb above the other.

Dragons always preferred to attack from above, Dany had learned. Should either get between the other and the sun, he would fold his wings and dive screaming, and they would tumble from the sky locked together in a tangled scaly ball, jaws snapping and tails lashing. The first time they had done it, she feared that they meant to kill each other, but it was only sport. No sooner would they splash into the sea than they would break apart and rise again, shrieking and hissing, the salt water steaming off them as their wings clawed at the air. Drogon was aloft as well, though not in sight; he would be miles ahead, or miles behind, hunting.

He was always hungry, her Drogon. *Hungry and growing fast. Another year, or perhaps two, and he may be large enough to ride. Then I shall have no need of ships to cross the great salt sea.*

But that time was not yet come. Rhaegal and Viserion were the size of small dogs, Drogon only a little larger, and any dog would have outweighed them; they were all wings and neck and tail, lighter than they looked. And so Daenerys Targaryen must rely on wood and wind and canvas to bear her home.

The wood and the canvas had served her well enough so far, but the fickle wind had turned traitor. For six days and six nights they had been becalmed, and now a seventh day had come, and still no breath of air to fill their sails. Fortunately, two of the ships that Magister Illyrio had sent after her were trading galleys, with two hundred oars apiece and crews of strong-armed oarsmen to row them. But the great cog *Balerion* was a song of a different key; a ponderous broad-beamed sow of a ship with immense holds and huge sails, but helpless in a calm. *Vhagar* and *Meraxes* had let out lines to tow her, but it made for painfully slow going. All three ships were crowded, and heavily laden.

"I cannot see Drogon," said Ser Jorah Mormont as he joined her on the forecastle. "Is he lost again?"

"We are the ones who are lost, ser. Drogon has no taste for this wet creeping, no more than I do." Bolder than the other two, her black dragon had been the first to try his wings above the water, the first to flutter from ship to ship, the first to lose himself in a passing cloud . . . and the first to kill. The flying fish no sooner broke the surface of the water than they were enveloped in a lance of flame, snatched up, and swallowed. "How big will he grow?" Dany asked curiously. "Do you know?"

"In the Seven Kingdoms, there are tales of dragons who grew so huge that they could pluck giant krakens from the seas."

Dany laughed. "That would be a wondrous sight to see."

"It is only a tale, *Khaleesi*," said her exile knight. "They talk of wise old dragons living a thousand years as well."

"Well, how long *does* a dragon live?" She looked up as Viserion swooped low over the ship, his wings beating slowly and stirring the limp sails.

Ser Jorah shrugged. "A dragon's natural span of days is many times as long as a man's, or so the songs would have us believe . . . but the dragons the Seven Kingdoms knew best were those of House Targaryen. They were bred for war, and in war they died. It is no easy thing to slay a dragon, but it can be done."

The squire Whitebeard, standing by the figurehead with one lean hand curled about his tall hardwood staff, turned toward them and said, "Balerion the Black Dread was two hundred years old when he died during the reign of Jaehaerys the Conciliator. He was so large he could swallow an aurochs whole. A dragon never stops growing, Your Grace, so long as he has food and freedom." His name was Arstan, but Strong Belwas had named him Whitebeard for his pale whiskers, and most everyone called him that now. He was taller than Ser Jorah, though not so muscular; his eyes were a pale blue, his long beard as white as snow and as fine as silk.

"Freedom?" asked Dany, curious. "What do you mean?"

"In King's Landing, your ancestors raised an immense domed castle for their dragons. The Dragonpit, it is called. It still stands atop the Hill of Rhaenys, though all in ruins now. That was where the royal dragons dwelt in days of yore, and a cavernous dwelling it was, with iron doors so wide that thirty knights could ride through them abreast. Yet even so, it was noted that none of the pit dragons ever reached the size of their ancestors. The maesters say it was because of the walls around them, and the great dome above their heads."

"If walls could keep us small, peasants would all be tiny and kings as large as giants," said Ser Jorah. "I've seen huge men born in hovels, and dwarfs who dwelt in castles."

"Men are men," Whitebeard replied. "Dragons are dragons."

Ser Jorah snorted his disdain. "How profound." The exile knight had no love for the old man, he'd made that plain from the first. "What do you know of dragons, anyway?"

"Little enough, that's true. Yet I served for a time in King's Landing in the days when King Aerys sat the Iron

Throne, and walked beneath the dragonskulls that looked down from the walls of his throne room."

"Viserys talked of those skulls," said Dany. "The Usurper took them down and hid them away. He could not bear them looking down on him upon his stolen throne." She beckoned Whitebeard closer. "Did you ever meet my royal father?" King Aerys II had died before his daughter was born.

"I had that great honor, Your Grace."

"Did you find him good and gentle?"

Whitebeard did his best to hide his feelings, but they were there, plain on his face. "His Grace was . . . often pleasant."

"Often?" Dany smiled. "But not always?"

"He could be very harsh to those he thought his enemies."

"A wise man never makes an enemy of a king," said Dany. "Did you know my brother Rhaegar as well?"

"It was said that no man ever knew Prince Rhaegar, truly. I had the privilege of seeing him in tourney, though, and often heard him play his harp with its silver strings."

Ser Jorah snorted. "Along with a thousand others at some harvest feast. Next you'll claim you squired for him."

"I make no such claim, ser. Myles Mooton was Prince Rhaegar's squire, and Richard Lonmouth after him. When they won their spurs, he knighted them himself, and they remained his close companions. Young Lord Connington was dear to the prince as well, but his oldest friend was Arthur Dayne."

"The Sword of the Morning!" said Dany, delighted. "Viserys used to talk about his wondrous white blade. He said Ser Arthur was the only knight in the realm who was our brother's peer."

Whitebeard bowed his head. "It is not my place to question the words of Prince Viserys."

"King," Dany corrected. "He was a king, though he never reigned. Viserys, the Third of His Name. But what do you mean?" His answer had not been one that she'd expected. "Ser Jorah named Rhaegar the last dragon once.

He had to have been a peerless warrior to be called that, surely?"

"Your Grace," said Whitebeard, "the Prince of Dragonstone was a most puissant warrior, but . . ."

"Go on," she urged. "You may speak freely to me."

"As you command." The old man leaned upon his hardwood staff, his brow furrowed. "A warrior without peer . . . those are fine words, Your Grace, but words win no battles."

"Swords win battles," Ser Jorah said bluntly. "And Prince Rhaegar knew how to use one."

"He did, ser, but . . . I have seen a hundred tournaments and more wars than I would wish, and however strong or fast or skilled a knight may be, there are others who can match him. A man will win one tourney, and fall quickly in the next. A slick spot in the grass may mean defeat, or what you ate for supper the night before. A change in the wind may bring the gift of victory." He glanced at Ser Jorah. "Or a lady's favor knotted round an arm."

Mormont's face darkened. "Be careful what you say, old man."

Arstan had seen Ser Jorah fight at Lannisport, Dany knew, in the tourney Mormont had won with a lady's favor knotted round his arm. He had won the lady too; Lynesse of House Hightower, his second wife, highborn and beautiful . . . but she had ruined him, and abandoned him, and the memory of her was bitter to him now. "Be gentle, my knight." She put a hand on Jorah's arm. "Arstan had no wish to give offense, I'm certain."

"As you say, *Khaleesi*." Ser Jorah's voice was grudging.

Dany turned back to the squire. "I know little of Rhaegar. Only the tales Viserys told, and he was a little boy when our brother died. What was he truly like?"

The old man considered a moment. "Able. That above all. Determined, deliberate, dutiful, single-minded. There is a tale told of him . . . but doubtless Ser Jorah knows it as well."

"I would hear it from you."

"As you wish," said Whitebeard. "As a young boy, the

Prince of Dragonstone was bookish to a fault. He was reading so early that men said Queen Rhaella must have swallowed some books and a candle whilst he was in her womb. Rhaegar took no interest in the play of other children. The maesters were awed by his wits, but his father's knights would jest sourly that Baelor the Blessed had been born again. Until one day Prince Rhaegar found something in his scrolls that changed him. No one knows what it might have been, only that the boy suddenly appeared early one morning in the yard as the knights were donning their steel. He walked up to Ser Willem Darry, the master-at-arms, and said, 'I will require sword and armor. It seems I must be a warrior.'"

"And he was!" said Dany, delighted.

"He was indeed." Whitebeard bowed. "My pardons, Your Grace. We speak of warriors, and I see that Strong Belwas has arisen. I must attend him."

Dany glanced aft. The eunuch was climbing through the hold amidships, nimble for all his size. Belwas was squat but broad, a good fifteen stone of fat and muscle, his great brown gut crisscrossed by faded white scars. He wore baggy pants, a yellow silk bellyband, and an absurdly tiny leather vest dotted with iron studs. "Strong Belwas is hungry!" he roared at everyone and no one in particular. "Strong Belwas will eat now!" Turning, he spied Arstan on the forecastle. "Whitebeard! You will bring food for Strong Belwas!"

"You may go," Dany told the squire. He bowed again, and moved off to tend the needs of the man he served.

Ser Jorah watched with a frown on his blunt honest face. Mormont was big and burly, strong of jaw and thick of shoulder. Not a handsome man by any means, but as true a friend as Dany had ever known. "You would be wise to take that old man's words well salted," he told her when Whitebeard was out of earshot.

"A queen must listen to all," she reminded him. "The highborn and the low, the strong and the weak, the noble and the venal. One voice may speak you false, but in many there is always truth to be found." She had read that in a book.

"Hear my voice then, Your Grace," the exile said. "This Arstan Whitebeard is playing you false. He is too old to be a squire, and too well spoken to be serving that oaf of a eunuch."

That does seem queer, Dany had to admit. Strong Belwas was an ex-slave, bred and trained in the fighting pits of Meereen. Magister Illyrio had sent him to guard her, or so Belwas claimed, and it was true that she needed guarding. The Usurper on his Iron Throne had offered land and lordship to any man who killed her. One attempt had been made already, with a cup of poisoned wine. The closer she came to Westeros, the more likely another attack became. Back in Qarth, the warlock Pyat Pree had sent a Sorrowful Man after her to avenge the Undying she'd burned in their House of Dust. Warlocks never forgot a wrong, it was said, and the Sorrowful Men never failed to kill. Most of the Dothraki would be against her as well. Khal Drogo's *ko*s led *khalasar*s of their own now, and none of them would hesitate to attack her own little band on sight, to slay and slave her people and drag Dany herself back to Vaes Dothrak to take her proper place among the withered crones of the *dosh khaleen*. She *hoped* that Xaro Xhoan Daxos was not an enemy, but the Qartheen merchant had coveted her dragons. And there was Quaithe of the Shadow, that strange woman in the red lacquer mask with all her cryptic counsel. Was she an enemy too, or only a dangerous friend? Dany could not say.

Ser Jorah saved me from the poisoner, and Arstan Whitebeard from the manticore. Perhaps Strong Belwas will save me from the next. He was huge enough, with arms like small trees and a great curved *arakh* so sharp he might have shaved with it, in the unlikely event of hair sprouting on those smooth brown cheeks. Yet he was childlike as well. *As a protector, he leaves much to be desired. Thankfully, I have Ser Jorah and my bloodriders. And my dragons, never forget.* In time, the dragons would be her most formidable guardians, just as they had been for Aegon the Conqueror and his sisters three hundred years ago. Just now, though, they brought her more danger than protection. In all the world there were but three living dragons, and those were hers; they were a wonder, and a terror, and beyond price.

She was pondering her next words when she felt a cool breath on the back of her neck, and a loose strand of her silver-gold hair stirred against her brow. Above, the canvas creaked and moved, and suddenly a great cry went up from all over *Balerion*. "Wind!" the sailors shouted. "The wind returns, the *wind!*"

Dany looked up to where the great cog's sails rippled and belled as the lines thrummed and tightened and sang the sweet song they had missed so for six long days. Captain Groleo rushed aft, shouting commands. The Pentoshi were scrambling up the masts, those that were not cheering. Even Strong Belwas let out a great bellow and did a little dance. "The gods are good!" Dany said. "You see, Jorah? We are on our way once more."

"Yes," he said, "but to what, my queen?"

All day the wind blew, steady from the east at first, and then in wild gusts. The sun set in a blaze of red. *I am still half a world from Westeros,* Dany reminded herself, *but every hour brings me closer.* She tried to imagine what it would feel like, when she first caught sight of the land she was born to rule. *It will be as fair a shore as I have ever seen, I know it. How could it be otherwise?*

But later that night, as *Balerion* plunged onward through the dark and Dany sat crosslegged on her bunk in the captain's cabin, feeding her dragons – "Even upon the sea," Groleo had said, so graciously, "queens take precedence over captains" – a sharp knock came upon the door.

Irri had been sleeping at the foot of her bunk (it was too narrow for three, and tonight was Jhiqui's turn to share the soft featherbed with her *khaleesi*), but the handmaid roused at the knock and went to the door. Dany pulled up a coverlet and tucked it in under her arms. She was naked, and had not expected a caller at this hour. "Come," she said when she saw Ser Jorah standing without, beneath a swaying lantern.

The exile knight ducked his head as he entered. "Your Grace. I am sorry to disturb your sleep."

"I was not sleeping, ser. Come and watch." She took a chunk of salt pork out of the bowl in her lap and held it up for her dragons to see. All three of them eyed it hungrily. Rhaegal spread green wings and stirred the air, and Viserion's neck swayed back and forth like a long pale snake's as he followed the movement of her hand. "Drogon," Dany said softly, "*dracarys*." And she tossed the pork in the air.

Drogon moved quicker than a striking cobra. Flame roared from his mouth, orange and scarlet and black, searing the meat before it began to fall. As his sharp black teeth snapped shut around it, Rhaegal's head darted close, as if to steal the prize from his brother's jaws, but Drogon swallowed and screamed, and the smaller green dragon could only *hiss* in frustration.

"Stop that, Rhaegal," Dany said in annoyance, giving his head a swat. "You had the last one. I'll have no greedy dragons." She smiled at Ser Jorah. "I won't need to char their meat over a brazier any longer."

"So I see. *Dracarys!*"

All three dragons turned their heads at the sound of that word, and Viserion let loose with a blast of pale gold flame that made Ser Jorah take a hasty step backward. Dany giggled. "Be careful with that word, ser, or they're like to singe your beard off. It means 'dragonfire' in High Valyrian. I wanted to choose a command that no one was like to utter by chance."

Mormont nodded. "Your Grace," he said, "I wonder if I might have a few private words?"

"Of course. Irri, leave us for a bit." She put a hand on Jhiqui's bare shoulder and shook the other handmaid awake. "You as well, sweetling. Ser Jorah needs to talk to me."

"Yes, *Khaleesi*." Jhiqui tumbled from the bunk, naked and yawning, her thick black hair tumbled about her head. She dressed quickly and left with Irri, closing the door behind them.

Dany gave the dragons the rest of the salt pork to squabble over, and patted the bed beside her. "Sit, good ser, and tell me what is troubling you."

"Three things." Ser Jorah sat. "Strong Belwas. This Arstan Whitebeard. And Illyrio Mopatis, who sent them."

Again? Dany pulled the coverlet higher and tugged one end over her shoulder. "And why is that?"

"The warlocks in Qarth told you that you would be betrayed three times," the exile knight reminded her, as Viserion and Rhaegal began to snap and claw at each other.

"Once for blood and once for gold and once for love." Dany was not like to forget. "Mirri Maz Duur was the first."

"Which means two traitors yet remain ... and now these two appear. I find that troubling, yes. Never forget, Robert offered a lordship to the man who slays you."

Dany leaned forward and yanked Viserion's tail, to pull him off his green brother. Her blanket fell away from her chest as she moved. She grabbed it hastily and covered herself again. "The Usurper is dead," she said.

"But his son rules in his place." Ser Jorah lifted his gaze, and his dark eyes met her own. "A dutiful son pays his father's debts. Even blood debts."

"This boy Joffrey might want me dead ... if he recalls that I'm alive. What has that to do with Belwas and Arstan Whitebeard? The old man does not even wear a sword. You've seen that."

"Aye. And I have seen how deftly he handles that staff of his. Recall how he killed that manticore in Qarth? It might as easily have been your throat he crushed."

"Might have been, but was not," she pointed out. "It was a stinging manticore meant to slay me. He saved my life."

"*Khaleesi*, has it occurred to you that Whitebeard and Belwas might have been in league with the assassin? It might all have been a ploy to win your trust."

Her sudden laughter made Drogon *hiss*, and sent Viserion flapping to his perch above the porthole. "The ploy worked well."

The exile knight did not return her smile. "These are Illyrio's ships, Illyrio's captains, Illyrio's sailors ... and Strong Belwas and Arstan are his men as well, not yours."

"Magister Illyrio has protected me in the past. Strong

Belwas says that he wept when he heard my brother was dead."

"Yes," said Mormont, "but did he weep for Viserys, or for the plans he had made with him?"

"His plans need not change. Magister Illyrio is a friend to House Targaryen, and wealthy . . ."

"He was not born wealthy. In the world as I have seen it, no man grows rich by kindness. The warlocks said the second treason would be for *gold*. What does Illyrio Mopatis love more than gold?"

"His skin." Across the cabin Drogon stirred restlessly, steam rising from his snout. "Mirri Maz Duur betrayed me. I burned her for it."

"Mirri Maz Duur was in your power. In Pentos, you shall be in Illyrio's power. It is not the same. I know the magister as well as you. He is a devious man, and clever – "

"I need clever men about me if I am to win the Iron Throne."

Ser Jorah snorted. "That wineseller who tried to poison you was a clever man as well. Clever men hatch ambitious schemes."

Dany drew her legs up beneath the blanket. "You will protect me. You, and my bloodriders."

"Four men? *Khaleesi*, you believe you know Illyrio Mopatis, very well. Yet you insist on surrounding yourself with men you do *not* know, like this puffed-up eunuch and the world's oldest squire. Take a lesson from Pyat Pree and Xaro Xhoan Daxos."

He means well, Dany reminded herself. *He does all he does for love.* "It seems to me that a queen who trusts no one is as foolish as a queen who trusts everyone. Every man I take into my service is a risk, I understand that, but how am I to win the Seven Kingdoms without such risks? Am I to conquer Westeros with one exile knight and three Dothraki bloodriders?"

His jaw set stubbornly. "Your path is dangerous, I will not deny that. But if you blindly trust in every liar and schemer who crosses it, you will end as your brothers did."

His obstinacy made her angry. *He treats me like some*

child. "Strong Belwas could not scheme his way to breakfast. And what lies has Arstan Whitebeard told me?"

"He is not what he pretends to be. He speaks to you more boldly than any squire would dare."

"He spoke frankly at my command. He knew my brother."

"A great many men knew your brother. Your Grace, in Westeros the Lord Commander of the Kingsguard sits on the small council, and serves the king with his wits as well as his steel. If I am the first of your Queensguard, I pray you, hear me out. I have a plan to put to you."

"What plan? Tell me."

"Illyrio Mopatis wants you back in Pentos, under his roof. Very well, go to him . . . but in your own time, and not alone. Let us see how loyal and obedient these new subjects of yours truly are. Command Groleo to change course for Slaver's Bay."

Dany was not certain she liked the sound of that at all. Everything she'd ever heard of the flesh marts in the great slave cities of Yunkai, Meereen, and Astapor was dire and frightening. "What is there for me in Slaver's Bay?"

"An army," said Ser Jorah. "If Strong Belwas is so much to your liking you can buy hundreds more like him out of the fighting pits of Meereen . . . but it is Astapor I'd set my sails for. In Astapor you can buy Unsullied."

"The slaves in the spiked bronze hats?" Dany had seen Unsullied guards in the Free Cities, posted at the gates of magisters, archons, and dynasts. "Why should I want Unsullied? They don't even ride horses, and most of them are fat."

"The Unsullied you may have seen in Pentos and Myr were household guards. That's soft service, and eunuchs tend to plumpness in any case. Food is the only vice allowed them. To judge all Unsullied by a few old household slaves is like judging all squires by Arstan Whitebeard, Your Grace. Do you know the tale of the Three Thousand of Qohor?"

"No." The coverlet slipped off Dany's shoulder, and she tugged it back into place.

"It was four hundred years ago or more, when the

Dothraki first rode out of the east, sacking and burning every town and city in their path. The *khal* who led them was named Temmo. His *khalasar* was not so big as Drogo's, but it was big enough. Fifty thousand, at the least. Half of them braided warriors with bells ringing in their hair.

"The Qohorik knew he was coming. They strengthened their walls, doubled the size of their own guard, and hired two free companies besides, the Bright Banners and the Second Sons. And almost as an afterthought, they sent a man to Astapor to buy three thousand Unsullied. It was a long march back to Qohor, however, and as they approached they saw the smoke and dust and heard the distant din of battle.

"By the time the Unsullied reached the city the sun had set. Crows and wolves were feasting beneath the walls on what remained of the Qohorik heavy horse. The Bright Banners and Second Sons had fled, as sellswords are wont to do in the face of hopeless odds. With dark falling, the Dothraki had retired to their own camps to drink and dance and feast, but none doubted that they would return on the morrow to smash the city gates, storm the walls, and rape, loot, and slave as they pleased.

"But when dawn broke and Temmo and his bloodriders led their *khalasar* out of camp, they found three thousand Unsullied drawn up before the gates with the Black Goat standard flying over their heads. So small a force could easily have been flanked, but you know Dothraki. These were men on foot, and men on foot are fit only to be ridden down.

"The Dothraki charged. The Unsullied locked their shields, lowered their spears, and stood firm. Against twenty thousand screamers with bells in their hair, they stood firm.

"Eighteen times the Dothraki charged, and broke themselves on those shields and spears like waves on a rocky shore. Thrice Temmo sent his archers wheeling past and arrows fell like rain upon the Three Thousand, but the Unsullied merely lifted their shields above their heads until the squall had passed. In the end only six hundred of them remained ... but more than twelve thousand Dothraki lay dead upon that field, including Khal Temmo, his bloodriders, his *kos*, and all his sons. On the morning of the fourth day, the new *khal* led the survivors past the city gates in a stately procession. One by one, each man cut off his braid and threw it down before the feet of the Three Thousand.

"Since that day, the city guard of Qohor has been made up solely of Unsullied, every one of whom carries a tall spear from which hangs a braid of human hair.

"*That* is what you will find in Astapor, Your Grace. Put ashore there, and continue on to Pentos overland. It will take longer, yes ... but when you break bread with Magister Illyrio, you will have a thousand swords behind you, not just four."

There is wisdom in this, yes, Dany thought, *but ...* "How am I to buy a thousand slave soldiers? All I have of value is the crown the Tourmaline Brotherhood gave me."

"Dragons will be as great a wonder in Astapor as they were in Qarth. It may be that the slavers will shower you with gifts, as the Qartheen did. If not ... these ships carry more than your Dothraki and their horses. They took on trade goods at Qarth, I've been through the holds and seen for myself. Bolts of silk and bales of tiger skin, amber and jade carvings, saffron, myrrh ... slaves are cheap, Your Grace. Tiger skins are costly."

"Those are *Illyrio*'s tiger skins," she objected.

"And Illyrio is a friend to House Targaryen."

"All the more reason not to steal his goods."

"What use are wealthy friends if they will not put their wealth at your disposal, my queen? If Magister Illyrio would deny you, he is only Xaro Xhoan Daxos with four chins. And if he is sincere in his devotion to your cause, he will not begrudge you three shiploads of trade goods. What better use for his tiger skins than to buy you the beginnings of an army?"

That's true. Dany felt a rising excitement. "There will be dangers on such a long march ..."

"There are dangers at sea as well. Corsairs and pirates hunt the southern route, and north of Valyria the Smoking

Sea is demon-haunted. The next storm could sink or scatter us, a kraken could pull us under . . . or we might find ourselves becalmed again, and die of thirst as we wait for the wind to rise. A march will have different dangers, my queen, but none greater."

"What if Captain Groleo refuses to change course, though? And Arstan, Strong Belwas, what will they do?"

Ser Jorah stood. "Perhaps it's time you found that out."

"Yes," she decided. "I'll do it!" Dany threw back the coverlets and hopped from the bunk. "I'll see the captain at once, command him to set course for Astapor." She bent over her chest, threw open the lid, and seized the first garment to hand, a pair of loose sandsilk trousers. "Hand me my medallion belt," she commanded Jorah as she pulled the sandsilk up over her hips. "And my vest – " she started to say, turning.

Ser Jorah slid his arms around her.

"Oh," was all Dany had time to say as he pulled her close and pressed his lips down on hers. He smelled of sweat and salt and leather, and the iron studs on his jerkin dug into her naked breasts as he crushed her hard against him. One hand held her by the shoulder while the other slid down her spine to the small of her back, and her mouth opened for his tongue, though she never told it to. *His beard is scratchy*, she thought, *but his mouth is sweet*. The Dothraki wore no beards, only long mustaches, and only Khal Drogo had ever kissed her before. *He should not be doing this. I am his queen, not his woman.*

It was a long kiss, though how long Dany could not have said. When it ended, Ser Jorah let go of her, and she took a quick step backward. "You . . . you should not have . . ."

"I should not have waited so long," he finished for her. "I should have kissed you in Qarth, in Vaes Tolorru. I should have kissed you in the red waste, every night and every day. You were made to be kissed, often and well." His eyes were on her breasts.

Dany covered them with her hands, before her nipples could betray her. "I . . . that was not fitting. I am your queen."

"My queen," he said, "and the bravest, sweetest, and most beautiful woman I have ever seen. Daenerys –"

"*Your Grace!*"

"Your Grace," he conceded, "*the dragon has three heads*, remember? You have wondered at that, ever since you heard it from the warlocks in the House of Dust. Well, here's your meaning: Balerion, Meraxes, and Vhagar, ridden by Aegon, Rhaenys, and Visenya. The three-headed dragon of House Targaryen – three dragons, and *three riders*."

"Yes," said Dany, "but my brothers are dead."

"Rhaenys and Visenya were Aegon's wives as well as his sisters. You have no brothers, but you can take husbands. And I tell you truly, Daenerys, there is no man in all the world who will ever be half so true to you as me."

BRAN

The ridge slanted sharply from the earth, a long fold of stone and soil shaped like a claw. Trees clung to its lower slopes, pines and hawthorn and ash, but higher up the ground was bare, the ridgeline stark against the cloudy sky.

He could feel the high stone calling him. Up he went, loping easy at first, then faster and higher, his strong legs eating up the incline. Birds burst from the branches overhead as he raced by, clawing and flapping their way into the sky. He could hear the wind sighing up amongst the leaves, the squirrels chittering to one another, even the sound a pinecone made as it tumbled to the forest floor. The smells were a song around him, a song that filled the good green world.

Gravel flew from beneath his paws as he gained the last few feet to stand upon the crest. The sun hung above the tall pines huge and red, and below him the trees and hills went on and on as far as he could see or smell. A kite was circling far above, dark against the pink sky.

Prince. The man-sound came into his head suddenly, yet he could feel the rightness of it. *Prince of the green, prince of the wolfswood.* He was strong and swift and fierce, and all that lived in the good green world went in fear of him.

Far below, at the base of the woods, something moved amongst the trees. A flash of grey, quick-glimpsed and gone again, but it was enough to make his ears prick up. Down there beside a swift green brook, another form slipped by, running. *Wolves*, he knew. His little cousins, chasing down some prey. Now the prince could see more of them, shadows on fleet grey paws. *A pack*.

He had a pack as well, once. Five they had been, and a sixth who stood aside. Somewhere down inside him were the sounds the men had given them to tell one from the other, but it was not by their sounds he knew them. He remembered their scents, his brothers and his sisters. They all had smelled alike, had smelled of *pack*, but each was different too.

His angry brother with the hot green eyes was near, the prince felt, though he had not seen him for many hunts. Yet with every sun that set he grew more distant, and he had been the last. The others were far scattered, like leaves blown by the wild wind.

Sometimes he could sense them, though, as if they were still with him, only hidden from his sight by a boulder or a stand of trees. He could not smell them, nor hear their howls by night, yet he felt their presence at his back . . . all but the sister they had lost. His tail drooped when he remembered her. *Four now, not five. Four and one more, the white who has no voice.*

These woods belonged to them, the snowy slopes and stony hills, the great green pines and the golden leaf oaks, the rushing streams and blue lakes fringed with fingers of white frost. But his sister had left the wilds, to walk in the halls of man-rock where other hunters ruled, and once within those halls it was hard to find the path back out. The wolf prince remembered.

The wind shifted suddenly.

Deer, and fear, and blood. The scent of prey woke the hunger in him. The prince sniffed the air again, turning, and then he was off, bounding along the ridgetop with jaws half-parted. The far side of the ridge was steeper than the one he'd come up, but he flew surefoot over stones and roots and rotting leaves, down the slope and through the trees, long strides eating up the ground. The scent pulled him onward, ever faster.

The deer was down and dying when he reached her, ringed by eight of his small grey cousins. The heads of the pack had begun to feed, the male first and then his female, taking turns tearing flesh from the red underbelly of their prey. The others waited patiently, all but the tail, who paced in a wary circle a few strides from the rest, his own tail tucked low. He would eat the last of all, whatever his brothers left him.

The prince was downwind, so they did not sense him until he leapt up upon a fallen log six strides from where they fed. The tail saw him first, gave a piteous whine, and slunk away. His pack brothers turned at the sound and bared their teeth, snarling, all but the head male and female.

The direwolf answered the snarls with a low warning growl and showed them his own teeth. He was bigger than his cousins, twice the size of the scrawny tail, half again as large as the two pack heads. He leapt down into their midst, and three of them broke, melting away into the brush. Another came at him, teeth snapping. He met the attack head on, caught the wolf's leg in his jaws when they met, and flung him aside yelping and limping.

And then there was only the head wolf to face, the great grey male with his bloody muzzle fresh from the prey's soft belly. There was white on his muzzle as well, to mark him as an old wolf, but when his mouth opened, red slaver ran from his teeth.

He has no fear, the prince thought, *no more than me*. It would be a good fight. They went for each other.

Long they fought, rolling together over roots and stones and fallen leaves and the scattered entrails of the prey, tearing at each other with tooth and claw, breaking apart, circling each round the other, and bolting in to fight again. The prince was larger, and much the stronger, but his cousin had a pack. The female prowled around them closely, snuffing and snarling, and would interpose herself whenever her mate broke off bloodied. From time to time the other wolves would dart in as well, to snap at a leg or an ear when the prince was turned the other way. One angered him so much that he whirled in a black fury and tore out the attacker's throat. After that the others kept their distance.

And as the last red light was filtering through green boughs and golden, the old wolf lay down weary in the dirt, and rolled over to expose his throat and belly. It was submission.

The prince sniffed at him and licked the blood from fur and torn flesh. When the old wolf gave a soft whimper, the direwolf turned away. He was very hungry now, and the prey was his.

"Hodor."

The sudden sound made him stop and snarl. The wolves regarded him with green and yellow eyes, bright with the last light of day. None of them had heard it. It was a queer wind that blew only in his ears. He buried his jaws in the deer's belly and tore off a mouthful of flesh.

"Hodor, hodor."

No, he thought. *No, I won't.* It was a boy's thought, not a direwolf's. The woods were darkening all about him, until only the shadows of the trees remained, and the glow of his cousins' eyes. And *through* those and behind those eyes, he saw a big man's grinning face, and a stone vault whose walls were spotted with niter. The rich warm taste of blood faded on his tongue. *No, don't, don't, I want to eat, I want to, I want . . .*

"Hodor, hodor, hodor, hodor, hodor," Hodor chanted as he shook him softly by the shoulders, back and forth and back and forth. He was trying to be gentle, he always tried, but Hodor was seven feet tall and stronger than he knew, and his huge hands rattled Bran's teeth together. "*NO!*" he shouted angrily. "Hodor, leave off, I'm here, I'm *here*."

Hodor stopped, looking abashed. "Hodor?"

The woods and wolves were gone. Bran was back again, down in the damp vault of some ancient watchtower that must have been abandoned thousands of years before. It wasn't much of a tower now. Even the tumbled stones were so overgrown with moss and ivy that you could hardly see them until you were right on top of them. "Tumbledown Tower", Bran had named the place; it was Meera who found the way down into the vault, however.

"You were gone too long." Jojen Reed was thirteen, only four years older than Bran. Jojen wasn't much bigger either, no more than two inches or maybe three, but he had a solemn way of talking that made him seem older and wiser than he really was. At Winterfell, Old Nan had dubbed him "little grandfather."

Bran frowned at him. "I wanted to eat."

"Meera will be back soon with supper."

"I'm sick of frogs." Meera was a frogeater from the Neck, so Bran couldn't really *blame* her for catching so many frogs, he supposed, but even so . . . "I wanted to eat the deer." For a moment he remembered the taste of it, the blood and the raw rich meat, and his mouth watered. *I won the fight for it. I won.*

"Did you mark the trees?"

Bran flushed. Jojen was always telling him to do things when he opened his third eye and put on Summer's skin. To claw the bark of a tree, to catch a rabbit and bring it back in his jaws uneaten, to push some rocks in a line. *Stupid things.* "I forgot," he said.

"You always forget."

It was true. He *meant* to do the things that Jojen asked, but once he was a wolf they never seemed important. There were always things to see and things to smell, a whole green world to hunt. And he could *run!* There was nothing better than running, unless it was running after prey. "I was a prince, Jojen," he told the older boy. "I was the prince of the woods."

"You are a prince," Jojen reminded him softly. "You remember, don't you? Tell me who you are."

"You *know*." Jojen was his friend and his teacher, but sometimes Bran just wanted to hit him.

"I want you to say the words. Tell me who you are."

"Bran," he said sullenly. *Bran the Broken.* "Brandon Stark." *The cripple boy.* "The Prince of Winterfell." Of Winterfell burned and tumbled, its people scattered and slain. The glass gardens were smashed, and hot water gushed from the cracked walls to steam beneath the sun. *How can you be the prince of someplace you might never see again?*

"And who is Summer?" Jojen prompted.

"My direwolf." He smiled. "Prince of the green."

"Bran the boy and Summer the wolf. You are two, then?"

"Two," he sighed, "and one." He hated Jojen when he got stupid like this. *At Winterfell he wanted me to dream my wolf dreams, and now that I know how he's always calling me back.*

"Remember that, Bran. Remember *yourself*, or the wolf will consume you. When you join, it is not enough to run and hunt and howl in Summer's skin."

It is for me, Bran thought. He liked Summer's skin better than his own. *What good is it to be a skinchanger if you can't wear the skin you like?*

"Will you remember? And next time, mark the tree. Any tree, it doesn't matter, so long as you do it."

"I will. I'll remember. I could go back and do it now, if you like. I won't forget this time." *But I'll eat my deer first, and fight with those little wolves some more.*

Jojen shook his head. "No. Best stay, and eat. With your own mouth. A warg cannot live on what his beast consumes."

How would you know? Bran thought resentfully. *You've never been a warg, you don't know what it's like.*

Hodor jerked suddenly to his feet, almost hitting his head on the barrel-vaulted ceiling. "HODOR!" he shouted, rushing to the door. Meera pushed it open just before he reached it, and stepped through into their refuge. "Hodor, hodor," the huge stableboy said, grinning.

Meera Reed was sixteen, a woman grown, but she stood no higher than her brother. All the crannogmen were small, she told Bran once when he asked why she wasn't taller. Brown-haired, green-eyed, and flat as a boy, she walked with a supple grace that Bran could only watch and envy. Meera wore a long sharp dagger, but her favorite way to fight was with a slender three-pronged frog spear in one hand and a woven net in the other.

"Who's hungry?" she asked, holding up her catch: two small silvery trout and six fat green frogs.

"I am," said Bran. *But not for frogs.* Back at Winterfell before all the bad things had happened, the Walders used to say that eating frogs would turn your teeth green and make moss grow under your arms. He wondered if the Walders were dead. He hadn't seen their corpses at Winterfell . . . but there had been a *lot* of corpses, and they hadn't looked inside the buildings.

"We'll just have to feed you, then. Will you help me clean the catch, Bran?"

He nodded. It was hard to sulk with Meera. She was much more cheerful than her brother, and always seemed to know how to make him smile. Nothing ever scared her or made her angry. *Well, except Jojen, sometimes . . .* Jojen Reed could scare most anyone. He dressed all in green, his eyes were murky as moss, and he had green dreams. What Jojen dreamed came true. *Except he dreamed me dead, and I'm not.* Only he was, in a way.

Jojen sent Hodor out for wood and built them a small fire while Bran and Meera were cleaning the fish and frogs. They used Meera's helm for a cooking pot, chopping up the catch into little cubes and tossing in some water and some wild onions Hodor had found to make a froggy stew. It wasn't as good as deer, but it wasn't bad either, Bran decided as he ate. "Thank you, Meera," he said. "My lady."

"You are most welcome, Your Grace."

"Come the morrow," Jojen announced, "we had best move on."

Bran could see Meera tense. "Have you had a green dream?"

"No," he admitted.

"Why leave, then?" his sister demanded. "Tumbledown Tower's a good place for us. No villages near, the woods are full of game, there's fish and frogs in the streams and lakes . . . and who is ever going to find us here?"

"This is not the place we are meant to be."

"It is safe, though."

"It *seems* safe, I know," said Jojen, "but for how long?

There was a battle at Winterfell, we saw the dead. Battles mean wars. If some army should take us unawares . . ."

"It might be Robb's army," said Bran. "Robb will come back from the south soon, I know he will. He'll come back with all his banners and chase the ironmen away."

"Your maester said naught of Robb when he lay dying," Jojen reminded him. "*Ironmen on the Stony Shore*, he said, and, *east, the Bastard of Bolton.* Moat Cailin and Deepwood Motte fallen, the heir to Cerwyn dead, and the castellan of Torrhen's Square. *War everywhere*, he said, *each man against his neighbor.*"

"We have plowed this field before," his sister said. "You want to make for the Wall, and your three-eyed crow. That's well and good, but the Wall is a very long way and Bran has no legs but Hodor. If we were mounted . . ."

"If we were eagles we might fly," said Jojen sharply, "but we have no wings, no more than we have horses."

"There are horses to be had," said Meera. "Even in the deep of the wolfswood there are foresters, crofters, hunters. Some will have horses."

"And if they do, should we steal them? Are we thieves? The last thing we need is men hunting us."

"We could buy them," she said. "Trade for them."

"Look at us, Meera. A crippled boy with a direwolf, a simpleminded giant, and two crannogmen a thousand leagues from the Neck. *We will be known.* And word will spread. So long as Bran remains dead, he is safe. Alive, he becomes prey for those who want him dead for good and true." Jojen went to the fire to prod the embers with a stick. "Somewhere to the north, the three-eyed crow awaits us. Bran has need of a teacher wiser than me."

"How, Jojen?" his sister asked. "*How?*"

"Afoot," he answered. "A step at a time."

"The road from Greywater to Winterfell went on forever, and we were mounted then. You want us to travel a longer road on foot, without even knowing where it ends. Beyond the Wall, you say. I haven't been there, no more than you, but I know that Beyond the Wall's a big place, Jojen. Are there many three-eyed crows, or only one? How do we find him?"

"Perhaps he will find us."

Before Meera could find a reply to that, they heard the sound, the distant howl of a wolf, drifting through the night. "Summer?" asked Jojen, listening.

"No." Bran knew the voice of his direwolf.

"Are you certain?" said the little grandfather.

"Certain." Summer had wandered far afield today, and would not be back till dawn. *Maybe Jojen dreams green, but he can't tell a wolf from a direwolf.* He wondered why they all listened to Jojen so much. He was not a prince like Bran, nor big and strong like Hodor, nor as good a hunter as Meera, yet somehow it was always Jojen telling them what to do. "We should steal horses like Meera wants," Bran said, "and ride to the Umbers up at Last Hearth." He thought a moment. "Or we could steal a boat and sail down the White Knife to White Harbor town. That fat Lord Manderly rules there, he was friendly at the harvest feast. He wanted to build ships. Maybe he built some, and we could sail to Riverrun and bring Robb home with all his army. Then it wouldn't matter who knew I was alive. Robb wouldn't let anyone hurt us."

"Hodor!" burped Hodor. "Hodor, hodor."

He was the only one who liked Bran's plan, though. Meera just smiled at him and Jojen frowned. They never listened to what he wanted, even though Bran was a Stark and a prince besides, and the Reeds of the Neck were Stark bannermen.

"Hoooodor," said Hodor, swaying. "Hooooooodor, hooooooodor, hoDOR, hoDOR, hoDOR." Sometimes he liked to do this, just saying his name different ways, over and over and over. Other times, he would stay so quiet you forgot he was there. There was never any knowing with Hodor. *"HODOR, HODOR, HODOR!"* he shouted.

He is not going to stop, Bran realized. "Hodor," he said, "why don't you go outside and train with your sword?"

The stableboy had forgotten about his sword, but now he remembered. "Hodor!" he burped. He went for his blade. They had three tomb swords taken from the crypts of Winterfell where Bran and his brother Rickon had hidden from Theon Greyjoy's ironmen. Bran claimed his uncle Brandon's sword, Meera the one she found upon the knees of his grandfather Lord Rickard. Hodor's blade was much older, a huge heavy piece of iron, dull from centuries of neglect and well spotted with rust. He could swing it for hours at a time. There was a rotted tree near the tumbled stones that he had hacked half to pieces.

Even when he went outside they could hear him through the walls, bellowing "HODOR!" as he cut and slashed at his tree. Thankfully the wolfswood was huge, and there was not like to be anyone else around to hear.

"Jojen, what did you mean about a teacher?" Bran asked. "*You're* my teacher. I know I never marked the tree, but I will the next time. My third eye is open like you wanted . . ."

"So wide open that I fear you may fall through it, and live all the rest of your days as a wolf of the woods."

"I won't, I promise."

"The boy promises. Will the wolf remember? You run with Summer, you hunt with him, kill with him . . . but you bend to his will more than him to yours."

"I just forget," Bran complained. "I'm only nine. I'll be better when I'm older. Even Florian the Fool and Prince Aemon the Dragonknight weren't great knights when they were *nine*."

"That is true," said Jojen, "and a wise thing to say, if the days were still growing longer . . . but they aren't. You are a summer child, I know. Tell me the words of House Stark."

"*Winter is coming.*" Just saying it made Bran feel cold.

Jojen gave a solemn nod. "I dreamed of a winged wolf bound to earth by chains of stone, and came to Winterfell to free him. The chains are off you now, yet still you do not fly."

"Then *you* teach me." Bran still feared the three-eyed crow who haunted his dreams sometimes, pecking endlessly at the skin between his eyes and telling him to fly. "You're a greenseer."

"No," said Jojen, "only a boy who dreams. The greenseers were more than that. They were wargs as well, as *you* are, and the greatest of them could wear the skins of *any* beast that flies or swims or crawls, and could look through the eyes of the weirwoods as well, and see the truth that lies beneath the world.

"The gods give many gifts, Bran. My sister is a hunter. It is given to her to run swiftly, and stand so still she seems to vanish. She has sharp ears, keen eyes, a steady hand with net and spear. She can breathe mud and fly through trees. I could not do these things, no more than you could. To me the gods gave the green dreams, and to you . . . you could be more than me, Bran. You are the winged wolf, and there is no saying how far and high you might fly . . . if you had someone to teach you. How can I help you master a gift I do not understand? We remember the First Men in the Neck, and the children of the forest who were their friends . . . but so much is forgotten, and so much we never knew."

Meera took Bran by the hand. "If we stay here, troubling no one, you'll be safe until the war ends. You will not learn, though, except what my brother can teach you, and you've heard what he says. If we leave this place to seek refuge at Last Hearth or beyond the Wall, we risk being taken. You are only a boy, I know, but you are our prince as well, our lord's son and our king's true heir. We have sworn you our faith by earth and water, bronze and iron, ice and fire. The risk is yours, Bran, as is the gift. The choice should be yours too, I think. We are your servants to command." She grinned. "At least in this."

"You mean," Bran said, "you'll do what *I* say? Truly?"

"Truly, my prince," the girl replied, "so consider well."

Bran tried to think it through, the way his father might have. The Greatjon's uncles Hother Whoresbane and Mors Crowfood were fierce men, but he thought they would be loyal. And the Karstarks, them too. Karhold was a strong castle, Father always said. *We would be safe with the Umbers or the Karstarks.*

Or they could go south to fat Lord Manderly. At Winterfell, he'd laughed a lot, and never seemed to look at Bran with so much pity as the other lords. Castle Cerwyn was closer than White Harbor, but Maester Luwin had said that Cley Cerwyn was dead. *The Umbers and the*

Karstarks and the Manderlys may all be dead as well, he realized. As he would be, if he was caught by the ironmen or the Bastard of Bolton.

If they stayed here, hidden down beneath Tumbledown Tower, no one would find them. He would stay alive. *And crippled.*

Bran realized he was crying. *Stupid baby,* he thought at himself. No matter where he went, to Karhold or White Harbor or Greywater Watch, he'd be a cripple when he got there. He balled his hands into fists. "I want to fly," he told them. "Please. Take me to the crow."

DAVOS

When he came up on deck, the long point of Driftmark was dwindling behind them while Dragonstone rose from the sea ahead. A pale grey wisp of smoke blew from the top of the mountain to mark where the island lay. *Dragonmont is restless this morning,* Davos thought, *or else Melisandre is burning someone else.*

Melisandre had been much in his thoughts as *Shayala's Dance* made her way across Blackwater Bay and through the Gullet, tacking against perverse contrary winds. The great fire that burned atop the Sharp Point watchtower at the end of Massey's Hook reminded him of the ruby she wore at her throat, and when the world turned red at dawn and sunset the drifting clouds turned the same color as the silks and satins of her rustling gowns.

She would be waiting on Dragonstone as well, waiting in all her beauty and all her power, with her god and her shadows and his king. The red priestess had always seemed loyal to Stannis, until now. *She has broken him, as a man breaks a horse. She would ride him to power if she could, and for that she gave my sons to the fire. I will cut the living heart from her breast and see how it burns.* He touched the hilt of the fine long Lysene dirk that the captain had given him.

The captain had been very kind to him. His name was

Khorane Sathmantes, a Lyseni like Salladhor Saan, whose ship this was. He had the pale blue eyes you often saw on Lys, set in a bony weatherworn face, but he had spent many years trading in the Seven Kingdoms. When he learned that the man he had plucked from the sea was the celebrated onion knight, he gave him the use of his own cabin and his own clothes, and a pair of new boots that almost fit. He insisted that Davos share his provisions as well, though that turned out badly. His stomach could not tolerate the snails and lampreys and other rich food Captain Khorane so relished, and after his first meal at the captain's table he spent the rest of the day with one end or the other dangling over the rail.

Dragonstone loomed larger with every stroke of the oars. Davos could see the shape of the mountain now, and on its side the great black citadel with its gargoyles and dragon towers. The bronze figurehead at the bow of *Shayala's Dance* sent up wings of salt spray as it cut the waves. He leaned his weight against the rail, grateful for its support. His ordeal had weakened him. If he stood too long his legs shook, and sometimes he fell prey to uncontrollable fits of coughing and brought up gobs of bloody phlegm. *It is nothing*, he told himself. *Surely the gods did not bring me safe through fire and sea only to kill me with a flux.*

As he listened to the pounding of the oarmaster's drum, the thrum of the sail, and the rhythmic swish and creak of the oars, he thought back to his younger days, when these same sounds woke dread in his heart on many a misty morn. They heralded the approach of old Ser Tristimun's sea watch, and the sea watch was death to smugglers when Aerys Targaryen sat the Iron Throne.

But that was another lifetime, he thought. *That was before the onion ship, before Storm's End, before Stannis shortened my fingers. That was before the war or the red comet, before I was a Seaworth or a knight. I was a different man in those days, before Lord Stannis raised me high.*

Captain Khorane had told him of the end of Stannis's hopes, on the night the river burned. The Lannisters had taken him from the flank, and his fickle bannermen had abandoned him by the hundreds in the hour of his greatest need. "King Renly's shade was seen as well," the captain said, "slaying right and left as he led the lion lord's van. It's said his green armor took a ghostly glow from the wildfire, and his antlers ran with golden flames."

Renly's shade. Davos wondered if his sons would return as shades as well. He had seen too many queer things on the sea to say that ghosts did not exist. "Did none keep faith?" he asked.

"Some few," the captain said. "The queen's kin, them in chief. We took off many who wore the fox-and-flowers, though many more were left ashore, with all manner of badges. Lord Florent is the King's Hand on Dragonstone now."

The mountain grew taller, crowned all in pale smoke. The sail sang, the drum beat, the oars pulled smoothly, and before very long the mouth of the harbor opened before them. *So empty,* Davos thought, remembering how it had been before, with the ships crowding every quay and rocking at anchor off the breakwater. He could see Salladhor Saan's flagship *Valyrian* moored at the quay where *Fury* and her sisters had once tied up. The ships on either side of her had striped Lysene hulls as well. In vain he looked for any sign of *Lady Marya* or *Wraith*.

They pulled down the sail as they entered the harbor, to dock on oars alone. The captain came to Davos as they were tying up. "My prince will wish to see you at once."

A fit of coughing seized Davos as he tried to answer. He clutched the rail for support and spat over the side. "The king," he wheezed. "I must go to the king." *For where the king is, I will find Melisandre.*

"No one goes to the king," Khorane Sathmantes replied firmly. "Salladhor Saan will tell you. Him first."

Davos was too weak to defy him. He could only nod.

Salladhor Saan was not aboard his *Valyrian*. They found him at another quay a quarter mile distant, down in the hold of a big-bellied Pentoshi cog named *Bountiful Harvest*, counting cargo with two eunuchs. One held a lantern, the other a wax tablet and stylus. "Thirty-seven, thirty-eight, thirty-nine," the old rogue was saying when Davos and the captain came down the hatch. Today he wore a wine-colored tunic and high boots of bleached white leather inlaid with silver scrollwork. Pulling the stopper from a jar, he sniffed, sneezed, and said, "A coarse grind, and of the second quality, my nose declares. The bill of lading is saying forty-three jars. Where have the others gotten to, I am wondering? These Pentoshi, do they think I am not counting?" When he saw Davos he stopped suddenly. "Is it pepper stinging my eyes, or tears? Is this the knight of the onions who stands before me? No, how can it be, my dear friend Davos died on the burning river, all agree. Why has he come to haunt me?"

"I am no ghost, Salla."

"What else? My onion knight was never so thin or so pale as you." Salladhor Saan threaded his way between the jars of spice and bolts of cloth that filled the hold of the merchanter, wrapped Davos in a fierce embrace, then kissed him once on each cheek and a third time on his forehead. "You are still warm, ser, and I feel your heart thumpety-thumping. Can it be true? The sea that swallowed you has spit you up again."

Davos was reminded of Patchface, Princess Shireen's lackwit fool. He had gone into the sea as well, and when he came out he was mad. *Am I mad as well?* He coughed into a gloved hand and said, "I swam beneath the chain and washed ashore on a spear of the merling king. I would have died there, if *Shayala's Dance* had not come upon me."

Salladhor Saan threw an arm around the captain's shoulders. "This was well done, Khorane. You will be having a fine reward, I am thinking. Meizo Mahr, be a good eunuch and take my friend Davos to the owner's cabin. Fetch him some hot wine with cloves, I am misliking the sound of that cough. Squeeze some lime in it as well. And bring white cheese and a bowl of those cracked green olives we counted earlier! Davos, I will join you soon, once I have bespoken our good captain. You will be forgiving me, I know. Do not eat all the olives, or I must be cross with you!"

Davos let the elder of the two eunuchs escort him to a large and lavishly furnished cabin at the stern of the ship. The carpets were deep, the windows stained glass, and any of the great leather chairs would have seated three of Davos quite comfortably. The cheese and olives arrived shortly, and a cup of steaming hot red wine. He held it between his hands and sipped it gratefully. The warmth felt soothing as it spread through his chest.

Salladhor Saan appeared not long after. "You must be forgiving me for the wine, my friend. These Pentoshi would drink their own water if it were purple."

"It will help my chest," said Davos. "Hot wine is better than a compress, my mother used to say."

"You shall be needing compresses as well, I am thinking. Sitting on a spear all this long time, oh my. How are you finding that excellent chair? He has fat cheeks, does he not?"

"Who?" asked Davos, between sips of hot wine.

"Illyrio Mopatis. A whale with whiskers, I am telling you truly. These chairs were built to his measure, though he is seldom bestirring himself from Pentos to sit in them. A fat man always sits comfortably, I am thinking, for he takes his pillow with him wherever he goes."

"How is it you come by a Pentoshi ship?" asked Davos. "Have you gone pirate again, my lord?" He set his empty cup aside.

"Vile calumny. Who has suffered more from pirates than Salladhor Saan? I ask only what is due me. Much gold is owed, oh yes, but I am not without reason, so in place of coin I have taken a handsome parchment, very crisp. It bears the name and seal of Lord Alester Florent, the Hand of the King. I am made Lord of Blackwater Bay, and no vessel may be crossing my lordly waters without my lordly leave, no. And when these outlaws are trying to steal past me in the night to avoid my lawful duties and customs, why, they are no better than smugglers, so I am well within my rights to seize them." The old pirate laughed. "I cut off no man's fingers, though. What good are bits of fingers? The ships I am taking, the cargoes, a few ransoms, nothing unreasonable." He gave Davos a sharp look. "You are unwell, my friend. That cough . . . and so thin, I am seeing your bones through your skin. And yet I am not seeing your little bag of fingerbones . . ."

Old habit made Davos reach for the leather pouch that was no longer there. "I lost it in the river." *My luck.*

"The river was terrible," Salladhor Saan said solemnly. "Even from the bay, I was seeing, and shuddering."

Davos coughed, spat, and coughed again. "I saw *Black Betha* burning, and *Fury* as well," he finally managed, hoarsely. "Did none of our ships escape the fire?" Part of him still hoped.

"*Lord Steffon, Ragged Jenna, Swift Sword, Laughing Lord,* and some others were upstream of the pyromancers' pissing, yes. They did not burn, but with the chain raised, neither could they be flying. Some few were surrendering. Most rowed far up the Blackwater, away from the battling, and then were sunk by their crews so they would not be falling into Lannister hands. *Ragged Jenna* and *Laughing Lord* are still playing pirate on the river, I have heard, but who can say if it is so?"

"*Lady Marya?*" Davos asked. "*Wraith?*"

Salladhor Saan put a hand on Davos's forearm and gave a squeeze. "No. Of them, no. I am sorry, my friend. They were good men, your Dale and Allard. But this comfort I can give you – your young Devan was among those we took off at the end. The brave boy never once left the king's side, or so they say."

For a moment he felt almost dizzy, his relief was so palpable. He had been afraid to ask about Devan. "The Mother is merciful. I must go to him, Salla. I must see him."

"Yes," said Salladhor Saan. "And you will be wanting to sail to Cape Wrath, I know, to see your wife and your two little ones. You must be having a new ship, I am thinking."

"His Grace will give me a ship," said Davos.

The Lyseni shook his head. "Of ships, His Grace has none, and Salladhor Saan has many. The king's ships burned up on the river, but not mine. You shall have one, old friend. You will sail for me, yes? You will dance into

Braavos and Myr and Volantis in the black of night, all unseen, and dance out again with silks and spices. We will be having fat purses, yes."

"You are kind, Salla, but my duty's to my king, not your purse. The war will go on. Stannis is still the rightful heir by all the laws of the Seven Kingdoms."

"All the laws are not helping when all the ships burn up, I am thinking. And your king, well, you will be finding him changed, I am fearing. Since the battle, he sees no one, but broods in his Stone Drum. Queen Selyse keeps court for him with her uncle the Lord Alester, who is naming himself the Hand. The king's seal she has given to this uncle, to fix to the letters he writes, even to my pretty parchment. But it is a little kingdom they are ruling, poor and rocky, yes. There is no gold, not even a little bit to pay faithful Salladhor Saan what is owed him, and only those knights that we took off at the end, and no ships but my little brave few."

A sudden racking cough bent Davos over. Salladhor Saan moved to help him, but he waved him off, and after a moment he recovered. "No one?" he wheezed. "What do you mean, he sees no one?" His voice sounded wet and thick, even in his own ears, and for a moment the cabin swam dizzily around him.

"No one but *her*," said Salladhor Saan, and Davos did not have to ask who he meant. "My friend, you tire yourself. It is a bed you are needing, not Salladhor Saan. A bed and many blankets, with a hot compress for your chest and more wine and cloves."

Davos shook his head. "I will be fine. Tell me, Salla, I must know. No one but Melisandre?"

The Lyseni gave him a long doubtful look, and continued reluctantly. "The guards keep all others away, even his queen and his little daughter. Servants bring meals that no one eats." He leaned forward and lowered his voice. "Queer talking I have heard, of hungry fires within the mountain, and how Stannis and the red woman go down together to watch the flames. There are shafts, they say, and secret stairs down into the mountain's heart, into hot places where only *she* may walk unburned. It is enough and more to give an old man such terrors that sometimes he can scarcely find the strength to eat."

Melisandre. Davos shivered. "The red woman did this to him," he said. "She sent the fire to consume us, to punish Stannis for setting her aside, to teach him that he could not hope to win without her sorceries."

The Lyseni chose a plump olive from the bowl between them. "You are not the first to be saying this, my friend. But if I am you, I am not saying it so loudly. Dragonstone crawls with these queen's men, oh yes, and they have sharp ears and sharper knives." He popped the olive into his mouth.

"I have a knife myself. Captain Khorane made me a gift of it." He pulled out the dirk and laid it on the table between them. "A knife to cut out Melisandre's heart. If she has one."

Salladhor Saan spit out an olive pit. "Davos, good Davos, you must not be saying such things, even in jest."

"No jest. I mean to kill her." *If she can be killed by mortal weapons.* Davos was not certain that she could. He had seen old Maester Cressen slip poison into her wine, with his own eyes he had seen it, but when they both drank from the poisoned cup it was the maester who died, not the red priestess. *A knife in the heart, though . . . even demons can be killed by cold iron, the singers say.*

"These are dangerous talkings, my friend," Salladhor Saan warned him. "I am thinking you are still sick from the sea. The fever has cooked your wits, yes. Best you are taking to your bed for a long resting, until you are stronger."

Until my resolve weakens, you mean. Davos got to his feet. He did feel feverish and a little dizzy, but it did not matter. "You are a treacherous old rogue, Salladhor Saan, but a good friend all the same."

The Lyseni stroked his pointed silver beard. "So with this great friend you will be staying, yes?"

"No, I will be going." He coughed.

"Go? Look at you! You cough, you tremble, you are thin and weak. Where will you be going?"

"To the castle. My bed is there, and my son."

"And the red woman," Salladhor Saan said suspiciously. "She is in the castle also."

"Her too." Davos slid the dirk back into its sheath.

"You are an onion smuggler, what do you know of skulkings and stabbings? And you are ill, you cannot even hold the dirk. Do you know what will be happening to you, if you are caught? While we were burning on the river, the queen was burning traitors. *Servants of the dark*, she named them, poor men, and the red woman sang as the fires were lit."

Davos was unsurprised. *I knew*, he thought, *I knew before he told me.* "She took Lord Sunglass from the dungeons," he guessed, "and Hubard Rambton's sons."

"Just so, and burned them, as she will burn you. If you kill the red woman, they will burn you for revenge, and if you fail to kill her, they will burn you for the trying. She will sing and you will scream, and then you will die. And you have only just come back to life!"

"And this is why," said Davos. "To do this thing. To make an end of Melisandre of Asshai and all her works. Why else would the sea have spit me out? You know Blackwater Bay as well as I do, Salla. No sensible captain would ever take his ship through the spears of the merling king and risk ripping out his bottom. *Shayala's Dance* should never have come near me."

"A wind," insisted Salladhor Saan loudly, "an ill wind, is all. A wind drove her too far to the south."

"And who sent the wind? Salla, the Mother spoke to me."

The old Lyseni blinked at him. "Your mother is dead . . ."

"*The* Mother. She blessed me with seven sons, and yet I let them burn her. She spoke to me. We *called* the fire, she said. We called the shadows too. I rowed Melisandre into the bowels of Storm's End and watched her birth a horror." He saw it still in his nightmares, the gaunt black hands pushing against her thighs as it wriggled free of her swollen womb. "She killed Cressen and Lord Renly and a brave man named Cortnay Penrose, and she killed my sons as well. Now it is time someone killed her."

"*Someone*," said Salladhor Saan. "Yes, just so, someone. But not you. You are weak as a child, and no warrior. Stay, I beg you, we will talk more and you will eat, and perhaps we will sail to Braavos and hire a Faceless Man to do this thing, yes? But you, no, you must sit and eat."

He is making this much harder, thought Davos wearily, *and it was perishingly hard to begin with*. "I have vengeance in my belly, Salla. It leaves no room for food. Let me go now. For our friendship, wish me luck and let me go."

Salladhor Saan pushed himself to his feet. "You are no true friend, I am thinking. When you are dead, who will be bringing your ashes and bones back to your lady wife and telling her that she has lost a husband and four sons? Only sad old Salladhor Saan. But so be it, brave ser knight, go rushing to your grave. I will gather your bones in a sack and give them to the sons you leave behind, to wear in little bags around their necks." He waved an angry hand, with rings on every finger. "Go, go, go, go, go."

Davos did not want to leave like this. "Salla –"

"*GO*. Or stay, better, but if you are going, go."

He went.

His walk up from the *Bountiful Harvest* to the gates of Dragonstone was long and lonely. The dockside streets where soldiers and sailors and smallfolk had thronged were empty and deserted. Where once he had stepped around squealing pigs and naked children, rats scurried. His legs felt like pudding beneath him, and thrice the coughing racked him so badly that he had to stop and rest. No one came to help him, nor even peered through a window to see what was the matter. The windows were shuttered, the doors barred, and more than half the houses displayed some mark of mourning. *Thousands sailed up the Blackwater Rush, and hundreds came back*, Davos reflected. *My sons did not die alone. May the Mother have mercy on them all*.

When he reached the castle gates, he found them shut as well. Davos pounded on the iron-studded wood with his fist. When there was no answer, he kicked at it, again and again. Finally a crossbowman appeared atop the barbican, peering down between two towering gargoyles. "Who goes there?"

He craned his head back and cupped his hands around his mouth. "Ser Davos Seaworth, to see His Grace."

"Are you drunk? Go away and stop that pounding."

Salladhor Saan had warned him. Davos tried a different tack. "Send for my son, then. Devan, the king's squire."

The guard frowned. "Who did you say you were?"

"Davos," he shouted. "The onion knight."

The head vanished, to return a moment later. "Be off with you. The onion knight died on the river. His ship burned."

"His ship burned," Davos agreed, "but he lived, and here he stands. Is Jate still captain of the gate?"

"Who?"

"Jate Blackberry. He knows me well enough."

"I never heard of him. Most like he's dead."

"Lord Chyttering, then."

"That one I know. He burned on the Blackwater."

"Hookface Will? Hal the Hog?"

"Dead and dead," the crossbowman said, but his face betrayed a sudden doubt. "You wait there." He vanished again.

Davos waited. *Gone, all gone*, he thought dully, remembering how fat Hal's white belly always showed beneath his grease-stained doublet, the long scar the fish hook had left across Will's face, the way Jate always doffed his cap at the women, be they five or fifty, highborn or low. *Drowned or burned, with my sons and a thousand others, gone to make a king in hell.*

Suddenly the crossbowman was back. "Go round to the sally port and they'll admit you."

Davos did as he was bid. The guards who ushered him inside were strangers to him. They carried spears, and on their breasts they wore the fox-and-flowers sigil of House Florent. They escorted him not to the Stone Drum, as he'd expected, but under the arch of the Dragon's Tail and down to Aegon's Garden. "Wait here," their sergeant told him.

"Does His Grace know that I've returned?" asked Davos.

"Bugger all if I know. Wait, I said." The man left, taking his spearmen with him.

Aegon's Garden had a pleasant piney smell to it, and tall dark trees rose on every side. There were wild roses as well, and towering thorny hedges, and a boggy spot where cranberries grew.

Why have they brought me here? Davos wondered.

Then he heard a faint ringing of bells, and a child's giggle, and suddenly the fool Patchface popped from the bushes, shambling along as fast as he could go with the Princess Shireen hot on his heels. "You come back now," she was shouting after him. "Patches, you come back."

When the fool saw Davos, he jerked to a sudden halt, the bells on his antlered tin helmet going *ting-a-ling, ting-a-ling*. Hopping from one foot to the other, he sang, "*Fool's blood, king's blood, blood on the maiden's thigh, but chains for the guests and chains for the bridegroom, aye aye aye.*" Shireen almost caught him then, but at the last instant he hopped over a patch of bracken and vanished among the trees. The princess was right behind him. The sight of them made Davos smile.

He had turned to cough into his gloved hand when another small shape crashed out of the hedge and bowled right into him, knocking him off his feet.

The boy went down as well, but he was up again almost at once. "What are you doing here?" he demanded as he brushed himself off. Jet-black hair fell to his collar, and his eyes were a startling blue. "You shouldn't get in my way when I'm running."

"No," Davos agreed. "I shouldn't." Another fit of coughing seized him as he struggled to his knees.

"Are you unwell?" The boy took him by the arm and pulled him to his feet. "Should I summon the maester?"

Davos shook his head. "A cough. It will pass."

The boy took him at his word. "We were playing monsters and maidens," he explained. "I was the monster. It's a childish game but my cousin likes it. Do you have a name?"

"Ser Davos Seaworth."

The boy looked him up and down dubiously. "Are you certain? You don't look very knightly."

"I am the knight of the onions, my lord."

The blue eyes blinked. "The one with the black ship?"

"You know that tale?"

"You brought my uncle Stannis fish to eat before I was born, when Lord Tyrell had him under siege." The boy drew himself up tall. "I am Edric Storm," he announced. "King Robert's son."

"Of course you are." Davos had known that almost at once. The lad had the prominent ears of a Florent, but the hair, the eyes, the jaw, the cheekbones, those were all Baratheon.

"Did you know my father?" Edric Storm demanded.

"I saw him many a time while calling on your uncle at court, but we never spoke."

"My father taught me to fight," the boy said proudly. "He came to see me almost every year, and sometimes we trained together. On my last name day he sent me a warhammer just like his, only smaller. They made me leave it at Storm's End, though. Is it true my uncle Stannis cut off your fingers?"

"Only the last joint. I still have fingers, only shorter."

"Show me."

Davos peeled his glove off. The boy studied his hand carefully. "He did not shorten your thumb?"

"No." Davos coughed. "No, he left me that."

"He should not have chopped any of your fingers," the lad decided. "That was ill done."

"I was a smuggler."

"Yes, but you smuggled him fish and onions."

"Lord Stannis knighted me for the onions, and took my fingers for the smuggling." He pulled his glove back on.

"... y father would not have chopped your fingers."

"... s you say, my lord." *Robert was a different man Stannis, true enough. The boy is like him. Aye, and Renly as well.* That thought made him anxious.

The boy was about to say something more when they ... ard steps. Davos turned. Ser Axell Florent was coming down the garden path with a dozen guards in quilted jerkins. On their breasts they wore the fiery heart of the Lord of Light. *Queen's men*, Davos thought. A cough came on him suddenly.

Ser Axell was short and muscular, with a barrel chest, thick arms, bandy legs, and hair growing from his ears. The queen's uncle, he had served as castellan of Dragonstone for a decade, and had always treated Davos courteously, knowing he enjoyed the favor of Lord Stannis. But there was neither courtesy nor warmth in his tone as he said, "Ser Davos, and undrowned. How can that be?"

"Onions float, ser. Have you come to take me to the king?"

"I have come to take you to the dungeon." Ser Axell waved his men forward. "Seize him, and take his dirk. He means to use it on our lady."

JAIME

Jaime was the first to spy the inn. The main building hugged the south shore where the river bent, its long low wings outstretched along the water as if to embrace travelers sailing downstream. The lower story was grey stone, the upper whitewashed wood, the roof slate. He could see stables as well, and an arbor heavy with vines. "No smoke from the chimneys," he pointed out as they approached. "Nor lights in the windows."

"The inn was still open when last I passed this way," said Ser Cleos Frey. "They brewed a fine ale. Perhaps there is still some to be had in the cellars."

"There may be people," Brienne said. "Hiding. Or dead."

"Frightened of a few corpses, wench?" Jaime said.

She glared at him. "My name is –"

"– Brienne, yes. Wouldn't you like to sleep in a bed for a night, Brienne? We'd be safer than on the open river, and it might be prudent to find what's happened here."

She gave no answer, but after a moment she pushed at the tiller to angle the skiff in toward the weathered wooden dock. Ser Cleos scrambled to take down the sail. When they bumped softly against the pier, he climbed out to tie them up. Jaime clambered after him, made awkward by his chains.

At the end of the dock, a flaking shingle swung from an iron post, painted with the likeness of a king upon his knees, his hands pressed together in the gesture of fealty. Jaime took one look and laughed aloud. "We could not have found a better inn."

"Is this some special place?" the wench asked, suspicious.

Ser Cleos answered. "This is the Inn of the Kneeling Man, my lady. It stands upon the very spot where the last King in the North knelt before Aegon the Conqueror to offer his submission. That's him on the sign, I suppose."

"Torrhen had brought his power south after the fall of the two kings on the Field of Fire," said Jaime, "but when he saw Aegon's dragon and the size of his host, he chose the path of wisdom and bent his frozen knees." He stopped at the sound of a horse's whinny. "Horses in the stable. One at least." *And one is all I need to put the wench behind me.* "Let's see who's home, shall we?" Without waiting for an answer, Jaime went clinking down the dock, put a shoulder to the door, shoved it open . . .

. . . and found himself eye to eye with a loaded crossbow. Standing behind it was a chunky boy of fifteen. "Lion, fish, or wolf?" the lad demanded.

"We were hoping for capon." Jaime heard his companions entering behind him. "The crossbow is a coward's weapon."

"It'll put a bolt through your heart all the same."

"Perhaps. But before you can wind it again my cousin here will spill your entrails on the floor."

"Don't be scaring the lad, now," Ser Cleos said.

"We mean no harm," the wench said. "And we have coin to pay for food and drink." She dug a silver piece from her pouch.

The boy looked suspiciously at the coin, and then at Jaime's manacles. "Why's this one in irons?"

"Killed some crossbowmen," said Jaime. "Do you have ale?"

"Yes." The boy lowered the crossbow an inch. "Undo your swordbelts and let them fall, and might be we'll feed you." He edged around to peer through the thick, diamond-shaped windowpanes and see if any more of them were outside. "That's a Tully sail."

"We come from Riverrun." Brienne undid the clasp on her belt and let it clatter to the floor. Ser Cleos followed suit.

A sallow man with a pocked doughy face stepped through the cellar door, holding a butcher's heavy cleaver. "Three, are you? We got horsemeat enough for three. The horse was old and tough, but the meat's still fresh."

"Is there bread?" asked Brienne.

"Hardbread and stale oatcakes."

Jaime grinned. "Now there's an honest innkeep. They'll all serve you stale bread and stringy meat, but most don't own up to it so freely."

"I'm no innkeep. I buried him out back, with his women."

"Did you kill them?"

"Would I tell you if I did?" The man spat. "Likely it were wolves' work, or maybe lions, what's the difference? The wife and I found them dead The way we see it, the place is ours now."

"Where is this wife of yours?" Ser Cleos asked.

The man gave him a suspicious squint. "And why would you be wanting to know that? She's not here . . . no more'n you three will be, unless I like the taste of your silver."

Brienne tossed the coin to him. He caught it in the air, bit it, and tucked it away.

"She's got more," the boy with the crossbow announced.

"So she does. Boy, go down and find me some onions."

The lad raised the crossbow to his shoulder, gave them one last sullen look, and vanished into the cellar.

"Your son?" Ser Cleos asked.

"Just a boy the wife and me took in. We had two sons, but the lions killed one and the other died of the flux. The boy lost his mother to the Bloody Mummers. These days, a man needs someone to keep watch while he sleeps." He waved the cleaver at the tables. "Might as well sit."

The hearth was cold, but Jaime picked the chair nearest

the ashes and stretched out his long legs under the table. The clink of his chains accompanied his every movement. *An irritating sound. Before this is done, I'll wrap these chains around the wench's throat, see how she likes them then.*

The man who wasn't an innkeep charred three huge horse steaks and fried the onions in bacon grease, which almost made up for the stale oatcakes. Jaime and Cleos drank ale, Brienne a cup of cider. The boy kept his distance, perching atop the cider barrel with his crossbow across his knees, cocked and loaded. The cook drew a tankard of ale and sat with them. "What news from Riverrun?" he asked Ser Cleos, taking him for their leader.

Ser Cleos glanced at Brienne before answering. "Lord Hoster is failing, but his son holds the fords of the Red Fork against the Lannisters. There have been battles."

"Battles everywhere. Where are you bound, ser?"

"King's Landing." Ser Cleos wiped grease off his lips.

Their host snorted. "Then you're three fools. Last I heard, King Stannis was outside the city walls. They say he has a hundred thousand men and a magic sword."

Jaime's hands wrapped around the chain that bound his wrists, and he twisted it taut, wishing for the strength to snap it in two. *Then I'd show Stannis where to sheathe his magic sword.*

"I'd stay well clear of that kingsroad, if I were you," the man went on. "It's worse than bad, I hear. Wolves and lions both, and bands of broken men preying on anyone they can catch."

"Vermin," declared Ser Cleos with contempt. "Such would never dare to trouble armed men."

"Begging your pardon, ser, but I see one armed man, traveling with a woman and a prisoner in chains."

Brienne gave the cook a dark look. *The wench does hate being reminded that she's a wench*, Jaime reflected, twisting at the chains again. The links were cold and hard against his flesh, the iron implacable. The manacles had chafed his wrists raw.

"I mean to follow the Trident to the sea," the wench told their host. "We'll find mounts at Maidenpool and ride by way of Duskendale and Rosby. That should keep us well away from the worst of the fighting."

Their host shook his head. "You'll never reach Maidenpool by river. Not thirty miles from here a couple boats burned and sank, and the channel's been silting up around them. There's a nest of outlaws there preying on anyone tries to come by, and more of the same downriver around the Skipping Stones and Red Deer Island. And the lightning lord's been seen in these parts as well. He crosses the river wherever he likes, riding this way and that way, never still."

"And who is this lightning lord?" demanded Ser Cleos Frey.

"Lord Beric, as it please you, ser. They call him that 'cause he strikes so sudden, like lightning from a clear sky. It's said he cannot die."

They all die when you shove a sword through them, Jaime thought. "Does Thoros of Myr still ride with him?"

"Aye. The red wizard. I've heard tell he has strange powers."

Well, he had the power to match Robert Baratheon drink for drink, and there were few enough who could say that. Jaime had once heard Thoros tell the king that he became a red priest because the robes hid the winestains so well. Robert had laughed so hard he'd spit ale all over Cersei's silken mantle. "Far be it from me to make objection," he said, "but perhaps the Trident is not our safest course."

"I'd say that's so," their cook agreed. "Even if you get past Red Deer Island and don't meet up with Lord Beric and the red wizard, there's still the ruby ford before you. Last I heard, it was the Leech Lord's wolves held the ford, but that was some time past. By now it could be lions again, or Lord Beric, or anyone."

"Or no one," Brienne suggested.

"If m'lady cares to wager her skin on that I won't stop her . . . but if I was you, I'd leave this here river, cut overland. If you stay off the main roads and shelter under the trees of a night, hidden as it were . . . well, I still wouldn't want to go with you, but you might stand a mummer's chance."

The big wench was looking doubtful. "We would need horses."

"There are horses here," Jaime pointed out. "I heard one in the stable."

"Aye, there are," said the innkeep, who wasn't an innkeep. "Three of them, as it happens, but they're not for sale."

Jaime had to laugh. "Of course not. But you'll show them to us anyway."

Brienne scowled, but the man who wasn't an innkeep met her eyes without blinking, and after a moment, reluctantly, she said, "Show me," and they all rose from the table.

The stables had not been mucked out in a long while, from the smell of them. Hundreds of fat black flies swarmed amongst the straw, buzzing from stall to stall and crawling over the mounds of horse dung that lay everywhere, but there were only the three horses to be seen. They made an unlikely trio; a lumbering brown plow horse, an ancient white gelding blind in one eye, and a knight's palfrey, dapple grey and spirited. "They're not for sale at any price," their alleged owner announced.

"How did you come by these horses?" Brienne wanted to know.

"The dray was stabled here when the wife and me come on the inn," the man said, "along with the one you just ate. The gelding come wandering up one night, and the boy caught the palfrey running free, still saddled and bridled. Here, I'll show you."

The saddle he showed them was decorated with silver inlay. The saddlecloth had originally been checkered pink and black, but now it was mostly brown. Jaime did not recognize the original colors, but he recognized bloodstains easily enough. "Well, her owner won't be coming to claim her anytime soon." He examined the palfrey's legs, counted the gelding's teeth. "Give him a gold piece for the grey, if he'll include the saddle," he advised Brienne. "A silver for the plow horse. He ought to pay us for taking the white off his hands."

"Don't speak discourteously of your horse, ser." The

wench opened the purse Lady Catelyn had given her and took out three golden coins. "I will pay you a dragon for each."

He blinked and reached for the gold, then hesitated and drew his hand back. "I don't know. I can't ride no golden dragon if I need to get away. Nor eat one if I'm hungry."

"You can have our skiff as well," she said. "Sail up the river or down, as you like."

"Let me have a taste o' that gold." The man took one of the coins from her palm and bit it. "Hm. Real enough, I'd say. Three dragons *and* the skiff?"

"He's robbing you blind, wench," Jaime said amiably.

"I'll want provisions too," Brienne told their host, ignoring Jaime. "Whatever you have that you can spare."

"There's more oatcakes." The man scooped the other two dragons from her palm and jingled them in his fist, smiling at the sound they made. "Aye, and smoked salt fish, but that will cost you silver. My beds will be costing as well. You'll be wanting to stay the night."

"No," Brienne said at once.

The man frowned at her. "Woman, you don't want to go riding at night through strange country on horses you don't know. You're like to blunder into some bog or break your horse's leg."

"The moon will be bright tonight," Brienne said. "We'll have no trouble finding our way."

Their host chewed on that. "If you don't have the silver, might be some coppers would buy you them beds, and a coverlet or two to keep you warm. It's not like I'm turning travelers away, if you get my meaning."

"That sounds more than fair," said Ser Cleos.

"The coverlets is fresh washed, too. My wife saw to that before she had to go off. Not a flea to be found neither, you have my word on that." He jingled the coins again, smiling.

Ser Cleos was plainly tempted. "A proper bed would do us all good, my lady," he said to Brienne. "We'd make better time on the morrow once refreshed." He looked to his cousin for support.

"No, coz, the wench is right. We have promises to keep, and long leagues before us. We ought ride on."

"But," said Cleos, "you said yourself – "

"Then." *When I thought the inn deserted.* "Now I have a full belly, and a moonlight ride will be just the thing." He smiled for the wench. "But unless you mean to throw me over the back of that plow horse like a sack of flour, someone had best do something about these irons. It's difficult to ride with your ankles chained together."

Brienne frowned at the chain. The man who wasn't an innkeep rubbed his jaw. "There's a smithy round back of the stable."

"Show me," Brienne said.

"Yes," said Jaime, "and the sooner the better. There's far too much horse shit about here for my taste. I would hate to step in it." He gave the wench a sharp look, wondering if she was bright enough to take his meaning.

He hoped she might strike the irons off his wrists as well, but Brienne was still suspicious. She split the ankle chain in the center with a half-dozen sharp blows from the smith's hammer delivered to the blunt end of a steel chisel. When he suggested that she break the wrist chain as well, she ignored him.

"Six miles downriver you'll see a burned village," their host said as he was helping them saddle the horses and load their packs. This time he directed his counsel at Brienne. "The road splits there. If you turn south, you'll come on Ser Warren's stone towerhouse. Ser Warren went off and died, so I couldn't say who holds it now, but it's a place best shunned. You'd do better to follow the track through the woods, south by east."

"We shall," she answered. "You have my thanks."

More to the point, he has your gold. Jaime kept the thought to himself. He was tired of being disregarded by this huge ugly cow of a woman.

She took the plow horse for herself and assigned the palfrey to Ser Cleos. As threatened, Jaime drew the one-eyed gelding, which put an end to any thoughts he might have had of giving his horse a kick and leaving the wench in his dust.

The man and the boy came out to watch them leave. The man wished them luck and told them to come back in better times, while the lad stood silent, his crossbow under his arm. "Take up the spear or maul," Jaime told him, "they'll serve you better." The boy stared at him distrustfully. *So much for friendly advice.* He shrugged, turned his horse, and never looked back.

Ser Cleos was all complaints as they rode out, still in mourning for his lost featherbed. They rode east, along the bank of the moonlit river. The Red Fork was very broad here, but shallow, its banks all mud and reeds. Jaime's mount plodded along placidly, though the poor old thing had a tendency to want to drift off to the side of his good eye. It felt good to be mounted once more. He had not been on a horse since Robb Stark's archers had killed his destrier under him in the Whispering Wood.

When they reached the burned village, a choice of equally unpromising roads confronted them; narrow tracks, deeply rutted by the carts of farmers hauling their grain to the river. One wandered off toward the southeast and soon vanished amidst the trees they could see in the distance, while the other, straighter and stonier, arrowed due south. Brienne considered them briefly, and then swung her horse onto the southern road. Jaime was pleasantly surprised; it was the same choice he would have made.

"But this is the road the innkeep warned us against," Ser Cleos objected.

"He was no innkeep." She hunched gracelessly in the saddle, but seemed to have a sure seat nonetheless. "The man took too great an interest in our choice of route, and those woods . . . such places are notorious haunts of outlaws. He may have been urging us into a trap."

"Clever wench." Jaime smiled at his cousin. "Our host has friends down that road, I would venture. The ones whose mounts gave that stable such a memorable aroma."

"He may have been lying about the river as well, to put us on these horses," the wench said, "but I could not take the risk. There will be soldiers at the ruby ford and the crossroads."

Well, she may be ugly but she's not entirely stupid. Jaime gave her a grudging smile.

The ruddy light from the upper windows of the stone towerhouse gave them warning of its presence a long way off, and Brienne led them off into the fields. Only when the stronghold was well to the rear did they angle back and find the road again.

Half the night passed before the wench allowed that it might be safe to stop. By then all three of them were drooping in their saddles. They sheltered in a small grove of oak and ash beside a sluggish stream. The wench would allow no fire, so they shared a midnight supper of stale oatcakes and salt fish. The night was strangely peaceful. The half-moon sat overhead in a black felt sky, surrounded by stars. Off in the distance, some wolves were howling. One of their horses whickered nervously. There was no other sound. *The war has not touched this place,* Jaime thought. He was glad to be here, glad to be alive, glad to be on his way back to Cersei.

"I'll take the first watch," Brienne told Ser Cleos, and Frey was soon snoring softly.

Jaime sat against the bole of an oak and wondered what Cersei and Tyrion were doing just now. "Do you have any siblings, my lady?" he asked.

Brienne squinted at him suspiciously. "No. I was my father's only s – child."

Jaime chuckled. "*Son,* you meant to say. Does he think of you as a son? You make a queer sort of daughter, to be sure."

Wordless, she turned away from him, her knuckles tight on her sword hilt. *What a wretched creature this one is.* She reminded him of Tyrion in some queer way, though at first blush two people could scarcely be any more dissimilar. Perhaps it was that thought of his brother that made him say, "I did not intend to give offense, Brienne. Forgive me."

"Your crimes are past forgiving, Kingslayer."

"That name again." Jaime twisted idly at his chains. "Why do I enrage you so? I've never done you harm that I know of."

"You've harmed others. Those you were sworn to protect. The weak, the innocent . . ."

". . . the king?" It always came back to Aerys. "Don't presume to judge what you do not understand, wench."

"My name is –"

"– Brienne, yes. Has anyone ever told you that you're as tedious as you are ugly?"

"You will not provoke me to anger, Kingslayer."

"Oh, I might, if I cared enough to try."

"Why did you take the oath?" she demanded. "Why don the white cloak if you meant to betray all it stood for?"

Why? What could he say that she might possibly understand? "I was a boy. Fifteen. It was a great honor for one so young."

"That is no answer," she said scornfully.

You would not like the truth. He had joined the Kingsguard for love, of course.

Their father had summoned Cersei to court when she was twelve, hoping to make her a royal marriage. He refused every offer for her hand, preferring to keep her with him in the Tower of the Hand while she grew older and more womanly and ever more beautiful. No doubt he was waiting for Prince Viserys to mature, or perhaps for Rhaegar's wife to die in childbed. Elia of Dorne was never the healthiest of women.

Jaime, meantime, had spent four years as squire to Ser Sumner Crakehall and earned his spurs against the Kingswood Brotherhood. But when he made a brief call at King's Landing on his way back to Casterly Rock, chiefly to see his sister, Cersei took him aside and whispered that Lord Tywin meant to marry him to Lysa Tully, had gone so far as to invite Lord Hoster to the city to discuss dower. But if Jaime took the white, he could be near her always. Old Ser Harlan Grandison had died in his sleep, as was only appropriate for one whose sigil was a sleeping lion. Aerys would want a young man to take his place, so why not a roaring lion in place of a sleepy one?

"Father will never consent," Jaime objected.

"The king won't ask him. And once it's done, Father

can't object, not openly. Aerys had Ser Ilyn Payne's tongue torn out just for boasting that it was the Hand who truly ruled the Seven Kingdoms. The captain of the Hand's guard, and yet Father dared not try and stop it! He won't stop this, either."

"But," Jaime said, "there's Casterly Rock . . ."

"Is it a rock you want? Or me?"

He remembered that night as if it were yesterday. They spent it in an old inn on Eel Alley, well away from watchful eyes. Cersei had come to him dressed as a simple serving wench, which somehow excited him all the more. Jaime had never seen her more passionate. Every time he went to sleep, she woke him again. By morning Casterly Rock seemed a small price to pay to be near her always. He gave his consent, and Cersei promised to do the rest.

A moon's turn later, a royal raven arrived at Casterly Rock to inform him that he had been chosen for the Kingsguard. He was commanded to present himself to the king during the great tourney at Harrenhal to say his vows and don his cloak.

Jaime's investiture freed him from Lysa Tully. Elsewise, nothing went as planned. His father had never been more furious. He could not object openly – Cersei had judged that correctly – but he resigned the Handship on some thin pretext and returned to Casterly Rock, taking his daughter with him. Instead of being together, Cersei and Jaime just changed places, and he found himself alone at court, guarding a mad king while four lesser men took their turns dancing on knives in his father's ill-fitting shoes. So swiftly did the Hands rise and fall that Jaime remembered their heraldry better than their faces. The horn-of-plenty Hand and the dancing griffins Hand had both been exiled, the mace-and-dagger Hand dipped in wildfire and burned alive. Lord Rossart had been the last. His sigil had been a burning torch; an unfortunate choice, given the fate of his predecessor, but the alchemist had been elevated largely because he shared the king's passion for fire. *I ought to have drowned Rossart instead of gutting him.*

Brienne was still awaiting his answer. Jaime said, "You

are not old enough to have known Aerys Targaryen . . ."

She would not hear it. "Aerys was mad and cruel, no one has ever denied that. He was still king, crowned and anointed. And you had sworn to protect him."

"I know what I swore."

"And what you did." She loomed above him, six feet of freckled, frowning, horse-toothed disapproval.

"Yes, and what *you* did as well. We're both kingslayers here, if what I've heard is true."

"I never harmed Renly. I'll kill the man who says I did."

"Best start with Cleos, then. And you'll have a deal of killing to do after that, the way he tells the tale."

"*Lies.* Lady Catelyn was there when His Grace was murdered, she saw. There was a shadow. The candles guttered and the air grew cold, and there was blood – "

"Oh, very good." Jaime laughed. "Your wits are quicker than mine, I confess it. When they found me standing over my dead king, I never thought to say, 'No, no, it wasn't me, it was a shadow, a terrible cold shadow.'" He laughed again. "Tell me true, one kingslayer to another – did the Starks pay you to slit his throat, or was it Stannis? Had Renly spurned you, was that the way of it? Or perhaps your moon's blood was on you. Never give a wench a sword when she's bleeding."

For a moment Jaime thought Brienne might strike him. *A step closer, and I'll snatch that dagger from her sheath and bury it up her womb.* He gathered a leg under him, ready to spring, but the wench did not move. "It is a rare and precious gift to be a knight," she said, "and even more so a knight of the Kingsguard. It is a gift given to few, a gift you scorned and soiled."

A gift you want desperately, wench, and can never have. "I earned my knighthood. Nothing was given to me. I won a tourney mêlée at thirteen, when I was yet a squire. At fifteen, I rode with Ser Arthur Dayne against the Kingswood Brotherhood, and he knighted me on the battlefield. It was that white cloak that soiled me, not the other way around. So spare me your envy. It was the gods who neglected to give you a cock, not me."

The look Brienne gave him then was full of loathing. *She would gladly hack me to pieces, but for her precious vow,* he reflected. *Good. I've had enough of feeble pieties and maidens' judgments.* The wench stalked off without saying a word. Jaime curled up beneath his cloak, hoping to dream of Cersei.

But when he closed his eyes, it was Aerys Targaryen he saw, pacing alone in his throne room, picking at his scabbed and bleeding hands. The fool was always cutting himself on the blades and barbs of the Iron Throne. Jaime had slipped in through the king's door, clad in his golden armor, sword in hand. *The golden armor, not the white, but no one ever remembers that. Would that I had taken off that damned cloak as well.*

When Aerys saw the blood on his blade, he demanded to know if it was Lord Tywin's. "I want him dead, the traitor. I want his head, you'll bring me his head, or you'll burn with all the rest. All the traitors. Rossart says they are *inside the walls!* He's gone to make them a warm welcome. Whose blood? *Whose?*"

"Rossart's," answered Jaime.

Those purple eyes grew huge then, and the royal mouth drooped open in shock. He lost control of his bowels, turned, and ran for the Iron Throne. Beneath the empty eyes of the skulls on the walls, Jaime hauled the last dragonking bodily off the steps, squealing like a pig and smelling like a privy. A single slash across his throat was all it took to end it. *So easy,* he remembered thinking. *A king should die harder than this.* Rossart at least had tried to make a fight of it, though if truth be told he fought like an alchemist. *Queer that they never ask who killed Rossart . . . but of course, he was no one, lowborn, Hand for a fortnight, just another mad fancy of the Mad King.*

Ser Elys Westerling and Lord Crakehall and others of his father's knights burst into the hall in time to see the last of it, so there was no way for Jaime to vanish and let some braggart steal the praise or blame. It would be blame, he knew at once when he saw the way they looked at him . . . though perhaps that was fear. Lannister or no, he was one of Aerys's seven.

"The castle is ours, ser, and the city," Roland Crakehall told him, which was half true. Targaryen loyalists were still dying on the serpentine steps and in the armory, Gregor Clegane and Amory Lorch were scaling the walls of Maegor's Holdfast, and Ned Stark was leading his northmen through the King's Gate even then, but Crakehall could not have known that. He had not seemed surprised to find Aerys slain; Jaime had been Lord Tywin's son long before he had been named to the Kingsguard.

"Tell them the Mad King is dead," he commanded. "Spare all those who yield and hold them captive."

"Shall I proclaim a new king as well?" Crakehall asked, and Jaime read the question plain: Shall it be your father, or Robert Baratheon, or do you mean to try to make a new dragonking? He thought for a moment of the boy Viserys, fled to Dragonstone, and of Rhaegar's infant son Aegon, still in Maegor's with his mother. A new Targaryen king, and my father as Hand. How the wolves will howl, and the storm lord choke with rage. For a moment he was tempted, until he glanced down again at the body on the floor, in its spreading pool of blood. His blood is in both of them, he thought. "Proclaim who you bloody well like," he told Crakehall. Then he climbed the Iron Throne and seated himself with his sword across his knees, to see who would come to claim the kingdom. As it happened, it had been Eddard Stark.

You had no right to judge me either, Stark.

In his dreams the dead came burning, gowned in swirling green flames. Jaime danced around them with a golden sword, but for every one he struck down two more arose to take his place.

Brienne woke him with a boot in the ribs. The world was still black, and it had begun to rain. They broke their fast on oatcakes, salt fish, and some blackberries that Ser Cleos had found, and were back in the saddle before the sun came up.

TYRION

The eunuch was humming tunelessly to himself as he came through the door, dressed in flowing robes of peach-colored silk and smelling of lemons. When he saw Tyrion seated by the hearth, he stopped and grew very still. "My lord Tyrion," came out in a squeak, punctuated by a nervous giggle.

"So you *do* remember me? I had begun to wonder."

"It is so *very* good to see you looking so strong and well." Varys smiled his slimiest smile. "Though I confess, I had not thought to find you in mine own humble chambers."

"They are humble. Excessively so, in truth." Tyrion had waited until Varys was summoned by his father before slipping in to pay him a visit. The eunuch's apartments were sparse and small, three snug windowless chambers under the north wall. "I'd hoped to discover bushel baskets of juicy secrets to while away the waiting, but there's not a paper to be found." He'd searched for hidden passages too, knowing the Spider must have ways of coming and going unseen, but those had proved equally elusive. "There was *water* in your flagon, gods have mercy," he went on, "your sleeping cell is no wider than a coffin, and that bed . . . is it actually made of stone, or does it only feel that way?"

Varys closed the door and barred it. "I am plagued with

backaches, my lord, and prefer to sleep upon a hard surface."

"I would have taken you for a featherbed man."

"I am full of surprises. Are you cross with me for abandoning you after the battle?"

"It made me think of you as one of my family."

"It was not for want of love, my good lord. I have such a delicate disposition, and your scar is so dreadful to look upon . . ." He gave an exaggerated shudder. "Your poor nose . . ."

Tyrion rubbed irritably at the scab. "Perhaps I should have a new one made of gold. What sort of nose would you suggest, Varys? One like yours, to smell out secrets? Or should I tell the goldsmith that I want my father's nose?" He smiled. "My noble father labors so diligently that I scarce see him anymore. Tell me, is it true that he's restoring Grand Maester Pycelle to the small council?"

"It is, my lord."

"Do I have my sweet sister to thank for that?" Pycelle had been his sister's creature; Tyrion had stripped the man of office, beard, and dignity, and flung him down into a black cell.

"Not at all, my lord. Thank the archmaesters of Oldtown, those who wished to insist on Pycelle's restoration on the grounds that only the Conclave may make or unmake a Grand Maester."

Bloody fools, thought Tyrion. "I seem to recall that Maegor the Cruel's headsman unmade three with his axe."

"Quite true," Varys said. "And the second Aegon fed Grand Maester Gerardys to his dragon."

"Alas, I am quite dragonless. I suppose I could have dipped Pycelle in wildfire and set him ablaze. Would the Citadel have preferred that?"

"Well, it would have been more in keeping with tradition." The eunuch tittered. "Thankfully, wiser heads prevailed, and the Conclave accepted the fact of Pycelle's dismissal and set about choosing his successor. After giving due consideration to Maester Turquin the cordwainer's son and Maester Erreck the hedge knight's bastard, and thereby demonstrating to their own satisfaction that ability counts for more than birth in their order, the Conclave was on the verge of sending us Maester Gormon, a Tyrell of Highgarden. When I told your lord father, he acted at once."

The Conclave met in Oldtown behind closed doors, Tyrion knew; its deliberations were supposedly a secret. *So Varys has little birds in the Citadel too.* "I see. So my father decided to nip the rose before it bloomed." He had to chuckle. "Pycelle is a toad. But better a Lannister toad than a Tyrell toad, no?"

"Grand Maester Pycelle has always been a good friend to your House," Varys said sweetly. "Perhaps it will console you to learn that Ser Boros Blount is also being restored."

Cersei had stripped Ser Boros of his white cloak for failing to die in the defense of Prince Tommen when Jacelyn Bywater had seized the boy on the Rosby road. The man was no friend of Tyrion's, but after that he likely hated Cersei almost as much. *I suppose that's something.* "Blount is a blustering coward," he said amiably.

"Is he? Oh dear. Still, the knights of the Kingsguard *do* serve for life, traditionally. Perhaps Ser Boros will prove braver in future. He will no doubt remain very loyal."

"To my father," said Tyrion pointedly.

"While we are on the subject of the Kingsguard . . . I wonder, could this delightfully unexpected visit of yours happen to concern Ser Boros's fallen brother, the gallant Ser Mandon Moore?" The eunuch stroked a powdered cheek. "Your man Bronn seems most interested in him of late."

Bronn had turned up all he could on Ser Mandon, but no doubt Varys knew a deal more . . . should he choose to share it. "The man seems to have been quite friendless," Tyrion said carefully.

"Sadly," said Varys, "oh, sadly. You might find some kin if you turned over enough stones back in the Vale, but here . . . Lord Arryn brought him to King's Landing and Robert gave him his white cloak, but neither loved him much, I fear. Nor was he the sort the smallfolk cheer in tourneys, despite his undoubted prowess. Why, even his brothers of the Kingsguard never warmed to him. Ser Barristan was once heard to say that the man had no friend but his sword and no life but duty . . . but you know, I do not think Selmy meant it altogether as praise. Which is queer when you consider it, is it not? Those are the very qualities we seek in our Kingsguard, it could be said – men who live not for themselves, but for their king. By those lights, our brave Ser Mandon was the perfect white knight. And he died as a knight of the Kingsguard ought, with sword in hand, defending one of the king's own blood." The eunuch gave him a slimy smile and watched him sharply.

Trying to murder one of the king's own blood, you mean. Tyrion wondered if Varys knew rather more than he was saying. Nothing he'd just heard was new to him; Bronn had brought back much the same reports. He needed a link to Cersei, some sign that Ser Mandon had been his sister's catspaw. *What we want is not always what we get*, he reflected bitterly, which reminded him . . .

"It is not Ser Mandon who brings me here."

"To be sure." The eunuch crossed the room to his flagon of water. "May I serve you, my lord?" he asked as he filled a cup.

"Yes. But not with water." He folded his hands together. "I want you to bring me Shae."

Varys took a drink. "Is that wise, my lord? The dear sweet child. It would be such a shame if your father hanged her."

It did not surprise him that Varys knew. "No, it's not wise, it's bloody madness. I want to see her one last time, before I send her away. I cannot abide having her so close."

"I understand."

How could you? Tyrion had seen her only yesterday, climbing the serpentine steps with a pail of water. He had watched as a young knight had offered to carry the heavy pail. The way she had touched his arm and smiled for him had tied Tyrion's guts into knots. They passed within inches of each other, him descending and her climbing, so close that he could smell the clean fresh scent of her hair. "M'lord," she'd said to him, with a little curtsy, and he wanted to reach out and grab her and kiss her right there, but all he could do was nod stiffly and waddle on past. "I have seen her several times," he told Varys, "but I dare not speak to her. I suspect that all my movements are being watched."

"You are wise to suspect so, my good lord."

"Who?" He cocked his head.

"The Kettleblacks report frequently to your sweet sister."

"When I think of how much coin I paid those wretched . . . do you think there's any chance that more gold might win them away from Cersei?"

"There is always a chance, but I should not care to wager on the likelihood. They are knights now, all three, and your sister has promised them further advancement." A wicked little titter burst from the eunuch's lips. "And the eldest, Ser Osmund of the Kingsguard, dreams of certain other . . . *favors* . . . as well. You can match the queen coin for coin, I have no doubt, but she has a second purse that is quite inexhaustible."

Seven hells, thought Tyrion. "Are you suggesting that Cersei's fucking Osmund Kettleblack?"

"Oh, dear me, no, that would be dreadfully dangerous, don't you think? No, the queen only *hints* . . . perhaps on the morrow, or when the wedding's done . . . and then a smile, a whisper, a ribald jest . . . a breast brushing lightly against his sleeve as they pass . . . and yet it seems to serve. But what would a eunuch know of such things?" The tip of his tongue ran across his lower lip like a shy pink animal.

If I could somehow push them beyond sly fondling, arrange for Father to catch them abed together . . . Tyrion fingered the scab on his nose. He did not see how it could be done, but perhaps some plan would come to him later. "Are the Kettleblacks the only ones?"

"Would that were true, my lord. I fear there are many eyes upon you. You are . . . how shall we say? *Conspicuous?* And not well loved, it grieves me to tell you. Janos Slynt's sons would gladly inform on you to avenge their father, and our sweet Lord Petyr has friends in half the brothels of King's Landing. Should you be so unwise as to visit any of them, he will know at once, and your lord father soon thereafter."

It's even worse than I feared. "And my father? Who does he have spying on me?"

This time the eunuch laughed aloud. "Why, me, my lord."

Tyrion laughed as well. He was not so great a fool as to trust Varys any further than he had to – but the eunuch already knew enough about Shae to get her well and thoroughly hanged. "You will bring Shae to me through the walls, hidden from all these eyes. As you have done before."

Varys wrung his hands. "Oh, my lord, nothing would please me more, but . . . King Maegor wanted no rats in his own walls, if you take my meaning. He did require a means of secret egress, should he ever be trapped by his enemies, but that door does not connect with any other passages. I can steal your Shae away from Lady Lollys for a time, to be sure, but I have no way to bring her to your bedchamber without us being seen."

"Then bring her somewhere else."

"But where? There is no safe place."

"There is." Tyrion grinned. "Here. It's time to put that rock-hard bed of yours to better use, I think."

The eunuch's mouth opened. Then he giggled. "Lollys tires easily these days. She is great with child. I imagine she will be safely asleep by moonrise."

Tyrion hopped down from the chair. "Moonrise, then. See that you lay in some wine. And two clean cups."

Varys bowed. "It shall be as my lord commands."

The rest of the day seemed to creep by as slow as a worm in molasses. Tyrion climbed to the castle library and tried to distract himself with Beldecar's *History of the Rhoynish Wars*, but he could hardly see the elephants for imagining Shae's smile. Come the afternoon, he put the book aside and called for a bath. He scrubbed himself until the water grew cool, and then had Pod even out his whiskers. His beard was a trial to him; a tangle of yellow, white, and black hairs, patchy and coarse, it was seldom less than unsightly, but it did serve to conceal some of his face, and that was all to the good.

When he was as clean and pink and trimmed as he was like to get, Tyrion looked over his wardrobe, and chose a pair of tight satin breeches in Lannister crimson and his best doublet, the heavy black velvet with the lion's head studs. He would have donned his chain of golden hands as well, if his father hadn't stolen it while he lay dying. It was not until he was dressed that he realized the depths of his folly. *Seven hells, dwarf, did you lose all your sense along with your nose? Anyone who sees you is going to wonder why you've put on your court clothes to visit the eunuch.* Cursing, Tyrion stripped and dressed again, in simpler garb; black woolen breeches, an old white tunic, and a faded brown leather jerkin. *It doesn't matter*, he told himself as he waited for moonrise. *Whatever you wear, you're still a dwarf. You'll never be as tall as that knight on the steps, him with his long straight legs and hard stomach and wide manly shoulders.*

The moon was peeping over the castle wall when he told Podrick Payne that he was going to pay a call on Varys. "Will you be long, my lord?" the boy asked.

"Oh, I hope so."

With the Red Keep so crowded, Tyrion could not hope to go unnoticed. Ser Balon Swann stood guard on the door, and Ser Loras Tyrell on the drawbridge. He stopped to exchange pleasantries with both of them. It was strange to see the Knight of Flowers all in white when before he had always been as colorful as a rainbow. "How old are you, Ser Loras?" Tyrion asked him.

"Seventeen, my lord."

Seventeen, and beautiful, and already a legend. Half the girls in the Seven Kingdoms want to bed him, and all the boys want to be him. "If you will pardon my asking, ser – why would anyone choose to join the Kingsguard at seventeen?"

"Prince Aemon the Dragonknight took his vows at seventeen," Ser Loras said, "and your brother Jaime was younger still."

"I know their reasons. What are yours? The honor of serving beside such paragons as Meryn Trant and Boros Blount?" He gave the boy a mocking grin. "To guard the

king's life, you surrender your own. You give up your lands
and titles, give up hope of marriage, children . . ."

"House Tyrell continues through my brothers," Ser
Loras said. "It is not necessary for a third son to wed, or
breed."

"Not necessary, but some find it pleasant. What of
love?"

"When the sun has set, no candle can replace it."

"Is that from a song?" Tyrion cocked his head, smiling.
"Yes, you are seventeen, I see that now."

Ser Loras tensed. "Do you mock me?"

A prickly lad. "No. If I've given offense, forgive me. I
had my own love once, and we had a song as well." *I loved
a maid as fair as summer, with sunlight in her hair.* He
bid Ser Loras a good evening and went on his way.

Near the kennels a group of men-at-arms were fighting
a pair of dogs. Tyrion stopped long enough to see the
smaller dog tear half the face off the larger one, and earned
a few coarse laughs by observing that the loser now
resembled Sandor Clegane. Then, hoping he had disarmed
their suspicions, he proceeded to the north wall and down
the short flight of steps to the eunuch's meager abode.
The door opened as he was lifting his hand to knock.

"Varys?" Tyrion slipped inside. "Are you there?" A
single candle lit the gloom, spicing the air with the scent
of jasmine.

"My lord." A woman sidled into the light; plump, soft,
matronly, with a round pink moon of a face and heavy
dark curls. Tyrion recoiled. "Is something amiss?" she
asked.

Varys, he realized with annoyance. "For one horrid
moment I thought you'd brought me Lollys instead of
Shae. Where is she?"

"Here, m'lord." She put her hands over his eyes from
behind. "Can you guess what I'm wearing?"

"Nothing?"

"Oh, you're so *smart*," she pouted, snatching her hands
away. "How did you know?"

"You're very beautiful in nothing."

"Am I?" she said. "Am I truly?"

"Oh yes."

"Then shouldn't you be fucking me instead of talking?"

"We need to rid ourselves of Lady Varys first. I am not the sort of dwarf who likes an audience."

"He's gone," Shae said.

Tyrion turned to look. It was true. The eunuch had vanished, skirts and all. *The hidden doors are here somewhere, they have to be.* That was as much as he had time to think, before Shae turned his head to kiss him. Her mouth was wet and hungry, and she did not even seem to see his scar, or the raw scab where his nose had been. Her skin was warm silk beneath his fingers. When his thumb brushed against her left nipple, it hardened at once. "Hurry," she urged, between kisses, as his fingers went to his laces, "oh, hurry, hurry, I want you in me, in me, in me." He did not even have time to undress properly. Shae pulled his cock out of his breeches, then pushed him down onto the floor and climbed atop him. She screamed as he pushed past her lips, and rode him wildly, moaning, "My giant, my giant, my giant," every time she slammed down on him. Tyrion was so eager that he exploded on the fifth stroke, but Shae did not seem to mind. She smiled wickedly when she felt him spurting, and leaned forward to kiss the sweat from his brow. "My giant of Lannister," she murmured. "Stay inside me, please. I like to feel you there."

So Tyrion did not move, except to put his arms around her. *It feels so good to hold her, and to be held,* he thought. *How can something this sweet be a crime worth hanging her for?* "Shae," he said, "sweetling, this must be our last time together. The danger is too great. If my lord father should find you . . ."

"I like your scar." She traced it with her finger. "It makes you look very fierce and strong."

He laughed. "Very ugly, you mean."

"M'lord will never be ugly in my eyes." She kissed the scab that covered the ragged stub of his nose.

"It's not my face that need concern you, it's my father –"

"He does not frighten me. Will m'lord give me back

my jewels and silks now? I asked Varys if I could have them when you were hurt in the battle, but he wouldn't give them to me. What would have become of them if you'd died?"

"I didn't die. Here I am."

"I know." Shae wriggled atop him, smiling. "Just where you belong." Her mouth turned pouty. "But how long must I go on with Lollys, now that you're well?"

"Have you been listening?" Tyrion said. "You can stay with Lollys if you like, but it would be best if you left the city."

"I don't want to leave. You promised you'd move me into a manse again after the battle." Her cunt gave him a little squeeze, and he started to stiffen again inside her. "A Lannister always pays his debts, you said."

"Shae, gods be damned, stop that. *Listen* to me. You have to go away. The city's full of Tyrells just now, and I am closely watched. You don't understand the dangers."

"Can I come to the king's wedding feast? Lollys won't go. I told her no one's like to rape her in the king's own throne room, but she's so *stupid*." When Shae rolled off, his cock slid out of her with a soft wet sound. "Symon says there's to be a singers' tourney, and tumblers, even a fools' joust."

Tyrion had almost forgotten about Shae's thrice-damned singer. "How is it you spoke to Symon?"

"I told Lady Tanda about him, and she hired him to play for Lollys. The music calms her when the baby starts to kick. Symon says there's to be a dancing bear at the feast, and wines from the Arbor. I've never seen a bear dance."

"They do it worse than I do." It was the singer who concerned him, not the bear. One careless word in the wrong ear, and Shae would hang.

"Symon says there's to be seventy-seven courses and a hundred doves baked into a great pie," Shae gushed. "When the crust's opened, they'll all burst out and fly."

"After which they will roost in the rafters and rain down birdshit on the guests." Tyrion had suffered such wedding pies before. The doves liked to shit on *him* especially, or so he had always suspected.

"Couldn't I dress in my silks and velvets and go as a lady instead of a maidservant? No one would know I wasn't."

Everyone would know you weren't, thought Tyrion. "Lady Tanda might wonder where Lollys's bedmaid found so many jewels."

"There's to be a thousand guests, Symon says. She'd never even see me. I'd find a place in some dark corner below the salt, but whenever you got up to go to the privy I could slip out and meet you." She cupped his cock and stroked it gently. "I won't wear any smallclothes under my gown, so m'lord won't even need to unlace me." Her fingers teased him, up and down. "Or if he liked, I could do this for him." She took him in her mouth.

Tyrion was soon ready again. This time he lasted much longer. When he finished Shae crawled back up him and curled up naked under his arm. "You'll let me come, won't you?"

"Shae," he groaned, "it *is not safe*."

For a time she said nothing at all. Tyrion tried to speak of other things, but he met a wall of sullen courtesy as icy and unyielding as the Wall he'd once walked in the north. *Gods be good*, he thought wearily as he watched the candle burn down and begin to gutter, *how could I let this happen again, after Tysha? Am I as great a fool as my father thinks?* Gladly would he have given her the promise she wanted, and gladly walked her back to his own bedchamber on his arm to let her dress in the silks and velvets she loved so much. Had the choice been his, she could have sat beside him at Joffrey's wedding feast, and danced with all the bears she liked. But he could not see her hang.

When the candle burned out, Tyrion disentangled himself and lit another. Then he made a round of the walls, tapping on each in turn, searching for the hidden door. Shae sat with her legs drawn up and her arms wrapped around them, watching him. Finally she said, "They're under the bed. The secret steps."

He looked at her, incredulous. "The bed? The bed is solid stone. It weighs half a ton."

"There's a place where Varys pushes, and it floats right up. I asked him how, and he said it was magic."

"Yes." Tyrion had to grin. "A counterweight spell."

Shae stood. "I should go back. Sometimes the baby kicks and Lollys wakes and calls for me."

"Varys should return shortly. He's probably listening to every word we say." Tyrion set the candle down. There was a wet spot on the front of his breeches, but in the darkness it ought to go unnoticed. He told Shae to dress and wait for the eunuch.

"I will," she promised. "You are my lion, aren't you? My giant of Lannister?"

"I am," he said. "And you're – "

" – your whore." She laid a finger to his lips. "I know. I'd be your lady, but I never can. Else you'd take me to the feast. It doesn't matter. I like being a whore for you, Tyrion. Just keep me, my lion, and keep me safe."

"I shall," he promised. *Fool, fool,* the voice inside him screamed. *Why did you say that? You came here to send her away!* Instead he kissed her once more.

The walk back seemed long and lonely. Podrick Payne was asleep in his trundle bed at the foot of Tyrion's, but he woke the boy. "Bronn," he said.

"Ser Bronn?" Pod rubbed the sleep from his eyes. "Oh. Should I get him? My lord?"

"Why no, I woke you up so we could have a little chat about the way he dresses," said Tyrion, but his sarcasm was wasted. Pod only gaped at him in confusion until he threw up his hands and said, "Yes, get him. Bring him. Now."

The lad dressed hurriedly and all but ran from the room. *Am I really so terrifying?* Tyrion wondered, as he changed into a bedrobe and poured himself some wine.

He was on his third cup and half the night was gone before Pod finally returned, with the sellsword knight in tow. "I hope the boy had a damn good reason dragging me out of Chataya's," Bronn said as he seated himself.

"*Chataya's?*" Tyrion said, annoyed.

"It's good to be a knight. No more looking for the cheaper brothels down the street." Bronn grinned. "Now it's Alayaya and Marei in the same featherbed, with Ser Bronn in the middle."

Tyrion had to bite back his annoyance. Bronn had as much right to bed Alayaya as any other man, but still . . . *I never touched her, much as I wanted to, but Bronn could not know that. He should have kept his cock out of her.* He dare not visit Chataya's himself. If he did, Cersei would see that his father heard of it, and 'Yaya would suffer more than a whipping. He'd sent the girl a necklace of silver and jade and a pair of matching bracelets by way of apology, but other than that . . .

This is fruitless. "There is a singer who calls himself Symon Silver Tongue," Tyrion said wearily, pushing his guilt aside. "He plays for Lady Tanda's daughter sometimes."

"What of him?"

Kill him, he might have said, but the man had done nothing but sing a few songs. *And fill Shae's sweet head with visions of doves and dancing bears.* "Find him," he said instead. "Find him before someone else does."

ARYA

She was grubbing for vegetables in a dead man's garden when she heard the singing.

Arya stiffened, still as stone, listening, the three stringy carrots in her hand suddenly forgotten. She thought of the Bloody Mummers and Roose Bolton's men, and a shiver of fear went down her back. *It's not fair, not when we finally found the Trident, not when we thought we were almost safe.*

Only why would the Mummers be singing?

The song came drifting up the river from somewhere beyond the little rise to the east. *"Off to Gulltown to see the fair maid, heigh-ho, heigh-ho . . ."*

Arya rose, carrots dangling from her hand. It sounded like the singer was coming up the river road. Over among the cabbages, Hot Pie had heard it too, to judge by the look on his face. Gendry had gone to sleep in the shade of the burned cottage, and was past hearing anything.

"I'll steal a sweet kiss with the point of my blade, heigh-ho, heigh-ho." She thought she heard a woodharp too, beneath the soft rush of the river.

"Do you hear?" Hot Pie asked in a hoarse whisper, as he hugged an armful of cabbages. "Someone's coming."

"Go wake Gendry," Arya told him. "Just shake him by the shoulder, don't make a lot of noise." Gendry was easy to wake, unlike Hot Pie, who needed to be kicked and shouted at.

"I'll make her my love and we'll rest in the shade, heigh-ho, heigh-ho." The song swelled louder with every word.

Hot Pie opened his arms. The cabbages fell to the ground with soft thumps. "We have to *hide.*"

Where? The burned cottage and its overgrown garden stood hard beside the banks of the Trident. There were a few willows growing along the river's edge and reed beds in the muddy shallows beyond, but most of the ground hereabouts was painfully open. *I knew we should never have left the woods,* she thought. They'd been so hungry, though, and the garden had been too much a temptation. The bread and cheese they had stolen from Harrenhal had given out six days ago, back in the thick of the woods. "Take Gendry and the horses behind the cottage," she decided. There was part of one wall still standing, big enough, maybe, to conceal two boys and three horses. *If the horses don't whinny, and that singer doesn't come poking around the garden.*

"What about you?"

"I'll hide by the tree. He's probably alone. If he bothers me, I'll kill him. *Go!*"

Hot Pie went, and Arya dropped her carrots and drew the stolen sword from over her shoulder. She had strapped the sheath across her back; the longsword was made for a man grown, and it bumped against the ground when she wore it on her hip. *It's too heavy besides,* she thought, missing Needle the way she did every time she took this clumsy thing in her hand. But it was a sword and she could kill with it, that was enough.

Lightfoot, she moved to the big old willow that grew beside the bend in the road and went to one knee in the grass and mud, within the veil of trailing branches. *You old gods,* she prayed as the singer's voice grew louder, *you tree gods, hide me, and make him go past.* Then a horse whickered, and the song broke off suddenly. *He's heard,* she knew, *but maybe he's alone, or if he's not, maybe they'll be as scared of us as we are of them.*

"Did you hear that?" a man's voice said. "There's something behind that wall, I would say."

"Aye," replied a second voice, deeper. "What do you think it might be, Archer?"

Two, then. Arya bit her lip. She could not see them from where she knelt, on account of the willow. But she could hear.

"A bear." A third voice, or the first one again?

"A lot of meat on a bear," the deep voice said. "A lot of fat as well, in fall. Good to eat, if it's cooked up right."

"Could be a wolf. Maybe a lion."

"With four feet, you think? Or two?"

"Makes no matter. Does it?"

"Not so I know. Archer, what do you mean to do with all them arrows?"

"Drop a few shafts over the wall. Whatever's hiding back there will come out quick enough, watch and see."

"What if it's some honest man back there, though? Or some poor woman with a little babe at her breast?"

"An honest man would come out and show us his face. Only an outlaw would skulk and hide."

"Aye, that's so. Go on and loose your shafts, then."

Arya sprang to her feet. *"Don't!"* She showed them her sword. There were three, she saw. *Only three.* Syrio could fight more than three, and she had Hot Pie and Gendry to stand with her, maybe. *But they're boys, and these are men.*

They were men afoot, travel-stained and mud-specked. She knew the singer by the woodharp he cradled against his jerkin, as a mother might cradle a babe. A small man, fifty from the look of him, he had a big mouth, a sharp nose, and thinning brown hair. His faded greens were mended here and there with old leather patches, and he wore a brace of throwing knives on his hip and a woodman's axe slung across his back.

The man beside him stood a good foot taller, and had the look of a soldier. A longsword and dirk hung from his studded leather belt, rows of overlapping steel rings were sewn onto his shirt, and his head was covered by a black iron halfhelm shaped like a cone. He had bad teeth and a bushy brown beard, but it was his hooded yellow cloak that drew the eye. Thick and heavy, stained here with grass and there with blood, frayed along the bottom and patched with deerskin on the right shoulder, the greatcloak gave the big man the look of some huge yellow bird.

The last of the three was a youth as skinny as his longbow, if not quite as tall. Red-haired and freckled, he wore a studded brigantine, high boots, fingerless leather gloves, and a quiver on his back. His arrows were fletched with grey goose feathers, and six of them stood in the ground before him, like a little fence.

The three men looked at her, standing there in the road with her blade in hand. Then the singer idly plucked a string. "Boy," he said, "put up that sword now, unless you're wanting to be hurt. It's too big for you, lad, and besides, Anguy here could put three shafts through you before you could hope to reach us."

"He could not," Arya said, "and I'm a *girl*."

"So you are." The singer bowed. "My pardons."

"You go on down the road. Just walk right past here, and you keep on singing, so we'll know where you are. Go away and leave us be and I won't kill you."

The freckle-faced archer laughed. "Lem, she won't kill us, did you hear?"

"I heard," said Lem, the big soldier with the deep voice.

"Child," said the singer, "put up that sword, and we'll take you to a safe place and get some food in that belly. There are wolves in these parts, and lions, and worse things. No place for a little girl to be wandering alone."

"She's not alone." Gendry rode out from behind the cottage wall, and behind him Hot Pie, leading her horse. In his chainmail shirt with a sword in his hand, Gendry looked almost a man grown, and dangerous. Hot Pie looked like Hot Pie. "Do like she says, and leave us be," warned Gendry.

"Two and three," the singer counted, "and is that all of you? And horses too, lovely horses. Where did you steal them?"

"They're ours." Arya watched them carefully. The

singer kept distracting her with his talk, but it was the archer who was the danger. *If he should pull an arrow from the ground . . .*

"Will you give us your names like honest men?" the singer asked the boys.

"I'm Hot Pie," Hot Pie said at once.

"Aye, and good for you." The man smiled. "It's not every day I meet a lad with such a tasty name. And what would your friends be called, Mutton Chop and Squab?"

Gendry scowled down from his saddle. "Why should I tell you my name? I haven't heard yours."

"Well, as to that, I'm Tom of Sevenstreams, but Tom Sevenstrings is what they call me, or Tom o' Sevens. This great lout with the brown teeth is Lem, short for Lemoncloak. It's yellow, you see, and Lem's a sour sort. And young fellow me lad over there is Anguy, or Archer as we like to call him."

"Now who are you?" demanded Lem, in the deep voice that Arya had heard through the branches of the willow.

She was not about to give up her true name as easy as that. "Squab, if you want," she said. "I don't care."

The big man laughed. "A squab with a sword," he said. "Now there's something you don't often see."

"I'm the Bull," said Gendry, taking his lead from Arya. She could not blame him for preferring Bull to Mutton Chop.

Tom Sevenstrings strummed his harp. "Hot Pie, Squab, and the Bull. Escaped from Lord Bolton's kitchen, did you?"

"How did you know?" Arya demanded, uneasy.

"You bear his sigil on your chest, little one."

She had forgotten that for an instant. Beneath her cloak, she still wore her fine page's doublet, with the flayed man of the Dreadfort sewn on her breast. "Don't call me little one!"

"Why not?" said Lem. "You're little enough."

"I'm bigger than I was. I'm not a *child*." Children didn't kill people, and she had.

"I can see that, Squab. You're none of you children, not if you were Bolton's."

"We never were." Hot Pie never knew when to keep quiet. "We were at Harrenhal before he came, that's all."

"So you're lion cubs, is that the way of it?" said Tom.

"Not that either. We're nobody's men. Whose men are you?"

Anguy the Archer said, "We're king's men."

Arya frowned. "Which king?"

"King Robert," said Lem, in his yellow cloak.

"That old drunk?" said Gendry scornfully. "He's dead, some boar killed him, everyone knows that."

"Aye, lad," said Tom Sevenstrings, "and more's the pity." He plucked a sad chord from his harp.

Arya didn't think they were king's men at all. They looked more like outlaws, all tattered and ragged. They didn't even have horses to ride. King's men would have had horses.

But Hot Pie piped up eagerly. "We're looking for Riverrun," he said. "How many days' ride is it, do you know?"

Arya could have killed him. "You be quiet, or I'll stuff rocks in your big stupid mouth."

"Riverrun is a long way upstream," said Tom. "A long hungry way. Might be you'd like a hot meal before you set out? There's an inn not far ahead kept by some friends of ours. We could share some ale and a bite of bread, instead of fighting one another."

"An inn?" The thought of hot food made Arya's belly rumble, but she didn't trust this Tom. Not everyone who spoke you friendly was really your friend. "It's near, you say?"

"Two miles upstream," said Tom. "A league at most."

Gendry looked as uncertain as she felt. "What do you mean, *friends?*" he asked warily.

"Friends. Have you forgotten what friends are?"

"Sharna is the innkeep's name," Tom put in. "She has a sharp tongue and a fierce eye, I'll grant you that, but her heart's a good one, and she's fond of little girls."

"I'm not a little girl," she said angrily. "Who else is there? You said *friends.*"

"Sharna's husband, and an orphan boy they took in. They won't harm you. There's ale, if you think you're old enough. Fresh bread and maybe a bit of meat." Tom glanced toward the cottage. "And whatever you stole from Old Pate's garden besides."

"We never stole," said Arya.

"Are you Old Pate's daughter, then? A sister? A wife? Tell me no lies, Squab. I buried Old Pate myself, right there under that willow where you were hiding, and you don't have his look." He drew a sad sound from his harp. "We've buried many a good man this past year, but we've no wish to bury you, I swear it on my harp. Archer, show her."

The archer's hand moved quicker than Arya would have believed. His shaft went hissing past her head within an inch of her ear and buried itself in the trunk of the willow behind her. By then the bowman had a second arrow notched and drawn. She'd thought she understood what Syrio meant by *quick as a snake* and *smooth as summer silk*, but now she knew she hadn't. The arrow thrummed behind her like a bee. "You missed," she said.

"More fool you if you think so," said Anguy. "They go where I send them."

"That they do," agreed Lem Lemoncloak.

There were a dozen steps between the archer and the point of her sword. *We have no chance*, Arya realized, wishing she had a bow like his, and the skill to use it. Glumly, she lowered her heavy longsword till the point touched the ground. "We'll come see this inn," she conceded, trying to hide the doubt in her heart behind bold words. "You walk in front and we'll ride behind, so we can see what you're doing."

Tom Sevenstrings bowed deeply and said, "Before, behind, it makes no matter. Come along, lads, let's show them the way. Anguy, best pull up those arrows, we won't be needing them here."

Arya sheathed her sword and crossed the road to where her friends sat on their horses, keeping her distance from the three strangers. "Hot Pie, get those cabbages," she said as she vaulted into her saddle. "And the carrots too."

For once he did not argue. They set off as she had wanted, walking their horses slowly down the rutted road a dozen paces behind the three on foot. But before very long, somehow they were riding right on top of them. Tom Sevenstrings walked slowly, and liked to strum his woodharp as he went. "Do you know any songs?" he asked them. "I'd dearly love someone to sing with, that I would. Lem can't carry a tune, and our longbow lad only knows marcher ballads, every one of them a hundred verses long."

"We sing real songs in the marches," Anguy said mildly.

"Singing is *stupid*," said Arya. "Singing makes noise. We heard you a long way off. We could have killed you."

Tom's smile said he did not think so. "There are worse things than dying with a song on your lips."

"If there were wolves hereabouts, we'd know it," groused Lem. "Or lions. These are our woods."

"You never knew we were there," said Gendry.

"Now, lad, you shouldn't be so certain of that," said Tom. "Sometimes a man knows more than he says."

Hot Pie shifted his seat. "I know the song about the bear," he said. "Some of it, anyhow."

Tom ran his fingers down his strings. "Then let's hear it, pie boy." He threw back his head and sang, "*A bear there was, a bear, a bear! All black and brown, and covered with hair . . .*"

Hot Pie joined in lustily, even bouncing in his saddle a little on the rhymes. Arya stared at him in astonishment. He had a good voice and he sang well. *He never did anything well, except bake*, she thought to herself.

A small brook flowed into the Trident a little farther on. As they waded across, their singing flushed a duck from among the reeds. Anguy stopped where he stood, unslung his bow, notched an arrow, and brought it down. The bird fell in the shallows not far from the bank. Lem took off his yellow cloak and waded in knee-deep to retrieve it, complaining all the while. "Do you think Sharna might have lemons down in that cellar of hers?" said Anguy to Tom as they watched Lem splash around, cursing. "A Dornish girl once cooked me duck with lemons." He sounded wistful.

Tom and Hot Pie resumed their song on the other side

of the brook, with the duck hanging from Lem's belt beneath his yellow cloak. Somehow the singing made the miles seem shorter. It was not very long at all until the inn appeared before them, rising from the riverbank where the Trident made a great bend to the north. Arya squinted at it suspiciously as they neared. It did not *look* like an outlaws' lair, she had to admit; it looked friendly, even homey, with its whitewashed upper story and slate roof and the smoke curling up lazy from its chimney. Stables and other outbuildings surrounded it, and there was an arbor in back, and apple trees, a small garden. The inn even had its own dock, thrusting out into the river, and . . .

"Gendry," she called, her voice low and urgent. "They have a boat. We could sail the rest of the way up to River-run. It would be faster than riding, I think."

He looked dubious. "Did you ever sail a boat?"

"You put up the sail," she said, "and the wind pushes it."

"What if the wind is blowing the wrong way?"

"Then there's oars to row."

"Against the current?" Gendry frowned. "Wouldn't that be slow? And what if the boat tips over and we fall into the water? It's not our boat anyway, it's the inn's."

We could take it. Arya chewed her lip and said nothing. They dismounted in front of stables. There were no other horses to be seen, but Arya noticed fresh manure in many of the stalls. "One of us should watch the horses," she said, wary.

Tom overheard her. "There's no need for that, Squab. Come eat, they'll be safe enough."

"I'll stay," Gendry said, ignoring the singer. "You can come get me after you've had some food."

Nodding, Arya set off after Hot Pie and Lem. Her sword was still in its sheath across her back, and she kept a hand close to the hilt of the dagger she had stolen from Roose Bolton, in case she didn't like whatever they found within.

The painted sign above the door showed a picture of some old king on his knees. Inside was the common room, where a very tall ugly woman with a knobby chin stood with her hands on her hips, glaring. "Don't just stand there, boy," she snapped. "Or are you a girl? Either one, you're blocking my door. Get in or get out. Lem, what did I tell you about my floor? You're all mud."

"We shot a duck." Lem held it out like a peace banner.

The woman snatched it from his hand. "Anguy shot a duck, is what you're meaning. Get your boots off, are you deaf or just stupid?" She turned away. "*Husband!*" she called loudly. "Get up here, the lads are back. *Husband!*"

Up the cellar steps came a man in a stained apron, grumbling. He was a head shorter than the woman, with a lumpy face and loose yellowish skin that still showed the marks of some pox. "I'm here, woman, quit your bellowing. What is it now?"

"Hang this," she said, handing him the duck.

Anguy shuffled his feet. "We were thinking we might eat it, Sharna. With lemons. If you had some."

"Lemons. And where would we get lemons? Does this look like Dorne to you, you freckled fool? Why don't you hop out back to the lemon trees and pick us a bushel, and some nice olives and pomegranates too." She shook a finger at him. "Now, I suppose I could cook it with Lem's cloak, if you like, but not till it's hung for a few days. You'll eat rabbit, or you won't eat. Roast rabbit on a spit would be quickest, if you've got a hunger. Or might be you'd like it stewed, with ale and onions."

Arya could almost taste the rabbit. "We have no coin, but we brought some carrots and cabbages we could trade you."

"Did you now? And where would they be?"

"Hot Pie, give her the cabbages," Arya said, and he did, though he approached the old woman as gingerly as if she were Rorge or Biter or Vargo Hoat.

The woman gave the vegetables a close inspection, and the boy a closer one. "Where is this *hot pie?*"

"Here. Me. It's my name. And she's . . . ah . . . Squab."

"Not under my roof. I give my diners and my dishes different names, so as to tell them apart. *Husband!*"

Husband had stepped outside, but at her shout he hurried back. "The duck's hung. What is it now, woman?"

"Wash these vegetables," she commanded. "The rest of you, sit down while I start the rabbits. The boy will bring you drink." She looked down her long nose at Arya and Hot Pie. "I am not in the habit of serving ale to children, but the cider's run out, there's no cows for milk, and the river water tastes of war, with all the dead men drifting downstream. If I served you a cup of soup full of dead flies, would you drink it?"

"'Arry would," said Hot Pie. "I mean, Squab."

"So would Lem," offered Anguy with a sly smile.

"Never you mind about Lem," Sharna said. "It's ale for all." She swept off toward the kitchen.

Anguy and Tom Sevenstrings took the table near the hearth while Lem was hanging his big yellow cloak on a peg. Hot Pie plopped down heavily on a bench at the table by the door, and Arya wedged herself in beside him.

Tom unslung his harp. *"A lonely inn on a forest road,"* he sang, slowly picking out a tune to go with the words. *"The innkeep's wife was plain as a toad."*

"Shut up with that now or we won't be getting no rabbit," Lem warned him. "You know how she is."

Arya leaned close to Hot Pie. "Can you sail a boat?" she asked. Before he could answer, a thickset boy of fifteen or sixteen appeared with tankards of ale. Hot Pie took his reverently in both hands, and when he sipped he smiled wider than Arya had ever seen him smile. "Ale," he whispered, "and *rabbit*."

"Well, here's to His Grace," Anguy the Archer called out cheerfully, lifting a toast. "Seven save the king!"

"All twelve o' them," Lem Lemoncloak muttered. He drank, and wiped the foam from his mouth with the back of his hand.

Husband came bustling in through the front door, with an apron full of washed vegetables. "There's strange horses in the stable," he announced, as if they hadn't known.

"Aye," said Tom, setting the woodharp aside, "and better horses than the three you gave away."

Husband dropped the vegetables on a table, annoyed. "I never gave them away. I *sold* them for a good price, and got us a skiff as well. Anyways, you lot were supposed to get them back."

I knew they were outlaws, Arya thought, listening. Her

hand went under the table to touch the hilt of her dagger, and make sure it was still there. *If they try to rob us, they'll be sorry.*

"They never came our way," said Lem.

"Well, I sent them. You must have been drunk, or asleep."

"Us? Drunk?" Tom drank a long draught of ale. "Never."

"You could have taken them yourself," Lem told Husband.

"What, with only the boy here? I told you twice, the old woman was up to Lambswold helping that Fern birth her babe. And like as not it was one o' you planted the bastard in the poor girl's belly." He gave Tom a sour look. "You, I'd wager, with that harp o' yours, singing all them sad songs just to get poor Fern out of her smallclothes."

"If a song makes a maid want to slip off her clothes and feel the good warm sun kiss her skin, why, is that the singer's fault?" asked Tom. "And 'twas Anguy she fancied, besides. 'Can I touch your bow?' I heard her ask him. 'Ooohh, it feels so smooth and hard. Could I give it a little pull, do you think?'"

Husband snorted. "You and Anguy, makes no matter which. You're as much to blame as me for them horses. They was three, you know. What can one man do against three?"

"Three," said Lem scornfully, "but one a woman and t'other in chains, you said so yourself."

Husband made a face. "A *big* woman, dressed like a man. And the one in chains . . . I didn't fancy the look of his eyes."

Anguy smiled over his ale. "When I don't fancy a man's eyes, I put an arrow through one."

Arya remembered the shaft that had brushed by her ear. She wished she knew how to shoot arrows.

Husband was not impressed. "You be quiet when your elders are talking. Drink your ale and mind your tongue, or I'll have the old woman take a spoon to you."

"My elders talk too much, and I don't need you to tell me to drink my ale." He took a big swallow, to show that it was so.

Arya did the same. After days of drinking from brooks and puddles, and then the muddy Trident, the ale tasted as good as the little sips of wine her father used to allow her. A smell was drifting out from the kitchen that made her mouth water, but her thoughts were still full of that boat. *Sailing it will be harder than stealing it. If we wait until they're all asleep . . .*

The serving boy reappeared with big round loaves of bread. Arya broke off a chunk hungrily and tore into it. It was hard to chew, though, sort of thick and lumpy, and burned on the bottom.

Hot Pie made a face as soon as he tasted it. "That's bad bread," he said. "It's burned, and tough besides."

"It's better when there's stew to sop up," said Lem.

"No, it isn't," said Anguy, "but you're less like to break your teeth."

"You can eat it or go hungry," said Husband. "Do I look like some bloody baker? I'd like to see you make better."

"I could," said Hot Pie. "It's easy. You kneaded the dough too much, that's why it's so hard to chew." He took another sip of ale, and began talking lovingly of breads and pies and tarts, all the things he loved. Arya rolled her eyes.

Tom sat down across from her. "Squab," he said, "or Arry, or whatever your true name might be, this is for you." He placed a dirty scrap of parchment on the wooden tabletop between them.

She looked at it suspiciously. "What is it?"

"Three golden dragons. We need to buy those horses."

Arya looked at him warily. "They're *our* horses."

"Meaning you stole them yourselves, is that it? No shame in that, girl. War makes thieves of many honest folk." Tom tapped the folded parchment with his finger. "I'm paying you a handsome price. More than any horse is worth, if truth be told."

Hot Pie grabbed the parchment and unfolded it. "There's no gold," he complained loudly. "It's only writing."

"Aye," said Tom, "and I'm sorry for that. But after the

war, we mean to make that good, you have my word as a king's man."

Arya pushed back from the table and got to her feet. "You're no king's men, you're robbers."

"If you'd ever met a true robber, you'd know they do not pay, not even in paper. It's not for us we take your horses, child, it's for the good of the realm, so we can get about more quickly and fight the fights that need fighting. The king's fights. Would you deny the king?"

They were all watching her; the Archer, big Lem, Husband with his sallow face and shifty eyes. Even Sharna, who stood in the door to the kitchen squinting. *They are going to take our horses no matter what I say*, she realized. *We'll need to walk to Riverrun, unless . . .* "We don't want paper." Arya slapped the parchment out of Hot Pie's hand. "You can have our horses for that boat outside. But only if you show us how to work it."

Tom Sevenstrings stared at her a moment, and then his wide homely mouth quirked into a rueful grin. He laughed aloud. Anguy joined in, and then they were all laughing, Lem Lemoncloak, Sharna and Husband, even the serving boy, who had stepped out from behind the casks with a crossbow under one arm. Arya wanted to scream at them, but instead she started to smile . . .

"*Riders!*" Gendry's shout was shrill with alarm. The door burst open and there he was. "*Soldiers*," he panted. "Coming down the river road, a dozen of them."

Hot Pie leapt up, knocking over his tankard, but Tom and the others were unpertubed. "There's no cause for spilling good ale on my floor," said Sharna. "Sit back down and calm yourself, boy, there's rabbit coming. You too, girl. Whatever harm's been done you, it's over and it's done and you're with king's men now. We'll keep you safe as best we can."

Arya's only answer was to reach over her shoulder for her sword, but before she had it halfway drawn Lem grabbed her wrist. "We'll have no more of that, now." He twisted her arm until her hand opened. His fingers were hard with callus and fearsomely strong. *Again!* Arya thought. *It's happening again, like it happened in the village, with Chiswyck and Raff and the Mountain That Rides.* They were going to steal her sword and turn her back into a mouse. Her free hand closed around her tankard, and she swung it at Lem's face. The ale sloshed over the rim and splashed into his eyes, and she heard his nose break and saw the spurt of blood. When he roared his hands went to his face, and she was free. *"Run!"* she screamed, bolting.

But Lem was on her again at once, with his long legs that made one of his steps equal to three of hers. She twisted and kicked, but he yanked her off her feet effortlessly and held her dangling while the blood ran down his face.

"Stop it, you little fool," he shouted, shaking her back and forth. "Stop it now!" Gendry moved to help her, until Tom Sevenstrings stepped in front of him with a dagger.

By then it was too late to flee. She could hear horses outside, and the sound of men's voices. A moment later a man came swaggering through the open door, a Tyroshi even bigger than Lem with a great thick beard, bright green at the ends but growing out grey. Behind came a pair of crossbowmen helping a wounded man between them, and then others . . .

A more ragged band Arya had never seen, but there was nothing ragged about the swords, axes, and bows they carried. One or two gave her curious glances as they entered, but no one said a word. A one-eyed man in a rusty pothelm sniffed the air and grinned, while an archer with a head of stiff yellow hair was shouting for ale. After them came a spearman in a lion-crested helm, an older man with a limp, a Braavosi sellsword, a . . .

"Harwin?" Arya whispered. *It was!* Under the beard and the tangled hair was the face of Hullen's son, who used to lead her pony around the yard, ride at quintain with Jon and Robb, and drink too much on feast days. He was thinner, harder somehow, and at Winterfell he had never worn a beard, but it was him – her father's man. *"Harwin!"* Squirming, she threw herself forward, trying to wrench free of Lem's iron grip. "It's me," she shouted, "Harwin, it's me, don't you know me, don't you?" The tears came, and she found herself weeping like a baby, just like some stupid little girl. "Harwin, *it's me!*"

Harwin's eyes went from her face to the flayed man on her doublet. "How do you know me?" he said, frowning suspiciously. "The flayed man . . . who are you, some serving boy to Lord Leech?"

For a moment she did not know how to answer. She'd had so many names. Had she only dreamed Arya Stark? "I'm a girl," she sniffed. "I was Lord Bolton's cupbearer but he was going to leave me for the goat, so I ran off with Gendry and Hot Pie. You *have* to know me! You used to lead my pony, when I was little."

His eyes went wide. "Gods be good," he said in a choked voice. "Arya Underfoot? Lem, let go of her."

"She broke my nose." Lem dumped her unceremoniously on the floor. "Who in seven hells is she supposed to be?"

"The Hand's daughter." Harwin went to one knee before her. "Arya Stark, of Winterfell."

CATELYN

Robb, she knew, the moment she heard the kennels erupt.

Her son had returned to Riverrun, and Grey Wind with him. Only the scent of the great grey direwolf could send the hounds into such a frenzy of baying and barking. *He will come to me*, she knew. Edmure had not returned after his first visit, preferring to spend his days with Marq Piper and Patrek Mallister, listening to Rymund the Rhymer's verses about the battle at the Stone Mill. *Robb is not Edmure, though. Robb will see me.*

It had been raining for days now, a cold grey downpour that well suited Catelyn's mood. Her father was growing weaker and more delirious with every passing day, waking only to mutter, "Tansy," and beg forgiveness. Edmure shunned her, and Ser Desmond Grell still denied her freedom of the castle, however unhappy it seemed to make him. Only the return of Ser Robin Ryger and his men, footweary and drenched to the bone, served to lighten her spirits. They had walked back, it seemed. Somehow the Kingslayer had contrived to sink their galley and escape, Maester Vyman confided. Catelyn asked if she might speak with Ser Robin to learn more of what had happened, but that was refused her.

Something else was wrong as well. On the day her brother returned, a few hours after their argument, she had heard angry voices from the yard below. When she climbed to the roof to see, there were knots of men gathered across the castle beside the main gate. Horses were being led from the stables, saddled and bridled, and there was shouting, though Catelyn was too far away to make out the words. One of Robb's white banners lay on the ground, and one of the knights turned his horse and trampled over the direwolf as he spurred toward the gate. Several others did the same. *Those are men who fought with Edmure on the fords*, she thought. *What could have made them so angry? Has my brother slighted them somehow, given them some insult?* She thought she recognized Ser Perwyn Frey, who had traveled with her to Bitterbridge and Storm's End and back, and his bastard half brother Martyn Rivers as well, but from this vantage it was hard to be certain. Close to forty men poured out through the castle gates, to what end she did not know.

They did not come back. Nor would Maester Vyman tell her who they had been, where they had gone, or what had made them so angry. "I am here to see to your father, and only that, my lady," he said. "Your brother will soon be Lord of Riverrun. What he wishes you to know, he must tell you."

But now Robb was returned from the west, returned in triumph. *He will forgive me*, Catelyn told herself. *He must forgive me, he is my own son, and Arya and Sansa are as much his blood as mine. He will free me from these rooms and then I will know what has happened.*

By the time Ser Desmond came for her, she had bathed and dressed and combed out her auburn hair. "King Robb has returned from the west, my lady," the knight said, "and commands that you attend him in the Great Hall."

It was the moment she had dreamt of and dreaded. *Have I lost two sons, or three?* She would know soon enough.

The hall was crowded when they entered. Every eye was on the dais, but Catelyn knew their backs: Lady Mormont's patched ringmail, the Greatjon and his son looming above every other head in the hall, Lord Jason Mallister white-haired with his winged helm in the crook of hi arm, Tytos Blackwood in his magnificent raven-feather cloak ... *Half of them will want to hang me now. The other half may only turn their eyes away.* She had the uneasy feeling that someone was missing, too.

Robb stood on the dais. *He is a boy no longer,* she realized with a pang. *He is sixteen now, a man grown. Just look at him.* War had melted all the softness from his face and left him hard and lean. He had shaved his beard away, but his auburn hair fell uncut to his shoulders. The recent rains had rusted his mail and left brown stains on the white of his cloak and surcoat. Or perhaps the stains were blood. On his head was the sword crown they had fashioned him of bronze and iron. *He bears it more comfortably now. He bears it like a king.*

Edmure stood below the crowded dais, head bowed modestly as Robb praised his victory. "... fell at the Stone Mill shall never be forgotten. Small wonder Lord Tywin ran off to fight Stannis. He'd had his fill of northmen and rivermen both." That brought laughter and approving shouts, but Robb raised a hand for quiet. "Make no mistake, though. The Lannisters will march again, and there will be other battles to win before the kingdom is secure."

The Greatjon roared out, "*King in the North!*" and thrust a mailed fist into the air. The river lords answered with a shout of "*King of the Trident!*" The hall grew thunderous with pounding fists and stamping feet.

Only a few noted Catelyn and Ser Desmond amidst the tumult, but they elbowed their fellows, and slowly a hush grew around her. She held her head high and ignored the eyes. *Let them think what they will. It is Robb's judgment that matters.*

The sight of Ser Brynden Tully's craggy face on the dais gave her comfort. A boy she did not know seemed to be acting as Robb's squire. Behind him stood a young knight in a sand-colored surcoat blazoned with seashells, and an older one who wore three black pepperpots on a saffron bend, across a field of green and silver stripes. Between them were a handsome older lady and a pretty maid who looked to be her daughter. There was another girl as well, near Sansa's age. The seashells were the sigil of some lesser house, Catelyn knew; the older man's she did not recognize. *Prisoners!* Why would Robb bring captives onto the dais!

Utherydes Wayn banged his staff on the floor as Ser Desmond escorted her forward. *If Robb looks at me as Edmure did, I do not know what I will do.* But it seemed to her that it was not anger she saw in her son's eyes, but something else . . . apprehension, perhaps? No, that made no sense. What should *he* fear? He was the Young Wolf, King of the Trident and the North.

Her uncle was the first to greet her. As black a fish as ever, Ser Brynden had no care for what others might think. He leapt off the dais and pulled Catelyn into his arms. When he said, "It is good to see you home, Cat," she had to struggle to keep her composure. "And you," she whispered.

"Mother."

Catelyn looked up at her tall kingly son. "Your Grace, I have prayed for your safe return. I had heard you were wounded."

"I took an arrow through the arm while storming the Crag," he said. "It's healed well, though. I had the best of care."

"The gods are good, then." Catelyn took a deep breath. *Say it. It cannot be avoided.* "They will have told you what I did. Did they tell you my reasons?"

"For the girls."

"I had five children. Now I have three."

"Aye, my lady." Lord Rickard Karstark pushed past the Greatjon, like some grim specter with his black mail and long ragged grey beard, his narrow face pinched and cold, "And I have one son, who once had three. You have robbed me of my vengeance."

Catelyn faced him calmly. "Lord Rickard, the Kingslayer's dying would not have bought life for your children. His living may buy life for mine."

The lord was unappeased. "Jaime Lannister has played you for a fool. You've bought a bag of empty words, no more. My Torrhen and my Eddard deserved better of you."

"Leave off, Karstark," rumbled the Greatjon, crossing

his huge arms against his chest. "It was a mother's folly. Women are made that way."

"A mother's folly?" Lord Karstark rounded on Lord Umber. "I name it treason."

"*Enough.*" For just an instant Robb sounded more like Brandon than his father. "No man calls my lady of Winterfell a traitor in my hearing, Lord Rickard." When he turned to Catelyn, his voice softened. "If I could wish the Kingslayer back in chains I would. You freed him without my knowledge or consent . . . but what you did, I know you did for love. For Arya and Sansa, and out of grief for Bran and Rickon. Love's not always wise, I've learned. It can lead us to great folly, but we follow our hearts . . . wherever they take us. Don't we, Mother?"

Is that what I did? "If my heart led me into folly, I would gladly make whatever amends I can to Lord Karstark and yourself."

Lord Rickard's face was implacable. "Will your *amends* warm Torrhen and Eddard in the cold graves where the Kingslayer laid them?" He shouldered between the Greatjon and Maege Mormont and left the hall.

Robb made no move to detain him. "Forgive him, Mother."

"If you will forgive me."

"I have. I know what it is to love so greatly you can think of nothing else."

Catelyn bowed her head. "Thank you." *I have not lost this child, at least.*

"We must talk," Robb went on. "You and my uncles. Of this and . . . other things. Steward, call an end."

Utherydes Wayn slammed his staff on the floor and shouted the dismissal, and river lords and northerners alike moved toward the doors. It was only then that Catelyn realized what was amiss. *The wolf. The wolf is not here. Where is Grey Wind?* She knew the direwolf had returned with Robb, she had heard the dogs, but he was not in the hall, not at her son's side where he belonged.

Before she could think to question Robb, however, she found herself surrounded by a circle of well-wishers. Lady Mormont took her hand and said, "My lady, if Cersei

Lannister held two of my daughters, I would have done the same." The Greatjon, no respecter of proprieties, lifted her off her feet and squeezed her arms with his huge hairy hands. "Your wolf pup mauled the Kingslayer once, he'll do it again if need be." Galbart Glover and Lord Jason Mallister were cooler, and Jonos Bracken almost icy, but their words were courteous enough. Her brother was the last to approach her. "I pray for your girls as well, Cat. I hope you do not doubt that."

"Of course not." She kissed him. "I love you for it."

When all the words were done, the Great Hall of Riverrun was empty save for Robb, the three Tullys, and the six strangers Catelyn could not place. She eyed them curiously. "My lady, sers, are you new to my son's cause?"

"New," said the younger knight, him of the seashells, "but fierce in our courage and firm in our loyalties, as I hope to prove to you, my lady."

Robb looked uncomfortable. "Mother," he said, "may I present the Lady Sybell, the wife of Lord Gawen Westerling of the Crag." The older woman came forward with solemn mien. "Her husband was one of those we took captive in the Whispering Wood."

Westerling, yes, Catelyn thought. *Their banner is six seashells, white on sand. A minor house sworn to the Lannisters.*

Robb beckoned the other strangers forward, each in turn. "Ser Rolph Spicer, Lady Sybell's brother. He was castellan at the Crag when we took it." The pepperpot knight inclined his head. A square-built man with a broken nose and a close-cropped grey beard, he looked doughty enough. "The children of Lord Gawen and Lady Sybell. Ser Raynald Westerling." The seashell knight smiled beneath a bushy mustache. Young, lean, rough-hewn, he had good teeth and a thick mop of chestnut hair. "Elenya." The little girl did a quick curtsy. "Rollam Westerling, my squire." The boy started to kneel, saw no one else was kneeling, and bowed instead.

"The honor is mine," Catelyn said. *Can Robb have won the Crag's allegiance?* If so, it was no wonder the

Westerlings were with him. Casterly Rock did not suffer such betrayals gently. Not since Tywin Lannister had been old enough to go to war . . .

The maid came forward last, and very shy. Robb took her hand. "Mother," he said, "I have the great honor to present you the Lady Jeyne Westerling. Lord Gawen's elder daughter, and my . . . ah . . . my lady wife."

The first thought that flew across Catelyn's mind was, *No, that cannot be, you are only a child.*

The second was, *And besides, you have pledged another.*

The third was, *Mother have mercy, Robb, what have you done?*

Only then came her belated remembrance. *Follies done for love? He has bagged me neat as a hare in a snare. I seem to have already forgiven him.* Mixed with her annoyance was a rueful admiration; the scene had been staged with the cunning worthy of a master mummer . . . or a king. Catelyn saw no choice but to take Jeyne Westerling's hands. "I have a new daughter," she said, more stiffly than she'd intended. She kissed the terrified girl on both cheeks. "Be welcome to our hall and hearth."

"Thank you, my lady. I shall be a good and true wife to Robb, I swear. And as wise a queen as I can."

Queen. Yes, this pretty little girl is a queen, I must remember that. She *was* pretty, undeniably, with her chestnut curls and heart-shaped face, and that shy smile. Slender, but with good hips, Catelyn noted. *She should have no trouble bearing children, at least.*

Lady Sybell took a hand before any more was said. "We are honored to be joined to House Stark, my lady, but we are also very weary. We have come a long way in a short time. Perhaps we might retire to our chambers, so you may visit with your son?"

"That would be best." Robb kissed his Jeyne. "The steward will find you suitable accommodations."

"I'll take you to him," Ser Edmure Tully volunteered.

"You are most kind," said Lady Sybell.

"Must I go too?" asked the boy, Rollam. "I'm your squire."

Robb laughed. "But I'm not in need of squiring just now."

"Oh."

"His Grace has gotten along for sixteen years without you, Rollam," said Ser Raynald of the seashells. "He will survive a few hours more, I think." Taking his little brother firmly by the hand, he walked him from the hall.

"Your wife is lovely," Catelyn said when they were out of earshot, "and the Westerlings seem worthy . . . though Lord Gawen is Tywin Lannister's sworn man, is he not?"

"Yes. Jason Mallister captured him in the Whispering Wood and has been holding him at Seagard for ransom. Of course I'll free him now, though he may not wish to join me. We wed without his consent, I fear, and this marriage puts him in dire peril. The Crag is not strong. For love of me, Jeyne may lose all."

"And you," she said softly, "have lost the Freys."

His wince told all. She understood the angry voices now, why Perwyn Frey and Martyn Rivers had left in such haste, trampling Robb's banner into the ground as they went.

"Dare I ask how many swords come with your bride, Robb?"

"Fifty. A dozen knights." His voice was glum, as well it might be. When the marriage contract had been made at the Twins, old Lord Walder Frey had sent Robb off with a thousand mounted knights and near three thousand foot. "Jeyne is bright as well as beautiful. And kind as well. She has a gentle heart."

It is swords you need, not gentle hearts. How could you do this, Robb? How could you be so heedless, so stupid? How could you be so . . . so very . . . young. Reproaches would not serve here, however. All she said was, "Tell me how this came to be."

"I took her castle and she took my heart." Robb smiled. "The Crag was weakly garrisoned, so we took it by storm one night. Black Walder and the Smalljon led scaling parties over the walls, while I broke the main gate with a ram. I took an arrow in the arm just before Ser Rolph yielded us the castle. It seemed nothing at first, but it festered. Jeyne had me taken to her own bed, and she nursed me until the fever passed. And she was with me when the Greatjon brought me the news of . . . of Winterfell. Bran and Rickon." He seemed to have trouble saying his brothers' names. "That night, she . . . she comforted me, Mother."

Catelyn did not need to be told what sort of comfort Jeyne Westerling had offered her son. "And you wed her the next day."

He looked her in the eyes, proud and miserable all at once. "It was the only honorable thing to do. She's gentle and sweet, Mother, she will make me a good wife."

"Perhaps. That will not appease Lord Frey."

"I know," her son said, stricken. "I've made a botch of everything but the battles, haven't I? I thought the battles would be the hard part, but . . . if I had listened to you and kept Theon as my hostage, I'd still rule the north, and Bran and Rickon would be alive and safe in Winterfell."

"Perhaps. Or not. Lord Balon might still have chanced war. The last time he reached for a crown, it cost him two sons. He might have thought it a bargain to lose only one this time." She touched his arm. "What happened with the Freys, after you wed?"

Robb shook his head. "With Ser Stevron, I might have been able to make amends, but Ser Ryman is dull-witted as a stone, and Black Walder . . . that one was not named for the color of his beard, I promise you. He went so far as to say that his sisters would not be loath to wed a widower. I would have killed him for that if Jeyne had not begged me to be merciful."

"You have done House Frey a grievous insult, Robb."

"I never meant to. Ser Stevron died for me, and Olyvar was as loyal a squire as any king could want. He asked to stay with me, but Ser Ryman took him with the rest. All their strength. The Greatjon urged me to attack them . . ."

"Fighting your own in the midst of your enemies?" she said. "It would have been the end of you."

"Yes. I thought perhaps we could arrange other matches for Lord Walder's daughters. Ser Wendel Manderly has offered to take one, and the Greatjon tells me his uncles wish to wed again. If Lord Walder will be reasonable – "

"He is *not* reasonable," said Catelyn. "He is proud, and prickly to a fault. You know that. He wanted to be grandfather to a king. You will not appease him with the offer of two hoary old brigands and the second son of the fattest man in the Seven Kingdoms. Not only have you broken your oath, but you've slighted the honor of the Twins by choosing a bride from a lesser house."

Robb bristled at that. "The Westerlings are better blood than the Freys. They're an ancient line, descended from the First Men. The Kings of the Rock sometimes wed Westerlings before the Conquest, and there was another Jeyne Westerling who was queen to King Maegor three hundred years ago."

"All of which will only salt Lord Walder's wounds. It has always rankled him that older houses look down on the Freys as upstarts. This insult is not the first he's borne, to hear him tell it. Jon Arryn was disinclined to foster his grandsons, and my father refused the offer of one of his daughters for Edmure." She inclined her head toward her brother as he rejoined them.

"Your Grace," Brynden Blackfish said, "perhaps we had best continue this in private."

"Yes." Robb sounded tired. "I would kill for a cup of wine. The audience chamber, I think."

As they started up the steps, Catelyn asked the question that had been troubling her since she entered the hall. "Robb, where is Grey Wind?"

"In the yard, with a haunch of mutton. I told the kennelmaster to see that he was fed."

"You always kept him with you before."

"A hall is no place for a wolf. He gets restless, you've seen. Growling and snapping. I should never have taken him into battle with me. He's killed too many men to fear them now. Jeyne's anxious around him, and he terrifies her mother."

And there's the heart of it, Catelyn thought. "He is part of you, Robb. To fear him is to fear you."

"I am not a wolf, no matter what they call me." Robb sounded cross. "Grey Wind killed a man at the Crag, another at Ashemark, and six or seven at Oxcross. If you had seen –"

"I saw Bran's wolf tear out a man's throat at Winterfell," she said sharply, "and loved him for it."

"That's different. The man at the Crag was a knight Jeyne had known all her life. You can't blame her for being afraid. Grey Wind doesn't like her uncle either. He bares his teeth every time Ser Rolph comes near him."

A chill went through her. "Send Ser Rolph away. At once."

"Where? Back to the Crag, so the Lannisters can mount his head on a spike? Jeyne loves him. He's her uncle, and a fair knight besides. I need more men like Rolph Spicer, not fewer. I am not going to banish him just because my wolf doesn't seem to like the way he smells."

"Robb." She stopped and held his arm. "I told you once to keep Theon Greyjoy close, and you did not listen. Listen now. *Send this man away.* I am not saying you must banish him. Find some task that requires a man of courage, some honorable duty, what it is matters not ... but *do not keep him near you.*"

He frowned. "Should I have Grey Wind sniff all my knights? There might be others whose smell he mislikes."

"Any man Grey Wind mislikes is a man I do not want close to you. These wolves are more than wolves, Robb. You *must* know that. I think perhaps the gods sent them to us. Your father's gods, the old gods of the north. Five wolf pups, Robb, five for five Stark children."

"Six," said Robb. "There was a wolf for Jon as well. I found them, remember? I know how many there were and where they came from. I used to think the same as you, that the wolves were our guardians, our protectors, until ..."

"Until?" she prompted.

Robb's mouth tightened. "... until they told me that Theon had murdered Bran and Rickon. Small good their wolves did them. I am no longer a boy, Mother. I'm a king, and I can protect myself." He sighed. "I will find some duty for Ser Rolph, some pretext to send him away. Not because of his smell, but to ease your mind. You have suffered enough."

Relieved, Catelyn kissed him lightly on the cheek before the others could come around the turn of the stair, and for a moment he was her boy again, and not her king.

Lord Hoster's private audience chamber was a small room above the Great Hall, better suited to intimate discussions. Robb took the high seat, removed his crown, and set it on the floor beside him as Catelyn rang for wine. Edmure was filling his uncle's ear with the whole story of the fight at the Stone Mill. It was only after the servants had come and gone that the Blackfish cleared his throat and said, "I think we've all heard sufficient of your boasting, Nephew."

Edmure was taken aback. "Boasting? What do you mean?"

"I *mean*," said the Blackfish, "that you owe His Grace your thanks for his forbearance. He played out that mummer's farce in the Great Hall so as not to shame you before your own people. Had it been me I would have flayed you for your stupidity rather than praising this folly of the fords."

"Good men died to defend those fords, Uncle." Edmure sounded outraged. "What, is no one to win victories but the Young Wolf? Did I steal some glory meant for you, Robb?"

"*Your Grace*," Robb corrected, icy. "You took me for your king, Uncle. Or have you forgotten that as well?"

The Blackfish said, "You were commanded to hold Riverrun, Edmure, no more."

"I held Riverrun, *and* I bloodied Lord Tywin's nose –"

"So you did," said Robb. "But a bloody nose won't win the war, will it? Did you ever think to ask yourself why we remained in the west so long after Oxcross? You knew I did not have enough men to threaten Lannisport or Casterly Rock."

"Why . . . there were other castles . . . gold, cattle . . ."

"You think we stayed for *plunder*?" Robb was incredulous. "Uncle, I wanted Lord Tywin to come west."

"We were all horsed," Ser Brynden said. "The Lannister

host was mainly foot. We planned to run Lord Tywin a merry chase up and down the coast, then slip behind him to take up a strong defensive position athwart the gold road, at a place my scouts had found where the ground would have been greatly in our favor. If he had come at us there, he would have paid a grievous price. But if he did not attack, he would have been trapped in the west, a thousand leagues from where he needed to be. All the while we would have lived off his land, instead of him living off ours."

"Lord Stannis was about to fall upon King's Landing," Robb said. "He might have rid us of Joffrey, the queen, and the Imp in one red stroke. Then we might have been able to make a peace."

Edmure looked from uncle to nephew. "You never told me."

"I *told* you to hold Riverrun," said Robb. "What part of that command did you fail to comprehend?"

"When you stopped Lord Tywin on the Red Fork," said the Blackfish, "you delayed him just long enough for riders out of Bitterbridge to reach him with word of what was happening to the east. Lord Tywin turned his host at once, joined up with Matthis Rowan and Randyll Tarly near the headwaters of the Blackwater, and made a forced march to Tumbler's Falls, where he found Mace Tyrell and two of his sons waiting with a huge host and a fleet of barges. They floated down the river, disembarked half a day's ride from the city, and took Stannis in the rear."

Catelyn remembered King Renly's court, as she had seen it at Bitterbridge. A thousand golden roses streaming in the wind, Queen Margaery's shy smile and soft words, her brother the Knight of Flowers with the bloody linen around his temples. *If you had to fall into a woman's arms, my son, why couldn't they have been Margaery Tyrell's?* The wealth and power of Highgarden could have made all the difference in the fighting yet to come. *And perhaps Grey Wind would have liked the smell of her as well.*

Edmure looked ill. "I never meant . . . *never*, Robb, you must let me make amends. I will lead the van in the next battle!"

For amends, Brother? Or for glory? Catelyn wondered.

"The next battle," Robb said. "Well, that will be soon enough. Once Joffrey is wed, the Lannisters will take the field against me once more, I don't doubt, and this time the Tyrells will march beside them. And I may need to fight the Freys as well, if Black Walder has his way . . ."

"So long as Theon Greyjoy sits in your father's seat with your brothers' blood on his hands, these other foes must wait," Catelyn told her son. "Your first duty is to defend your own people, win back Winterfell, and hang Theon in a crow's cage to die slowly. Or else put off that crown for good, Robb, for men will know that you are no true king at all."

From the way Robb looked at her, she could tell that it had been a long while since anyone had dared speak to him so bluntly. "When they told me Winterfell had fallen, I wanted to go north at once," he said, with a hint of defensiveness. "I wanted to free Bran and Rickon, but I thought . . . I never dreamed that Theon could harm them, truly. If I had . . ."

"It is too late for *if*s, and too late for rescues," Catelyn said. "All that remains is vengeance."

"The last word we had from the north, Ser Rodrik had defeated a force of ironmen near Torrhen's Square, and was assembling a host at Castle Cerwyn to retake Winterfell," said Robb. "By now he may have done it. There has been no news for a long while. And what of the Trident, if I turn north? I can't ask the river lords to abandon their own people."

"No," said Catelyn. "Leave them to guard their own, and win back the north with northmen."

"How will you get the northmen to the north?" her brother Edmure asked. "The ironmen control the sunset sea. The Greyjoys hold Moat Cailin as well. No army has ever taken Moat Cailin from the south. Even to march against it is madness. We could be trapped on the causeway, with the ironborn before us and angry Freys at our backs."

"We must win back the Freys," said Robb. "With them, we still have some chance of success, however small.

Without them, I see no hope. I am willing to give Lord Walder whatever he requires . . . apologies, honors, lands, gold . . . there must be *something* that would soothe his pride . . ."

"Not something," said Catelyn. "Some*one*."

JON

"**B**ig enough for you?" Snowflakes speckled Tormund's broad face, melting in his hair and beard. The giants swayed slowly atop the mammoths as they rode past two by two. Jon's garron shied, frightened by such strangeness, but whether it was the mammoths or their riders that scared him it was hard to say. Even Ghost backed off a step, baring his teeth in a silent snarl. The direwolf was big, but the mammoths were a deal bigger, and there were many and more of them.

Jon took the horse in hand and held him still, so he could count the giants emerging from the blowing snow and pale mists that swirled along the Milkwater. He was well beyond fifty when Tormund said something and he lost the count. *There must be hundreds*. No matter how many went past, they just seemed to keep coming.

In Old Nan's stories, giants were outsized men who lived in colossal castles, fought with huge swords, and walked about in boots a boy could hide in. These were something else, more bearlike than human, and as wooly as the mammoths they rode. Seated, it was hard to say how big they truly were. *Ten feet tall maybe, or twelve*, Jon thought. *Maybe fourteen, but no taller*. Their sloping chests might have passed for those of men, but their arms hung down too far, and their lower torsos looked half again as wide as their upper. Their legs were shorter than their arms, but very thick, and they wore no boots at all; their feet were broad splayed things, hard and horny and black. Neckless, their huge heavy heads thrust forward from between their shoulder blades, and their faces were squashed and brutal. Rats' eyes no larger than beads were almost lost within folds of horny flesh, but they snuffled constantly, smelling as much as they saw.

They're not wearing skins, Jon realized. *That's hair.* Shaggy pelts covered their bodies, thick below the waist, sparser above. The stink that came off them was choking, but perhaps that was the mammoths. *And Joramun blew the Horn of Winter, and woke giants from the earth.* He looked for great swords ten feet long, but saw only clubs. Most were just the limbs of dead trees, some still trailing shattered branches. A few had stone balls lashed to the ends to make colossal mauls. *The song never says if the horn can put them back to sleep.*

One of the giants coming up on them looked older than the rest. His pelt was grey and streaked with white, and the mammoth he rode, larger than any of the others, was grey and white as well. Tormund shouted something up to him as he passed, harsh clanging words in a tongue that Jon did not comprehend. The giant's lips split apart to reveal a mouth full of huge square teeth, and he made a sound half belch and half rumble. After a moment Jon realized he was laughing. The mammoth turned its massive head to regard the two of them briefly, one huge tusk passing over the top of Jon's head as the beast lumbered by, leaving huge footprints in the soft mud and fresh snow along the river. The giant shouted down something in the same coarse tongue that Tormund had used.

"Was that their king?" asked Jon.

"Giants have no kings, no more'n mammoths do, nor snow bears, nor the great whales o' the grey sea. That was Mag Mar Tun Doh Weg. Mag the Mighty. You can kneel to him if you like, he won't mind. I know your kneeler's knees must be itching, for want of some king to bend to. Watch out he don't step on you, though. Giants have bad eyes, and might be he wouldn't see some little crow all the way down there by his feet."

"What did you say to him? Was that the Old Tongue?"

"Aye. I asked him if that was his father he was forking, they looked so much alike, except his father had a better smell."

"And what did he say to you?"

Tormund Thunderfist cracked a gap-toothed smile. "He asked me if that was my daughter riding there beside me, with her smooth pink cheeks." The wildling shook snow from his arm and turned his horse about. "It may be he never saw a man without a beard before. Come, we start back. Mance grows sore wroth when I'm not found in my accustomed place."

Jon wheeled and followed Tormund back toward the head of the column, his new cloak hanging heavy from his shoulders. It was made of unwashed sheepskins, worn fleece side in, as the wildlings suggested. It kept the snow off well enough, and at night it was good and warm, but he kept his black cloak as well, folded up beneath his saddle. "Is it true you killed a giant once?" he asked Tormund as they rode. Ghost loped silently beside them, leaving paw prints in the new-fallen snow.

"Now why would you doubt a mighty man like me? It was winter and I was half a boy, and stupid the way boys are. I went too far and my horse died and then a storm caught me. A *true* storm, not no little dusting such as this. Har! I knew I'd freeze to death before it broke. So I found me a sleeping giant, cut open her belly, and crawled up right inside her. Kept me warm enough, she did, but the stink near did for me. The worst thing was, she woke up when the spring come and took me for her babe. Suckled me for three whole moons before I could get away. Har! There's times I miss the taste o' giant's milk, though."

"If she nursed you, you couldn't have killed her."

"I never did, but see you don't go spreading that about. Tormund Giantsbane has a better ring to it than Tormund Giantsbabe, and that's the honest truth o' it."

"So how did you come by your other names?" Jon asked. "Mance called you the Horn-Blower, didn't he? Mead-king of Ruddy Hall, Husband to Bears, Father to

Hosts?" It was the horn blowing he particularly wanted to hear about, but he dared not ask too plainly. *And Joramun blew the Horn of Winter, and woke giants from the earth.* Is that where they had come from, them and their mammoths? Had Mance Rayder found the Horn of Joramun, and given it to Tormund Thunderfist to blow?

"Are all crows so curious?" asked Tormund. "Well, here's a tale for you. It were another winter, colder even than the one I spent inside that giant, and snowing day and night, snowflakes as big as your head, not these little things. It snowed so hard the whole village was half buried. I was in me Ruddy Hall, with only a cask o' mead to keep me company and nothing to do but drink it. The more I drank the more I got to thinking about this woman lived close by, a fine strong woman with the biggest pair of teats you ever saw. She had a temper on her, that one, but oh, she could be warm too, and in the deep of winter a man needs his warmth.

"The more I drank the more I thought about her, and the more I thought the harder me member got, till I couldn't suffer it no more. Fool that I was, I bundled meself up in furs from head to heels, wrapped a winding wool around me face, and set off to find her. The snow was coming down so hard I got turned around once or twice, and the wind blew right through me and froze me bones, but finally I come on her, all bundled up like I was.

"The woman had a terrible temper, and she put up quite the fight when I laid hands on her. It was all I could do to carry her home and get her out o' them furs, but when I did, oh, she was hotter even than I remembered, and we had a fine old time, and then I went to sleep. Next morning when I woke the snow had stopped and the sun was shining, but I was in no fit state to enjoy it. All ripped and torn I was, and half me member bit right off, and there on me floor was a she-bear's pelt. And soon enough the free folk were telling tales o' this bald bear seen in the woods, with the queerest pair o' cubs behind her. Har!" He slapped a meaty thigh. "Would that I could find her again. She was fine to lay with, that bear. Never was a woman gave me such a fight, nor such strong sons neither."

"What could you do if you *did* find her?" Jon asked, smiling. "You said she bit your member off."

"Only half. And half me member is twice as long as any other man's." Tormund snorted. "Now as to you . . . is it true they cut your members off when they take you for the Wall?"

"No," Jon said, affronted.

"I think it must be true. Else why refuse Ygritte? She'd hardly give you any fight at all, seems to me. The girl wants you in her, that's plain enough to see."

Too bloody plain, thought Jon, *and it seems that half the column has seen it.* He studied the falling snow so Tormund might not see him redden. *I am a man of the Night's Watch*, he reminded himself. So why did he feel like some blushing maid?

He spent most of his days in Ygritte's company, and most nights as well. Mance Rayder had not been blind to Rattleshirt's mistrust of the "crow-come-over," so after he had given Jon his new sheepskin cloak he had suggested that he might want to ride with Tormund Giantsbane instead. Jon had happily agreed, and the very next day Ygritte and Longspear Ryk left Rattleshirt's band for Tormund's as well. "Free folk ride with who they want," the girl told him, "and we had a bellyful of Bag o' Bones."

Every night when they made camp, Ygritte threw her sleeping skins down beside his own, no matter if he was near the fire or well away from it. Once he woke to find her nestled against him, her arm across his chest. He lay listening to her breathe for a long time, trying to ignore the tension in his groin. Rangers often shared skins for warmth, but warmth was not all Ygritte wanted, he suspected. After that he had taken to using Ghost to keep her away. Old Nan used to tell stories about knights and their ladies who would sleep in a single bed with a blade between them for honor's sake, but he thought this must be the first time where a direwolf took the place of the sword.

Even then, Ygritte persisted. The day before last, Jon had made the mistake of wishing he had hot water for a bath. "Cold is better," she had said at once, "if you've got someone to warm you up after. The river's only part ice yet, go on."

Jon laughed. "You'd freeze me to death."

"Are all crows afraid of gooseprickles? A little ice won't kill you. I'll jump in with you t'prove it so."

"And ride the rest of the day with wet clothes frozen to our skins?" he objected.

"Jon Snow, you know nothing. You don't go in with clothes."

"I don't go in at all," he said firmly, just before he heard Tormund Thunderfist bellowing for him (he hadn't, but never mind).

The wildlings seemed to think Ygritte a great beauty because of her hair; red hair was rare among the free folk, and those who had it were said to be kissed by fire, which was supposed to be lucky. Lucky it might be, and red it certainly was, but Ygritte's hair was such a tangle that Jon was tempted to ask her if she only brushed it at the changing of the seasons.

At a lord's court the girl would never have been considered anything but common, he knew. She had a round peasant face, a pug nose, and slightly crooked teeth, and her eyes were too far apart. Jon had noticed all that the first time he'd seen her, when his dirk had been at her throat. Lately, though, he was noticing some other things. When she grinned, the crooked teeth didn't seem to matter. And maybe her eyes were too far apart, but they were a pretty blue-grey color, and lively as any eyes he knew. Sometimes she sang in a low husky voice that stirred him. And sometimes by the cookfire when she sat hugging her knees with the flames waking echoes in her red hair, and looked at him, just smiling ... well, *that* stirred some things as well.

But he was a man of the Night's Watch, he had taken a vow. I shall take no wife, hold no lands, father no children. He had said the words before the weirwood, before his father's gods. He could not unsay them ... no more than he could admit the reason for his reluctance to Tormund Thunderfist, Father to Bears.

"Do you mislike the girl?" Tormund asked him as they

passed another twenty mammoths, these bearing wildlings in tall wooden towers instead of giants.

"No, but I . . ." *What can I say that he will believe?* "I
am still too young to wed."

"Wed?" Tormund laughed. "Who spoke of wedding? In
the south, must a man wed every girl he beds?"

Jon could feel himself turning red again. "She spoke for
me when Rattleshirt would have killed me. I would not
dishonor her."

"You are a free man now, and Ygritte is a free woman.
What dishonor if you lay together?"

"I might get her with child."

"Aye, I'd hope so. A strong son or a lively laughing girl
kissed by fire, and where's the harm in that?"

Words failed him for a moment. "The boy . . . the child
would be a bastard."

"Are bastards weaker than other children? More sickly,
more like to fail?"

"No, but –"

"You're bastard-born yourself. And if Ygritte does not
want a child, she will go to some woods witch and drink
a cup o' moon tea. You do not come into it, once the seed
is planted."

"I will *not* father a bastard."

Tormund shook his shaggy head. "What fools you kneelers be. Why did you steal the girl if you don't want her?"

"*Steal?* I never . . ."

"You did," said Tormund. "You slew the two she was
with and carried her off, what do you call it?"

"I took her prisoner."

"You made her yield to you."

"Yes, but . . . Tormund, I swear, I've never touched
her."

"Are you *certain* they never cut your member off?"
Tormund gave a shrug, as if to say he would never understand such madness. "Well, you are a free man now, but
if you will not have the girl, best find yourself a she-bear.
If a man does not use his member it grows smaller and
smaller, until one day he wants to piss and cannot find
it."

Jon had no answer for that. Small wonder that the Seven Kingdoms thought the free folk scarcely human. *They have no laws, no honor, not even simple decency. They steal endlessly from each other, breed like beasts, prefer rape to marriage, and fill the world with baseborn children.* Yet he was growing fond of Tormund Giantsbane, great bag of wind and lies though he was. Longspear as well. *And Ygritte . . . no, I will not think about Ygritte.*

Along with the Tormunds and the Longspears rode other sorts of wildlings, though; men like Rattleshirt and the Weeper who would as soon slit you as spit on you. There was Harma Dogshead, a squat keg of a woman with cheeks like slabs of white meat, who hated dogs and killed one every fortnight to make a fresh head for her banner; earless Styr, Magnar of Thenn, whose own people thought him more god than lord; Varamyr Sixskins, a small mouse of a man whose steed was a savage white snow bear that stood thirteen feet tall on its hind legs. And wherever the bear and Varamyr went, three wolves and a shadowcat came following. Jon had been in his presence only once, and once had been enough; the mere sight of the man had made him bristle, even as the fur on the back of Ghost's neck had bristled at the sight of the bear and that long black-and-white 'cat.

And there were folks fiercer even than Varamyr, from the northernmost reaches of the haunted forest, the hidden valleys of the Frostfangs, and even queerer places: the men of the Frozen Shore who rode in chariots made of walrus bones pulled along by packs of savage dogs, the terrible ice-river clans who were said to feast on human flesh, the cave dwellers with their faces dyed blue and purple and green. With his own eyes Jon had beheld the Hornfoot men trotting along in column on bare soles as hard as boiled leather. He had not seen any snarks or grumpkins, but for all he knew Tormund would be having some to supper.

Half the wildling host had lived all their lives without so much as a glimpse of the Wall, Jon judged, and most of those spoke no word of the Common Tongue. It did not matter. Mance Rayder spoke the Old Tongue, even sang in it, fingering his lute and filling the night with strange wild music.

Mance had spent years assembling this vast plodding host, talking to this clan mother and that magnar, winning one village with sweet words and another with a song and a third with the edge of his sword, making peace between Harma Dogshead and the Lord o' Bones, between the Hornfoots and the Nightrunners, between the walrus men of the Frozen Shore and the cannibal clans of the great ice rivers, hammering a hundred different daggers into one great spear, aimed at the heart of the Seven Kingdoms. He had no crown nor scepter, no robes of silk and velvet, but it was plain to Jon that Mance Rayder *was* a king in more than name.

Jon had joined the wildlings at Qhorin Halfhand's command. "Ride with them, eat with them, fight with them," the ranger had told him, the night before he died. "And *watch*." But all his watching had learned him little. The Halfhand had suspected that the wildlings had gone up into the bleak and barren Frostfangs in search of some weapon, some power, some fell sorcery with which to break the Wall . . . but if they had found any such, no one was boasting of it openly, or showing it to Jon. Nor had Mance Rayder confided any of his plans or strategies. Since that first night, he had hardly seen the man save at a distance.

I will kill him if I must. The prospect gave Jon no joy; there would be no honor in such a killing, and it would mean his own death as well. Yet he could not let the wildlings breach the Wall, to threaten Winterfell and the north, the barrowlands and the Rills, White Harbor and the Stony Shore, even the Neck. For eight thousand years the men of House Stark had lived and died to protect their people against such ravagers and reavers . . . and bastard-born or no, the same blood ran in his veins. *Bran and Rickon are still at Winterfell besides. Maester Luwin, Ser Rodrik, Old Nan, Farlen the kennelmaster, Mikken at his forge and Gage by his ovens . . . everyone I ever knew, everyone I ever loved.* If Jon must slay a man he half admired and almost liked to save them from the mercies of Rattleshirt and Harma Dogshead and the earless Magnar of Thenn, that was what he meant to do.

Still, he prayed his father's gods might spare him that bleak task. The host moved but slowly, burdened as it was by all the wildlings' herds and children and mean little treasures, and the snows had slowed its progress even more. Most of the column was out of the foothills now, oozing down along the west bank of the Milkwater like honey on a cold winter's morning, following the course of the river into the heart of the haunted forest.

And somewhere close ahead, Jon knew, the Fist of the First Men loomed above the trees, home to three hundred black brothers of the Night's Watch, armed, mounted, and waiting. The Old Bear had sent out other scouts besides the Halfhand, and surely Jarman Buckwell or Thoren Smallwood would have returned by now with word of what was coming down out of the mountains.

Mormont will not run, Jon thought. *He is too old and he has come too far. He will strike, and damn the numbers.* One day soon he would hear the sound of warhorns, and see a column of riders pounding down on them with black cloaks flapping and cold steel in their hands. Three hundred men could not hope to kill a hundred times their number, of course, but Jon did not think they would need to. *He need not slay a thousand, only one. Mance is all that keeps them together.*

The King-beyond-the-Wall was doing all he could, yet the wildlings remained hopelessly undisciplined, and that made them vulnerable. Here and there within the leagues-long snake that was their line of march were warriors as fierce as any in the Watch, but a good third of them were grouped at either end of the column, in Harma Dogshead's van and the savage rearguard with its giants, aurochs, and fire flingers. Another third rode with Mance himself near the center, guarding the wayns and sledges and dog carts that held the great bulk of the host's provisions and supplies, all that remained of the last summer harvest. The rest, divided into small bands under the likes of Rattleshirt, Jarl, Tormund Giantsbane, and the Weeper, served as outriders, foragers, and whips, galloping up and down the column endlessly to keep it moving in a more or less orderly fashion.

And even more telling, only one in a hundred wildlings was mounted. *The Old Bear will go through them like an axe through porridge.* And when that happened, Mance must give chase with his center, to try and blunt the threat. If he should fall in the fight that must follow, the Wall would be safe for another hundred years, Jon judged. *And if not . . .*

He flexed the burned fingers of his sword hand. Longclaw was slung to his saddle, the carved stone wolf's-head pommel and soft leather grip of the great bastard sword within easy reach.

The snow was falling heavily by the time they caught Tormund's band, several hours later. Ghost departed along the way, melting into the forest at the scent of prey. The direwolf would return when they made camp for the night, by dawn at the latest. However far he prowled, Ghost always came back . . . and so, it seemed, did Ygritte.

"So," the girl called when she saw him, "d'you believe us now, Jon Snow? Did you see the giants on their mammoths?"

"Har!" shouted Tormund, before Jon could reply. "The crow's in love! He means to marry one!"

"A giantess?" Longspear Ryk laughed.

"No, a *mammoth*!" Tormund bellowed. "Har!"

Ygritte trotted beside Jon as he slowed his garron to a walk. She claimed to be three years older than him, though she stood half a foot shorter; however old she might be, the girl was a tough little thing. Stonesnake had called her a "spearwife" when they'd captured her in the Skirling Pass. She wasn't wed and her weapon of choice was a short curved bow of horn and weirwood, but "spearwife" fit her all the same. She reminded him a little of his sister Arya, though Arya was younger and probably skinnier. It was hard to tell how plump or thin Ygritte might be, with all the furs and skins she wore.

"Do you know 'The Last of the Giants'?" Without waiting for an answer Ygritte said, "You need a deeper voice than mine to do it proper." Then she sang, "*Ooooooh, I*

*am the last of the giants, my people are gone from the
earth."*

Tormund Giantsbane heard the words and grinned.
*"The last of the great mountain giants, who ruled all the
world at my birth,"* he bellowed back through the snow.

Longspear Ryk joined in, singing, *"Oh, the smallfolk
have stolen my forests, they've stolen my rivers and
hills."*

*"And they've built a great wall through my valleys,
and fished all the fish from my rills,"* Ygritte and Tormund
sang back at him in turn, in suitably gigantic voices.

Tormund's sons Toregg and Dormund added their deep
voices as well, then his daughter Munda and all the rest.
Others began to bang their spears on leathern shields to
keep rough time, until the whole war band was singing
as they rode.

> *In stone halls they burn their great fires,*
> > *in stone halls they forge their sharp spears.*
> *Whilst I walk alone in the mountains,*
> > *with no true companion but tears.*
> *They hunt me with dogs in the daylight,*
> > *they hunt me with torches by night.*
> *For these men who are small can never stand tall,*
> > *whilst giants still walk in the light.*
> *Ooooooh, I am the LAST of the giants,*
> > *so learn well the words of my song.*
> *For when I am gone the singing will fade,*
> > *and the silence shall last long and long.*

There were tears on Ygritte's cheeks when the song
ended.

"Why are you weeping?" Jon asked. "It was only a song.
There are hundreds of giants, I've just seen them."

"Oh, hundreds," she said furiously. "You know nothing, Jon Snow. You – *JON!"*

Jon turned at the sudden sound of wings. Blue-grey
feathers filled his eyes, as sharp talons buried themselves
in his face. Red pain lanced through him sudden and fierce
as pinions beat round his head. He saw the beak, but there

was no time to get a hand up or reach for a weapon. Jon reeled backward, his foot lost the stirrup, his garron broke in panic, and then he was falling. And still the eagle clung to his face, its talons tearing at him as it flapped and shrieked and pecked. The world turned upside down in a chaos of feathers and horseflesh and blood, and then the ground came up to smash him.

The next he knew, he was on his face with the taste of mud and blood in his mouth and Ygritte kneeling over him protectively, a bone dagger in her hand. He could still hear wings, though the eagle was not in sight. Half his world was black. "My eye," he said in sudden panic, raising a hand to his face.

"It's only blood, Jon Snow. He missed the eye, just ripped your skin up some."

His face was throbbing. Tormund stood over them bellowing, he saw from his right eye as he rubbed blood from his left. Then there were hoofbeats, shouts, and the clacking of old dry bones.

"Bag o' Bones," roared Tormund, "call off your hellcrow!"

"There's your hellcrow!" Rattleshirt pointed at Jon. "Bleeding in the mud like a faithless dog!" The eagle came flapping down to land atop the broken giant's skull that served him for his helm. "I'm here for him."

"Come take him then," said Tormund, "but best come with sword in hand, for that's where you'll find mine. Might be I'll boil *your* bones, and use your skull to piss in. Har!"

"Once I prick you and let the air out, you'll shrink down smaller'n that girl. Stand aside, or Mance will hear o' this."

Ygritte stood. "What, is it *Mance* who wants him?"

"I said so, didn't I? Get him up on those black feet."

Tormund frowned down at Jon. "Best go, if it's the Mance who's wanting you."

Ygritte helped pull him up. "He's bleeding like a butchered boar. Look what Orell did t' his sweet face."

Can a bird hate? Jon had slain the wildling Orell, but some part of the man remained within the eagle. The golden eyes looked out on him with cold malevolence. "I'll come," he said. The blood kept running down into his right eye, and his cheek was a blaze of pain. When he touched it his black gloves came away stained with red. "Let me catch my garron." It was not the horse he wanted so much as Ghost, but the direwolf was nowhere to be seen. *He could be leagues away by now, ripping out the throat of some elk*. Perhaps that was just as well.

The garron shied away from him when he approached, no doubt frightened by the blood on his face, but Jon calmed him with a few quiet words and finally got close enough to take the reins. As he swung back into the saddle his head whirled. *I will need to get this tended*, he thought, *but not just now. Let the King-beyond-the-Wall see what his eagle did to me*. His right hand opened and closed, and he reached down for Longclaw and slung the bastard sword over a shoulder before he wheeled to trot back to where the Lord of Bones and his band were waiting.

Ygritte was waiting too, sitting on her horse with a fierce look on her face. "I am coming too."

"Be gone." The bones of Rattleshirt's breastplate clattered together. "I was sent for the crow-come-down, none other."

"A free woman rides where she will," Ygritte said.

The wind was blowing snow into Jon's eyes. He could feel the blood freezing on his face. "Are we talking or riding?"

"Riding," said the Lord of Bones.

It was a grim gallop. They rode two miles down the column through swirling snows, then cut through a tangle of baggage wayns to splash across the Milkwater where it took a great loop toward the east. A crust of thin ice covered the river shallows; with every step their horses' hooves crashed through, until they reached the deeper water ten yards out. The snow seemed be falling even faster on the eastern bank, and the drifts were deeper too. *Even the wind is colder*. And night was falling too.

But even through the blowing snow, the shape of the great white hill that loomed above the trees was unmistakable. *The Fist of the First Men*. Jon heard the scream of the eagle overhead. A raven looked down from a soldier pine and *quork*ed as he went past. *Had the Old Bear made his attack?* Instead of the clash of steel and the thrum of arrows taking flight, Jon heard only the soft crunch of frozen crust beneath his garron's hooves.

In silence they circled round to the south slope, where the approach was easiest. It was there at the bottom that Jon saw the dead horse, sprawled at the base of the hill, half buried in the snow. Entrails spilled from the belly of the animal like frozen snakes, and one of its legs was gone. *Wolves*, was Jon's first thought, but that was wrong. Wolves eat their kill.

More garrons were strewn across the slope, legs twisted grotesquely, blind eyes staring in death. The wildlings crawled over them like flies, stripping them of saddles, bridles, packs, and armor, and hacking them apart with stone axes.

"Up," Rattleshirt told Jon. "Mance is up top."

Outside the ringwall they dismounted to squeeze through a crooked gap in the stones. The carcass of a shaggy brown garron was impaled upon the sharpened stakes the Old Bear had placed inside every entrance. *He was trying to get out, not in.* There was no sign of a rider.

Inside was more, and worse. Jon had never seen pink snow before. The wind gusted around him, pulling at his heavy sheepskin cloak. Ravens flapped from one dead horse to the next. *Are those wild ravens, or our own?* Jon could not tell. He wondered where poor Sam was now. And *what* he was.

A crust of frozen blood crunched beneath the heel of his boot. The wildlings were stripping the dead horses of every scrap of steel and leather, even prying the horseshoes off their hooves. A few were going through packs they'd turned up, looking for weapons and food. Jon passed one of Chett's dogs, or what remained of him, lying in a sludgy pool of half-frozen blood.

A few tents were still standing on the far side of the camp, and it was there they found Mance Rayder. Beneath his slashed cloak of black wool and red silk he wore black ringmail and shaggy fur breeches, and on his head was a great bronze-and-iron helm with raven wings at either temple. Jarl was with him, and Harma the Dogshead; Styr as well, and Varamyr Sixskins with his wolves and his shadowcat.

The look Mance gave Jon was grim and cold. "What happened to your face?"

Ygritte said, "Orell tried to take his eye out."

"It was him I asked. Has he lost his tongue? Perhaps he should, to spare us further lies."

Styr the Magnar drew a long knife. "The boy might see more clear with one eye, instead of two."

"Would you like to keep your eye, Jon?" asked the King-beyond-the-Wall. "If so, tell me how many they were. And try and speak the truth this time, Bastard of Winterfell."

Jon's throat was dry. "My lord . . . what . . ."

"I am not your lord," said Mance. "And the *what* is plain enough. Your brothers died. The question is, how many?"

Jon's face was throbbing, the snow kept coming down, and it was hard to think. *You must not balk, whatever is asked of you*, Qhorin had told him. The words stuck in his throat, but he made himself say, "There were three hundred of us."

"Us?" Mance said sharply.

"Them. Three hundred of them." *Whatever is asked, the Halfhand said. So why do I feel so craven?* "Two hundred from Castle Black, and one hundred from the Shadow Tower."

"There's a truer song than the one you sang in my tent." Mance looked to Harma Dogshead. "How many horses have we found?"

"More'n a hundred," that huge woman replied, "less than two. There's more dead to the east, under the snow, hard t' know how many." Behind her stood her banner bearer, holding a pole with a dog's head on it, fresh enough to still be leaking blood.

"You should never have lied to me, Jon Snow," said Mance.

"I . . . I know that." *What could he say?*

The wildling king studied his face. "Who had the command here? And tell me true. Was it Rykker? Smallwood? Not Wythers, he's too feeble. Whose tent was this?"

I have said too much. "You did not find his body?"

Harma snorted, her disdain frosting from her nostrils. "What fools these black crows be."

"The next time you answer me with a question, I will give you to my Lord of Bones," Mance Rayder promised Jon. He stepped closer. "Who led here?"

One more step, thought Jon. *Another foot.* He moved his hand closer to Longclaw's hilt. *If I hold my tongue . . .*

"Reach up for that bastard sword and I'll have your bastard head off before it clears the scabbard," said Mance. "I am fast losing patience with you, crow."

"Say it," Ygritte urged. "He's dead, whoever he was."

His frown cracked the blood on his cheek. *This is too hard*, Jon thought in despair. *How do I play the turncloak without becoming one?* Qhorin had not told him that. But the second step is always easier than the first. "The Old Bear."

"That old man?" Harma's tone said she did not believe it. "He came himself? Then who commands at Castle Black?"

"Bowen Marsh." This time Jon answered at once. *You must not balk, whatever is asked of you.*

Mance laughed. "If so, our war is won. Bowen knows a deal more about counting swords than he's ever known about using them."

"The Old Bear commanded," said Jon. "This place was high and strong, and he made it stronger. He dug pits and planted stakes, laid up food and water. He was ready for . . ."

". . . me?" finished Mance Rayder. "Aye, he was. Had I been fool enough to storm this hill, I might have lost five men for every crow I slew and still counted myself lucky." His mouth grew hard. "But when the dead walk, walls and stakes and swords mean nothing. You cannot fight the dead, Jon Snow. No man knows that half so well as me." He gazed up at the darkening sky and said, "The crows may have helped us more than they know. I'd wondered why we'd suffered no attacks. But there's still a hundred leagues to go, and the cold is rising. Varamyr, send your wolves sniffing after the wights, I won't have them taking us unawares. My Lord of Bones, double all the patrols, and make certain every man has torch and flint. Styr, Jarl, you ride at first light."

"Mance," Rattleshirt said, "I want me some crow bones."

Ygritte stepped in front of Jon. "You can't kill a man for lying to protect them as was his brothers."

"They are still his brothers," declared Styr.

"They're *not*," insisted Ygritte. "He never killed me, like they told him. And he slew the Halfhand, we all saw."

Jon's breath misted the air. *If I lie to him, he'll know.* He looked Mance Rayder in the eyes, opened and closed his burned hand. "I wear the cloak you gave me, Your Grace."

"A sheepskin cloak!" said Ygritte. "And there's many a night we dance beneath it, too!"

Jarl laughed, and even Harma Dogshead smirked. "Is that the way of it, Jon Snow?" asked Mance Rayder, mildly. "Her and you?"

It was easy to lose your way beyond the Wall. Jon did not know that he could tell honor from shame anymore, or right from wrong. *Father forgive me.* "Yes," he said.

Mance nodded. "Good. You'll go with Jarl and Styr on the morrow, then. Both of you. Far be it from me to separate two hearts that beat as one."

"Go where?" said Jon.

"Over the Wall. It's past time you proved your faith with something more than words, Jon Snow."

The Magnar was not pleased. "What do I want with a crow?"

"He knows the Watch and he knows the Wall," said Mance, "and he knows Castle Black better than any raider ever could. You'll find a use for him, or you're a fool."

Styr scowled. "His heart may still be black."

"Then cut it out." Mance turned to Rattleshirt. "My Lord of Bones, keep the column moving at all costs. If we reach the Wall before Mormont, we've won."

"They'll move." Rattleshirt's voice was thick and angry.

Mance nodded, and walked away, Harma and Sixskins beside him. Varamyr's wolves and shadowcat followed behind. Jon and Ygritte were left with Jarl, Rattleshirt, and the Magnar. The two older wildlings looked at Jon with ill-concealed rancor as Jarl said, "You heard, we ride at daybreak. Bring all the food you can, there'll be no time to hunt. And have your face seen to, crow. You look a bloody mess."

"I will," said Jon.

"You best not be lying, girl," Rattleshirt said to Ygritte, his eyes shiny behind the giant's skull.

Jon drew Longclaw. "Get away from us, unless you want what Qhorin got."

"You got no wolf to help you here, boy." Rattleshirt reached for his own sword.

"Sure o' that, are you?" Ygritte laughed.

Atop the stones of the ringwall, Ghost hunched with white fur bristling. He made no sound, but his dark red eyes spoke blood. The Lord of Bones moved his hand slowly away from his sword, backed off a step, and left them with a curse.

Ghost padded beside their garrons as Jon and Ygritte descended the Fist. It was not until they were halfway across the Milkwater that Jon felt safe enough to say, "I never asked you to lie for me."

"I never did," she said. "I left out part, is all."

"You said –"

"– that we fuck beneath your cloak many a night. I never said when we started, though." The smile she gave him was almost shy. "Find another place for Ghost to sleep tonight, Jon Snow. It's like Mance said. Deeds is truer than words."

SANSA

"A new gown?" she said, as wary as she was astonished.

"More lovely than any you have worn, my lady," the old woman promised. She measured Sansa's hips with a length of knotted string. "All silk and Myrish lace, with satin linings. You will be very beautiful. The queen herself has commanded it."

"Which queen?" Margaery was not yet Joff's queen, but she had been Renly's. Or did she mean the Queen of Thorns? Or . . .

"The Queen Regent, to be sure."

"Queen *Cersei*?"

"None other. She has honored me with her custom for many a year." The old woman laid her string along the inside of Sansa's leg. "Her Grace said to me that you are a woman now, and should not dress like a little girl. Hold out your arm."

Sansa lifted her arm. She needed a new gown, that was true. She had grown three inches in the past year, and most of her old wardrobe had been ruined by the smoke when she'd tried to burn her mattress on the day of her first flowering

"Your bosom will be as lovely as the queen's," the old woman said as she looped her string around Sansa's chest. "You should not hide it so."

The comment made her blush. Yet the last time she'd gone riding, she could not lace her jerkin all the way to the top, and the stableboy gaped at her as he helped her mount. Sometimes she caught grown men looking at her chest as well, and some of her tunics were so tight she could scarce breathe in them.

"What color will it be?" she asked the seamstress.

"Leave the colors to me, my lady. You will be pleased, I know you will. You shall have smallclothes and hose as well, kirtles and mantles and cloaks, and all else befitting a . . . a lovely young lady of noble birth."

"Will they be ready in time for the king's wedding?"

"Oh, sooner, much sooner, Her Grace insists. I have six seamstresses and twelve apprentice girls, and we have set all our other work aside for this. Many ladies will be cross with us, but it was the queen's command."

"Thank Her Grace kindly for her thoughtfulness," Sansa said politely. "She is too good to me."

"Her Grace is most generous," the seamstress agreed, as she gathered up her things and took her leave.

But why? Sansa wondered when she was alone. It made her uneasy. *I'll wager this gown is Margaery's doing somehow, or her grandmother's.*

Margaery's kindness had been unfailing, and her presence changed everything. Her ladies welcomed Sansa as well. It had been so long since she had enjoyed the company of other women, she had almost forgotten how pleasant it could be. Lady Leonette gave her lessons on the high harp, and Lady Janna shared all the choice gossip. Merry Crane always had an amusing story, and little Lady Bulwer reminded her of Arya, though not so fierce.

Closest to Sansa's own age were the cousins Elinor, Alla, and Megga, Tyrells from junior branches of the House. "Roses from lower on the bush," quipped Elinor, who was witty and willowy. Megga was round and loud, Alla shy and pretty, but Elinor ruled the three by right of womanhood; she was a maiden flowered, whereas Megga and Alla were mere girls.

The cousins took Sansa into their company as if they had known her all their lives. They spent long afternoons doing needlework and talking over lemon cakes and honeyed wine, played at tiles of an evening, sang together in the castle sept . . . and often one or two of them would be chosen to share Margaery's bed, where they would whisper half the night away. Alla had a lovely voice, and when coaxed would play the woodharp and sing songs of chivalry and lost loves. Megga couldn't sing, but she was mad to be kissed. She and Alla played a kissing game sometimes, she confessed, but it wasn't the same as kissing a man, much less a king. Sansa wondered what Megga would think about kissing the Hound, as she had. He'd come to her the night of the battle stinking of wine and blood. *He kissed me and threatened to kill me, and made me sing him a song.*

"King Joffrey has such beautiful lips," Megga gushed, oblivious, "oh, poor Sansa, how your heart must have broken when you lost him. Oh, how you must have wept!"

Joffrey made me weep more often than you know, she wanted to say, but Butterbumps was not on hand to drown out her voice, so she pressed her lips together and held her tongue.

As for Elinor, she was promised to a young squire, a son of Lord Ambrose; they would be wed as soon as he won his spurs. He had worn her favor in the Battle of the Blackwater, where he'd slain a Myrish crossbowman and a Mullendore man-at-arms. "Alyn said her favor made him fearless," said Megga. "He says he shouted her name for his battle cry, isn't that ever so gallant? Someday I want some champion to wear my favor, and kill a hundred men." Elinor told her to hush, but looked pleased all the same.

They are children, Sansa thought. *They are silly little girls, even Elinor. They've never seen a battle, they've never seen a man die, they know nothing.* Their dreams were full of songs and stories, the way hers had been before Joffrey cut her father's head off. Sansa pitied them. Sansa envied them.

Margaery was different, though. Sweet and gentle, yet there was a little of her grandmother in her, too. The day before last she'd taken Sansa hawking. It was the first time she had been outside the city since the battle. The dead had been burned or buried, but the Mud Gate was scarred and splintered where Lord Stannis's rams had battered it, and the hulls of smashed ships could be seen along both sides of the Blackwater, charred masts poking from the shallows like gaunt black fingers. The only traffic was the flat-bottomed ferry that took them across the river, and when they reached the kingswood they found a wilderness of ash and charcoal and dead trees. But the waterfowl teemed in the marshes along the bay, and Sansa's merlin brought down three ducks while Margaery's peregrine took a heron in full flight.

"Willas has the best birds in the Seven Kingdoms," Margaery said when the two of them were briefly alone. "He flies an eagle sometimes. You will see, Sansa." She took her by the hand and gave it a squeeze. "Sister."

Sister. Sansa had once dreamt of having a sister like Margaery; beautiful and gentle, with all the world's graces at her command. Arya had been entirely unsatisfactory as sisters went. *How can I let my sister marry Joffrey?* she thought, and suddenly her eyes were full of tears. "Margaery, please," she said, "you mustn't." It was hard to get the words out. "You *mustn't* marry him. He's not like he seems, he's not. He'll hurt you."

"I shouldn't think so." Margaery smiled confidently. "It's brave of you to warn me, but you need not fear. Joff's spoiled and vain and I don't doubt that he's as cruel as you say, but Father forced him to name Loras to his Kingsguard before he would agree to the match. I shall have the finest knight in the Seven Kingdoms protecting me night and day, as Prince Aemon protected Naerys. So our little lion had best behave, hadn't he?" She laughed, and said, "Come, sweet sister, let's race back to the river. It will drive our guards quite mad." And without waiting for an answer, she put her heels into her horse and flew.

She is so brave, Sansa thought, galloping after her . . . and yet, her doubts still gnawed at her. Ser Loras was a great knight, all agreed. But Joffrey had other Kingsguard, and gold cloaks and red cloaks besides, and when he was older he would command armies of his own. Aegon the

Unworthy had never harmed Queen Naerys, perhaps for fear of their brother the Dragonknight ... but when another of his Kingsguard fell in love with one of his mistresses, the king had taken both their heads.

Ser Loras is a Tyrell, Sansa reminded herself. *That other knight was only a Toyne. His brothers had no armies, no way to avenge him but with swords.* Yet the more she thought about it all, the more she wondered. *Joff might restrain himself for a few turns, perhaps as long as a year, but soon or late he will show his claws, and when he does ...* The realm might have a second Kingslayer, and there would be war *inside* the city, as the men of the lion and the men of the rose made the gutters run red.

Sansa was surprised that Margaery did not see it too. *She is older than me, she must be wiser. And her father, Lord Tyrell, he knows what he is doing, surely. I am just being silly.*

When she told Ser Dontos that she was going to Highgarden to marry Willas Tyrell, she thought he would be relieved and pleased for her. Instead he had grabbed her arm and said, "You *cannot!*" in a voice as thick with horror as with wine. "I tell you, these Tyrells are only Lannisters with flowers. I beg of you, forget this folly, give your Florian a kiss, and promise you'll go ahead as we have planned. The night of Joffrey's wedding, that's not so long, wear the silver hair net and do as I told you, and afterward we make our escape." He tried to plant a kiss on her cheek.

Sansa slipped from his grasp and stepped away from him. "I won't. I can't. Something would go wrong. When I *wanted* to escape you wouldn't take me, and now I don't need to."

Dontos stared at her stupidly. "But the arrangements are made, sweetling. The ship to take you home, the boat to take you to the ship, your Florian did it all for his sweet Jonquil."

"I am sorry for all the trouble I put you to," she said, "but I have no need of boats and ships now."

"But it's all to see you *safe.*"

"I will be safe in Highgarden. Willas will keep me safe."

"But he does not know you," Dontos insisted, "and he will not love you. Jonquil, Jonquil, open your sweet eyes, these Tyrells care nothing for you. It's your *claim* they mean to wed."

"My claim?" She was lost for a moment.

"Sweetling," he told her, "you are heir to Winterfell." He grabbed her again, pleading that she must not do this thing, and Sansa wrenched free and left him swaying beneath the heart tree. She had not visited the godswood since.

But she had not forgotten his words, either. *The heir to Winterfell*, she would think as she lay abed at night. *It's your claim they mean to wed.* Sansa had grown up with three brothers. She never thought to have a claim, but with Bran and Rickon dead ... *It doesn't matter, there's still Robb, he's a man grown now, and soon he'll wed and have a son. Anyway, Willas Tyrell will have Highgarden, what would he want with Winterfell?*

Sometimes she would whisper his name into her pillow just to hear the sound of it. "Willas, Willas, Willas." Willas was as good a name as Loras, she supposed. They even sounded the same, a little. What did it matter about his leg? Willas would be Lord of Highgarden and she would be his lady.

She pictured the two of them sitting together in a garden with puppies in their laps, or listening to a singer strum upon a lute while they floated down the Mander on a pleasure barge. *If I give him sons, he may come to love me.* She would name them Eddard and Brandon and Rickon, and raise them all to be as valiant as Ser Loras. *And to hate Lannisters, too.* In Sansa's dreams, her children looked just like the brothers she had lost. Sometimes there was even a girl who looked like Arya.

She could never hold a picture of Willas long in her head, though; her imaginings kept turning him back into Ser Loras, young and graceful and beautiful. *You must not think of him like that*, she told herself. *Or else he may see the disappointment in your eyes when you meet, and how could he marry you then, knowing it was his brother you loved?* Willas Tyrell was twice her age, she reminded herself constantly, and lame as well, and perhaps even plump and red-faced like his father. But comely or no, he might be the only champion she would ever have.

Once she dreamed it was still her marrying Joff, not Margaery, and on their wedding night he turned into the headsman Ilyn Payne. She woke trembling. She did not want Margaery to suffer as she had, but she dreaded the thought that the Tyrells might refuse to go ahead with the wedding. *I warned her, I did, I told her the truth of him*. Perhaps Margaery did not believe her. Joff always played the perfect knight with her, as once he had with Sansa. *She will see his true nature soon enough. After the wedding if not before*. Sansa decided that she would light a candle to the Mother Above the next time she visited the sept, and ask her to protect Margaery from Joffrey's cruelty. And perhaps a candle to the Warrior as well, for Loras.

She would wear her new gown for the ceremony at the Great Sept of Baelor, she decided as the seamstress took her last measurement. *That must be why Cersei is having it made for me, so I will not look shabby at the wedding*. She really ought to have a different gown for the feast afterward but she supposed one of her old ones would do. She did not want to risk getting food or wine on the new one. *I must take it with me to Highgarden*. She wanted to look beautiful for Willas Tyrell. *Even if Dontos was right, and it is Winterfell he wants and not me, he still may come to love me for myself*. Sansa hugged herself tightly, wondering how long it would be before the gown was ready. She could scarcely wait to wear it.

ARYA

The rains came and went, but there was more grey sky than blue, and all the streams were running high. On the morning of the third day, Arya noticed that the moss was growing mostly on the wrong side of the trees. "We're going the wrong way," she said to Gendry, as they rode past an especially mossy elm. "We're going south. See how the moss is growing on the trunk?"

He pushed thick black hair from eyes and said, "We're following the road, that's all. The road goes south here."

We've been going south all day, she wanted to tell him. *And yesterday too, when we were riding along that streambed.* But she hadn't been paying close attention yesterday, so she couldn't be certain. "I think we're lost," she said in a low voice. "We shouldn't have left the river. All we had to do was follow it."

"The river bends and loops," said Gendry. "This is just a shorter way, I bet. Some secret outlaw way. Lem and Tom and them have been living here for years."

That was true. Arya bit her lip. "But the moss . . ."

"The way it's raining, we'll have moss growing from our ears before long," Gendry complained.

"Only from our *south* ear," Arya declared stubbornly. There was no use trying to convince the Bull of anything. Still, he was the only true friend she had, now that Hot Pie had left them.

"Sharna says she needs me to bake bread," he'd told her, the day they rode. "Anyhow I'm tired of rain and saddlesores and being scared all the time. There's ale here, and rabbit to eat, and the bread will be better when I make it. You'll see, when you come back. You will come back, won't you? When the war's done?" He remembered who she was then, and added, "My lady," reddening.

Arya didn't know if the war would ever be done, but she had nodded. "I'm sorry I beat you that time," she said. Hot Pie was stupid and craven, but he'd been with her all the way from King's Landing and she'd gotten used to him. "I broke your nose."

"You broke Lem's too." Hot Pie grinned. "That was good."

"Lem didn't think so," Arya said glumly. Then it was time to go. When Hot Pie asked if he might kiss milady's hand, she punched his shoulder. "Don't call me that. You're Hot Pie, and I'm Arry."

"I'm not Hot Pie here. Sharna just calls me Boy. The same as she calls the other boy. It's going to be confusing."

She missed him more than she thought she would, but Harwin made up for it some. She had told him about his father Hullen, and how she'd found him dying by the stables in the Red Keep, the day she fled. "He always said he'd die in a stable," Harwin said, "but we all thought some bad-tempered stallion would be his death, not a pack of lions." Arya told of Yoren and their escape from King's Landing as well, and much that had happened since, but she left out the stableboy she'd stabbed with Needle, and the guard whose throat she'd cut to get out of Harrenhal. Telling Harwin would be almost like telling her father, and there were some things that she could not bear having her father know.

Nor did she speak of Jaqen H'ghar and the three deaths he'd owed and paid. The iron coin he'd given her Arya kept tucked away beneath her belt, but sometimes at night she would take it out and remember how his face had melted and changed when he ran his hand across it. "*Valar morghulis*," she would say under her breath. "Ser Gregor, Dunsen, Polliver, Raff the Swectling. The

Tickler and the Hound. Ser Ilyn, Ser Meryn, Queen Cersei, King Joffrey."

Only six Winterfell men remained of the twenty her father had sent west with Beric Dondarrion, Harwin told her, and they were scattered. "It was a trap, milady. Lord Tywin sent his Mountain across the Red Fork with fire and sword, hoping to draw your lord father. He planned for Lord Eddard to come west himself to deal with Gregor Clegane. If he had he would have been killed, or taken prisoner and traded for the Imp, who was your lady mother's captive at the time. Only the Kingslayer never knew Lord Tywin's plan, and when he heard about his brother's capture he attacked your father in the streets of King's Landing."

"I remember," said Arya. "He killed Jory." Jory had always smiled at her, when he wasn't telling her to get from underfoot.

"He killed Jory," Harwin agreed, "and your father's leg was broken when his horse fell on him. So Lord Eddard *couldn't* go west. He sent Lord Beric instead, with twenty of his own men and twenty from Winterfell, me among them. There were others besides. Thoros and Ser Raymun Darry and their men, Ser Gladden Wylde, a lord named Lothar Mallery. But Gregor was waiting for us at the Mummer's Ford, with men concealed on both banks. As we crossed he fell upon us from front and rear.

"I saw the Mountain slay Raymun Darry with a single blow so terrible that it took Darry's arm off at the elbow and killed the horse beneath him too. Gladden Wylde died there with him, and Lord Mallery was ridden down and drowned. We had lions on every side, and I thought I was doomed with the rest, but Alyn shouted commands and restored order to our ranks, and those still ahorse rallied around Thoros and cut our way free. Six score we'd been that morning. By dark no more than two score were left, and Lord Beric was gravely wounded. Thoros drew a foot of lance from his chest that night, and poured boiling wine into the hole it left.

"Every man of us was certain his lordship would be dead by daybreak. But Thoros prayed with him all night beside the fire, and when dawn came, he was still alive, and stronger than he'd been. It was a fortnight before he could mount a horse, but his courage kept us strong. He told us that our war had not ended at the Mummer's Ford, but only begun there, and that every man of ours who'd fallen would be avenged tenfold.

"By then the fighting had passed by us. The Mountain's men were only the van of Lord Tywin's host. They crossed the Red Fork in strength and swept up into the riverlands, burning everything in their path. We were so few that all we could do was harry their rear, but we told each other that we'd join up with King Robert when he marched west to crush Lord Tywin's rebellion. Only then we heard that Robert was dead, and Lord Eddard as well, and Cersei Lannister's whelp had ascended the Iron Throne.

"That turned the whole world on its head. We'd been sent out by the King's Hand to deal with outlaws, you see, but now we *were* the outlaws, and Lord Tywin was the Hand of the King. There was some wanted to yield then, but Lord Beric wouldn't hear of it. We were still king's men, he said, and these were the king's people the lions were savaging. If we could not fight for Robert, we would fight for them, until every man of us was dead. And so we did, but as we fought something queer happened. For every man we lost, two showed up to take his place. A few were knights or squires, of gentle birth, but most were common men – fieldhands and fiddlers and innkeeps, servants and shoemakers, even two septons. Men of all sorts, and women too, children, dogs . . ."

"*Dogs?*" said Arya.

"Aye." Harwin grinned. "One of our lads keeps the meanest dogs you'd ever want to see."

"I wish I had a good mean dog," said Arya wistfully. "A lion-killing dog." She'd had a direwolf once, Nymeria, but she'd thrown rocks at her until she fled, to keep the queen from killing her. *Could a direwolf kill a lion?* she wondered.

It rained again that afternoon, and long into the evening. Thankfully the outlaws had secret friends all over, so they did not need to camp out in the open or seek shelter beneath some leaky bower, as she and Hot Pie and Gendry had done so often.

That night they sheltered in a burned, abandoned village. At least it *seemed* to be abandoned, until Jack-Be-Lucky blew two short blasts and two long ones on his hunting horn. Then all sorts of people came crawling out of the ruins and up from secret cellars. They had ale and dried apples and some stale barley bread, and the outlaws had a goose that Anguy had brought down on the ride, so supper that night was almost a feast.

Arya was sucking the last bit of meat off a wing when one of the villagers turned to Lem Lemoncloak and said, "There were men through here not two days past, looking for the Kingslayer."

Lem snorted. "They'd do better looking in Riverrun. Down in the deepest dungeons, where it's nice and damp." His nose looked like a squashed apple, red and raw and swollen, and his mood was foul.

"No," another villager said. "He's escaped."

The Kingslayer. Arya could feel the hair on the back of her neck prickling. She held her breath to listen.

"Could that be true?" Tom o' Sevens said.

"I'll not believe it," said the one-eyed man in the rusty pothelm. The other outlaws called him Jack-Be-Lucky, though losing an eye didn't seem very lucky to Arya. "I've had me a taste o' them dungeons. How could he escape?"

The villagers could only shrug at that. Greenbeard stroked his thick grey-and-green whiskers and said, "The wolves will drown in blood if the Kingslayer's loose again. Thoros must be told. The Lord of Light will show him Lannister in the flames."

"There's a fine fire burning here," said Anguy, smiling.

Greenbeard laughed, and cuffed the archer's ear. "Do I look a priest to you, Archer? When Pello of Tyrosh peers into the fire, the cinders singe his beard."

Lem cracked his knuckles and said, "Wouldn't Lord Beric love to capture Jaime Lannister, though . . ."

"Would he hang him, Lem?" one of the village women asked. "It'd be half a shame to hang a man as pretty as that one."

"A trial first!" said Anguy. "Lord Beric always gives them a trial, you know that." He smiled. "*Then* he hangs them."

There was laughter all around. Then Tom drew his fingers across the strings of his woodharp and broke into soft song.

> The brothers of the Kingswood,
> > they were an outlaw band.
> The forest was their castle,
> > but they roamed across the land.
> No man's gold was safe from them,
> > nor any maiden's hand.
> Oh, the brothers of the Kingswood,
> > that fearsome outlaw band . . .

Warm and dry in a corner between Gendry and Harwin, Arya listened to the singing for a time, then closed her eyes and drifted off to sleep. She dreamt of home; not Riverrun, but Winterfell. It was not a good dream, though. She was alone outside the castle, up to her knees in mud. She could see the grey walls ahead of her, but when she tried to reach the gates every step seemed harder than the one before, and the castle faded before her, until it looked more like smoke than granite. And there were wolves as well, gaunt grey shapes stalking through the trees all around her, their eyes shining. Whenever she looked at them, she remembered the taste of blood.

The next morning they left the road to cut across the fields. The wind was gusting, sending dry brown leaves swirling around the hooves of their horses, but for once it did not rain. When the sun came out from behind a cloud, it was so bright Arya had to pull her hood forward to keep it out of her eyes.

She reined up very suddenly. "We *are* going the wrong way!"

Gendry groaned. "What is it, moss again?"

"Look at the *sun*," she said. "We're going *south!*" Arya rummaged in her saddlebag for the map, so she could show them. "We should never have left the Trident. See." She unrolled the map on her leg. All of them were looking at her now. "See, there's Riverrun, between the rivers."

"As it happens," said Jack-Be-Lucky, "we know where Riverrun is. Every man o' us."

"You're not going to Riverrun," Lem told her bluntly.

I was almost there, Arya thought. *I should have let them take our horses. I could have walked the rest of the way.* She remembered her dream then, and bit her lip.

"Ah, don't look so hurt, child," said Tom Sevenstrings. "No harm will come to you, you have my word on that."

"The word of a *liar!*"

"No one lied," said Lem. "We made no promises. It's not for us to say what's to be done with you."

Lem was not the leader, though, no more than Tom; that was Greenbeard, the Tyroshi. Arya turned to face him. "Take me to Riverrun and you'll be rewarded," she said desperately.

"Little one," Greenbeard answered, "a peasant may skin a common squirrel for his pot, but if he finds a gold squirrel in his tree he takes it to his lord, or he will wish he did."

"I'm not a squirrel," Arya insisted.

"You are." Greenbeard laughed. "A little gold squirrel who's off to see the lightning lord, whether she wills it or not. He'll know what's to be done with you. I'll wager he sends you back to your lady mother, just as you wish."

Tom Sevenstrings nodded. "Aye, that's like Lord Beric. He'll do right by you, see if he don't."

Lord Beric Dondarrion. Arya remembered all she'd heard at Harrenhal, from the Lannisters and the Bloody Mummers alike. Lord Beric the wisp o' the wood. Lord Beric who'd been killed by Vargo Hoat and before that by Ser Amory Lorch, and twice by the Mountain That Rides. *If he won't send me home maybe I'll kill him too.* "Why do I have to see Lord Beric?" she asked quietly.

"We bring him all our highborn captives," said Anguy.

Captive. Arya took a breath to still her soul. *Calm as still water.* She glanced at the outlaws on their horses, and turned her horse's head. *Now, quick as a snake*, she thought, as she slammed her heels into the courser's flank.

Right between Greenbeard and Jack-Be-Lucky she flew, and caught one glimpse of Gendry's startled face as his mare moved out of her way. And then she was in the open field, and running.

North or south, east or west, that made no matter now. She could find the way to Riverrun later, once she'd lost them. Arya leaned forward in the saddle and urged the horse to a gallop. Behind her the outlaws were cursing and shouting at her to come back. She shut her ears to the calls, but when she glanced back over her shoulder four of them were coming after her, Anguy and Harwin and Greenbeard racing side by side with Lem farther back, his big yellow cloak flapping behind him as he rode. "Swift as a deer," she told her mount. "Run, now, *run.*"

Arya dashed across brown weedy fields, through waist-high grass and piles of dry leaves that flurried and flew when her horse galloped past. There were woods to her left, she saw. *I can lose them there.* A dry ditch ran along one side of the field, but she leapt it without breaking stride, and plunged in among the stand of elm and yew and birch trees. A quick peek back showed Anguy and Harwin still hard on her heels. Greenbeard had fallen behind, though, and she could not see Lem at all. "Faster," she told her horse, "you can, you *can.*"

Between two elms she rode, and never paused to see which side the moss was growing on. She leapt a rotten log and swung wide around a monstrous deadfall, jagged with broken branches. Then up a gentle slope and down the other side, slowing and speeding up again, her horse's shoes striking sparks off the flintstones underfoot. At the top of the hill she glanced back. Harwin had pushed ahead of Anguy, but both were coming hard. Greenbeard had fallen further back and seemed to be flagging.

A stream barred her way. She splashed down into it, through water choked with wet brown leaves. Some clung to her horse's legs as they climbed the other side. The undergrowth was thicker here, the ground so full of roots and rocks that she had to slow, but she kept as good a pace as she dared. Another hill before her, this one steeper. Up she went, and down again. *How big are these woods?*

she wondered. She had the faster horse, she knew that, she had stolen one of Roose Bolton's best from the stables at Harrenhal, but his speed was wasted here. *I need to find the fields again. I need to find a road.* Instead she found a game trail. It was narrow and uneven, but it was something. She raced along it, branches whipping at her face. One snagged her hood and yanked it back, and for half a heartbeat she feared they had caught her. A vixen burst from the brush as she passed, startled by the fury of her flight. The game trail brought her to another stream. Or was it the same one? Had she gotten turned around? There was no time to puzzle it out, she could hear their horses crashing through the trees behind her. Thorns scratched at her face like the cats she used to chase in King's Landing. Sparrows exploded from the branches of an alder. But the trees were thinning now, and suddenly she was out of them. Broad level fields stretched before her, all weeds and wild wheat, sodden and trampled. Arya kicked her horse back to a gallop. *Run*, she thought, *run for Riverrun, run for home.* Had she lost them? She took one quick look, and there was Harwin six yards back and gaining. *No*, she thought, *no, he can't, not him, it isn't fair.*

Both horses were lathered and flagging by the time he came up beside her, reached over, and grabbed her bridle. Arya was breathing hard herself then. She knew the fight was done. "You ride like a northman, milady," Harwin said when he'd drawn them to a halt. "Your aunt was the same. Lady Lyanna. But my father was master of horse, remember."

The look she gave him was full of hurt. "I thought you were my father's man."

"Lord Eddard's dead, milady. I belong to the lightning lord now, and to my brothers."

"What brothers?" Old Hullen had fathered no other sons that Arya could remember.

"Anguy, Lem, Tom o' Sevens, Jack and Greenbeard, all of them. We mean your brother Robb no ill, milady ... but it's not him we fight for. He has an army all his own, and many a great lord to bend the knee. The smallfolk have only us." He gave her a searching look. "Can you understand what I am telling you?"

"Yes." That he was not Robb's man, she understood well enough. And that she was his captive. *I could have stayed with Hot Pie. We could have taken the little boat and sailed it up to Riverrun.* She had been better off as Squab. No one would take Squab captive, or Nan, or Weasel, or Arry the orphan boy. *I was a wolf,* she thought, *but now I'm just some stupid little lady again.*

"Will you ride back peaceful now," Harwin asked her, "or must I tie you up and throw you across your horse?"

"I'll ride peaceful," she said sullenly. *For now.*

SAMWELL

Sobbing, Sam took another step. *This is the last one, the very last, I can't go on, I can't.* But his feet moved again. One and then the other. They took a step, and then another, and he thought, *They're not my feet, they're someone else's, someone else is walking, it can't be me.*

When he looked down he could see them stumbling through the snow; shapeless things, and clumsy. His boots had been black, he seemed to remember, but the snow had caked around them, and now they were misshapen white balls. Like two clubfeet made of ice.

It would not stop, the snow. The drifts were up past his knees, and a crust covered his lower legs like a pair of white greaves. His steps were dragging, lurching. The heavy pack he carried made him look like some monstrous hunchback. And he was tired, so tired. *I can't go on. Mother have mercy, I can't.*

Every fourth or fifth step he had to reach down and tug up his swordbelt. He had lost the sword on the Fist, but the scabbard still weighed down the belt. He did have two knives; the dragonglass dagger Jon had given him and the steel one he cut his meat with. All that weight dragged heavy, and his belly was so big and round that if he forgot to tug the belt slipped right off and tangled round his ankles, no matter how tight he cinched it. He had tried belting it *above* his belly once, but then it came almost to his armpits. Grenn had laughed himself sick at the sight of it, and Dolorous Edd had said, "I knew a man once who wore his sword on a chain around his neck like that. One day he stumbled, and the hilt went up his nose."

Sam was stumbling himself. There were rocks beneath the snow, and the roots of trees, and sometimes deep holes in the frozen ground. Black Bernarr had stepped in one and broken his ankle three days past, or maybe four, or . . . he did not know how long it had been, truly. The Lord Commander had put Bernarr on a horse after that.

Sobbing, Sam took another step. It felt more like he was falling down than walking, falling endlessly but never hitting the ground, just falling forward and forward. *I have to stop, it hurts too much. I'm so cold and tired, I need to sleep, just a little sleep beside a fire, and a bite to eat that isn't frozen.*

But if he stopped he died. He knew that. They all knew that, the few who were left. They had been fifty when they fled the Fist, maybe more, but some had wandered off in the snow, a few wounded had bled to death . . . and sometimes Sam heard shouts behind him, from the rear guard, and once an *awful* scream. When he heard that he had run, twenty yards or thirty, as fast and as far as he could, his half-frozen feet kicking up the snow. He would be running still if his legs were stronger. *They are behind us, they are still behind us, they are taking us one by one.*

Sobbing, Sam took another step. He had been cold so long he was forgetting what it was like to feel warm. He wore three pairs of hose, two layers of smallclothes beneath a double lambswool tunic, and over that a thick quilted coat that padded him against the cold steel of his chainmail. Over the hauberk he had a loose surcoat, over *that* a triple-thick cloak with a bone button that fastened tight under his chins. Its hood flopped forward over his forehead. Heavy fur mitts covered his hands over thin wool-and-leather gloves, a scarf was wrapped snugly about the lower half of his face, and he had a tight-fitting fleece-lined cap to pull down over his ears beneath the hood. And still the cold was in him. His feet especially. He couldn't even feel them now, but only yesterday they had hurt so bad he could hardly bear to stand on them, let alone walk. Every step made him want to scream. Was that yesterday? He could not remember. He had not slept since the Fist, not once since the horn had blown. Unless it was while he was walking. Could a man walk while he was sleeping? Sam did not know, or else he had forgotten.

Sobbing, he took another step. The snow swirled down around him. Sometimes it fell from a white sky, and sometimes from a black, but that was all that remained of day and night. He wore it on his shoulders like a second cloak, and it piled up high atop the pack he carried and made it even heavier and harder to bear. The small of his back hurt abominably, as if someone had shoved a knife in there and was wiggling it back and forth with every step. His shoulders were in agony from the weight of the mail. He would have given most anything to take it off, but he was afraid to. Anyway he would have needed to remove his cloak and surcoat to get at it, and then the cold would have him.

If only I was stronger . . . He wasn't, though, and it was no good wishing. Sam was weak, and fat, so very fat, he could hardly bear his own weight, the mail was much too much for him. It felt as though it was rubbing his shoulders raw, despite the layers of cloth and quilt between the steel and skin. The only thing he could do was cry, and when he cried the tears froze on his cheeks.

Sobbing, he took another step. The crust was broken where he set his feet, otherwise he did not think he could have moved at all. Off to the left and right, half-seen through the silent trees, torches turned to vague orange haloes in the falling snow. When he turned his head he could see them, slipping silent through the wood, bobbing up and down and back and forth. *The Old Bear's ring of fire,* he reminded himself, *and woe to him who leaves it.* As he walked, it seemed as if he were chasing the torches ahead of him, but they had legs as well, longer and stronger than his, so he could never catch them.

Yesterday he begged for them to let him be one of the torchbearers, even if it meant walking outside of the column with the darkness pressing close. He wanted the fire, dreamed of the fire. *If I had the fire, I would not be cold.* But someone reminded him that he'd *had* a torch at the start, but he'd dropped it in the snow and snuffed the fire out. Sam didn't remember dropping any torch, but he supposed it was true. He was too weak to hold his arm up for long. Was it Edd who reminded him about the torch, or Grenn? He couldn't remember that either. *Fat and weak and useless, even my wits are freezing now.* He took another step.

He had wrapped his scarf over his nose and mouth, but it was covered with snot now, and so stiff he feared it must be frozen to his face. Even breathing was hard, and the air was so cold it hurt to swallow it. "Mother have mercy," he muttered in a hushed husky voice beneath the frozen mask. "Mother have mercy, Mother have mercy, Mother have mercy." With each prayer he took another step, dragging his legs through the snow. "Mother have mercy, Mother have mercy, Mother have mercy."

His own mother was a thousand leagues south, safe with his sisters and his little brother Dickon in the keep at Horn Hill. *She can't hear me, no more than the Mother Above.* The Mother was merciful, all the septons agreed, but the Seven had no power beyond the Wall. This was where the old gods ruled, the nameless gods of the trees and the wolves and the snows. "Mercy," he whispered then, to whatever might be listening, old gods or new, or demons too, "oh, mercy, mercy me, mercy me."

Maslyn screamed for mercy. Why had he suddenly remembered that? It was nothing he wanted to remember. The man had stumbled backward, dropping his sword, pleading, yielding, even yanking off his thick black glove and thrusting it up before him as if it were a gauntlet. He was still shrieking for quarter as the wight lifted him in the air by the throat and near ripped the head off him. *The dead have no mercy left in them, and the Others . . . no, I mustn't think of that, don't think, don't remember, just walk, just walk, just walk.*

Sobbing, he took another step.

A root beneath the crust caught his toe, and Sam tripped

and fell heavily to one knee, so hard he bit his tongue. He could taste the blood in his mouth, warmer than anything he had tasted since the Fist. *This is the end*, he thought. Now that he had fallen he could not seem to find the strength to rise again. He groped for a tree branch and clutched it tight, trying to pull himself back to his feet, but his stiff legs would not support him. The mail was too heavy, and he was too fat besides, and too weak, and too tired.

"Back on your feet, Piggy," someone growled as he went past, but Sam paid him no mind. *I'll just lie down in the snow and close my eyes.* It wouldn't be so bad, dying here. He couldn't possibly be any colder, and after a little while he wouldn't be able to feel the ache in his lower back or the terrible pain in his shoulders, no more than he could feel his feet. *I won't be the first to die, they can't say I was.* Hundreds had died on the Fist, they had died all around him, and more had died after, he'd seen them. Shivering, Sam released his grip on the tree and eased himself down in the snow. It was cold and wet, he knew, but he could scarcely feel it through all his clothing. He stared upward at the pale white sky as snowflakes drifted down upon his stomach and his chest and his eyelids. *The snow will cover me like a thick white blanket. It will be warm under the snow, and if they speak of me they'll have to say I died a man of the Night's Watch. I did. I did. I did my duty. No one can say I forswore myself. I'm fat and I'm weak and I'm craven, but I did my duty.*

The ravens had been his responsibility. That was why they had brought him along. He hadn't wanted to go, he'd told them so, he'd told them all what a big coward he was. But Maester Aemon was very old and blind besides, so they had to send Sam to tend to the ravens. The Lord Commander had given him his orders when they made their camp on the Fist. "You're no fighter. We both know that, boy. If it happens that we're attacked, don't go trying to prove otherwise, you'll just get in the way. You're to send a message. And don't come running to ask what the letter should say. Write it out yourself, and send one bird to Castle Black and another to the Shadow Tower." The Old Bear pointed a gloved finger right in Sam's face. "I don't care if you're so scared you foul your breeches, and I don't care if a thousand wildlings are coming over the walls howling for your blood, *you get those birds off*, or I swear I'll hunt you through all seven hells and make you damn sorry that you didn't." And Mormont's own raven had bobbed its head up and down and croaked, "*Sorry, sorry, sorry.*"

Sam *was* sorry; sorry he hadn't been braver, or stronger, or good with swords, that he hadn't been a better son to his father and a better brother to Dickon and the girls. He was sorry to die too, but better men had died on the Fist, good men and true, not squeaking fat boys like him. At least he would not have the Old Bear hunting him through hell, though. *I got the birds off. I did that right, at least.* He had written out the messages ahead of time, short messages and simple, telling of an attack on the Fist of the First Men, and then he had tucked them away safe in his parchment pouch, hoping he would never need to send them.

When the horns blew Sam had been sleeping. He thought he was dreaming them at first, but when he opened his eyes snow was falling on the camp and the black brothers were all grabbing bows and spears and running toward the ringwall. Chett was the only one nearby, Maester Aemon's old steward with the face full of boils and the big wen on his neck. Sam had never seen so much fear on a man's face as he saw on Chett's when that third blast came moaning through the trees. "Help me get the birds off," he pleaded, but the other steward had turned and run off, dagger in hand. *He has the dogs to care for,* Sam remembered. Probably the Lord Commander had given him some orders as well.

His fingers had been so stiff and clumsy in the gloves, and he was shaking from fear and cold, but he found the parchment pouch and dug out the messages he'd written. The ravens were shrieking furiously, and when he opened the Castle Black cage one of them flew right in his face. Two more escaped before Sam could catch one, and when he did it pecked him through his glove, drawing blood. Yet somehow he held on long enough to attach the little roll of parchment. The warhorn had fallen silent by then, but the Fist rang with shouted commands and the clatter of steel. *"Fly!"* Sam called as he tossed the raven into the air.

The birds in the Shadow Tower cage were screaming and fluttering about so madly that he was afraid to open the door, but he made himself do it anyway. This time he caught the first raven that tried to escape. A moment later, it was clawing its way up through the falling snow, bearing word of the attack.

His duty done, he finished dressing with clumsy, frightened fingers, donning his cap and surcoat and hooded cloak and buckling on his swordbelt, buckling it real tight so it wouldn't fall down. Then he found his pack and stuffed all his things inside, spare smallclothes and dry socks, the dragonglass arrowheads and spearhead Jon had given him and the old horn too, his parchments, inks, and quills, the maps he'd been drawing, and a rock-hard garlic sausage he'd been saving since the Wall. He tied it all up and shouldered the pack onto his back. *The Lord Commander said I wasn't to rush to the ringwall*, he recalled, *but he said I shouldn't come running to him either.* Sam took a deep breath and realized that he did not know what to do next.

He remembered turning in a circle, lost, the fear growing inside him as it always did. There were dogs barking and horses trumpeting, but the snow muffled the sounds and made them seem far away. Sam could see nothing beyond three yards, not even the torches burning along the low stone wall that ringed the crown of the hill. *Could the torches have gone out?* That was too scary to think about. *The horn blew thrice long, three long blasts means Others.* The white walkers of the wood, the cold shadows, the monsters of the tales that made him squeak and tremble as a boy, riding their giant ice-spiders, hungry for blood . . .

Awkwardly he drew his sword, and plodded heavily through the snow holding it. A dog ran past barking, and he saw some of the men from the Shadow Tower, big bearded men with longaxes and eight-foot spears. He felt safer for their company, so he followed them to the wall. When he saw the torches still burning atop the ring of stones a shudder of relief went through him.

The black brothers stood with swords and spears in hand, watching the snow fall, waiting. Ser Mallador Locke went by on his horse, wearing a snow-speckled helm. Sam stood well back behind the others, looking for Grenn or Dolorous Edd. *If I have to die, let me die beside my friends*, he remembered thinking. But all the men around him were strangers, Shadow Tower men under the command of the ranger named Blane.

"Here they come," he heard a brother say.

"Notch," said Blane, and twenty black arrows were pulled from as many quivers, and notched to as many bowstrings.

"Gods be good, there's hundreds," a voice said softly.

"Draw," Blane said, and then, "Hold." Sam could not see and did not want to see. The men of the Night's Watch stood behind their torches, waiting with arrows pulled back to their ears, as *something* came up that dark, slippery slope through the snow. "Hold," Blane said again, "hold, hold." And then, "Loose."

The arrows whispered as they flew.

A ragged cheer went up from the men along the ring-wall, but it died quickly. "They're not stopping, m'lord," a man said to Blane, and another shouted, "*More!* Look there, coming from the trees," and yet another said, "Gods ha' mercy, they's crawling. They's almost here, *they's on us!*" Sam had been backing away by then, shaking like the last leaf on the tree when the wind kicks up, as much from cold as from fear. It had been very cold that night. *Even colder than now. The snow feels almost warm. I feel better now. A little rest was all I needed. Maybe in a little while I'll be strong enough to walk again. In a little while.*

A horse stepped past his head, a shaggy grey beast with snow in its mane and hooves crusted with ice. Sam watched it come and watched it go. Another appeared from out of the falling snow, with a man in black leading it. When he saw Sam in his path he cursed him and led the horse around. *I wish I had a horse*, he thought. *If I had a horse I could keep going. I could sit, and even sleep some in the saddle.* Most of their mounts had been lost at the Fist, though, and those that remained carried their food, their torches, and their wounded. Sam wasn't wounded. *Only fat and weak, and the greatest craven in the Seven Kingdoms.*

He was *such* a coward. Lord Randyll, his father, had always said so, and he had been right. Sam was his heir, but he had never been worthy, so his father had sent him away to the Wall. His little brother Dickon would inherit the Tarly lands and castle, and the greatsword Heartsbane that the lords of Horn Hill had borne so proudly for centuries. He wondered whether Dickon would shed a tear for his brother who died in the snow, somewhere off beyond the edge of the world. *Why should he? A coward's not worth weeping over.* He had heard his father tell his mother as much, half a hundred times. The Old Bear knew it too.

"Fire arrows," the Lord Commander roared that night on the Fist, when he appeared suddenly astride his horse, "give them flame." It was then he noticed Sam there quaking. "*Tarly!* Get out of here! Your place is with the ravens."

"I . . . I . . . I got the messages away."

"Good." On Mormont's shoulder his own raven echoed, "*Good, good.*" The Lord Commander looked huge in fur and mail. Behind his black iron visor, his eyes were fierce. "You're in the way here. Go back to your cages. If I need to send another message, I don't want to have to find you first. See that the birds are ready." He did not wait for a response, but turned his horse and trotted around the ring, shouting, "Fire! Give them fire!"

Sam did not need to be told twice. He went back to the birds, as fast as his fat legs could carry him. *I should write the message ahead of time*, he thought, *so we can get the birds away as fast as need be.* It took him longer than it should have to light his little fire, to warm the frozen ink.

He sat beside it on a rock with quill and parchment, and wrote his messages.

Attacked amidst snow and cold, but we've thrown them back with fire arrows, he wrote, as he heard Thoren Smallwood's voice ring out with a command of, "Notch, draw . . . loose." The flight of arrows made a sound as sweet as a mother's prayer. "Burn, you dead bastards, burn," Dywen sang out, cackling. The brothers cheered and cursed. *All safe,* he wrote. *We remain on the Fist of the First Men.* Sam hoped they were better archers than him.

He put that note aside and found another blank parchment. *Still fighting on the Fist, amidst heavy snow,* he wrote when someone shouted, "They're still coming." *Result uncertain.* "Spears," someone said. It might have been Ser Mallador, but Sam could not swear to it. *Wights attacked us on the Fist, in snow,* he wrote, *but we drove them off with fire.* He turned his head. Through the drifting snow, all he could see was the huge fire at the center of the camp, with mounted men moving restlessly around it. The reserve, he knew, ready to ride down anything that breached the ringwall. They had armed themselves with torches in place of swords, and were lighting them in the flames.

Wights all around us, he wrote, when he heard the shouts from the north face. *Coming up from north and south at once. Spears and swords don't stop them, only fire.* "Loose, loose, loose," a voice screamed in the night, and another shouted, "Bloody huge," and a third voice said, "A giant!" and a fourth insisted, "A bear, a *bear!*" A horse shrieked and the hounds began to bay, and there was so much shouting that Sam couldn't make out the voices anymore. He wrote faster, note after note. *Dead wildlings, and a giant, or maybe a bear, on us, all around.* He heard the crash of steel on wood, which could only mean one thing. *Wights over the ringwall. Fighting inside the camp.* A dozen mounted brothers pounded past him toward the east wall, burning brands streaming flames in each rider's hand. *Lord Commander Mormont is meeting them with fire. We've won. We're winning. We're holding our own. We're cutting our way free and retreating for the Wall. We're trapped on the Fist, hard pressed.*

One of the Shadow Tower men came staggering out of the darkness to fall at Sam's feet. He crawled within a foot of the fire before he died. *Lost,* Sam wrote, *the battle's lost. We're all lost.*

Why must he remember the fight at the Fist? He didn't want to remember. Not *that.* He tried to make himself remember his mother, or his little sister Talla, or that girl Gilly at Craster's Keep. Someone was shaking him by the shoulder. "Get up," a voice said. "Sam, you can't go to sleep here. Get up and keep walking."

I wasn't asleep, I was remembering. "Go away," he said, his words frosting in the cold air. "I'm well. I want to rest."

"Get up." Grenn's voice, harsh and husky. He loomed over Sam, his blacks crusty with snow. "There's no resting, the Old Bear said. You'll die."

"Grenn." He smiled. "No, truly, I'm good here. You just go on. I'll catch you after I've rested a bit longer."

"You won't." Grenn's thick brown beard was frozen all around his mouth. It made him look like some old man. "You'll freeze, or the Others will get you. Sam, *get up!*"

The night before they left the Wall, Pyp had teased Grenn the way he did, Sam remembered, smiling and saying how Grenn was a good choice for the ranging, since he was too stupid to be terrified. Grenn hotly denied it until he realized what he was saying. He was stocky and thick-necked and strong – Ser Alliser Thorne had called him "Aurochs," the same way he called Sam "Ser Piggy" and Jon "Lord Snow" – but he had always treated Sam nice enough. *That was only because of Jon, though. If it weren't for Jon, none of them would have liked me.* And now Jon was gone, lost in the Skirling Pass with Qhorin Halfhand, most likely dead. Sam would have cried for him, but those tears would only freeze as well, and he could scarcely keep his eyes open now.

A tall brother with a torch stopped beside them, and for a wonderful moment Sam felt the warmth on his face. "Leave him," the man said to Grenn. "If they can't walk, they're done. Save your strength for yourself, Grenn."

"He'll get up," Grenn replied. "He only needs a hand."

The man moved on, taking the blessed warmth with him. Grenn tried to pull Sam to his feet. "That hurts," he complained. "Stop it. Grenn, you're hurting my arm. Stop it."

"You're too bloody heavy." Grenn jammed his hands into Sam's armpits, gave a grunt, and hauled him upright. But the moment he let go, the fat boy sat back down in the snow. Grenn kicked him, a solid thump that cracked the crust of snow around his boot and sent it flying everywhere. "Get *up!*" He kicked him again. "Get up and walk. You have to walk."

Sam fell over sideways, curling up into a tight ball to protect himself from the kicks. He hardly felt them through all his wool and leather and mail, but even so, they hurt. *I thought Grenn was my friend. You shouldn't kick your friends. Why won't they let me be? I just need to rest, that's all, to rest and sleep some, and maybe die a little.*

"If you take the torch, I can take the fat boy."

Suddenly he was jerked up into the cold air, away from his sweet soft snow; he was floating. There was an arm under his knees, and another one under his back. Sam raised his head and blinked. A face loomed close, a broad brutal face with a flat nose and small dark eyes and a thicket of coarse brown beard. He had seen the face before, but it took him a moment to remember. *Paul. Small Paul.* Melting ice ran down into his eyes from the heat of the torch. "Can you carry him?" he heard Grenn ask.

"I carried a calf once was heavier than him. I carried him down to his mother so he could get a drink of milk."

Sam's head bobbed up and down with every step that Small Paul took. "Stop it," he muttered, "put me down, I'm not a baby. I'm a man of the Night's Watch." He sobbed. "Just let me die."

"Be quiet, Sam," said Grenn. "Save your strength. Think about your sisters and brother. Maester Aemon. Your favorite foods. Sing a song if you like."

"Aloud?"

"In your head."

Sam knew a hundred songs, but when he tried to think of one he couldn't. The words had all gone from his head. He sobbed again and said, "I don't know any songs, Grenn. I did know some, but now I don't."

"Yes you do," said Grenn. "How about 'The Bear and the Maiden Fair,' everybody knows that one. *A bear there was, a bear, a bear! All black and brown and covered with hair!*"

"No, not that one," Sam pleaded. The bear that had come up the Fist had no hair left on its rotted flesh. He didn't want to think about bears. "No songs. Please, Grenn."

"Think about your ravens, then."

"They were never mine." *They were the Lord Commander's ravens, the ravens of the Night's Watch.* "They belonged to Castle Black and the Shadow Tower."

Small Paul frowned. "Chett said I could have the Old Bear's raven, the one that talks. I saved food for it and everything." He shook his head. "I forgot, though. I left the food where I hid it." He plodded onward, pale white breath coming from his mouth with every step, then suddenly said, "Could I have one of your ravens? Just the one. I'd never let Lark eat it."

"They're gone," said Sam. "I'm sorry." *So sorry.* "They're flying back to the Wall now." He had set the birds free when he'd heard the warhorns sound once more, calling the Watch to horse. *Two short blasts and a long one, that was the call to mount up.* But there was no reason to mount, unless to abandon the Fist, and that meant the battle was lost. The fear bit him so strong then that it was all Sam could do to open the cages. Only as he watched the last raven flap up into the snowstorm did he realize that he had forgotten to send any of the messages he'd written.

"No," he'd squealed, "oh, no, oh, no." The snow fell and the horns blew; *ahooo ahooo ahoooooooooooooo-ooooooo,* they cried, *to horse, to horse, to horse.* Sam saw two ravens perched on a rock and ran after them, but the birds flapped off lazily through the swirling snow, in opposite directions. He chased one, his breath puffing out his nose in thick white clouds, stumbled, and found himself ten feet from the ringwall.

After that . . . he remembered the dead coming over the stones with arrows in their faces and through their throats. Some were all in ringmail and some were almost naked . . . wildlings, most of them, but a few wore faded blacks. He remembered one of the Shadow Tower men shoving his spear through a wight's pale soft belly and out his back, and how the thing staggered right up the shaft and reached out his black hands and twisted the brother's head around until blood came out his mouth. That was when his bladder let go the first time, he was almost sure.

He did not remember running, but he must have, because the next he knew he was near the fire half a camp away, with old Ser Ottyn Wythers and some archers. Ser Ottyn was on his knees in the snow, staring at the chaos around them, until a riderless horse came by and kicked him in the face. The archers paid him no mind. They were loosing fire arrows at shadows in the dark. Sam saw one wight hit, saw the flames engulf it, but there were a dozen more behind it, and a huge pale shape that must have been the bear, and soon enough the bowmen had no arrows.

And then Sam found himself on a horse. It wasn't his own horse, and he never recalled mounting up either. Maybe it was the horse that had smashed Ser Ottyn's face in. The horns were still blowing, so he kicked the horse and turned him toward the sound.

In the midst of carnage and chaos and blowing snow, he found Dolorous Edd sitting on his garron with a plain black banner on a spear. "Sam," Edd said when he saw him, "would you wake me, please? I am having this terrible nightmare."

More men were mounting up every moment. The warhorns called them back. *Ahooo ahooo ahooooooooooooooooooooo.* "They're over the west wall, m'lord," Thoren Smallwood screamed at the Old Bear, as he fought to control his horse. "I'll send reserves . . ."

"*NO!*" Mormont had to bellow at the top of his lungs to be heard over the horns. "Call them back, we have to cut our way out." He stood in his stirrups, his black cloak snapping in the wind, the fire shining off his armor. "*Spearhead!*" he roared. "Form wedge, we ride. Down the south face, then east!"

"My lord, the south slope's crawling with them!"

"The others are too steep," Mormont said. "We have –"

His garron screamed and reared and almost threw him as the bear came staggering through the snow. Sam pissed himself all over again. *I didn't think I had any more left inside me.* The bear was dead, pale and rotting, its fur and skin all sloughed off and half its right arm burned to bone, yet still it came on. Only its eyes lived. *Bright blue, just as Jon said.* They shone like frozen stars. Thoren Smallwood charged, his longsword shining all orange and red from the light of the fire. His swing near took the bear's head off. And then the bear took his.

"*RIDE!*" the Lord Commander shouted, wheeling.

They were at the gallop by the time they reached the ring. Sam had always been too frightened to jump a horse before, but when the low stone wall loomed up before him he knew he had no choice. He kicked and closed his eyes and whimpered, and the garron took him over, somehow, *somehow*, the garron took him over. The rider to his right came crashing down in a tangle of steel and leather and screaming horseflesh, and then the wights were swarming over him and the wedge was closing up. They plunged down the hillside at a run, through clutching black hands and burning blue eyes and blowing snow. Horses stumbled and rolled, men were swept from their saddles, torches spun through the air, axes and swords hacked at dead flesh, and Samwell Tarly sobbed, clutching desperately to his horse with a strength he never knew he had.

He was in the middle of the flying spearhead with brothers on either side, and before and behind him as well. A dog ran with them for a ways, bounding down the snowy slope and in and out among the horses, but it could not keep up. The wights stood their ground and were ridden down and trampled underhoof. Even as they fell they clutched at swords and stirrups and the legs of passing horses. Sam saw one claw open a garron's belly with its right hand while it clung to the saddle with its left.

Suddenly the trees were all about them, and Sam was splashing through a frozen stream with the sounds of slaughter dwindling behind. He turned, breathless with relief ... until a man in black leapt from the brush and yanked him out of the saddle. Who he was, Sam never saw; he was up in an instant, and galloping away the next. When he tried to run after the horse, his feet tangled in a root and he fell hard on his face and lay weeping like a baby until Dolorous Edd found him there.

That was his last coherent memory of the Fist of the First Men. Later, hours later, he stood shivering among the other survivors, half mounted and half afoot. They were miles from the Fist by then, though Sam did not remember how. Dywen had led down five packhorses, heavy laden with food and oil and torches, and three had made it this far. The Old Bear made them redistribute the loads, so the loss of any one horse and its provisions would not be such a catastrophe. He took garrons from the healthy men and gave them to the wounded, organized the walkers, and set torches to guard their flanks and rear. *All I need do is walk*, Sam told himself, as he took that first step toward home. But before an hour was gone he had begun to struggle, and to lag ...

They were lagging now as well, he saw. He remembered Pyp saying once how Small Paul was the strongest man in the Watch. *He must be, to carry me.* Yet even so, the snow was growing deeper, the ground more treacherous, and Paul's strides had begun to shorten. More horsemen passed, wounded men who looked at Sam with dull incurious eyes. Some torch bearers went by as well. "You're falling behind," one told them. The next agreed. "No one's like to wait for you, Paul. Leave the pig for the dead men."

"He promised I could have a bird," Small Paul said, even though Sam hadn't, not truly. *They aren't mine to give.* "I want me a bird that talks, and eats corn from my hand."

"Bloody fool," the torch man said. Then he was gone.

It was a while after when Grenn stopped suddenly.

"We're alone," he said in a hoarse voice. "I can't see the other torches. Was that the rear guard?"

Small Paul had no answer for him. The big man gave a grunt and sank to his knees. His arms trembled as he lay Sam gently in the snow. "I can't carry you no more. I would, but I can't." He shivered violently.

The wind sighed through the trees, driving a fine spray of snow into their faces. The cold was so bitter that Sam felt naked. He looked for the other torches, but they were gone, every one of them. There was only the one Grenn carried, the flames rising from it like pale orange silks. He could see through them, to the black beyond. *That torch will burn out soon*, he thought, *and we are all alone, without food or friends or fire.*

But that was wrong. They weren't alone at all.

The lower branches of the great green sentinel shed their burden of snow with a soft wet *plop*. Grenn spun, thrusting out his torch. "Who goes there?" A horse's head emerged from the darkness. Sam felt a moment's relief, until he saw the horse. Hoarfrost covered it like a sheen of frozen sweat, and a nest of stiff black entrails dragged from its open belly. On its back was a rider pale as ice. Sam made a whimpery sound deep in his throat. He was so scared he might have pissed himself all over again, but the cold was in him, a cold so savage that his bladder felt frozen solid. The Other slid gracefully from the saddle to stand upon the snow. Sword-slim it was, and milky white. Its armor rippled and shifted as it moved, and its feet did not break the crust of the new-fallen snow.

Small Paul unslung the long-hafted axe strapped across his back. "Why'd you hurt that horse? That was Mawney's horse."

Sam groped for the hilt of his sword, but the scabbard was empty. He had lost it on the Fist, he remembered too late.

"Get away!" Grenn took a step, thrusting the torch out before him. "*Away*, or you burn." He poked at it with the flames.

The Other's sword gleamed with a faint blue glow. It moved toward Grenn, lightning quick, slashing. When the

ice blue blade brushed the flames, a screech stabbed Sam's
ears sharp as a needle. The head of the torch tumbled
sideways to vanish beneath a deep drift of snow, the fire
snuffed out at once. And all Grenn held was a short
wooden stick. He flung it at the Other, cursing, as Small
Paul charged in with his axe.

The fear that filled Sam then was worse than any fear
he had ever felt before, and Samwell Tarly knew every
kind of fear. "Mother have mercy," he wept, forgetting
the old gods in his terror. "Father protect me, oh oh . . ."
His fingers found his dagger and he filled his hand with
that.

The wights had been slow clumsy things, but the Other
was light as snow on the wind. It slid away from Paul's
axe, armor rippling, and its crystal sword twisted and spun
and slipped between the iron rings of Paul's mail, through
leather and wool and bone and flesh. It came out his back
with a *hisssssssssssss* and Sam heard Paul say, "Oh," as he
lost the axe. Impaled, his blood smoking around the sword,
the big man tried to reach his killer with his hands and
almost had before he fell. The weight of him tore the
strange pale sword from the Other's grip.

*Do it now. Stop crying and fight, you baby. Fight,
craven.* It was his father he heard, it was Alliser Thorne, it
was his brother Dickon and the boy Rast. *Craven, craven,
craven.* He giggled hysterically, wondering if they would
make a wight of him, a huge fat white wight always tripping over its own dead feet. *Do it, Sam.* Was that Jon,
now? Jon was dead. *You can do it, you can, just do it.*
And then he was stumbling forward, falling more than
running, really, closing his eyes and shoving the dagger
blindly out before him with both hands. He heard a *crack*,
like the sound ice makes when it breaks beneath a man's
foot, and then a screech so shrill and sharp that he went
staggering backward with his hands over his muffled ears,
and fell hard on his arse.

When he opened his eyes the Other's armor was running down its legs in rivulets as pale blue blood hissed
and steamed around the black dragonglass dagger in its
throat. It reached down with two bone-white hands to pull

out the knife, but where its fingers touched the obsidian they *smoked*.

Sam rolled onto his side, eyes wide as the Other shrank and puddled, dissolving away. In twenty heartbeats its flesh was gone, swirling away in a fine white mist. Beneath were bones like milkglass, pale and shiny, and they were melting too. Finally only the dragonglass dagger remained, wreathed in steam as if it were alive and sweating. Grenn bent to scoop it up and flung it down again at once. "Mother, that's *cold*."

"Obsidian." Sam struggled to his knees. "Dragonglass, they call it. Dragonglass. *Dragon* glass." He giggled, and cried, and doubled over to heave his courage out onto the snow.

Grenn pulled Sam to his feet, checked Small Paul for a pulse and closed his eyes, then snatched up the dagger again. This time he was able to hold it.

"You keep it," Sam said. "You're not craven like me."

"So craven you killed an Other." Grenn pointed with the knife. "Look there, through the trees. Pink light. Dawn, Sam. Dawn. That must be east. If we head that way, we should catch Mormont."

"If you say." Sam kicked his left foot against a tree, to knock off all the snow. Then the right. "I'll try." Grimacing, he took a step. "I'll try hard." And then another.

TYRION

Lord Tywin's chain of hands made a golden glitter against the deep wine velvet of his tunic. The Lords Tyrell, Redwyne, and Rowan gathered round him as he entered. He greeted each in turn, spoke a quiet word to Varys, kissed the High Septon's ring and Cersei's cheek, clasped the hand of Grand Maester Pycelle, and seated himself in the king's place at the head of the long table, between his daughter and his brother.

Tyrion had claimed Pycelle's old place at the foot, propped up by cushions so he could gaze down the length of the table. Dispossessed, Pycelle had moved up next to Cersei, about as far from the dwarf as he could get without claiming the king's seat. The Grand Maester was a shambling skeleton, leaning heavily on a twisted cane and shaking as he walked, a few white hairs sprouting from his long chicken's neck in place of his once-luxuriant white beard. Tyrion gazed at him without remorse.

The others had to scramble for seats: Lord Mace Tyrell, a heavy, robust man with curling brown hair and a spade-shaped beard well salted with white; Paxter Redwyne of the Arbor, stoop-shouldered and thin, his bald head fringed by tufts of orange hair; Mathis Rowan, Lord of Goldengrove, clean-shaven, stout, and sweating; the High Septon, a frail man with wispy white chin hair. *Too many strange faces*, Tyrion thought, *too many new players. The game changed while I lay rotting in my bed, and no one will tell me the rules.*

Oh, the lords had been courteous enough, though he could tell how uncomfortable it made them to look at him. "That chain of yours, that was cunning," Mace Tyrell had said in a jolly tone, and Lord Redwyne nodded and said, "Quite so, quite so, my lord of Highgarden speaks for all of us," and very cheerfully too.

Tell it to the people of this city, Tyrion thought bitterly. *Tell it to the bloody singers, with their songs of Renly's ghost.*

His uncle Kevan had been the warmest, going so far as to kiss his cheek and say, "Lancel has told me how brave you were, Tyrion. He speaks very highly of you."

He'd better, or I'll have a few things to say of him. He made himself smile and say, "My good cousin is too kind. His wound is healing, I trust?"

Ser Kevan frowned. "One day he seems stronger, the next . . . it is worrisome. Your sister often visits his sickbed, to lift his spirits and pray for him."

But is she praying that he lives, or dies? Cersei had made shameless use of their cousin, both in and out of bed, a little secret she no doubt hoped Lancel would carry to his grave now that Father was here and she no longer had need of him. *Would she go so far as to murder him, though?* To look at her today, you would never suspect Cersei was capable of such ruthlessness. She was all charm, flirting with Lord Tyrell as they spoke of Joffrey's wedding feast, complimenting Lord Redwyne on the valor of his twins, softening gruff Lord Rowan with jests and smiles, making pious noises at the High Septon. "Shall we begin with the wedding arrangements?" she asked as Lord Tywin took his seat.

"No," their father said. "With the war. Varys."

The eunuch smiled a silken smile. "I have such *delicious* tidings for you all, my lords. Yesterday at dawn our brave Lord Randyll caught Robett Glover outside Duskendale and trapped him against the sea. Losses were heavy on both sides, but in the end our loyal men prevailed. Ser Helman Tallhart is reported dead, with a thousand others. Robett Glover leads the survivors back toward Harrenhal in bloody disarray, little dreaming he will find valiant Ser Gregor and his stalwarts athwart his path."

"Gods be praised!" said Paxter Redwyne. "A great victory for King Joffrey!"

What did Joffrey have to do with it? thought Tyrion.

"And a terrible defeat for the north, certainly," observed Littlefinger, "yet one in which Robb Stark played no part. The Young Wolf remains unbeaten in the field."

"What do we know of Stark's plans and movements?" asked Mathis Rowan, ever blunt and to the point.

"He has run back to Riverrun with his plunder, abandoning the castles he took in the west," announced Lord Tywin. "Our cousin Ser Daven is reforming the remnants of his late father's army at Lannisport. When they are ready he shall join Ser Forley Prester at the Golden Tooth. As soon as the Stark boy starts north, Ser Forley and Ser Daven will descend on Riverrun."

"You are certain Lord Stark means to go north?" Lord Rowan asked. "Even with the ironmen at Moat Cailin?"

Mace Tyrell spoke up. "Is there anything as pointless as a king without a kingdom? No, it's plain, the boy must abandon the riverlands, join his forces to Roose Bolton's once more, and throw all his strength against Moat Cailin. That is what *I* would do."

Tyrion had to bite his tongue at that. Robb Stark had won more battles in a year than the Lord of Highgarden had in twenty. Tyrell's reputation rested on one indecisive victory over Robert Baratheon at Ashford, in a battle largely won by Lord Tarly's van before the main host had even arrived. The siege of Storm's End, where Mace Tyrell actually did hold the command, had dragged on a year to no result, and after the Trident was fought, the Lord of Highgarden had meekly dipped his banners to Eddard Stark.

"I ought to write Robb Stark a stern letter," Littlefinger was saying. "I understand his man Bolton is stabling goats in *my* high hall, it's really quite unconscionable."

Ser Kevan Lannister cleared his throat. "As regards the

Starks . . . Balon Greyjoy, who now styles himself King of the Isles and the North, has written to us offering terms of alliance."

"He ought to be offering fealty," snapped Cersei. "By what right does he call himself king?"

"By right of conquest," Lord Tywin said. "King Balon has strangler's fingers round the Neck. Robb Stark's heirs are dead, Winterfell is fallen, and the ironmen hold Moat Cailin, Deepwood Motte, and most of the Stony Shore. King Balon's longships command the sunset sea, and are well placed to menace Lannisport, Fair Isle, and even Highgarden, should we provoke him."

"And if we accept this alliance?" inquired Lord Mathis Rowan. "What terms does he propose?"

"That we recognize his kingship and grant him everything north of the Neck."

Lord Redwyne laughed. "What is there north of the Neck that any sane man would want? If Greyjoy will trade swords and sails for stone and snow, I say do it, and count ourselves lucky."

"Truly," agreed Mace Tyrell. "That's what I would do. Let King Balon finish the northmen whilst we finish Stannis."

Lord Tywin's face gave no hint as to his feelings. "There is Lysa Arryn to deal with as well. Jon Arryn's widow, Hoster Tully's daughter, Catelyn Stark's sister . . . whose husband was conspiring with Stannis Baratheon at the time of his death."

"Oh," said Mace Tyrell cheerfully, "women have no stomach for war. Let her be, I say, she's not like to trouble us."

"I agree," said Redwyne. "The Lady Lysa took no part in the fighting, nor has she committed any overt acts of treason."

Tyrion stirred. "She did throw me in a cell and put me on trial for my life," he pointed out, with a certain amount of rancor. "Nor has she returned to King's Landing to swear fealty to Joff, as she was commanded. My lords, grant me the men, and I will sort out Lysa Arryn." He could think of nothing he would enjoy more, except perhaps strangling Cersei. Sometimes he still dreamed of the Eyrie's sky cells, and woke drenched in cold sweat.

Mace Tyrell's smile was jovial, but behind it Tyrion sensed contempt. "Perhaps you'd best leave the fighting to fighters," said the Lord of Highgarden. "Better men than you have lost great armies in the Mountains of the Moon, or shattered them against the Bloody Gate. We know your worth, my lord, no need to tempt fate."

Tyrion pushed off his cushions, bristling, but his father spoke before he could lash back. "I have other tasks in mind for Tyrion. I believe Lord Petyr may hold the key to the Eyrie."

"Oh, I do," said Littlefinger, "I have it here between my legs." There was mischief in his grey-green eyes. "My lords, with your leave, I propose to travel to the Vale and there woo and win Lady Lysa Arryn. Once I am her consort, I shall deliver you the Vale of Arryn without a drop of blood being spilled."

Lord Rowan looked doubtful. "Would Lady Lysa have you?"

"She's had me a few times before, Lord Mathis, and voiced no complaints."

"Bedding," said Cersei, "is not wedding. Even a cow like Lysa Arryn might be able to grasp the difference."

"To be sure. It would not have been fitting for a daughter of Riverrun to marry one so far below her." Littlefinger spread his hands. "Now, though . . . a match between the Lady of the Eyrie and the Lord of Harrenhal is not so unthinkable, is it?"

Tyrion noted the look that passed between Paxter Redwyne and Mace Tyrell. "It might serve," Lord Rowan said, "if you are certain that you can keep the woman loyal to the King's Grace."

"My lords," pronounced the High Septon, "autumn is upon us, and all men of good heart are weary of war. If Lord Baelish can bring the Vale back into the king's peace without more shedding of blood, the gods will surely bless him."

"But can he?" asked Lord Redwyne. "Jon Arryn's son is Lord of the Eyrie now. The Lord Robert."

"Only a boy," said Littlefinger. "I will see that he grows to be Joffrey's most loyal subject, and a fast friend to us all."

Tyrion studied the slender man with the pointed beard and irreverent grey-green eyes. *Lord of Harrenhal an empty honor? Bugger that, Father. Even if he never sets foot in the castle, the title makes this match possible, as he's known all along.*

"We have no lack of foes," said Ser Kevan Lannister. "If the Eyrie can be kept out of the war, all to the good. I am of a mind to see what Lord Petyr can accomplish."

Ser Kevan was his brother's vanguard in council, Tyrion knew from long experience; he never had a thought that Lord Tywin had not had first. *It has all been settled beforehand*, he concluded, *and this discussion's no more than show.*

The sheep were bleating their agreement, unaware of how neatly they'd been shorn, so it fell to Tyrion to object. "How will the crown pay its debts without Lord Petyr? He is our wizard of coin, and we have no one to replace him."

Littlefinger smiled. "My little friend is too kind. All I do is count coppers, as King Robert used to say. Any clever tradesman could do as well . . . and a Lannister, blessed with the golden touch of Casterly Rock, will no doubt far surpass me."

"A Lannister?" Tyrion had a bad feeling about this.

Lord Tywin's gold-flecked eyes met his son's mismatched ones. "You are admirably suited to the task, I believe."

"Indeed!" Ser Kevan said heartily. "I've no doubt you'll make a splendid master of coin, Tyrion."

Lord Tywin turned back to Littlefinger. "If Lysa Arryn will take you for a husband and return to the king's peace, we shall restore the Lord Robert to the honor of Warden of the East. How soon might you leave?"

"On the morrow, if the winds permit. There's a Braavosi galley standing out past the chain, taking on cargo by boat. The *Merling King*. I'll see her captain about a berth."

"You will miss the king's wedding," said Mace Tyrell.

Petyr Baelish gave a shrug. "Tides and brides wait on no man, my lord. Once the autumn storms begin the voyage will be much more hazardous. Drowning would definitely diminish my charms as a bridegroom."

Lord Tyrell chuckled. "True. Best you do not linger."

"May the gods speed you on your way," the High Septon said. "All King's Landing shall pray for your success."

Lord Redwyne pinched at his nose. "May we return to the matter of the Greyjoy alliance? In my view, there is much to be said for it. Greyjoy's longships will augment my own fleet and give us sufficient strength at sea to assault Dragonstone and end Stannis Baratheon's pretensions."

"King Balon's longships are occupied for the nonce," Lord Tywin said politely, "as are we. Greyjoy demands half the kingdom as the price of alliance, but what will he do to earn it? Fight the Starks? He is doing that already. Why should we pay for what he has given us for free? The best thing to do about our lord of Pyke is nothing, in my view. Granted enough time, a better option may well present itself. One that does not require the king to give up half his kingdom."

Tyrion watched his father closely. *There's something he's not saying.* He remembered those important letters Lord Tywin had been writing, the night Tyrion had demanded Casterly Rock. *What was it he said? Some battles are won with swords and spears, others with quills and ravens . . .* He wondered who the "better option" was, and what sort of price he was demanding.

"Perhaps we ought move on to the wedding," Ser Kevan said.

The High Septon spoke of the preparations being made at the Great Sept of Baelor, and Cersei detailed the plans she had been making for the feast. They would feed a thousand in the throne room, but many more outside in the yards. The outer and middle wards would be tented in silk, with tables of food and casks of ale for all those who could not be accommodated within the hall.

"Your Grace," said Grand Maester Pycelle, "in regard

to the number of guests ... we have had a raven from
Sunspear. Three hundred Dornishmen are riding toward
King's Landing as we speak, and hope to arrive before the
wedding."

"How do they come?" asked Mace Tyrell gruffly. "They
have not asked leave to cross *my* lands." His thick neck
had turned a dark red, Tyrion noted. Dornishmen and
Highgardeners had never had great love for one another;
over the centuries, they had fought border wars beyond
count, and raided back and forth across mountains and
marches even when at peace. The enmity had waned a bit
after Dorne had become part of the Seven Kingdoms ...
until the Dornish prince they called the Red Viper had
crippled the young heir of Highgarden in a tourney. *This
could be ticklish*, the dwarf thought, waiting to see how
his father would handle it.

"Prince Doran comes at my son's invitation," Lord
Tywin said calmly, "not only to join in our celebration,
but to claim his seat on this council, and the justice Robert
denied him for the murder of his sister Elia and her
children."

Tyrion watched the faces of the Lords Tyrell, Redwyne,
and Rowan, wondering if any of the three would be bold
enough to say, "But Lord Tywin, wasn't it *you* who presented the bodies to Robert, all wrapped up in Lannister
cloaks?" None of them did, but it was there on their faces
all the same. *Redwyne does not give a fig*, he thought, *but
Rowan looks fit to gag*.

"When the king is wed to your Margaery and Myrcella
to Prince Trystane, we shall all be one great House," Ser
Kevan reminded Mace Tyrell. "The enmities of the past
should remain there, would you not agree, my lord?"

"This is *my daughter's wedding –*"

"– and my grandson's," said Lord Tywin firmly. "No
place for old quarrels, surely?"

"I have no quarrel with *Doran* Martell," insisted Lord
Tyrell, though his tone was more than a little grudging.
"If he wishes to cross the Reach in peace, he need only
ask my leave."

Small chance of that, thought Tyrion. *He'll climb the*

Bonway, turn east near Summerhall, and come up the kingsroad.

"Three hundred Dornishmen need not trouble our plans," said Cersei. "We can feed the men-at-arms in the yard, squeeze some extra benches into the throne room for the lordlings and highborn knights, and find Prince Doran a place of honor on the dais."

Not by me, was the message Tyrion saw in Mace Tyrell's eyes, but the Lord of Highgarden made no reply but a curt nod.

"Perhaps we can move to a more pleasant task," said Lord Tywin. "The fruits of victory await division."

"What could be sweeter?" said Littlefinger, who had already swallowed his own fruit, Harrenhal.

Each lord had his own demands; this castle and that village, tracts of lands, a small river, a forest, the wardship of certain minors left fatherless by the battle. Fortunately, these fruits were plentiful, and there were orphans and castles for all. Varys had lists. Forty-seven lesser lordlings and six hundred nineteen knights had lost their lives beneath the fiery heart of Stannis and his Lord of Light, along with several thousand common men-at-arms. Traitors all, their heirs were disinherited, their lands and castles granted to those who had proved more loyal.

Highgarden reaped the richest harvest. Tyrion eyed Mace Tyrell's broad belly and thought, *He has a prodigious appetite, this one.* Tyrell demanded the lands and castles of Lord Alester Florent, his own bannerman, who'd had the singular ill judgment to back first Renly and then Stannis. Lord Tywin was pleased to oblige. Brightwater Keep and all its lands and incomes were granted to Lord Tyrell's second son, Ser Garlan, transforming him into a great lord in the blink of an eye. His elder brother, of course, stood to inherit Highgarden itself.

Lesser tracts were granted to Lord Rowan, and set aside for Lord Tarly, Lady Oakheart, Lord Hightower, and other worthies not present. Lord Redwyne asked only for thirty years' remission of the taxes that Littlefinger and his wine factors had levied on certain of the Arbor's finest vintages. When that was granted, he pronounced himself well satisfied and suggested that they send for a cask of Arbor gold, to toast good King Joffrey and his wise and benevolent Hand. At that Cersei lost patience. "It's swords Joff needs, not toasts," she snapped. "His realm is still plagued with would-be usurpers and self-styled kings."

"But not for long, I think," said Varys unctuously.

"A few more items remain, my lords." Ser Kevan consulted his papers. "Ser Addam has found some crystals from the High Septon's crown. It appears certain now that the thieves broke up the crystals and melted down the gold."

"Our Father Above knows their guilt and will sit in judgment on them all," the High Septon said piously.

"No doubt he will," said Lord Tywin. "All the same, you must be crowned at the king's wedding. Cersei, summon your goldsmiths, we must see to a replacement." He did not wait for her reply, but turned at once to Varys. "You have reports?"

The eunuch drew a parchment from his sleeve. "A kraken has been seen off the Fingers." He giggled. "Not a Greyjoy, mind you, a true kraken. It attacked an Ibbenese whaler and pulled it under. There is fighting on the Stepstones, and a new war between Tyrosh and Lys seems likely. Both hope to win Myr as olly. Sailors back from the Jade Sea report that a three-headed dragon has hatched in Qarth, and is the wonder of that city."

"Dragons and krakens do not interest me, regardless of the number of their heads," said Lord Tywin. "Have your whisperers perchance found some trace of my brother's son?"

"Alas, our beloved Tyrek has quite vanished, the poor brave lad." Varys sounded close to tears.

"Tywin," Ser Kevan said, before Lord Tywin could vent his obvious displeasure, "some of the gold cloaks who deserted during the battle have drifted back to barracks, thinking to take up duty once again. Ser Addam wishes to know what to do with them."

"They might have endangered Joff with their cowardice," Cersei said at once. "I want them put to death."

Varys sighed. "They have surely earned death, Your

Grace, none can deny it. And yet, perhaps we might be wiser to send them to the Night's Watch. We have had disturbing messages from the Wall of late. Of wildlings astir . . ."

"Wildlings, krakens, and dragons." Mace Tyrell chuckled. "Why, is there anyone *not* stirring?"

Lord Tywin ignored that. "The deserters serve us best as a lesson. Break their knees with hammers. They will not run again. Nor will any man who sees them begging in the streets." He glanced down the table to see if any of the other lords disagreed.

Tyrion remembered his own visit to the Wall, and the crabs he'd shared with old Lord Mormont and his officers. He remembered the Old Bear's fears as well. "Perhaps we might break the knees of a few to make our point. Those who killed Ser Jacelyn, say. The rest we can send to Marsh. The Watch is grievously under strength. If the Wall should fail . . ."

". . . the wildlings will flood the north," his father finished, "and the Starks and Greyjoys will have another enemy to contend with. They no longer wish to be subject to the Iron Throne, it would seem, so by what right do they look to the Iron Throne for aid? King Robb and King Balon both claim the north. Let *them* defend it, if they can. And if not, this Mance Rayder might even prove a useful ally." Lord Tywin looked to his brother. "Is there more?"

Ser Kevan shook his head. "We are done. My lords, His Grace King Joffrey would no doubt wish to thank you all for your wisdom and good counsel."

"I should like private words with my children," said Lord Tywin as the others rose to leave. "You as well, Kevan."

Obediently, the other councillors made their farewells, Varys the first to depart and Tyrell and Redwyne the last. When the chamber was empty but for the four Lannisters, Ser Kevan closed the door.

"*Master of coin?*" said Tyrion in a thin strained voice. "Whose notion was that, pray?"

"Lord Petyr's," his father said, "but it serves us well

to have the treasury in the hands of a Lannister. You have asked for important work. Do you fear you might be incapable of the task?"

"No," said Tyrion, "I fear a trap. Littlefinger is subtle and ambitious. I do not trust him. Nor should you."

"He won Highgarden to our side . . ." Cersei began.

". . . and sold you Ned Stark, I know. He will sell us just as quick. A coin is as dangerous as a sword in the wrong hands."

His uncle Kevan looked at him oddly. "Not to us, surely. The gold of Casterly Rock . . ."

". . . is dug from the ground. Littlefinger's gold is made from thin air, with a snap of his fingers."

"A more useful skill than any of yours, sweet brother," purred Cersei, in a voice sweet with malice.

"Littlefinger is a liar –"

"– and black as well, said the raven of the crow."

Lord Tywin slammed his hand down on the table. "*Enough!* I will have no more of this unseemly squabbling. You are both Lannisters, and will comport yourselves as such."

Ser Kevan cleared his throat. "I would sooner have Petyr Baelish ruling the Eyrie than any of Lady Lysa's other suitors. Yohn Royce, Lyn Corbray, Horton Redfort . . . these are dangerous men, each in his own way. And proud. Littlefinger may be clever, but he has neither high birth nor skill at arms. The lords of the Vale will never accept such as their liege." He looked to his brother. When Lord Tywin nodded, he continued. "And there is this – Lord Petyr continues to demonstrate his loyalty. Only yesterday he brought us word of a Tyrell plot to spirit Sansa Stark off to Highgarden for a 'visit,' and there marry her to Lord Mace's eldest son, Willas."

"*Littlefinger* brought you word?" Tyrion leaned against the table. "Not our master of whisperers? How interesting."

Cersei looked at their uncle in disbelief. "Sansa is my hostage. She goes *nowhere* without my leave."

"Leave you must perforce grant, should Lord Tyrell ask," their father pointed out. "To refuse him would be tantamount to declaring that we did not trust him. He would take offense."

"Let him. What do we care?"

Bloody fool, thought Tyrion. "Sweet sister," he explained patiently, "offend Tyrell and you offend Redwyne, Tarly, Rowan, and Hightower as well, and perhaps start them wondering whether Robb Stark might not be more accommodating of their desires."

"I will not have the rose and the direwolf in bed together," declared Lord Tywin. "We must forestall him."

"How?" asked Cersei.

"By marriage. Yours, to begin with."

It came so suddenly that Cersei could only stare for a moment. Then her cheeks reddened as if she had been slapped. "No. Not again. I will not."

"Your Grace," said Ser Kevan, courteously, "you are a young woman, still fair and fertile. Surely you cannot wish to spend the rest of your days alone? And a new marriage would put to rest this talk of incest for good and all."

"So long as you remain unwed, you allow Stannis to spread his disgusting slander," Lord Tywin told his daughter. "You must have a new husband in your bed, to father children on you."

"Three children is quite sufficient. I am Queen of the Seven Kingdoms, not a brood mare! The Queen *Regent*!"

"You are my daughter, and will do as I command."

She stood. "I will not sit here and listen to this –"

"You will if you wish to have any voice in the choice of your next husband," Lord Tywin said calmly.

When she hesitated, then sat, Tyrion knew she was lost, despite her loud declaration of, "I will *not* marry again!"

"You will marry and you will breed. Every child you birth makes Stannis more a liar." Their father's eyes seemed to pin her to her chair. "Mace Tyrell, Paxter Redwyne, and Doran Martell are wed to younger women likely to outlive them. Balon Greyjoy's wife is elderly and failing, but such a match would commit us to an alliance with the Iron Islands, and I am still uncertain whether that would be our wisest course."

"No," Cersei said from between white lips. "No, no, no."

Tyrion could not quite suppress the grin that came to his lips at the thought of packing his sister off to Pyke. *Just when I was about to give up praying, some sweet god gives me this.*

Lord Tywin went on. "Oberyn Martell might suit, but the Tyrells would take that very ill. So we must look to the sons. I assume you do not object to wedding a man younger than yourself?"

"I object to wedding *any* –"

"I have considered the Redwyne twins, Theon Greyjoy, Quentyn Martell, and a number of others. But our alliance with Highgarden was the sword that broke Stannis. It should be tempered and made stronger. Ser Loras has taken the white and Ser Garlan is wed to one of the Fossoways, but there remains the eldest son, the boy they scheme to wed to Sansa Stark."

Willas Tyrell. Tyrion was taking a wicked pleasure in Cersei's helpless fury. "That would be the cripple," he said.

Their father chilled him with a look. "Willas is heir to Highgarden, and by all reports a mild and courtly young man, fond of reading books and looking at the stars. He has a passion for breeding animals as well, and owns the finest hounds, hawks, and horses in the Seven Kingdoms."

A perfect match, mused Tyrion. *Cersei also has a passion for breeding.* He pitied poor Willas Tyrell, and did not know whether he wanted to laugh at his sister or weep for her.

"The Tyrell heir would be my choice," Lord Tywin concluded, "but if you would prefer another, I will hear your reasons."

"That is so very kind of you, Father," Cersei said with icy courtesy. "It is such a difficult choice you give me. Who would I sooner take to bed, the old squid or the crippled dog boy? I shall need a few days to consider. Do I have your leave to go?"

You are the queen, Tyrion wanted to tell her. *He ought to be begging leave of you.*

"Go," their father said. "We shall talk again after you have composed yourself. Remember your duty."

Cersei swept stiffly from the room, her rage plain to see. *Yet in the end she will do as Father bid.* She had proved that with Robert. *Though there is Jaime to consider.* Their brother had been much younger when Cersei wed the first time; he might not acquiesce to a second marriage quite so easily. The unfortunate Willas Tyrell was like to contract a sudden fatal case of sword-through-bowels, which could rather sour the alliance between Highgarden and Casterly Rock. *I should say something, but what? Pardon me, Father, but it's our brother she wants to marry?*

"Tyrion."

He gave a resigned smile. "Do I hear the herald summoning me to the lists?"

"Your whoring is a weakness in you," Lord Tywin said without preamble, "but perhaps some share of the blame is mine. Since you stand no taller than a boy, I have found it easy to forget that you are in truth a man grown, with all of a man's baser needs. It is past time you were wed."

I was wed, or have you forgotten? Tyrion's mouth twisted, and the noise emerged that was half laugh and half snarl.

"Does the prospect of marriage amuse you?"

"Only imagining what a bugger-all handsome bridegroom I'll make." A wife might be the very thing he needed. If she brought him lands and a keep, it would give him a place in the world apart from Joffrey's court . . . and away from Cersei and their father.

On the other hand, there was Shae. *She will not like this, for all she swears that she is content to be my whore.*

That was scarcely a point to sway his father, however, so Tyrion squirmed higher in his seat and said, "You mean to wed me to Sansa Stark. But won't the Tyrells take the match as an affront, if they have designs on the girl?"

"Lord Tyrell will not broach the matter of the Stark girl until after Joffrey's wedding. If Sansa is wed before that, how can he take offense, when he gave us no hint of his intentions?"

"Quite so," said Ser Kevan, "and any lingering resentments should be soothed by the offer of Cersei for his Willas."

Tyrion rubbed at the raw stub of his nose. The scar tissue itched abominably sometimes. "His Grace the royal pustule has made Sansa's life a misery since the day her father died, and now that she is finally rid of Joffrey you propose to marry her to me. That seems singularly cruel. Even for you, Father."

"Why, do you plan to mistreat her?" His father sounded more curious than concerned. "The girl's happiness is not my purpose, nor should it be yours. Our alliances in the south may be as solid as Casterly Rock, but there remains the north to win, and the key to the north is Sansa Stark."

"She is no more than a child."

"Your sister swears she's flowered. If so, she is a woman, fit to be wed. You must needs take her maidenhead, so no man can say the marriage was not consummated. After that, if you prefer to wait a year or two before bedding her again, you would be within your rights as her husband."

Shae is all the woman I need just now, he thought, *and Sansa's a girl, no matter what you say.* "If your purpose here is to keep her from the Tyrells, why not return her to her mother? Perhaps that would convince Robb Stark to bend the knee."

Lord Tywin's look was scornful. "Send her to Riverrun and her mother will match her with a Blackwood or a Mallister to shore up her son's alliances along the Trident. Send her north, and she will be wed to some Manderly or Umber before the moon turns. Yet she is no less dangerous here at court, as this business with the Tyrells should prove. She must marry a Lannister, and soon."

"The man who weds Sansa Stark can claim Winterfell in her name," his uncle Kevan put in. "Had that not occurred to you?"

"If you will not have the girl, we shall give her to one of your cousins," said his father. "Kevan, is Lancel strong enough to wed, do you think?"

Ser Kevan hesitated. "If we bring the girl to his bedside, he could say the words . . . but to consummate, no . . . I would suggest one of the twins, but the Starks hold them both at Riverrun. They have Genna's boy Tion as well, else he might serve."

Tyrion let them have their byplay; it was all for his benefit, he knew. *Sansa Stark*, he mused. Soft-spoken sweet-smelling Sansa, who loved silks, songs, chivalry and tall gallant knights with handsome faces. He felt as though he was back on the bridge of boats, the deck shifting beneath his feet.

"You asked me to reward you for your efforts in the battle," Lord Tywin reminded him forcefully. "This is a chance for you, Tyrion, the best you are ever likely to have." He drummed his fingers impatiently on the table. "I once hoped to marry your brother to Lysa Tully, but Aerys named Jaime to his Kingsguard before the arrangements were complete. When I suggested to Lord Hoster that Lysa might be wed to you instead, he replied that he wanted a whole man for his daughter."

So he wed her to Jon Arryn, who was old enough to be her grandfather. Tyrion was more inclined to be thankful than angry, considering what Lysa Arryn had become.

"When I offered you to Dorne I was told that the suggestion was an insult," Lord Tywin continued. "In later years I had similar answers from Yohn Royce and Leyton Hightower. I finally stooped so low as to suggest you might take the Florent girl Robert deflowered in his brother's wedding bed, but her father preferred to give her to one of his own household knights.

"If you will not have the Stark girl, I shall find you another wife. Somewhere in the realm there is doubtless some little lordling who'd gladly part with a daughter to win the friendship of Casterly Rock. Lady Tanda has offered Lollys . . ."

Tyrion gave a shudder of dismay. "I'd sooner cut it off and feed it to the goats."

"Then open your eyes. The Stark girl is young, nubile, tractable, of the highest birth, and still a maid. She is not uncomely. Why would you hesitate?"

Why indeed? "A quirk of mine. Strange to say, I would prefer a wife who wants me in her bed."

"If you think your whores want you in their bed, you are an even greater fool than I suspected," said Lord Tywin. "You disappoint me, Tyrion. I had hoped this match would please you."

"Yes, we all know how important my pleasure is to you, Father. But there's more to this. The key to the north, you say? The Greyjoys hold the north now, and King Balon has a daughter. Why Sansa Stark, and not her?" He looked into his father's cool green eyes with their bright flecks of gold.

Lord Tywin steepled his fingers beneath his chin. "Balon Greyjoy thinks in terms of plunder, not rule. Let him enjoy an autumn crown and suffer a northern winter. He will give his subjects no cause to love him. Come spring, the northmen will have had a bellyful of krakens. When you bring Eddard Stark's grandson home to claim his birthright, lords and little folk alike will rise as one to place him on the high seat of his ancestors. You *are* capable of getting a woman with child, I hope?"

"I believe I am," he said, bristling. "I confess, I cannot prove it. Though no one can say I have not tried. Why, I plant my little seeds just as often as I can . . ."

"In the gutters and the ditches," finished Lord Tywin, "and in common ground where only bastard weeds take root. It is past time you kept your own garden." He rose to his feet. "You shall never have Casterly Rock, I promise you. But wed Sansa Stark, and it is just possible that you might win Winterfell."

Tyrion Lannister, Lord Protector of Winterfell. The prospect gave him a queer chill. "Very good, Father," he said slowly, "but there's a big ugly roach in your rushes. Robb Stark is as *capable* as I am, presumably, and sworn to marry one of those fertile Freys. And once the Young Wolf sires a litter, any pups that Sansa births are heirs to nothing."

Lord Tywin was unconcerned. "Robb Stark will father no children on his fertile Frey, you have my word. There is a bit of news I have not yet seen fit to share with the council, though no doubt the good lords will hear it soon enough. The Young Wolf has taken Gawen Westerling's eldest daughter to wife."

For a moment Tyrion could not believe he'd heard his father right. "He broke his sworn word?" he said, incredulous. "He threw away the Freys for . . ." Words failed him.

"A maid of sixteen years, named Jeyne," said Ser Kevan. "Lord Gawen once suggested her to me for Willem or Martyn, but I had to refuse him. Gawen is a good man, but his wife is Sybell Spicer. He should never have wed her. The Westerlings always did have more honor than sense. Lady Sybell's grandfather was a trader in saffron and pepper, almost as lowborn as that smuggler Stannis keeps. And the grandmother was some woman he'd brought back from the east. A frightening old crone, supposed to be a priestess. *Maegi*, they called her. No one could pronounce her real name. Half of Lannisport used to go to her for cures and love potions and the like." He shrugged. "She's long dead, to be sure. And Jeyne seemed a sweet child, I'll grant you, though I only saw her once. But with such doubtful blood . . ."

Having once married a whore, Tyrion could not entirely share his uncle's horror at the thought of wedding a girl whose great grandfather sold cloves. Even so . . . *A sweet child*, Ser Kevan had said, but many a poison was sweet as well. The Westerlings were old blood, but they had more pride than power. It would not surprise him to learn that Lady Sybell had brought more wealth to the marriage than her highborn husband. The Westerling mines had failed years ago, their best lands had been sold off or lost, and the Crag was more ruin than stronghold. *A romantic ruin, though, jutting up so brave above the sea.* "I am surprised," Tyrion had to confess. "I thought Robb Stark had better sense."

"He is a boy of sixteen," said Lord Tywin. "At that age, sense weighs for little, against lust and love and honor."

"He forswore himself, shamed an ally, betrayed a solemn promise. Where is the honor in that?"

Ser Kevan answered. "He chose the girl's honor over his own. Once he had deflowered her, he had no other course."

"It would have been kinder to leave her with a bastard in her belly," said Tyrion bluntly. The Westerlings stood to lose everything here; their lands, their castle, their very lives. *A Lannister always pays his debts.*

"Jeyne Westerling is her mother's daughter," said Lord Tywin, "and Robb Stark is his father's son."

This Westerling betrayal did not seem to have enraged his father as much as Tyrion would have expected. Lord Tywin did not suffer disloyalty in his vassals. He had extinguished the proud Reynes of Castamere and the ancient Tarbecks of Tarbeck Hall root and branch when he was still half a boy. The singers had even made a rather gloomy song of it. Some years later, when Lord Farman of Faircastle grew truculent, Lord Tywin sent an envoy bearing a lute instead of a letter. But once he'd heard "The Rains of Castamere" echoing through his hall, Lord Farman gave no further trouble. And if the song were not enough, the shattered castles of the Reynes and Tarbecks still stood as mute testimony to the fate that awaited those who chose to scorn the power of Casterly Rock. "The Crag is not so far from Tarbeck Hall and Castamere," Tyrion pointed out. "You'd think the Westerlings might have ridden past and seen the lesson there."

"Mayhaps they have," Lord Tywin said. "They are well aware of Castamere, I promise you."

"Could the Westerlings and Spicers be such great fools as to believe the wolf can defeat the lion?"

Every once in a very long while, Lord Tywin Lannister would actually threaten to smile; he never did, but the threat alone was terrible to behold. "The greatest fools are ofttimes more clever than the men who laugh at them," he said, and then, "You will marry Sansa Stark, Tyrion. And soon."

CATELYN

They carried the corpses in upon their shoulders and laid them beneath the dais. A silence fell across the torchlit hall, and in the quiet Catelyn could hear Grey Wind howling half a castle away. *He smells the blood*, she thought, *through stone walls and wooden doors, through night and rain, he still knows the scent of death and ruin.*

She stood at Robb's left hand beside the high seat, and for a moment felt almost as if she were looking down at her own dead, at Bran and Rickon. These boys had been much older, but death had shrunken them. Naked and wet, they seemed such little things, so still it was hard to remember them living.

The blond boy had been trying to grow a beard. Pale yellow peach fuzz covered his cheeks and jaw above the red ruin the knife had made of his throat. His long golden hair was still wet, as if he had been pulled from a bath. By the look of him, he had died peacefully, perhaps in sleep, but his brown-haired cousin had fought for life. His arms bore slashes where he'd tried to block the blades, and red still trickled slowly from the stab wounds that covered his chest and belly and back like so many tongue-less mouths, though the rain had washed him almost clean.

Robb had donned his crown before coming to the hall,

and the bronze shone darkly in the torchlight. Shadows hid his eyes as he looked upon the dead. *Does he see Bran and Rickon as well?* She might have wept, but there were no tears left in her. The dead boys were pale from long imprisonment, and both had been fair; against their smooth white skin, the blood was shockingly red, unbearable to look upon. *Will they lay Sansa down naked beneath the Iron Throne after they have killed her? Will her skin seem as white, her blood as red?* From outside came the steady wash of rain and the restless howling of a wolf.

Her brother Edmure stood to Robb's right, one hand upon the back of his father's seat, his face still puffy from sleep. They had woken him as they had her, pounding on his door in the black of night to yank him rudely from his dreams. *Were they good dreams, brother? Do you dream of sunlight and laughter and a maiden's kisses? I pray you do.* Her own dreams were dark and laced with terrors.

Robb's captains and lords bannermen stood about the hall, some mailed and armed, others in various states of dishevelment and undress. Ser Raynald and his uncle Ser Rolph were among them, but Robb had seen fit to spare his queen this ugliness. *The Crag is not far from Casterly Rock,* Catelyn recalled. *Jeyne may well have played with these boys when all of them were children.*

She looked down again upon the corpses of the squires Tion Frey and Willem Lannister, and waited for her son to speak.

It seemed a very long time before Robb lifted his eyes from the bloody dead. "Smalljon," he said, "tell your father to bring them in." Wordless, Smalljon Umber turned to obey, his steps echoing in the great stone hall.

As the Greatjon marched his prisoners through the doors, Catelyn made note of how some other men stepped back to give them room, as if treason could somehow be passed by a touch, a glance, a cough. The captors and the captives looked much alike; big men, every one, with thick beards and long hair. Two of the Greatjon's men were wounded, and three of their prisoners. Only the fact that some had spears and others empty scabbards served to set them apart. All were clad in mail hauberks or shirts of sewn rings, with heavy boots and thick cloaks, some of wool and some of fur. *The north is hard and cold, and has no mercy*, Ned had told her when she first came to Winterfell a thousand years ago.

"Five," said Robb when the prisoners stood before him, wet and silent. "Is that all of them?"

"There were eight," rumbled the Greatjon. "We killed two taking them, and a third is dying now."

Robb studied the faces of the captives. "It required eight of you to kill two unarmed squires."

Edmure Tully spoke up. "They murdered two of my men as well, to get into the tower. Delp and Elwood."

"It was no murder, ser," said Lord Rickard Karstark, no more discomfited by the ropes about his wrists than by the blood that trickled down his face. "Any man who steps between a father and his vengeance asks for death."

His words rang against Catelyn's ears, harsh and cruel as the pounding of a war drum. Her throat was dry as bone. *I did this. These two boys died so my daughters might live.*

"I saw your sons die, that night in the Whispering Wood," Robb told Lord Karstark. "Tion Frey did not kill Torrhen. Willem Lannister did not slay Eddard. How then can you call this vengeance? This was folly, and bloody murder. Your sons died honorably on a battlefield, with swords in their hands."

"They *died*," said Rickard Karstark, yielding no inch of ground. "The Kingslayer cut them down. These two were of his ilk. Only blood can pay for blood."

"The blood of children?" Robb pointed at the corpses. "How old were they? Twelve, thirteen? *Squires*."

"Squires die in every battle."

"Die fighting, yes. Tion Frey and Willem Lannister gave up their swords in the Whispering Wood. They were captives, locked in a cell, asleep, unarmed . . . boys. *Look at them!*"

Lord Karstark looked instead at Catelyn. "Tell your mother to look at them," he said. "She slew them, as much as I."

Catelyn put a hand on the back of Robb's seat. The hall seemed to spin about her. She felt as though she might retch.

"My mother had naught to do with this," Robb said angrily. "This was your work. Your murder. Your *treason*."

"How can it be treason to kill Lannisters, when it is not treason to free them?" asked Karstark harshly. "Has Your Grace forgotten that we are at war with Casterly Rock? In war you kill your enemies. Didn't your father teach you that, boy?"

"*Boy?*" The Greatjon dealt Rickard Karstark a buffet with a mailed fist that sent the other lord to his knees.

"Leave him!" Robb's voice rang with command. Umber stepped back away from the captive.

Lord Karstark spit out a broken tooth. "Yes, Lord Umber, leave me to the king. He means to give me a scolding before he forgives me. That's how he deals with treason, our King in the North." He smiled a wet red smile. "Or should I call you the King Who Lost the North, Your Grace?"

The Greatjon snatched a spear from the man beside him and jerked it to his shoulder. "Let me spit him, sire. Let me open his belly so we can see the color of his guts."

The doors of the hall crashed open, and the Blackfish entered with water running from his cloak and helm. Tully men-at-arms followed him in, while outside lightning cracked across the sky and a hard black rain pounded against the stones of Riverrun. Ser Brynden removed his helm and went to one knee. "Your Grace," was all he said, but the grimness of his tone spoke volumes.

"I will hear Ser Brynden privily, in the audience chamber." Robb rose to his feet. "Greatjon, keep Lord Karstark here till I return, and hang the other seven."

The Greatjon lowered the spear. "Even the dead ones?"

"Yes. I will not have such fouling my lord uncle's rivers. Let them feed the crows."

One of the captives dropped to his knees. "Mercy, sire. I killed no one, I only stood at the door to watch for guards."

Robb considered that a moment. "Did you know what

Lord Rickard intended? Did you see the knives drawn? Did you hear the shouts, the screams, the cries for mercy?"

"Aye, I did, but I took no part. I was only the watcher, I swear it . . ."

"Lord Umber," said Robb, "this one was only the watcher. Hang him last, so he may watch the others die. Mother, Uncle, with me, if you please." He turned away as the Greatjon's men closed upon the prisoners and drove them from the hall at spearpoint. Outside the thunder crashed and boomed, so loud it sounded as if the castle were coming down about their ears. *Is this the sound of a kingdom falling?* Catelyn wondered.

It was dark within the audience chamber, but at least the sound of the thunder was muffled by another thickness of wall. A servant entered with an oil lamp to light the fire, but Robb sent him away and kept the lamp. There were tables and chairs, but only Edmure sat, and he rose again when he realized that the others had remainded standing. Robb took off his crown and placed it on the table before him.

The Blackfish shut the door. "The Karstarks are gone."

"All?" Was it anger or despair that thickened Robb's voice like that? Even Catelyn was not certain.

"All the fighting men," Ser Brynden replied. "A few camp followers and serving men were left with their wounded. We questioned as many as we needed, to be certain of the truth. They started leaving at nightfall, stealing off in ones and twos at first, and then in larger groups. The wounded men and servants were told to keep the campfires lit so no one would know they'd gone, but once the rains began it didn't matter."

"Will they re-form, away from Riverrun?" asked Robb.

"No. They've scattered, hunting. Lord Karstark has sworn to give the hand of his maiden daughter to any man highborn or low who brings him the head of the Kingslayer."

Gods be good. Catelyn felt ill again.

"Near three hundred riders and twice as many mounts, melted away in the night." Robb rubbed his temples, where the crown had left its mark in the soft skin above his ears. "All the mounted strength of Karhold, lost."

Lost by me. By me, may the gods forgive me. Catelyn did not need to be a soldier to grasp the trap Robb was in. For the moment he held the riverlands, but his kingdom was surrounded by enemies to every side but east, where Lysa sat aloof on her mountaintop. Even the Trident was scarce secure so long as the Lord of the Crossing withheld his allegiance. *And now to lose the Karstarks as well . . .*

"No word of this must leave Riverrun," her brother Edmure said. "Lord Tywin would . . . the Lannisters pay their debts, they are always saying that. Mother have mercy, when he hears."

Sansa. Catelyn's nails dug into the soft flesh of her palms, so hard did she close her hand.

Robb gave Edmure a look that chilled. "Would you make me a liar as well as a murderer, Uncle?"

"We need speak no falsehood. Only say nothing. Bury the boys and hold our tongues till the war's done. Willem was son to Ser Kevan Lannister, and Lord Tywin's nephew. Tion was Lady Genna's, *and* a Frey. We must keep the news from the Twins as well, until . . ."

"Until we can bring the murdered dead back to life?" said Brynden Blackfish sharply. "The truth escaped with the Karstarks, Edmure. It is too late for such games."

"I owe their fathers truth," said Robb. "And justice. I owe them that as well." He gazed at his crown, the dark gleam of bronze, the circle of iron swords. "Lord Rickard defied me. Betrayed me. I have no choice but to condemn him. Gods know what the Karstark foot with Roose Bolton will do when they hear I've executed their liege for a traitor. Bolton must be warned."

"Lord Karstark's heir was at Harrenhal as well," Ser Brynden reminded him. "The eldest son, the one the Lannisters took captive on the Green Fork."

"Harrion. His name is Harrion." Robb laughed bitterly. "A king had best know the names of his enemies, don't you think?"

The Blackfish looked at him shrewdly. "You know that for a certainty? That this will make young Karstark your enemy?"

"What else would he be? I am about to kill his father, he's not like to thank me."

"He might. There are sons who hate their fathers, and in a stroke you will make him Lord of Karhold."

Robb shook his head. "Even if Harrion were that sort, he could never openly forgive his father's killer. His own men would turn on him. These are *northmen*, Uncle. The north remembers."

"Pardon him, then," urged Edmure Tully.

Robb stared at him in frank disbelief.

Under that gaze, Edmure's face reddened. "Spare his life, I mean. I don't like the taste of it any more than you, sire. He slew my men as well. Poor Delp had only just recovered from the wound Ser Jaime gave him. Karstark must be punished, certainly. Keep him in chains, I say."

"A hostage?" said Catelyn. *It might be best . . .*

"Yes, a hostage!" Her brother seized on her musing as agreement. "Tell the son that so long as he remains loyal, his father will not be harmed. Otherwise . . . we have no hope of the Freys now, not if I offered to marry *all* Lord Walder's daughters and carry his litter besides. If we should lose the Karstarks as well, what hope is there?"

"What hope . . ." Robb let out a breath, pushed his hair back from his eyes, and said, "We've had naught from Ser Rodrik in the north, no response from Walder Frey to our new offer, only silence from the Eyrie." He appealed to his mother. "Will your sister never answer us? How many times must I write her? I will not believe that *none* of the birds have reached her."

Her son wanted comfort, Catelyn realized; he wanted to hear that it would be all right. But her king needed truth. "The birds have reached her. Though she may tell you they did not, if it ever comes to that. Expect no help from that quarter, Robb.

"Lysa was never brave. When we were girls together, she would run and hide whenever she'd done something wrong. Perhaps she thought our lord father would forget to be wroth with her if he could not find her. It is no different now. She ran from King's Landing for fear, to the safest place she knows, and she sits on her mountain hoping everyone will forget her."

"The knights of the Vale could make all the difference in this war," said Robb, "but if she will not fight, so be it. I've asked only that she open the Bloody Gate for us, and provide ships at Gulltown to take us north. The high road would be hard, but not so hard as fighting our way up the Neck. If I could land at White Harbor I could flank Moat Cailin and drive the ironmen from the north in half a year."

"It will not happen, sire," said the Blackfish. "Cat is right. Lady Lysa is too fearful to admit an army to the Vale. *Any* army. The Bloody Gate will remain closed."

"The Others can take her, then," Robb cursed, in a fury of despair. "Bloody Rickard Karstark as well. And Theon Greyjoy, Walder Frey, Tywin Lannister, and all the rest of them. Gods be good, why would any man ever want to be king? When everyone was shouting *King in the North, King in the North*, I told myself . . . *swore* to myself . . . that I would be a good king, as honorable as Father, strong, just, loyal to my friends and brave when I faced my enemies . . . now I can't even tell one from the other. How did it all get so *confused?* Lord Rickard's fought at my side in half a dozen battles. His sons died for me in the Whispering Wood. Tion Frey and Willem Lannister were my *enemies*. Yet now I have to kill my dead friends' father for their sakes." He looked at them all. "Will the Lannisters thank me for Lord Rickard's head? Will the Freys?"

"No," said Brynden Blackfish, blunt as ever.

"All the more reason to spare Lord Rickard's life and keep him hostage," Edmure urged.

Robb reached down with both hands, lifted the heavy bronze-and-iron crown, and set it back atop his head, and suddenly he was a king again. "Lord Rickard dies."

"But *why?*" said Edmure. "You said yourself – "

"I know what I said, Uncle. It does not change what I must do." The swords in his crown stood stark and black against his brow. "In battle I might have slain Tion and Willem myself, but this was no battle. They were asleep in their beds, naked and unarmed, in a cell where I put them. Rickard Karstark killed more than a Frey and a Lannister. *He killed my honor*. I shall deal with him at dawn."

When day broke, grey and chilly, the storm had diminished to a steady, soaking rain, yet even so the godswood was crowded. River lords and northmen, highborn and low, knights and sellswords and stableboys, they stood amongst the trees to see the end of the night's dark dance. Edmure had given commands, and a headsman's block had been set up before the heart tree. Rain and leaves fell all around them as the Greatjon's men led Lord Rickard Karstark through the press, hands still bound. His men already hung from Riverrun's high walls, slumping at the end of long ropes as the rain washed down their darkening faces.

Long Lew waited beside the block, but Robb took the poleaxe from his hand and ordered him to step aside. "This is my work," he said. "He dies at my word. He must die by my hand."

Lord Rickard Karstark dipped his head stiffly. "For that much, I thank you. But for naught else." He had dressed for death in a long black wool surcoat emblazoned with the white sunburst of his House. "The blood of the First Men flows in my veins as much as yours, boy. You would do well to remember that. I was named for your grandfather. I raised my banners against King Aerys for your father, and against King Joffrey for you. At Oxcross and the Whispering Wood and in the Battle of the Camps, I rode beside you, and I stood with Lord Eddard on the Trident. We are kin, Stark and Karstark."

"This kinship did not stop you from betraying me," Robb said. "And it will not save you now. Kneel, my lord."

Lord Rickard had spoken truly, Catelyn knew. The Karstarks traced their descent to Karlon Stark, a younger son of Winterfell who had put down a rebel lord a thousand years ago, and been granted lands for his valor. The castle he built had been named Karl's Hold, but that soon became Karhold, and over the centuries the Karhold Starks had become Karstarks.

"Old gods or new, it makes no matter," Lord Rickard

told her son, "no man is so accursed as the kinslayer."

"Kneel, traitor," Robb said again. "Or must I have them force your head onto the block?"

Lord Karstark knelt. "The gods shall judge you, as you have judged me." He laid his head upon the block.

"Rickard Karstark, Lord of Karhold." Robb lifted the heavy axe with both hands. "Here in sight of gods and men, I judge you guilty of murder and high treason. In mine own name I condemn you. With mine own hand I take your life. Would you speak a final word?"

"Kill me, and be cursed. You are no king of mine."

The axe crashed down. Heavy and well-honed, it killed at a single blow, but it took three to sever the man's head from his body, and by the time it was done both living and dead were drenched in blood. Robb flung the poleaxe down in disgust, and turned wordless to the heart tree. He stood shaking with his hands half-clenched and the rain running down his cheeks. *Gods forgive him*, Catelyn prayed in silence. *He is only a boy, and he had no other choice.*

That was the last she saw of her son that day. The rain continued all through the morning, lashing the surface of the rivers and turning the godswood grass into mud and puddles. The Blackfish assembled a hundred men and rode out after Karstarks, but no one expected he would bring back many. "I only pray I do not need to hang them," he said as he departed. When he was gone, Catelyn retreated to her father's solar, to sit once more beside Lord Hoster's bed.

"It will not be much longer," Maester Vyman warned her, when he came that afternoon. "His last strength is going, though still he tries to fight."

"He was ever a fighter," she said. "A sweet stubborn man."

"Yes," the maester said, "but this battle he cannot win. It is time he lay down his sword and shield. Time to yield."

To yield, she thought, *to make a peace.* Was it her father the maester was speaking of, or her son?

At evenfall, Jeyne Westerling came to see her. The

young queen entered the solar timidly. "Lady Catelyn, I do not mean to disturb you . . ."

"You are most welcome here, Your Grace." Catelyn had been sewing, but she put the needle aside now.

"Please. Call me Jeyne. I don't feel like a Grace."

"You are one, nonetheless. Please, come sit, Your Grace."

"Jeyne." She sat by the hearth and smoothed her skirt out anxiously.

"As you wish. How might I serve you, Jeyne?"

"It's Robb," the girl said. "He's so miserable, so . . . so angry and disconsolate. I don't know what to do."

"It is a hard thing to take a man's life."

"I know. I told him, he should use a headsman. When Lord Tywin sends a man to die, all he does is give the command. It's easier that way, don't you think?"

"Yes," said Catelyn, "but my lord husband taught his sons that killing should never be easy."

"Oh." Queen Jeyne wet her lips. "Robb has not eaten all day. I had Rollam bring him a nice supper, boar's ribs and stewed onions and ale, but he never touched a bite of it. He spent all morning writing a letter and told me not to disturb him, but when the letter was done he burned it. Now he is sitting and looking at maps. I asked him what he was looking for, but he never answered. I don't think he ever heard me. He wouldn't even change out of his clothes. They were damp all day, and bloody. I want to be a good wife to him, I do, but I don't know how to help. To cheer him, or comfort him. I don't know what he *needs*. Please, my lady, you're his mother, tell me what I should do."

Tell me what I should do. Catelyn might have asked the same, if her father had been well enough to ask. But Lord Hoster was gone, or near enough. Her Ned as well. *Bran and Rickon too, and Mother, and Brandon so long ago.* Only Robb remained to her, Robb and the fading hope of her daughters.

"Sometimes," Catelyn said slowly, "the best thing you can do is nothing. When I first came to Winterfell, I was hurt whenever Ned went to the godswood to sit beneath his heart tree. Part of his soul was in that tree, I knew, a part I would never share. Yet without that part, I soon realized, he would not have been Ned. Jeyne, child, you have wed the north, as I did . . . and in the north, the winters will come." She tried to smile. "Be patient. Be understanding. He loves you and he needs you, and he will come back to you soon enough. This very night, perhaps. Be there when he does. That is all I can tell you."

The young queen listened raptly. "I will," she said when Catelyn was done. "I'll be there." She got to her feet. "I should go back. He might have missed me. I'll see. But if he's still at his maps, I'll be patient."

"Do," said Catelyn, but when the girl was at the door, she thought of something else. "Jeyne," she called after, "there's one more thing Robb needs from you, though he may not know it yet himself. A king must have an heir."

The girl smiled at that. "My mother says the same. She makes a posset for me, herbs and milk and ale, to help make me fertile, I drink it every morning. I told Robb I'm sure to give him twins. An Eddard and a Brandon. He liked that, I think. We . . . we try most every day, my lady. Sometimes twice or more." The girl blushed very prettily. "I'll be with child soon, I promise. I pray to our Mother Above, every night."

"Very good. I will add my prayers as well. To the old gods *and the new*."

When the girl had gone, Catelyn turned back to her father and smoothed the thin white hair across his brow. "An Eddard and a Brandon," she sighed softly. "And perhaps in time a Hoster. Would *you* like that?" He did not answer, but she had never expected that he would. As the sound of the rain on the roof mingled with her father's breathing, she thought about Jeyne. The girl did seem to have a good heart, just as Robb had said. *And good hips, which might be more important.*

JAIME

Two days' ride to either side of the kingsroad, they passed through a wide swath of destruction, miles of blackened fields and orchards where the trunks of dead trees jutted into the air like archers' stakes. The bridges were burnt as well, and the streams swollen by autumn rains, so they had to range along the banks in search of fords. The nights were alive with howling of wolves, but they saw no people.

At Maidenpool, Lord Mooton's red salmon still flew above the castle on its hill, but the town walls were deserted, the gates smashed, half the homes and shops burned or plundered. They saw nothing living but a few feral dogs that went slinking away at the sound of their approach. The pool from which the town took its name, where legend said that Florian the Fool had first glimpsed Jonquil bathing with her sisters, was so choked with rotting corpses that the water had turned into a murky grey-green soup.

Jaime took one look and burst into song. *"Six maids there were in a spring-fed pool . . ."*

"What are you *doing*?" Brienne demanded.

"Singing. 'Six Maids in a Pool,' I'm sure you've heard it. And shy little maids they were, too. Rather like you. Though somewhat prettier, I'll warrant."

"Be quiet," the wench said, with a look that suggested

she would love to leave him floating in the pool among the corpses.

"Please, Jaime," pleaded cousin Cleos. "Lord Mooton is sworn to Riverrun, we don't want to draw him out of his castle. And there may be other enemies hiding in the rubble . . ."

"Hers or ours? They are not the same, coz. I have a yen to see if the wench can use that sword she wears."

"If you won't be quiet, you leave me no choice but to gag you, Kingslayer."

"Unchain my hands and I'll play mute all the way to King's Landing. What could be fairer than that, wench?"

"*Brienne!* My name is *Brienne!*" Three crows went flapping into the air, startled at the sound.

"Care for a bath, Brienne?" He laughed. "You're a maiden and there's the pool. I'll wash your back." He used to scrub Cersei's back, when they were children together at Casterly Rock.

The wench turned her horse's head and trotted away. Jaime and Ser Cleos followed her out of the ashes of Maidenpool. A half mile on, green began to creep back into the world once more. Jaime was glad. The burned lands reminded him too much of Aerys.

"She's taking the Duskendale road," Ser Cleos muttered. "It would be safer to follow the coast."

"Safer but slower. I'm for Duskendale, coz. If truth be told, I'm bored with your company." *You may be half Lannister, but you're a far cry from my sister.*

He could never bear to be long apart from his twin. Even as children, they would creep into each other's beds and sleep with their arms entwined. *Even in the womb.* Long before his sister's flowering or the advent of his own manhood, they had seen mares and stallions in the fields and dogs and bitches in the kennels and played at doing the same. Once their mother's maid had caught them at it . . . he did not recall just what they had been doing, but whatever it was had horrified Lady Joanna. She'd sent the maid away, moved Jaime's bedchamber to the other side of Casterly Rock, set a guard outside Cersei's, and told them that they must *never* do that again or she would have no choice but to tell their lord father. They need not have feared, though. It was not long after that she died birthing Tyrion. Jaime barely remembered what his mother had looked like.

Perhaps Stannis Baratheon and the Starks had done him a kindness. They had spread their tale of incest all over the Seven Kingdoms, so there was nothing left to hide. *Why shouldn't I marry Cersei openly and share her bed every night? The dragons always married their sisters.* Septons, lords, and smallfolk had turned a blind eye to the Targaryens for hundreds of years, let them do the same for House Lannister. It would play havoc with Joffrey's claim to the crown, to be sure, but in the end it had been swords that had won the Iron Throne for Robert, and swords could keep Joffrey there as well, regardless of whose seed he was. *We could marry him to Myrcella, once we've sent Sansa Stark back to her mother. That would show the realm that the Lannisters are above their laws, like gods and Targaryens.*

Jaime had decided that he *would* return Sansa, and the younger girl as well if she could be found. It was not like to win him back his lost honor, but the notion of keeping faith when they all expected betrayal amused him more than he could say.

They were riding past a trampled wheatfield and a low stone wall when Jaime heard a soft *thrum* from behind, as if a dozen birds had taken flight at once. *"Down!"* he shouted, throwing himself against the neck of his horse. The gelding screamed and reared as an arrow took him in the rump. Other shafts went hissing past. Jaime saw Ser Cleos lurch from the saddle, twisting as his foot caught in the stirrup. His palfrey bolted, and Frey was dragged past shouting, head bouncing against the ground.

Jaime's gelding lumbered off ponderously, blowing and snorting in pain. He craned around to look for Brienne. She was still ahorse, an arrow lodged in her back and another in her leg, but she seemed not to feel them. He saw her pull her sword and wheel in a circle, searching for the bowmen. *"Behind the wall,"* Jaime called, fighting to turn his half-blind mount back toward the fight. The reins were tangled in his damned chains, and the air was full of arrows again. "*At them!*" he shouted, kicking to show her how it was done. The old sorry horse found a burst of speed from somewhere. Suddenly they were racing across the wheatfield, throwing up clouds of chaff. Jaime had just enough time to think, *The wench had better follow before they realize they're being charged by an unarmed man in chains.* Then he heard her coming hard behind. "Evenfall!" she shouted as her plow horse thundered by. She brandished her longsword. "Tarth! Tarth!"

A few last arrows sped harmlessly past; then the bowmen broke and ran, the way unsupported bowmen always broke and ran before the charge of knights. Brienne reined up at the wall. By the time Jaime reached her, they had all melted into the wood twenty yards away. "Lost your taste for battle?"

"They were running."

"That's the best time to kill them."

She sheathed her sword. "Why did you charge?"

"Bowmen are fearless so long as they can hide behind walls and shoot at you from afar, but if you come at them, they run. They know what will happen when you reach them. You have an arrow in your back, you know. And another in your leg. You ought to let me tend them."

"You?"

"Who else? The last I saw of cousin Cleos, his palfrey was using his head to plow a furrow. Though I suppose we ought to find him. He *is* a Lannister of sorts."

They found Cleos still tangled in his stirrup. He had an arrow through his right arm and a second in his chest, but it was the ground that had done for him. The top of his head was matted with blood and mushy to the touch, pieces of broken bone moving under the skin beneath the pressure of Jaime's hand.

Brienne knelt and held his hand. "He's still warm."

"He'll cool soon enough. I want his horse and his clothes. I'm weary of rags and fleas."

"He was your cousin." The wench was shocked.

"*Was*," Jaime agreed. "Have no fear, I am amply provisioned in cousins. I'll have his sword as well. You need someone to share the watches."

"You can stand a watch without weapons." She rose.

"Chained to a tree? Perhaps I could. Or perhaps I could make my own bargain with the next lot of outlaws and let them slit that thick neck of yours, wench."

"I will not arm you. And my name is – "

" – Brienne, I know. I'll swear an oath not to harm you, if that will ease your girlish fears."

"Your oaths are worthless. You swore an oath to Aerys."

"You haven't cooked anyone in their armor so far as I know. And we both want me safe and whole in King's Landing, don't we?" He squatted beside Cleos and began to undo his swordbelt.

"Step away from him. Now. Stop that."

Jaime was tired. Tired of her suspicions, tired of her insults, tired of her crooked teeth and her broad spotty face and that limp thin hair of hers. Ignoring her protests, he grasped the hilt of his cousin's longsword with both hands, held the corpse down with his foot, and pulled. As the blade slid from the scabbard, he was already pivoting, bringing the sword around and up in a swift deadly arc. Steel met steel with a ringing, bone-jarring *clang*. Somehow Brienne had gotten her own blade out in time. Jaime laughed. "Very good, wench."

"Give me the sword, Kingslayer."

"Oh, I will." He sprang to his feet and drove at her, the longsword alive in his hands. Brienne jumped back, parrying, but he followed, pressing the attack. No sooner did she turn one cut than the next was upon her. The swords kissed and sprang apart and kissed again. Jaime's blood was singing. This was what he was meant for; he never felt so alive as when he was fighting, with death balanced on every stroke. *And with my wrists chained together, the wench may even give me a contest for a time.* His chains forced him to use a two-handed grip, though of course the weight and reach were less than if the blade had been a true two-handed greatsword, but what did it matter? His cousin's sword was long enough to write an end to this Brienne of Tarth.

High, low, overhand, he rained down steel upon her. Left, right, backslash, swinging so hard that sparks flew when the swords came together, upswing, sideslash, overhand, always attacking, moving into her, step and slide, strike and step, step and strike, hacking, slashing, faster, faster, faster . . .

. . . until, breathless, he stepped back and let the point of the sword fall to the ground, giving her a moment of respite. "Not half bad," he acknowledged. "For a wench."

She took a slow deep breath, her eyes watching him warily. "I would not hurt you, Kingslayer."

"As if you could." He whirled the blade back up above his head and flew at her again, chains rattling.

Jaime could not have said how long he pressed the attack. It might have been minutes or it might have been hours; time slept when swords woke. He drove her away from his cousin's corpse, drove her across the road, drove her into the trees. She stumbled once on a root she never saw, and for a moment he thought she was done, but she went to one knee instead of falling, and never lost a beat. Her sword leapt up to block a downcut that would have opened her from shoulder to groin, and then she cut at *him*, again and again, fighting her way back to her feet stroke by stroke.

The dance went on. He pinned her against an oak, cursed as she slipped away, followed her through a shallow brook half-choked with fallen leaves. Steel rang, steel sang, steel screamed and sparked and scraped, and the woman started grunting like a sow at every crash, yet somehow he could not reach her. It was as if she had an iron cage around her that stopped every blow.

"Not bad at all," he said when he paused for a second to catch his breath, circling to her right.

"For a wench?"

"For a squire, say. A green one." He laughed a ragged, breathless laugh. "Come on, come on, my sweetling, the music's still playing. Might I have this dance, my lady?"

Grunting, she came at him, blade whirling, and suddenly it was Jaime struggling to keep steel from skin. One of her slashes raked across his brow, and blood ran down into his right eye. *The Others take her, and Riverrun as well!* His skills had gone to rust and rot in that bloody dungeon, and the chains were no great help either. His eye closed, his shoulders were going numb from the jarring they'd taken, and his wrists ached from the weight of chains, manacles, and sword. His longsword grew heavier with every blow, and Jaime knew he was not swinging it as quickly as he'd done earlier, nor raising it as high.

She is stronger than I am.

The realization chilled him. Robert had been stronger than him, to be sure. The White Bull Gerold Hightower as well, in his heyday, and Ser Arthur Dayne. Amongst the living, Greatjon Umber was stronger, Strongboar of Crakehall most likely, both Cleganes for a certainty. The Mountain's strength was like nothing human. It did not matter. With speed and skill, Jaime could beat them all. But this was a *woman.* A huge cow of a woman, to be sure, but even so . . . by rights, she should be the one wearing down.

Instead she forced him back into the brook again, shouting, "Yield! Throw down the sword!"

A slick stone turned under Jaime's foot. As he felt himself falling, he twisted the mischance into a diving lunge. His point scraped past her parry and bit into her upper thigh. A red flower blossomed, and Jaime had an instant to savor the sight of her blood before his knee slammed into a rock. The pain was blinding. Brienne splashed into him and kicked away his sword. *"YIELD!"*

Jaime drove his shoulder into her legs, bringing her down on top of him. They rolled, kicking and punching until finally she was sitting astride him. He managed to jerk her dagger from its sheath, but before he could plunge it into her belly she caught his wrist and slammed his hands back on a rock so hard he thought she'd wrenched an arm from its socket. Her other hand spread across his face. "Yield!" She shoved his head down, held it under, pulled it up. *"Yield!"* Jaime spit water into her face. A shove, a splash, and he was under again, kicking uselessly, fighting to breathe. Up again. *"Yield, or I'll drown you!"*

"And break your oath?" he snarled. "Like me?"

She let him go, and he went down with a splash.

And the woods rang with coarse laughter.

Brienne lurched to her feet. She was all mud and blood below the waist, her clothing askew, her face red. *She looks as if they caught us fucking instead of fighting.* Jaime crawled over the rocks to shallow water, wiping the blood from his eye with his chained hands. Armed men lined both sides of the brook. *Small wonder, we were making enough noise to wake a dragon.* "Well met, friends," he called to them amiably. "My pardons if I disturbed you. You caught me chastising my wife."

"Seemed to me she was doing the *chastising.*" The man who spoke was thick and powerful, and the nasal bar of his iron halfhelm did not wholly conceal his lack of a nose.

These were not the outlaws who had killed Ser Cleos, Jaime realized suddenly. The scum of the earth surrounded them: swarthy Dornishmen and blond Lyseni, Dothraki with bells in their braids, hairy Ibbenese, coal-black Summer Islanders in feathered cloaks. He knew them. *The Brave Companions.*

Brienne found her voice. "I have a hundred stags –"

A cadaverous man in a tattered leather cloak said, "We'll take that for a start, m'lady."

"Then we'll have your cunt," said the noseless man. "It can't be as ugly as the rest of you."

"Turn her over and rape her arse, Rorge," urged a Dornish spearman with a red silk scarf wound about his helm. "That way you won't need to look at her."

"And rob her o' the pleasure o' looking at *me?*" noseless said, and the others laughed.

Ugly and stubborn though she might be, the wench deserved better than to be gang raped by such refuse as these. "Who commands here?" Jaime demanded loudly.

"I have that honor, Ser Jaime." The cadaver's eyes were rimmed in red, his hair thin and dry. Dark blue veins could be seen through the pallid skin of his hands and face. "Urswyck I am. Called Urswyck the Faithful."

"You know who I am?"

The sellsword inclined his head. "It takes more than a beard and a shaved head to deceive the Brave Companions."

The Bloody Mummers, you mean. Jaime had no more use for these than he did for Gregor Clegane or Amory Lorch. *Dogs*, his father called them all, and he used them like dogs, to hound his prey and put fear in their hearts. "If you know me, Urswyck, you know you'll have your reward. A Lannister always pays his debts. As for the wench, she's highborn, and worth a good ransom."

The other cocked his head. "Is it so? How fortunate."

There was something sly about the way Urswyck was smiling that Jaime did not like. "You heard me. Where's the goat?"

"A few hours distant. He will be pleased to see you, I have no doubt, but I would not call him a goat to his face. *Lord* Vargo grows prickly about his dignity."

Since when has that slobbering savage had dignity? "I'll be sure and remember that, when I see him. Lord of what, pray?"

"Harrenhal. It has been promised."

Harrenhal? Has my father taken leave of his senses? Jaime raised his hands. "I'll have these chains off."

Urswyck's chuckle was papery dry.

Something is very wrong here. Jaime gave no sign of his discomfiture, but only smiled. "Did I say something amusing?"

Noseless grinned. "You're the funniest thing I seen since Biter chewed that septa's teats off."

"You and your father lost too many battles," offered the Dornishman. "We had to trade our lion pelts for wolfskins."

Urswyck spread his hands. "What Timeon means to say is that the Brave Companions are no longer in the hire of House Lannister. We now serve Lord Bolton, and the King in the North."

Jaime gave him a cold, contemptuous smile. "And men say *I* have shit for honor?"

Urswyck was unhappy with that comment. At his signal, two of the Mummers grasped Jaime by the arms and Rorge drove a mailed fist into his stomach. As he doubled over grunting, he heard the wench protesting, "Stop, he's not to be harmed! Lady Catelyn sent us, an exchange of captives, he's under my protection . . ." Rorge hit him again, driving the air from his lungs. Brienne dove for her sword beneath the waters of the brook, but the Mummers were on her before she could lay hands on it. Strong as she was, it took four of them to beat her into submission.

By the end the wench's face was as swollen and bloody as Jaime's must have been, and they had knocked out two of her teeth. It did nothing to improve her appearance. Stumbling and bleeding, the two captives were dragged back through the woods to the horses, Brienne limping from the thigh wound he'd given her in the brook. Jaime felt sorry for her. She would lose her maidenhood tonight, he had no doubt. That noseless bastard would have her for a certainty, and some of the others would likely take a turn.

The Dornishman bound them back to back atop Brienne's plow horse while the other Mummers were stripping Cleos Frey to his skin to divvy up his possessions. Rorge won the bloodstained surcoat with its proud Lannister and Frey quarterings. The arrows had punched holes through lions and towers alike.

"I hope you're pleased, wench," Jaime whispered at Brienne. He coughed, and spat out a mouthful of blood. "If you'd armed me, we'd never have been taken." She made no answer. *There's a pig-stubborn bitch*, he thought. *But brave, yes.* He could not take that from her. "When we make camp for the night, you'll be raped, and more than once," he warned her. "You'd be wise not to resist. If you fight them, you'll lose more than a few teeth."

He felt Brienne's back stiffen against his. "Is that what *you* would do, if you were a woman?"

If I were a woman I'd be Cersei. "If I were a woman, I'd make them kill me. But I'm not." Jaime kicked their horse to a trot. "*Urswyck!* A word!"

The cadaverous sellsword in the ragged leather cloak

reined up a moment, then fell in beside him. "What would you have of me, ser? And mind your tongue, or I'll chastise you again."

"Gold," said Jaime. "You do like gold?"

Urswyck studied him through reddened eyes. "It has its uses, I do confess."

Jaime gave Urswyck a knowing smile. "All the gold in Casterly Rock. Why let the goat enjoy it? Why not take us to King's Landing, and collect my ransom for yourself? Hers as well, if you like. Tarth is called the Sapphire Isle, a maiden told me once." The wench squirmed at that, but said nothing.

"Do you take me for a turncloak?"

"Certainly. What else?"

For half a heartbeat Urswyck considered the proposition. "King's Landing is a long way, and your father is there. Lord Tywin may resent us for selling Harrenhal to Lord Bolton."

He's cleverer than he looks. Jaime had been been looking forward to hanging the wretch while his pockets bulged with gold. "Leave me to deal with my father. I'll get you a royal pardon for any crimes you have committed. I'll get you a knighthood."

"Ser Urswyck," the man said, savoring the sound. "How proud my dear wife would be to hear it. If only I hadn't killed her." He sighed. "And what of brave Lord Vargo?"

"Shall I sing you a verse of 'The Rains of Castamere'? The goat won't be quite so brave when my father gets hold of him."

"And how will he do that? Are your father's arms so long that they can reach over the walls of Harrenhal and pluck us out?"

"If need be." King Harren's monstrous folly had fallen before, and it could fall again. "Are you such a fool as to think the goat can outfight the lion?"

Urswyck leaned over and slapped him lazily across the face. The sheer casual *insolence* of it was worse than the blow itself. *He does not fear me*, Jaime realized, with a chill. "I have heard enough, Kingslayer. I would have to be a great fool indeed to believe the promises of an oathbreaker like you." He kicked his horse and galloped smartly ahead.

Aerys, Jaime thought resentfully. *It always turns on Aerys.* He swayed with the motion of his horse, wishing for a sword. *Two swords would be even better. One for the wench and one for me. We'd die, but we'd take half of them down to hell with us.* "Why did you tell him Tarth was the Sapphire Isle?" Brienne whispered when Urswyck was out of earshot. "He's like to think my father's rich in gemstones . . ."

"You best pray he does."

"Is every word you say a lie, Kingslayer? Tarth is called the Sapphire Isle for the blue of its waters."

"Shout it a little louder, wench, I don't think Urswyck heard you. The sooner they know how little you're worth in ransom, the sooner the rapes begin. Every man here will mount you, but what do you care? Just close your eyes, open your legs, and pretend they're all Lord Renly."

Mercifully, that shut her mouth for a time.

The day was almost done by the time they found Vargo Hoat, sacking a small sept with another dozen of his Brave Companions. The leaded windows had been smashed, the carved wooden gods dragged out into the sunlight. The fattest Dothraki Jaime had ever seen was sitting on the Mother's chest when they rode up, prying out her chalcedony eyes with the point of his knife. Nearby, a skinny balding septon hung upside down from the limb of a spreading chestnut tree. Three of the Brave Companions were using his corpse for an archery butt. One of them must have been good; the dead man had arrows through both of his eyes.

When the sellswords spied Urswyck and the captives, a cry went up in half a dozen tongues. The goat was seated by a cookfire eating a half-cooked bird off a skewer, grease and blood running down his fingers into his long stringy beard. He wiped his hands on his tunic and rose. "*Kingthlayer*," he slobbered. "You are my captifth."

"My lord, I am Brienne of Tarth," the wench called

out. "Lady Catelyn Stark commanded me to deliver Ser Jaime to his brother at King's Landing."

The goat gave her an uninterested glance. "Thilence her."

"Hear me," Brienne entreated as Rorge cut the ropes that bound her to Jaime, "in the name of the King in the North, the king you serve, please, listen – "

Rorge dragged her off the horse and began to kick her. "See that you don't break any bones," Urswyck called out to him. "The horse-faced bitch is worth her weight in sapphires."

The Dornishman Timeon and a foul-smelling Ibbenese pulled Jaime down from the saddle and shoved him roughly toward the cookfire. It would not have been hard for him to have grasped one of their sword hilts as they manhandled him, but there were too many, and he was still in fetters. He might cut down one or two, but in the end he would die for it. Jaime was not ready to die just yet, and certainly not for the likes of Brienne of Tarth.

"Thith ith a thweet day," Vargo Hoat said. Around his neck hung a chain of linked coins, coins of every shape and size, cast and hammered, bearing the likenesses of kings, wizards, gods and demons, and all manner of fanciful beasts.

Coins from every land where he has fought, Jaime remembered. Greed was the key to this man. *If he was turned once, he can be turned again.* "Lord Vargo, you were foolish to leave my father's service, but it is not too late to make amends. He will pay well for me, you know it."

"Oh yeth," said Vargo Hoat. "Half the gold in Cathterly Rock, I thall have. But firth I mutht thend him a methage." He said something in his slithery goatish tongue.

Urswyck shoved him in the back, and a jester in green and pink motley kicked his legs out from under him. When he hit the ground one of the archers grabbed the chain between Jaime's wrists and used it to yank his arms out in front of him. The fat Dothraki put aside his knife to unsheathe a huge curved *arakh*, the wickedly sharp scythe-sword the horselords loved.

They mean to scare me. The fool hopped on Jaime's back, giggling, as the Dothraki swaggered toward him. *The goat wants me to piss my breeches and beg his mercy, but he'll never have that pleasure.* He was a Lannister of Casterly Rock, Lord Commander of the Kingsguard; no sellsword would make him scream.

Sunlight ran silver along the edge of the *arakh* as it came shivering down, almost too fast to see. And Jaime screamed.

ARYA

The small square keep was half a ruin, and so too the great grey knight who lived there. He was so old he did not understand their questions. No matter what was said to him, he would only smile and mutter, "I held the bridge against Ser Maynard. Red hair and a black temper, he had, but he could not move me. Six wounds I took before I killed him. Six!"

The maester who cared for him was a young man, thankfully. After the old knight had drifted to sleep in his chair, he took them aside and said, "I fear you seek a ghost. We had a bird, ages ago, half a year at least. The Lannisters caught Lord Beric near the Gods Eye. He was hanged."

"Aye, hanged he was, but Thoros cut him down before he died." Lem's broken nose was not so red or swollen as it had been, but it was healing crooked, giving his face a lopsided look. "His lordship's a hard man to kill, he is."

"And a hard man to find, it would seem," the maester said. "Have you asked the Lady of the Leaves?"

"We shall," said Greenbeard.

The next morning, as they crossed the little stone bridge behind the keep, Gendry wondered if this was the bridge the old man had fought over. No one knew. "Most like it is," said Jack-Be-Lucky. "Don't see no other bridges."

"You'd know for certain if there was a song," said Tom

Sevenstrings. "One good song, and we'd know who Ser Maynard used to be and why he wanted to cross this bridge so bad. Poor old Lychester might be as far famed as the Dragonknight if he'd only had sense enough to keep a singer."

"Lord Lychester's sons died in Robert's Rebellion," grumbled Lem. "Some on one side, some on t'other. He's not been right in the head since. No bloody song's like to help any o' that."

"What did the maester mean, about asking the Lady of the Leaves?" Arya asked Anguy as they rode.

The archer smiled. "Wait and see."

Three days later, as they rode through a yellow wood, Jack-Be-Lucky unslung his horn and blew a signal, a different one than before. The sounds had scarcely died away when rope ladders unrolled from the limbs of trees. "Hobble the horses and up we go," said Tom, half singing the words. They climbed to a hidden village in the upper branches, a maze of rope walkways and little moss-covered houses concealed behind walls of red and gold, and were taken to the Lady of the Leaves, a stick-thin white-haired woman dressed in roughspun. "We cannot stay here much longer, with autumn on us," she told them. "A dozen wolves went down the Hayford road nine days past, hunting. If they'd chanced to look up they might have seen us."

"You've not seen Lord Beric?" asked Tom Sevenstrings.

"He's dead." The woman sounded sick. "The Mountain caught him, and drove a dagger through his eye. A begging brother told us. He had it from the lips of a man who saw it happen."

"That's an old stale tale, and false," said Lem. "The lightning lord's not so easy to kill. Ser Gregor might have put his eye out, but a man don't die o' that. Jack could tell you."

"Well, I never did," said one-eyed Jack-Be-Lucky. "My father got himself good and hanged by Lord Piper's bailiff, my brother Wat got sent to the Wall, and the Lannisters killed my other brothers. An eye, that's nothing."

"You swear he's not dead?" The woman clutched Lem's

arm. "Bless you, Lem, that's the best tidings we've had in half a year. May the Warrior defend him, and the red priest too."

The next night they found shelter beneath the scorched shell of a sept, in a burned village called Sallydance. Only shards remained of its windows of leaded glass, and the aged septon who greeted them said the looters had even made off with the Mother's costly robes, the Crone's gilded lantern, and the silver crown the Father had worn. "They hacked the Maiden's breasts off too, though those were only wood," he told them. "And the eyes, the eyes were jet and lapis and mother-of-pearl, they pried them out with their knives. May the Mother have mercy on them all."

"Whose work was this?" said Lem Lemoncloak. "Mummers?"

"No," the old man said. "Northmen, they were. Savages who worship trees. They wanted the Kingslayer, they said."

Arya heard him, and chewed her lip. She could feel Gendry looking at her. It made her angry and ashamed.

There were a dozen men living in the vault beneath the sept, amongst cobwebs and roots and broken wine casks, but they had no word of Beric Dondarrion either. Not even their leader, who wore soot-blackened armor and a crude lightning bolt on his cloak. When Greenbeard saw Arya staring at him, he laughed and said, "The lightning lord is everywhere and nowhere, skinny squirrel."

"I'm not a squirrel," she said. "I'll almost be a woman soon. I'll be one-and-ten."

"Best watch out I don't marry you, then!" He tried to tickle her under the chin, but Arya slapped his stupid hand away.

Lem and Gendry played tiles with their hosts that night, while Tom Sevenstrings sang a silly song about Big Belly Ben and the High Septon's goose. Anguy let Arya try his longbow, but no matter how hard she bit her lip she could not draw it. "You need a lighter bow, milady," the freckled bowman said. "If there's seasoned wood at Riverrun, might be I'll make you one."

Tom overheard him, and broke off his song. "You're a young fool, Archer. If we go to Riverrun it will only be to collect her ransom, won't be no time for you to sit about making bows. Be thankful if you get out with your hide. Lord Hoster was hanging outlaws before you were shaving. And that son of his . . . a man who hates music can't be trusted, I always say."

"It's not music he hates," said Lem. "It's you, fool."

"Well, he has no cause. The wench was willing to make a man of him, is it my fault he drank too much to do the deed?"

Lem snorted through his broken nose. "Was it you who made a song of it, or some other bloody arse in love with his own voice?"

"I only sang it the once," Tom complained. "And who's to say the song was about him? 'Twas a song about a fish."

"A floppy fish," said Anguy, laughing.

Arya didn't care what Tom's stupid songs were about. She turned to Harwin. "What did he mean about ransom?"

"We have sore need of horses, milady. Armor as well. Swords, shields, spears. All the things coin can buy. Aye, and seed for planting. Winter is coming, remember?" He touched her under the chin. "You will not be the first highborn captive we've ransomed. Nor the last, I'd hope."

That much was true, Arya knew. Knights were captured and ransomed all the time, and sometimes women were too. *But what if Robb won't pay their price?* She wasn't a famous knight, and kings were supposed to put the realm before their sisters. And her lady mother, what would she say? Would she still want her back, after all the things she'd done? Arya chewed her lip and wondered.

The next day they rode to a place called High Heart, a hill so lofty that from atop it Arya felt as though she could see half the world. Around its brow stood a ring of huge pale stumps, all that remained of a circle of once-mighty weirwoods. Arya and Gendry walked around the hill to count them. There were thirty-one, some so wide that she could have used them for a bed.

High Heart had been sacred to the children of the forest, Tom Sevenstrings told her, and some of their magic lingered here still. "No harm can ever come to those as sleep here," the singer said. Arya thought that must be true; the hill was so high and the surrounding lands so flat that no enemy could approach unseen.

The smallfolk hereabouts shunned the place, Tom told her; it was said to be haunted by the ghosts of the children of the forest who had died here when the Andal king named Erreg the Kinslayer had cut down their grove. Arya knew about the children of the forest, and about the Andals too, but ghosts did not frighten her. She used to hide in the crypts of Winterfell when she was little, and play games of come-into-my-castle and monsters and maidens amongst the stone kings on their thrones.

Yet even so, the hair on the back of her neck stood up that night. She had been asleep, but the storm woke her. The wind pulled the coverlet right off her and sent it swirling into the bushes. When she went after it she heard voices.

Beside the embers of their campfire, she saw Tom, Lem, and Greenbeard talking to a tiny little woman, a foot shorter than Arya and older than Old Nan, all stooped and wrinkled and leaning on a gnarled black cane. Her white hair was so long it came almost to the ground. When the wind gusted it blew about her head in a fine cloud. Her flesh was whiter, the color of milk, and it seemed to Arya that her eyes were red, though it was hard to tell from the bushes. "The old gods stir and will not let me sleep," she heard the woman say. "I dreamt I saw a shadow with a burning heart butchering a golden stag, aye. I dreamt of a man without a face, waiting on a bridge that swayed and swung. On his shoulder perched a drowned crow with seaweed hanging from his wings. I dreamt of a roaring river and a woman that was a fish. Dead she drifted, with red tears on her cheeks, but when her eyes did open, *oh*, I woke from terror. All this I dreamt, and more. Do you have gifts for me, to pay me for my dreams?"

"Dreams," grumbled Lem Lemoncloak, "what good are dreams? Fish women and drowned crows. I had a dream myself last night. I was kissing this tavern wench I used to know. Are you going to pay me for that, old woman?"

"The wench is dead," the woman hissed. "Only worms may kiss her now." And then to Tom Sevenstrings she said, "I'll have my song or I'll have you gone."

So the singer played for her, so soft and sad that Arya only heard snatches of the words, though the tune was half-familiar. *Sansa would know it, I bet.* Her sister had known all the songs, and she could even play a little, and sing so sweetly. *All I could ever do was shout the words.*

The next morning the little white woman was nowhere to be seen. As they saddled their horses, Arya asked Tom Sevenstrings if the children of the forest still dwelled on High Heart. The singer chuckled. "Saw her, did you?"

"Was she a ghost?"

"Do ghosts complain of how their joints creak? No, she's only an old dwarf woman. A queer one, though, and evil-eyed. But she knows things she has no business knowing, and sometimes she'll tell you if she likes the look of you."

"Did she like the look of *you?*" Arya asked doubtfully.

The singer laughed. "The sound of me, at least. She always makes me sing the same bloody song, though. Not a bad song, mind you, but I know others just as good." He shook his head. "What matters is, we have the scent now. You'll soon be seeing Thoros and the lightning lord, I'll wager."

"If you're their men, why do they hide from you?"

Tom Sevenstrings rolled his eyes at that, but Harwin gave her an answer. "I wouldn't call it hiding, milady, but it's true, Lord Beric moves about a lot, and seldom lets on what his plans are. That way no one can betray him. By now there must be hundreds of us sworn to him, maybe thousands, but it wouldn't do for us all to trail along behind him. We'd eat the country bare, or get butchered in a battle by some bigger host. The way we're scattered in little bands, we can strike in a dozen places at once, and be off somewhere else before they know. And when one of us is caught and put to the question, well, we can't tell them where to find Lord Beric no matter what they do to us." He hesitated. "You know what it means, to be put to the question?"

Arya nodded. "Tickling, they called it. Polliver and Raff and all." She told them about the village by the Gods Eye where she and Gendry had been caught, and the questions that the Tickler had asked. "Is there gold hidden in the village?" he would always begin. "Silver, gems? Is there food? Where is Lord Beric? Which of you village folk helped him? Where did he go? How many men did he have with him? How many knights? How many bowmen? How many were horsed? How are they armed? How many wounded? Where did they go, did you say?" Just thinking of it, she could hear the shrieks again, and smell the stench of blood and shit and burning flesh. "He always asked the same questions," she told the outlaws solemnly, "but he changed the tickling every day."

"No child should be made to suffer that," Harwin said when she was done. "The Mountain lost half his men at the Stone Mill, we hear. Might be this Tickler's floating down the Red Fork even now, with fish biting at his face. If not, well, it's one more crime they'll answer for. I've heard his lordship say this war began when the Hand sent him out to bring the king's justice to Gregor Clegane, and that's how he means for it to end." He gave her shoulder a reassuring pat. "You best mount up, milady. It's a long day's ride to Acorn Hall, but at the end of it we'll have a roof above our heads and a hot supper in our bellies."

It *was* a long day's ride, but as dusk was settling they forded a brook and came up on Acorn Hall, with its stone curtain walls and great oaken keep. Its master was away fighting in the retinue of *his* master, Lord Vance, the castle gates closed and barred in his absence. But his lady wife was an old friend of Tom Sevenstrings, and Anguy said they'd once been lovers. Anguy often rode beside her; he was closer to her in age than any of them but Gendry, and he told her droll tales of the Dornish Marches. He never fooled her, though. *He's not my friend. He's only staying close to watch me and make sure I don't ride off again.* Well, Arya could watch as well. Syrio Forel had taught her how.

Lady Smallwood welcomed the outlaws kindly enough, though she gave them a tongue lashing for dragging a young girl through the war. She became even more wroth when Lem let slip that Arya was highborn. "Who dressed the poor child in those Bolton rags?" she demanded of them. "That badge ... there's many a man who would hang her in half a heartbeat for wearing a flayed man on her breast." Arya promptly found herself marched upstairs, forced into a tub, and doused with scalding hot water. Lady Smallwood's maidservants scrubbed her so hard it felt like they were flaying her themselves. They even dumped in some stinky-sweet stuff that smelled like flowers.

And afterward, they insisted she dress herself in girl's things, brown woolen stockings and a light linen shift, and over that a light green gown with acorns embroidered all over the bodice in brown thread, and more acorns bordering the hem. "My great-aunt is a septa at a motherhouse in Oldtown," Lady Smallwood said as the women laced the gown up Arya's back. "I sent my daughter there when the war began. She'll have outgrown these things by the time she returns, no doubt. Are you fond of dancing, child? My Carellen's a lovely dancer. She sings beautifully as well. What do you like to do?"

She scuffed a toe amongst the rushes. "Needlework."

"Very restful, isn't it?"

"Well," said Arya, "not the way I do it."

"No? I have always found it so. The gods give each of us our little gifts and talents, and it is meant for us to use them, my aunt always says. Any act can be a prayer, if done as well as we are able. Isn't that a lovely thought? Remember that the next time you do your needlework. Do you work at it every day?"

"I did till I lost Needle. My new one's not as good."

"In times like these, we all must make do as best we can." Lady Smallwood fussed at the bodice of the gown. "Now you look a proper young lady."

I'm not a lady, Arya wanted to tell her, *I'm a wolf*.

"I do not know who you are, child," the woman said, "and it may be that's for the best. Someone important, I fear." She smoothed down Arya's collar. "In times like these, it is better to be insignificant. Would that I could keep you here with me. That would not be safe, though. I have walls, but too few men to hold them." She sighed.

Supper was being served in the hall by the time Arya was all washed and combed and dressed. Gendry took one look and laughed so hard that wine came out his nose, until Harwin gave him a *thwack* alongside his ear. The meal was plain but filling; mutton and mushrooms, brown bread, pease pudding, and baked apples with yellow cheese. When the food had been cleared and the servants sent away, Greenbeard lowered his voice to ask if her ladyship had word of the lightning lord.

"Word?" She smiled. "They were here not a fortnight past. Them and a dozen more, driving sheep. I could scarcely believe my eyes. Thoros gave me three as thanks. You've eaten one tonight."

"Thoros herding sheep?" Anguy laughed aloud.

"I grant you it was an odd sight, but Thoros claimed that as a priest he knew how to tend a flock."

"Aye, and shear them too," chuckled Lem Lemoncloak.

"Someone could make a rare fine song of that." Tom plucked a string on his woodharp.

Lady Smallwood gave him a withering look. "Someone who doesn't rhyme *carry on* with *Dondarrion*, perhaps. Or play 'Oh, Lay My Sweet Lass Down in the Grass' to every milkmaid in the shire and leave two of them with big bellies."

"It was 'Let Me Drink Your Beauty,'" said Tom defensively, "and milkmaids are always glad to hear it. As was a certain highborn lady I do recall. I play to please."

Her nostrils flared. "The riverlands are full of maids you've pleased, all drinking tansy tea. You'd think a man as old as you would know to spill his seed on their bellies. Men will be calling you Tom Sevensons before much longer."

"As it happens," said Tom, "I passed seven many years ago. And fine boys they are too, with voices sweet as nightingales." Plainly he did not care for the subject.

"Did his lordship say where he was bound, milady?" asked Harwin.

"Lord Beric never shares his plans, but there's hunger

down near Stoney Sept and the Threepenny Wood. I should look for him there." She took a sip of wine. "You'd best know, I've had less pleasant callers as well. A pack of wolves came howling around my gates, thinking I might have Jaime Lannister in here."

Tom stopped his plucking. "Then it's true, the Kingslayer is loose again?"

Lady Smallwood gave him a scornful look. "I hardly think they'd be hunting him if he was chained up under Riverrun."

"What did m'lady tell them?" asked Jack-Be-Lucky.

"Why, that I had Ser Jaime naked in my bed, but I'd left him much too exhausted to come down. One of them had the effrontery to call me a liar, so we saw them off with a few quarrels. I believe they made for Blackbottom Bend."

Arya squirmed restlessly in her seat. "What northmen was it, who came looking after the Kingslayer?"

Lady Smallwood seemed surprised that she'd spoken. "They did not give their names, child, but they wore black, with the badge of a white sun on the breast."

A white sun on black was the sigil of Lord Karstark, Arya thought. *Those were Robb's men.* She wondered if they were still close. If she could give the outlaws the slip and find them, maybe they would take her to her mother at Riverrun . . .

"Did they say how Lannister came to escape?" Lem asked.

"They did," said Lady Smallwood. "Not that I believe a word of it. They claimed that Lady Catelyn set him free."

That startled Tom so badly he snapped a string. "Go on with you," he said. "That's madness."

It's not true, thought Arya. *It couldn't be true.*

"I thought the same," said Lady Smallwood.

That was when Harwin remembered Arya. "Such talk is not for your ears, milady."

"No, I want to hear."

The outlaws were adamant. "Go on with you, skinny squirrel," said Greenbeard. "Be a good little lady and go play in the yard while we talk, now."

Arya stalked away angry, and would have slammed the door if it hadn't been so heavy. Darkness had settled over Acorn Hall. A few torches burned along the walls, but that was all. The gates of the little castle were closed and barred. She had promised Harwin that she would not try and run away again, she knew, but that was before they started telling lies about her mother.

"Arya?" Gendry had followed her out. "Lady Smallwood said there's a smithy. Want to have a look?"

"If you want." She had nothing else to do.

"This Thoros," Gendry said as they walked past the kennels, "is he the same Thoros who lived in the castle at King's Landing? A red priest, fat, with a shaved head?"

"I think so." Arya had never spoken to Thoros at King's Landing that she could recall, but she knew who he was. He and Jalabhar Xho had been the most colorful figures at Robert's court, and Thoros was a great friend of the king as well.

"He won't remember me, but he used to come to our forge." The Smallwood forge had not been used in some time, though the smith had hung his tools neatly on the wall. Gendry lit a candle and set it on the anvil while he took down a pair of tongs. "My master always scolded him about his flaming swords. It was no way to treat good steel, he'd say, but this Thoros never used good steel. He'd just dip some cheap sword in wildfire and set it alight. It was only an alchemist's trick, my master said, but it scared the horses and some of the greener knights."

She screwed up her face, trying to remember if her father had ever talked about Thoros. "He isn't very priestly, is he?"

"No," Gendry admitted. "Master Mott said Thoros could outdrink even King Robert. They were peas in a pod, he told me, both gluttons and sots."

"You shouldn't call the king a sot." Maybe King Robert had drunk a lot, but he'd been her father's friend.

"I was talking about Thoros." Gendry reached out with the tongs as if to pinch her face, but Arya swatted them away. "He liked feasts and tourneys, that was why King Robert was so fond of him. And this Thoros was brave.

When the walls of Pyke crashed down, he was the first through the breach. He fought with one of his flaming swords, setting ironmen afire with every slash."

"I wish I had a flaming sword." Arya could think of lots of people she'd like to set on fire.

"It's only a trick, I told you. The wildfire ruins the steel. My master sold Thoros a new sword after every tourney. Every time they would have a fight about the price." Gendry hung the tongs back up and took down the heavy hammer. "Master Mott said it was time I made my first longsword. He gave me a sweet piece of steel, and I knew just how I wanted to shape the blade. Only Yoren came, and took me away for the Night's Watch."

"You can still make swords if you want," said Arya. "You can make them for my brother Robb when we get to Riverrun."

"Riverrun." Gendry put the hammer down and looked at her. "You look different now. Like a proper little girl."

"I look like an oak tree, with all these stupid acorns."

"Nice, though. A nice oak tree." He stepped closer, and *sniffed* at her. "You even smell nice for a change."

"You don't. You *stink*." Arya shoved him back against the anvil and made to run, but Gendry caught her arm. She stuck a foot between his legs and tripped him, but he yanked her down with him, and they rolled across the floor of the smithy. He was very strong, but she was quicker. Every time he tried to hold her still she wriggled free and punched him. Gendry only laughed at the blows, which made her mad. He finally caught both her wrists in one hand and started to tickle her with the other, so Arya slammed her knee between his legs, and wrenched free. Both of them were covered in dirt, and one sleeve was torn on her stupid acorn dress. "I bet I don't look so nice *now*," she shouted.

Tom was singing when they returned to the hall.

> *My featherbed is deep and soft,*
> *   and there I'll lay you down,*
> *I'll dress you all in yellow silk,*
> *   and on your head a crown.*

For you shall be my lady love,
            and I shall be your lord.
I'll always keep you warm and safe,
            and guard you with my sword.

Harwin took one look at them and burst out laughing, and Anguy smiled one of his stupid freckly smiles and said, "Are we *certain* this one is a highborn lady?" But Lem Lemoncloak gave Gendry a clout alongside the head. "You want to fight, fight with me! She's a girl, and half your age! You keep your hands off o' her, you hear me?"

"I started it," said Arya. "Gendry was just talking."

"Leave the boy, Lem," said Harwin. "Arya did start it, I have no doubt. She was much the same at Winterfell."

Tom winked at her as he sang:

And how she smiled and how she laughed,
            the maiden of the tree.
She spun away and said to him,
            no featherbed for me.
I'll wear a gown of golden leaves,
            and bind my hair with grass,
But you can be my forest love,
            and me your forest lass.

"I have no gowns of leaves," said Lady Smallwood with a small fond smile, "but Carellen left some other dresses that might serve. Come, child, let us go upstairs and see what we can find."

It was even worse than before; Lady Smallwood insisted that Arya take *another* bath, and cut and comb her hair besides; the dress she put her in this time was sort of lilac-colored, and decorated with little baby pearls. The only good thing about it was that it was so delicate that no one could expect her to ride in it. So the next morning as they broke their fast, Lady Smallwood gave her breeches, belt, and tunic to wear, and a brown doeskin jerkin dotted with iron studs. "They were my son's things," she said. "He died when he was seven."

"I'm sorry, my lady." Arya suddenly felt bad for her,

and ashamed. "I'm sorry I tore the acorn dress too. It was pretty."

"Yes, child. And so are you. Be brave."

DAENERYS

In the center of the Plaza of Pride stood a red brick fountain whose waters smelled of brimstone, and in the center of the fountain a monstrous harpy made of hammered bronze. Twenty feet tall she reared. She had a woman's face, with gilded hair, ivory eyes, and pointed ivory teeth. Water gushed yellow from her heavy breasts. But in place of arms she had the wings of a bat or a dragon, her legs were the legs of an eagle, and behind she wore a scorpion's curled and venomous tail.

The harpy of Ghis, Dany thought. Old Ghis had fallen five thousand years ago, if she remembered true; its legions shattered by the might of young Valyria, its brick walls pulled down, its streets and buildings turned to ash and cinder by dragonflame, its very fields sown with salt, sulfur, and skulls. The gods of Ghis were dead, and so too its people; these Astapori were mongrels, Ser Jorah said. Even the Ghiscari tongue was largely forgotten; the slave cities spoke the High Valyrian of their conquerors, or what they had made of it.

Yet the symbol of the Old Empire still endured here, though this bronze monster had a heavy chain dangling from her talons, an open manacle at either end. *The harpy of Ghis had a thunderbolt in her claws. This is the harpy of Astapor.*

"Tell the Westerosi whore to lower her eyes," the slaver

Kraznys mo Nakloz complained to the slave girl who spoke for him. "I deal in meat, not metal. The bronze is not for sale. Tell her to look at the soldiers. Even the dim purple eyes of a sunset savage can see how magnificent my creatures are, surely."

Kraznys's High Valyrian was twisted and thickened by the characteristic growl of Ghis, and flavored here and there with words of slaver argot. Dany understood him well enough, but she smiled and looked blankly at the slave girl, as if wondering what he might have said.

"The Good Master Kraznys asks, are they not magnificent?" The girl spoke the Common Tongue well, for one who had never been to Westeros. No older than ten, she had the round flat face, dusky skin, and golden eyes of Naath. *The Peaceful People*, her folk were called. All agreed that they made the best slaves.

"They might be adequate to my needs," Dany answered. It had been Ser Jorah's suggestion that she speak only Dothraki and the Common Tongue while in Astapor. *My bear is more clever than he looks.* "Tell me of their training."

"The Westerosi woman is pleased with them, but speaks no praise, to keep the price down," the translator told her master. "She wishes to know how they were trained."

Kraznys mo Nakloz bobbed his head. He smelled as if he'd bathed in raspberries, this slaver, and his jutting red-black beard glistened with oil. *He has larger breasts than I do*, Dany reflected. She could see them through the thin sea-green silk of the gold-fringed *tokar* he wound about his body and over one shoulder. His left hand held the *tokar* in place as he walked, while his right clasped a short leather whip. "Are all Westerosi pigs so ignorant?" he complained. "All the world knows that the Unsullied are masters of spear and shield and shortsword." He gave Dany a broad smile. "Tell her what she would know, slave, and be quick about it. The day is hot."

That much at least is no lie. A matched pair of slave girls stood behind them, holding a striped silk awning over their heads, but even in the shade Dany felt light-headed, and Kraznys was perspiring freely. The Plaza of Pride had been baking in the sun since dawn. Even through the thickness of her sandals, she could feel the warmth of the red bricks underfoot. Waves of heat rose off them shimmering to make the stepped pyramids of Astapor around the plaza seem half a dream.

If the Unsullied felt the heat, however, they gave no hint of it. *They could be made of brick themselves, the way they stand there.* A thousand had been marched out of their barracks for her inspection; drawn up in ten ranks of one hundred before the fountain and its great bronze harpy, they stood stiffly at attention, their stony eyes fixed straight ahead. They wore nought but white linen clouts knotted about their loins, and conical bronze helms topped with a sharpened spike a foot tall. Kraznys had commanded them to lay down their spears and shields, and doff their swordbelts and quilted tunics, so the Queen of Westeros might better inspect the lean hardness of their bodies.

"They are chosen young, for size and speed and strength," the slave told her. "They begin their training at five. Every day they train from dawn to dusk, until they have mastered the shortsword, the shield, and the three spears. The training is most rigorous, Your Grace. Only one boy in three survives it. This is well known. Among the Unsullied it is said that on the day they win their spiked cap, the worst is done with, for no duty that will ever fall to them could be as hard as their training."

Kraznys mo Nakloz supposedly spoke no word of the Common Tongue, but he bobbed his head as he listened, and from time to time gave the slave girl a poke with the end of his lash. "Tell her that these have been standing here for a day and a night, with no food nor water. Tell her that they will stand until they drop if I should command it, and when nine hundred and ninety-nine have collapsed to die upon the bricks, the last will stand there still, and never move until his own death claims him. Such is their courage. Tell her that."

"I call that madness, not courage," said Arstan Whitebeard, when the solemn little scribe was done. He tapped the end of his hardwood staff against the bricks, *tap tap*, as if to tell his displeasure. The old man had not wanted to sail to Astapor; nor did he favor buying this slave army. A queen should hear all sides before reaching a decision. That was why Dany had brought him with her to the Plaza of Pride, not to keep her safe. Her bloodriders would do that well enough. Ser Jorah Mormont she had left aboard *Balerion* to guard her people and her dragons. Much against her inclination, she had locked the dragons belowdecks. It was too dangerous to let them fly freely over the city; the world was all too full of men who would gladly kill them for no better reason than to name themselves *dragonslayer*.

"What did the smelly old man say?" the slaver demanded of his translator. When she told him, he smiled and said, "Inform the savages that we call this *obedience*. Others may be stronger or quicker or larger than the Unsullied. Some few may even equal their skill with sword and spear and shield. But nowhere between the seas will you ever find any more obedient."

"Sheep are obedient," said Arstan when the words had been translated. He had some Valyrian as well, though not so much as Dany, but like her he was feigning ignorance.

Kraznys mo Nakloz showed his big white teeth when that was rendered back to him. "A word from me and these sheep would spill his stinking old bowels on the bricks," he said, "but do not say that. Tell them that these creatures are more dogs than sheep. Do they eat dogs or horse in these Seven Kingdoms?"

"They prefer pigs and cows, your worship."

"Beef. Pfag. Food for unwashed savages."

Ignoring them all, Dany walked slowly down the line of slave soldiers. The girls followed close behind with the silk awning, to keep her in the shade, but the thousand men before her enjoyed no such protection. More than half had the copper skins and almond eyes of Dothraki and Lhazerene, but she saw men of the Free Cities in the ranks as well, along with pale Qartheen, ebon-faced Summer Islanders, and others whose origins she could not guess. And some had skins of the same amber hue as

Kraznys mo Nakloz, and the bristly red-black hair that marked the ancient folk of Ghis, who named themselves the harpy's sons. *They sell even their own kind.* It should not have surprised her. The Dothraki did the same, when *khalasar* met *khalasar* in the sea of grass.

Some of the soldiers were tall and some were short. They ranged in age from fourteen to twenty, she judged. Their cheeks were smooth, and their eyes all the same, be they black or brown or blue or grey or amber. *They are like one man,* Dany thought, until she remembered that they were no men at all. The Unsullied were eunuchs, every one of them. "Why do you cut them?" she asked Kraznys through the slave girl. "Whole men are stronger than eunuchs, I have always heard."

"A eunuch who is cut young will never have the brute strength of one of your Westerosi knights, this is true," said Kraznys mo Nakloz when the question was put to him. "A bull is strong as well, but bulls die every day in the fighting pits. A girl of nine killed one not three days past in Jothiel's Pit. The Unsullied have something better than strength, tell her. They have discipline. We fight in the fashion of the Old Empire, yes. They are the lockstep legions of Old Ghis come again, absolutely obedient, absolutely loyal, and utterly without fear."

Dany listened patiently to the translation.

"Even the bravest men fear death and maiming," Arstan said when the girl was done.

Kraznys smiled again when he heard that. "Tell the old man that he smells of piss, and needs a stick to hold him up."

"Truly, your worship?"

He poked her with his lash. "No, not truly, are you a girl or a goat, to ask such folly? Say that Unsullied are not men. Say that death means nothing to them, and maiming less than nothing." He stopped before a thickset man who had the look of Lhazar about him and brought his whip up sharply, laying a line of blood across one copper cheek. The eunuch blinked, and stood there, bleeding. "Would you like another?" asked Kraznys.

"If it please your worship."

It was hard to pretend not to understand. Dany laid a hand on Kraznys's arm before he could raise the whip again. "Tell the Good Master that I see how strong his Unsullied are, and how bravely they suffer pain."

Kraznys chuckled when he heard her words in Valyrian. "Tell this ignorant whore of a westerner that courage has nothing to do with it."

"The Good Master says that was not courage, Your Grace."

"Tell her to open those slut's eyes of hers."

"He begs you attend this carefully, Your Grace."

Kraznys moved to the next eunuch in line, a towering youth with the blue eyes and flaxen hair of Lys. "Your sword," he said. The eunuch knelt, unsheathed the blade, and offered it up hilt first. It was a shortsword, made more for stabbing than for slashing, but the edge looked razor-sharp. "Stand," Kraznys commanded.

"Your worship." The eunuch stood, and Kraznys mo Nakloz slid the sword slowly up his torso, leaving a thin red line across his belly and between his ribs. Then he jabbed the swordpoint in beneath a wide pink nipple and began to work it back and forth.

"What is he doing?" Dany demanded of the girl, as the blood ran down the man's chest.

"Tell the cow to stop her bleating," said Kraznys, without waiting for the translation. "This will do him no great harm. Men have no need of nipples, eunuchs even less so." The nipple hung by a thread of skin. He slashed, and sent it tumbling to the bricks, leaving behind a round red eye copiously weeping blood. The eunuch did not move, until Kraznys offered him back his sword, hilt first. "Here, I'm done with you."

"This one is pleased to have served you."

Kraznys turned back to Dany. "They feel no pain, you see."

"How can that be?" she demanded through the scribe.

"*The wine of courage*," was the answer he gave her. "It is no true wine at all, but made from deadly nightshade, bloodfly larva, black lotus root, and many secret things. They drink it with every meal from the day they are cut, and with each passing year feel less and less. It makes them fearless in battle. Nor can they be tortured. Tell the savage her secrets are safe with the Unsullied. She may set them to guard her councils and even her bedchamber, and never a worry as to what they might overhear.

"In Yunkai and Meereen, eunuchs are often made by removing a boy's testicles, but leaving the penis. Such a creature is infertile, yet often still capable of erection. Only trouble can come of this. We remove the penis as well, leaving nothing. The Unsullied are the purest creatures on the earth." He gave Dany and Arstan another of his broad white smiles. "I have heard that in the Sunset Kingdoms men take solemn vows to keep chaste and father no children, but live only for their duty. Is it not so?"

"It is," Arstan said, when the question was put. "There are many such orders. The maesters of the Citadel, the septons and septas who serve the Seven, the silent sisters of the dead, the Kingsguard and the Night's Watch . . ."

"Poor things," growled the slaver, after the translation. "Men were not made to live thus. Their days are a torment of temptation, any fool must see, and no doubt most succumb to their baser selves. Not so our Unsullied. They are wed to their swords in a way that your Sworn Brothers cannot hope to match. No woman can ever tempt them, nor any man."

His girl conveyed the essence of his speech, more politely. "There are other ways to tempt men, besides the flesh," Arstan Whitebeard objected, when she was done.

"Men, yes, but not Unsullied. Plunder interests them no more than rape. They own nothing but their weapons. We do not even permit them names."

"No names?" Dany frowned at the little scribe. "Can that be what the Good Master said? They have no names?"

"It is so, Your Grace."

Kraznys stopped in front of a Ghiscari who might have been his taller fitter brother, and flicked his lash at a small bronze disk on the swordbelt at his feet. "There is his name. Ask the whore of Westeros whether she can read Ghiscari glyphs." When Dany admitted that she could not, the slaver turned to the Unsullied. "What is your name?" he demanded.

"This one's name is Red Flea, your worship."

The girl repeated their exchange in the Common Tongue.

"And yesterday, what was it?"

"Black Rat, your worship."

"The day before?"

"Brown Flea, your worship."

"Before that?"

"This one does not recall, your worship. Blue Toad, perhaps. Or Blue Worm."

"Tell her all their names are such," Kraznys commanded the girl. "It reminds them that by themselves they are vermin. The name disks are thrown in an empty cask at duty's end, and each dawn plucked up again at random."

"More madness," said Arstan, when he heard. "How can any man possibly remember a new name every day?"

"Those who cannot are culled in training, along with those who cannot run all day in full pack, scale a mountain in the black of night, walk across a bed of coals, or slay an infant."

Dany's mouth surely twisted at that. *Did he see, or is he blind as well as cruel?* She turned away quickly, trying to keep her face a mask until she heard the translation. Only then did she allow herself to say, "Whose infants do they slay?"

"To win his spiked cap, an Unsullied must go to the slave marts with a silver mark, find some wailing newborn, and kill it before its mother's eyes. In this way, we make certain that there is no weakness left in them."

She was feeling faint. *The heat,* she tried to tell herself. "You take a babe from its mother's arms, kill it as she watches, and pay for her pain with a silver coin?"

When the translation was made for him, Kraznys mo Nakloz laughed aloud. "What a soft mewling fool this one is. Tell the whore of Westeros that the mark is for the child's owner, not the mother. The Unsullied are not permitted to steal." He tapped his whip against his leg. "Tell her that few ever fail that test. The dogs are harder for them, it must be said. We give each boy a puppy on the day that he is cut. At the end of the first year, he is required to strangle it. Any who cannot are killed, and fed to the surviving dogs. It makes for a good strong lesson, we find."

Arstan Whitebeard tapped the end of his staff on the bricks as he listened to that. *Tap tap tap.* Slow and steady. *Tap tap tap.* Dany saw him turn his eyes away, as if he could not bear to look at Kraznys any longer.

"The Good Master has said that these eunuchs cannot be tempted with coin or flesh," Dany told the girl, "but if some enemy of mine should offer them *freedom* for betraying me . . ."

"They would kill him out of hand and bring her his head, tell her that," the slaver answered. "Other slaves may steal and hoard up silver in hopes of buying freedom, but an Unsullied would not take it if the little mare offered it as a gift. They have no life outside their duty. They are *soldiers*, and that is all."

"It is soldiers I need," Dany admitted.

"Tell her it is well she came to Astapor, then. Ask her how large an army she wishes to buy."

"How many Unsullied do you have to sell?"

"Eight thousand fully trained and available at present. We sell them only by the unit, she should know. By the thousand or the century. Once we sold by the ten, as household guards, but that proved unsound. Ten is too few. They mingle with other slaves, even freemen, and forget who and what they are." Kraznys waited for that to be rendered in the Common Tongue, and then continued. "This beggar queen must understand, such wonders do not come cheaply. In Yunkai and Meereen, slave swordsmen can be had for less than the price of their swords, but Unsullied are the finest foot in all the world, and each represents many years of training. Tell her they are like Valyrian steel, folded over and over and hammered for years on end, until they are stronger and more resilient than any metal on earth."

"I know of Valyrian steel," said Dany. "Ask the Good Master if the Unsullied have their own officers."

"You must set your own officers over them. We train them to obey, not to think. If it is wits she wants, let her buy scribes."

"And their gear?"

"Sword, shield, spear, sandals, and quilted tunic are included," said Kraznys. "And the spiked caps, to be sure. They will wear such armor as you wish, but you must provide it."

Dany could think of no other questions. She looked at Arstan. "You have lived long in the world, Whitebeard. Now that you have seen them, what do you say?"

"I say *no*, Your Grace," the old man answered at once.

"Why?" she asked. "Speak freely." Dany thought she knew what he would say, but she wanted the slave girl to hear, so Kraznys mo Nakloz might hear later.

"My queen," said Arstan, "there have been no slaves in the Seven Kingdoms for thousands of years. The old gods and the new alike hold slavery to be an abomination. Evil. If you should land in Westeros at the head of a slave army, many good men will oppose you for no other reason than that. You will do great harm to your cause, and to the honor of your House."

"Yet I must have some army," Dany said. "The boy Joffrey will not give me the Iron Throne for asking politely."

"When the day comes that you raise your banners, half of Westeros will be with you," Whitebeard promised. "Your brother Rhaegar is still remembered, with great love."

"And my father?" Dany said.

The old man hesitated before saying, "King Aerys is also remembered. He gave the realm many years of peace. Your Grace, you have no need of slaves. Magister Illyrio can keep you safe while your dragons grow, and send secret envoys across the narrow sea on your behalf, to sound out the high lords for your cause."

"Those same high lords who abandoned my father to the Kingslayer and bent the knee to Robert the Usurper?"

"Even those who bent their knees may yearn in their hearts for the return of the dragons."

"*May*," said Dany. That was such a slippery word, *may*.
In any language. She turned back to Kraznys mo Nakloz
and his slave girl. "I must consider carefully."

The slaver shrugged. "Tell her to consider quickly.
There are many other buyers. Only three days past I
showed these same Unsullied to a corsair king who hopes
to buy them all."

"The corsair wanted only a hundred, your worship,"
Dany heard the slave girl say.

He poked her with the end of the whip. "Corsairs are
all liars. He'll buy them all. Tell her that, girl."

Dany knew she would take more than a hundred, if she
took any at all. "Remind your Good Master of who I am.
Remind him that I am Daenerys Stormborn, Mother of
Dragons, the Unburnt, trueborn queen of the Seven King-
doms of Westeros. My blood is the blood of Aegon the
Conqueror, and of old Valyria before him."

Yet her words did not move the plump perfumed slaver,
even when rendered in his own ugly tongue. "Old Ghis
ruled an empire when the Valyrians were still fucking
sheep," he growled at the poor little scribe, "and we are
the sons of the harpy." He gave a shrug. "My tongue is
wasted wagging at women. East or west, it makes no matter, they cannot decide until they have been pampered and
flattered and stuffed with sweetmeats. Well, if this is my
fate, so be it. Tell the whore that if she requires a guide
to our sweet city, Kraznys mo Nakloz will gladly serve
her . . . and service her as well, if she is more woman than
she looks."

"Good Master Kraznys would be most pleased to show
you Astapor while you ponder, Your Grace," the translator
said.

"I will feed her jellied dog brains, and a fine rich stew
of red octopus and unborn puppy." He wiped his lips.

"Many delicious dishes can be had here, he says."

"Tell her how pretty the pyramids are at night," the
slaver growled. "Tell her I will lick honey off her breasts,
or allow her to lick honey off mine if she prefers."

"Astapor is most beautiful at dusk, Your Grace," said
the slave girl. "The Good Masters light silk lanterns on

every terrace, so all the pyramids glow with colored lights.
Pleasure barges ply the Worm, playing soft music and calling at the little islands for food and wine and other
delights."

"Ask her if she wishes to view our fighting pits," Kraznys added. "Douquor's Pit has a fine folly scheduled for
the evening. A bear and three small boys. One boy will
be rolled in honey, one in blood, and one in rotting fish,
and she may wager on which the bear will eat first."

Tap tap tap, Dany heard. Arstan Whitebeard's face was
still, but his staff beat out his rage. *Tap tap tap.* She made
herself smile. "I have my own bear on *Balerion*," she told
the translator, "and he may well eat me if I do not return
to him."

"See," said Kraznys when her words were translated.
"It is not the woman who decides, it is this man she runs
to. As ever!"

"Thank the Good Master for his patient kindness,"
Dany said, "and tell him that I will think on all I learned
here." She gave her arm to Arstan Whitebeard, to lead her
back across the plaza to her litter. Aggo and Jhogo fell in
to either side of them, walking with the bowlegged swag-
ger all the horselords affected when forced to dismount
and stride the earth like common mortals.

Dany climbed into her litter frowning, and beckoned
Arstan to climb in beside her. A man as old as him should
not be walking in such heat. She did not close the curtains
as they got under way. With the sun beating down so
fiercely on this city of red brick, every stray breeze was
to be cherished, even if it did come with a swirl of fine
red dust. *Besides, I need to see.*

Astapor was a queer city, even to the eyes of one who
had walked within the House of Dust and bathed in the
Womb of the World beneath the Mother of Mountains.
All the streets were made of the same red brick that had
paved the plaza. So too were the stepped pyramids, the
deep-dug fighting pits with their rings of descending seats,
the sulfurous fountains and gloomy wine caves, and the
ancient walls that encircled them. *So many bricks,* she
thought, *and so old and crumbling.* Their fine red dust

was everywhere, dancing down the gutters at each gust of wind. Small wonder so many Astapori women veiled their faces; the brick dust stung the eyes worse than sand.

"Make way!" Jhogo shouted as he rode before her litter. "Make way for the Mother of Dragons!" But when he uncoiled the great silver-handled whip that Dany had given him, and made to crack it in the air, she leaned out and told him nay. "Not in this place, blood of my blood," she said, in his own tongue. "These bricks have heard too much of the sound of whips."

The streets had been largely deserted when they had set out from the port that morning, and scarcely seemed more crowded now. An elephant lumbered past with a latticework litter on its back. A naked boy with peeling skin sat in a dry brick gutter, picking his nose and staring sullenly at some ants in the street. He lifted his head at the sound of hooves, and gaped as a column of mounted guards trotted by in a cloud of red dust and brittle laughter. The copper disks sewn to their cloaks of yellow silk glittered like so many suns, but their tunics were embroidered linen, and below the waist they wore sandals and pleated linen skirts. Bareheaded, each man had teased and oiled and twisted his stiff red-black hair into some fantastic shape, horns and wings and blades and even grasping hands, so they looked like some troupe of demons escaped from the seventh hell. The naked boy watched them for a bit, along with Dany, but soon enough they were gone, and he went back to his ants, and a knuckle up his nose.

An old city, this, she reflected, *but not so populous as it was in its glory, nor near so crowded as Qarth or Pentos or Lys.*

Her litter came to a sudden halt at the cross street, to allow a coffle of slaves to shuffle across her path, urged along by the crack of an overseer's lash. These were no Unsullied, Dany noted, but a more common sort of men, with pale brown skins and black hair. There were women among them, but no children. All were naked. Two Astapori rode behind them on white asses, a man in a red silk *tokar* and a veiled woman in sheer blue linen decorated with flakes of lapis lazuli. In her red-black hair she wore an ivory comb. The man laughed as he whispered to her, paying no more mind to Dany than to his slaves, nor the overseer with his twisted five-thonged lash, a squat broad Dothraki who had the harpy and chains tattooed proudly across his muscular chest.

"Bricks and blood built Astapor," Whitebeard murmured at her side, "and bricks and blood her people."

"What is that?" Dany asked him, curious.

"An old rhyme a maester taught me, when I was a boy. I never knew how true it was. The bricks of Astapor are red with the blood of the slaves who make them."

"I can well believe that," said Dany.

"Then leave this place before your heart turns to brick as well. Sail this very night, on the evening tide."

Would that I could, thought Dany. "When I leave Astapor it must be with an army, Ser Jorah says."

"Ser Jorah was a slaver himself, Your Grace," the old man reminded her. "There are sellswords in Pentos and Myr and Tyrosh you can hire. A man who kills for coin has no honor, but at least they are no slaves. Find your army there, I beg you."

"My brother visited Pentos, Myr, Braavos, near all the Free Cities. The magisters and archons fed him wine and promises, but his soul was starved to death. A man cannot sup from the beggar's bowl all his life and stay a man. I had my taste in Qarth, that was enough. I will not come to Pentos bowl in hand."

"Better to come a beggar than a slaver," Arstan said.

"There speaks one who has been neither." Dany's nostrils flared. "Do you know what it is like to be *sold*, squire? I do. My brother sold me to Khal Drogo for the promise of a golden crown. Well, Drogo crowned him in gold, though not as he had wished, and I . . . my sun-and-stars made a queen of me, but if he had been a different man, it might have been much otherwise. Do you think I have forgotten how it felt to be afraid?"

Whitebeard bowed his head. "Your Grace, I did not mean to give offense."

"Only lies offend me, never honest counsel." Dany patted Arstan's spotted hand to reassure him. "I have a dragon's temper, that's all. You must not let it frighten you."

"I shall try and remember." Whitebeard smiled.

He has a good face, and great strength to him, Dany thought. She could not understand why Ser Jorah mistrusted the old man so. *Could he be jealous that I have found another man to talk to?* Unbidden, her thoughts went back to the night on *Balerion* when the exile knight had kissed her. *He should never have done that. He is thrice my age, and of too low a birth for me, and I never gave him leave. No true knight would ever kiss a queen without her leave.* She had taken care never to be alone with Ser Jorah after that, keeping her handmaids with her aboard ship, and sometimes her bloodriders. *He wants to kiss me again, I see it in his eyes.*

What Dany wanted she could not begin to say, but Jorah's kiss had woken something in her, something that been sleeping since Khal Drogo died. Lying abed in her narrow bunk, she found herself wondering how it would be to have a man squeezed in beside her in place of her handmaid, and the thought was more exciting than it should have been. Sometimes she would close her eyes and dream of him, but it was never Jorah Mormont she dreamed of; her lover was always younger and more comely, though his face remained a shifting shadow.

Once, so tormented she could not sleep, Dany slid a hand down between her legs, and gasped when she felt how wet she was. Scarce daring to breathe, she moved her fingers back and forth between her lower lips, slowly so as not to wake Irri beside her, until she found one sweet spot and lingered there, touching herself lightly, timidly at first and then faster. Still, the relief she wanted seemed to recede before her, until her dragons stirred, and one screamed out across the cabin, and Irri woke and saw what she was doing.

Dany knew her face was flushed, but in the darkness Irri surely could not tell. Wordless, the handmaid put a hand on her breast, then bent to take a nipple in her mouth. Her other hand drifted down across the soft curve of belly, through the mound of fine silvery-gold hair, and went to work between Dany's thighs. It was no more than a few moments until her legs twisted and her breasts heaved and her whole body shuddered. She screamed then. Or perhaps that was Drogon. Irri never said a thing, only curled back up and went back to sleep the instant the thing was done.

The next day, it all seemed a dream. And what did Ser Jorah have to do with it, if anything? *It is Drogo I want, my sun-and-stars,* Dany reminded herself. *Not Irri, and not Ser Jorah, only Drogo.* Drogo was dead, though. She'd thought these feelings had died with him there in the red waste, but one treacherous kiss had somehow brought them back to life. *He should never have kissed me. He presumed too much, and I permitted it. It must never happen again.* She set her mouth grimly and gave her head a shake, and the bell in her braid chimed softly.

Closer to the bay, the city presented a fairer face. The great brick pyramids lined the shore, the largest four hundred feet high. All manner of trees and vines and flowers grew on their broad terraces, and the winds that swirled around them smelled green and fragrant. Another gigantic harpy stood atop the gate, this one made of baked red clay and crumbling visibly, with no more than a stub of her scorpion's tail remaining. The chain she grasped in her clay claws was old iron, rotten with rust. It was cooler down by the water, though. The lapping of the waves against the rotting pilings made a curiously soothing sound.

Aggo helped Dany down from her litter. Strong Belwas was seated on a massive piling, eating a great haunch of brown roasted meat. "Dog," he said happily when he saw Dany. "Good dog in Astapor, little queen. Eat?" He offered it with a greasy grin.

"That is kind of you, Belwas, but no." Dany had eaten dog in other places, at other times, but just now all she could think of was the Unsullied and their stupid puppies. She swept past the huge eunuch and up the plank onto the deck of *Balerion*.

Ser Jorah Mormont stood waiting for her. "Your Grace," he said, bowing his head. "The slavers have come and gone. Three of them, with a dozen scribes and as many slaves to lift and fetch. They crawled over every foot of our holds and made note of all we had." He walked her aft. "How many men do they have for sale?"

"None." Was it Mormont she was angry with, or this city with its sullen heat, its stinks and sweats and crumbling bricks? "They sell eunuchs, not men. Eunuchs made of brick, like the rest of Astapor. Shall I buy eight thousand brick eunuchs with dead eyes that never move, who kill suckling babes for the sake of a spiked hat and strangle their own dogs? They don't even have names. So don't call them *men*, ser."

"*Khaleesi*," he said, taken aback by her fury, "the Unsullied are chosen as boys, and trained –"

"I have heard all I care to of their *training*." Dany could feel tears welling in her eyes, sudden and unwanted. Her hand flashed up and cracked Ser Jorah hard across the face. It was either that, or cry.

Mormont touched the cheek she'd slapped. "If I have displeased my queen –"

"You *have*. You've displeased me greatly, ser. If you were my true knight, you would never have brought me to this vile sty." *If you were my true knight, you would never have kissed me, or looked at my breasts the way you did, or . . .*

"As Your Grace commands. I shall tell Captain Groleo to make ready to sail on the evening tide, for some sty less vile."

"No," said Dany. Groleo watched them from the forecastle, and his crew was watching too. Whitebeard, her bloodriders, Jhiqui, every one had stopped what they were doing at the sound of the slap. "I want to sail *now*, not on the tide, I want to sail far and fast and never look back. But I can't, can I? There are eight thousand brick eunuchs for sale, and I must find some way to buy them." And with that she left him, and went below.

Behind the carved wooden door of the captain's cabin, her dragons were restless. Drogon raised his head and screamed, pale smoke venting from his nostrils, and Viserion flapped at her and tried to perch on her shoulder, as he had when he was smaller. "No," Dany said, trying to shrug him off gently. "You're too big for that now, sweetling." But the dragon coiled his white and gold tail around one arm and dug black claws into the fabric of her sleeve, clinging tightly. Helpless, she sank into Groleo's great leather chair, giggling.

"They have been wild while you were gone, *Khaleesi*," Irri told her. "Viserion clawed splinters from the door, do you see? And Drogon made to escape when the slaver men came to see them. When I grabbed his tail to hold him back, he turned and bit me." She showed Dany the marks of his teeth on her hand.

"Did any of them try to burn their way free?" That was the thing that frightened Dany the most.

"No, *Khaleesi*. Drogon breathed his fire, but in the empty air. The slaver men feared to come near him."

She kissed Irri's hand where Drogon had bitten it. "I'm sorry he hurt you. Dragons are not meant to be locked up in a small ship's cabin."

"Dragons are like horses in this," Irri said. "And riders, too. The horses scream below, *Khaleesi*, and kick at the wooden walls. I hear them. And Jhiqui says the old women and the little ones scream too, when you are not here. They do not like this water cart. They do not like the black salt sea."

"I know," Dany said. "I do, I know."

"My *khaleesi* is sad?"

"Yes," Dany admitted. *Sad and lost.*

"Should I pleasure the *khaleesi*?"

Dany stepped away from her. "No. Irri, you do not need to do that. What happened that night, when you woke . . . you're no bed slave, I freed you, remember? You . . ."

"I am handmaid to the Mother of Dragons," the girl said. "It is great honor to please my *khaleesi*."

"I don't want that," she insisted. "I don't." She turned away sharply. "Leave me now. I want to be alone. To think."

Dusk had begun to settle over the waters of Slaver's Bay before Dany returned to the deck. She stood by the rail and looked out over Astapor. *From here it looks almost beautiful*, she thought. The stars were coming out above, and the silk lanterns below, just as Kraznys's translator had promised. The brick pyramids were all glimmery with light. *But it is dark below, in the streets and plazas and fighting pits. And it is darkest of all in the barracks, where some little boy is feeding scraps to the puppy they gave him when they took away his manhood.*

There was a soft step behind her. "*Khaleesi.*" His voice. "Might I speak frankly?"

Dany did not turn. She could not bear to look at him just now. If she did, she might well slap him again. Or cry. Or kiss him. And never know which was right and which was wrong and which was madness. "Say what you will, ser."

"When Aegon the Dragon stepped ashore in Westeros, the kings of Vale and Rock and Reach did not rush to hand him their crowns. If you mean to sit his Iron Throne, you must win it as he did, with steel and dragonfire. And that will mean blood on your hands before the thing is done."

Blood and fire, thought Dany. The words of House Targaryen. She had known them all her life. "The blood of my enemies I will shed gladly. The blood of innocents is another matter. Eight thousand Unsullied they would offer me. Eight thousand dead babes. Eight thousand strangled dogs."

"Your Grace," said Jorah Mormont, "I saw King's Landing after the Sack. Babes were butchered that day as well, and old men, and children at play. More women were raped than you can count. There is a savage beast in every man, and when you hand that man a sword or spear and send him forth to war, the beast stirs. The scent of blood is all it takes to wake him. Yet I have never heard of these Unsullied raping, nor putting a city to the sword, nor even plundering, save at the express command of those who lead them. Brick they may be, as you say, but if you buy them henceforth the only dogs they'll kill are those *you* want dead. And you do have some dogs you want dead, as I recall."

The Usurper's dogs. "Yes." Dany gazed off at the soft colored lights and let the cool salt breeze caress her. "You speak of sacking cities. Answer me this, ser – why have the Dothraki never sacked *this* city?" She pointed. "Look at the walls. You can see where they've begun to crumble. There, and there. Do you see any guards on those towers? I don't. Are they hiding, ser? I saw these sons of the harpy today, all their proud highborn warriors. They dressed in linen skirts, and the fiercest thing about them was their hair. Even a modest *khalasar* could crack this Astapor like a nut and spill out the rotted meat inside. So tell me, why is that ugly harpy not sitting beside the godsway in Vaes Dothrak among the other stolen gods?"

"You have a dragon's eye, *Khaleesi*, that's plain to see."

"I wanted an answer, not a compliment."

"There are two reasons. Astapor's brave defenders are so much chaff, it's true. Old names and fat purses who dress up as Ghiscari scourges to pretend they still rule a vast empire. Every one is a high officer. On feastdays they fight mock wars in the pits to demonstrate what brilliant commanders they are, but it's the eunuchs who do the dying. All the same, any enemy wanting to sack Astapor would have to know that they'd be facing Unsullied. The slavers would turn out the whole garrison in the city's defense. The Dothraki have not ridden against Unsullied since they left their braids at the gates of Qohor."

"And the second reason?" Dany asked.

"Who would attack Astapor?" Ser Jorah asked. "Meereen and Yunkai are rivals but not enemies, the Doom destroyed Valyria, the folk of the eastern hinterlands are all Ghiscari, and beyond the hills lies Lhazar. The Lamb Men, as your Dothraki call them, a notably unwarlike people."

"Yes," she agreed, "but *north* of the slave cities is the Dothraki sea, and two dozen mighty *khals* who like nothing more than sacking cities and carrying off their people into slavery."

"Carrying them off *where?* What good are slaves once you've killed the slavers? Valyria is no more, Qarth lies beyond the red waste, and the Nine Free Cities are thousands of leagues to the west. And you may be sure the sons of the harpy give lavishly to every passing *khal*, just as the magisters do in Pentos and Norvos and Myr. They know that if they feast the horselords and give them gifts, they will soon ride on. It's cheaper than fighting, and a deal more certain."

Cheaper than fighting, Dany thought. *Yes, it might be.* If only it could be that easy for her. How pleasant it would be to sail to King's Landing with her dragons, and pay the boy Joffrey a chest of gold to make him go away.

"Khaleesi?" Ser Jorah prompted, when she had been silent for a long time. He touched her elbow lightly.

Dany shrugged him off. "Viserys would have bought as many Unsullied as he had the coin for. But you once said I was like Rhaegar . . ."

"I remember, Daenerys."

"Your Grace," she corrected. "Prince Rhaegar led free men into battle, not slaves. Whitebeard said he dubbed his squires himself, and made many other knights as well."

"There was no higher honor than to receive your knighthood from the Prince of Dragonstone."

"Tell me, then – when he touched a man on the shoulder with his sword, what did he say? 'Go forth and kill the weak'? Or 'Go forth and defend them'? At the Trident, those brave men Viserys spoke of who died beneath our dragon banners – did they give their lives because they *believed* in Rhaegar's cause, or because they had been bought and paid for?" Dany turned to Mormont, crossed her arms, and waited for an answer.

"My queen," the big man said slowly, "all you say is true. But Rhaegar lost on the Trident. He lost the battle, he lost the war, he lost the kingdom, and he lost his life. His blood swirled downriver with the rubies from his breastplate, and Robert the Usurper rode over his corpse to steal the Iron Throne. Rhaegar fought valiantly, Rhaegar fought nobly, Rhaegar fought honorably. And Rhaegar *died*."

BRAN

No roads ran through the twisted mountain valleys where they walked now. Between the grey stone peaks lay still blue lakes, long and deep and narrow, and the green gloom of endless piney woods. The russet and gold of autumn leaves grew less common when they left the wolfswood to climb amongst the old flint hills, and vanished by the time those hills had turned to mountains. Giant grey-green sentinels loomed above them now, and spruce and fir and soldier pines in endless profusion. The undergrowth was sparse beneath them, the forest floor carpeted in dark green needles.

When they lost their way, as happened once or twice, they need only wait for a clear cold night when the clouds did not intrude, and look up in the sky for the Ice Dragon. The blue star in the dragon's eye pointed the way north, as Osha told him once. Thinking of Osha made Bran wonder where she was. He pictured her safe in White Harbor with Rickon and Shaggydog, eating eels and fish and hot crab pie with fat Lord Manderly. Or maybe they were warming themselves at the Last Hearth before the Greatjon's fires. But Bran's life had turned into endless chilly days on Hodor's back, riding his basket up and down the slopes of mountains.

"Up and down," Meera would sigh sometimes as they walked, "then down and up. Then up and down again. I hate these stupid mountains of yours, Prince Bran."

"Yesterday you said you loved them."

"Oh, I do. My lord father told me about mountains, but I never saw one till now. I love them more than I can say."

Bran made a face at her. "But you just said you hated them."

"Why can't it be both?" Meera reached up to pinch his nose.

"Because they're *different*," he insisted. "Like night and day, or ice and fire."

"If ice can burn," said Jojen in his solemn voice, "then love and hate can mate. Mountain or marsh, it makes no matter. The land is one."

"One," his sister agreed, "but over wrinkled."

The high glens seldom did them the courtesy of running north and south, so often they found themselves going long leagues in the wrong direction, and sometimes they were forced to double back the way they'd come. "If we took the kingsroad we could be at the Wall by now," Bran would remind the Reeds. He wanted to find the three-eyed crow, so he could learn to fly. Half a hundred times he said it if he said it once, until Meera started teasing by saying it along with him.

"If we took the kingsroad we wouldn't be so hungry either," he started saying then. Down in the hills they'd had no lack of food. Meera was a fine huntress, and even better at taking fish from streams with her three-pronged frog spear. Bran liked to watch her, admiring her quickness, the way she sent the spear lancing down and pulled it back with a silvery trout wriggling on the end of it. And they had Summer hunting for them as well. The direwolf vanished most every night as the sun went down, but he was always back again before dawn, most often with something in his jaws, a squirrel or a hare.

But here in the mountains, the streams were smaller and more icy, and the game scarcer. Meera still hunted and fished when she could, but it was harder, and some nights even Summer found no prey. Often they went to sleep with empty bellies.

But Jojen remained stubbornly determined to stay well

away from roads. "Where you find roads you find travelers," he said in that way he had, "and travelers have
eyes to see, and mouths to spread tales of the crippled boy,
his giant, and the wolf that walks beside them." No one
could get as stubborn as Jojen, so they struggled on through
the wild, and every day climbed a little higher, and moved
a little farther north.

Some days it rained, some days were windy, and once
they were caught in a sleet storm so fierce that even Hodor
bellowed in dismay. On the clear days, it often seemed as
if they were the only living things in all the world. "Does
no one live up here?" Meera Reed asked once, as they made
their way around a granite upthrust as large as Winterfell.

"There's people," Bran told her. "The Umbers are
mostly east of the kingsroad, but they graze their sheep
in the high meadows in summer. There are Wulls west of
the mountains along the Bay of Ice, Harclays back behind
us in the hills, and Knotts and Liddles and Norreys and
even some Flints up here in the high places." His father's
mother's mother had been a Flint of the mountains. Old
Nan once said that it was her blood in him that made
Bran such a fool for climbing before his fall. She had died
years and years and years before he was born, though, even
before his father had been born.

"Wull?" said Meera. "Jojen, wasn't there a Wull who
rode with Father during the war?"

"Theo Wull." Jojen was breathing hard from the climb.
"Buckets, they used to call him."

"That's their sigil," said Bran. "Three brown buckets
on a blue field, with a border of white and grey checks.
Lord Wull came to Winterfell once, to do his fealty and
talk with Father, and he had the buckets on his shield.
He's no true lord, though. Well, he is, but they call him
just *the Wull*, and there's the Knott and the Norrey and
the Liddle too. At Winterfell we called them lords, but
their own folk don't."

Jojen Reed stopped to catch his breath. "Do you think
these mountain folk know we're here?"

"They know." Bran had seen them watching; not with
his own eyes, but with Summer's sharper ones, that

missed so little. "They won't bother us so long as we don't try and make off with their goats or horses."

Nor did they. Only once did they encounter any of the mountain people, when a sudden burst of freezing rain sent them looking for shelter. Summer found it for them, sniffing out a shallow cave behind the grey-green branches of a towering sentinel tree, but when Hodor ducked beneath the stony overhang, Bran saw the orange glow of fire farther back and realized they were not alone. "Come in and warm yourselves," a man's voice called out. "There's stone enough to keep the rain off all our heads."

He offered them oatcakes and blood sausage and a swallow of ale from a skin he carried, but never his name; nor did he ask theirs. Bran figured him for a Liddle. The clasp that fastened his squirrelskin cloak was gold and bronze and wrought in the shape of a pinecone, and the Liddles bore pinecones on the white half of their green-and-white shields.

"Is it far to the Wall?" Bran asked him as they waited for the rain to stop.

"Not so far as the raven flies," said the Liddle, if that was who he was. "Farther, for them as lacks wings."

Bran started, "I'd bet we'd be there if . . ."

". . . we took the kingsroad," Meera finished with him.

The Liddle took out a knife and whittled at a stick. "When there was a Stark in Winterfell, a maiden girl could walk the kingsroad in her name-day gown and still go unmolested, and travelers could find fire, bread, and salt at many an inn and holdfast. But the nights are colder now, and doors are closed. There's squids in the wolfswood, and flayed men ride the kingsroad asking after strangers."

The Reeds exchanged a look. "Flayed men?" said Jojen.

"The Bastard's boys, aye. He was dead, but now he's not. And paying good silver for wolfskins, a man hears, and maybe gold for word of certain other walking dead." He looked at Bran when he said that, and at Summer stretched out beside him. "As to that Wall," the man went on, "it's not a place that I'd be going. The Old Bear took the Watch into the haunted woods, and all that come back was his ravens, with hardly a message between them.

Dark wings, dark words, me mother used to say, but when the birds fly silent, seems to me that's even darker." He poked at the fire with his stick. "It was different when there was a Stark in Winterfell. But the old wolf's dead and young one's gone south to play the game of thrones, and all that's left us is the ghosts."

"The wolves will come again," said Jojen solemnly.

"And how would you be knowing, boy?"

"I dreamed it."

"Some nights I dream of me mother that I buried nine years past," the man said, "but when I wake, she's not come back to us."

"There are dreams and dreams, my lord."

"Hodor," said Hodor.

They spent that night together, for the rain did not let up till well past dark, and only Summer seemed to want to leave the cave. When the fire had burned down to embers, Bran let him go. The direwolf did not feel the damp as people did, and the night was calling him. Moonlight painted the wet woods in shades of silver and turned the grey peaks white. Owls hooted through the dark and flew silently between the pines, while pale goats moved along the mountainsides. Bran closed his eyes and gave himself up to the wolf dream, to the smells and sounds of midnight.

When they woke the next morning, the fire had gone out and the Liddle was gone, but he'd left a sausage for them, and a dozen oatcakes folded up neatly in a green and white cloth. Some of the cakes had pinenuts baked in them and some had blackberries. Bran ate one of each, and still did not know which sort he liked the best. One day there would be Starks in Winterfell again, he told himself, and then he'd send for the Liddles and pay them back a hundredfold for every nut and berry.

The trail they followed was a little easier that day, and by noon the sun came breaking through the clouds. Bran sat in his basket up on Hodor's back and felt almost content. He dozed off once, lulled to sleep by the smooth swing of the big stableboy's stride and the soft humming sound he made sometimes when he walked. Meera woke him up with a light touch on his arm. "Look," she said, pointing at the sky with her frog spear, "an eagle."

Bran lifted his head and saw it, its grey wings spread and still as it floated on the wind. He followed it with his eyes as it circled higher, wondering what it would be like to soar about the world so effortlessly. *Better than climbing, even.* He tried to reach the eagle, to leave his stupid crippled body and rise into the sky to join it, the way he joined with Summer. *The greenseers could do it. I should be able to do it too.* He tried and tried, until the eagle vanished in the golden haze of the afternoon. "It's gone," he said, disappointed.

"We'll see others," said Meera. "They live up here."

"I suppose."

"Hodor," said Hodor.

"Hodor," Bran agreed.

Jojen kicked a pinecone. "Hodor likes it when you say his name, I think."

"Hodor's not his true name," Bran explained. "It's just some word he says. His real name is Walder, Old Nan told me. She was his grandmother's grandmother or something." Talking about Old Nan made him sad. "Do you think the ironmen killed her?" They hadn't seen her body at Winterfell. He didn't remember seeing any women dead, now that he thought back. "She never hurt no one, not even Theon. She just told stories. Theon wouldn't hurt someone like that. Would he?"

"Some people hurt others just because they can," said Jojen.

"And it wasn't Theon who did the killing at Winterfell," said Meera. "Too many of the dead were ironmen." She shifted her frog spear to her other hand. "Remember Old Nan's stories, Bran. Remember the way she told them, the sound of her voice. So long as you do that, part of her will always be alive in you."

"I'll remember," he promised. They climbed without speaking for a long time, following a crooked game trail over the high saddle between two stony peaks. Scrawny soldier pines clung to the slopes around them. Far ahead Bran could see the icy glitter of a stream where it tumbled

down a mountainside. He found himself listening to
Jojen's breathing and the crunch of pine needles under
Hodor's feet. "Do you know any stories?" he asked the
Reeds all of a sudden.

Meera laughed. "Oh, a few."

"A few," her brother admitted.

"Hodor," said Hodor, humming.

"You could tell one," said Bran. "While we walked.
Hodor likes stories about knights. I do, too."

"There are no knights in the Neck," said Jojen.

"Above the water," his sister corrected. "The bogs are
full of dead ones, though."

"That's true," said Jojen. "Andals and ironmen, Freys
and other fools, all those proud warriors who set out to
conquer Greywater. Not one of them could find it. They
ride into the Neck, but not back out. And sooner or later
they blunder into the bogs and sink beneath the weight
of all that steel and drown there in their armor."

The thought of drowned knights under the water gave
Bran the shivers. He didn't object, though; he *liked* the
shivers.

"There was one knight," said Meera, "in the year of
the false spring. The Knight of the Laughing Tree, they
called him. He might have been a crannogman, that one."

"Or not." Jojen's face was dappled with green shadows.
"Prince Bran has heard that tale a hundred times, I'm
sure."

"No," said Bran. "I haven't. And if I have it doesn't
matter. Sometimes Old Nan would tell the same story
she'd told before, but we never minded, if it was a good
story. Old stories are like old friends, she used to say. You
have to visit them from time to time."

"That's true." Meera walked with her shield on her
back, pushing an occasional branch out of the way with
her frog spear. Just when Bran began to think that she
wasn't going to tell the story after all, she began, "Once
there was a curious lad who lived in the Neck. He was
small like all crannogmen, but brave and smart and strong
as well. He grew up hunting and fishing and climbing
trees, and learned all the magics of my people."

Bran was almost certain he had never heard this story. "Did he have green dreams like Jojen?"

"No," said Meera, "but he could breathe mud and run on leaves, and change earth to water and water to earth with no more than a whispered word. He could talk to trees and weave words and make castles appear and disappear."

"I wish I could," Bran said plaintively. "When does he meet the tree knight?"

Meera made a face at him. "Sooner if a certain prince would be quiet."

"I was just asking."

"The lad knew the magics of the crannogs," she continued, "but he wanted more. Our people seldom travel far from home, you know. We're a small folk, and our ways seem queer to some, so the big people do not always treat us kindly. But this lad was bolder than most, and one day when he had grown to manhood he decided he would leave the crannogs and visit the Isle of Faces."

"No one visits the Isle of Faces," objected Bran. "That's where the green men live."

"It was the green men he meant to find. So he donned a shirt sewn with bronze scales, like mine, took up a leathern shield and a three-pronged spear, like mine, and paddled a little skin boat down the Green Fork."

Bran closed his eyes to try and see the man in his little skin boat. In his head, the crannogman looked like Jojen, only older and stronger and dressed like Meera.

"He passed beneath the Twins by night so the Freys would not attack him, and when he reached the Trident he climbed from the river and put his boat on his head and began to walk. It took him many a day, but finally he reached the Gods Eye, threw his boat in the lake, and paddled out to the Isle of Faces."

"Did he meet the green men?"

"Yes," said Meera, "but that's another story, and not for me to tell. My prince asked for knights."

"Green men are good too."

"They are," she agreed, but said no more about them. "All that winter the crannogman stayed on the isle, but when the spring broke he heard the wide world calling and knew the time had come to leave. His skin boat was just where he'd left it, so he said his farewells and paddled off toward shore. He rowed and rowed, and finally saw the distant towers of a castle rising beside the lake. The towers reached ever higher as he neared shore, until he realized that this must be the greatest castle in all the world."

"Harrenhal!" Bran knew at once. "It was Harrenhal!"

Meera smiled. "Was it? Beneath its walls he saw tents of many colors, bright banners cracking in the wind, and knights in mail and plate on barded horses. He smelled roasting meats, and heard the sound of laughter and the blare of heralds' trumpets. A great tourney was about to commence, and champions from all over the land had come to contest it. The king himself was there, with his son the dragon prince. The White Swords had come, to welcome a new brother to their ranks. The storm lord was on hand, and the rose lord as well. The great lion of the rock had quarreled with the king and stayed away, but many of his bannermen and knights attended all the same. The crannogman had never seen such pageantry, and knew he might never see the like again. Part of him wanted nothing so much as to be part of it."

Bran knew that feeling well enough. When he'd been little, all he had ever dreamed of was being a knight. But that had been before he fell and lost his legs.

"The daughter of the great castle reigned as queen of love and beauty when the tourney opened. Five champions had sworn to defend her crown; her four brothers of Harrenhal, and her famous uncle, a white knight of the Kingsguard."

"Was she a fair maid?"

"She was," said Meera, hopping over a stone, "but there were others fairer still. One was the wife of the dragon prince, who'd brought a dozen lady companions to attend her. The knights all begged them for favors to tie about their lances."

"This isn't going to be one of those *love* stories, is it?" Bran asked suspiciously. "Hodor doesn't like those so much."

"Hodor," said Hodor agreeably.

"He likes the stories where the knights fight monsters."

"Sometimes the knights are the monsters, Bran. The little crannogman was walking across the field, enjoying the warm spring day and harming none, when he was set upon by three squires. They were none older than fifteen, yet even so they were bigger than him, all three. This was *their* world, as they saw it, and he had no right to be there. They snatched away his spear and knocked him to the ground, cursing him for a frogeater."

"Were they Walders?" It sounded like something Little Walder Frey might have done.

"None offered a name, but he marked their faces well so he could revenge himself upon them later. They shoved him down every time he tried to rise, and kicked him when he curled up on the ground. But then they heard a roar. 'That's my father's man you're kicking,' howled the she-wolf."

"A wolf on four legs, or two?"

"Two," said Meera. "The she-wolf laid into the squires with a tourney sword, scattering them all. The crannog-man was bruised and bloodied, so she took him back to her lair to clean his cuts and bind them up with linen. There he met her pack brothers: the wild wolf who led them, the quiet wolf beside him, and the pup who was youngest of the four.

"That evening there was to be a feast in Harrenhal, to mark the opening of the tourney, and the she-wolf insisted that the lad attend. He was of high birth, with as much a right to a place on the bench as any other man. She was not easy to refuse, this wolf maid, so he let the young pup find him garb suitable to a king's feast, and went up to the great castle.

"Under Harren's roof he ate and drank with the wolves, and many of their sworn swords besides, barrowdown men and moose and bears and mermen. The dragon prince sang a song so sad it made the wolf maid sniffle, but when her pup brother teased her for crying she poured wine over his head. A black brother spoke, asking the knights to

join the Night's Watch. The storm lord drank down the
knight of skulls and kisses in a wine-cup war. The crannogman saw a maid with laughing purple eyes dance with
a white sword, a red snake, and the lord of griffins, and
lastly with the quiet wolf . . . but only after the wild wolf
spoke to her on behalf of a brother too shy to leave his
bench.

"Amidst all this merriment, the little crannogman
spied the three squires who'd attacked him. One served a
pitchfork knight, one a porcupine, while the last attended
a knight with two towers on his surcoat, a sigil all crannogmen know well."

"The Freys," said Bran. "The Freys of the Crossing."

"Then, as now," she agreed. "The wolf maid saw them
too, and pointed them out to her brothers. 'I could find
you a horse, and some armor that might fit,' the pup
offered. The little crannogman thanked him, but gave no
answer. His heart was torn. Crannogmen are smaller than
most, but just as proud. The lad was no knight, no more
than any of his people. We sit a boat more often than a
horse, and our hands are made for oars, not lances. Much
as he wished to have his vengeance, he feared he would
only make a fool of himself and shame his people. The
quiet wolf had offered the little crannogman a place in his
tent that night, but before he slept he knelt on the
lakeshore, looking across the water to where the Isle of
Faces would be, and said a prayer to the old gods of north
and Neck . . ."

"You never heard this tale from your father?" asked
Jojen.

"It was Old Nan who told the stories. Meera, go on,
you can't stop there."

Hodor must have felt the same. "Hodor," he said, and
then, "Hodor hodor hodor hodor."

"Well," said Meera, "if you would hear the rest . . ."

"Yes. *Tell* it."

"Five days of jousting were planned," she said. "There
was a great seven-sided mêlée as well, and archery and
axe-throwing, a horse race and tourney of singers . . ."

"Never mind about all that." Bran squirmed

impatiently in his basket on Hodor's back. "Tell about the jousting."

"As my prince commands. The daughter of the castle was the queen of love and beauty, with four brothers and an uncle to defend her, but all four sons of Harrenhal were defeated on the first day. Their conquerors reigned briefly as champions, until they were vanquished in turn. As it happened, the end of the first day saw the porcupine knight win a place among the champions, and on the morning of the second day the pitchfork knight and the knight of the two towers were victorious as well. But late on the afternoon of that second day, as the shadows grew long, a mystery knight appeared in the lists."

Bran nodded sagely. Mystery knights would oft appear at tourneys, with helms concealing their faces, and shields that were either blank or bore some strange device. Sometimes they were famous champions in disguise. The Dragonknight once won a tourney as the Knight of Tears, so he could name his sister the queen of love and beauty in place of the king's mistress. And Barristan the Bold twice donned a mystery knight's armor, the first time when he was only ten. "It was the little crannogman, I bet."

"No one knew," said Meera, "but the mystery knight was short of stature, and clad in ill-fitting armor made up of bits and pieces. The device upon his shield was a heart tree of the old gods, a white weirwood with a laughing red face."

"Maybe he came from the Isle of Faces," said Bran. "Was he green?" In Old Nan's stories, the guardians had dark green skin and leaves instead of hair. Sometimes they had antlers too, but Bran didn't see how the mystery knight could have worn a helm if he had antlers. "I bet the old gods sent him."

"Perhaps they did. The mystery knight dipped his lance before the king and rode to the end of the lists, where the five champions had their pavilions. You know the three he challenged."

"The porcupine knight, the pitchfork knight, and the knight of the twin towers." Bran had heard enough stories to know *that*. "He was the little crannogman, I told you."

"Whoever he was, the old gods gave strength to his arm. The porcupine knight fell first, then the pitchfork knight, and lastly the knight of the two towers. None were well loved, so the common folk cheered lustily for the Knight of the Laughing Tree, as the new champion soon was called. When his fallen foes sought to ransom horse and armor, the Knight of the Laughing Tree spoke in a booming voice through his helm, saying, '*Teach your squire honor, that shall be ransom enough.*' Once the defeated knights chastised their squires sharply, their horses and armor were returned. And so the little crannogman's prayer was answered . . . by the green men, or the old gods, or the children of the forest, who can say?"

It was a good story, Bran decided after thinking about it a moment or two. "Then what happened? Did the Knight of the Laughing Tree win the tourney and marry a princess?"

"No," said Meera. "That night at the great castle, the storm lord and the knight of skulls and kisses each swore they would unmask him, and the king himself urged men to challenge him, declaring that the face behind that helm was no friend of his. But the next morning, when the heralds blew their trumpets and the king took his seat, only two champions appeared. The Knight of the Laughing Tree had vanished. The king was wroth, and even sent his son the dragon prince to seek the man, but all they ever found was his painted shield, hanging abandoned in a tree. It was the dragon prince who won that tourney in the end."

"Oh." Bran thought about the tale awhile. "That was a good story. But it should have been the three bad knights who hurt him, not their squires. Then the little crannogman could have killed them all. The part about the ransoms was stupid. And the mystery knight should win the tourney, defeating every challenger, and name the wolf maid the queen of love and beauty."

"She was," said Meera, "but that's a sadder story."

"Are you certain you never heard this tale before, Bran?" asked Jojen. "Your lord father never told it to you?"

Bran shook his head. The day was growing old by then, and long shadows were creeping down the mountainsides to send black fingers through the pines. *If the little crannogman could visit the Isle of Faces, maybe I could too.* All the tales agreed that the green men had strange magic powers. Maybe they could help him walk again, even turn him into a knight. *They turned the little crannogman into a knight, even if it was only for a day*, he thought. *A day would be enough.*

DAVOS

The cell was warmer than any cell had a right to be. It was dark, yes. Flickering orange light fell through the ancient iron bars from the torch in the sconce on the wall outside, but the back half of the cell remained drenched in gloom. It was dank as well, as might be expected on an isle such as Dragonstone, where the sea was never far. And there were rats, as many as any dungeon could expect to have and a few more besides.

But Davos could not complain of chill. The smooth stony passages beneath the great mass of Dragonstone were always warm, and Davos had often heard it said they grew warmer the farther down one went. He was well below the castle, he judged, and the wall of his cell often felt warm to his touch when he pressed a palm against it. Perhaps the old tales were true, and Dragonstone was built with the stones of hell.

He was sick when they first brought him here. The cough that had plagued him since the battle grew worse, and a fever took hold of him as well. His lips broke with blood blisters, and the warmth of the cell did not stop his shivering. *I will not linger long*, he remembered thinking. *I will die soon, here in the dark.*

Davos soon found that he was wrong about that, as about so much else. Dimly he remembered gentle hands and a firm voice, and young Maester Pylos looking down on him. He was given hot garlic broth to drink, and milk of the poppy to take away his aches and shivers. The poppy made him sleep and while he slept they leeched him to drain off the bad blood. Or so he surmised, by the leech marks on his arms when he woke. Before very long the coughing stopped, the blisters vanished, and his broth had chunks of whitefish in it, and carrots and onions as well. And one day he realized that he felt stronger than he had since *Black Betha* shattered beneath him and flung him in the river.

He had two gaolers to tend him. One was broad and squat, with thick shoulders and huge strong hands. He wore a leather brigantine dotted with iron studs, and once a day brought Davos a bowl of oaten porridge. Sometimes he sweetened it with honey or poured in a bit of milk. The other gaoler was older, stooped and sallow, with greasy unwashed hair and pebbled skin. He wore a doublet of white velvet with a ring of stars worked upon the breast in golden thread. It fit him badly, being both too short and too loose, and was soiled and torn besides. He would bring Davos plates of meat and mash, or fish stew, and once even half a lamprey pie. The lamprey was so rich he could not keep it down, but even so, it was a rare treat for a prisoner in a dungeon.

Neither sun nor moon shone in the dungeons; no windows pierced the thick stone walls. The only way to tell day from night was by his gaolers. Neither man would speak to him, though he knew they were no mutes; sometimes he heard them exchange a few brusque words as the watch was changing. They would not even tell him their names, so he gave them names of his own. The short strong one he called Porridge, the stooped sallow one Lamprey, for the pie. He marked the passage of days by the meals they brought, and by the changing of the torches in the sconce outside his cell.

A man grows lonely in the dark, and hungers for the sound of a human voice. Davos would talk to the gaolers whenever they came to his cell, whether to bring him food or change his slops pail. He knew they would be deaf to pleas for freedom or mercy; instead he asked them questions, hoping perhaps one day one might answer. "What news of the war?" he asked, and "Is the king well?" He asked after his son Devan, and the Princess Shireen, and Salladhor Saan. "What is the weather like?" he asked, and "Have the autumn storms begun yet? Do ships still sail the narrow sea?"

It made no matter what he asked; they never answered, though sometimes Porridge gave him a look, and for half a heartbeat Davos would think that he was about to speak. With Lamprey there was not even that much. *I am not a man to him*, Davos thought, *only a stone that eats and shits and speaks.* He decided after a while that he liked Porridge much the better. Porridge at least seemed to know he was alive, and there was a queer sort of kindness to the man. Davos suspected that he fed the rats; that was why there were so many. Once he thought he heard the gaoler talking to them as if they were children, but perhaps he'd only dreamed that.

They do not mean to let me die, he realized. *They are keeping me alive, for some purpose of their own.* He did not like to think what that might be. Lord Sunglass had been confined in the cells beneath Dragonstone for a time, as had Ser Hubard Rambton's sons; all of them had ended on the pyre. *I should have given myself to the sea*, Davos thought as he sat staring at the torch beyond the bars. *Or let the sail pass me by, to perish on my rock. I would sooner feed crabs than flames.*

Then one night as he was finishing his supper, Davos felt a queer flush come over him. He glanced up through the bars, and there she stood in shimmering scarlet with her great ruby at her throat, her red eyes gleaming as bright as the torch that bathed her. "Melisandre," he said, with a calm he did not feel.

"Onion Knight," she replied, just as calmly, as if the two of them had met on a stair or in the yard, and were exchanging polite greetings. "Are you well?"

"Better than I was."

"Do you lack for anything?"

"My king. My son. I lack for them." He pushed the bowl aside and stood. "Have you come to burn me?"

Her strange red eyes studied him through the bars. "This is a bad place, is it not? A dark place, and foul. The good sun does not shine here, nor the bright moon." She lifted a hand toward the torch in the wall sconce. "This is all that stands between you and the darkness, Onion Knight. This little fire, this gift of R'hllor. Shall I put it out?"

"No." He moved toward the bars. "Please." He did not think he could bear that, to be left alone in utter blackness with no one but the rats for company.

The red woman's lips curved upward in a smile. "So you have come to love the fire, it would seem."

"I need the torch." His hands opened and closed. *I will not beg her. I will not.*

"I am like this torch, Ser Davos. We are both instruments of R'hllor. We were made for a single purpose – to keep the darkness at bay. Do you believe that?"

"No." Perhaps he should have lied, and told her what she wanted to hear, but Davos was too accustomed to speaking truth. "You are the mother of darkness. I saw that under Storm's End, when you gave birth before my eyes."

"Is the brave Ser Onions so frightened of a passing shadow? Take heart, then. Shadows only live when given birth by light, and the king's fires burn so low I dare not draw off any more to make another son. It might well kill him." Melisandre moved closer. "With another man, though . . . a man whose flames still burn hot and high . . . if you truly wish to serve your king's cause, come to my chamber one night. I could give you pleasure such as you have never known, and with your life-fire I could make . . ."

". . . a horror." Davos retreated from her. "I want no part of you, my lady. Or your god. May the Seven protect me."

Melisandre sighed. "They did not protect Guncer Sunglass. He prayed thrice each day, and bore seven seven-pointed stars upon his shield, but when R'hllor reached out his hand his prayers turned to screams, and he burned. Why cling to these false gods?"

"I have worshiped them all my life."

"All your life, Davos Seaworth? As well say *it was so yesterday.*" She shook her head sadly. "You have never feared to speak the truth to kings, why do you lie to yourself? Open your eyes, ser knight."

"What is it you would have me see?"

"The way the world is made. The truth is all around you, plain to behold. The night is dark and full of terrors, the day bright and beautiful and full of hope. One is black, the other white. There is ice and there is fire. Hate and love. Bitter and sweet. Male and female. Pain and pleasure. Winter and summer. Evil and good." She took a step toward him. *"Death and life.* Everywhere, opposites. Everywhere, the war."

"The war?" asked Davos.

"The war," she affirmed. *"There are two,* Onion Knight. Not seven, not one, not a hundred or a thousand. *Two!* Do you think I crossed half the world to put yet another vain king on yet another empty throne? The war has been waged since time began, and before it is done, all men must choose where they will stand. On one side is R'hllor, the Lord of Light, the Heart of Fire, the God of Flame and Shadow. Against him stands the Great Other whose name may not be spoken, the Lord of Darkness, the Soul of Ice, the God of Night and Terror. Ours is not a choice between Baratheon and Lannister, between Greyjoy and Stark. It is death we choose, or life. Darkness, or light." She clasped the bars of his cell with her slender white hands. The great ruby at her throat seemed to pulse with its own radiance. "So tell me, Ser Davos Seaworth, and tell me truly – does your heart burn with the shining light of R'hllor? Or is it black and cold and full of worms?" She reached through the bars and laid three fingers upon his breast, as if to feel the truth of him through flesh and wool and leather.

"My heart," Davos said slowly, "is full of doubts."

Melisandre sighed. "Ahhhh, Davos. The good knight is honest to the last, even in his day of darkness. It is well you did not lie to me. I would have known. The Other's servants oft hide black hearts in gaudy light, so R'hllor gives his priests the power to see through falsehoods." She stepped lightly away from the cell. "Why did you mean to kill me?"

"I will tell you," said Davos, "if you will tell me who betrayed me." It could only have been Salladhor Saan, and yet even now he prayed it was not so.

The red woman laughed. "No one betrayed you, onion knight. I saw your purpose in my flames."

The flames. "If you can see the future in these flames, how is it that we burned upon the Blackwater? You gave my sons to the fire . . . my sons, my ship, my men, all burning . . ."

Melisandre shook her head. "You wrong me, onion knight. Those were no fires of mine. Had I been with you, your battle would have had a different ending. But His Grace was surrounded by unbelievers, and his pride proved stronger than his faith. His punishment was grievous, but he has learned from his mistake."

Were my sons no more than a lesson for a king, then? Davos felt his mouth tighten.

"It is night in your Seven Kingdoms now," the red woman went on, "but soon the sun will rise again. The war continues, Davos Seaworth, and some will soon learn that even an ember in the ashes can still ignite a great blaze. The old maester looked at Stannis and saw only a man. You see a king. You are both wrong. He is the Lord's chosen, the warrior of fire. I have seen him leading the fight against the dark, I have seen it in the flames. The flames do not lie, else you would not be here. It is written in prophecy as well. When the red star bleeds and the darkness gathers, Azor Ahai shall be born again amidst smoke and salt to wake dragons out of stone. The bleeding star has come and gone, and Dragonstone is the place of smoke and salt. Stannis Baratheon is Azor Ahai reborn!" Her red eyes blazed like twin fires, and seemed to stare deep into his soul. "You do not believe me. You doubt the truth of R'hllor even now . . . yet have served him all the same, and will serve him again. I shall leave you here to think on all that I have told you. And because R'hllor is the source of all good, I shall leave the torch as well."

With a smile and swirl of scarlet skirts, she was gone. Only her scent lingered after. That, and the torch. Davos lowered himself to the floor of the cell and wrapped his arms about his knees. The shifting torchlight washed over him. Once Melisandre's footsteps faded away, the only sound was the scrabbling of rats. *Ice and fire*, he thought. *Black and white. Dark and light.* Davos could not deny the power of her god. He had seen the shadow crawling from Melisandre's womb, and the priestess knew things she had no way of knowing. *She saw my purpose in her flames.* It was good to learn that Salla had not sold him, but the thought of the red woman spying out his secrets with her fires disquieted him more than he could say. *And what did she mean when she said that I had served her god and would serve him again?* He did not like that either.

He lifted his eyes to stare up at the torch. He looked for a long time, never blinking, watching the flames shift and shimmer. He tried to see beyond them, to peer through the fiery curtain and glimpse whatever lived back there . . . but there was nothing, only fire, and after a time his eyes began to water.

God-blind and tired, Davos curled up on the straw and gave himself to sleep.

Three days later – well, Porridge had come thrice, and Lamprey twice – Davos heard voices outside his cell. He sat up at once, his back to the stone wall, listening to the sounds of struggle. This was new, a change in his unchanging world. The noise was coming from the left, where the steps led up to daylight. He could hear a man's voice, pleading and shouting.

". . . *madness!*" the man was saying as he came into view, dragged along between two guardsmen with fiery hearts on their breasts. Porridge went before them, jangling a ring of keys, and Ser Axell Florent walked behind. "Axell," the prisoner said desperately, "for the love you bear me, *unhand me! You* cannot do this, I'm no traitor." He was an older man, tall and slender, with silvery grey hair, a pointed beard, and a long elegant face twisted in fear. "Where is Selyse, where is the queen? I demand to see her. The Others take you all! *Release me!*"

The guards paid no mind to his outcries. "Here?" Porridge asked in front of the cell. Davos got to his feet. For an instant he considered trying to rush them when the door was opened, but that was madness. There were too many, the guards wore swords, and Porridge was strong as a bull.

Ser Axell gave the gaoler a curt nod. "Let the traitors enjoy each other's company."

"*I am no traitor!*" screeched the prisoner as Porridge was unlocking the door. Though he was plainly dressed, in grey wool doublet and black breeches, his speech marked him as highborn. *His birth will not serve him here*, thought Davos.

Porridge swung the bars wide, Ser Axell gave a nod, and the guards flung their charge in headlong. The man stumbled and might have fallen, but Davos caught him. At once he wrenched away and staggered back toward the door, only to have it slammed in his pale, pampered face. "*No*," he shouted. "*Nooooo*." All the strength suddenly left his legs, and he slid slowly to the floor, clutching at the iron bars. Ser Axell, Porridge, and the guards had already turned to leave. "You cannot do this," the prisoner shouted at their retreating backs. "*I am the King's Hand!*"

It was then that Davos knew him. "You are Alester Florent."

The man turned his head. "Who . . . ?"

"Ser Davos Seaworth."

Lord Alester blinked. "Seaworth . . . the onion knight. You tried to murder Melisandre."

Davos did not deny it. "At Storm's End you wore red-gold armor, with inlaid lapis flowers on your breastplate." He reached down a hand to help the other man to his feet.

Lord Alester brushed the filthy straw from his clothing. "I . . . I must apologize for my appearance, ser. My chests were lost when the Lannisters overran our camp. I escaped with no more than the mail on my back and the rings on my fingers."

He still wears those rings, noted Davos, who had lacked even all of his fingers.

"No doubt some cook's boy or groom is prancing

around King's Landing just now in my slashed velvet doublet and jeweled cloak," Lord Alester went on, oblivious. "But war has its horrors, as all men know. No doubt you suffered your own losses."

"My ship," said Davos. "All my men. Four of my sons."

"May the . . . may the Lord of Light lead them through the darkness to a better world," the other man said.

May the Father judge them justly, and the Mother grant them mercy, Davos thought, but he kept his prayer to himself. The Seven had no place on Dragonstone now.

"My own son is safe at Brightwater," the lord went on, "but I lost a nephew on the *Fury*. Ser Imry, my brother Ryam's son."

It had been Ser Imry Florent who led them blindly up the Blackwater Rush with all oars pulling, paying no heed to the small stone towers at the mouth of the river. Davos was not like to forget him. "My son Maric was your nephew's oarmaster." He remembered his last sight of *Fury*, engulfed in wildfire. "Has there been any word of survivors?"

"The *Fury* burned and sank with all hands," his lordship said. "Your son and my nephew were lost, with countless other good men. The war itself was lost that day, ser."

This man is defeated. Davos remembered Melisandre's talk of embers in the ashes igniting great blazes. *Small wonder he ended here.* "His Grace will never yield, my lord."

"Folly, that's folly." Lord Alester sat on the floor again, as if the effort of standing for a moment had been too much for him. "Stannis Baratheon will never sit the Iron Throne. Is it treason to say the truth? A bitter truth, but no less true for that. His fleet is gone, save for the Lyseni, and Salladhor Saan will flee at the first sight of a Lannister sail. Most of the lords who supported Stannis have gone over to Joffrey or died . . ."

"Even the lords of the narrow sea? The lords sworn to Dragonstone?"

Lord Alester waved his hand feebly. "Lord Celtigar was captured and bent the knee. Monford Velaryon died with his ship, the red woman burned Sunglass, and Lord Bar

Emmon is fifteen, fat, and feeble. Those are your lords of the narrow sea. Only the strength of House Florent is left to Stannis, against all the might of Highgarden, Sunspear, and Casterly Rock, and now most of the storm lords as well. The best hope that remains is to try and salvage something with a peace. That is all I meant to do. Gods be good, how can they call it *treason?*"

Davos stood frowning. "My lord, what did you do?"

"Not treason. Never treason. I love His Grace as much as any man. My own niece is his queen, and I remained loyal to him when wiser men fled. I am his *Hand*, the Hand of the King, how can I be a traitor? I only meant to save our lives, and . . . honor . . . yes." He licked his lips. "I penned a letter. Salladhor Saan swore that he had a man who could get it to King's Landing, to Lord Tywin. His lordship is a . . . a man of reason, and my terms . . . the terms were fair . . . more than fair."

"What terms were these, my lord?"

"It is filthy here," Lord Alester said suddenly. "And that odor . . . what is that odor?"

"The pail," said Davos, gesturing. "We have no privy here. What terms?"

His lordship stared at the pail in horror. "That Lord Stannis give up his claim to the Iron Throne and retract all he said of Joffrey's bastardy, on the condition that he be accepted back into the king's peace and confirmed as Lord of Dragonstone and Storm's End. I vowed to do the same, for the return of Brightwater Keep and all our lands. I thought . . . Lord Tywin would see the sense in my proposal. He still has the Starks to deal with, and the ironmen as well. I offered to seal the bargain by wedding Shireen to Joffrey's brother Tommen." He shook his head. "The terms . . . they are as good as we are ever like to get. Even you can see that, surely?"

"Yes," said Davos, "even me." Unless Stannis should father a son, such a marriage would mean that Dragonstone and Storm's End would one day pass to Tommen, which would doubtless please Lord Tywin. Meanwhile, the Lannisters would have Shireen as hostage to make certain Stannis raised no new rebellions. "And what did

His Grace say when you proposed these terms to him?"

"He is always with the red woman, and . . . he is not in his right mind, I fear. This talk of a stone dragon . . . madness, I tell you, sheer madness. Did we learn nothing from Aerion Brightfire, from the nine mages, from the alchemists? Did we learn nothing from *Summerhall?* No good has ever come from these dreams of dragons, I told Axell as much. My way was better. Surer. And Stannis gave me his seal, he gave me leave to rule. The Hand speaks with the king's voice."

"Not in this." Davos was no courtier, and he did not even try to blunt his words. "It is not in Stannis to yield, so long as he knows his claim is just. No more than he can unsay his words against Joffrey, when he believes them true. As for the marriage, Tommen was born of the same incest as Joffrey, and His Grace would sooner see Shireen dead than wed to such."

A vein throbbed in Florent's forehead. "*He has no choice.*"

"You are wrong, my lord. He can choose to die a king."

"And us with him? Is that what you desire, Onion Knight?"

"No. But I am the king's man, and I will make no peace without his leave."

Lord Alester stared at him helplessly for a long moment, and then began to weep.

JON

The last night fell black and moonless, but for once the sky was clear. "I am going up the hill to look for Ghost," he told the Thenns at the cave mouth, and they grunted and let him pass.

So many stars, he thought as he trudged up the slope through pines and firs and ash. Maester Luwin had taught him his stars as a boy in Winterfell; he had learned the names of the twelve houses of heaven and the rulers of each; he could find the seven wanderers sacred to the Faith; he was old friends with the Ice Dragon, the Shadowcat, the Moonmaid, and the Sword of the Morning. All those he shared with Ygritte, but not some of the others. *We look up at the same stars, and see such different things.* The King's Crown was the Cradle, to hear her tell it; the Stallion was the Horned Lord; the red wanderer that septons preached was sacred to their Smith up here was called the Thief. And when the Thief was in the Moonmaid, that was a propitious time for a man to steal a woman, Ygritte insisted. "Like the night you stole me. The Thief was bright that night."

"I never meant to steal you," he said. "I never knew you were a girl until my knife was at your throat."

"If you kill a man, and never mean t', he's just as dead," Ygritte said stubbornly. Jon had never met anyone so stubborn, except maybe for his little sister Arya. *Is she still my sister?* he wondered. *Was she ever?* He had never truly been a Stark, only Lord Eddard's motherless bastard, with no more place at Winterfell than Theon Greyjoy. And even that he'd lost. When a man of the Night's Watch said his words, he put aside his old family and joined a new one, but Jon Snow had lost those brothers too.

He found Ghost atop the hill, as he thought he might. The white wolf never howled, yet something drew him to the heights all the same, and he would squat there on his hindquarters, hot breath rising in a white mist as his red eyes drank the stars.

"Do you have names for them as well?" Jon asked, as he went to one knee beside the direwolf and scratched the thick white fur on his neck. "The Hare? The Doe? The She-Wolf?" Ghost licked his face, his rough wet tongue rasping against the scabs where the eagle's talons had ripped Jon's cheek. *The bird marked both of us*, he thought. "Ghost," he said quietly, "on the morrow we go over. There's no steps here, no cage-and-crane, no way for me to get you to the other side. We have to part. Do you understand?"

In the dark, the direwolf's red eyes looked black. He nuzzled at Jon's neck, silent as ever, his breath a hot mist. The wildlings called Jon Snow a warg, but if so he was a poor one. He did not know how to put on a wolf skin, the way Orell had with his eagle before he'd died. Once Jon had dreamed that he was Ghost, looking down upon the valley of the Milkwater where Mance Rayder had gathered his people, and that dream had turned out to be true. But he was not dreaming now, and that left him only words.

"You cannot come with me," Jon said, cupping the wolf's head in his hands and looking deep into those eyes. "You have to go to Castle Black. Do you understand? *Castle Black.* Can you find it? The way home? Just follow the ice, east and east, into the sun, and you'll find it. They will know you at Castle Black, and maybe your coming will warn them." He had thought of writing out a warning for Ghost to carry, but he had no ink, no parchment, not even a writing quill, and the risk of discovery was too great. "I will meet you again at Castle Black, but you have to get there by yourself. We must each hunt alone for a time. *Alone.*"

The direwolf twisted free of Jon's grasp, his ears pricked up. And suddenly he was bounding away. He loped through a tangle of brush, leapt a deadfall, and raced down the hillside, a pale streak among the trees. *Off to Castle Black?* Jon wondered. *Or off after a hare?* He wished he knew. He feared he might prove just as poor a warg as a sworn brother and a spy.

A wind sighed through the trees, rich with the smell of pine needles, tugging at his faded blacks. Jon could see the Wall looming high and dark to the south, a great shadow blocking out the stars. The rough hilly ground made him think they must be somewhere between the Shadow Tower and Castle Black, and likely closer to the former. For days they had been wending their way south between deep lakes that stretched like long thin fingers along the floors of narrow valleys, while flint ridges and pine-clad hills jostled against one another to either side. Such ground made for slow riding, but offered easy concealment for those wishing to approach the Wall unseen.

For wildling raiders, he thought. *Like us. Like me.*

Beyond that Wall lay the Seven Kingdoms, and everything he had sworn to protect. He had said the words, had pledged his life and honor, and by rights he should be up there standing sentry. He should be raising a horn to his lips to rouse the Night's Watch to arms. He had no horn, though. It would not be hard to steal one from the wildlings, he suspected, but what would that accomplish? Even if he blew it, there was no one to hear. The Wall was a hundred leagues long and the Watch sadly dwindled. All but three of the strongholds had been abandoned; there might not be a brother within forty miles of here, but for Jon. If he was a brother still . . .

I should have tried to kill Mance Rayder on the Fist, even if it meant my life. That was what Qhorin Halfhand would have done. But Jon had hesitated, and the chance passed. The next day he had ridden off with Styr the Magnar, Jarl, and more than a hundred picked Thenns and raiders. He told himself that he was only biding his time, that when the moment came he would slip away and ride for Castle Black. The moment never came. They rested most nights in empty wildling villages, and Styr always set a dozen of his Thenns to guard the horses. Jarl watched him suspiciously. And Ygritte was never far, day or night.

Two hearts that beat as one. Mance Rayder's mocking words rang bitter in his head. Jon had seldom felt so confused. *I have no choice*, he'd told himself the first time, when she slipped beneath his sleeping skins. *If I refuse her, she will know me for a turncloak. I am playing the part the Halfhand told me to play.*

His body had played the part eagerly enough. His lips on hers, his hand sliding under her doeskin shirt to find a breast, his manhood stiffening when she rubbed her mound against it through their clothes. *My vows*, he'd thought, remembering the weirwood grove where he had said them, the nine great white trees in a circle, the carved red faces watching, listening. But her fingers were undoing his laces and her tongue was in his mouth and her hand slipped inside his smallclothes and brought him out, and he could not see the weirwoods anymore, only her. She bit his neck and he nuzzled hers, burying his nose in her thick red hair. *Lucky*, he thought, *she is lucky, fire-kissed.* "Isn't that good?" she whispered as she guided him inside her. She was sopping wet down there, and no maiden, that was plain, but Jon did not care. His vows, her maidenhood, none of it mattered, only the heat of her, the mouth on his, the finger that pinched at his nipple. "Isn't that sweet?" she said again. "Not so fast, oh, slow, yes, like that. There now, there now, yes, sweet, sweet. You know nothing, Jon Snow, but I can show you. Harder now. Yessss."

A part, he tried to remind himself afterward. *I am playing a part. I had to do it once, to prove I'd abandoned my vows. I had to make her trust me.* It need never happen again. He was still a man of the Night's Watch, and a son of Eddard Stark. He had done what needed to be done, proved what needed to be proven.

The proving had been so sweet, though, and Ygritte had gone to sleep beside him with her head against his chest, and that was sweet as well, dangerously sweet. He thought of the weirwoods again, and the words he'd said before them. *It was only once, and it had to be. Even my father stumbled once, when he forgot his marriage vows and sired a bastard.* Jon vowed to himself that it would be the same with him. *It will never happen again.*

It happened twice more that night, and again in the morning, when she woke to find him hard. The wildlings were stirring by then, and several could not help but notice what was going on beneath the pile of furs. Jarl told them to be quick about it, before he had to throw a pail of water over them. *Like a pair of rutting dogs*, Jon thought afterward. Was that what he'd become? *I am a man of the Night's Watch*, a small voice inside insisted, but every night it seemed a little fainter, and when Ygritte kissed his ears or bit his neck, he could not hear it at all. *Was this how it was for my father?* he wondered. *Was he as weak as I am, when he dishonored himself in my mother's bed?*

Something was coming up the hill behind him, he realized suddenly. For half a heartbeat he thought it might be Ghost come back, but the direwolf never made so much noise. Jon drew Longclaw in a single smooth motion, but it was only one of the Thenns, a broad man in a bronze helm. "Snow," the intruder said. "Come. Magnar wants." The men of Thenn spoke the Old Tongue, and most had only a few words of the Common.

Jon did not much care what the Magnar wanted, but there was no use arguing with someone who could scarcely understand him, so he followed the man back down the hill.

The mouth of the cave was a cleft in the rock barely wide enough for a horse, half concealed behind a soldier pine. It opened to the north, so the glows of the fires within would not be visible from the Wall. Even if by some mischance a patrol should happen to pass atop the Wall tonight, they would see nothing but hills and pines and the icy sheen of starlight on a half-frozen lake. Mance Rayder had planned his thrust well.

Within the rock, the passage descended twenty feet

before it opened out onto a space as large as Winterfell's Great Hall. Cookfires burned amongst the columns, their smoke rising to blacken the stony ceiling. The horses had been hobbled along one wall, beside a shallow pool. A sinkhole in the center of the floor opened on what might have been an even greater cavern below, though the darkness made it hard to tell. Jon could hear the soft rushing sound of an underground stream somewhere below as well.

Jarl was with the Magnar; Mance had given them the joint command. Styr was none too pleased by that, Jon had noted early on. Mance Rayder had called the dark youth a "pet" of Val, who was sister to Dalla, his own queen, which made Jarl a sort of good brother once removed to the King-beyond-the-Wall. The Magnar plainly resented sharing his authority. He had brought a hundred Thenns, five times as many men as Jarl, and often acted as if he had the sole command. But it would be the younger man who got them over the ice, Jon knew. Though he could not have been older than twenty, Jarl had been raiding for eight years, and had gone over the Wall a dozen times with the likes of Alfyn Crowkiller and the Weeper, and more recently with his own band.

The Magnar was direct. "Jarl has warned me of crows, patrolling on high. Tell me all you know of these patrols."

Tell me, Jon noted, not *tell us,* though Jarl stood right beside him. He would have liked nothing better than to refuse the brusque demand, but he knew Styr would put him to death at the slightest disloyalty, and Ygritte as well, for the crime of being his. "There are four men in each patrol, two rangers and two builders," he said. "The builders are supposed to make note of cracks, melting, and other structural problems, while the rangers look for signs of foes. They ride mules."

"Mules?" The earless man frowned. "Mules are slow."

"Slow, but more surefooted on the ice. The patrols often ride atop the Wall, and aside from Castle Black, the paths up there have not been graveled for long years. The mules are bred at Eastwatch, and specially trained to their duty."

"They *often* ride atop the Wall? Not always?"

"No. One patrol in four follows the base instead, to search for cracks in the foundation ice or signs of tunneling."

The Magnar nodded. "Even in far Thenn we know the tale of Arson Iceaxe and his tunnel."

Jon knew the tale as well. Arson Iceaxe had been halfway through the Wall when his tunnel was found by rangers from the Nightfort. They did not trouble to disturb him at his digging, only sealed the way behind with ice and stone and snow. Dolorous Edd used to say that if you pressed your ear flat to the Wall, you could still hear Arson chipping away with his axe.

"When do these patrols go out? How often?"

Jon shrugged. "It changes. I've heard that Lord Commander Qorgyle used to send them out every third day from Castle Black to Eastwatch-by-the-Sea, and every second day from Castle Black to the Shadow Tower. The Watch had more men in his day, though. Lord Commander Mormont prefers to vary the number of patrols and the days of their departure, to make it more difficult for anyone to know their comings and goings. And sometimes the Old Bear will even send a larger force to one of the abandoned castles for a fortnight or a moon's turn." His uncle had originated that tactic, Jon knew. Anything to make the enemy unsure.

"Is Stonedoor manned at present?" asked Jarl. "Greyguard?"

So we're between those two, are we? Jon kept his face carefully blank. "Only Eastwatch, Castle Black, and the Shadow Tower were manned when I left the Wall. I can't speak to what Bowen Marsh or Ser Denys might have done since."

"How many crows remain within the castles?" asked Styr.

"Five hundred at Castle Black. Two hundred at Shadow Tower, perhaps three hundred at Eastwatch." Jon added three hundred men to the count. *If only it were that easy . . .*

Jarl was not fooled, however. "He's lying," he told Styr. "Or else including those they lost on the Fist."

"Crow," the Magnar warned, "do not take me for Mance Rayder. If you lie to me, I will have your tongue."

"I'm no crow, and won't be called a liar." Jon flexed the fingers of his sword hand.

The Magnar of Thenn studied Jon with his chilly grey eyes. "We shall learn their numbers soon enough," he said after a moment. "Go. I will send for you if I have further questions."

Jon bowed his head stiffly, and went. *If all the wildlings were like Styr, it would be easier to betray them.* The Thenns were not like other free folk, though. The Magnar claimed to be the last of the First Men, and ruled with an iron hand. His little land of Thenn was a high mountain valley hidden amongst the northernmost peaks of the Frostfangs, surrounded by cave dwellers, Hornfoot men, giants, and the cannibal clans of the ice rivers. Ygritte said the Thenns were savage fighters, and that their Magnar was a god to them. Jon could believe that. Unlike Jarl and Harma and Rattleshirt, Styr commanded absolute obedience from his men, and that discipline was no doubt part of why Mance had chosen him to go over the Wall.

He walked past the Thenns, sitting atop their rounded bronze helms about their cookfires. *Where did Ygritte get herself to?* He found her gear and his together, but no sign of the girl herself. "She took a torch and went off that way," Grigg the Goat told him, pointing toward the back of the cavern.

Jon followed his finger, and found himself in a dim back room wandering through a maze of columns and stalactites. *She can't be here*, he was thinking, when he heard her laugh. He turned toward the sound, but within ten paces he was in a dead end, facing a blank wall of rose and white flowstone. Baffled, he made his way back the way he'd come, and then he saw it: a dark hole under an outthrust of wet stone. He knelt, listened, heard the faint sound of water. "Ygritte?"

"In here," her voice came back, echoing faintly.

Jon had to crawl a dozen paces before the cave opened up around him. When he stood again, it took his eyes a moment to adjust. Ygritte had brought a torch, but there was no other light. She stood beside a little waterfall that fell from a cleft in the rock down into a wide dark pool. The orange and yellow flames shone against the pale green water.

"What are you doing here?" he asked her.

"I heard water. I wanted t'see how deep the cave went." She pointed with the torch. "There's a passage goes down further. I followed it a hundred paces before I turned back."

"A dead end?"

"You know nothing, Jon Snow. It went on and on and on. There are hundreds o' caves in these hills, and down deep they all connect. There's even a way under your Wall. Gorne's Way."

"Gorne," said Jon. "Gorne was King-beyond-the-Wall."

"Aye," said Ygritte. "Together with his brother Gendel, three thousand years ago. They led a host o' free folk through the caves, and the Watch was none the wiser. But when they come out, the wolves o' Winterfell fell upon them."

"There was a battle," Jon recalled. "Gorne slew the King in the North, but his son picked up his banner and took the crown from his head, and cut down Gorne in turn."

"And the sound o' swords woke the crows in their castles, and they rode out all in black to take the free folk in the rear."

"Yes. Gendel had the king to the south, the Umbers to the east, and the Watch to the north of him. He died as well."

"You know nothing, Jon Snow. Gendel did not die. He cut his way free, *through* the crows, and led his people back north with the wolves howling at their heels. Only Gendel did not know the caves as Gorne had, and took a wrong turn." She swept the torch back and forth, so the shadows jumped and moved. "Deeper he went, and deeper, and when he tried t' turn back the ways that seemed familiar ended in stone rather than sky. Soon his torches began t' fail, one by one, till finally there was naught but dark. Gendel's folk were never seen again, but on a still night you can hear their children's children's children sobbing under the hills, still looking for the way back up. Listen? Do you hear them?"

All Jon could hear was the falling water and the faint crackle of flames. "This way under the Wall was lost as well?"

"Some have searched for it. Them that go too deep find Gendel's children, and Gendel's children are always hungry." Smiling, she set the torch carefully in a notch of rock, and came toward him. "There's naught to eat in the dark but flesh," she whispered, biting at his neck.

Jon nuzzled her hair and filled his nose with the smell of her. "You sound like Old Nan, telling Bran a monster story."

Ygritte punched his shoulder. "An old woman, am I?"

"You're older than me."

"Aye, and wiser. You know nothing, Jon Snow." She pushed away from him, and shrugged out of her rabbitskin vest.

"What are you doing?"

"Showing you how old I am." She unlaced her doeskin shirt, tossed it aside, pulled her three woolen undershirts up over her head all at once. "I want you should see me."

"We shouldn't –"

"We *should*." Her breasts bounced as she stood on one leg to pull one boot, then hopped onto her other foot to attend to the other. Her nipples were wide pink circles. "You as well," Ygritte said as she yanked down her sheepskin breeches. "If you want to look you have to show. You know nothing, Jon Snow."

"I know I want you," he heard himself say, all his vows and all his honor forgotten. She stood before him naked as her name day, and he was as hard as the rock around them. He had been in her half a hundred times by now, but always beneath the furs, with others all around them. He had never seen how beautiful she was. Her legs were skinny but well muscled, the hair at the juncture of her thighs a brighter red than that on her head. *Does that make it even luckier?* He pulled her close. "I love the smell of you," he said. "I love your red hair. I love your mouth, and the way you kiss me. I love your smile. I love your teats." He kissed them, one and then the other. "I love your skinny legs, and what's between them." He knelt to kiss her there, lightly on her mound at first, but Ygritte moved her legs apart a little, and he saw the pink inside and kissed that as well, and tasted her. She gave a little gasp. "If you love me all so much, why are you still dressed?" she whispered. "You know nothing, Jon Snow. *Noth – oh. Oh. OHHH.*"

Afterward, she was almost shy, or as shy as Ygritte ever got. "That thing you did," she said, when they lay together on their piled clothes. "With your . . . mouth." She hesitated. "Is that . . . is it what lords do to their ladies, down in the south?"

"I don't think so." No one had ever told Jon just what lords did with their ladies. "I only . . . wanted to kiss you there, that's all. You seemed to like it."

"Aye. I . . . I liked it some. No one taught you such?"

"There's been no one," he confessed. "Only you."

"A maid," she teased. "You were a maid."

He gave her closest nipple a playful pinch. "I was a man of the Night's Watch." *Was*, he heard himself say. What was he now? He did not want to look at that. "Were you a maid?"

Ygritte pushed herself onto an elbow. "I am nineteen, and a spearwife, and kissed by fire. How could I be maiden?"

"Who was he?"

"A boy at a feast, five years past. He'd come trading with his brothers, and he had hair like mine, kissed by fire, so I thought he would be lucky. But he was weak. When he came back t' try and steal me, Longspear broke his arm and ran him off, and he never tried again, not once."

"It wasn't Longspear, then?" Jon was relieved. He liked Longspear, with his homely face and friendly ways.

She punched him. "That's vile. Would you bed your sister?"

"Longspear's not your brother."

"He's of my village. You know nothing, Jon Snow. A true man steals a woman from afar, t' strengthen the clan.

Women who bed brothers or fathers or clan kin offend the gods, and are cursed with weak and sickly children. Even monsters."

"Craster weds his daughters," Jon pointed out.

She punched him again. "Craster's more your kind than ours. His father was a crow who stole a woman out of Whitetree village, but after he had her he flew back t' his Wall. She went t' Castle Black once t' show the crow his son, but the brothers blew their horns and run her off. Craster's blood is black, and he bears a heavy curse." She ran her fingers lightly across his stomach. "I feared you'd do the same once. Fly back to the Wall. You never knew what t' do after you stole me."

Jon sat up. "Ygritte, I never stole you."

"Aye, you did. You jumped down the mountain and killed Orell, and afore I could get my axe you had a knife at my throat. I thought you'd have me then, or kill me, or maybe both, but you never did. And when I told you the tale o' Bael the Bard and how he plucked the rose o' Winterfell, I thought you'd know to pluck me then for certain, but you didn't. You know *nothing*, Jon Snow." She gave him a shy smile. "You might be learning some, though."

The light was shifting all about her, Jon noticed suddenly. He looked around. "We had best go up. The torch is almost done."

"Is the crow afeared o' Gendel's children?" she said, with a grin. "It's only a little way up, and I'm not done with you, Jon Snow." She pushed him back down on the clothes and straddled him. "Would you . . ." She hesitated.

"What?" he prompted, as the torch began to gutter.

"Do it again?" Ygritte blurted. "With your mouth? The lord's kiss? And I . . . I could see if you liked it any."

By the time the torch burned out, Jon Snow no longer cared.

His guilt came back afterward, but weaker than before. *If this is so wrong*, he wondered, *why did the gods make it feel so good?*

The grotto was pitch-dark by the time they finished. The only light was the dim glow of the passage back up to the larger cavern, where a score of fires burned. They were soon fumbling and bumping into each other as they tried to dress in the dark. Ygritte stumbled into the pool and screeched at the cold of the water. When Jon laughed, she pulled him in too. They wrestled and splashed in the dark, and then she was in his arms again, and it turned out they were not finished after all.

"Jon Snow," she told him, when he'd spent his seed inside her, "don't move now, sweet. I like the feel of you in there, I do. Let's not go back t' Styr and Jarl. Let's go down inside, and join up with Gendel's children. I don't ever want t' leave this cave, Jon Snow. Not ever."

DAENERYS

" *A* ll?" The slave girl sounded wary. "Your Grace, did this one's worthless ears mishear you?"

Cool green light filtered down through the diamond-shaped panes of colored glass set in the sloping triangular walls, and a breeze was blowing gently through the terrace doors, carrying the scents of fruit and flowers from the garden beyond. "Your ears heard true," said Dany. "I want to buy them all. Tell the Good Masters, if you will."

She had chosen a Qartheen gown today. The deep violet silk brought out the purple of her eyes. The cut of it bared her left breast. While the Good Masters of Astapor conferred among themselves in low voices, Dany sipped tart persimmon wine from a tall silver flute. She could not quite make out all that they were saying, but she could hear the greed.

Each of the eight brokers was attended by two or three body slaves . . . though one Grazdan, the eldest, had six. So as not to seem a beggar, Dany had brought her own attendants; Irri and Jhiqui in their sandsilk trousers and painted vests, old Whitebeard and mighty Belwas, her bloodriders. Ser Jorah stood behind her sweltering in his green surcoat with the black bear of Mormont embroidered upon it. The smell of his sweat was an earthy answer to the sweet perfumes that drenched the Astapori.

"All," growled Kraznys mo Nakloz, who smelled of peaches today. The slave girl repeated the word in the Common Tongue of Westeros. "Of thousands, there are eight. Is this what she means by *all*? There are also six centuries, who shall be part of a ninth thousand when complete. Would she have them too?"

"I would," said Dany when the question was put to her. "The eight thousands, the six centuries . . . and the ones still in training as well. The ones who have not earned the spikes."

Kraznys turned back to his fellows. Once again they conferred among themselves. The translator had told Dany their names, but it was hard to keep them straight. Four of the men seemed to be named Grazdan, presumably after Grazdan the Great who had founded Old Ghis in the dawn of days. They all looked alike; thick fleshy men with amber skin, broad noses, dark eyes. Their wiry hair was black, or a dark red, or that queer mixture of red and black that was peculiar to Ghiscari. All wrapped themselves in *tokars*, a garment permitted only to freeborn men of Astapor.

It was the fringe on the *tokar* that proclaimed a man's status, Dany had been told by Captain Groleo. In this cool green room atop the pyramid, two of the slavers wore *tokars* fringed in silver, five had gold fringes, and one, the oldest Grazdan, displayed a fringe of fat white pearls that clacked together softly when he shifted in his seat or moved an arm.

"We cannot sell half-trained boys," one of the silver-fringe Grazdans was saying to the others.

"We can, if her gold is good," said a fatter man whose fringe was gold.

"They are not Unsullied. They have not killed their sucklings. If they fail in the field, they will shame us. And even if we cut five thousand raw boys tomorrow, it would be ten years before they are fit for sale. What would we tell the next buyer who comes seeking Unsullied?"

"We will tell him that he must wait," said the fat man. "Gold in my purse is better than gold in my future."

Dany let them argue, sipping the tart persimmon wine

and trying to keep her face blank and ignorant. *I will have them all, no matter the price,* she told herself. The city had a hundred slave traders, but the eight before her were the greatest. When selling bed slaves, fieldhands, scribes, craftsmen, and tutors, these men were rivals, but their ancestors had allied one with the other for the purpose of making and selling the Unsullied. *Brick and blood built Astapor, and brick and blood her people.*

It was Kraznys who finally announced their decision. "Tell her that the eight thousands she shall have, if her gold proves sufficient. And the six centuries, if she wishes. Tell her to come back in a year, and we will sell her another two thousand."

"In a year I shall be in Westeros," said Dany when she had heard the translation. "My need is *now*. The Unsullied are well trained, but even so, many will fall in battle. I shall need the boys as replacements to take up the swords they drop." She put her wine aside and leaned toward the slave girl. "Tell the Good Masters that I will want even the little ones who still have their puppies. Tell them that I will pay as much for the boy they cut yesterday as for an Unsullied in a spiked helm."

The girl told them. The answer was still no.

Dany frowned in annoyance. "Very well. Tell them I will pay double, so long as I get them all."

"Double?" The fat one in the gold fringe all but drooled.

"This little whore is a fool, truly," said Khaznys mo Nakloz. "Ask her for triple, I say. She is desperate enough to pay. Ask for ten times the price of every slave, yes."

The tall Grazdan with the spiked beard spoke in the Common Tongue, though not so well as the slave girl. "Your Grace," he growled, "Westeros is being wealthy, yes, but you are not being queen now. Perhaps will never being queen. Even Unsullied may be losing battles to savage steel knights of Seven Kingdoms. I am reminding, the Good Masters of Astapor are not selling flesh for promisings. Are you having gold and trading goods sufficient to be paying for all these eunuchs you are wanting?"

"You know the answer to that better than I, Good Master," Dany replied. "Your men have gone through my ships and tallied every bead of amber and jar of saffron. How much do I have?"

"Sufficient to be buying one of thousands," the Good Master said, with a contemptuous smile. "Yet you are paying double, you are saying. Five centuries, then, is all you buy."

"Your pretty crown might buy another century," said the fat one in Valyrian. "Your crown of the three dragons."

Dany waited for his words to be translated. "My crown is not for sale." When Viserys sold their mother's crown, the last joy had gone from him, leaving only rage. "Nor will I enslave my people, nor sell their goods and horses. But my ships you can have. The great cog *Balerion* and the galleys *Vhagar* and *Meraxes*." She had warned Groleo and the other captains it might come to this, though they had protested the necessity of it furiously. "Three good ships should be worth more than a few paltry eunuchs."

The fat Grazdan turned to the others. They conferred in low voices once again. "Two of the thousands," the one with the spiked beard said when he turned back. "It is too much, but the Good Masters are being generous and your need is being great."

Two thousand would never serve for what she meant to do. *I must have them all.* Dany knew what she must do now, though the taste of it was so bitter that even the persimmon wine could not cleanse it from her month. She had considered long and hard and found no other way. *It is my only choice.* "Give me all," she said, "and you may have a dragon."

There was the sound of indrawn breath from Jhiqui beside her. Kraznys smiled at his fellows. "Did I not tell you? Anything, she would give us."

Whitebeard stared in shocked disbelief. His hand trembled where it grasped the staff. *"No."* He went to one knee before her. "Your Grace, I beg you, win your throne with dragons, not slaves. You must not do this thing –"

"You must not presume to instruct me. Ser Jorah, remove Whitebeard from my presence."

Mormont seized the old man roughly by an elbow,

yanked him back to his feet, and marched him out onto the terrace.

"Tell the Good Masters I regret this interruption," said Dany to the slave girl. "Tell them I await their answer."

She knew the answer, though; she could see it in the glitter of their eyes and the smiles they tried so hard to hide. Astapor had thousands of eunuchs, and even more slave boys waiting to be cut, but there were only three living dragons in all the great wide world. *And the Ghiscari lust for dragons.* How could they not? Five times had Old Ghis contended with Valyria when the world was young, and five times gone down to bleak defeat. For the Freehold had dragons, and the Empire had none.

The oldest Grazdan stirred in his seat, and his pearls clacked together softly. "A dragon of our choice," he said in a thin, hard voice. "The black one is largest and healthiest."

"His name is Drogon." She nodded.

"All your goods, save your crown and your queenly raiment, which we will allow you to keep. The three ships. And Drogon."

"Done," she said, in the Common Tongue.

"Done," the old Grazdan answered in his thick Valyrian.

The others echoed that old man of the pearl fringe. "Done," the slave girl translated, "and done, and done, eight times done."

"The Unsullied will learn your savage tongue quick enough," added Kraznys mo Nakloz, when all the arrangements had been made, "but until such time you will need a slave to speak to them. Take this one as our gift to you, a token of a bargain well struck."

"I shall," said Dany.

The slave girl rendered his words to her, and hers to him. If she had feelings about being given for a token, she took care not to let them show.

Arstan Whitebeard held his tongue as well, when Dany swept by him on the terrace. He followed her down the steps in silence, but she could hear his hardwood staff *tap tap*ping on the red bricks as they went. She did not blame him for his fury. It was a wretched thing she did. *The Mother of Dragons has sold her strongest child.* Even the thought made her ill.

Yet down in the Plaza of Pride, standing on the hot red bricks between the slavers' pyramid and the barracks of the eunuchs, Dany turned on the old man. "Whitebeard," she said, "I want your counsel, and you should never fear to speak your mind with me . . . when we are alone. But *never* question me in front of strangers. Is that understood?"

"Yes, Your Grace," he said unhappily.

"I am not a child," she told him. "I am a queen."

"Yet even queens can err. The Astapori have cheated you, Your Grace. A dragon is worth more than any army. Aegon proved that three hundred years ago, upon the Field of Fire."

"I know what Aegon proved. I mean to prove a few things of my own." Dany turned away from him, to the slave girl standing meekly beside her litter. "Do you have a name, or must you draw a new one every day from some barrel?"

"That is only for Unsullied," the girl said. Then she realized the question had been asked in High Valyrian. Her eyes went wide. "Oh."

"Your name is Oh?"

"No. Your Grace, forgive this one her outburst. Your slave's name is Missandei, but . . ."

"Missandei is no longer a slave. I free you, from this instant. Come ride with me in the litter, I wish to talk." Rakharo helped them in, and Dany drew the curtains shut against the dust and heat. "If you stay with me you will serve as one of my handmaids," she said as they set off. "I shall keep you by my side to speak for me as you spoke for Kraznys. But you may leave my service whenever you choose, if you have father or mother you would sooner return to."

"This one will stay," the girl said. "This one . . . I . . . there is no place for me to go. This . . . I will serve you, gladly."

"I can give you freedom, but not safety," Dany warned.

"I have a world to cross and wars to fight. You may go hungry. You may grow sick. You may be killed."

"*Valar morghulis*," said Missandei, in High Valyrian.

"All men must die," Dany agreed, "but not for a long while, we may pray." She leaned back on the pillows and took the girl's hand. "Are these Unsullied truly fearless?"

"Yes, Your Grace."

"You serve me now. Is it true they feel no pain?"

"The wine of courage kills such feelings. By the time they slay their sucklings, they have been drinking it for years."

"And they are obedient?"

"Obedience is all they know. If you told them not to breathe, they would find that easier than not to obey."

Dany nodded. "And when I am done with them?"

"Your Grace?"

"When I have won my war and claimed the throne that was my father's, my knights will sheathe their swords and return to their keeps, to their wives and children and mothers . . . to their *lives*. But these eunuchs have no lives. What am I to do with eight thousand eunuchs when there are no more battles to be fought?"

"The Unsullied make fine guards and excellent watchmen, Your Grace," said Missandei. "And it is never hard to find a buyer for such fine well-blooded troops."

"Men are not bought and sold in Westeros, they tell me."

"With all respect, Your Grace, Unsullied are not men."

"If I did resell them, how would I know they could not be used against me?" Dany asked pointedly. "Would they do that? Fight *against* me, even do me harm?"

"If their master commanded. They do not question, Your Grace. All the questions have been culled from them. They obey." She looked troubled. "When you are . . . when you are done with them . . . Your Grace might command them to fall upon their swords."

"And even that, they would do?"

"Yes." Missandei's voice had grown soft. "Your Grace."

Dany squeezed her hand. "You would sooner I did not ask it of them, though. Why is that? Why do you care?"

"This one does not . . . I . . . Your Grace . . ."

"Tell me."

The girl lowered her eyes. "Three of them were my brothers once, Your Grace."

Then I hope your brothers are as brave and clever as you. Dany leaned back into her pillow, and let the litter bear her onward, back to *Balerion* one last time to set her world in order. *And back to Drogon.* Her mouth set grimly.

It was a long, dark, windy night that followed. Dany fed her dragons as she always did, but found she had no appetite herself. She cried awhile, alone in her cabin, then dried her tears long enough for yet another argument with Groleo. "Magister Illyrio is not here," she finally had to tell him, "and if he was, he could not sway me either. I need the Unsullied more than I need these ships, and I will hear no more about it."

The anger burned the grief and fear from her, for a few hours at the least. Afterward she called her bloodriders to her cabin, with Ser Jorah. They were the only ones she truly trusted.

She meant to sleep afterward, to be well rested for the morrow, but an hour of restless tossing in the stuffy confines of the cabin soon convinced her that was hopeless. Outside her door she found Aggo fitting a new string to his bow by the light of a swinging oil lamp. Rakharo sat crosslegged on the deck beside him, sharpening his *arakh* with a whetstone. Dany told them both to keep on with what they were doing, and went up on deck for a taste of the cool night air. The crew left her alone as they went about their business, but Ser Jorah soon joined her by the rail. *He is never far*, Dany thought. *He knows my moods too well.*

"*Khaleesi.* You ought to be asleep. Tomorrow will be hot and hard, I promise you. You'll need your strength."

"Do you remember Eroeh?" she asked him.

"The Lhazareen girl?"

"They were raping her, but I stopped them and took her under my protection. Only when my sun-and-stars was dead Mago took her back, used her again, and killed her. Aggo said it was her fate."

"I remember," Ser Jorah said.

"I was alone for a long time, Jorah. All alone but for my brother. I was such a small scared thing. Viserys should have protected me, but instead he hurt me and scared me worse. He shouldn't have done that. He wasn't just my brother, he was my *king*. Why do the gods make kings and queens, if not to protect the ones who can't protect themselves?"

"Some kings make themselves. Robert did."

"He was no true king," Dany said scornfully. "He did no justice. Justice . . . that's what kings are *for*."

Ser Jorah had no answer. He only smiled, and touched her hair, so lightly. It was enough.

That night she dreamt that she was Rhaegar, riding to the Trident. But she was mounted on a dragon, not a horse. When she saw the Usurper's rebel host across the river they were armored all in ice, but she bathed them in dragonfire and they melted away like dew and turned the Trident into a torrent. Some small part of her knew that she was dreaming, but another part exulted. *This is how it was meant to be. The other was a nightmare, and I have only now awakened.*

She woke suddenly in the darkness of her cabin, still flush with triumph. *Balerion* seemed to wake with her, and she heard the faint creak of wood, water lapping against the hull, a footfall on the deck above her head. And something else.

Someone was in the cabin with her.

"Irri? Jhiqui? Where are you?" Her handmaids did not respond. It was too black to see, but she could hear them breathing. "Jorah, is that you?"

"They sleep," a woman said. "They all sleep." The voice was very close. "Even dragons must sleep."

She is standing over me. "Who's there?" Dany peered into the darkness. She thought she could see a shadow, the faintest outline of a shape. "What do you want of me?"

"Remember. To go north, you must journey south. To reach the west, you must go east. To go forward you must go back, and to touch the light you must pass beneath the shadow."

"Quaithe?" Dany sprung from the bed and threw open the door. Pale yellow lantern light flooded the cabin, and Irri and Jhiqui sat up sleepily. *"Khaleesi!"* murmured Jhiqui, rubbing her eyes. Viserion woke and opened his jaws, and a puff of flame brightened even the darkest corners. There was no sign of a woman in a red lacquer mask. *"Khaleesi,* are you unwell?" asked Jhiqui.

"A dream." Dany shook her head. "I dreamed a dream, no more. Go back to sleep. All of us, go back to sleep." Yet try as she might, sleep would not come again.

If I look back I am lost, Dany told herself the next morning as she entered Astapor through the harbor gates. She dared not remind herself how small and insignificant her following truly was, or she would lose all courage. Today she rode her silver, clad in horsehair pants and painted leather vest, a bronze medallion belt about her waist and two more crossed between her breasts. Irri and Jhiqui had braided her hair and hung it with a tiny silver bell whose chime sang of the Undying of Qarth, burned in their Palace of Dust.

The red brick streets of Astapor were almost crowded this morning. Slaves and servants lined the ways, while the slavers and their women donned their *tokars* to look down from their stepped pyramids. *They are not so different from Qartheen after all,* she thought. *They want a glimpse of dragons to tell their children of, and their children's children.* It made her wonder how many of them would ever have children.

Aggo went before her with his great Dothraki bow. Strong Belwas walked to the right of her mare, the girl Missandei to her left. Ser Jorah Mormont was behind in mail and surcoat, glowering at anyone who came too near. Rakharo and Jhogo protected the litter. Dany had commanded that the top be removed, so her three dragons might be chained to the platform. Irri and Jhiqui rode with them, to try and keep them calm. Yet Viserion's tail lashed back and forth, and smoke rose angry from his nostrils. Rhaegal could sense something wrong as well. Thrice he tried to take wing, only to be pulled down by the heavy chain in Jhiqui's hand. Drogon coiled into a ball, wings and tail tucked tight. Only his eyes remained to tell that he was not asleep.

The rest of her people followed: Groleo and the other captains and their crews, and the eighty-three Dothraki who remained to her of the hundred thousand who had once ridden in Drogo's *khalasar*. She put the oldest and weakest on the inside of the column, with the nursing women and those with child, and the little girls, and the boys too young to braid their hair. The rest – her warriors, such as they were – rode outside and moved their dismal herd along, the hundred-odd gaunt horses that had survived both red waste and black salt sea.

I ought to have a banner sewn, she thought as she led her tattered band up along Astapor's meandering river. She closed her eyes to imagine how it would look: all flowing black silk, and on it the red three-headed dragon of Targaryen, breathing golden flames. *A banner such as Rhaegar might have borne.* The river's banks were strangely tranquil. The Worm, the Astapori called the stream. It was wide and slow and crooked, dotted with tiny wooded islands. She glimpsed children playing on one of them, darting amongst elegant marble statues. On another island two lovers kissed in the shade of tall green trees, with no more shame than Dothraki at a wedding. Without clothing, she could not tell if they were slave or free.

The Plaza of Pride with its great bronze harpy was too small to hold all the Unsullied she had bought. Instead they had been assembled in the Plaza of Punishment, fronting on Astapor's main gate, so they might be marched directly from the city once Daenerys had taken them in hand. There were no bronze statues here; only a wooden platform where rebellious slaves were racked, and flayed, and hanged. "The Good Masters place them so they will be the first thing a new slave sees upon entering the city," Missandei told her as they came to the plaza.

At first glimpse, Dany thought their skin was striped like the zorses of the Jogos Nhai. Then she rode her silver nearer and saw the raw red flesh beneath the crawling black stripes. *Flies. Flies and maggots.* The rebellious slaves had been peeled like a man might peel an apple, in a long curling strip. One man had an arm black with flies from fingers to elbow, and red and white beneath. Dany reined in beneath him. "What did this one do?"

"He raised a hand against his owner."

Her stomach roiling, Dany wheeled her silver about and trotted toward the center of the plaza, and the army she had bought so dear. Rank on rank on rank they stood, her stone halfmen with their hearts of brick; eight thousand and six hundred in the spiked bronze caps of fully trained Unsullied, and five thousand odd behind them, bareheaded, yet armed with spears and shortswords. The ones farthest to the back were only boys, she saw, but they stood as straight and still as all the rest.

Kraznys mo Nakloz and his fellows were all there to greet her. Other well-born Astapori stood in knots behind them, sipping wine from silver flutes as slaves circulated among them with trays of olives and cherries and figs. The elder Grazdan sat in a sedan chair supported by four huge copper-skinned slaves. Half a dozen mounted lancers rode along the edges of the plaza, keeping back the crowds who had come to watch. The sun flashed blinding bright off the polished copper disks sewn to their cloaks, but she could not help but notice how nervous their horses seemed. *They fear the dragons. And well they might.*

Kraznys had a slave help her from her saddle. His own hands were full; one clutched his *tokar*, while the other held an ornate whip. "Here they are." He looked at Missandei. "Tell her they are hers . . . if she can pay."

"She can," the girl said.

Ser Jorah barked a command, and the trade goods were brought forward. Six bales of tiger skins, three hundred bolts of fine silk. Jars of saffron, jars of myrrh, jars of pepper and curry and cardamom, an onyx mask, twelve jade monkeys, casks of ink in red and black and green, a box of rare black amethysts, a box of pearls, a cask of pitted olives stuffed with maggots, a dozen casks of pickled cave fish, a great brass gong and a hammer to beat it with, seventeen ivory eyes, and a huge chest full of books written in tongues that Dany could not read. And more, and more, and more. Her people stacked it all before the slavers.

While the payment was being made, Kraznys mo Nakloz favored her with a few final words on the handling of her troops. "They are green as yet," he said through Missandei. "Tell the whore of Westeros she would be wise to blood them early. There are many small cities between here and there, cities ripe for sacking. Whatever plunder she takes will be hers alone. Unsullied have no lust for gold or gems. And should she take captives, a few guards will suffice to march them back to Astapor. We'll buy the healthy ones, and for a good price. And who knows? In ten years, some of the boys she sends us may be Unsullied in their turn. Thus all shall prosper."

Finally there were no more trade goods to add to the pile. Her Dothraki mounted their horses once more, and Dany said, "This was all we could carry. The rest awaits you on the ships, a great quantity of amber and wine and black rice. And you have the ships themselves. So all that remains is . . ."

". . . the dragon," finished the Grazdan with the spiked beard, who spoke the Common Tongue so thickly.

"And here he waits." Ser Jorah and Belwas walked beside her to the litter, where Drogon and his brothers lay basking in the sun. Jhiqui unfastened one end of the chain, and handed it down to her. When she gave a yank, the black dragon raised his head, hissing, and unfolded wings of night and scarlet. Kraznys mo Nakloz smiled broadly as their shadow fell across him.

Dany handed the slaver the end of Drogon's chain. In return he presented her with the whip. The handle was black dragonbone, elaborately carved and inlaid with gold. Nine long thin leather lashes trailed from it, each one tipped by a gilded claw. The gold pommel was a woman's head, with pointed ivory teeth. "The harpy's fingers," Kraznys named the scourge.

Dany turned the whip in her hand. *Such a light thing, to bear such weight.* "Is it done, then? Do they belong to me?"

"It is done," he agreed, giving the chain a sharp pull to bring Drogon down from the litter.

Dany mounted her silver. She could feel her heart

thumping in her chest. She felt desperately afraid. *Was this what my brother would have done?* She wondered if Prince Rhaegar had been this anxious when he saw the Usurper's host formed up across the Trident with all their banners floating on the wind.

She stood in her stirrups and raised the harpy's fingers above her head for all the Unsullied to see. *"IT IS DONE!"* she cried at the top of her lungs. *"YOU ARE MINE!"* She gave the mare her heels and galloped along the first rank, holding the fingers high. *"YOU ARE THE DRAGON'S NOW! YOU'RE BOUGHT AND PAID FOR! IT IS DONE! IT IS DONE!"*

She glimpsed old Grazdan turn his grey head sharply. *He hears me speak Valyrian.* The other slavers were not listening. They crowded around Kraznys and the dragon, shouting advice. Though the Astapori yanked and tugged, Drogon would not budge off the litter. Smoke rose grey from his open jaws, and his long neck curled and straightened as he snapped at the slaver's face.

It is time to cross the Trident, Dany thought, as she wheeled and rode her silver back. Her bloodriders moved in close around her. "You are in difficulty," she observed.

"He will not come," Kraznys said.

"There is a reason. A dragon is no slave." And Dany swept the lash down as hard as she could across the slaver's face. Kraznys screamed and staggered back, the blood running red down his cheeks into his perfumed beard. The harpy's fingers had torn his features half to pieces with one slash, but she did not pause to contemplate the ruin. "Drogon," she sang out loudly, sweetly, all her fear forgotten. *"Dracarys."*

The black dragon spread his wings and roared.

A lance of swirling dark flame took Kraznys full in the face. His eyes melted and ran down his cheeks, and the oil in his hair and beard burst so fiercely into fire that for an instant the slaver wore a burning crown twice as tall as his head. The sudden stench of charred meat overwhelmed even his perfume, and his wail seemed to drown all other sound.

Then the Plaza of Punishment blew apart into blood

and chaos. The Good Masters were shrieking, stumbling, shoving one another aside and tripping over the fringes of their *tokars* in their haste. Drogon flew almost lazily at Kraznys, black wings beating. As he gave the slaver another taste of fire, Irri and Jhiqui unchained Viserion and Rhaegal, and suddenly there were three dragons in the air. When Dany turned to look, a third of Astapor's proud demon-horned warriors were fighting to stay atop their terrified mounts, and another third were fleeing in a bright blaze of shiny copper. One man kept his saddle long enough to draw a sword, but Jhogo's whip coiled about his neck and cut off his shout. Another lost a hand to Rakharo's *arakh* and rode off reeling and spurting blood. Aggo sat calmly notching arrows to his bowstring and sending them at *tokars*. Silver, gold, or plain, he cared nothing for the fringe. Strong Belwas had his *arakh* out as well, and he spun it as he charged.

"*Spears!*" Dany heard one Astapori shout. It was Grazdan, old Grazdan in his tokar heavy with pearls. "*Unsullied! Defend us, stop them, defend your masters! Spears! Swords!*"

When Rakharo put an arrow through his mouth, the slaves holding his sedan chair broke and ran, dumping him unceremoniously on the ground. The old man crawled to the first rank of eunuchs, his blood pooling on the bricks. The Unsullied did not so much as look down to watch him die. Rank on rank on rank, they stood.

And did not move. *The gods have heard my prayer.*

"*Unsullied!*" Dany galloped before them, her silvergold braid flying behind her, her bell chiming with every stride. "Slay the Good Masters, slay the soldiers, slay every man who wears a *tokar* or holds a whip, but harm no child under twelve, and strike the chains off every slave you see." She raised the harpy's fingers in the air . . . and then she flung the scourge aside. "*Freedom!*" she sang out. "*Dracarys! Dracarys!*"

"*Dracarys!*" they shouted back, the sweetest word she'd ever heard. "*Dracarys! Dracarys!*" And all around them slavers ran and sobbed and begged and died, and the dusty air was filled with spears and fire.

SANSA

O n the morning her new gown was to be ready, the
serving girls filled Sansa's tub with steaming hot
water and scrubbed her head to toe until she
glowed pink. Cersei's own bedmaid trimmed her nails and
brushed and curled her auburn hair so it fell down her
back in soft ringlets. She brought a dozen of the queen's
favorite scents as well. Sansa chose a sharp sweet fragrance
with a hint of lemon in it under the smell of flowers. The
maid dabbed some on her finger and touched Sansa behind
each ear, and under her chin, and then lightly on her
nipples.

Cersei herself arrived with the seamstress, and watched
as they dressed Sansa in her new clothes. The smallclothes
were all silk, but the gown itself was ivory samite and
cloth-of-silver, and lined with silvery satin. The points of
the long dagged sleeves almost touched the ground when
she lowered her arms. And it was a woman's gown, not a
little girl's, there was no doubt of that. The bodice was
slashed in front almost to her belly, the deep vee covered
over with a panel of ornate Myrish lace in dove-grey. The
skirts were long and full, the waist so tight that Sansa had
to hold her breath as they laced her into it. They brought
her new shoes as well, slippers of soft grey doeskin that
hugged her feet like lovers. "You are very beautiful, my
lady," the seamstress said when she was dressed.

"I am, aren't I?" Sansa giggled, and spun, her skirts swirling around her. "Oh, I *am*." She could not wait for Willas to see her like this. *He will love me, he will, he must . . . he will forget Winterfell when he sees me, I'll see that he does.*

Queen Cersei studied her critically. "A few gems, I think. The moonstones Joffrey gave her."

"At once, Your Grace," her maid replied.

When the moonstones hung from Sansa's ears and about her neck, the queen nodded. "Yes. The gods have been kind to you, Sansa. You are a lovely girl. It seems almost obscene to squander such sweet innocence on that gargoyle."

"What gargoyle?" Sansa did not understand. Did she mean Willas? *How could she know?* No one knew, but her and Margaery and the Queen of Thorns . . . oh, and Dontos, but he didn't count.

Cersei Lannister ignored the question. "The cloak," she commanded, and the women brought it out: a long cloak of white velvet heavy with pearls. A fierce direwolf was embroidered upon it in silver thread. Sansa looked at it with sudden dread. "Your father's colors," said Cersei, as they fastened it about her neck with a slender silver chain.

A maiden's cloak. Sansa's hand went to her throat. She would have torn the thing away if she had dared.

"You're prettier with your mouth closed, Sansa," Cersei told her. "Come along now, the septon is waiting. And the wedding guests as well."

"No," Sansa blurted. "*No.*"

"Yes. You are a ward of the crown. The king stands in your father's place, since your brother is an attainted traitor. That means he has every right to dispose of your hand. You are to marry my brother Tyrion."

My claim, she thought, sickened. Dontos the Fool was not so foolish after all; he had seen the truth of it. Sansa backed away from the queen. "I won't." *I'm to marry Willas, I'm to be the lady of Highgarden, please . . .*

"I understand your reluctance. Cry if you must. In your place, I would likely rip my hair out. He's a loathsome little imp, no doubt of it, but marry him you shall."

"You can't make me."

"Of course we can. You may come along quietly and say your vows as befits a lady, or you may struggle and scream and make a spectacle for the stableboys to titter over, but you will end up wedded and bedded all the same." The queen opened the door. Ser Meryn Trant and Ser Osmund Kettleblack were waiting without, in the white scale armor of the Kingsguard. "Escort Lady Sansa to the sept," she told them. "Carry her if you must, but try not to tear the gown, it was very costly."

Sansa tried to run, but Cersei's handmaid caught her before she'd gone a yard. Ser Meryn Trant gave her a look that made her cringe, but Kettleblack touched her almost gently and said, "Do as you're told, sweetling, it won't be so bad. Wolves are supposed to be brave, aren't they?"

Brave. Sansa took a deep breath. *I am a Stark, yes, I can be brave.* They were all looking at her, the way they had looked at her that day in the yard when Ser Boros Blount had torn her clothes off. It had been the Imp who saved her from a beating that day, the same man who was waiting for her now. *He is not so bad as the rest of them,* she told herself. "I'll go."

Cersei smiled. "I knew you would."

Afterward, she could not remember leaving the room or descending the steps or crossing the yard. It seemed to take all her attention just to put one foot down in front of the other. Ser Meryn and Ser Osmund walked beside her, in cloaks as pale as her own, lacking only the pearls and the direwolf that had been her father's. Joffrey himself was waiting for her on the steps of the castle sept. The king was resplendent in crimson and gold, his crown on his head. "I'm your father today," he announced.

"You're not," she flared. "You'll never be."

His face darkened. "I am. I'm your father, and I can marry you to whoever I like. To *anyone.* You'll marry the pig boy if I say so, and bed down with him in the sty." His green eyes glittered with amusement. "Or maybe I should give you to Ilyn Payne, would you like him better?"

Her heart lurched. "Please, Your Grace," she begged.

"If you ever loved me even a little bit, don't make me marry your –"

" – uncle?" Tyrion Lannister stepped through the doors of the sept. "Your Grace," he said to Joffrey. "Grant me a moment alone with Lady Sansa, if you would be so kind?"

The king was about to refuse, but his mother gave him a sharp look. They drew off a few feet.

Tyrion wore a doublet of black velvet covered with golden scrollwork, thigh-high boots that added three inches to his height, a chain of rubies and lions' heads. But the gash across his face was raw and red, and his nose was a hideous scab. "You are very beautiful, Sansa," he told her.

"It is good of you to say so, my lord." She did not know what else to say. *Should I tell him he is handsome? He'll think me a fool or a liar.* She lowered her gaze and held her tongue.

"My lady, this is no way to bring you to your wedding. I am sorry for that. And for making this so sudden, and so secret. My lord father felt it necessary, for reasons of state. Else I would have come to you sooner, as I wished." He waddled closer. "You did not ask for this marriage, I know. No more than I did. If I had refused you, however, they would have wed you to my cousin Lancel. Perhaps you would prefer that. He is nearer your age, and fairer to look upon. If that is your wish, say so, and I will end this farce."

I don't want any Lannister, she wanted to say. *I want Willas, I want Highgarden and the puppies and the barge, and sons named Eddard and Bran and Rickon.* But then she remembered what Dontos had told her in the godswood. *Tyrell or Lannister, it makes no matter, it's not me they want, only my claim.* "You are kind, my lord," she said, defeated. "I am a ward of the throne and my duty is to marry as the king commands."

He studied her with his mismatched eyes. "I know I am not the sort of husband young girls dream of, Sansa," he said softly, "but neither am I Joffrey."

"No," she said. "You were kind to me. I remember."

Tyrion offered her a thick, blunt-fingered hand. "Come, then. Let us do our duty."

So she put her hand in his, and he led her to the marriage altar, where the septon waited between the Mother and the Father to join their lives together. She saw Dontos in his fool's motley, looking at her with big round eyes. Ser Balon Swann and Ser Boros Blount were there in Kingsguard white, but not Ser Loras. *None of the Tyrells are here*, she realized suddenly. But there were other witnesses aplenty; the eunuch Varys, Ser Addam Marbrand, Lord Philip Foote, Ser Bronn, Jalabhar Xho, a dozen others. Lord Gyles was coughing, Lady Ermesande was at the breast, and Lady Tanda's pregnant daughter was sobbing for no apparent reason. *Let her sob*, Sansa thought. *Perhaps I shall do the same before this day is done.*

The ceremony passed as in a dream. Sansa did all that was required of her. There were prayers and vows and singing, and tall candles burning, a hundred dancing lights that the tears in her eyes transformed into a thousand. Thankfully no one seemed to notice that she was crying as she stood there, wrapped in her father's colors; or if they did, they pretended not to. In what seemed no time at all, they came to the changing of the cloaks.

As father of the realm, Joffrey took the place of Lord Eddard Stark. Sansa stood stiff as a lance as his hands came over her shoulders to fumble with the clasp of her cloak. One of them brushed her breast and lingered to give it a little squeeze. Then the clasp opened, and Joff swept her maiden's cloak away with a kingly flourish and a grin.

His uncle's part went less well. The bride's cloak he held was huge and heavy, crimson velvet richly worked with lions and bordered with gold satin and rubies. No one had thought to bring a stool, however, and Tyrion stood a foot and a half shorter than his bride. As he moved behind her, Sansa felt a sharp tug on her skirt. *He wants me to kneel*, she realized, blushing. She was mortified. It was not supposed to be this way. She had dreamed of her wedding a thousand times, and always she had pictured how her betrothed would stand behind her tall and strong, sweep the cloak of his protection over her shoulders, and tenderly kiss her cheek as he leaned forward to fasten the clasp.

She felt another tug at her skirt, more insistent. *I won't. Why should I spare his feelings, when no one cares about mine?*

The dwarf tugged at her a third time. Stubbornly she pressed her lips together and pretended not to notice. Someone behind them tittered. *The queen*, she thought, but it didn't matter. They were all laughing by then, Joffrey the loudest. "Dontos, down on your hands and knees," the king commanded. "My uncle needs a boost to climb his bride."

And so it was that her lord husband cloaked her in the colors of House Lannister whilst standing on the back of a fool.

When Sansa turned, the little man was gazing up at her, his mouth tight, his face as red as her cloak. Suddenly she was ashamed of her stubbornness. She smoothed her skirts and knelt in front of him, so their heads were on the same level. "With this kiss I pledge my love, and take you for my lord and husband."

"With this kiss I pledge my love," the dwarf replied hoarsely, "and take you for my lady and wife." He leaned forward, and their lips touched briefly.

He is so ugly, Sansa thought when his face was close to hers. *He is even uglier than the Hound.*

The septon raised his crystal high, so the rainbow light fell down upon them. "Here in the sight of gods and men," he said, "I do solemnly proclaim Tyrion of House Lannister and Sansa of House Stark to be man and wife, one flesh, one heart, one soul, now and forever, and cursed be the one who comes between them."

She had to bite her lip to keep from sobbing.

The wedding feast was held in the Small Hall. There were perhaps fifty guests; Lannister retainers and allies for the most part, joining those who had been at the wedding. And here Sansa found the Tyrells. Margaery gave her such a sad look, and when the Queen of Thorns tottered in between Left and Right, she never looked at her at all.

Elinor, Alla, and Megga seemed determined not to know her. *My friends*, Sansa thought bitterly.

Her husband drank heavily and ate but little. He listened whenever someone rose to make a toast and sometimes nodded a curt acknowledgment, but otherwise his face might have been made of stone. The feast seemed to go on forever, though Sansa tasted none of the food. She wanted it to be done, and yet she dreaded its end. For after the feast would come the bedding. The men would carry her up to her wedding bed, undressing her on the way and making rude jokes about the fate that awaited her between the sheets, while the women did Tyrion the same honors. Only after they had been bundled naked into bed would they be left alone, and even then the guests would stand outside the bridal chamber, shouting ribald suggestions through the door. The bedding had seemed wonderfully wicked and exciting when Sansa was a girl, but now that the moment was upon her she felt only dread. She did not think she could bear for them to rip off her clothes, and she was certain she would burst into tears at the first randy jape.

When the musicians began to play, she timidly laid her hand on Tyrion's and said, "My lord, should we lead the dance?"

His mouth twisted. "I think we have already given them sufficent amusement for one day, don't you?"

"As you say, my lord." She pulled her hand back.

Joffrey and Margaery led in their place. *How can a monster dance so beautifully?* Sansa wondered. She had often daydreamed of how she would dance at her wedding, with every eye upon her and her handsome lord. In her dreams they had all been smiling. *Not even my husband is smiling.*

Other guests soon joined the king and his betrothed on the floor. Elinor danced with her young squire, and Megga with Prince Tommen. Lady Merryweather, the Myrish beauty with the black hair and the big dark eyes, spun so provocatively that every man in the hall was soon watching her. Lord and Lady Tyrell moved more sedately. Ser Kevan Lannister begged the honor of Lady Janna Fossoway,

Lord Tyrell's sister. Merry Crane took the floor with the exile prince Jalabhar Xho, gorgeous in his feathered finery. Cersei Lannister partnered first Lord Redwyne, then Lord Rowan, and finally her own father, who danced with smooth unsmiling grace.

Sansa sat with her hands in her lap, watching how the queen moved and laughed and tossed her blonde curls. *She charms them all*, she thought dully. *How I hate her.* She looked away, to where Moon Boy danced with Dontos.

"Lady Sansa." Ser Garlan Tyrell stood beside the dais. "Would you honor me? If your lord consents?"

The Imp's mismatched eyes narrowed. "My lady can dance with whomever she pleases."

Perhaps she ought to have remained beside her husband, but she wanted to dance so badly . . . and Ser Garlan was brother to Margaery, to Willas, to her Knight of Flowers. "I see why they name you Garlan the Gallant, ser," she said, as she took his hand.

"My lady is gracious to say so. My brother Willas gave me that name, as it happens. To protect me."

"To protect you?" She gave him a puzzled look.

Ser Garlan laughed. "I was a plump little boy, I fear, and we do have an uncle called Garth the Gross. So Willas struck first, though not before threatening me with Garlan the Greensick, Garlan the Galling, and Garlan the Gargoyle."

It was so sweet and silly that Sansa had to laugh, despite everything. Afterward she was absurdly grateful. Somehow the laughter made her hopeful again, if only for a little while. Smiling, she let the music take her, losing herself in the steps, in the sound of flute and pipes and harp, in the rhythm of the drum . . . and from time to time in Ser Garlan's arms, when the dance brought them together. "My lady wife is most concerned for you," he said quietly, one such time.

"Lady Leonette is too sweet. Tell her I am well."

"A bride at her wedding should be more than *well*." His voice was not unkind. "You seemed close to tears."

"Tears of joy, ser."

"Your eyes give the lie to your tongue." Ser Garlan

turned her, drew her close to his side. "My lady, I have seen how you look at my brother. Loras is valiant and handsome, and we all love him dearly ... but your Imp will make a better husband. He is a bigger man than he seems, I think."

The music spun them apart before Sansa could think of a reply. It was Mace Tyrell opposite her, red-faced and sweaty, and then Lord Merryweather, and then Prince Tommen. "I want to be married too," said the plump little princeling, who was all of nine. "I'm taller than my uncle!"

"I know you are," said Sansa, before the partners changed again. Ser Kevan told her she was beautiful, Jalabhar Xho said something she did not understand in the Summer Tongue, and Lord Redwyne wished her many fat children and long years of joy. And then the dance brought her face-to-face with Joffrey.

Sansa stiffened as his hand touched hers, but the king tightened his grip and drew her closer. "You shouldn't look so sad. My uncle is an ugly little thing, but you'll still have me."

"You're to marry Margaery!"

"A king can have other women. Whores. My father did. One of the Aegons did too. The third one, or the fourth. He had lots of whores and lots of bastards." As they whirled to the music, Joff gave her a moist kiss. "My uncle will bring you to my bed whenever I command it."

Sansa shook her head. "He won't."

"He will, or I'll have his head. That King Aegon, he had any woman he wanted, whether they were married or no."

Thankfully, it was time to change again. Her legs had turned to wood, though, and Lord Rowan, Ser Tallad, and Elinor's squire all must have thought her a very clumsy dancer. And then she was back with Ser Garlan once more, and soon, blessedly, the dance was over.

Her relief was short-lived. No sooner had the music died than she heard Joffrey say, "It's time to bed them! Let's get the clothes off her, and have a look at what the she-wolf's got to give my uncle!" Other men took up the cry, loudly.

Her dwarf husband lifted his eyes slowly from his wine cup. "I'll have no bedding."

Joffrey seized Sansa's arm. "You will if I command it."

The Imp slammed his dagger down in the table, where it stood quivering. "Then you'll service your own bride with a wooden prick. I'll geld you, I swear it."

A shocked silence fell. Sansa pulled away from Joffrey, but he had a grip on her, and her sleeve ripped. No one even seemed to hear. Queen Cersei turned to her father. "Did you hear him?"

Lord Tywin rose from his seat. "I believe we can dispense with the bedding. Tyrion, I am certain you did not mean to threaten the king's royal person."

Sansa saw a spasm of rage pass across her husband's face. "I misspoke," he said. "It was a bad jape, sire."

"You threatened to *geld* me!" Joffrey said shrilly.

"I did, Your Grace," said Tyrion, "but only because I envied your royal manhood. Mine own is so small and stunted." His face twisted into a leer. "And if you take my tongue, you will leave me no way at all to pleasure this sweet wife you gave me."

Laughter burst from the lips of Ser Osmund Kettleblack. Someone else sniggered. But Joff did not laugh, nor Lord Tywin. "Your Grace," he said, "my son is drunk, you can see that."

"I am," the Imp confessed, "but not so drunk that I cannot attend to my own bedding." He hopped down from the dais and grabbed Sansa roughly. "Come, wife, time to smash your portcullis. I want to play come-into-the-castle."

Red-faced, Sansa went with him from the Small Hall. *What choice do I have?* Tyrion waddled when he walked, especially when he walked as quickly as he did now. The gods were merciful, and neither Joffrey nor any of the others moved to follow.

For their wedding night, they had been granted the use of an airy bedchamber high in the Tower of the Hand. Tyrion kicked the door shut behind them. "There is a flagon of good Arbor gold on the sideboard, Sansa. Will you be so kind as to pour me a cup?"

"Is that wise, my lord?"

"Nothing was ever wiser. I am not truly drunk, you see. But I mean to be."

Sansa filled a goblet for each of them. *It will be easier if I am drunk as well.* She sat on the edge of the great curtained bed and drained half her cup in three long swallows. No doubt it was very fine wine, but she was too nervous to taste it. It made her head swim. "Would you have me undress, my lord?"

"Tyrion." He cocked his head. "My name is Tyrion, Sansa."

"Tyrion. My lord. Should I take off my gown, or do you want to undress me?" She took another swallow of wine.

The Imp turned away from her. "The first time I wed, there was us and a drunken septon, and some pigs to bear witness. We ate one of our witnesses at our wedding feast. Tysha fed me crackling and I licked the grease off her fingers, and we were laughing when we fell into bed."

"You were wed before? I . . . I had forgotten."

"You did not forget. You never knew."

"Who was she, my lord?" Sansa was curious despite herself.

"Lady Tysha." His mouth twisted. "Of House Silverfist. Their arms have one gold coin and a hundred silver, upon a bloody sheet. Ours was a very short marriage . . . as befits a very short man, I suppose."

Sansa stared down at her hands and said nothing.

"How old are you, Sansa?" asked Tyrion, after a moment.

"Thirteen," she said, "when the moon turns."

"Gods have mercy." The dwarf took another swallow of wine. "Well, talk won't make you older. Shall we get on with this, my lady? If it please you?"

"It will please me to please my lord husband."

That seemed to anger him. "You hide behind courtesy as if it were a castle wall."

"Courtesy is a lady's armor," Sansa said. Her septa had always told her that.

"I am your husband. You can take off your armor now."

"And my clothing?"

"That too." He waved his wine cup at her. "My lord father has commanded me to consummate this marriage."

Her hands trembled as she began fumbling at her clothes. She had ten thumbs instead of fingers, and all of them were broken. Yet somehow she managed the laces and buttons, and her cloak and gown and girdle and undersilk slid to the floor, until finally she was stepping out of her smallclothes. Gooseprickles covered her arms and legs. She kept her eyes on the floor, too shy to look at him, but when she was done she glanced up and found him staring. There was hunger in his green eye, it seemed to her, and fury in the black. Sansa did not know which scared her more.

"You're a child," he said.

She covered her breasts with her hands. "I've flowered."

"A child," he repeated, "but I want you. Does that frighten you, Sansa?"

"Yes."

"Me as well. I know I am ugly –"

"No, my –"

He pushed himself to his feet. "Don't lie, Sansa. I am malformed, scarred, and small, but . . ." she could see him groping ". . . abed, when the candles are blown out, I am made no worse than other men. In the dark, I am the Knight of Flowers." He took a draught of wine. "I am generous. Loyal to those who are loyal to me. I've proven I'm no craven. And I am cleverer than most, surely wits count for something. I can even be kind. Kindness is not a habit with us Lannisters, I fear, but I know I have some somewhere. I could be . . . I could be good to you."

He is as frightened as I am, Sansa realized. Perhaps that should have made her feel more kindly toward him, but it did not. All she felt was pity, and pity was death to desire. He was looking at her, waiting for her to say something, but all her words had withered. She could only stand there trembling.

When he finally realized that she had no answer for him, Tyrion Lannister drained the last of his wine. "I understand," he said bitterly. "Get in the bed, Sansa. We need to do our duty."

She climbed onto the featherbed, conscious of his stare. A scented beeswax candle burned on the bedside table and rose petals had been strewn between the sheets. She had started to pull up a blanket to cover herself when she heard him say, "No."

The cold made her shiver, but she obeyed. Her eyes closed, and she waited. After a moment she heard the sound of her husband pulling off his boots, and the rustle of clothing as he undressed himself. When he hopped up on the bed and put his hand on her breast, Sansa could not help but shudder. She lay with her eyes closed, every muscle tense, dreading what might come next. Would he touch her again? Kiss her? Should she open her legs for him now? She did not know what was expected of her.

"Sansa." The hand was gone. "Open your eyes."

She had promised to obey; she opened her eyes. He was sitting by her feet, naked. Where his legs joined, his man's staff poked up stiff and hard from a thicket of coarse yellow hair, but it was the only thing about him that was straight.

"My lady," Tyrion said, "you are lovely, make no mistake, but . . . I cannot do this. My father be damned. We will wait. The turn of a moon, a year, a season, however long it takes. Until you have come to know me better, and perhaps to trust me a little." His smile might have been meant to be reassuring, but without a nose it only made him look more grotesque and sinister.

Look at him, Sansa told herself, *look at your husband, at all of him. Septa Mordane said all men are beautiful, find his beauty, try.* She stared at the stunted legs, the swollen brutish brow, the green eye and the black one, the raw stump of his nose and crooked pink scar, the coarse tangle of black and gold hair that passed for his beard. Even his manhood was ugly, thick and veined, with a bulbous purple head. *This is not right, this is not fair, how have I sinned that the gods would do this to me, how?*

"On my honor as a Lannister," the Imp said, "I will not touch you until you want me to."

It took all the courage that was in her to look in those

mismatched eyes and say, "And if I never want you to, my lord?"

His mouth jerked as if she had slapped him. "Never?"

Her neck was so tight she could scarcely nod.

"Why," he said, "that is why the gods made whores for imps like me." He closed his short blunt fingers into a fist, and climbed down off the bed.

ARYA

S toney Sept was the biggest town Arya had seen since King's Landing, and Harwin said her father had won a famous battle here.

"The Mad King's men had been hunting Robert, trying to catch him before he could rejoin your father," he told her as they rode toward the gate. "He was wounded, being tended by some friends, when Lord Connington the Hand took the town with a mighty force and started searching house by house. Before they could find him, though, Lord Eddard and your grandfather came down on the town and stormed the walls. Lord Connington fought back fierce. They battled in the streets and alleys, even on the rooftops, and all the septons rang their bells so the smallfolk would know to lock their doors. Robert came out of hiding to join the fight when the bells began to ring. He slew six men that day, they say. One was Myles Mooton, a famous knight who'd been Prince Rhaegar's squire. He would have slain the Hand too, but the battle never brought them together. Connington wounded your grandfather Tully sore, though, and killed Ser Denys Arryn, the darling of the Vale. But when he saw the day was lost, he flew off as fast as the griffins on his shield. The Battle of the Bells, they called it after. Robert always said your father won it, not him."

More recent battles had been fought here as well, Arya

thought from the look of the place. The town gates were made of raw new wood; outside the walls a pile of charred planks remained to tell what had happened to the old ones.

Stoney Sept was closed up tight, but when the captain of the gate saw who they were, he opened a sally port for them. "How you fixed for food?" Tom asked as they entered.

"Not so bad as we were. The Huntsman brought in a flock o' sheep, and there's been some trading across the Blackwater. The harvest wasn't burned south o' the river. Course, there's plenty want to take what we got. Wolves one day, Mummers the next. Them that's not looking for food are looking for plunder, or women to rape, and them that's not out for gold or wenches are looking for the bloody Kingslayer. Talk is, he slipped right through Lord Edmure's fingers."

"*Lord* Edmure?" Lem frowned. "Is Lord Hoster dead, then?"

"Dead or dying. Think Lannister might be making for the Blackwater? It's the quickest way to King's Landing, the Huntsman swears." The captain did not wait for an answer. "He took his dogs out for a sniff round. If Ser Jaime's hereabouts, they'll find him. I've seen them dogs rip bears apart. Think they'll like the taste of lion blood?"

"A chewed-up corpse's no good to no one," said Lem. "The Huntsman bloody well knows that, too."

"When the westermen came through they raped the Huntsman's wife and sister, put his crops to the torch, ate half his sheep, and killed the other half for spite. Killed six dogs too, and threw the carcasses down his well. A chewed-up corpse would be plenty good enough for him, I'd say. Me as well."

"He'd best not," said Lem. "That's all I got to say. He'd best not, and you're a bloody fool."

Arya rode between Harwin and Anguy as the outlaws moved down the streets where her father once had fought. She could see the sept on its hill, and below it a stout strong holdfast of grey stone that looked much too small for such a big town. But every third house they passed was a blackened shell, and she saw no people. "Are all the townfolk dead?"

"Only shy." Anguy pointed out two bowmen on a roof, and some boys with sooty faces crouched in the rubble of an alehouse. Farther on, a baker threw open a shuttered window and shouted down to Lem. The sound of his voice brought more people out of hiding, and Stoney Sept slowly seemed to come to life around them.

In the market square at the town's heart stood a fountain in the shape of a leaping trout, spouting water into a shallow pool. Women were filling pails and flagons there. A few feet away, a dozen iron cages hung from creaking wooden posts. *Crow cages*, Arya knew. The crows were mostly outside the cages, splashing in the water or perched atop the bars; inside were men. Lem reined up scowling. "What's this, now?"

"Justice," answered a woman at the fountain.

"What, did you run short o' hempen rope?"

"Was this done at Ser Wilbert's decree?" asked Tom.

A man laughed bitterly. "The lions killed Ser Wilbert a year ago. His sons are all off with the Young Wolf, getting fat in the west. You think they give a damn for the likes of us? It was the Mad Huntsman caught these wolves."

Wolves. Arya went cold. *Robb's men, and my father's.* She felt drawn toward the cages. The bars allowed so little room that prisoners could neither sit nor turn; they stood naked, exposed to sun and wind and rain. The first three cages held dead men. Carrion crows had eaten out their eyes, yet the empty sockets seemed to follow her. The fourth man in the row stirred as she passed. Around his mouth his ragged beard was thick with blood and flies. They exploded when he spoke, buzzing around his head. "*Water.*" The word was a croak. "Please . . . water . . ."

The man in the next cage opened his eyes at the sound. "Here," he said. "Here, me." An old man, he was; his beard was grey and his scalp was bald and mottled brown with age.

There was another dead man beyond the old one, a big red-bearded man with a rotting grey bandage covering his left ear and part of his temple. But the worst thing was between his legs, where nothing remained but a crusted brown hole crawling with maggots. Farther down was a fat man. The crow cage was so cruelly narrow it was hard to see how they'd ever gotten him inside. The iron dug painfully into his belly, squeezing bulges out between the bars. Long days baking in the sun had burned him a painful red from head to heel. When he shifted his weight, his cage creaked and swayed, and Arya could see pale white stripes where the bars had shielded his flesh from the sun.

"Whose men were you?" she asked them.

At the sound of her voice, the fat man opened his eyes. The skin around them was so red they looked like boiled eggs floating in a dish of blood. "Water . . . a drink . . ."

"Whose?" she said again.

"Pay them no mind, boy," the townsman told her. "They're none o' your concern. Ride on by."

"What did they do?" she asked him.

"They put eight people to the sword at Tumbler's Falls," he said. "They wanted the Kingslayer, but he wasn't there so they did some rape and murder." He jerked a thumb toward the corpse with maggots where his manhood ought to be. "That one there did the raping. Now move along."

"A swallow," the fat one called down. "Ha' mercy, boy, a swallow." The old one slid an arm up to grasp the bars. The motion made his cage swing violently. "Water," gasped the one with the flies in his beard.

She looked at their filthy hair and scraggly beards and reddened eyes, at their dry, cracked, bleeding lips. *Wolves,* she thought again. *Like me.* Was this her pack? *How could they be Robb's men?* She wanted to hit them. She wanted to hurt them. She wanted to cry. They all seemed to be looking at her, the living and the dead alike. The old man had squeezed three fingers out between the bars. "Water," he said, "water."

Arya swung down from her horse. *They can't hurt me, they're dying.* She took her cup from her bedroll and went to the fountain. "What do you think you're doing, boy?" the townsman snapped. "They're no concern o' yours." She raised the cup to the fish's mouth. The water splashed

across her fingers and down her sleeve, but Arya did not
move until the cup was brimming over. When she turned
back toward the cages, the townsman moved to stop her.
"You get away from them, boy – "

"She's a girl," said Harwin. "Leave her be."

"Aye," said Lem. "Lord Beric don't hold with caging
men to die of thirst. Why don't you hang them decent?"

"There was nothing decent 'bout them things they did
at Tumbler's Falls," the townsman growled right back at
him.

The bars were too narrow to pass a cup through, but
Harwin and Gendry offered her a leg up. She planted a
foot in Harwin's cupped hands, vaulted onto Gendry's
shoulders, and grabbed the bars on top of the cage. The
fat man turned his face up and pressed his cheek to the
iron, and Arya poured the water over him. He sucked at
it eagerly and let it run down over his head and cheeks
and hands, and then he licked the dampness off the bars.
He would have licked Arya's fingers if she hadn't snatched
them back. By the time she served the other two the same,
a crowd had gathered to watch her. "The Mad Huntsman
will hear of this," a man threatened. "He won't like it.
No, he won't."

"He'll like this even less, then." Anguy strung his longbow, slid an arrow from his quiver, nocked, drew, loosed.
The fat man shuddered as the shaft drove up between his
chins, but the cage would not let him fall. Two more
arrows ended the other two northmen. The only sound in
the market square was the splash of falling water and the
buzzing of flies.

Valar morghulis, Arya thought.

On the east side of the market square stood a modest
inn with whitewashed walls and broken windows. Half
its roof had burnt off recently, but the hole had been
patched over. Above the door hung a wooden shingle
painted as a peach, with a big bite taken out of it. They
dismounted at the stables sitting catty-corner, and
Greenbeard bellowed for grooms.

The buxom red-haired innkeep howled with pleasure
at the sight of them, then promptly set to tweaking them.

"Greenbeard, is it? Or Greybeard? Mother take mercy, when did you get so old? Lem, is that you? Still wearing the same ratty cloak, are you? I know why you never wash it, I do. You're afraid all the piss will wash out and we'll see you're really a knight o' the Kingsguard! And Tom o' Sevens, you randy old goat! You come to see that son o' yours? Well, you're too late, he's off riding with that bloody Huntsman. And don't tell me he's not yours!"

"He hasn't got my voice," Tom protested weakly.

"He's got your nose, though. Aye, and t'other parts as well, to hear the girls talk." She spied Gendry then, and pinched him on the cheek. "Look at this fine young ox. Wait till Alyce sees those arms. Oh, and he blushes like a maid, too. Well, Alyce will fix that for you, boy, see if she don't."

Arya had never seen Gendry turn so red. "Tansy, you leave the Bull alone, he's a good lad," said Tom Sevenstrings. "All we need from you is safe beds for a night."

"Speak for yourself, singer." Anguy slid his arm around a strapping young serving girl as freckly as he was.

"Beds we got," said red-haired Tansy. "There's never been no lack o' beds at the Peach. But you'll all climb in a tub first. Last time you lot stayed under my roof you left your fleas behind." She poked Greenbeard in the chest. "And yours was green, too. You want food?"

"If you can spare it, we won't say no," Tom conceded.

"Now when did you ever say no to anything, Tom?" the woman hooted. "I'll roast some mutton for your friends, and an old dry rat for you. It's more than you deserve, but if you gargle me a song or three, might be I'll weaken. I always pity the afflicted. Come on, come on. Cass, Lanna, put some kettles on. Jyzene, help me get the clothes off them, we'll need to boil those too."

She made good on all her threats. Arya tried to tell them that she'd been bathed *twice* at Acorn Hall, not a fortnight past, but the red-haired woman was having none of it. Two serving wenches carried her up the stairs bodily, arguing about whether she was a girl or a boy. The one called Helly won, so the other had to fetch the hot water and scrub Arya's back with a stiff bristly brush that almost took her skin off. Then they stole all the clothes that Lady Smallwood had given her and dressed her up like one of Sansa's dolls in linen and lace. But at least when they were done she got to go down and eat.

As she sat in the common room in her stupid girl clothes, Arya remembered what Syrio Forel had told her, the trick of looking and seeing what was there. When she looked, she saw more serving wenches than any inn could want, and most of them young and comely. And come evenfall, lots of men started coming and going at the Peach. They did not linger long in the common room, not even when Tom took out his woodharp and began to sing "Six Maids in a Pool." The wooden steps were old and steep, and creaked something fierce whenever one of the men took a girl upstairs. "I bet this is a brothel," she whispered to Gendry.

"You don't even know what a brothel is."

"I do so," she insisted. "It's like an inn, with girls."

He was turning red again. "What are you doing here, then?" he demanded. "A brothel's no fit place for no bloody highborn lady, everybody knows that."

One of the girls sat down on the bench beside him. "Who's a highborn lady? The little skinny one?" She looked at Arya and laughed. "I'm a king's daughter myself."

Arya knew she was being mocked. "You are not."

"Well, I might be." When the girl shrugged, her gown slipped off one shoulder. "They say King Robert fucked my mother when he hid here, back before the battle. Not that he didn't have all the other girls too, but Leslyn says he liked my ma the best."

The girl *did* have hair like the old king's, Arya thought; a great thick mop of it, as black as coal. *That doesn't mean anything, though. Gendry has the same kind of hair too. Lots of people have black hair.*

"I'm named Bella," the girl told Gendry. "For the battle. I bet I could ring *your* bell, too. You want to?"

"No," he said gruffly.

"I bet you do." She ran a hand along his arm. "I don't

cost nothing to friends of Thoros and the lightning lord."

"*No*, I said." Gendry rose abruptly and stalked away from the table out into the night.

Bella turned to Arya. "Don't he like girls?"

Arya shrugged. "He's just stupid. He likes to polish helmets and beat on swords with hammers."

"Oh." Bella tugged her gown back over her shoulder and went to talk with Jack-Be-Lucky. Before long she was sitting in his lap, giggling and drinking wine from his cup. Greenbeard had two girls, one on each knee. Anguy had vanished with his freckle-faced wench, and Lem was gone as well. Tom Sevenstrings sat by the fire, singing, "The Maids that Bloom in Spring." Arya sipped at the cup of watered wine the red-haired woman had allowed her, listening. Across the square the dead men were rotting in their crow cages, but inside the Peach everyone was jolly. Except it seemed to her that some of them were laughing too hard, somehow.

It would have been a good time to sneak away and steal a horse, but Arya couldn't see how that would help her. She could only ride as far as the city gates. *That captain would never let me pass, and if he did, Harwin would come after me, or that Huntsman with his dogs.* She wished she had her map, so she could see how far Stoney Sept was from Riverrun.

By the time her cup was empty, Arya was yawning. Gendry hadn't come back. Tom Sevenstrings was singing "Two Hearts that Beat as One," and kissing a different girl at the end of every verse. In the corner by the window Lem and Harwin sat talking to red-haired Tansy in low voices. ". . . spent the night in Jaime's cell," she heard the woman say. "Her and this other wench, the one who slew Renly. All three o' them together, and come the morn Lady Catelyn cut him loose for love." She gave a throaty chuckle.

It's not true, Arya thought. *She never would.* She felt sad and angry and lonely, all at once.

An old man sat down beside her. "Well, aren't you a pretty little peach?" His breath smelled near as foul as the dead men in the cages, and his little pig eyes were crawling up and down her. "Does my sweet peach have a name?"

For half a heartbeat she forgot who she was supposed to be. She wasn't any peach, but she couldn't be Arya Stark either, not here with some smelly drunk she did not know. "I'm . . ."

"She's my sister." Gendry put a heavy hand on the old man's shoulder, and squeezed. "Leave her be."

The man turned, spoiling for a quarrel, but when he saw Gendry's size he thought better of it. "Your sister, is she? What kind of brother are you? I'd never bring no sister of mine to the Peach, that I wouldn't." He got up from the bench and moved off muttering, in search of a new friend.

"Why did you say that?" Arya hopped to her feet. "You're not my brother."

"That's right," he said angrily. "I'm too bloody lowborn to be kin to m'lady high."

Arya was taken aback by the fury in his voice. "That's not the way I meant it."

"Yes it is." He sat down on the bench, cradling a cup of wine between his hands. "Go away. I want to drink this wine in peace. Then maybe I'll go find that black-haired girl and ring her bell for her."

"But . . ."

"I said, *go away*. M'lady."

Arya whirled and left him there. *A stupid bullheaded bastard boy, that's all he is.* He could ring all the bells he wanted, it was nothing to her.

Their sleeping room was at the top of the stairs, under the eaves. Maybe the Peach had no lack of beds, but there was only one to spare for the likes of them. It was a *big* bed, though. It filled the whole room, just about, and the musty straw-stuffed mattress looked large enough for all of them. Just now, though, she had it to herself. Her real clothes were hanging from a peg on the wall, between Gendry's stuff and Lem's. Arya took off the linen and lace, pulled her tunic over her head, climbed up into the bed, and burrowed under the blankets. "Queen Cersei," she whispered into the pillow. "King Joffrey, Ser Ilyn, Ser Meryn. Dunsen, Raff, and Polliver. The Tickler, the

Hound, and Ser Gregor the Mountain." She liked to mix up the order of the names sometimes. It helped her remember who they were and what they'd done. *Maybe some of them are dead*, she thought. *Maybe they're in iron cages someplace, and the crows are picking out their eyes.*

Sleep came as quick as she closed her eyes. She dreamed of wolves that night, stalking through a wet wood with the smell of rain and rot and blood thick in the air. Only they were good smells in the dream, and Arya knew she had nothing to fear. She was strong and swift and fierce, and her pack was all around her, her brothers and her sisters. They ran down a frightened horse together, tore its throat out, and feasted. And when the moon broke through the clouds, she threw back her head and *howled*.

But when the day came, she woke to the barking of dogs.

Arya sat up yawning. Gendry was stirring on her left and Lem Lemoncloak snoring loudly to her right, but the baying outside all but drowned him out. *There must be half a hundred dogs out there.* She crawled from under the blankets and hopped over Lem, Tom, and Jack-Be-Lucky to the window. When she opened the shutters wide, wind and wet and cold all came flooding in together. The day was grey and overcast. Down below, in the square, the dogs were barking, running in circles, growling and howling. There was a pack of them, great black mastiffs and lean wolfhounds and black-and-white sheepdogs and kinds Arya did not know, shaggy brindled beasts with long yellow teeth. Between the inn and the fountain, a dozen riders sat astride their horses, watching the townsmen open the fat man's cage and tug his arm until his swollen corpse spilled out onto the ground. The dogs were at him at once, tearing chunks of flesh off his bones.

Arya heard one of the riders laugh. "Here's your new castle, you bloody Lannister bastard," he said. "A little snug for the likes o' you, but we'll squeeze you in, never fret." Beside him a prisoner sat sullen, with coils of hempen rope tight around his wrists. Some of the townsmen were throwing dung at him, but he never flinched. "You'll *rot* in them cages," his captor was shouting. "The crows will be picking out your eyes while we're spending all that good Lannister gold o' yours! And when them crows are done, we'll send what's left o' you to your bloody brother. Though I doubt he'll know you."

The noise had woken half the Peach. Gendry squeezed into the window beside Arya, and Tom stepped up behind them naked as his name day. "What's all that bloody shouting?" Lem complained from bed. "A man's trying to get some bloody sleep."

"Where's Greenbeard?" Tom asked him.

"Abed with Tansy," Lem said. "Why?"

"Best find him. Archer too. The Mad Huntsman's come back, with another man for the cages."

"Lannister," said Arya. "I heard him say *Lannister.*"

"Have they caught the Kingslayer?" Gendry wanted to know.

Down in the square, a thrown stone caught the captive on the cheek, turning his head. *Not the Kingslayer*, Arya thought, when she saw his face. The gods had heard her prayers after all.

JON

Ghost was gone when the wildlings led their horses from the cave. *Did he understand about Castle Black?* Jon took a breath of the crisp morning air and allowed himself to hope. The eastern sky was pink near the horizon and pale grey higher up. The Sword of the Morning still hung in the south, the bright white star in its hilt blazing like a diamond in the dawn, but the blacks and greys of the darkling forest were turning once again to greens and golds, reds and russets. And above the soldier pines and oaks and ash and sentinels stood the Wall, the ice pale and glimmering beneath the dust and dirt that pocked its surface.

The Magnar sent a dozen men riding west and a dozen more east, to climb the highest hills they could find and watch for any sign of rangers in the wood or riders on the high ice. The Thenns carried bronze-banded warhorns to give warning should the Watch be sighted. The other wildlings fell in behind Jarl, Jon and Ygritte with the rest. This was to be the young raider's hour of glory.

The Wall was often said to stand seven hundred feet high, but Jarl had found a place where it was both higher and lower. Before them, the ice rose sheer from out of the trees like some immense cliff, crowned by wind-carved battlements that loomed at least eight hundred feet high, perhaps nine hundred in spots. But that was deceptive,

Jon realized as they drew closer. Brandon the Builder had laid his huge foundation blocks along the heights wherever feasible, and hereabouts the hills rose wild and rugged.

He had once heard his uncle Benjen say that the Wall was a sword east of Castle Black, but a snake to the west. It was true. Sweeping in over one huge humped hill, the ice dipped down into a valley, climbed the knife edge of a long granite ridgeline for a league or more, ran along a jagged crest, dipped again into a valley deeper still, and then rose higher and higher, leaping from hill to hill as far as the eye could see, into the mountainous west.

Jarl had chosen to assault the stretch of ice along the ridge. Here, though the top of the Wall loomed eight hundred feet above the forest floor, a good third of that height was earth and stone rather than ice; the slope was too steep for their horses, almost as difficult a scramble as the Fist of the First Men, but still vastly easier to ascend than the sheer vertical face of the Wall itself. And the ridge was densely wooded as well, offering easy concealment. Once brothers in black had gone out every day with axes to cut back the encroaching trees, but those days were long past, and here the forest grew right up to the ice.

The day promised to be damp and cold, and damper and colder by the Wall, beneath those tons of ice. The closer they got, the more the Thenns held back. *They have never seen the Wall before, not even the Magnar*, Jon realized. *It frightens them*. In the Seven Kingdoms it was said that the Wall marked the end of the world. *That is true for them as well*. It was all in where you stood.

And where do I stand? Jon did not know. To stay with Ygritte, he would need to become a wildling heart and soul. If he abandoned her to return to his duty, the Magnar might cut her heart out. And if he took her with him ... assuming she would go, which was far from certain ... well, he could scarcely bring her back to Castle Black to live among the brothers. A deserter and a wildling could expect no welcome anywhere in the Seven Kingdoms. *We could go look for Gendel's children, I suppose. Though they'd be more like to eat us than to take us in.*

The Wall did not awe Jarl's raiders, Jon saw. *They have*

done this before, every man of them. Jarl called out names when they dismounted beneath the ridge, and eleven gathered round him. All were young. The oldest could not have been more than five-and-twenty, and two of the ten were younger than Jon. Every one was lean and hard, though; they had a look of sinewy strength that reminded him of Stonesnake, the brother the Halfhand had sent off afoot when Rattleshirt was hunting them.

In the very shadow of the Wall the wildlings made ready, winding thick coils of hempen rope around one shoulder and down across their chests, and lacing on queer boots of supple doeskin. The boots had spikes jutting from the toes; iron, for Jarl and two others, bronze for some, but most often jagged bone. Small stone-headed hammers hung from one hip, a leathern bag of stakes from the other. Their ice axes were antlers with sharpened tines, bound to wooden hafts with strips of hide. The eleven climbers sorted themselves into three teams of four; Jarl himself made the twelfth man. "Mance promises swords for every man of the first team to reach the top," he told them, his breath misting in the cold air. "Southron swords of castle-forged steel. And your name in the song he'll make of this, that too. What more could a free man ask? *Up*, and the Others take the hindmost!"

The Others take them all, thought Jon, as he watched them scramble up the steep slope of the ridge and vanish beneath the trees. It would not be the first time wildlings had scaled the Wall, not even the hundred and first. The patrols stumbled on climbers two or three times a year, and rangers sometimes came on the broken corpses of those who had fallen. Along the east coast the raiders most often built boats to slip across the Bay of Seals. In the west they would descend into the black depths of the Gorge to make their way around the Shadow Tower. But in between the only way to defeat the Wall was to go over it, and many a raider had. *Fewer come back, though*, he thought with a certain grim pride. Climbers must of necessity leave their mounts behind, and many younger, greener raiders began by taking the first horses they found. Then a hue and cry would go up, ravens would fly, and as often as not the Night's Watch would hunt them down and hang them before they could get back with their plunder and stolen women. Jarl would not make that mistake, Jon knew, but he wondered about Styr. *The Magnar is a ruler, not a raider. He may not know how the game is played.*

"There they are," Ygritte said, and Jon glanced up to see the first climber emerge above the treetops. It was Jarl. He had found a sentinel tree that leaned against the Wall, and led his men up the trunk to get a quicker start. *The wood should never have been allowed to creep so close. They're three hundred feet up, and they haven't touched the ice itself yet.*

He watched the wildling move carefully from wood to Wall, hacking out a handhold with short sharp blows of his ice axe, then swinging over. The rope around his waist tied him to the second man in line, still edging up the tree. Step by slow step, Jarl moved higher, kicking out toeholds with his spiked boots when there were no natural ones to be found. When he was ten feet above the sentinel, he stopped upon a narrow icy ledge, slung his axe from his belt, took out his hammer, and drove an iron stake into a cleft. The second man moved onto the Wall behind him while the third was scrambling to the top of the tree.

The other two teams had no happily placed trees to give them a leg up, and before long the Thenns were wondering whether they had gotten lost climbing the ridge. Jarl's party were all on the Wall and eighty feet up before the leading climbers from the other groups came into view. The teams were spaced a good twenty yards apart. Jarl's four were in the center. To the right of them was a team headed up by Grigg the Goat, whose long blond braid made him easy to spot from below. To the left a very thin man named Errok led the climbers.

"So slow," the Magnar complained loudly, as he watched them edge their way upward. "Has he forgotten the crows? He should climb faster, afore we are discovered."

Jon had to hold his tongue. He remembered the Skirling Pass all too well, and the moonlight climb he'd made with Stonesnake. He had swallowed his heart a half-dozen times that night, and by the end his arms and legs had been aching and his fingers were half frozen. *And that was stone, not ice.* Stone was solid. Ice was treacherous stuff at the best of times, and on a day like this, when the Wall was weeping, the warmth of a climber's hand might be enough to melt it. The huge blocks could be frozen rock-hard inside, but their outer surface would be slick, with runnels of water trickling down, and patches of rotten ice where the air had gotten in. *Whatever else the wildlings are, they're brave.*

All the same, Jon found himself hoping that Styr's fears proved well founded. *If the gods are good, a patrol will chance by and put an end to this.* "No wall can keep you safe," his father had told him once, as they walked the walls of Winterfell. "A wall is only as strong as the men who defend it." The wildlings might have a hundred and twenty men, but four defenders would be enough to see them off, with a few well-placed arrows and perhaps a pail of stones.

No defenders appeared, however; not four, not even one. The sun climbed the sky and the wildlings climbed the Wall. Jarl's four remained well ahead till noon, when they hit a pitch of bad ice. Jarl had looped his rope around a wind-carved pinnace and was using it to support his weight when the whole jagged thing suddenly crumbled and came crashing down, and him with it. Chunks of ice as big as a man's head bombarded the three below, but they clung to the handholds and the stakes held, and Jarl jerked to a sudden halt at the end of the rope.

By the time his team had recovered from that mischance, Grigg the Goat had almost drawn even with them. Errok's four remained well behind. The face where they were climbing looked smooth and unpitted, covered with a sheet of icemelt that glistened wetly where the sun brushed it. Grigg's section was darker to the eye, with more obvious features; long horizontal ledges where a block had been imperfectly positioned atop the block below, cracks and crevices, even chimneys along the vertical joins, where wind and water had eaten holes large enough for a man to hide in.

Jarl soon had his men edging upward again. His four and Grigg's moved almost side by side, with Errok's fifty feet below. Deerhorn axes chopped and hacked, sending showers of glittery shards cascading down onto the trees. Stone hammers pounded stakes deep into the ice to serve as anchors for the ropes; the iron stakes ran out before they were halfway up, and after that the climbers used horn and sharpened bone. And the men kicked, driving the spikes on their boots against the hard unyielding ice again and again and again and again to make one foothold. *Their legs must be numb,* Jon thought by the fourth hour. *How long can they keep on with that?* He watched as restless as the Magnar, listening for the distant moan of a Thenn warhorn. But the horns stayed silent, and there was no sign of the Night's Watch.

By the sixth hour, Jarl had moved ahead of Grigg the Goat again, and his men were widening the gap. "The Mance's pet must want a sword," the Magnar said, shading his eyes. The sun was high in the sky, and the upper third of the Wall was a crystalline blue from below, reflecting so brilliantly that it hurt the eyes to look on it. Jarl's four and Grigg's were all but lost in the glare, though Errok's team was still in shadow. Instead of moving upward they were edging their way sideways at about five hundred feet, making for a chimney. Jon was watching them inch along when he heard the sound – a sudden *crack* that seemed to roll along the ice, followed by a shout of alarm. And then the air was full of shards and shrieks and falling men, as a sheet of ice a foot thick and fifty feet square broke off from the Wall and came tumbling, crumbling, rumbling, sweeping all before it. Even down at the foot of the ridge, some chunks came spinning through the trees and rolling down the slope. Jon grabbed Ygritte and pulled her down to shield her, and one of the Thenns was struck in the face by a chunk that broke his nose.

And when they looked up Jarl and his team were gone. Men, ropes, stakes, all gone; nothing remained above six hundred feet. There was a wound in the Wall where the climbers had clung half a heartbeat before, the ice within as smooth and white as polished marble and shining in the sun. Far far below there was a faint red smear where someone had smashed against a frozen pinnace.

The Wall defends itself, Jon thought as he pulled Ygritte back to her feet.

They found Jarl in a tree, impaled upon a splintered branch and still roped to the three men who lay broken beneath him. One was still alive, but his legs and spine were shattered, and most of his ribs as well. "Mercy," he said when they came upon him. One of the Thenns smashed his head in with a big stone mace. The Magnar gave orders, and his men began to gather fuel for a pyre.

The dead were burning when Grigg the Goat reached the top of the Wall. By the time Errok's four had joined them, nothing remained of Jarl and his team but bone and ash.

The sun had begun to sink by then, so the climbers wasted little time. They unwound the long coils of hemp they'd had looped around their chests, tied them all together, and tossed down one end. The thought of trying to climb five hundred feet up that rope filled Jon with dread, but Mance had planned better than that. The raiders Jarl had left below uncasked a huge ladder, with rungs of woven hemp as thick as a man's arm, and tied it to the climbers' rope. Errok and Grigg and their men grunted and heaved, pulled it up, staked it to the top, then lowered the rope again to haul up a second ladder. There were five altogether.

When all of them were in place, the Magnar shouted a brusque command in the Old Tongue, and five of his Thenns started up together. Even with the ladders, it was no easy climb. Ygritte watched them struggle for a while. "I hate this Wall," she said in a low angry voice. "Can you feel how *cold* it is?"

"It's made of ice," Jon pointed out.

"You know nothing, Jon Snow. This wall is made o' blood."

Nor had it drunk its fill. By sunset, two of the Thenns had fallen from the ladder to their deaths, but they were the last. It was near midnight before Jon reached the top. The stars were out again, and Ygritte was trembling from the climb. "I almost fell," she said, with tears in her eyes. "Twice. Thrice. The Wall was trying t' shake me off, I could feel it." One of the tears broke free and trickled slowly down her cheek.

"The worst is behind us." Jon tried to sound confident. "Don't be frightened." He tried to put an arm around her.

Ygritte slammed the heel of her hand into his chest, so hard it stung even through his layers of wool, mail, and boiled leather. "I wasn't *frightened*. You know nothing, Jon Snow."

"Why are you crying, then?"

"Not for fear!" She kicked savagely at the ice beneath her with a heel, chopping out a chunk. "I'm crying because we never found the Horn of Winter. We opened half a hundred graves and let all those shades loose in the world, and never found the Horn of Joramun to bring this cold thing down!"

JAIME

His hand burned.

Still, *still*, long after they had snuffed out the torch they'd used to sear his bloody stump, days after, he could still feel the fire lancing up his arm, and his fingers twisting in the flames, the fingers he no longer had.

He had taken wounds before, but never like this. He had never known there could be such pain. Sometimes, unbidden, old prayers bubbled from his lips, prayers he learned as a child and never thought of since, prayers he had first prayed with Cersei kneeling beside him in the sept at Casterly Rock. Sometimes he even wept, until he heard the Mummers laughing. Then he made his eyes go dry and his heart go dead, and prayed for his fever to burn away his tears. *Now I know how Tyrion has felt, all those times they laughed at him.*

After the second time he fell from the saddle, they bound him tight to Brienne of Tarth and made them share a horse again. One day, instead of back to front, they bound them face-to-face. "The lovers," Shagwell sighed loudly, "and what a lovely sight they are. 'Twould be cruel to separate the good knight and his lady." Then he laughed that high shrill laugh of his, and said, "Ah, but which one is the knight and which one is the lady?"

If I had my hand, you'd learn that soon enough, Jaime

thought. His arms ached and his legs were numb from the ropes, but after a while none of that mattered. His world shrunk to the throb of agony that was his phantom hand, and Brienne pressed against him. *She's warm, at least,* he consoled himself, though the wench's breath was as foul as his own.

His hand was always between them. Urswyck had hung it about his neck on a cord, so it dangled down against his chest, slapping Brienne's breasts as Jaime slipped in and out of consciousness. His right eye was swollen shut, the wound inflamed where Brienne had cut him during their fight, but it was his hand that hurt the most. Blood and pus seeped from his stump, and the missing hand throbbed every time the horse took a step.

His throat was so raw that he could not eat, but he drank wine when they gave it to him, and water when that was all they offered. Once they handed him a cup and he quaffed it straight away, trembling, and the Brave Companions burst into laughter so loud and harsh it hurt his ears. "That's horse piss you're drinking, Kingslayer," Rorge told him. Jaime was so thirsty he drank it anyway, but afterward he retched it all back up. They made Brienne wash the vomit out of his beard, just as they made her clean him up when he soiled himself in the saddle.

One damp cold morning when he was feeling slightly stronger, a madness took hold of him and he reached for the Dornishman's sword with his left hand and wrenched it clumsily from its scabbard. *Let them kill me,* he thought, *so long as I die fighting, a blade in hand.* But it was no good. Shagwell came hopping from leg to leg, dancing nimbly aside when Jaime slashed at him. Unbalanced, he staggered forward, hacking wildly at the fool, but Shagwell spun and ducked and darted until all the Mummers were laughing at Jaime's futile efforts to land a blow. When he tripped over a rock and stumbled to his knees, the fool leapt in and planted a wet kiss atop his head.

Rorge finally flung him aside and kicked the sword from Jaime's feeble fingers as he tried to bring it up. "That wath amuthing, Kingthlayer," said Vargo Hoat, "but if you try it again, I thall take your other hand, or perhapth a foot."

Jaime lay on his back afterward, staring at the night sky, trying not to feel the pain that snaked up his right arm every time he moved it. The night was strangely beautiful. The moon was a graceful crescent, and it seemed as though he had never seen so many stars. The King's Crown was at the zenith, and he could see the Stallion rearing, and there the Swan. The Moonmaid, shy as ever, was half-hidden behind a pine tree. *How can such a night be beautiful?* he asked himself. *Why would the stars want to look down on such as me?*

"Jaime," Brienne whispered, so faintly he thought he was dreaming it. "Jaime, what are you doing?"

"Dying," he whispered back.

"No," she said, "no, you must live."

He wanted to laugh. "Stop telling me what do, wench. I'll die if it pleases me."

"Are you so craven?"

The word shocked him. He was Jaime Lannister, a knight of the Kingsguard, he was the Kingslayer. No man had ever called him craven. Other things they called him, yes; oathbreaker, liar, murderer. They said he was cruel, treacherous, reckless. But never craven. "What else can I do, but die?"

"Live," she said, "live, and fight, and take revenge." But she spoke too loudly. Rorge heard her voice, if not her words, and came over to kick her, shouting at her to hold her bloody tongue if she wanted to keep it.

Craven, Jaime thought, as Brienne fought to stifle her moans. *Can it be? They took my sword hand. Was that all I was, a sword hand? Gods be good, is it true?*

The wench had the right of it. He could not die. Cersei was waiting for him. She would have need of him. And Tyrion, his little brother, who loved him for a lie. And his enemies were waiting too; the Young Wolf who had beaten him in the Whispering Wood and killed his men around him, Edmure Tully who had kept him in darkness and chains, these Brave Companions.

When morning came, he made himself eat. They fed

him a mush of oats, horse food, but he forced down every spoon. He ate again at evenfall, and the next day. *Live,* he told himself harshly, when the mush was like to gag him, *live for Cersei, live for Tyrion. Live for vengeance. A Lannister always pays his debts.* His missing hand throbbed and burned and stank. *When I reach King's Landing I'll have a new hand forged, a golden hand, and one day I'll use it to rip out Vargo Hoat's throat.*

The days and the nights blurred together in a haze of pain. He would sleep in the saddle, pressed against Brienne, his nose full of the stink of his rotting hand, and then at night he would lie awake on the hard ground, caught in a waking nightmare. Weak as he was, they always bound him to a tree. It gave him some cold consolation to know that they feared him that much, even now.

Brienne was always bound beside him. She lay there in her bonds like a big dead cow, saying not a word. *The wench has built a fortress inside herself. They will rape her soon enough, but behind her walls they cannot touch her.* But Jaime's walls were gone. They had taken his hand, they had taken his *sword hand,* and without it he was nothing. The other was no good to him. Since the time he could walk, his left arm had been his shield arm, no more. It was his right hand that made him a knight; his right arm that made him a man.

One day, he heard Urswyck say something about Harrenhal, and remembered that was to be their destination. That made him laugh aloud, and *that* made Timeon slash his face with a long thin whip. The cut bled, but beside his hand he scarcely felt it. "Why did you laugh?" the wench asked him that night, in a whisper.

"Harrenhal was where they gave me the white cloak," he whispered back. "Whent's great tourney. He wanted to show us all his big castle and his fine sons. I wanted to show them too. I was only fifteen, but no one could have beaten me that day. Aerys never let me joust." He laughed again. "He sent me away. But now I'm coming back."

They heard the laugh. That night it was Jaime who got the kicks and punches. He hardly felt them either, until

Rorge slammed a boot into his stump, and then he fainted.

It was the next night when they finally came, three of the worst; Shagwell, noseless Rorge, and the fat Dothraki Zollo, the one who'd cut his hand off. Zollo and Rorge were arguing about who would go first as they approached; there seemed to be no question but that the fool would be going last. Shagwell suggested that they should both go first, and take her front and rear. Zollo and Rorge liked that notion, only then they began to fight about who would get the front and who the rear.

They will leave her a cripple too, but inside, where it does not show. "Wench," he whispered as Zollo and Rorge were cursing one another, "let them have the meat, and you go far away. It will be over quicker, and they'll get less pleasure from it."

"They'll get no pleasure from what I'll give them," she whispered back, defiant.

Stupid stubborn brave bitch. She was going to get herself good and killed, he knew it. *And what do I care if she does? If she hadn't been so pigheaded, I'd still have a hand.* Yet he heard himself whisper, "Let them do it, and go away inside." That was what he'd done, when the Starks had died before him, Lord Rickard cooking in his armor while his son Brandon strangled himself trying to save him. "Think of Renly, if you loved him. Think of Tarth, mountains and seas, pools, waterfalls, whatever you have on your Sapphire Isle, think . . ."

But Rorge had won the argument by then. "You're the ugliest woman I ever seen," he told Brienne, "but don't think I can't make you uglier. You want a nose like mine? Fight me, and you'll get one. And two eyes, that's too many. One scream out o' you, and I'll pop one out and make you eat it, and then I'll pull your fucking teeth out one by one."

"Oh, do it, Rorge," pleaded Shagwell. "Without her teeth, she'll look just like my dear old mother." He cackled. "And I *always* wanted to fuck my dear old mother up the arse."

Jaime chuckled. "There's a funny fool. I have a riddle for you, Shagwell. Why do you care if she screams? Oh, wait, I know." He shouted, "SAPPHIRES," as loudly as he could.

Cursing, Rorge kicked at his stump again. Jaime howled. *I never knew there was such agony in the world*, was the last thing he remembered thinking. It was hard to say how long he was gone, but when the pain spit him out, Urswyck was there, and Vargo Hoat himself. "Thee'th not to be touched," the goat screamed, spraying spittle all over Zollo. "Thee hath to be a maid, you foolth! Thee'th worth a bag of thapphireth!" And from then on, every night Hoat put guards on them, to protect them from his own.

Two nights passed in silence before the wench finally found the courage to whisper, "Jaime? Why did you shout out?"

"Why did I shout 'sapphires,' you mean? Use your wits, wench. Would this lot have cared if I shouted 'rape'?"

"You did not need to shout at all."

"You're hard enough to look at *with* a nose. Besides, I wanted to make the goat say 'thapphireth.'" He chuckled. "A good thing for you I'm such a liar. An honorable man would have told the truth about the Sapphire Isle."

"All the same," she said. "I thank you, ser."

His hand was throbbing again. He ground his teeth and said, "A Lannister pays his debts. That was for the river, and those rocks you dropped on Robin Ryger."

The goat wanted to make a show of parading him in, so Jaime was made to dismount a mile from the gates of Harrenhal. A rope was looped around his waist, a second around Brienne's wrists; the ends were tied to the pommel of Vargo Hoat's saddle. They stumbled along side by side behind the Qohorik's striped zorse.

Jaime's rage kept him walking. The linen that covered the stump was grey and stinking with pus. His phantom fingers screamed with every step. *I am stronger than they know*, he told himself. *I am still a Lannister. I am still a knight of the Kingsguard*. He would reach Harrenhal, and then King's Landing. He would live. *And I will pay this debt with interest*.

As they approached the clifflike walls of Black Harren's

monstrous castle, Brienne squeezed his arm. "Lord Bolton holds this castle. The Boltons are bannermen to the Starks."

"The Boltons skin their enemies." Jaime remembered that much about the northman. Tyrion would have known all there was to know about the Lord of the Dreadfort, but Tyrion was a thousand leagues away, with Cersei. *I cannot die while Cersei lives*, he told himself. *We will die together as we were born together.*

The castleton outside the walls had been burned to ash and blackened stone, and many men and horses had recently encamped beside the lakeshore, where Lord Whent had staged his great tourney in the year of the false spring. A bitter smile touched Jaime's lips as they crossed that torn ground. Someone had dug a privy trench in the very spot where he'd once knelt before the king to say his vows. *I never dreamed how quick the sweet would turn to sour. Aerys would not even let me savor that one night. He honored me, and then he spat on me.*

"The banners," Brienne observed. "Flayed man and twin towers, see. King Robb's sworn men. There, above the gatehouse, grey on white. They fly the direwolf."

Jaime twisted his head upward for a look. "That's your bloody wolf, true enough," he granted her. "And those are heads to either side of it."

Soldiers, servants, and camp followers gathered to hoot at them. A spotted bitch followed them through the camps barking and growling until one of the Lyseni impaled her on a lance and galloped to the front of the column. "I am bearing Kingslayer's banner," he shouted, shaking the dead dog above Jaime's head.

The walls of Harrenhal were so thick that passing beneath them was like passing through a stone tunnel. Vargo Hoat had sent two of his Dothraki ahead to inform Lord Bolton of their coming, so the outer ward was full of the curious. They gave way as Jaime staggered past, the rope around his waist jerking and pulling at him whenever he slowed. "I give you the *Kingthlayer*," Vargo Hoat proclaimed in that thick slobbery voice of his. A spear jabbed at the small of Jaime's back, sending him sprawling.

Instinct made him put out his hands to stop his fall. When his stump smashed against the ground the pain was blinding, yet somehow he managed to fight his way back to one knee. Before him, a flight of broad stone steps led up to the entrance of one of Harrenhal's colossal round towers. Five knights and a northman stood looking down on him; the one pale-eyed in wool and fur, the five fierce in mail and plate, with the twin towers sigil on their surcoats. "A fury of Freys," Jaime declared. "Ser Danwell, Ser Aenys, Ser Hosteen." He knew Lord Walder's sons by sight; his aunt had married one, after all. "You have my condolences."

"For what, ser?" Ser Danwell Frey asked.

"Your brother's son, Ser Cleos," said Jaime. "He was with us until outlaws filled him full of arrows. Urswyck and this lot took his goods and left him for the wolves."

"*My lords!*" Brienne wrenched herself free and pushed forward. "I saw your banners. Hear me for your oath!"

"Who speaks?" demanded Ser Aenys Frey.

"Lannither'th wet nurth."

"I am Brienne of Tarth, daughter to Lord Selwyn the Evenstar, and sworn to House Stark even as you are."

Ser Aenys spit at her feet. "That's for your oaths. We trusted the word of Robb Stark, and he repaid our faith with betrayal."

Now this is interesting. Jaime twisted to see how Brienne might take the accusation, but the wench was as singleminded as a mule with a bit between his teeth. "I know of no betrayal." She chafed at the ropes around her wrists. "Lady Catelyn commanded me to deliver Lannister to his brother at King's Landing –"

"She was trying to drown him when we found them," said Urswyck the Faithful.

She reddened. "In anger I forgot myself, but I would never have killed him. If he dies the Lannisters will put my lady's daughters to the sword."

Ser Aenys was unmoved. "Why should that trouble us?"

"Ransom him back to Riverrun," urged Ser Danwell.

"Casterly Rock has more gold," one brother objected.

"Kill him!" said another. "His head for Ned Stark's!"

Shagwell the Fool somersaulted to the foot of the steps in his grey and pink motley and began to sing. *"There once was a lion who danced with a bear, oh my, oh my . . ."*

"Thilenth, fool." Vargo Hoat cuffed the man. "The Kingthlayer ith not for the bear. He ith mine."

"He is no one's should he die." Roose Bolton spoke so softly that men quieted to hear him. "And pray recall, my lord, you are not master of Harrenhal till I march north."

Fever made Jaime as fearless as he was lightheaded. "Can this be the Lord of the Dreadfort? When last I heard, my father had sent you scampering off with your tail betwixt your legs. When did you stop running, my lord?"

Bolton's silence was a hundred times more threatening than Vargo Hoat's slobbering malevolence. Pale as morning mist, his eyes concealed more than they told. Jaime misliked those eyes. They reminded him of the day at King's Landing when Ned Stark had found him seated on the Iron Throne. The Lord of the Dreadfort finally pursed his lips and said, "You have lost a hand."

"No," said Jaime, "I have it here, hanging round my neck."

Roose Bolton reached down, snapped the cord, and flung the hand at Hoat. "Take this away. The sight of it offends me."

"I will thend it to hith lord father. I will tell him he muth pay one hundred thouthand dragonth, or we thall return the Kingthlayer to him pieth by pieth. And when we hath hith gold, we thall deliver Ther Jaime to Karthark, and collect a maiden too!" A roar of laughter went up from the Brave Companions.

"A fine plan," said Roose Bolton, the same way he might say, "A fine wine," to a dinner companion, "though Lord Karstark will not be giving you his daughter. King Robb has shortened him by a head, for treason and murder. As to Lord Tywin, he remains at King's Landing, and there he will stay till the new year, when his grandson takes for bride a daughter of Highgarden."

"Winterfell," said Brienne. "You mean Winterfell. King Joffrey is betrothed to Sansa Stark."

"No longer. The Battle of the Blackwater changed all. The rose and the lion joined there, to shatter Stannis Baratheon's host and burn his fleet to ashes."

I warned you, Urswyck, Jaime thought, *and you, goat. When you bet against the lions, you lose more than your purse.* "Is there word of my sister?" he asked.

"She is well. As is your . . . nephew." Bolton paused before he said *nephew*, a pause that said *I know.* "Your brother also lives, though he took a wound in the battle." He beckoned to a dour northman in a studded brigantine. "Escort Ser Jaime to Qyburn. And unbind this woman's hands." As the rope between Brienne's wrists was slashed in two, he said, "Pray forgive us, my lady. In such troubled times it is hard to know friend from foe."

Brienne rubbed inside her wrist where the hemp had scraped her skin bloody. "My lord, these men tried to rape me."

"Did they?" Lord Bolton turned his pale eyes on Vargo Hoat. "I am displeased. By that, and this of Ser Jaime's hand."

There were five northmen and as many Freys in the yard for every Brave Companion. The goat might not be as clever as some, but he could count that high at least. He held his tongue.

"They took my sword," Brienne said, "my armor . . ."

"You shall have no need of armor here, my lady," Lord Bolton told her. "In Harrenhal, you are under my protection. Amabel, find suitable rooms for the Lady Brienne. Walton, you will see to Ser Jaime at once." He did not wait for an answer, but turned and climbed the steps, his fur-trimmed cloak swirling behind. Jaime had only enough time to exchange a quick look with Brienne before they were marched away, separately.

In the maester's chambers beneath the rookery, a grey-haired, fatherly man named Qyburn sucked in his breath when he cut away the linen from the stump of Jaime's hand.

"That bad? Will I die?"

Qyburn pushed at the wound with a finger, and ⸱⸱kled his nose at the gush of pus. "No. Though in a few more days . . ." He sliced away Jaime's sleeve. "The corruption has spread. See how tender the flesh is? I must cut it all away. The safest course would be to take the arm off."

"Then *you'll* die," Jaime promised. "Clean the stump and sew it up. I'll take my chances."

Qyburn frowned. "I can leave you the upper arm, make the cut at your elbow, but . . ."

"Take any part of my arm, and you'd best chop off the other one as well, or I'll strangle you with it afterward."

Qyburn looked in his eyes. Whatever he saw there gave him pause. "Very well. I will cut away the rotten flesh, no more. Try to burn out the corruption with boiling wine and a poultice of nettle, mustard seed, and bread mold. Mayhaps that will suffice. It is on your head. You will want milk of the poppy – "

"No." Jaime dare not let himself be put to sleep; he might be short an arm when he woke, no matter what the man said.

Qyburn was taken aback. "There will be pain."

"I'll scream."

"A great deal of pain."

"I'll scream very loudly."

"Will you take some wine at least?"

"Does the High Septon ever pray?"

"Of that I am not certain. I shall bring the wine. Lie back, I must needs strap down your arm."

With a bowl and a sharp blade, Qyburn cleaned the stump while Jaime gulped down strongwine, spilling it all over himself in the process. His left hand did not seem to know how to find his mouth, but there was something to be said for that. The smell of wine in his sodden beard helped disguise the stench of pus.

Nothing helped when the time came to pare away the rotten flesh. Jaime did scream then, and pounded his table with his good fist, over and over and over again. He screamed again when Qyburn poured boiling wine over what remained of his stump. Despite all his vows and all his fears, he lost consciousness for a time. When he woke, the maester was sewing at his arm with needle and catgut. "I left a flap of skin to fold back over your wrist."

"You have done this before," muttered Jaime, weakly. He could taste blood in his mouth where he'd bitten his tongue.

"No man who serves with Vargo Hoat is a stranger to stumps. He makes them wherever he goes."

Qyburn did not look a monster, Jaime thought. He was spare and soft-spoken, with warm brown eyes. "How does a maester come to ride with the Brave Companions?"

"The Citadel took my chain." Qyburn put away his needle. "I should do something about that wound above your eye as well. The flesh is badly inflamed."

Jaime closed his eyes and let the wine and Qyburn do their work. "Tell me of the battle." As keeper of Harrenhal's ravens, Qyburn would have been the first to hear the news.

"Lord Stannis was caught between your father and the fire. It's said the Imp set the river itself aflame."

Jaime saw green flames reaching up into the sky higher than the tallest towers, as burning men screamed in the streets. *I have dreamed this dream before*. It was almost funny, but there was no one to share the joke.

"Open your eye." Qyburn soaked a cloth in warm water and dabbed at the crust of dried blood. The eyelid was swollen, but Jaime found he could force it open halfway. Qyburn's face loomed above. "How did you come by this one?" the maester asked.

"A wench's gift."

"Rough wooing, my lord?"

"This wench is bigger than me and uglier than you. You'd best see to her as well. She's still limping on the leg I pricked when we fought."

"I will ask after her. What is this woman to you?"

"My protector." Jaime had to laugh, no matter how it hurt.

"I'll grind some herbs you can mix with wine to bring down your fever. Come back on the morrow and I'll put a leech on your eye to drain the bad blood."

"A leech. Lovely."

"Lord Bolton is very fond of leeches," Qyburn said primly.

"Yes," said Jaime. "He would be."

TYRION

Nothing remained beyond the King's Gate but mud and ashes and bits of burned bone, yet already there were people living in the shadow of the city walls, and others selling fish from barrows and barrels. Tyrion felt their eyes on him as he rode past; chilly eyes, angry and unsympathetic. No one dared speak to him, or try to bar his way; not with Bronn beside him in oiled black mail. *If I were alone, though, they would pull me down and smash my face in with a cobblestone, as they did for Aron Santagar.*

"They come back quicker than the rats," he complained. "We burned them out once, you'd think they'd take that as a lesson."

"Give me a few dozen gold cloaks and I'll kill them all," said Bronn. "Once they're dead they don't come back."

"No, but others come in their place. Leave them be . . . but if they start throwing up hovels against the wall again, pull them down at once. The war's not done yet, no matter what these fools may think." He spied the Mud Gate up ahead. "I have seen enough for now. We'll return on the morrow with the guild masters to go over their plans." He sighed. *Well, I burned most of this, I suppose it's only just that I rebuild it.*

That task was to have been his uncle's, but solid, steady, tireless Ser Kevan Lannister had not been himself since the raven had come from Riverrun with word of his son's murder. Willem's twin Martyn had been taken captive by Robb Stark as well, and their elder brother Lancel was still abed, beset by an ulcerating wound that would not heal. With one son dead and two more in mortal danger, Ser Kevan was consumed by grief and fear. Lord Tywin had always relied on his brother, but now he had no choice but to turn again to his dwarf son.

The cost of rebuilding was going to be ruinous, but there was no help for that. King's Landing was the realm's principal harbor, rivaled only by Oldtown. The river had to be reopened, and the sooner the better. *And where am I going to find the bloody coin?* It was almost enough to make him miss Littlefinger, who had sailed north a fortnight past. *While he beds Lysa Arryn and rules the Vale beside her, I get to clean up the mess he left behind him.* Though at least his father was giving him significant work to do. *He won't name me heir to Casterly Rock, but he'll make use of me wherever he can,* Tyrion thought, as a captain of gold cloaks waved them through the Mud Gate.

The Three Whores still dominated the market square inside the gate, but they stood idle now, and the boulders and barrels of pitch had all been trundled away. There were children climbing the towering wooden structures, swarming up like monkeys in roughspun to perch on the throwing arms and hoot at each other.

"Remind me to tell Ser Addam to post some gold cloaks here," Tyrion told Bronn as they rode between two of the trebuchets. "Some fool boy's like to fall off and break his back." There was a shout from above, and a clod of manure exploded on the ground a foot in front of them. Tyrion's mare reared and almost threw him. "On second thoughts," he said when he had the horse in hand, "let the poxy brats splatter on the cobbles like overripe melons."

He was in a black mood, and not just because a few low street urchins wanted to pelt him with dung. His marriage was a daily agony. Sansa Stark remained a maiden, and half the castle seemed to know it. When they had saddled up this morning, he'd heard two of the stableboys sniggering behind his back. He could almost imagine that the horses were sniggering as well. He'd risked his skin to avoid the bedding ritual, hoping to preserve the privacy of his bedchamber, but that hope had been dashed quick enough. Either Sansa had been stupid enough to confide in one of her bedmaids, every one of whom was a spy for Cersei, or Varys and his little birds were to blame.

What difference did it make? They were laughing at him all the same. The only person in the Red Keep who didn't seem to find his marriage a source of amusement was his lady wife.

Sansa's misery was deepening every day. Tyrion would gladly have broken through her courtesy to give her what solace he might, but it was no good. No words would ever make him fair in her eyes. *Or any less a Lannister.* This was the wife they had given him, for all the rest of his life, and she hated him.

And their nights together in the great bed were another source of torment. He could no longer bear to sleep naked, as had been his custom. His wife was too well trained ever to say an unkind word, but the revulsion in her eyes whenever she looked on his body was more than he could bear. Tyrion had commanded Sansa to wear a sleeping shift as well. *I want her*, he realized. *I want Winterfell, yes, but I want her as well, child or woman or whatever she is. I want to comfort her. I want to hear her laugh. I want her to come to me willingly, to bring me her joys and her sorrows and her lust.* His mouth twisted in a bitter smile. *Yes, and I want to be tall as Jaime and as strong as Ser Gregor the Mountain too, for all the bloody good it does.*

Unbidden, his thoughts went to Shae. Tyrion had not wanted her to hear the news from any lips but his own, so he had commanded Varys to bring her to him the night before his wedding. They met again in the eunuch's chambers, and when Shae began to undo the laces of his jerkin, he'd caught her by the wrist and pushed her away. "Wait," he said, "there is something you must hear. On the morrow I am to be wed . . ."

". . . to Sansa Stark. I know."

He was speechless for an instant. Even *Sansa* did not

know, not then. "How could you know? Did Varys tell you?"

"Some page was telling Ser Tallad about it when I took Lollys to the sept. He had it from this serving girl who heard Ser Kevan talking to your father." She wriggled free of his grasp and pulled her dress up over her head. As ever, she was naked underneath. "I don't care. She's only a little girl. You'll give her a big belly and come back to me."

Some part of him had hoped for less indifference. *Had hoped*, he jeered bitterly, *but now you know better, dwarf. Shae is all the love you're ever like to have.*

Muddy Way was crowded, but soldiers and townfolk alike made way for the Imp and his escort. Hollow-eyed children swarmed underfoot, some looking up in silent appeal whilst others begged noisily. Tyrion pulled a big fistful of coppers from his purse and tossed them in the air, and the children went running for them, shoving and shouting. The lucky ones might be able to buy a heel of stale bread tonight. He had never seen markets so crowded, and for all the food the Tyrells were bringing in, prices remained shockingly high. Six coppers for a melon, a silver stag for a bushel of corn, a dragon for a side of beef or six skinny piglets. Yet there seemed no lack of buyers. Gaunt men and haggard women crowded around every wagon and stall, while others even more ragged looked on sullenly from the mouths of alleys.

"This way," Bronn said, when they reached the foot of the Hook. "If you still mean to . . . ?"

"I do." The riverfront had made a convenient excuse, but Tyrion had another purpose today. It was not a task he relished, but it must be done. They turned away from Aegon's High Hill, into the maze of smaller streets that clustered around the foot of Visenya's. Bronn led the way. Once or twice Tyrion glanced back over his shoulder to see if they were being followed, but there was nothing to be seen except the usual rabble: a carter beating his horse, an old woman throwing nightsoil from her window, two little boys fighting with sticks, three gold cloaks escorting a captive . . . they all looked innocent, but any one of them could be his undoing. Varys had informers everywhere.

They turned at a corner, and again at the next, and rode slowly through a crowd of women at a well. Bronn led him along a curving wynd, through an alley, under a broken archway. They cut through the rubble where a house had burned and walked their horses up a shallow flight of stone steps. The buildings were close and poor. Bronn halted at the mouth of a crooked alley, too narrow for two to ride abreast. "There's two jags and then a dead end. The sink is in the cellar of the last building."

Tyrion swung down off his horse. "See that no one enters or leaves till I return. This won't take long." His hand went into his cloak, to make certain the gold was still there in the hidden pocket. Thirty dragons. *A bloody fortune, for a man like him.* He waddled up the alley quickly, anxious to be done with this.

The wine sink was a dismal place, dark and damp, walls pale with niter, the ceiling so low that Bronn would have had to duck to keep from hitting his head on the beams. Tyrion Lannister had no such problem. At this hour, the front room was empty but for a dead-eyed woman who sat on a stool behind a rough plank bar. She handed him a cup of sour wine and said, "In the back."

The back room was even darker. A flickering candle burned on a low table, beside a flagon of wine. The man behind it scarce looked a danger; a short man – though all men were tall to Tyrion – with thinning brown hair, pink cheeks, and a little pot pushing at the bone buttons of his doeskin jerkin. In his soft hands he held a twelve-stringed woodharp more deadly than a longsword.

Tyrion sat across from him. "Symon Silver Tongue."

The man inclined his head. He was bald on top. "My lord Hand," he said.

"You mistake me. My father is the King's Hand. I am no longer even a finger, I fear."

"You shall rise again, I am sure. A man like you. My sweet lady Shae tells me you are newly wed. Would that you had sent for me earlier. I should have been honored to sing at your feast."

"The last thing my wife needs is more songs," said Tyrion. "As for Shae, we both know she is no lady, and

I would thank you never to speak her name aloud."

"As the Hand commands," Symon said.

The last time Tyrion had seen the man, a sharp word had been enough to set him sweating, but it seemed the singer had found some courage somewhere. *Most like in that flagon.* Or perhaps Tyrion himself was to blame for this new boldness. *I threatened him, but nothing ever came of the threat, so now he believes me toothless.* He sighed. "I am told you are a very gifted singer."

"You are most kind to say so, my lord."

Tyrion gave him a smile. "I think it is time you brought your music to the Free Cities. They are great lovers of song in Braavos and Pentos and Lys, and generous with those who please them." He took a sip of wine. It was foul stuff, but strong. "A tour of all nine cities would be best. You wouldn't want to deny anyone the joy of hearing you sing. A year in each should suffice." He reached inside his cloak, to where the gold was hidden. "With the port closed, you will need to go to Duskendale to take ship, but my man Bronn will find a horse for you, and I would be honored if you would let me pay your passage . . ."

"But my lord," the man objected, "you have never heard me sing. Pray listen a moment." His fingers moved deftly over the strings of the woodharp, and soft music filled the cellar. Symon began to sing.

> *He rode through the streets of the city,*
> > *down from his hill on high,*
> *O'er the wynds and the steps and the cobbles,*
> > *he rode to a woman's sigh.*
> *For she was his secret treasure,*
> > *she was his shame and his bliss.*
> *And a chain and a keep are nothing,*
> > *compared to a woman's kiss.*

"There's more," the man said as he broke off. "Oh, a good deal more. The refrain is especially nice, I think. *For hands of gold are always cold, but a woman's hands are warm . . .*"

"Enough." Tyrion slid his fingers from his cloak,

empty. "That's not a song I would care to hear again. Ever."

"No?" Symon Silver Tongue put his harp aside and took a sip of wine. "A pity. Still, each man has his song, as my old master used to say when he was teaching me to play. Others might like my tune better. The queen, perhaps. Or your lord father."

Tyrion rubbed the scar over his nose, and said, "My father has no time for singers, and my sister is not as generous as one might think. A wise man could earn more from silence than from song." He could not put it much plainer than that.

Symon seemed to take his meaning quick enough. "You will find my price modest, my lord."

"That's good to know." This would not be a matter of thirty golden dragons, Tyrion feared. "Tell me."

"At King Joffrey's wedding feast," the man said, "there is to be a tournament of singers."

"And jugglers, and jesters, and dancing bears."

"Only one dancing bear, my lord," said Symon, who had plainly attended Cersei's arrangements with far more interest than Tyrion had, "but seven singers. Galyeon of Cuy, Bethany Fair-fingers, Aemon Costayne, Alaric of Eysen, Hamish the Harper, Collio Quaynis, and Orland of Oldtown will compete for a gilded lute with silver strings . . . yet unaccountably, no invitation has been forthcoming for one who is master of them all."

"Let me guess. Symon Silver Tongue?"

Symon smiled modestly. "I am prepared to prove the truth of my boast before king and court. Hamish is old, and oft forgets what he is singing. And Collio, with that absurd Tyroshi accent! If you understand one word in three, count yourself fortunate."

"My sweet sister has arranged the feast. Even if I could secure you this invitation, it might look queer. Seven king-doms, seven vows, seven challenges, seventy-seven dishes . . . but *eight* singers? What would the High Septon think?"

"You did not strike me as a pious man, my lord."

"Piety is not the point. Certain forms must be observed."

Symon took a sip of wine. "Still . . . a singer's life is not without peril. We ply our trade in alehouses and wine sinks, before unruly drunkards. If one of your sister's seven should suffer some mishap, I hope you might consider me to fill his place." He smiled slyly, inordinately pleased with himself.

"Six singers would be as unfortunate as eight, to be sure. I will inquire after the health of Cersei's seven. If any of them should be indisposed, my man Bronn will find you."

"Very good, my lord." Symon might have left it at that, but flushed with triumph, he added, "I *shall* sing the night of King Joffrey's wedding. Should it happen that I am called to court, why, I will want to offer the king my very best compositions, songs I have sung a thousand times that are certain to please. If I should find myself singing in some dreary winesink, though . . . well, that would be an apt occasion to try my new song. *For hands of gold are always cold, but a woman's hands are warm.*"

"That will not be necessary," said Tyrion. "You have my word as a Lannister, Bronn will call upon you soon."

"Very *good*, my lord." The balding kettle-bellied singer took up his woodharp again.

Bronn was waiting with the horses at the mouth of the alley. He helped Tyrion into his saddle. "When do I take the man to Duskendale?"

"You don't." Tyrion turned his horse. "Give him three days, then inform him that Hamish the Harper has broken his arm. Tell him that his clothes will never serve for court, so he must be fitted for new garb at once. He'll come with you quick enough." He grimaced. "You may want his tongue, I understand it's made of silver. The rest of him should never be found."

Bronn grinned. "There's a pot shop I know in Flea Bottom makes a savory bowl of brown. All kinds of meat in it, I hear."

"Make certain I never eat there." Tyrion spurred to a trot. He wanted a bath, and the hotter the better.

Even that modest pleasure was denied him, however; no sooner had he returned to his chambers than Podrick

Payne informed him that he had been summoned to the Tower of the Hand. "His lordship wants to see you. The Hand. Lord Tywin."

"I recall who the Hand is, Pod," Tyrion said. "I lost my nose, not my wits."

Bronn laughed. "Don't bite the boy's head off now."

"Why not? He never uses it." Tyrion wondered what he'd done now. *Or more like, what I have failed to do.* A summons from Lord Tywin always had teeth; his father never sent for him just to share a meal or a cup of wine, that was for certain.

As he entered his lord father's solar a few moments later, he heard a voice saying, ". . . cherrywood for the scabbards, bound in red leather and ornamented with a row of lion's-head studs in pure gold. Perhaps with garnets for the eyes . . ."

"Rubies," Lord Tywin said. "Garnets lack the fire."

Tyrion cleared his throat. "My lord. You sent for me?"

His father glanced up. "I did. Come have a look at this." A bundle of oilcloth lay on the table between them, and Lord Tywin had a longsword in his hand. "A wedding gift for Joffrey," he told Tyrion. The light streaming through the diamond-shaped panes of glass made the blade shimmer black and red as Lord Tywin turned it to inspect the edge, while the pommel and crossguard flamed gold. "With this fool's jabber of Stannis and his magic sword, it seemed to me that we had best give Joffrey something extraordinary as well. A king should bear a kingly weapon."

"That's much too much sword for Joff," Tyrion said.

"He will grow into it. Here, feel the weight of it." He offered the weapon hilt first.

The sword was much lighter than he had expected. As he turned it in his hand he saw why. Only one metal could be beaten so thin and still have strength enough to fight with, and there was no mistaking those ripples, the mark of steel that has been folded back on itself many thousands of times. "Valyrian steel?"

"Yes," Lord Tywin said, in a tone of deep satisfaction. *At long last, Father!* Valyrian steel blades were scarce and costly, yet thousands remained in the world, perhaps two hundred in the Seven Kingdoms alone. It had always irked his father that none belonged to House Lannister. The old Kings of the Rock had owned such a weapon, but the greatsword Brightroar had been lost when the second King Tommen carried it back to Valyria on his fool's quest. He had never returned; nor had Uncle Gery, the youngest and most reckless of his father's brothers, who had gone seeking after the lost sword some eight years past.

Thrice at least Lord Tywin had offered to buy Valyrian longswords from impoverished lesser houses, but his advances had always been firmly rebuffed. The little lord-lings would gladly part with their daughters should a Lannister come asking, but they cherished their old family swords.

Tyrion wondered where the metal for this one had come from. A few master armorers could rework old Valyr-ian steel, but the secrets of its making had been lost when the Doom came to old Valyria. "The colors are strange," he commented as he turned the blade in the sunlight. Most Valyrian steel was a grey so dark it looked almost black, as was true here as well. But blended into the folds was a red as deep as the grey. The two colors lapped over one another without ever touching, each ripple distinct, like waves of night and blood upon some steely shore. "How did you get this patterning? I've never seen anything like it."

"Not I, my lord," said the armorer. "I confess, these colors were not what I intended, and I do not know that I could duplicate them. Your lord father had asked for the crimson of your House, and it was that color I set out to infuse into the metal. But Valyrian steel is stubborn. These old swords remember, it is said, and they do not change easily. I worked half a hundred spells and brightened the red time and time again, but always the color would darken, as if the blade was drinking the sun from it. And some folds would not take the red at all, as you can see. If my lords of Lannister are displeased, I will of course try again, as many times as you should require, but – "

"No need," Lord Tywin said. "This will serve."

"A crimson sword might flash prettily in the sun, but if truth be told I like these colors better," said Tyrion. "They have an ominous beauty . . . and they make this blade unique. There is no other sword like it in all the world, I should think."

"There is one." The armorer bent over the table and unfolded the bundle of oilcloth, to reveal a second longsword.

Tyrion put down Joffrey's sword and took up the other. If not twins, the two were at least close cousins. This one was thicker and heavier, a half-inch wider and three inches longer, but they shared the same fine clean lines and the same distinctive color, the ripples of blood and night. Three fullers, deeply incised, ran down the second blade from hilt to point; the king's sword had only two. Joff's hilt was a good deal more ornate, the arms of its crossguard done as lions' paws with ruby claws unsheathed, but both swords had grips of finely tooled red leather and gold lions' heads for pommels.

"Magnificent." Even in hands as unskilled as Tyrion's, the blade felt alive. "I have never felt better balance."

"It is meant for my son."

No need to ask which son. Tyrion placed Jaime's sword back on the table beside Joffrey's, wondering if Robb Stark would let his brother live long enough to wield it. *Our father must surely think so, else why have this blade forged?*

"You have done good work, Master Mott," Lord Tywin told the armorer. "My steward will see to your payment. And remember, rubies for the scabbards."

"I shall, my lord. You are most generous." The man folded the swords up in the oilcloth, tucked the bundle under one arm, and went to his knee. "It is an honor to serve the King's Hand. I shall deliver the swords the day before the wedding."

"See that you do."

When the guards had seen the armorer out, Tyrion clambered up onto a chair. "So . . . a sword for Joff, a sword for Jaime, and not even a dagger for the dwarf. Is that the way of it, Father?"

"The steel was sufficient for two blades, not three. If you have need of a dagger, take one from the armory. Robert left a hundred when he died. Gerion gave him a gilded dagger with an ivory grip and a sapphire pommel for a wedding gift, and half the envoys who came to court tried to curry favor by presenting His Grace with jewel-encrusted knives and silver inlay swords."

Tyrion smiled. "They'd have pleased him more if they'd presented him with their daughters."

"No doubt. The only blade he ever used was the hunting knife he had from Jon Arryn, when he was a boy." Lord Tywin waved a hand, dismissing King Robert and all his knives. "What did you find at the riverfront?"

"Mud," said Tyrion, "and a few dead things no one's bothered to bury. Before we can open the port again, the Blackwater's going to have to be dredged, the sunken ships broken up or raised. Three-quarters of the quays need repair, and some may have to be torn down and rebuilt. The entire fish market is gone, and both the River Gate and the King's Gate are splintered from the battering Stannis gave them and should be replaced. I shudder to think of the cost." *If you do shit gold, Father, find a privy and get busy*, he wanted to say, but he knew better.

"You will find whatever gold is required."

"Will I? Where? The treasury is empty, I've told you that. We're not done paying the alchemists for all that wildfire, or the smiths for my chain, and Cersei's pledged the crown to pay half the costs of Joff's wedding – seventy-seven bloody courses, a thousand guests, a pie full of doves, singers, jugglers . . ."

"Extravagance has its uses. We must demonstrate the power and wealth of Casterly Rock for all the realm to see."

"Then perhaps Casterly Rock should pay."

"Why? I have seen Littlefinger's accounts. Crown incomes are ten times higher than they were under Aerys."

"As are the crown's expenses. Robert was as generous with his coin as he was with his cock. Littlefinger borrowed heavily. From you, amongst others. Yes, the incomes are considerable, but they are barely sufficient to cover the usury on Littlefinger's loans. Will you forgive the throne's debt to House Lannister?"

"Don't be absurd."

"Then perhaps seven courses would suffice. Three hundred guests instead of a thousand. I understand that a marriage can be just as binding *without* a dancing bear."

"The Tyrells would think us niggardly. I will have the wedding *and* the waterfront. If you cannot pay for them, say so, and I shall find a master of coin who can."

The disgrace of being dismissed after so short a time was not something Tyrion cared to suffer. "I will find your money."

"You will," his father promised, "and while you are about it, see if you can find your wife's bed as well."

So the talk has reached even him. "I have, thank you. It's that piece of furniture between the window and the hearth, with the velvet canopy and the mattress stuffed with goose down."

"I am pleased you know of it. Now perhaps you ought to try and know the woman who shares it with you."

Woman? Child, you mean. "Has a spider been whispering in your ear, or do I have my sweet sister to thank?" Considering the things that went on beneath Cersei's blankets, you would think she'd have the decency to keep her nose out of his. "Tell me, why is it that all of Sansa's maids are women in Cersei's service? I am sick of being spied upon in my own chambers."

"If you mislike your wife's servants, dismiss them and hire ones more to your liking. That is your right. It is your wife's maidenhood that concerns me, not her maids. This . . . delicacy puzzles me. You seem to have no difficulty bedding whores. Is the Stark girl made differently?"

"Why do you take so much bloody interest in where I put my cock?" Tyrion demanded. "Sansa is too young."

"She is old enough to be Lady of Winterfell once her brother is dead. Claim her maidenhood and you will be one step closer to claiming the north. Get her with child, and the prize is all but won. Do I need to remind you that a marriage that has not been consummated can be set aside?"

"By the High Septon or a Council of Faith. Our present High Septon is a trained seal who barks prettily on command. Moon Boy is more like to annul my marriage than he is."

"Perhaps I should have married Sansa Stark to Moon Boy. He might have known what to do with her."

Tyrion's hands clenched on the arms of his chair. "I have heard all I mean to hear on the subject of my wife's maidenhead. But so long as we are discussing marriage, why is it that I hear nothing of my sister's impending nuptials? As I recall –"

Lord Tywin cut him off. "Mace Tyrell has refused my offer to marry Cersei to his heir Willas."

"*Refused* our sweet Cersei?" That put Tyrion in a *much* better mood.

"When I first broached the match to him, Lord Tyrell seemed well enough disposed," his father said. "A day later, all was changed. The old woman's work. She hectors her son unmercifully. Varys claims she told him that your sister was too old and too *used* for this precious one-legged grandson of hers."

"Cersei must have loved that." He laughed.

Lord Tywin gave him a chilly look. "She does not know. Nor will she. It is better for all of us if the offer was never made. See that you remember that, Tyrion. *The offer was never made.*"

"What offer?" Tyrion rather suspected that Lord Tyrell might come to regret this rebuff.

"Your sister *will* be wed. The question is, to whom? I have several thoughts –" Before he could get to them, there was a rap at the door and a guardsman stuck in his head to announce Grand Maester Pycelle. "He may enter," said Lord Tywin.

Pycelle tottered in on a cane, and stopped long enough to give Tyrion a look that would curdle milk. His once-magnificent white beard, which someone had unaccountably shaved off, was growing back sparse and wispy, leaving him with unsightly pink wattles to dangle beneath his neck. "My lord Hand," the old man said, bowing as deeply as he could without falling, "there has been another bird from Castle Black. Mayhaps we could consult privily?"

"There's no need for that." Lord Tywin waved Grand Maester Pycelle to a seat. "Tyrion may stay."

Oooooh, may I? He rubbed his nose, and waited.

Pycelle cleared his throat, which involved a deal of coughing and hawking. "The letter is from the same Bowen Marsh who sent the last. The castellan. He writes that Lord Mormont has sent word of wildlings moving south in vast numbers."

"The lands beyond the Wall cannot support vast numbers," said Lord Tywin firmly. "This warning is not new."

"This last is, my lord. Mormont sent a bird from the haunted forest, to report that he was under attack. More ravens have returned since, but none with letters. This Bowen Marsh fears Lord Mormont slain, with all his strength."

Tyrion had rather liked old Jeor Mormont, with his gruff manner and talking bird. "Is this certain?" he asked.

"It is not," Pycelle admitted, "but none of Mormont's men has returned as yet. Marsh fears the wildlings have killed them, and that the Wall itself may be attacked next." He fumbled in his robe and found the paper. "Here is his letter, my lord, a plea to all five kings. He wants men, as many men as we can send him."

"Five kings?" His father was annoyed. "There is one king in Westeros. Those fools in black might try and remember that if they wish His Grace to heed them. When you reply, tell him that Renly is dead and the others are traitors and pretenders."

"No doubt they will be glad to learn it. The Wall is a world apart, and news oft reaches them late." Pycelle bobbed his head up and down. "What shall I tell Marsh concerning the men he begs for? Shall we convene the council . . ."

"There is no need. The Night's Watch is a pack of thieves, killers, and baseborn churls, but it occurs to me that they *could* prove otherwise, given proper discipline. If Mormont is indeed dead, the black brothers must choose a new Lord Commander."

Pycelle gave Tyrion a sly glance. "An excellent thought, my lord. I know the very man. Janos Slynt."

Tyrion liked that notion not at all. "The black brothers choose their own commander," he reminded them. "Lord Slynt is new to the Wall. I know, I sent him there. Why should they pick *him* over a dozen more senior men?"

"Because," his father said, in a tone that suggested Tyrion was quite the simpleton, "if they do not vote as they are told, their Wall will melt before it sees another man."

Yes, that would work. Tyrion hitched forward. "Janos Slynt is the wrong man, Father. We'd do better with the commander of the Shadow Tower. Or Eastwatch-by-the-Sea."

"The commander of the Shadow Tower is a Mallister of Seagard. Eastwatch is held by an ironman." Neither would serve his purposes, Lord Tywin's tone said clear enough.

"Janos Slynt is a butcher's son," Tyrion reminded his father forcefully. "You yourself told me –"

"I recall what I told you. Castle Black is not Harrenhal, however. The Night's Watch is not the king's council. There is a tool for every task, and a task for every tool."

Tyrion's anger flashed. "Lord Janos is a hollow suit of armor who will sell himself to the highest bidder."

"I count that a point in his favor. Who is like to bid higher than us?" He turned to Pycelle. "Send a raven. Write that King Joffrey was deeply saddened to hear of Lord Commander Mormont's death, but regrets that he can spare no men just now, whilst so many rebels and usurpers remain in the field. Suggest that matters might be quite different once the throne is secure ... provided the king has full confidence in the leadership of the Watch. In closing, ask Marsh to pass along His Grace's fondest regards to his faithful friend and servant, Lord Janos Slynt."

"Yes, my lord." Pycelle bobbed his withered head once

more. "I shall write as the Hand commands. With great pleasure."

I should have trimmed his head, not his beard, Tyrion reflected. *And Slynt should have gone for a swim with his dear friend Allar Deem.* At least he had not made the same foolish mistake with Symon Silver Tongue. *See there, Father!* he wanted to shout. *See how fast I learn my lessons!*

SAMWELL

Up in the loft a woman was giving birth noisily, while below a man lay dying by the fire. Samwell Tarly could not say which frightened him more.

They'd covered poor Bannen with a pile of furs and stoked the fire high, yet all he could say was, "I'm cold. Please. I'm so cold." Sam was trying to feed him onion broth, but he could not swallow. The broth dribbled over his lips and down his chin as fast as Sam could spoon it in.

"That one's dead." Craster eyed the man with indifference as he worried at a sausage. "Be kinder to stick a knife in his chest than that spoon down his throat, you ask me."

"I don't recall as we did." Giant was no more than five feet tall – his true name was Bedwyck – but a fierce little man for all that. "Slayer, did you ask Craster for his counsel?"

Sam cringed at the name, but shook his head. He filled another spoon, brought it to Bannen's mouth, and tried to ease it between his lips.

"Food and fire," Giant was saying, "that was all we asked of you. And you grudge us the food."

"Be glad I didn't grudge you fire too." Craster was a thick man made thicker by the ragged smelly sheepskins he wore day and night. He had a broad flat nose, a mouth that drooped to one side, and a missing ear. And though

his matted hair and tangled beard might be grey going
white, his hard knuckly hands still looked strong enough
to hurt. "I fed you what I could, but you crows are always
hungry. I'm a godly man, else I would have chased you
off. You think I need the likes of him, dying on my floor?
You think I need all your mouths, little man?" The
wildling spat. "Crows. When did a black bird ever bring
good to a man's hall, I ask you? Never. Never."

More broth ran from the corner of Bannen's mouth.
Sam dabbed it away with a corner of his sleeve. The
ranger's eyes were open but unseeing. "I'm cold," he said
again, so faintly. A maester might have known how to
save him, but they had no maester. Kedge Whiteye had
taken Bannen's mangled foot off nine days past, in a gout
of pus and blood that made Sam sick, but it was too little,
too late. "I'm so cold," the pale lips repeated.

About the hall, a ragged score of black brothers squatted
on the floor or sat on rough-hewn benches, drinking cups
of the same thin onion broth and gnawing on chunks of
hardbread. A couple were wounded worse than Bannen,
to look at them. Fornio had been delirious for days, and
Ser Byam's shoulder was oozing a foul yellow pus. When
they'd left Castle Black, Brown Bernarr had been carrying
bags of Myrish fire, mustard salve, ground garlic, tansy,
poppy, kingscopper, and other healing herbs. Even sweets-
leep, which gave the gift of painless death. But Brown
Bernarr had died on the Fist and no one had thought to
search for Maester Aemon's medicines. Hake had known
some herblore as well, being a cook, but Hake was also
lost. So it was left to the surviving stewards to do what
they could for the wounded, which was little enough. *At
least they are dry here, with a fire to warm them. They
need more food, though.*

They all needed more food. The men had been grumbling for days. Clubfoot Karl kept saying how Craster had
to have a hidden larder, and Garth of Oldtown had begun
to echo him, when he was out of the Lord Commander's
hearing. Sam had thought of begging for something more
nourishing for the wounded men at least, but he did not
have the courage. Craster's eyes were cold and mean, and

whenever the wildling looked his way his hands twitched a little, as if they wanted to curl up into fists. *Does he know I spoke to Gilly, the last time we were here?* he wondered. *Did she tell him I said we'd take her? Did he beat it out of her?*

"I'm cold," said Bannen. "Please. I'm cold."

For all the heat and smoke in Craster's hall, Sam felt cold himself. *And tired, so tired.* He needed sleep, but whenever he closed his eyes he dreamed of blowing snow and dead men shambling toward him with black hands and bright blue eyes.

Up in the loft, Gilly let out a shuddering sob that echoed down the long low windowless hall. "Push," he heard one of Craster's older wives tell her. "Harder. *Harder.* Scream if it helps." She did, so loud it made Sam wince.

Craster turned his head to glare. "I've had a bellyful o' that shrieking," he shouted up. "Give her a rag to bite down on, or I'll come up there and give her a taste o' my hand."

He would too, Sam knew. Craster had nineteen wives, but none who'd dare interfere once he started up that ladder. No more than the black brothers had two nights past, when he was beating one of the younger girls. There had been mutterings, to be sure. "He's killing her," Garth of Greenaway had said, and Clubfoot Karl laughed and said, "If he don't want the little sweetmeat he could give her to me." Black Bernarr cursed in a low angry voice, and Alan of Rosby got up and went outside so he wouldn't have to hear. "His roof, his rule," the ranger Ronnel Harclay had reminded them. "Craster's a friend to the Watch."

A friend, thought Sam, as he listened to Gilly's muffled shrieks. Craster was a brutal man who ruled his wives and daughters with an iron hand, but his keep was a refuge all the same. "Frozen crows," Craster sneered when they straggled in, those few who had survived the snow, the wights, and the bitter cold. "And not so big a flock as went north, neither." Yet he had given them space on his floor, a roof to keep the snow off, a fire to dry them out, and his wives had brought them cups of hot wine to put some warmth in their bellies. "Bloody crows," he called them, but he'd fed them too, meager though the fare might be.

We are guests, Sam reminded himself. *Gilly is his. His daughter, his wife. His roof, his rule.*

The first time he'd seen Craster's Keep, Gilly had come begging for help, and Sam had lent her his black cloak to conceal her belly when she went to find Jon Snow. *Knights are supposed to defend women and children.* Only a few of the black brothers were knights, but even so . . . *We all say the words*, Sam thought. *I am the shield that guards the realms of men.* A woman was a woman, even a wildling woman. *We should help her. We should.* It was her child Gilly feared for; she was frightened that it might be a boy. Craster raised up his daughters to be his wives, but there were neither men nor boys to be seen about his compound. Gilly had told Jon that Craster gave his sons to the gods. *If the gods are good, they will send her a daughter*, Sam prayed.

Up in the loft, Gilly choked back a scream. "That's it," a woman said. "Another push, now. Oh, I see his head."

Hers, Sam thought miserably. *Her head, hers.*

"Cold," said Bannen, weakly. "Please. I'm so cold." Sam put the bowl and spoon aside, tossed another fur across the dying man, put another stick on the fire. Gilly gave a shriek, and began to pant. Craster gnawed on his hard black sausage. He had sausages for himself and his wives, he said, but none for the Watch. "Women," he complained. "The way they wail . . . I had me a fat sow once birthed a litter of eight with no more'n a grunt." Chewing, he turned his head to squint contemptuously at Sam. "She was near as fat as you, boy. Slayer." He laughed.

It was more than Sam could stand. He stumbled away from the firepit, stepping awkwardly over and around the men sleeping and squatting and dying upon the hard-packed earthen floor. The smoke and screams and moans were making him feel faint. Bending his head, he pushed through the hanging deerhide flaps that served Craster for a door and stepped out into the afternoon.

The day was cloudy, but still bright enough to blind him after the gloom of the hall. Some patches of snow weighed down the limbs of surrounding trees and blanketed the gold and russet hills, but fewer than there had been. The storm had passed on, and the days at Craster's Keep had been . . . well, not warm perhaps, but not so bitter cold. Sam could hear the soft *drip-drip-drip* of water melting off the icicles that bearded the edge of the thick sod roof. He took a deep shuddering breath and looked around.

To the west Ollo Lophand and Tim Stone were moving through the horselines, feeding and watering the remaining garrons.

Downwind, other brothers were skinning and butchering the animals deemed too weak to go on. Spearmen and archers walked sentry behind the earthen dikes that were Craster's only defense against whatever hid in the wood beyond, while a dozen firepits sent up thick fingers of blue-grey smoke. Sam could hear the distant echoes of axes at work in the forest, where a work detail was harvesting enough wood to keep the blazes burning all through the night. Nights were the bad time. When it got dark. And *cold*.

There had been no attacks while they had been at Craster's, neither wights nor Others. Nor would there be, Craster said. "A godly man got no cause to fear such. I said as much to that Mance Rayder once, when he come sniffing round. He never listened, no more'n you crows with your swords and your bloody fires. That won't help you none when the white cold comes. Only the gods will help you then. You best get right with the gods."

Gilly had spoken of the white cold as well, and she'd told them what sort of offerings Craster made to his gods. Sam had wanted to kill him when he heard. *There are no laws beyond the Wall,* he reminded himself, *and Craster's a friend to the Watch.*

A ragged shout went up from behind the daub-and-wattle hall. Sam went to take a look. The ground beneath his feet was a slush of melting snow and soft mud that Dolorous Edd insisted was made of Craster's shit. It was thicker than shit, though; it sucked at Sam's boots so hard he felt one pull loose.

Back of a vegetable garden and empty sheepfold, a dozen black brothers were loosing arrows at a butt they'd built of hay and straw. The slender blond steward they called Sweet Donnel had laid a shaft just off the bull's eye at fifty yards. "Best that, old man," he said.

"Aye. I will." Ulmer, stooped and grey-bearded and loose of skin and limb, stepped to the mark and pulled an arrow from the quiver at his waist. In his youth he had been an outlaw, a member of the infamous Kingswood Brotherhood. He claimed he'd once put an arrow through the hand of the White Bull of the Kingsguard to steal a kiss from the lips of a Dornish princess. He had stolen her jewels too, and a chest of golden dragons, but it was the kiss he liked to boast of in his cups.

He notched and drew, all smooth as summer silk, then let fly. His shaft struck the butt an inch inside of Donnel Hill's. "Will that do, lad?" he asked, stepping back.

"Well enough," said the younger man, grudgingly. "The crosswind helped you. It blew more strongly when I loosed."

"You ought to have allowed for it, then. You have a good eye and a steady hand, but you'll need a deal more to best a man of the kingswood. Fletcher Dick it was who showed me how to bend the bow, and no finer archer ever lived. Have I told you about old Dick, now?"

"Only three hundred times." Every man at Castle Black had heard Ulmer's tales of the great outlaw band of yore; of Simon Toyne and the Smiling Knight, Oswyn Longneck the Thrice-Hanged, Wenda the White Fawn, Fletcher Dick, Big Belly Ben, and all the rest. Searching for escape, Sweet Donnel looked about and spied Sam standing in the muck. "*Slayer*," he called. "Come, show us how you slew the Other." He held out the tall yew longbow.

Sam turned red. "It wasn't an arrow, it was a dagger, dragonglass . . ." He knew what would happen if he took the bow. He would miss the butt and send the arrow sailing over the dike off into the trees. Then he'd hear the laughter.

"No matter," said Alan of Rosby, another fine bowman. "We're all keen to see the Slayer shoot. Aren't we, lads?"

He could not face them; the mocking smiles, the mean little jests, the contempt in their eyes. Sam turned to go back the way he'd come, but his right foot sank deep in the muck, and when he tried to pull it out his boot came off. He had to kneel to wrench it free, laughter ringing in his ears. Despite all his socks, the snowmelt had soaked through to his toes by the time he made his escape. *Useless*, he thought miserably. *My father saw me true. I have no right to be alive when so many brave men are dead.*

Grenn was tending the firepit south of the compound gate, stripped to the waist as he split logs. His face was red with exertion, the sweat steaming off his skin. But he grinned as Sam came chuffing up. "The Others get your boot, Slayer?"

Him too? "It was the mud. Please don't call me that."

"Why not?" Grenn sounded honestly puzzled. "It's a good name, and you came by it fairly."

Pyp always teased Grenn about being thick as a castle wall, so Sam explained patiently. "It's just a different way of calling me a coward," he said, standing on his left leg and wriggling back into his muddy boot. "They're mocking me, the same way they mock Bedwyck by calling him 'Giant.'"

"He's not a giant, though," said Grenn, "and Paul was never small. Well, maybe when he was a babe at the breast, but not after. You *did* slay the Other, though, so it's not the same."

"I just . . . I never . . . I was *scared!*"

"No more than me. It's only Pyp who says I'm too dumb to be frightened. I get as frightened as anyone." Grenn bent to scoop up a split log, and tossed it into the fire. "I used to be scared of Jon, whenever I had to fight him. He was so quick, and he fought like he meant to kill me." The green damp wood sat in the flames, smoking before it took fire. "I never said, though. Sometimes I think everyone is just pretending to be brave, and none of us really are. Maybe pretending is how you *get* brave, I don't know. Let them call you Slayer, who cares?"

"You never liked Ser Alliser to call you Aurochs."

"He was saying I was big and stupid." Grenn scratched at his beard. "If Pyp wanted to call me Aurochs, though, he could. Or you, or Jon. An aurochs is a fierce strong beast, so that's not so bad, and I *am* big, and getting bigger. Wouldn't you rather be Sam the Slayer than Ser Piggy?"

"Why can't I just be Samwell Tarly?" He sat down heavily on a wet log that Grenn had yet to split. "It was the dragonglass that slew it. Not me, the dragonglass."

He had told them. He had told them all. Some of them didn't believe him, he knew. Dirk had shown Sam his dirk and said, "I got iron, what do I want with glass?" Black Bernarr and the three Garths made it plain that they doubted his whole story, and Rolley of Sisterton came right out and said, "More like you stabbed some rustling bushes and it turned out to be Small Paul taking a shit, so you came up with a lie."

But Dywen listened, and Dolorous Edd, and they made Sam and Grenn tell the Lord Commander. Mormont frowned all through the tale and asked pointed questions, but he was too cautious a man to shun any possible advantage. He asked Sam for all the dragonglass in his pack, though that was little enough. Whenever Sam thought of the cache Jon had found buried beneath the Fist, it made him want to cry. There'd been dagger blades and spearheads, and two or three hundred arrowheads at least. Jon had made daggers for himself, Sam, and Lord Commander Mormont, and he'd given Sam a spearhead, an old broken horn, and some arrowheads. Grenn had taken a handful of arrowheads as well, but that was all.

So now all they had was Mormont's dagger and the one Sam had given Grenn, plus nineteen arrows and a tall hardwood spear with a black dragonglass head. The sentries passed the spear along from watch to watch, while Mormont had divided the arrows among his best bowmen. Muttering Bill, Garth Greyfeather, Ronnel Harclay, Sweet Donnel Hill, and Alan of Rosby had three apiece, and Ulmer had four. But even if they made every shaft tell, they'd soon be down to fire arrows like all the rest. They had loosed hundreds of fire arrows on the Fist, yet still the wights kept coming.

It will not be enough, Sam thought. Craster's sloping palisades of mud and melting snow would hardly slow the wights, who'd climbed the much steeper slopes of the Fist to swarm over the ringwall. And instead of three hundred brothers drawn up in disciplined ranks to meet them, the wights would find forty-one ragged survivors, nine too badly hurt to fight. Forty-four had come straggling into Craster's out of the storm, out of the sixty-odd who'd cut their way free of the Fist, but three of those had died of their wounds, and Bannen would soon make four.

"Do you think the wights are gone?" Sam asked Grenn. "Why don't they come finish us?"

"They only come when it's cold."

"*Yes,*" said Sam, "but is it the cold that brings the wights, or the wights that bring the cold?"

"Who cares?" Grenn's axe sent wood chips flying. "They come together, that's what matters. Hey, now that we know that dragonglass kills them, maybe they won't come at all. Maybe they're frightened of *us* now!"

Sam wished he could believe that, but it seemed to him *that when you were dead, fear had no more meaning than pain or love or duty.* He wrapped his hands around his legs, sweating under his layers of wool and leather and fur. The dragonglass dagger had melted the pale thing in the woods, true . . . but Grenn was talking like it would do the same to the wights. *We don't know that,* he thought. *We don't know anything, really. I wish Jon was here.* He liked Grenn, but he couldn't talk to him the same way. *Jon wouldn't call me Slayer, I know. And I could talk to him about Gilly's baby. Jon had ridden off with Qhorin Halfhand, though, and they'd had no word of him since. He had a dragonglass dagger too, but did he think to use it? Is he lying dead and frozen in some ravine . . . or worse, is he dead and walking?*

He could not understand why the gods would want to take Jon Snow and Bannen and leave him, craven and clumsy as he was. He *should* have died on the Fist, where he'd pissed himself three times and lost his sword besides.

And he *would* have died in the woods if Small Paul had not come along to carry him. *I wish it was all a dream. Then I could wake up.* How fine that would be, to wake back on the Fist of the First Men with all his brothers still around him, even Jon and Ghost. Or even better, to wake in Castle Black behind the Wall and go to the common room for a bowl of Three-Finger Hobb's thick cream of wheat, with a big spoon of butter melting in the middle and a dollop of honey besides. Just the thought of it made his empty stomach rumble.

"*Snow.*"

Sam glanced up at the sound. Lord Commander Mormont's raven was circling the fire, beating the air with wide black wings.

"*Snow*," the bird cawed. "*Snow, snow.*"

Wherever the raven went, Mormont soon followed. The Lord Commander emerged from beneath the trees, mounted on his garron between old Dywen and the fox-faced ranger Ronnel Harclay, who'd been raised to Thoren Smallwood's place. The spearmen at the gate shouted a challenge, and the Old Bear returned a gruff, "Who in seven hells do you *think* goes there? Did the Others take your eyes?" He rode between the gateposts, one bearing a ram's skull and the other the skull of a bear, then reined up, raised a fist, and whistled. The raven came flapping down at his call.

"My lord," Sam heard Ronnel Harclay say, "we have only twenty-two mounts, and I doubt half will reach the Wall."

"I know that," Mormont grumbled. "We must go all the same. Craster's made that plain." He glanced to the west, where a bank of dark clouds hid the sun. "The gods gave us a respite, but for how long?" Mormont swung down from the saddle, jolting his raven back into the air. He saw Sam then, and bellowed, "*Tarly!*"

"Me?" Sam got awkwardly to his feet.

"*Me?*" The raven landed on the old man's head. "*Me?*"

"Is your name Tarly? Do you have a brother hereabouts? Yes, you. Close your mouth and come with me."

"With you?" The words tumbled out in a squeak.

Lord Commander Mormont gave him a withering look. "You are a man of the Night's Watch. Try not to soil your smallclothes every time I look at you. Come, I said." His boots made squishing sounds in the mud, and Sam had to hurry to keep up. "I've been thinking about this dragonglass of yours."

"It's not *mine*," Sam said.

"Jon Snow's dragonglass, then. If dragonglass daggers are what we need, why do we have only two of them? Every man on the Wall should be armed with one the day he says his words."

"We never knew . . ."

"*We never knew!* But we must have known once. The Night's Watch has forgotten its true purpose, Tarly. You don't build a wall seven hundred feet high to keep savages in skins from stealing women. The Wall was made *to guard the realms of men* . . . and not against other men, which is all the wildlings are when you come right down to it. Too many years, Tarly, too many hundreds and thousands of years. We lost sight of the true enemy. And now he's here, but we don't know how to fight him. Is dragonglass made by dragons, as the smallfolk like to say?"

"The m-maesters think not," Sam stammered. "The maesters say it comes from the fires of the earth. They call it obsidian."

Mormont snorted. "They can call it lemon pie for all I care. If it kills as you claim, I want more of it."

Sam stumbled. "Jon found more on the Fist. Hundreds of arrowheads, spearheads as well . . ."

"So you said. Small good it does us there. To reach the Fist again we'd need to be armed with the weapons we won't have until we reach the bloody Fist. And there are still the wildlings to deal with. We need to find dragonglass someplace else."

Sam had almost forgotten about the wildlings, so much had happened since. "The children of the forest used dragonglass blades," he said. "They'd know where to find obsidian."

"The children of the forest are all dead," said Mormont. "The First Men killed half of them with bronze blades, and the Andals finished the job with iron. Why a glass dagger should –"

The Old Bear broke off as Craster emerged from between the deerhide flaps of his door. The wildling smiled, revealing a mouth of brown rotten teeth. "I have a son."

"*Son,*" cawed Mormont's raven. "*Son, son, son.*"

The Lord Commander's face was stiff. "I'm glad for you."

"Are you, now? Me, I'll be glad when you and yours are gone. Past time, I'm thinking."

"As soon as our wounded are strong enough . . ."

"They're strong as they're like to get, old crow, and both of us know it. Them that's dying, you know them too, cut their bloody throats and be done with it. Or leave them, if you don't have the stomach, and I'll sort them out myself."

Lord Commander Mormont bristled. "Thoren Smallwood claimed you were a friend to the Watch –"

"Aye," said Craster. "I gave you all I could spare, but winter's coming on, and now the girl's stuck me with another squalling mouth to feed."

"We could take him," someone squeaked.

Craster's head turned. His eyes narrowed. He spat on Sam's foot. "What did you say, Slayer?"

Sam opened and closed his mouth. "I . . . I . . . I only meant . . . if you didn't want him . . . his mouth to feed . . . with winter coming on, we . . . we could take him, and . . ."

"My son. My blood. You think I'd give him to you crows?"

"I only thought . . ." *You have no sons, you expose them, Gilly said as much, you leave them in the woods, that's why you have only wives here, and daughters who grow up to be wives.*

"Be quiet, Sam," said Lord Commander Mormont. "You've said enough. Too much. Inside."

"M-my lord –"

"*Inside!*"

Red-faced, Sam pushed through the deerhides, back into the gloom of the hall. Mormont followed. "How great a fool are you?" the old man said within, his voice choked and angry. "Even if Craster gave us the child, he'd be dead before we reached the Wall. We need a newborn babe to care for near as much as we need more snow. Do you have milk to feed him in those big teats of yours? Or did you mean to take the mother too?"

"She wants to come," Sam said. "She begged me . . ."

Mormont raised a hand. "I will hear no more of this, Tarly. You've been told and *told* to stay well away from Craster's wives."

"She's his daughter," Sam said feebly.

"Go see to Bannen. Now. Before you make me wroth."

"Yes, my lord." Sam hurried off quivering.

But when he reached the fire, it was only to find Giant pulling a fur cloak up over Bannen's head. "He said he was cold," the small man said. "I hope he's gone some-place warm, I do."

"His wound . . ." said Sam.

"Bugger his wound." Dirk prodded the corpse with his foot. "His *foot* was hurt. I knew a man back in my village lost a foot. He lived to nine-and-forty."

"The cold," said Sam. "He was never warm."

"He was never *fed*," said Dirk. "Not proper. That bas-tard Craster starved him dead."

Sam looked around anxiously, but Craster had not returned to the hall. If he had, things might have grown ugly. The wildling hated bastards, though the rangers said he was baseborn himself, fathered on a wildling woman by some long-dead crow.

"Craster's got his own to feed," said Giant. "All these women. He's given us what he can."

"Don't you bloody believe it. The day we leave, he'll tap a keg o' mead and sit down to feast on ham and honey. And *laugh* at us, out starving in the snow. He's a bloody wildling, is all he is. There's none o' them friends of the Watch." He kicked at Bannen's corpse. "Ask him if you don't believe me."

They burned the ranger's corpse at sunset, in the fire
that Grenn had been feeding earlier that day. Tim Stone
and Garth of Oldtown carried out the naked corpse and
swung him twice between them before heaving him into
the flames. The surviving brothers divided up his clothes,
his weapons, his armor, and everything else he owned. At
Castle Black, the Night's Watch buried its dead with all
due ceremony. They were not at Castle Black, though.
And bones do not come back as wights.

"His name was Bannen," Lord Commander Mormont
said, as the flames took him. "He was a brave man, a
good ranger. He came to us from . . . where did he come
from?"

"Down White Harbor way," someone called out.

Mormont nodded. "He came to us from White Harbor,
and never failed in his duty. He kept his vows as best he
could, rode far, fought fiercely. We shall never see his like
again."

"*And now his watch is ended*," the black brothers said,
in solemn chant.

"And now his watch is ended," Mormont echoed.

"*Ended*," cried his raven. "*Ended*."

Sam was red-eyed and sick from the smoke. When
he looked at the fire, he thought he saw Bannen sitting up, his hands coiling into fists as if to fight off the
flames that were consuming him, but it was only for an
instant, before the swirling smoke hid all. The worst thing
was the *smell*, though. If it had been a foul unpleasant
smell he might have stood it, but his burning brother
smelled so much like roast pork that Sam's mouth began
to water, and that was so horrible that as soon as the bird
squawked "*Ended*" he ran behind the hall to throw up in
the ditch.

He was there on his knees in the mud when Dolorous
Edd came up. "Digging for worms, Sam? Or are you just
sick?"

"Sick," said Sam weakly, wiping his mouth with the
back of his hand. "The smell . . ."

"Never knew Bannen could smell so good." Edd's tone
was as morose as ever. "I had half a mind to carve a slice

off him. If we had some applesauce, I might have done it. Pork's always best with applesauce, I find." Edd undid his laces and pulled out his cock. "You best not die, Sam, or I fear I might succumb. There's bound to be more crackling on you than Bannen ever had, and I never could resist a bit of crackling." He sighed as his piss arced out, yellow and steaming. "We ride at first light, did you hear? Sun or snow, the Old Bear tells me."

Sun or snow. Sam glanced up anxiously at the sky. "Snow?" he squeaked. "We . . . ride? All of us?"

"Well, no, some will need to walk." He shook himself. "Dywen now, he says we need to learn to ride dead horses, like the Others do. He claims it would save on feed. How much could a dead horse eat?" Edd laced himself back up. "Can't say I fancy the notion. Once they figure a way to work a dead horse, we'll be next. Likely I'll be the first too. 'Edd,' they'll say, 'dying's no excuse for lying down no more, so get on up and take this spear, you've got the watch tonight.' Well, I shouldn't be so gloomy. Might be I'll die before they work it out."

Might be we'll all die, and sooner than we'd like, Sam thought, as he climbed awkwardly to his feet.

When Craster learned that his unwanted guests would be departing on the morrow, the wildling became almost amiable, or as close to amiable as Craster ever got. "Past time," he said, "you don't belong here, I told you that. All the same, I'll see you off proper, with a feast. Well, a feed. My wives can roast them horses you slaughtered, and I'll find some beer and bread." He smiled his brown smile. "Nothing better than beer and horsemeat. If you can't ride 'em, eat 'em, that's what I say."

His wives and daughters dragged out the benches and the long log tables, and cooked and served as well. Except for Gilly, Sam could hardly tell the women apart. Some were old and some were young and some were only girls, but a lot of them were Craster's daughters as well as his wives, and they all looked sort of alike. As they went about their work, they spoke in soft voices to each other, but never to the men in black.

Craster owned but one chair. He sat in it, clad in a

sleeveless sheepskin jerkin. His thick arms were covered with white hair, and about one wrist was a twisted ring of gold. Lord Commander Mormont took the place at the top of the bench to his right, while the brothers crowded in knee to knee; a dozen remained outside to guard the gate and tend the fires.

Sam found a place between Grenn and Orphan Oss, his stomach rumbling. The charred horsemeat dripped with grease as Craster's wives turned the spits above the firepit, and the smell of it set his mouth to watering again, but that reminded him of Bannen. Hungry as he was, Sam knew he would retch if he so much as tried a bite. How could they eat the poor faithful garrons who had carried them so far? When Craster's wives brought onions, he seized one eagerly. One side was black with rot, but he cut that part off with his dagger and ate the good half raw. There was bread as well, but only two loaves. When Ulmer asked for more, the woman only shook her head. That was when the trouble started.

"Two loaves?" Clubfoot Karl complained from down the bench. "How stupid are you women? We need more bread than this!"

Lord Commander Mormont gave him a hard look. "Take what you're given, and be thankful. Would you sooner be out in the storm eating snow?"

"We'll be there soon enough." Clubfoot Karl did not flinch from the Old Bear's wrath. "I'd sooner eat what Craster's hiding, my lord."

Craster narrowed his eyes. "I gave you crows enough. I got me women to feed."

Dirk speared a chunk of horsemeat. "Aye. So you admit you got a secret larder. How else to make it through a winter?"

"I'm a godly man . . ." Craster started.

"You're a niggardly man," said Karl, "and a liar."

"Hams," Garth of Oldtown said, in a reverent voice. "There were pigs, last time we come. I bet he's got hams hid someplace. Smoked and salted hams, and bacon too."

"Sausage," said Dirk. "Them long black ones, they're

the rocks, they keep for years. I bet he's got a hundred hangin in some cellar."

"Oats," suggested Ollo Lophand. "Corn. Barley."

"Corn," said Mormont's raven, with a flap of the wings. "Corn, corn, corn, corn, corn."

"Enough," said Lord Commander Mormont over the bird's raucous calls. "Be quiet, all of you. This is folly."

"Apples," said Garth of Greenaway. "Barrels and barrels of crisp autumn apples. There are apple trees out there, I saw 'em."

"Dried berries. Cabbages. Pine nuts."

"Corn. Corn. Corn."

"Salt mutton. There's a sheepfold. He's got casks and casks of mutton laid by, you know he does."

Craster looked fit to spit them all by then. Lord Commander Mormont rose. "Silence. I'll hear no more such talk."

"Then stuff bread in your ears, old man." Clubfoot Karl pushed back from the table. "Or did you swallow your bloody crumb already?"

Sam saw the Old Bear's face go red. "Have you forgotten who I am? Sit, eat, and be silent. That is a command."

No one spoke. No one moved. All eyes were on the Lord Commander and the big clubfooted ranger, as the two of them stared at each other across the table. It seemed to Sam that Karl broke first, and was about to sit, though sullenly . . .

. . . but Craster stood, and his axe was in his hand. The big black steel axe that Mormont had given him as a guest gift. "No," he growled. "You'll not sit. No one who calls me niggard will sleep beneath my roof nor eat at my board. Out with you, cripple. And you and you and you." He jabbed the head of the axe toward Dirk and Garth and Garth in turn. "Go sleep in the cold with empty bellies, the lot o' you, or . . ."

"Bloody bastard!" Sam heard one of the Garths curse. He never saw which one.

"Who calls me bastard?" Craster roared, sweeping platter and meat and wine cups from the table with his left hand while lifting the axe with his right.

"It's no more than all men know," Karl answered.

Craster moved quicker than Sam would have believed possible, vaulting across the table with axe in hand. A woman screamed, Garth Greenaway and Orphan Oss drew knives, Karl stumbled back and tripped over Ser Byam lying wounded on the floor. One instant Craster was coming after him spitting curses. The next he was spitting blood. Dirk had grabbed him by the hair, yanked his head back, and opened his throat ear to ear with one long slash. Then he gave him a rough shove, and the wildling fell forward, crashing face first across Ser Byam. Byam screamed in agony as Craster drowned in his own blood, the axe slipping from his fingers. Two of Craster's wives were wailing, a third cursed, a fourth flew at Sweet Donnel and tried to scratch his eyes out. He knocked her to the floor. The Lord Commander stood over Craster's corpse, dark with anger. "The gods will curse us," he cried. "There is no crime so foul as for a guest to bring murder into a man's hall. By all the laws of the hearth, we –"

"There are no laws beyond the Wall, old man. Remember?" Dirk grabbed one of Craster's wives by the arm, and shoved the point of his bloody dirk up under her chin. "Show us where he keeps the food, or you'll get the same as he did, woman."

"Unhand her." Mormont took a step. "I'll have your head for this, you –"

Garth of Greenaway blocked his path, and Ollo Lophand yanked him back. They both had blades in hand. "Hold your tongue," Ollo warned. Instead the Lord Commander grabbed for his dagger. Ollo had only one hand, but that was quick. He twisted free of the old man's grasp, shoved the knife into Mormont's belly, and yanked it out again, all red. And then the world went mad.

Later, much later, Sam found himself sitting cross-legged on the floor, with Mormont's head in his lap. He did not remember how they'd gotten there, or much of anything else that had happened after the Old Bear was stabbed. Garth of Greenaway had killed Garth of Oldtown, he recalled, but not why. Rolley of Sisterton had fallen from the loft and broken his neck after climbing the ladder to have a taste of Craster's wives. Grenn . . .

Grenn had shouted and slapped him, and then he'd run away with Giant and Dolorous Edd and some others. Craster still sprawled across Ser Byam, but the wounded knight no longer moaned. Four men in black sat on the bench eating chunks of burned horsemeat while Ollo coupled with a weeping woman on the table.

"Tarly." When he tried to speak, the blood dribbled from the Old Bear's mouth down into his beard. "Tarly, go. *Go.*"

"Where, my lord?" His voice was flat and lifeless. *I am not afraid.* It was a queer feeling. "There's no place to go."

"The Wall. Make for the Wall. Now."

"*Now,*" squawked the raven. "*Now. Now.*" The bird walked up the old man's arm to his chest, and plucked a hair from his beard.

"You must. Must tell them."

"Tell them what, my lord?" Sam asked politely.

"All. The Fist. The wildlings. Dragonglass. This. *All.*" His breathing was very shallow now, his voice a whisper. "Tell my son. Jorah. Tell him, take the black. My wish. Dying wish."

"*Wish?*" The raven cocked its head, beady black eyes shining. "*Corn?*" the bird asked.

"No corn," said Mormont feebly. "Tell Jorah. Forgive him. My son. Please. Go."

"It's too far," said Sam. "I'll never reach the Wall, my lord." He was so very tired. All he wanted was to sleep, to sleep and sleep and never wake, and he knew that if he just stayed here soon enough Dirk or Ollo Lophand or Clubfoot Karl would get angry with him and grant his wish, just to see him die. "I'd sooner stay with you. See, I'm not frightened anymore. Of you, or . . . of anything."

"You should be," said a woman's voice.

Three of Craster's wives were standing over them. Two were haggard old women he did not know, but Gilly was between them, all bundled up in skins and cradling a bundle of brown and white fur that must have held her baby. "We're not supposed to talk to Craster's wives," Sam told them. "We have orders."

"That's done now," said the old woman on the right.

"The blackest crows are down in the cellar, gorging," said the old woman on the left, "or up in the loft with the young ones. They'll be back soon, though. Best you be gone when they do. The horses run off, but Dyah's caught two."

"You said you'd help me," Gilly reminded him.

"I said Jon would help you. Jon's brave, and he's a good fighter, but I think he's dead now. I'm a craven. And fat. Look how fat I am. Besides, Lord Mormont's hurt. Can't you see? I couldn't leave the Lord Commander."

"Child," said the other old woman, "that old crow's gone before you. Look."

Mormont's head was still in his lap, but his eyes were open and staring and his lips no longer moved. The raven cocked its head and squawked, then looked up at Sam. "*Corn?*"

"No corn. He has no corn." Sam closed the Old Bear's eyes and tried to think of a prayer, but all that came to mind was, "Mother have mercy. Mother have mercy. Mother have mercy."

"Your mother can't help you none," said the old woman on the left. "That dead old man can't neither. You take his sword and you take that big warm fur cloak o' his and you take his horse if you can find him. And you go."

"The girl don't lie," the old woman on the right said. "She's my girl, and I beat the lying out of her early on. You said you'd help her. Do what Ferny says, boy. Take the girl and be quick about it."

"*Quick,*" the raven said. "*Quick quick quick.*"

"Where?" asked Sam, puzzled. "Where should I take her?"

"Someplace warm," the two old women said as one.

Gilly was crying. "Me and the babe. Please. I'll be your wife, like I was Craster's. Please, ser crow. He's a boy, just like Nella said he'd be. If you don't take him, *they* will."

"They?" said Sam, and the raven cocked its black head and echoed, "*They. They. They.*"

"The boy's brothers," said the old woman on the left. "Craster's sons. The white cold's rising out there, crow. I can feel it in my bones. These poor old bones don't lie. They'll be here soon, the sons."

ARYA

Her eyes had grown accustomed to blackness. When Harwin pulled the hood off her head, the ruddy glare inside the hollow hill made Arya blink like some stupid owl.

A huge firepit had been dug in the center of the earthen floor, and its flames rose swirling and crackling toward the smoke-stained ceiling. The walls were equal parts stone and soil, with huge white roots twisting through them like a thousand slow pale snakes. People were emerging from between those roots as she watched; edging out from the shadows for a look at the captives, stepping from the mouths of pitch-black tunnels, popping out of crannies and crevices on all sides. In one place on the far side of the fire, the roots formed a kind of stairway up to a hollow in the earth where a man sat almost lost in the tangle of weirwood.

Lem unhooded Gendry. "What is this place?" he asked.

"An old place, deep and secret. A refuge where neither wolves nor lions come prowling."

Neither wolves nor lions. Arya's skin prickled. She remembered the dream she'd had, and the taste of blood when she tore the man's arm from his shoulder.

Big as the fire was, the cave was bigger; it was hard to tell where it began and where it ended. The tunnel mouths might have been two feet deep or gone on two miles.

Arya saw men and women and little children, all of them watching her warily.

Greenbeard said, "Here's the wizard, skinny squirrel. You'll get your answers now." He pointed toward the fire, where Tom Sevenstrings stood talking to a tall thin man with oddments of old armor buckled on over his ratty pink robes. *That can't be Thoros of Myr.* Arya remembered the red priest as fat, with a smooth face and a shiny bald head. This man had a droopy face and a full head of shaggy grey hair. Something Tom said made him look at her, and Arya thought he was about to come over to her. Only then the Mad Huntsman appeared, shoving his captive down into the light, and she and Gendry were forgotten.

The Huntsman had turned out to be a stocky man in patched tan leathers, balding and weak-chinned and quarrelsome. At Stoney Sept she had thought that Lem and Greenbeard might be torn to pieces when they faced him at the crow cages to claim his captive for the lightning lord. The hounds had been all around them, sniffing and snarling. But Tom o' Sevens soothed them with his playing, Tansy marched across the square with her apron full of bones and fatty mutton, and Lem pointed out Anguy in the brothel window, standing with an arrow notched. The Mad Huntsman had cursed them all for lickspittles, but finally he had agreed to take his prize to Lord Beric for judgment.

They had bound his wrists with hempen rope, strung a noose around his neck, and pulled a sack down over his head, but even so there was danger in the man. Arya could feel it across the cave. Thoros – if that *was* Thoros – met captor and captive halfway to the fire. "How did you take him?" the priest asked.

"The dogs caught the scent. He was sleeping off a drunk under a willow tree, if you believe it."

"Betrayed by his own kind." Thoros turned to the prisoner and yanked his hood off. "Welcome to our humble hall, dog. It is not so grand as Robert's throne room, but the company is better."

The shifting flames painted Sandor Clegane's burned face with orange shadows, so he looked even more terrible than he did in daylight. When he pulled at the rope that bound his wrists, flakes of dry blood fell off. The Hound's mouth twitched. "I know you," he said to Thoros.

"You did. In mêlées, you'd curse my flaming sword, though thrice I overthrew you with it."

"Thoros of Myr. You used to shave your head."

"To betoken a humble heart, but in truth my heart was vain. Besides, I lost my razor in the woods." The priest slapped his belly. "I am less than I was, but more. A year in the wild will melt the flesh off a man. Would that I could find a tailor to take in my skin. I might look young again, and pretty maids would shower me with kisses."

"Only the blind ones, priest."

The outlaws hooted, none so loud as Thoros. "Just so. Yet I am not the false priest you knew. The Lord of Light has woken in my heart. Many powers long asleep are waking, and there are forces moving in the land. I have seen them in my flames."

The Hound was unimpressed. "Bugger your flames. And you as well." He looked around at the others. "You keep queer company for a holy man."

"These are my brothers," Thoros said simply.

Lem Lemoncloak pushed forward. He and Greenbeard were the only men there tall enough to look the Hound in the eye. "Be careful how you bark, dog. We hold your life in our hands."

"Best wipe the shit off your fingers, then." The Hound laughed. "How long have you been hiding in this hole?"

Anguy the Archer bristled at the suggestion of cowardice. "Ask the goat if we've hidden, Hound. Ask your brother. Ask the lord of leeches. We've bloodied them all."

"You lot? Don't make me laugh. You look more swineherds than soldiers."

"Some of us was swineherds," said a short man Arya did not know. "And some was tanners or singers or masons. But that was before the war come."

"When we left King's Landing we were men of Winterfell and men of Darry and men of Blackhaven, Mallery ͡men and Wylde men. We were knights and squires and ͡t-arms, lords and commoners, bound together only by our purpose." The voice came from the man seated amongst the weirwood roots halfway up the wall. "Six score of us set out to bring the king's justice to your brother." The speaker was descending the tangle of steps toward the floor. "Six score brave men and true, led by a fool in a starry cloak." A scarecrow of a man, he wore a ragged black cloak speckled with stars and an iron breast-plate dinted by a hundred battles. A thicket of red-gold hair hid most of his face, save for a bald spot above his left ear where his head had been smashed in. "More than eighty of our company are dead now, but others have taken up the swords that fell from their hands." When he reached the floor, the outlaws moved aside to let him pass. One of his eyes was gone, Arya saw, the flesh about the socket scarred and puckered, and he had a dark black ring all around his neck. "With their help, we fight on as best we can, for Robert and the realm."

"Robert?" rasped Sandor Clegane, incredulous.

"Ned Stark sent us out," said pothelmed Jack-Be-Lucky, "but he was sitting the Iron Throne when he gave us our commands, so we were never truly his men, but Robert's."

"Robert is the king of the worms now. Is that why you're down in the earth, to keep his court for him?"

"The king is dead," the scarecrow knight admitted, "but we are still king's men, though the royal banner we bore was lost at the Mummer's Ford when your brother's butchers fell upon us." He touched his breast with a fist. "Robert is slain, but his realm remains. And we defend her."

"*Her?*" The Hound snorted. "Is she your mother, Dondarrion? Or your whore?"

Dondarrion? Beric Dondarrion had been handsome; Sansa's friend Jeyne had fallen in love with him. Even Jeyne Poole was not so blind as to think this man was fair. Yet when Arya looked at him again, she saw it; the remains of a forked purple lightning bolt on the cracked enamel of his breastplate.

"Rocks and trees and rivers, that's what your realm is made of," the Hound was saying. "Do the rocks need defending? Robert wouldn't have thought so. If he couldn't fuck it, fight it, or drink it, it bored him, and so would you . . . you *brave companions*."

Outrage swept the hollow hill. "Call us that name again, dog, and you'll swallow that tongue." Lem drew his longsword.

The Hound stared at the blade with contempt. "Here's a brave man, baring steel on a bound captive. Untie me, why don't you? We'll see how brave you are then." He glanced at the Mad Huntsman behind him. "How about you? Or did you leave all your courage in your kennels?"

"No, but I should have left you in a crow cage." The Huntsman drew a knife. "I might still."

The Hound laughed in his face.

"We are brothers here," Thoros of Myr declared. "Holy brothers, sworn to the realm, to our god, and to each other."

"The brotherhood without banners." Tom Sevenstrings plucked a string. "The knights of the hollow hill."

"*Knights?*" Clegane made the word a sneer. "Dondarrion's a knight, but the rest of you are the sorriest lot of outlaws and broken men I've ever seen. I shit better men than you."

"Any knight can make a knight," said the scarecrow that was Beric Dondarrion, "and every man you see before you has felt a sword upon his shoulder. We are the forgotten fellowship."

"Send me on my way and I'll forget you too," Clegane rasped. "But if you mean to murder me, then bloody well get on with it. You took my sword, my horse, and my gold, so take my life and be done with it . . . but spare me this pious bleating."

"You will die soon enough, dog," promised Thoros, "but it shan't be murder, only justice."

"Aye," said the Mad Huntsman, "and a kinder fate than you deserve for all your kind have done. Lions, you call yourselves. At Sherrer and the Mummer's Ford, girls of six and seven years were raped, and babes still on the breast were cut in two while their mothers watched. No lion ever killed so cruel."

"I was not at Sherrer, nor the Mummer's Ford," the Hound told him. "Lay your dead children at some other door."

Thoros answered him. "Do you deny that House Clegane was built upon dead children? I saw them lay Prince Aegon and Princess Rhaenys before the Iron Throne. By rights your arms should bear two bloody infants in place of those ugly dogs."

The Hound's mouth twitched. "Do you take me for my brother? Is being born Clegane a crime?"

"Murder is a crime."

"Who did I murder?"

"Lord Lothar Mallery and Ser Gladden Wylde," said Harwin.

"My brothers Lister and Lennocks," declared Jack-Be-Lucky.

"Goodman Beck and Mudge the miller's son, from Donnelwood," an old woman called from the shadows.

"Merriman's widow, who loved so sweet," added Greenbeard.

"Them septons at Sludgy Pond."

"Ser Andrey Charlton. His squire Lucas Roote. Every man, woman, and child in Fieldstone and Mousedown Mill."

"Lord and Lady Deddings, that was so rich."

Tom Sevenstrings took up the count. "Alyn of Winterfell, Joth Quickbow, Little Matt and his sister Randa, Anvil Ryn. Ser Ormond. Ser Dudley. Pate of Mory, Pate of Lancewood, Old Pate, and Pate of Shermer's Grove. Blind Wyl the Whittler. Goodwife Maeric. Maerie the Whore. Becca the Baker. Ser Raymun Darry, Lord Darry, young Lord Darry. The Bastard of Bracken. Fletcher Will. Harsley. Goodwife Nolla – "

"*Enough.*" The Hound's face was tight with anger. "You're making noise. These names mean nothing. Who were they?"

"People," said Lord Beric. "People great and small, young and old. Good people and bad people, who died on the points of Lannister spears or saw their bellies opened by Lannister swords."

"It wasn't *my* sword in their bellies. Any man who says it was is a bloody liar."

"You serve the Lannisters of Casterly Rock," said Thoros.

"Once. Me and thousands more. Is each of us guilty of the crimes of the others?" Clegane spat. "Might be you *are* knights after all. You lie like knights, maybe you murder like knights."

Lem and Jack-Be-Lucky began to shout at him, but Dondarrion raised a hand for silence. "Say what you mean, Clegane."

"A knight's a sword with a horse. The rest, the vows and the sacred oils and the lady's favors, they're silk ribbons tied round the sword. Maybe the sword's prettier with ribbons hanging off it, but it will kill you just as dead. Well, bugger your ribbons, and shove your swords up your arses. I'm the same as you. The only difference is, I don't lie about what I am. So kill me, but don't call me a murderer while you stand there telling each other that your shit don't stink. *You hear me?*"

Arya squirted past Greenbeard so fast he never saw her. "You *are* a murderer!" she screamed. "You killed *Mycah*, don't say you never did. You *murdered* him!"

The Hound stared at her with no flicker of recognition. "And who was this Mycah, boy?"

"I'm not a boy! But Mycah was. He was a butcher's boy and you *killed* him. Jory said you cut him near in half, and he never even had a sword." She could feel them looking at her now, the women and the children and the men who called themselves the knights of the hollow hill. "Who's this now?" someone asked.

The Hound answered. "*Seven hells.* The little sister. The brat who tossed Joff's pretty sword in the river." He gave a bark of laughter. "Don't you know you're dead?"

"No, *you're* dead," she threw back at him.

Harwin took her arm to draw her back as Lord Beric said, "The girl has named you a murderer. Do you deny killing this butcher's boy, Mycah?"

The big man shrugged. "I was Joffrey's sworn shield. The butcher's boy attacked a prince of the blood."

"That's a *lie!*" Arya squirmed in Harwin's grip. "It was *me*. I hit Joffrey and threw Lion's Paw in the river. Mycah just ran away, like I told him."

"Did you see the boy attack Prince Joffrey?" Lord Beric Dondarrion asked the Hound.

"I heard it from the royal lips. It's not my place to question princes." Clegane jerked his hands toward Arya. "This one's own sister told the same tale when she stood before your precious Robert."

"Sansa's just a liar," Arya said, furious at her sister all over again. "It wasn't like she said. It *wasn't*."

Thoros drew Lord Beric aside. The two men stood talking in low whispers while Arya seethed. *They have to kill him. I prayed for him to die, hundreds and hundreds of times.*

Beric Dondarrion turned back to the Hound. "You stand accused of murder, but no one here knows the truth or falsehood of the charge, so it is not for us to judge you. Only the Lord of Light may do that now. I sentence you to trial by battle."

The Hound frowned suspiciously, as if he did not trust his ears. "Are you a fool or a madman?"

"Neither. I am a just lord. Prove your innocence with a blade, and you shall be free to go."

"No," Arya cried, before Harwin covered her mouth. *No, they can't, he'll go free.* The Hound was deadly with a sword, everyone knew that. *He'll laugh at them,* she thought.

And so he did, a long rasping laugh that echoed off the cave walls, a laugh choking with contempt. "So who will it be?" He looked at Lem Lemoncloak. "The brave man in the piss-yellow cloak? No? How about you, Huntsman? You've kicked dogs before, try me." He saw Greenbeard. "You're big enough, Tyrosh, step forward. Or do you mean to make the little girl fight me herself?" He laughed again. "Come on, who wants to die?"

"It's me you'll face," said Lord Beric Dondarrion.

Arya remembered all the tales. *He can't be killed,* she thought, hoping against hope. The Mad Huntsman sliced apart the ropes that bound Sandor Clegane's hands together. "I'll need sword and armor." The Hound rubbed a torn wrist.

"Your sword you shall have," declared Lord Beric, "but your innocence must be your armor."

Clegane's mouth twitched. "My innocence against your breastplate, is that the way of it?"

"Ned, help me remove my breastplate."

Arya got goosebumps when Lord Beric said her father's name, but this Ned was only a boy, a fair-haired squire no more than ten or twelve. He stepped up quickly to undo the clasps that fastened the battered steel about the Marcher lord. The quilting beneath was rotten with age and sweat, and fell away when the metal was pulled loose. Gendry sucked in his breath. "Mother have mercy."

Lord Beric's ribs were outlined starkly beneath his skin. A puckered crater scarred his breast just above his left nipple, and when he turned to call for sword and shield, Arya saw a matching scar upon his back. *The lance went through him.* The Hound had seen it too. *Is he scared?* Arya wanted him to be scared before he died, as scared as Mycah must have been.

Ned fetched Lord Beric his swordbelt and a long black surcoat. It was meant to be worn over armor, so it draped his body loosely, but across it crackled the forked purple lightning of his House. He unsheathed his sword and gave the belt back to his squire.

Thoros brought the Hound his swordbelt. "Does a dog have honor?" the priest asked. "Lest you think to cut your way free of here, or seize some child for a hostage ... Anguy, Dennet, Kyle, feather him at the first sign of treachery." Only when the three bowmen had notched their shafts did Thoros hand Clegane the belt.

The Hound ripped the sword free and threw away the scabbard. The Mad Huntsman gave him his oaken shield, all studded with iron and painted yellow, the three black dogs of Clegane emblazoned upon it. The boy Ned helped Lord Beric with his own shield, so hacked and battered that the purple lightning and the scatter of stars upon it had almost been obliterated.

But when the Hound made to step toward his foe,

Thoros of Myr stopped him. "First we pray." He turned toward the fire and lifted his arms. "Lord of Light, look down upon us."

All around the cave, the brotherhood without banners lifted their own voices in response. *"Lord of Light, defend us."*

"Lord of Light, protect us in the darkness."

"Lord of Light, shine your face upon us."

"Light your flame among us, R'hllor," said the red priest. "Show us the truth or falseness of this man. Strike him down if he is guilty, and give strength to his sword if he is true. Lord of Light, give us wisdom."

"For the night is dark," the others chanted, Harwin and Anguy loud as all the rest, *"and full of terrors."*

"This cave is dark too," said the Hound, "but I'm the terror here. I hope your god's a sweet one, Dondarrion. You're going to meet him shortly."

Unsmiling, Lord Beric laid the edge of his longsword against the palm of his left hand, and drew it slowly down. Blood ran dark from the gash he made, and washed over the steel.

And then the sword took fire.

Arya heard Gendry whisper a prayer.

"Burn in seven hells," the Hound cursed. "You, and Thoros too." He threw a glance at the red priest. "When I'm done with him you'll be next, Myr."

"Every word you say proclaims your guilt, dog," answered Thoros, while Lem and Greenbeard and Jack-Be-Lucky shouted threats and curses. Lord Beric himself waited silent, calm as still water, his shield on his left arm and his sword burning in his right hand. *Kill him,* Arya thought, *please, you have to kill him.* Lit from below, his face was a death mask, his missing eye a red and angry wound. The sword was aflame from point to crossguard, but Dondarrion seemed not to feel the heat. He stood so still he might have been carved of stone.

But when the Hound charged him, he moved fast enough.

The flaming sword leapt up to meet the cold one, long streamers of fire trailing in its wake like the ribbons the

Hound had spoken of. Steel rang on steel. No sooner was his first slash blocked than Clegane made another, but this time Lord Beric's shield got in the way, and wood chips flew from the force of the blow. Hard and fast the cuts came, from low and high, from right and left, and each one Dondarrion blocked. The flames swirled about his sword and left red and yellow ghosts to mark its passage. Each move Lord Beric made fanned them and made them burn the brighter, until it seemed as though the lightning lord stood within a cage of fire. "Is it wildfire?" Arya asked Gendry.

"No. This is different. This is . . ."

". . . magic?" she finished as the Hound edged back. Now it was Lord Beric attacking, filling the air with ropes of fire, driving the bigger man back on his heels. Clegane caught one blow high on his shield, and a painted dog lost a head. He countercut, and Dondarrion interposed his own shield and launched a fiery backslash. The outlaw brotherhood shouted on their leader. "*He's yours!*" Arya heard, and "*At him! At him! At him!*" The Hound parried a cut at his head, grimacing as the heat of the flames beat against his face. He grunted and cursed and reeled away.

Lord Beric gave him no respite. Hard on the big man's heels he followed, his arm never still. The swords clashed and sprang apart and clashed again, splinters flew from the lightning shield while swirling flames kissed the dogs once, and twice, and thrice. The Hound moved to his right, but Dondarrion blocked him with a quick sidestep and drove him back the other way . . . toward the sullen red blaze of the firepit. Clegane gave ground until he felt the heat at his back. A quick glance over his shoulder showed him what was behind him, and almost cost him his head when Lord Beric attacked anew.

Arya could see the whites of Sandor Clegane's eyes as he bulled his way forward again. Three steps up and two back, a move to the left that Lord Beric blocked, two more forward and one back, *clang* and *clang*, and the big oaken shields took blow after blow after blow. The Hound's lank dark hair was plastered to his brow in a sheen of sweat. *Wine sweat*, Arya thought, remembering that he'd been taken drunk. She thought she could see the beginnings of fear wake in his eyes. *He's going to lose*, she told herself, exulting, as Lord Beric's flaming sword whirled and slashed. In one wild flurry, the lightning lord took back all the ground the Hound had gained, sending Clegane staggering to the very edge of the firepit once more. *He is, he is, he's going to die.* She stood on her toes for a better look.

"*Bloody bastard!*" the Hound screamed as he felt the fire licking against the back of his thighs. He charged, swinging the heavy sword harder and harder, trying to smash the smaller man down with brute force, to break blade or shield or arm. But the flames of Dondarrion's parries snapped at his eyes, and when the Hound jerked away from them, his foot went out from under him and he staggered to one knee. At once Lord Beric closed, his downcut screaming through the air trailing pennons of fire. Panting from exertion, Clegane jerked his shield up over his head just in time, and the cave rang with the loud *crack* of splintering oak.

"His shield is afire," Gendry said in a hushed voice. Arya saw it in the same instant. The flames had spread across the chipped yellow paint, and the three black dogs were engulfed.

Sandor Clegane had fought his way back to his feet with a reckless counterattack. Not until Lord Beric retreated a pace did the Hound seem to realize that the fire that roared so near his face was his own shield, burning. With a shout of revulsion, he hacked down savagely on the broken oak, completing its destruction. The shield shattered, one piece of it spinning away, still afire, while the other clung stubbornly to his forearm. His efforts to free himself only fanned the flames. His sleeve caught, and now his whole left arm was ablaze. "*Finish him!*" Greenbeard urged Lord Beric, and other voices took up the chant of "*Guilty!*" Arya shouted with the rest. "*Guilty, guilty, kill him, guilty!*"

Smooth as summer silk, Lord Beric slid close to make an end of the man before him. The Hound gave a rasping scream, raised his sword in both hands and brought it crashing down with all his strength. Lord Beric blocked the cut easily . . .

"*Noooooo*," Arya shrieked.

. . . but the burning sword snapped in two, and the Hound's cold steel plowed into Lord Beric's flesh where his shoulder joined his neck and clove him clean down to the breastbone. The blood came rushing out in a hot black gush.

Sandor Clegane jerked backward, still burning. He ripped the remnants of his shield off and flung them away with a curse, then rolled in the dirt to smother the fire running along his arm.

Lord Beric's knees folded slowly, as if for prayer. When his mouth opened only blood came out. The Hound's sword was still in him as he toppled face forward. The dirt drank his blood. Beneath the hollow hill there was no sound but the soft crackling of flames and the whimper the Hound made when he tried to rise. Arya could only think of Mycah and all the stupid prayers she'd prayed for the Hound to die. *If there were gods, why didn't Lord Beric win?* She *knew* the Hound was guilty.

"Please," Sandor Clegane rasped, cradling his arm. "I'm burned. Help me. Someone. Help me." He was crying. "*Please*."

Arya looked at him in astonishment. *He's crying like a little baby*, she thought.

"Melly, see to his burns," said Thoros. "Lem, Jack, help me with Lord Beric. Ned, you'd best come too." The red priest wrenched the Hound's sword from the body of his fallen lord and thrust the point of it down in the blood-soaked earth. Lem slid his big hands under Dondarrion's arms, while Jack-Be-Lucky took his feet. They carried him around the firepit, into the darkness of one of the tunnels. Thoros and the boy Ned followed after.

The Mad Huntsman spat. "I say we take him back to Stoney Sept and put him in a crow cage."

"Yes," Arya said. "He murdered Mycah. He *did*."

"Such an angry squirrel," murmured Greenbeard.

Harwin sighed. "R'hllor has judged him innocent."

"Who's *Rulore*?" She couldn't even say it.

"The Lord of Light. Thoros has taught us – "

She didn't care what Thoros had taught them. She yanked Greenbeard's dagger from its sheath and spun away before he could catch her. Gendry made a grab for her as well, but she had always been too fast for Gendry.

Tom Sevenstrings and some woman were helping the Hound to his feet. The sight of his arm shocked her speechless. There was a strip of pink where the leather strap had clung, but above and below the flesh was cracked and red and bleeding from elbow to wrist. When his eyes met hers, his mouth twitched. "You want me dead that bad? Then do it, wolf girl. Shove it in. It's cleaner than fire." Clegane tried to stand, but as he moved a piece of burned flesh sloughed right off his arm, and his knees went out from under him. Tom caught him by his good arm and held him up.

His arm, Arya thought, and *his face*. But he was the Hound. He deserved to burn in a fiery hell. The knife felt heavy in her hand. She gripped it tighter. "You killed Mycah," she said once more, daring him to deny it. "Tell them. You did. You *did*."

"I did." His whole face twisted. "I rode him down and cut him in half, and laughed. I watched them beat your sister bloody too, watched them cut your father's head off."

Lem grabbed her wrist and twisted, wrenching the dagger away. She kicked at him, but he would not give it back. "You go to hell, Hound," she screamed at Sandor Clegane in helpless empty-handed rage. "*You just go to hell!*"

"He has," said a voice scarce stronger than a whisper.

When Arya turned, Lord Beric Dondarrion was standing behind her, his bloody hand clutching Thoros by the shoulder.

CATELYN

L *et the kings of winter have their cold crypt under the earth*, Catelyn thought. The Tullys drew their strength from the river, and it was to the river they returned when their lives had run their course.

They laid Lord Hoster in a slender wooden boat, clad in shining silver armor, plate-and-mail. His cloak was spread beneath him, rippling blue and red. His surcoat was divided blue-and-red as well. A trout, scaled in silver and bronze, crowned the crest of the greathelm they placed beside his head. On his chest they placed a painted wooden sword, his fingers curled about its hilt. Mail gauntlets hid his wasted hands, and made him look almost strong again. His massive oak-and-iron shield was set by his left side, his hunting horn to his right. The rest of the boat was filled with driftwood and kindling and scraps of parchment, and stones to make it heavy in the water. His banner flew from the prow, the leaping trout of Riverrun.

Seven were chosen to push the funereal boat to the water, in honor of the seven faces of god. Robb was one, Lord Hoster's liege lord. With him were the Lords Bracken, Blackwood, Vance, and Mallister, Ser Marq Piper . . . and Lame Lothar Frey, who had come down from the Twins with the answer they had awaited. Forty soldiers rode in his escort, commanded by Walder Rivers, the eldest of Lord Walder's bastard brood, a stern, grey-haired man with a formidable reputation as a warrior. Their arrival, coming within hours of Lord Hoster's passing, had sent Edmure into a rage. "Walder Frey should be flayed and quartered!" he'd shouted. "He sends a cripple and a bastard to treat with us, tell me there is no insult meant by that."

"I have no doubt that Lord Walder chose his envoys with care," she replied. "It was a peevish thing to do, a petty sort of revenge, but remember who we are dealing with. The Late Lord Frey, Father used to call him. The man is ill-tempered, envious, and above all *prideful.*"

Blessedly, her son had shown better sense than her brother. Robb had greeted the Freys with every courtesy, found barracks space for the escort, and quietly asked Ser Desmond Grell to stand aside so Lothar might have the honor of helping to send Lord Hoster on his last voyage. *He has learned a rough wisdom beyond his years, my son.* House Frey might have abandoned the King in the North, but the Lord of the Crossing remained the most powerful of Riverrun's bannermen, and Lothar was here in his stead.

The seven launched Lord Hoster from the water stair, wading down the steps as the portcullis was winched upward. Lothar Frey, a soft-bodied portly man, was breathing heavily as they shoved the boat out into the current. Jason Mallister and Tytos Blackwood, at the prow, stood chest deep in the river to guide it on its way.

Catelyn watched from the battlements, waiting and watching as she had waited and watched so many times before. Beneath her, the swift wild Tumblestone plunged like a spear into the side of the broad Red Fork, its blue-white current churning the muddy red-brown flow of the greater river. A morning mist hung over the water, as thin as gossamer and the wisps of memory.

Bran and Rickon will be waiting for him, Catelyn thought sadly, *as once I used to wait.*

The slim boat drifted out from under the red stone arch of the Water Gate, picking up speed as it was caught in the headlong rush of the Tumblestone and pushed out into the tumult where the waters met. As the boat emerged from beneath the high sheltering walls of the castle, its square sail filled with wind, and Catelyn saw sunlight flashing on her father's helm. Lord Hoster Tully's rudder held true, and he sailed serenely down the center of the channel, into the rising sun.

"Now," her uncle urged. Beside him, her brother Edmure – *Lord* Edmure now in truth, and how long would that take to grow used to? – nocked an arrow to his bowstring. His squire held a brand to its point. Edmure waited until the flame caught, then lifted the great bow, drew the string to his ear, and let fly. With a deep *thrum*, the arrow sped upward. Catelyn followed its flight with her eyes and heart, until it plunged into the water with a soft *hiss*, well astern of Lord Hoster's boat.

Edmure cursed softly. "The wind," he said, pulling a second arrow. "Again." The brand kissed the oil-soaked rag behind the arrowhead, the flames went licking up, Edmure lifted, pulled, and released. High and far the arrow flew. Too far. It vanished in the river a dozen yards beyond the boat, its fire winking out in an instant. A flush was creeping up Edmure's neck, red as his beard. "Once more," he commanded, taking a third arrow from the quiver. *He is as tight as his bowstring*, Catelyn thought.

Ser Brynden must have seen the same thing. "Let me, my lord," he offered.

"I can do it," Edmure insisted. He let them light the arrow, jerked the bow up, took a deep breath, drew back the arrow. For a long moment he seemed to hesitate while the fire crept up the shaft, crackling. Finally he released. The arrow flashed up and up, and finally curved down again, falling, falling . . . and hissing past the billowing sail.

A narrow miss, no more than a handspan, and yet a miss. "The Others take it!" her brother swore. The boat was almost out of range, drifting in and out among the river mists. Wordless, Edmure thrust the bow at his uncle.

"Swiftly," Ser Brynden said. He nocked an arrow, held it steady for the brand, drew and released before Catelyn was quite sure that the fire had caught . . . but as the shot rose, she saw the flames trailing through the air, a pale orange pennon. The boat had vanished in the mists. Falling, the flaming arrow was swallowed up as well . . . but only to a heartbeat. Then, sudden as hope, they saw the red bloom flower. The sails took fire, and the fog glowed pink and orange. For a moment Catelyn saw the outline of the boat clearly, wreathed in leaping flames.

Watch for me, little cat, she could hear him whisper.

Catelyn reached out blindly, groping for her brother's hand, but Edmure had moved away, to stand alone on the highest point of the battlements. Her uncle Brynden took her hand instead, twining his strong fingers through hers. Together they watched the little fire grow smaller as the burning boat receded in the distance.

And then it was gone . . . drifting downriver still, perhaps, or broken up and sinking. The weight of his armor would carry Lord Hoster down to rest in the soft mud of the riverbed, in the watery halls where the Tullys held eternal court, with schools of fish their last attendants.

No sooner had the burning boat vanished from their sight than Edmure walked off. Catelyn would have liked to embrace him, if only for a moment; to sit for an hour or a night or the turn of a moon to speak of the dead and mourn. Yet she knew as well as he that this was not the time; he was Lord of Riverrun now, and his knights were falling in around him, murmuring condolences and promises of fealty, walling him off from something as small as a sister's grief. Edmure listened, hearing none of the words.

"It is no disgrace to miss your shot," her uncle told her quietly. "Edmure should hear that. The day my own lord father went downriver, Hoster missed as well."

"With his first shaft." Catelyn had been too young to remember, but Lord Hoster had often told the tale. "His second found the sail." She sighed. Edmure was not as strong as he seemed. Their father's death had been a mercy when it came at last, but even so her brother had taken it hard.

Last night in his cups he had broken down and wept, full of regrets for things undone and words unsaid. He ought never to have ridden off to fight his battle on the fords, he told her tearfully; he should have stayed at their father's bedside. "I should have been with him, as you were," he said. "Did he speak of me at the end? Tell me true, Cat. Did he ask for me?"

Lord Hoster's last word had been *"Tansy,"* but Catelyn could not bring herself to tell him that. "He whispered your name," she lied, and her brother had nodded gratefully and kissed her hand. *If he had not tried to drown his grief and guilt, he might have been able to bend a bow,* she thought to herself, sighing, but that was something else she dare not say.

The Blackfish escorted her down from the battlements to where Robb stood among his bannermen, his young queen at his side. When he saw her, her son took her silently in his arms.

"Lord Hoster looked as noble as a king, my lady," murmured Jeyne. "Would that I had been given the chance to know him."

"And I to know him better," added Robb.

"He would have wished that too," said Catelyn. "There were too many leagues between Riverrun and Winterfell." *And too many mountains and rivers and armies between Riverrun and the Eyrie, it would seem.* Lysa had made no reply to her letter.

And from King's Landing came only silence as well. By now she had hoped that Brienne and Ser Cleos would have reached the city with their captive. It might even be that Brienne was on her way back, and the girls with her. *Ser Cleos swore he would make the Imp send a raven once the trade was made. He swore it!* Ravens did not always win through. Some bowman could have brought the bird down and roasted him for supper. The letter that would have set her heart at ease might even now be lying by the ashes of some campfire beside a pile of raven bones.

Others were waiting to offer Robb their consolations, so Catelyn stood aside patiently while Lord Jason Mallister, the Greatjon, and Ser Rolph Spicer spoke to him each in turn. But when Lothar Frey approached, she gave his sleeve a tug. Robb turned, and waited to hear what Lothar would say.

"Your Grace." A plump man in his middle thirties, Lothar Frey had close-set eyes, a pointed beard, and dark hair that fell to his shoulders in ringlets. A leg twisted at birth had earned him the name *Lame Lothar*. He had served as his father's steward for the past dozen years. "We are loath to intrude upon your grief, but perhaps you might grant us audience tonight?"

"It would be my pleasure," said Robb. "It was never my wish to sow enmity between us."

"Nor mine to be the cause of it," said Queen Jeyne.

Lothar Frey smiled. "I understand, as does my lord father. He instructed me to say that he was young once, and well remembers what it is like to lose one's heart to beauty."

Catelyn doubted very much that Lord Walder had said any such thing, or that he had ever lost his heart to beauty. The Lord of the Crossing had outlived seven wives and was now wed to his eighth, but he spoke of them only as bedwarmers and brood mares. Still, the words were fairly spoken, and she could scarce object to the compliment. Nor did Robb. "Your father is most gracious," he said. "I shall look forward to our talk."

Lothar bowed, kissed the queen's hand, and withdrew. By then a dozen others had gathered for a word. Robb spoke with them each, giving a thanks here, a smile there, as needed. Only when the last of them was done did he turn back to Catelyn. "There is something we must speak of. Will you walk with me?"

"As you command, Your Grace."

"That wasn't a command, Mother."

"It will be my pleasure, then." Her son had treated her kindly enough since returning to Riverrun, yet he seldom sought her out. If he was more comfortable with his young queen, she could scarcely blame him. *Jeyne makes him smile, and I have nothing to share with him but grief.* He seemed to enjoy the company of his bride's brothers, as well; young Rollam his squire and Ser Raynald his standard-bearer. *They are standing in the boots of those he's lost*, Catelyn realized when she watched them together. *Rollam has taken Bran's place, and Raynald is part Theon and part Jon Snow.* Only with the Westerlings did she see Robb smile, or hear him laugh like the boy he was. To the others he was always the King in the North, head bowed beneath the weight of the crown even when his brows were bare.

Robb kissed his wife gently, promised to see her in their chambers, and went off with his lady mother. His steps led them toward the godswood. "Lothar seemed amiable, that's a hopeful sign. We need the Freys."

"That does not mean we shall have them."

He nodded, and there was glumness to his face and a slope to his shoulders that made her heart go out to him. *The crown is crushing him*, she thought. *He wants so much to be a good king, to be brave and honorable and clever, but the weight is too much for a boy to bear.* Robb was doing all he could, yet still the blows kept falling, one after the other, relentless. When they brought him word of the battle at Duskendale, where Lord Randyll Tarly had shattered Robett Glover and Ser Helman Tallhart, he might have been expected to rage. Instead he'd stared in dumb disbelief and said, "Duskendale, on the narrow sea? Why would they go to Duskendale?" He'd shook his head, bewildered. "A third of my foot, lost for *Duskendale!*"

"The ironmen have my castle and now the Lannisters hold my brother," Galbart Glover said, in a voice thick with despair. Robett Glover had survived the battle, but had been captured near the kingsroad not long after.

"Not for long," her son promised. "I will offer them Martyn Lannister in exchange. Lord Tywin will have to accept, for his brother's sake." Martyn was Ser Kevan's son, a twin to the Willem that Lord Karstark had butchered. Those murders still haunted her son, Catelyn knew. He had tripled the guard around Martyn, but still feared for his safety.

"I should have traded the Kingslayer for Sansa when you first urged it," Robb said as they walked the gallery. "If I'd offered to wed her to the Knight of Flowers, the Tyrells might be ours instead of Joffrey's. I should have thought of that."

"Your mind was on your battles, and rightly so. Even a king cannot think of everything."

"Battles," muttered Robb as he led her out beneath the

trees. "I have won every battle, yet somehow I'm losing the war." He looked up, as if the answer might be written on the sky. "The ironmen hold Winterfell, and Moat Cailin too. Father's dead, and Bran and Rickon, maybe Arya. And now your father too."

She could not let him despair. She knew the taste of that draught too well herself. "My father has been dying for a long time. You could not have changed that. You have made mistakes, Robb, but what king has not? Ned would have been proud of you."

"Mother, there is something you must know."

Catelyn's heart skipped a beat. *This is something he hates. Something he dreads to tell me.* All she could think of was Brienne and her mission. "Is it the Kingslayer?"

"No. It's Sansa."

She's dead, Catelyn thought at once. *Brienne failed, Jaime is dead, and Cersei has killed my sweet girl in retribution.* For a moment she could barely speak. "Is . . . is she gone, Robb?"

"Gone?" He looked startled. "Dead? Oh, Mother, no, not that, they haven't harmed her, not that way, only . . . a bird came last night, but I couldn't bring myself to tell you, not until your father was sent to his rest." Robb took her hand. "They married her to Tyrion Lannister."

Catelyn's fingers clutched at his. "The Imp."

"Yes."

"He swore to trade her for his brother," she said numbly. "Sansa and Arya both. We would have them back if we returned his precious Jaime, he swore it before the whole court. How could he marry her, after saying that in sight of gods and men?"

"He's the Kingslayer's brother. Oathbreaking runs in their blood." Robb's fingers brushed the pommel of his sword. "If I could I'd take his ugly head off. Sansa would be a widow then, and free. There's no other way that I can see. They made her speak the vows before a septon and don a crimson cloak."

Catelyn remembered the twisted little man she had seized at the crossroads inn and carried all the way to the Eyrie. "I should have let Lysa push him out her Moon

Door. My poor sweet Sansa . . . why would anyone do this to her?"

"For Winterfell," Robb said at once. "With Bran and Rickon dead, Sansa is my heir. If anything should happen to me . . ."

She clutched tight at his hand. "Nothing will happen to you. *Nothing.* I could not stand it. They took Ned, and your sweet brothers. Sansa is married, Arya is lost, my father's dead . . . if anything befell you, I would go mad, Robb. You are all I have left. You are all the *north* has left."

"I am not dead yet, Mother."

Suddenly Catelyn was full of dread. "Wars need not be fought until the last drop of blood." Even she could hear the desperation in her voice. "You would not be the first king to bend the knee, nor even the first Stark."

His mouth tightened. "No. Never."

"There is no shame in it. Balon Greyjoy bent the knee to Robert when his rebellion failed. Torrhen Stark bent the knee to Aegon the Conqueror rather than see his army face the fires."

"Did Aegon kill King Torrhen's father?" He pulled his hand from hers. "Never, I said."

He is playing the boy now, not the king. "The Lannisters do not need the north. They will require homage and hostages, no more . . . and the Imp will keep Sansa no matter what we do, so they have their hostage. The ironmen will prove a more implacable enemy, I promise you. To have any hope of holding the north, the Greyjoys must leave no single sprig of House Stark alive to dispute their right. Theon's murdered Bran and Rickon, so now all they need do is kill you . . . *and* Jeyne, yes. Do you think Lord Balon can afford to let her live to bear you heirs?"

Robb's face was cold. "Is that why you freed the Kingslayer? To make a peace with the Lannisters?"

"I freed Jaime for Sansa's sake . . . and Arya's, if she still lives. You know that. But if I nurtured some hope of buying peace as well, was that so ill?"

"Yes," he said. "The Lannisters killed my father."

"Do you think I have forgotten that?"

"I don't know. Have you?"

Catelyn had never struck her children in anger, but she almost struck Robb then. It was an effort to remind herself how frightened and alone he must feel. "You are King in the North, the choice is yours. I only ask that you think on what I've said. The singers make much of kings who die valiantly in battle, but your life is worth more than a song. To me at least, who gave it to you." She lowered her head. "Do I have your leave to go?"

"Yes." He turned away and drew his sword. What he meant to do with it, she could not say. There was no enemy there, no one to fight. Only her and him, amongst tall trees and fallen leaves. *There are fights no sword can win*, Catelyn wanted to tell him, but she feared the king was deaf to such words.

Hours later, she was sewing in her bedchamber when young Rollam Westerling came running with the summons to supper. *Good*, Catelyn thought, relieved. She had not been certain that her son would want her there, after their quarrel. "A dutiful squire," she said to Rollam gravely. *Bran would have been the same.*

If Robb seemed cool at table and Edmure surly, Lame Lothar made up for them both. He was the model of courtesy, reminiscing warmly about Lord Hoster, offering Catelyn gentle condolences on the loss of Bran and Rickon, praising Edmure for the victory at Stone Mill, and thanking Robb for the "swift sure justice" he had meted out to Rickard Karstark. Lothar's bastard brother Walder Rivers was another matter; a harsh sour man with old Lord Walder's suspicious face, he spoke but seldom and devoted most of his attention to the meat and mead that was set before him.

When all the empty words were said, the queen and the other Westerlings excused themselves, the remains of the meal were cleared away, and Lothar Frey cleared his throat. "Before we turn to the business that brings us here, there is another matter," he said solemnly. "A grave matter, I fear. I had hoped it would not fall to me to bring you these tidings, but it seems I must. My lord father has had a letter from his grandsons."

Catelyn had been so lost in grief for her own that she had almost forgotten the two Freys she had agreed to foster. *No more*, she thought. *Mother have mercy, how many more blows can we bear?* Somehow she knew the next words she heard would plunge yet another blade into her heart. "The grandsons at Winterfell?" she made herself ask. "My wards?"

"Walder and Walder, yes. But they are presently at the Dreadfort, my lady. I grieve to tell you this, but there has been a battle. Winterfell is burned."

"*Burned?*" Robb's voice was incredulous.

"Your northern lords tried to retake it from the ironmen. When Theon Greyjoy saw that his prize was lost, he put the castle to the torch."

"We have heard naught of any battle," said Ser Brynden.

"My nephews are young, I grant you, but they were there. Big Walder wrote the letter, though his cousin signed as well. It was a bloody bit of business, by their account. Your castellan was slain. Ser Rodrik, was that his name?"

"Ser Rodrik Cassel," said Catelyn numbly. *That dear brave loyal old soul.* She could almost see him, tugging on his fierce white whiskers. "What of our other people?"

"The ironmen put many of them to the sword, I fear."

Wordless with rage, Robb slammed a fist down on the table and turned his face away, so the Freys would not see his tears.

But his mother saw them. *The world grows a little darker every day.* Catelyn's thoughts went to Ser Rodrik's little daughter Beth, to tireless Maester Luwin and cheerful Septon Chayle, Mikken at the forge, Farlen and Palla in the kennels, Old Nan and simple Hodor. Her heart was sick. "Please, not *all*."

"No," said Lame Lothar. "The women and children hid, my nephews Walder and Walder among them. With Winterfell in ruins, the survivors were carried back to the Dreadfort by this son of Lord Bolton's."

"Bolton's *son*?" Robb's voice was strained.

Walder Rivers spoke up. "A bastard son, I believe."

"Not Ramsay Snow? Does Lord Roose have another

bastard?" Robb scowled. "This Ramsay was a monster and a murderer, and he died a coward. Or so I was told."

"I cannot speak to that. There is much confusion in any war. Many false reports. All I can tell you is that my nephews claim it was this bastard son of Bolton's who saved the women of Winterfell, and the little ones. They are safe at the Dreadfort now, all those who remain."

"Theon," Robb said suddenly. "What happened to Theon Greyjoy? Was he slain?"

Lame Lothar spread his hands. "That I cannot say, Your Grace. Walder and Walder made no mention of his fate. Perhaps Lord Bolton might know, if he has had word from this son of his."

Ser Brynden said, "We will be certain to ask him."

"You are all distraught, I see. I am sorry to have brought you such fresh grief. Perhaps we should adjourn until the morrow. Our business can wait until you have composed yourselves . . ."

"No," said Robb, "I want the matter settled."

Her brother Edmure nodded. "Me as well. Do you have an answer to our offer, my lord?"

"I do." Lothar smiled. "My lord father bids me tell Your Grace that he will agree to this new marriage alliance between our houses and renew his fealty to the King in the North, upon the condition that the King's Grace apologize for the insult done to House Frey, in his royal person, face to face."

An apology was a small enough price to pay, but Catelyn misliked this petty condition of Lord Walder's at once.

"I am pleased," Robb said cautiously. "It was never my wish to cause this rift between us, Lothar. The Freys have fought valiantly for my cause. I would have them at my side once more."

"You are too kind, Your Grace. As you accept these terms, I am then instructed to offer Lord Tully the hand of my sister, the Lady Roslin, a maid of sixteen years. Roslin is my lord father's youngest daughter by Lady Bethany of House Rosby, his sixth wife. She has a gentle nature and a gift for music."

Edmure shifted in his seat. "Might not it be better if I first met –"

"You'll meet when you're wed," said Walder Rivers curtly. "Unless Lord Tully feels a need to count her teeth first?"

Edmure kept his temper. "I will take your word so far as her teeth are concerned, but it would be pleasant if I might gaze upon her face before I espoused her."

"You must accept her now, my lord," said Walder Rivers. "Else my father's offer is withdrawn."

Lame Lothar spread his hands. "My brother has a soldier's bluntness, but what he says is true. It is my lord father's wish that this marriage take place at once."

"*At once?*" Edmure sounded so unhappy that Catelyn had the unworthy thought that perhaps he had been entertaining notions of breaking the betrothal after the fighting was done.

"Has Lord Walder forgotten that we are fighting a war?" Brynden Blackfish asked sharply.

"Scarcely," said Lothar. "That is why he insists that the marriage take place now, ser. Men die in war, even men who are young and strong. What would become of our alliance should Lord Edmure fall before he took Roslin to bride? And there is my father's age to consider as well. He is past ninety and not like to see the end of this struggle. It would put his noble heart at peace if he could see his dear Roslin safely wed before the gods take him, so he might die with the knowledge that the girl had a strong husband to cherish and protect her."

We all want Lord Walder to die happy. Catelyn was growing less and less comfortable with this arrangement. "My brother has just lost his own father. He needs time to mourn."

"Roslin is a cheerful girl," said Lothar. "She may be the very thing Lord Edmure needs to help him through his grief."

"And my grandfather has come to mislike lengthy betrothals," the bastard Walder Rivers added. "I cannot imagine why."

Robb gave him a chilly look. "I take your meaning, Rivers. Pray excuse us."

"As Your Grace commands." Lame Lothar rose, and his bastard brother helped him hobble from the room.

Edmure was seething. "They're as much as saying that my promise is worthless. Why should I let that old weasel choose my bride? Lord Walder has other daughters besides this Roslin. Granddaughters as well. I should be offered the same choice you were. I'm his liege lord, he should be overjoyed that I'm willing to wed *any* of them."

"He is a proud man, and we've wounded him," said Catelyn.

"The Others take his pride! I will not be shamed in my own hall. My answer is no."

Robb gave him a weary look. "I will not command you. Not in this. But if you refuse, Lord Frey will take it for another slight, and any hope of putting this arights will be gone."

"You cannot know that," Edmure insisted. "Frey has wanted me for one of his daughters since the day I was born. He will not let a chance like this slip between those grasping fingers of his. When Lothar brings him our answer, he'll come wheedling back and accept a betrothal . . . and to a daughter of *my* choosing."

"Perhaps, in time," said Brynden Blackfish. "But can we wait, while Lothar rides back and forth with offers and counters?"

Robb's hands curled into fists. "I must get back to the north. My brothers dead, Winterfell burned, my smallfolk put to the sword . . . the gods only know what this bastard of Bolton's is about, or whether Theon is still alive and on the loose. I can't sit here waiting for a wedding that might or might not happen."

"It *must* happen," said Catelyn, though not gladly. "I have no more wish to suffer Walder Frey's insults and complaints than you do, Brother, but I see little choice here. Without this wedding, Robb's cause is lost. Edmure, we must accept."

"*We* must accept?" he echoed peevishly. "I don't see you offering to become the ninth Lady Frey, Cat."

"The eighth Lady Frey is still alive and well, so far as

I know," she replied. *Thankfully*. Otherwise it might well have come to that, knowing Lord Walder.

The Blackfish said, "I am the last man in the Seven Kingdoms to tell anyone who they must wed, Nephew. Nonetheless, you *did* say something of making amends for your Battle of the Fords."

"I had in mind a different sort of amends. Single combat with the Kingslayer. Seven years of penance as a begging brother. Swimming the sunset sea with my legs tied." When he saw that no one was smiling, Edmure threw up his hands. "The Others take you all! Very well, I'll wed the wench. As *amends*."

DAVOS

Lord Alester looked up sharply. "Voices," he said. "Do you hear, Davos? Someone is coming for us."

"Lamprey," said Davos. "It's time for our supper, or near enough." Last night Lamprey had brought them half a beef-and-bacon pie, and a flagon of mead as well. Just the thought of it made his belly start to rumble.

"No, there's more than one."

He's right. Davos heard two voices at least, and footsteps, growing louder. He got to his feet and moved to the bars.

Lord Alester brushed the straw from his clothes. "The king has sent for me. Or the queen, yes, Selyse would never let me rot here, her own blood."

Outside the cell, Lamprey appeared with a ring of keys in hand. Ser Axell Florent and four guardsmen followed close behind him. They waited beneath the torch while Lamprey searched for the correct key.

"Axell," Lord Alester said. "Gods be good. Is it the king who sends for me, or the queen?"

"No one has sent for you, traitor," Ser Axell said.

Lord Alester recoiled as if he'd been slapped. "No, I swear to you, I committed no treason. Why won't you listen? If His Grace would only let me explain—"

Lamprey thrust a great iron key into the lock, turned

it, and pulled open the cell. The rusted hinges screamed in protest. "You," he said to Davos. "Come."

"Where?" Davos looked to Ser Axell. "Tell me true, ser, do you mean to burn me?"

"You are sent for. Can you walk?"

"I can walk." Davos stepped from the cell. Lord Alester gave a cry of dismay as Lamprey slammed the door shut once more.

"Take the torch," Ser Axell commanded the gaoler. "Leave the traitor to the darkness."

"No," his brother said. "Axell, please, don't take the light . . . gods have mercy . . ."

"Gods? There is only R'hllor, and the Other." Ser Axell gestured sharply, and one of his guardsmen pulled the torch from its sconce and led the way to the stair.

"Are you taking me to Melisandre?" Davos asked.

"She will be there," Ser Axell said. "She is never far from the king. But it is His Grace himself who asked for you."

Davos lifted his hand to his chest, where once his luck had hung in a leather bag on a thong. *Gone now*, he remembered, *and the ends of four fingers as well*. But his hands were still long enough to wrap about a woman's throat, he thought, especially a slender throat like hers.

Up they went, climbing the turnpike stair in single file. The walls were rough dark stone, cool to the touch. The light of the torches went before them, and their shadows marched beside them on the walls. At the third turn they passed an iron gate that opened on blackness, and another at the fifth turn. Davos guessed that they were near the surface by then, perhaps even above it. The next door they came to was made of wood, but still they climbed. Now the walls were broken by arrow slits, but no shafts of sunlight pried their way through the thickness of the stone. It was night outside.

His legs were aching by the time Ser Axell thrust open a heavy door and gestured him through. Beyond, a high stone bridge arched over emptiness to the massive central tower called the Stone Drum. A sea wind blew restlessly through the arches that supported the roof, and Davos could smell the salt water as they crossed. He took a deep breath, filling his lungs with the clean cold air. *Wind and water, give me strength*, he prayed. A huge nightfire burned in the yard below, to keep the terrors of the dark at bay, and the queen's men were gathered around it, singing praises to their new red god.

They were in the center of the bridge when Ser Axell stopped suddenly. He made a brusque gesture with his hand, and his men moved out of earshot. "Were it my choice, I would burn you with my brother Alester," he told Davos. "You are both traitors."

"Say what you will. I would never betray King Stannis."

"You would. You will. I see it in your face. And I have seen it in the flames as well. R'hllor has blessed me with that gift. Like Lady Melisandre, he shows me the future in the fire. Stannis Baratheon *will* sit the Iron Throne. I have seen it. And I know what must be done. His Grace must make me his Hand, in place of my traitor brother. And you will tell him so."

Will I? Davos said nothing.

"The queen has urged my appointment," Ser Axell went on. "Even your old friend from Lys, the pirate Saan, he says the same. We have made a plan together, him and me. Yet His Grace does not act. The defeat gnaws inside him, a black worm in his soul. It is up to us who love him to show him what to do. If you are as devoted to his cause as you claim, smuggler, you will join your voice to ours. Tell him that I am the only Hand he needs. Tell him, and when we sail I shall see that you have a new ship."

A ship. Davos studied the other man's face. Ser Axell had big Florent ears, much like the queen's. Coarse hair grew from them, as from his nostrils; more sprouted in tufts and patches beneath his double chin. His nose was broad, his brow beetled, his eyes close-set and hostile. *He would sooner give me a pyre than a ship, he said as much, but if I do him this favor . . .*

"If you think to betray me," Ser Axell said, "pray remember that I have been castellan of Dragonstone a good long time. The garrison is mine. Perhaps I cannot burn you without the king's consent, but who is to say you might not suffer a fall." He laid a meaty hand on the back of Davos's neck and shoved him bodily against the waist-high side of the bridge, then shoved a little harder to force his face out over the yard. "Do you hear me?"

"I hear," said Davos. *And you dare name me traitor?*

Ser Axell released him. "Good." He smiled. "His Grace awaits. Best we do not keep him."

At the very top of Stone Drum, within the great round room called the Chamber of the Painted Table, they found Stannis Baratheon standing behind the artifact that gave the hall its name, a massive slab of wood carved and painted in the shape of Westeros as it had been in the time of Aegon the Conqueror. An iron brazier stood beside the king, its coals glowing a ruddy orange. Four tall pointed windows looked out to north, south, east, and west. Beyond was the night and the starry sky. Davos could hear the wind moving, and fainter, the sounds of the sea.

"Your Grace," Ser Axell said, "as it please you, I have brought the onion knight."

"So I see." Stannis wore a grey wool tunic, a dark red mantle, and a plain black leather belt from which his sword and dagger hung. A red-gold crown with flame-shaped points encircled his brows. The look of him was a shock. He seemed ten years older than the man that Davos had left at Storm's End when he set sail for the Blackwater and the battle that would be their undoing. The king's close-cropped beard was spiderwebbed with grey hairs, and he had dropped two stone or more of weight. He had never been a fleshy man, but now the bones moved beneath his skin like spears, fighting to cut free. Even his crown seemed too large for his head. His eyes were blue pits lost in deep hollows, and the shape of a skull could be seen beneath his face.

Yet when he saw Davos, a faint smile brushed his lips. "So the sea has returned me my knight of the fish and onions."

"It did, Your Grace." *Does he know that he had me in his dungeon?* Davos went to one knee.

"Rise, Ser Davos," Stannis commanded. "I have missed you, ser. I have need of good counsel, and you never gave me less. So tell me true – what is the penalty for treason?"

The word hung in the air. *A frightful word*, thought Davos. Was he being asked to condemn his cellmate? Or himself, perchance? *Kings know the penalty for treason better than any man.* "Treason?" he finally managed, weakly.

"What else would you call it, to deny your king and seek to steal his rightful throne. I ask you again – what is the penalty for treason under the law?"

Davos had no choice but to answer. "Death," he said. "The penalty is death, Your Grace."

"It has always been so. I am *not* . . . I am not a cruel man, Ser Davos. You know me. Have known me long. This is not my decree. It has always been so, since Aegon's day and before. Daemon Blackfyre, the brothers Toyne, the Vulture King, Grand Maester Hareth . . . traitors have always paid with their lives . . . even Rhaenyra Targaryen. She was daughter to one king and mother to two more, yet she died a traitor's death for trying to usurp her brother's crown. It is law. *Law*, Davos. Not cruelty."

"Yes, Your Grace." *He does not speak of me.* Davos felt a moment's pity for his cellmate down in the dark. He knew he should keep silent, but he was tired and sick at heart, and he heard himself say, "Sire, Lord Florent meant no treason."

"Do smugglers have another name for it? I made him Hand, and he would have sold my rights for a bowl of pease porridge. He would even have given them Shireen. Mine only child, he would have wed to a bastard born of incest." The king's voice was thick with anger. "My brother had a gift for inspiring loyalty. Even in his foes. At Summerhall he won three battles in a single day, and brought Lords Grandison and Cafferen back to Storm's End as prisoners. He hung their banners in the hall as trophies. Cafferen's white fawns were spotted with blood and Grandison's sleeping lion was torn near in two. Yet they would sit beneath those banners of a night, drinking and feasting with Robert. He even took them hunting. 'These men meant to deliver you to Aerys to be burned,' I told him after I saw them throwing axes in the yard.

'You should not be putting axes in their hands.' Robert only laughed. I would have thrown Grandison and Caff- eren into a dungeon, but he turned them into friends. Lord Cafferen died at Ashford Castle, cut down by Randyll Tarly whilst fighting *for* Robert. Lord Grandison was wounded on the Trident and died of it a year after. My brother made them love him, but it would seem that I inspire only betrayal. Even in mine own blood and kin. Brother, grandfather, cousins, good uncle . . .''

"Your Grace," said Ser Axell, "I beg you, give me the chance to prove to you that not all Florents are so feeble."

"Ser Axell would have me resume the war," King Stannis told Davos. "The Lannisters think I am done and beaten, and my sworn lords have forsaken me, near every one. Even Lord Estermont, my own mother's father, has bent his knee to Joffrey. The few loyal men who remain to me are losing heart. They waste their days drinking and gambling, and lick their wounds like beaten curs.'

"Battle will set their hearts ablaze once more, Your Grace," Ser Axell said. "Defeat is a disease, and victory is the cure."

"Victory." The king's mouth twisted. "There are vic- tories and victories, ser. But tell your plan to Ser Davos. I would hear his views on what you propose."

Ser Axell turned to Davos, with a look on his face much like the look that proud Lord Belgrave must have worn, the day King Baelor the Blessed had commanded him to wash the beggar's ulcerous feet. Nonetheless, he obeyed.

The plan Ser Axell had devised with Salladhor Saan was simple. A few hours' sail from Dragonstone lay Claw Isle, ancient sea-girt seat of House Celtigar. Lord Ardrian Celtigar had fought beneath the fiery heart on the Black- water, but once taken, he had wasted no time in going over to Joffrey. He remained in King's Landing even now. "Too frightened of His Grace's wrath to come near Dragonstone, no doubt," Ser Axell declared. "And wisely so. The man has betrayed his rightful king."

Ser Axell proposed to use Salladhor Saan's fleet and the men who had escaped the Blackwater – Stannis still had some fifteen hundred on Dragonstone, more than half of them Florents – to exact retribution for Lord Celtigar's defection. Claw Isle was but lightly garrisoned, its castle reputedly stuffed with Myrish carpets, Volantene glass, gold and silver plate, jeweled cups, magnificent hawks, an axe of Valyrian steel, a horn that could summon monsters from the deep, chests of rubies, and more wines than a man could drink in a hundred years. Though Celtigar had shown the world a niggardly face, he had never stinted on his own comforts. "Put his castle to the torch and his people to the sword, I say," Ser Axell concluded. "Leave Claw Isle a desolation of ash and bone, fit only for carrion crows, so the realm might see the fate of those who bed with Lannisters."

Stannis listened to Ser Axell's recitation in silence, grinding his jaw slowly from side to side. When it was done, he said, "It could be done, I believe. The risk is small. Joffrey has no strength at sea until Lord Redwyne sets sail from the Arbor. The plunder might serve to keep that Lysene pirate Salladhor Saan loyal for a time. By itself Claw Isle is worthless, but its fall would serve notice to Lord Tywin that my cause is not yet done." The king turned back to Davos. "Speak truly, ser. What do you make of Ser Axell's proposal?"

Speak truly, ser. Davos remembered the dark cell he had shared with Lord Alester, remembered Lamprey and Porridge. He thought of the promises that Ser Axell had made on the bridge above the yard. *A ship or a shove, what shall it be?* But this was Stannis asking. "Your Grace," he said slowly, "I make it folly . . . aye, and cowardice."

"*Cowardice!*" Ser Axell all but shouted. "No man calls me craven before my king!"

"Silence," Stannis commanded. "Ser Davos, speak on, I would hear your reasons."

Davos turned to face Ser Axell. "You say we ought to show the realm we are not done. Strike a blow. Make war, aye . . . but on what enemy? You will find no Lannisters on Claw Isle."

"We will find *traitors*," said Ser Axell, "though it may be I could find some closer to home. Even in this very room."

Davos ignored the jibe. "I don't doubt Lord Celtigar bent the knee to the boy Joffrey. He is an old done man, who wants no more than to end his days in his castle, drinking his fine wine out of his jeweled cups." He turned back to Stannis. "Yet he came when you called, sire. Came, with his ships and swords. He stood by you at Storm's End when Lord Renly came down on us, and his ships sailed up the Blackwater. His men fought for you, killed for you, *burned* for you. Claw Isle is weakly held, yes. Held by women and children and old men. And why is that? Because their husbands and sons and fathers died on the Blackwater, that's why. Died at their oars, or with swords in their hands, fighting beneath our banners. Yet Ser Axell proposes we swoop down on the homes they left behind, to rape their widows and put their children to the sword. These smallfolk are no traitors . . ."

"They *are*," insisted Ser Axell. "Not all of Celtigar's men were slain on the Blackwater. Hundreds were taken with their lord, and bent the knee when he did."

"*When he did*," Davos repeated. "They were his men. His sworn men. What choice were they given?"

"Every man has choices. They might have refused to kneel. Some did, and died for it. Yet they died true men, and loyal."

"Some men are stronger than others." It was a feeble answer, and Davos knew it. Stannis Baratheon was a man of iron will who neither understood nor forgave weakness in others. *I am losing*, he thought, despairing.

"It is every man's duty to remain loyal to his rightful king, even if the lord he serves proves false," Stannis declared in a tone that brooked no argument.

A desperate folly took hold of Davos, a recklessness akin to madness. "As you remained loyal to King Aerys when your brother raised his banners?" he blurted.

Shocked silence followed, until Ser Axell cried, "*Treason!*" and snatched his dagger from its sheath. "Your Grace, he speaks his infamy to your face!"

Davos could hear Stannis grinding his teeth. A vein bulged, blue and swollen, in the king's brow. Their eyes met. "Put up your knife, Ser Axell. And leave us."

"As it please Your Grace – "

"It would please me for you to leave," said Stannis. "Take yourself from my presence, and send me Melisandre."

"As you command." Ser Axell slid the knife away, bowed, and hurried toward the door. His boots rang against the floor, angry.

"You have always presumed on my forbearance," Stannis warned Davos when they were alone. "I can shorten your tongue as easy as I did your fingers, smuggler."

"I am your man, Your Grace. So it is your tongue, to do with as you please."

"It is," he said, calmer. "And I would have it speak the truth. Though the truth is a bitter draught at times. *Aerys?* If you only knew . . . that was a hard choosing. My blood or my liege. My brother or my king." He grimaced. "Have you ever seen the Iron Throne? The barbs along the back, the ribbons of twisted steel, the jagged ends of swords and knives all tangled up and melted? It is not a *comfortable* seat, ser. Aerys cut himself so often men took to calling him King Scab, and Maegor the Cruel was murdered in that chair. *By* that chair, to hear some tell it. It is not a seat where a man can rest at ease. Ofttimes I wonder why my brothers wanted it so desperately."

"Why would *you* want it, then?" Davos asked him.

"It is not a question of wanting. The throne is mine, as Robert's heir. That is law. After me, it must pass to my daughter, unless Selyse should finally give me a son." He ran three fingers lightly down the table, over the layers of smooth hard varnish, dark with age. "I *am* king. Wants do not enter into it. I have a duty to my daughter. To the realm. Even to Robert. He loved me but little, I know, yet he was my brother. The Lannister woman gave him horns and made a motley fool of him. She may have murdered him as well, as she murdered Jon Arryn and Ned Stark. For such crimes there must be justice. Starting with Cersei and her abominations. But only starting. I mean to scour that court clean. As Robert should have done, after the Trident. Ser Barristan once told me that the rot in King

Aerys's reign began with Varys. The eunuch should never have been pardoned. No more than the Kingslayer. At the least, Robert should have stripped the white cloak from Jaime and sent him to the Wall, as Lord Stark urged. He listened to Jon Arryn instead. I was still at Storm's End, under siege and unconsulted." He turned abruptly, to give Davos a hard shrewd look. "The truth, now. Why did you wish to murder Lady Melisandre?"

So he does know. Davos could not lie to him. "Four of my sons burned on the Blackwater. She gave them to the flames."

"You wrong her. Those fires were no work of hers. Curse the Imp, curse the pyromancers, curse that fool of Florent who sailed my fleet into the jaws of a trap. Or curse me for my stubborn pride, for sending her away when I needed her most. But not Melisandre. She remains my faithful servant."

"Maester Cressen was your faithful servant. She slew him, as she killed Ser Cortnay Penrose and your brother Renly."

"Now you sound a fool," the king complained. "She *saw* Renly's end in the flames, yes, but she had no more part in it than I did. The priestess was with me. Your Devan would tell you so. Ask him, if you doubt me. She would have spared Renly if she could. It was Melisandre who urged me to meet with him, and give him one last chance to amend his treason. And it was Melisandre who told me to send for you when Ser Axell wished to give you to R'hllor." He smiled thinly. "Does that surprise you?"

"Yes. She knows I am no friend to her or her red god."

"But you are a friend to me. She knows that as well." He beckoned Davos closer. "The boy is sick. Maester Pylos has been leeching him."

"The boy?" His thoughts went to his Devan, the king's squire. "My son, sire?"

"Devan? A good boy. He has much of you in him. It is Robert's bastard who is sick, the boy we took at Storm's End."

Edric Storm. "I spoke with him in Aegon's Garden."

"As she wished. As she saw." Stannis sighed. "Did the boy charm you? He has that gift. He got it from his father, with the blood. He knows he is a king's son, but chooses to forget that he is bastard-born. And he worships Robert, as Renly did when he was young. My royal brother played the fond father on his visits to Storm's End, and there were gifts . . . swords and ponies and fur-trimmed cloaks. The eunuch's work, every one. The boy would write the Red Keep full of thanks, and Robert would laugh and ask Varys what he'd sent this year. Renly was no better. He left the boy's upbringing to castellans and maesters, and every one fell victim to his charm. Penrose chose to die rather than give him up." The king ground his teeth together. "It still angers me. How could he think I would hurt the boy? I chose Robert, did I not? When that hard day came, I chose blood over honor."

He does not use the boy's name. That made Davos very uneasy. "I hope young Edric will recover soon."

Stannis waved a hand, dismissing his concern. "It is a chill, no more. He coughs, he shivers, he has a fever. Maester Pylos will soon set him right. By himself the boy is nought, you understand, but in his veins flows my brother's blood. There is power in a king's blood, she says."

Davos did not have to ask who she was.

Stannis touched the Painted Table. "Look at it, onion knight. My realm, by rights. My Westeros." He swept a hand across it. "This talk of Seven Kingdoms is a folly. Aegon saw that three hundred years ago when he stood where we are standing. They painted this table at his command. Rivers and bays they painted, hills and mountains, castles and cities and market towns, lakes and swamps and forests . . . but no borders. *It is all one.* One realm, for one king to rule alone."

"One king," agreed Davos. "One king means peace."

"I shall bring justice to Westeros. A thing Ser Axell understands as little as he does war. Claw Isle would gain me nought . . . and it was evil, just as you said. Celtigar must pay the traitor's price himself, in his own person. And when I come into my kingdom, he shall. Every man shall reap what he has sown, from the highest lord to the lowest gutter rat. And some will lose more than the tips off their fingers, I promise you. They have made my kingdom bleed, and I do not forget that." King Stannis turned from the table. "On your knees, Onion Knight."

"Your Grace?"

"For your onions and fish, I made you a knight once. For this, I am of a mind to raise you to lord."

This? Davos was lost. "I am content to be your knight, Your Grace. I would not know how to begin being lordly."

"Good. To be lordly is to be false. I have learned that lesson hard. Now, *kneel*. Your king commands."

Davos knelt, and Stannis drew his longsword. *Lightbringer*, Melisandre had named it; the red sword of heroes, drawn from the fires where the seven gods were consumed. The room seemed to grow brighter as the blade slid from its scabbard. The steel had a glow to it; now orange, now yellow, now red. The air shimmered around it, and no jewel had ever sparkled so brilliantly. But when Stannis touched it to Davos's shoulder, it felt no different than any other longsword. "Ser Davos of House Seaworth," the king said, "are you my true and honest liege man, now and forever?"

"I am, Your Grace."

"And do you swear to serve me loyally all your days, to give me honest counsel and swift obedience, to defend my rights and my realm against all foes in battles great and small, to protect my people and punish my enemies?"

"I do, Your Grace."

"Then rise again, Davos Seaworth, and rise as Lord of the Rainwood, Admiral of the Narrow Sea, and Hand of the King."

For a moment Davos was too stunned to move. *I woke this morning in his dungeon.* "Your Grace, you cannot . . . I am no fit man to be a King's Hand."

"There is no man fitter." Stannis sheathed Lightbringer, gave Davos his hand, and pulled him to his feet.

"I am lowborn," Davos reminded him. "An upjumped smuggler. Your lords will never obey me."

"Then we will make new lords."

"But . . . I cannot read . . . nor write . . ."

"Maester Pylos can read for you. As to writing, my last Hand wrote the head off his shoulders. All I ask of you are the things you've always given me. Honesty. Loyalty. Service."

"Surely there is someone better . . . some great lord . . ."

Stannis snorted. "Bar Emmon, that boy? My faithless grandfather? Celtigar has abandoned me, the new Velaryon is six years old, and the new Sunglass sailed for Volantis after I burned his brother." He made an angry gesture. "A few good men remain, it's true. Ser Gilbert Farring holds Storm's End for me still, with two hundred loyal men. Lord Morrigen, the Bastard of Nightsong, young Chyttering, my cousin Andrew . . . but I trust none of them as I trust you, my lord of Rainwood. You will be my Hand. It is you I want beside me for the battle."

Another battle will be the end of all of us, thought Davos. *Lord Alester saw that much true enough.* "Your Grace asked for honest counsel. In honesty then . . . we lack the strength for another battle against the Lannisters."

"It is the great battle His Grace is speaking of," said a woman's voice, rich with the accents of the east. Melisandre stood at the door in her red silks and shimmering satins, holding a covered silver dish in her hands. "These little wars are no more than a scuffle of children before what is to come. The one whose name may not be spoken is marshaling his power, Davos Seaworth, a power fell and evil and strong beyond measure. Soon comes the cold, and the night that never ends." She placed the silver dish on the Painted Table. "Unless true men find the courage to fight it. Men whose hearts are fire."

Stannis stared at the silver dish. "She has shown it to me, Lord Davos. In the flames."

"*You* saw it, sire?" It was not like Stannis Baratheon to lie about such a thing.

"With mine own eyes. After the battle, when I was lost to despair, the Lady Melisandre bid me gaze into the hearthfire. The chimney was drawing strongly, and bits of ash were rising from the fire. I stared at them, feeling half a fool, but she bid me look deeper, and . . . the ashes were white, rising in the updraft, yet all at once it seemed as if they were falling. *Snow*, I thought. Then the sparks in the air seemed to circle, to become a ring of torches, and I was looking *through* the fire down on some high hill in a forest. The cinders had become men in black behind the torches, and there were shapes moving through the snow. For all the heat of the fire, I felt a cold so terrible I shivered, and when I did the sight was gone, the fire but a fire once again. But what I saw was real, I'd stake my kingdom on it."

"And have," said Melisandre.

The conviction in the king's voice frightened Davos to the core. "A hill in a forest . . . shapes in the snow . . . I don't . . ."

"It means that the battle is begun," said Melisandre. "The sand is running through the glass more quickly now, and man's hour on earth is almost done. We must act boldly, or all hope is lost. Westeros must unite beneath her one true king, the prince that was promised, Lord of Dragonstone and chosen of R'hllor."

"R'hllor chooses queerly, then." The king grimaced, as if he'd tasted something foul. "Why me, and not my brothers? Renly and his peach. In my dreams I see the juice running from his mouth, the blood from his throat. If he had done his duty by his brother, we would have smashed Lord Tywin. A victory even Robert could be proud of. Robert . . ." His teeth ground side to side. "He is in my dreams as well. Laughing. Drinking. Boasting. Those were the things he was best at. Those, and fighting. I never bested him at anything. The Lord of Light should have made Robert his champion. Why me?"

"Because you are a righteous man," said Melisandre.

"A righteous man." Stannis touched the covered silver platter with a finger. "With leeches."

"Yes," said Melisandre, "but I must tell you once more, this is not the way."

"You swore it would work." The king looked angry.

"It will . . . and it will not."

"Which?"

"Both."

"Speak sense to me, woman."

"When the fires speak more plainly, so shall I. There is truth in the flames, but it is not always easy to see." The great ruby at her throat drank fire from the glow of the brazier. "Give me the boy, Your Grace. It is the surer way. The better way. Give me the boy and I shall wake the stone dragon."

"I have told you, no."

"He is only one baseborn boy, against all the boys of Westeros, and all the girls as well. Against all the children that might ever be born, in all the kingdoms of the world."

"The boy is innocent."

"The boy defiled your marriage bed, else you would surely have sons of your own. He shamed you."

"*Robert* did that. Not the boy. My daughter has grown fond of him. And he is mine own blood."

"Your brother's blood," Melisandre said. "A king's blood. Only a king's blood can wake the stone dragon."

Stannis ground his teeth. "I'll hear no more of this. The dragons are done. The Targaryens tried to bring them back half a dozen times. And made fools of themselves, or corpses. Patchface is the only fool we need on this godsforsaken rock. You have the leeches. Do your work."

Melisandre bowed her head stiffly, and said, "As my king commands." Reaching up her left sleeve with her right hand, she flung a handful of powder into the brazier. The coals roared. As pale flames writhed atop them, the red woman retrieved the silver dish and brought it to the king. Davos watched her lift the lid. Beneath were three large black leeches, fat with blood.

The boy's blood, Davos knew. *A king's blood.*

Stannis stretched forth a hand, and his fingers closed around one of the leeches.

"Say the name," Melisandre commanded.

The leech was twisting in the king's grip, trying to attach itself to one of his fingers. "The usurper," he said. "Joffrey Baratheon." When he tossed the leech into the fire, it curled up like an autumn leaf amidst the coals, and burned.

Stannis grasped the second. "The usurper," he declared,

louder this time. "Balon Greyjoy." He flipped it lightly onto the brazier, and its flesh split and cracked. The blood burst from it, hissing and smoking.

The last was in the king's hand. This one he studied a moment as it writhed between his fingers. "The usurper," he said at last. "Robb Stark." And he threw it on the flames.

JAIME

Harrenhal's bathhouse was a dim, steamy, low-ceilinged room filled with great stone tubs. When they led Jaime in, they found Brienne seated in one of them, scrubbing her arm almost angrily.

"Not so hard, wench," he called. "You'll scrub the skin off." She dropped her brush and covered her teats with hands as big as Gregor Clegane's. The pointy little buds she was so intent on hiding would have looked more natural on some ten-year-old than they did on her thick muscular chest.

"What are you doing here?" she demanded.

"Lord Bolton insists I sup with him, but he neglected to invite my fleas." Jaime tugged at his guard with his left hand. "Help me out of these stinking rags." One-handed, he could not so much as unlace his breeches. The man obeyed grudgingly, but he obeyed. "Now leave us," Jaime said when his clothes lay in a pile on the wet stone floor. "My lady of Tarth doesn't want the likes of you scum gaping at her teats." He pointed his stump at the hatchet-faced woman attending Brienne. "You too. Wait without. There's only the one door, and the wench is too big to try and shinny up a chimney."

The habit of obedience went deep. The woman followed his guard out, leaving the bathhouse to the two of them. The tubs were large enough to hold six or seven, after the fashion of the Free Cities, so Jaime climbed in with the wench, awkward and slow. Both his eyes were open, though the right remained somewhat swollen, despite Qyburn's leeches. Jaime felt a hundred and nine years old, which was a deal better than he had been feeling when he came to Harrenhal.

Brienne shrunk away from him. "There are other tubs."

"This one suits me well enough." Gingerly, he immersed himself up to the chin in the steaming water. "Have no fear, wench. Your thighs are purple and green, and I'm not interested in what you've got between them." He had to rest his right arm on the rim, since Qyburn had warned him to keep the linen dry. He could feel the tension drain from his legs, but his head spun. "If I faint, pull me out. No Lannister has ever drowned in his bath and I don't mean to be the first."

"Why should I care how you die?"

"You swore a solemn vow." He smiled as a red flush crept up the thick white column of her neck. She turned her back to him. "Still the shy maiden? What is it that you think I haven't seen?" He groped for the brush she had dropped, caught it with his fingers, and began to scrub himself desultorily. Even that was difficult, awkward. *My left hand is good for nothing.*

Still, the water darkened as the caked dirt dissolved off his skin. The wench kept her back to him, the muscles in her great shoulders hunched and hard.

"Does the sight of my stump distress you so?" Jaime asked. "You ought to be pleased. I've lost the hand I killed the king with. The hand that flung the Stark boy from that tower. The hand I'd slide between my sister's thighs to make her wet." He thrust his stump at her face. "No wonder Renly died, with you guarding him."

She jerked to her feet as if he'd struck her, sending a wash of hot water across the tub. Jaime caught a glimpse of the thick blonde bush at the juncture of her thighs as she climbed out. She was much hairier than his sister. Absurdly, he felt his cock stir beneath the bathwater. *Now I know I have been too long away from Cersei.* He averted his eyes, troubled by his body's response. "That was unworthy," he mumbled. "I'm a maimed man, and bitter. Forgive me, wench. You protected me as well as any man could have, and better than most."

She wrapped her nakedness in a towel. "Do you mock me?"

That pricked him back to anger. "Are you as thick as a castle wall? That was an apology. I am tired of fighting with you. What say we make a truce?"

"Truces are built on trust. Would you have me trust – "

"The Kingslayer, yes. The oathbreaker who murdered poor sad Aerys Targaryen." Jaime snorted. "It's not Aerys I rue, it's Robert. 'I hear they've named you Kingslayer,' he said to me at his coronation feast. 'Just don't think to make it a habit.' And he laughed. Why is it that no one names Robert oathbreaker? He tore the realm apart, yet *I* am the one with shit for honor."

"Robert did all he did for love." Water ran down Brienne's legs and pooled beneath her feet.

"Robert did all he did for pride, a cunt, and a pretty face." He made a fist . . . or would have, if he'd had a hand. Pain lanced up his arm, cruel as laughter.

"He rode to save the realm," she insisted.

To save the realm. "Did you know that my brother set the Blackwater Rush afire? Wildfire will burn on water. Aerys would have bathed in it if he'd dared. The Targaryens were all mad for fire." Jaime felt light-headed. *It is the heat in here, the poison in my blood, the last of my fever. I am not myself.* He eased himself down until the water reached his chin. "Soiled my white cloak . . . I wore my gold armor that day, but . . ."

"Gold armor?" Her voice sounded far off, faint.

He floated in heat, in memory. "After dancing griffins lost the Battle of the Bells, Aerys exiled him." *Why am I telling this absurd ugly child?* "He had finally realized that Robert was no mere outlaw lord to be crushed at whim, but the greatest threat House Targaryen had faced since Daemon Blackfyre. The king reminded Lewyn Martell gracelessly that he held Elia and sent him to take command of the ten thousand Dornishmen coming up the kingsroad. Jon Darry and Barristan Selmy rode to Stoney

Sept to rally what they could of griffins' men, and Prince
Rhaegar returned from the south and persuaded his father
to swallow his pride and summon my father. But no raven
returned from Casterly Rock, and that made the king even
more afraid. He saw traitors everywhere, and Varys was
always there to point out any he might have missed. So
His Grace commanded his alchemists to place caches of
wildfire all over King's Landing. Beneath Baelor's Sept and
the hovels of Flea Bottom, under stables and storehouses,
at all seven gates, even in the cellars of the Red Keep itself.

"Everything was done in the utmost secrecy by a handful of master pyromancers. They did not even trust their
own acolytes to help. The queen's eyes had been closed
for years, and Rhaegar was busy marshaling an army. But
Aerys's new mace-and-dagger Hand was not utterly stupid,
and with Rossart, Belis, and Garigus coming and going
night and day, he became suspicious. Chelsted, that was
his name, Lord Chelsted." It had come back to him suddenly, with the telling. "I'd thought the man craven, but
the day he confronted Aerys he found some courage somewhere. He did all he could to dissuade him. He reasoned,
he jested, he threatened, and finally he begged. When that
failed he took off his chain of office and flung it down on
the floor. Aerys burnt him alive for that, and hung his
chain about the neck of Rossart, his favorite pyromancer.
The man who had cooked Lord Rickard Stark in his own
armor. And all the time, I stood by the foot of the Iron
Throne in my white plate, still as a corpse, guarding my
liege and all his sweet secrets.

"My Sworn Brothers were all away, you see, but Aerys
liked to keep me close. I was my father's son, so he did
not trust me. He wanted me where Varys could watch me,
day and night. So I heard it all." He remembered how
Rossart's eyes would shine when he unrolled his maps to
show where *the substance* must be placed. Garigus and
Belis were the same. "Rhaegar met Robert on the Trident,
and you know what happened there. When the word
reached court, Aerys packed the queen off to Dragonstone
with Prince Viserys. Princess Elia would have gone as well,
but he forbade it. Somehow he had gotten it in his head

that Prince Lewyn must have betrayed Rhaegar on the Trident, but he thought he could keep Dorne loyal so long as he kept Elia and Aegon by his side. *The traitors want my city,* I heard him tell Rossart, *but I'll give them nought but ashes. Let Robert be king over charred bones and cooked meat.* The Targaryens never bury their dead, they burn them. Aerys meant to have the greatest funeral pyre of them all. Though if truth be told, I do not believe he truly expected to die. Like Aerion Brightfire before him, Aerys thought the fire would transform him . . . that he would rise again, reborn as a dragon, and turn all his enemies to ash.

"Ned Stark was racing south with Robert's van, but my father's forces reached the city first. Pycelle convinced the king that his Warden of the West had come to defend him, so he opened the gates. The one time he *should* have heeded Varys, and he ignored him. My father had held back from the war, brooding on all the wrongs Aerys had done him and determined that House Lannister should be on the winning side. The Trident decided him.

"It fell to me to hold the Red Keep, but I knew we were lost. I sent to Aerys asking his leave to make terms. My man came back with a royal command. *'Bring me your father's head, if you are no traitor.'* Aerys would have no yielding. Lord Rossart was with him, my messenger said. I knew what *that* meant.

"When I came on Rossart, he was dressed as a common man-at-arms, hurrying to a postern gate. I slew him first. Then I slew Aerys, before he could find someone else to carry his message to the pyromancers. Days later, I hunted down the others and slew them as well. Belis offered me gold, and Garigus wept for mercy. Well, a sword's more merciful than fire, but I don't think Garigus much appreciated the kindness I showed him."

The water had grown cool. When Jaime opened his eyes, he found himself staring at the stump of his sword hand. *The hand that made me Kingslayer.* The goat had robbed him of his glory and his shame, both at once. *Leaving what? Who am I now?*

The wench looked ridiculous, clutching her towel

her meager teats with her thick white legs sticking out beneath. "Has my tale turned you speechless? Come, curse me or kiss me or call me a liar. *Something*."

"If this is true, how is it no one knows?"

"The knights of the Kingsguard are sworn to keep the king's secrets. Would you have me break my oath?" Jaime laughed. "Do you think the noble Lord of Winterfell wanted to hear my feeble explanations? Such an *honorable* man. He only had to look at me to judge me guilty." Jaime lurched to his feet, the water running cold down his chest. "By what right does the wolf judge the lion? *By what right?*" A violent shiver took him, and he smashed his stump against the rim of the tub as he tried to climb out.

Pain shuddered through him . . . and suddenly the bath-house was spinning. Brienne caught him before he could fall. Her arm was all gooseflesh, clammy and chilled, but she was strong, and gentler than he would have thought. *Gentler than Cersei*, he thought as she helped him from the tub, his legs wobbly as a limp cock. "*Guards!*" he heard the wench shout. "The Kingslayer!"

Jaime, he thought, *my name is Jaime*.

The next he knew, he was lying on the damp floor with the guards and the wench and Qyburn all standing over him looking concerned. Brienne was naked, but she seemed to have forgotten that for the moment. "The heat of the tubs will do it," Maester Qyburn was telling them. *No, he's not a maester, they took his chain.* "There's still poison in his blood as well, and he's malnourished. What have you been feeding him?"

"Worms and piss and grey vomit," offered Jaime.

"Hardbread and water and oat porridge," insisted the guard. "He don't hardly eat it, though. What should we do with him?"

"Scrub him and dress him and carry him to Kingspyre, if need be," Qyburn said. "Lord Bolton insists he will sup with him tonight. The time is growing short."

"Bring me clean garb for him," Brienne said, "I'll see that he's washed and dressed."

The others were all too glad to give her the task. They ʹfted him to his feet and sat him on a stone bench by the wall. Brienne went away to retrieve her towel, and returned with a stiff brush to finish scrubbing him. One of the guards gave her a razor to trim his beard. Qyburn returned with roughspun smallclothes, clean black woolen breeches, a loose green tunic, and a leather jerkin that laced up the front. Jaime was feeling less dizzy by then, though no less clumsy. With the wench's help he managed to dress himself. "Now all I need is a silver looking glass."

The Bloody Maester had brought fresh clothing for Brienne as well; a stained pink satin gown and a linen undertunic. "I am sorry, my lady. These were the only women's garments in Harrenhal large enough to fit you."

It was obvious at once that the gown had been cut for someone with slimmer arms, shorter legs, and much fuller breasts. The fine Myrish lace did little to conceal the bruising that mottled Brienne's skin. All in all, the garb made the wench look ludicrous. *She has thicker shoulders than I do, and a bigger neck,* Jaime thought. *Small wonder she prefers to dress in mail.* Pink was not a kind color for her either. A dozen cruel japes leaped into his head, but for once he kept them there. Best not to make her angry; he was no match for her one-handed.

Qyburn had brought a flask as well. "What is it?" Jaime demanded when the chainless maester pressed him to drink.

"Licorice steeped in vinegar, with honey and cloves. It will give you some strength and clear your head."

"Bring me the potion that grows new hands," said Jaime. "That's the one I want."

"Drink it," Brienne said, unsmiling, and he did.

It was half an hour before he felt strong enough to stand. After the dim wet warmth of the bathhouse, the air outside was a slap across the face. "M'lord will be looking for him by now," a guard told Qyburn. "Her too. Do I need to carry him?"

"I can still walk. Brienne, give me your arm."

Clutching her, Jaime let them herd him across the yard to a vast draughty hall, larger even than the throne room in King's Landing. Huge hearths lined the walls, one every ten feet or so, more than he could count, but no fires had been lit, so the chill between the walls went bone-deep. A dozen spearmen in fur cloaks guarded the doors and the steps that led up to the two galleries above. And in the center of that immense emptiness, at a trestle table surrounded by what seemed like acres of smooth slate floor, the Lord of the Dreadfort waited, attended only by a cupbearer.

"My lord," said Brienne, when they stood before him.

Roose Bolton's eyes were paler than stone, darker than milk, and his voice was spider soft. "I am pleased that you are strong enough to attend me, ser. My lady, do be seated." He gestured at the spread of cheese, bread, cold meat, and fruit that covered the table. "Will you drink red or white? Of indifferent vintage, I fear. Ser Amory drained Lady Whent's cellars nearly dry."

"I trust you killed him for it." Jaime slid into the offered seat quickly, so Bolton could not see how weak he was. "White is for Starks. I'll drink red like a good Lannister."

"I would prefer water," said Brienne.

"Elmar, the red for Ser Jaime, water for the Lady Brienne, and hippocras for myself." Bolton waved a hand at their escort, dismissing them, and the men beat a silent retreat.

Habit made Jaime reach for his wine with his right hand. His stump rocked the goblet, spattering his clean linen bandages with bright red spots and forcing him to catch the cup with his left hand before it fell, but Bolton pretended not to notice his clumsiness. The northman helped himself to a prune and ate it with small sharp bites. "Do try these, Ser Jaime. They are most sweet, and help move the bowels as well. Lord Vargo took them from an inn before he burnt it."

"My bowels move fine, that goat's no lord, and your prunes don't interest me half so much as your intentions."

"Regarding you?" A faint smile touched Roose Bolton's lips. "You are a perilous prize, ser. You sow dissension wherever you go. Even here, in my happy house of Harrenhal." His voice was a whisker above a whisper. "And in Riverrun as well, it seems. Do you know, Edmure Tully has offered a thousand golden dragons for your recapture?"

Is that all? "My sister will pay ten times as much."

"Will she?" That smile again, there for an instant, gone as quick. "Ten thousand dragons is a formidable sum. Of course, there is Lord Karstark's offer to consider as well. He promises the hand of his daughter to the man who brings him your head."

"Leave it to your goat to get it backward," said Jaime.

Bolton gave a soft chuckle. "Harrion Karstark was captive here when we took the castle, did you know? I gave him all the Karhold men still with me and sent him off with Glover. I do hope nothing ill befell him at Duskendale ... else Alys Karstark would be all that remains of Lord Rickard's progeny." He chose another prune. "Fortunately for you, I have no need of a wife. I wed the Lady Walda Frey whilst I was at the Twins."

"Fair Walda?" Awkwardly, Jaime tried to hold the bread with his stump while tearing it with his left hand.

"Fat Walda. My lord of Frey offered me my bride's weight in silver for a dowry, so I chose accordingly. Elmar, break off some bread for Ser Jaime."

The boy tore a fist-sized chunk off one end of the loaf and handed it to Jaime. Brienne tore her own bread. "Lord Bolton," she asked, "it's said you mean to give Harrenhal to Vargo Hoat."

"That was his price," Lord Bolton said. "The Lannisters are not the only men who pay their debts. I must take my leave soon in any case. Edmure Tully is to wed the Lady Roslin Frey at the Twins, and my king commands my attendance."

"*Edmure* weds?" said Jaime. "Not Robb Stark?"

"His Grace King Robb is wed." Bolton spit a prune pit into his hand and put it aside. "To a Westerling of the Crag. I am told her name is Jeyne. No doubt you know her, ser. Her father is your father's bannerman."

"My father has a good many bannermen, and most of them have daughters." Jaime groped one-handed for his goblet, trying to recall this Jeyne. The Westerlings were an old house, with more pride than power.

"This cannot be true," Brienne said stubbornly. "King

Robb was sworn to wed a Frey. He would never break faith, he – "

"His Grace is a boy of sixteen," said Roose Bolton mildly. "And I would thank you not to question my word, my lady."

Jaime felt almost sorry for Robb Stark. *He won the war on the battlefield and lost it in a bedchamber, poor fool.* "How does Lord Walder relish dining on trout in place of wolf?" he asked.

"Oh, trout makes for a tasty supper." Bolton lifted a pale finger toward his cupbearer. "Though my poor Elmar is bereft. He was to wed Arya Stark, but my good father of Frey had no choice but to break the betrothal when King Robb betrayed him."

"Is there word of Arya Stark?" Brienne leaned forward. "Lady Catelyn had feared that . . . is the girl still alive?"

"Oh, yes," said the Lord of the Dreadfort.

"You have certain knowledge of that, my lord?"

Roose Bolton shrugged. "Arya Stark was lost for a time, it was true, but now she has been found. I mean to see her returned safely to the north."

"Her and her sister both," said Brienne. "Tyrion Lannister has promised us both girls for his brother."

That seemed to amuse the Lord of the Dreadfort. "My lady, has no one told you? Lannisters lie."

"Is that a slight on the honor of my House?" Jaime picked up the cheese knife with his good hand. "A rounded point, and dull," he said, sliding his thumb along the edge of the blade, "but it will go through your eye all the same." Sweat beaded his brow. He could only hope he did not look as feeble as he felt.

Lord Bolton's little smile paid another visit to his lips. "You speak boldly for a man who needs help to break his bread. My guards are all around us, I remind you."

"All around us, and half a league away." Jaime glanced down the vast length of the hall. "By the time they reach us, you'll be as dead as Aerys."

" 'Tis scarcely chivalrous to threaten your host over his own cheese and olives," the Lord of the Dreadfort scolded. "In the north, we hold the laws of hospitality sacred still."

"I'm a captive here, not a guest. Your goat cut off my hand. If you think some prunes will make me overlook that, you're bloody well mistaken."

That took Roose Bolton aback. "Perhaps I am. Perhaps I ought to make a wedding gift of you to Edmure Tully ... or strike your head off, as your sister did for Eddard Stark."

"I would not advise it. Casterly Rock has a long memory."

"A thousand leagues of mountain, sea, and bog lie between my walls and your rock. Lannister enmity means little to Bolton."

"Lannister friendship could mean much." Jaime thought he knew the game they were playing now. *But does the wench know as well?* He dare not look to see.

"I am not certain you are the sort of friends a wise man would want." Roose Bolton beckoned to the boy. "Elmar, carve our guests a slice off the roast."

Brienne was served first, but made no move to eat. "My lord," she said, "Ser Jaime is to be exchanged for Lady Catelyn's daughters. You must free us to continue on our way."

"The raven that came from Riverrun told of an escape, not an exchange. And if you helped this captive slip his bonds, you are guilty of treason, my lady."

The big wench rose to her feet. "I serve Lady Stark."

"And I the King in the North. Or the King Who Lost the North, as some now call him. Who never wished to trade Ser Jaime back to the Lannisters."

"Sit down and eat, Brienne," Jaime urged, as Elmar placed a slice of roast before him, dark and bloody. "If Bolton meant to kill us, he wouldn't be wasting his precious prunes on us, at such peril to his bowels." He stared at the meat and realized there was no way to cut it, one-handed. *I am worth less than a girl now,* he thought. *The goat's evened the trade, though I doubt Lady Catelyn will thank him when Cersei returns her whelps in like condition.* The thought made him grimace. *I will get the blame for that as well, I'll wager.*

Roose Bolton cut his meat methodically, the blood running across his plate. "Lady Brienne, will you sit if I tell you that I hope to send Ser Jaime on, just as you and Lady Stark desire?"

"I . . . you'd send us on?" The wench sounded wary, but she sat. "That is good, my lord."

"It is. However, Lord Vargo has created me one small . . . difficulty." He turned his pale eyes on Jaime. "Do you know why Hoat cut off your hand?"

"He enjoys cutting off hands." The linen that covered Jaime's stump was spotted with blood and wine. "He enjoys cutting off feet as well. He doesn't seem to need a reason."

"Nonetheless, he had one. Hoat is more cunning than he appears. No man commands a company such as the Brave Companions for long unless he has some wits about him." Bolton stabbed a chunk of meat with the point of his dagger, put it in his mouth, chewed thoughtfully, swallowed. "Lord Vargo abandoned House Lannister because I offered him Harrenhal, a reward a thousand times greater than any he could hope to have from Lord Tywin. As a stranger to Westeros, he did not know the prize was poisoned."

"The curse of Harren the Black?" mocked Jaime.

"The curse of Tywin Lannister." Bolton held out his goblet and Elmar refilled it silently. "Our goat should have consulted the Tarbecks or the Reynes. They might have warned him how your lord father deals with betrayal."

"There are no Tarbecks or Reynes," said Jaime.

"My point precisely. Lord Vargo doubtless hoped that Lord Stannis would triumph at King's Landing, and thence confirm him in his possession of this castle in gratitude for his small part in the downfall of House Lannister." He gave a dry chuckle. "He knows little of Stannis Baratheon either, I fear. That one might have given him Harrenhal for his service . . . but he would have given him a noose for his crimes as well."

"A noose is kinder than what he'll get from my father."

"By now he has come to the same realization. With Stannis broken and Renly dead, only a Stark victory can save him from Lord Tywin's vengeance, but the chances of that grow pershingly slim."

"King Robb has won every battle," Brienne said stoutly, as stubbornly loyal of speech as she was of deed.

"Won every battle, while losing the Freys, the Karstarks, Winterfell, and the north. A pity the wolf is so young. Boys of sixteen always believe they are immortal and invincible. An older man would bend the knee, I'd think. After a war there is always a peace, and with peace there are pardons . . . for the Robb Starks, at least. Not for the likes of Vargo Hoat." Bolton gave him a small smile. "Both sides have made use of him, but neither will shed a tear at his passing. The Brave Companions did not fight in the Battle of the Blackwater, yet they died there all the same."

"You'll forgive me if I don't mourn?"

"You have no pity for our wretched doomed goat? Ah, but the gods must . . . else why deliver you into his hands?" Bolton chewed another chunk of meat. "Karhold is smaller and meaner than Harrenhal, but it lies well beyond the reach of the lion's claws. Once wed to Alys Karstark, Hoat might be a lord in truth. If he could collect some gold from your father so much the better, but he would have delivered you to Lord Rickard no matter how much Lord Tywin paid. His price would be the maid, and safe refuge.

"But to sell you he must keep you, and the riverlands are full of those who would gladly steal you away. Glover and Tallhart were broken at Duskendale, but remnants of their host are still abroad, with the Mountain slaughtering the stragglers. A thousand Karstarks prowl the lands south and east of Riverrun, hunting you. Elsewhere are Darry men left lordless and lawless, packs of four-footed wolves, and the lightning lord's outlaw bands. Dondarrion would gladly hang you and the goat together from the same tree." The Lord of the Dreadfort sopped up some of the blood with a chunk of bread. "Harrenhal was the only place Lord Vargo could hope to hold you safe, but here his Brave Companions are much outnumbered by my own men, and by Ser Aenys and his Freys. No doubt he feared I might return you to Ser Edmure at Riverrun . . . or worse, send you on to your father.

"By maiming you, he meant to remove your sword as a threat, gain himself a grisly token to send to your father, and diminish your value to me. For he is my man, as I am King Robb's man. Thus his crime is mine, or may seem so in your father's eyes. And therein lies my . . . small difficulty." He gazed at Jaime, his pale eyes unblinking, expectant, chill.

I see. "You want me to absolve you of blame. To tell my father that this stump is no work of yours." Jaime laughed. "My lord, send me to Cersei, and I'll sing as sweet a song as you could want, of how gently you treated me." Any other answer, he knew, and Bolton would give him back to the goat. "Had I a hand, I'd write it out. How I was maimed by the sellsword my own father brought to Westeros, and saved by the noble Lord Bolton."

"I will trust to your word, ser."

There's something I don't often hear. "How soon might we be permitted to leave? And how do you mean to get me past all these wolves and brigands and Karstarks?"

"You will leave when Qyburn says you are strong enough, with a strong escort of picked men under the command of my captain, Walton. Steelshanks, he is called. A soldier of iron loyalty. Walton will see you safe and whole to King's Landing."

"Provided Lady Catelyn's daughters are delivered safe and whole as well," said the wench. "My lord, your man Walton's protection is welcome, but the girls are *my* charge."

The Lord of the Dreadfort gave her an uninterested glance. "The girls need not concern you any further, my lady. The Lady Sansa is the dwarf's wife, only the gods can part them now."

"His wife?" Brienne said, appalled. "The Imp? But . . . he swore, before the whole court, in sight of gods and men . . ."

She is such an innocent. Jaime was almost as surprised, if truth be told, but he hid it better. *Sansa Stark, that ought to put a smile on Tyrion's face.* He remembered

The sellsword knight shaded his eyes. "Eight . . . no, nine."

Tyrion turned in his saddle. "Pod, come up here. Describe the arms you see, and tell me which houses they represent."

Podrick Payne edged his gelding closer. He was carrying the royal standard, Joffrey's great stag-and-lion, and struggling with its weight. Bronn bore Tyrion's own banner, the lion of Lannister gold on crimson.

He's getting taller, Tyrion realized as Pod stood in his stirrups for a better look. *He'll soon tower over me like all the rest.* The lad had been making a diligent study of Dornish heraldry, at Tyrion's command, but as ever he was nervous. "I can't see. The wind is flapping them."

"Bronn, tell the boy what you see."

Bronn looked very much the knight today, in his new doublet and cloak, the flaming chain across his chest. "A red sun on orange," he called, "with a spear through its back."

"Martell," Podrick Payne said at once, visibly relieved. "House Martell of Sunspear, my lord. The Prince of Dorne."

"My horse would have known that one," said Tyrion dryly. "Give him another, Bronn."

"There's a purple flag with yellow balls."

"Lemons?" Pod said hopefully. "A purple field strewn with lemons? For House Dalt? Of, of Lemonwood."

"Might be. Next's a big black bird on yellow. Something pink or white in its claws, hard to say with the banner flapping."

"The vulture of Blackmont grasps a baby in its talons," said Pod. "House Blackmont of Blackmont, ser."

Bronn laughed. "Reading books again? Books will ruin your sword eye, boy. I see a skull too. A black banner."

"The crowned skull of House Manwoody, bone and gold on black." Pod sounded more confident with every correct answer. "The Manwoodys of Kingsgrave."

"Three black spiders?"

"They're scorpions, ser. House Qorgyle of Sandstone, three scorpions black on red."

"Red and yellow, a jagged line between."

"The flames of Hellholt. House Uller."

Tyrion was impressed. *The boy's not half stupid, once he gets his tongue untied.* "Go on, Pod," he urged. "If you get them all, I'll make you a gift."

"A pie with red and black slices," said Bronn. "There's a gold hand in the middle."

"House Allyrion of Godsgrace."

"A red chicken eating a snake, looks like."

"The Gargalens of Salt Shore. A cockatrice. Ser. Pardon. Not a chicken. Red, with a black snake in its beak."

"Very good!" exclaimed Tyrion. "One more, lad."

Bronn scanned the ranks of the approaching Dornishmen. "The last's a golden feather on green checks."

"A golden quill, ser. Jordayne of the Tor."

Tyrion laughed. "Nine, and well done. I could not have named them all myself." That was a lie, but it would give the boy some pride, and that he badly needed.

Martell brings some formidable companions, it would seem. Not one of the houses Pod had named was small or insignificant. Nine of the greatest lords of Dorne were coming up the kingsroad, them or their heirs, and somehow Tyrion did not think they had come all this way just to see the dancing bear. There was a message here. *And not one I like.* He wondered if it had been a mistake to ship Myrcella down to Sunspear.

"My lord," Pod said, a little timidly, "there's no litter."

Tyrion turned his head sharply. The boy was right.

"Doran Martell always travels in a litter," the boy said. "A carved litter with silk hangings, and suns on the drapes."

Tyrion had heard the same talk. Prince Doran was past fifty, and gouty. *He may have wanted to make faster time,* he told himself. *He may have feared his litter would make too tempting a target for brigands, or that it would prove too cumbersome in the high passes of the Boneway. Perhaps his gout is better.*

So why did he have such a bad feeling about this?

This waiting was intolerable. "Banners forward," he snapped. "We'll meet them." He kicked his horse. Bronn

and Pod followed, one to either side. When the Dornishmen saw them coming, they spurred their own mounts,
banners rippling as they rode. From their ornate saddles
were slung the round metal shields they favored, and many
carried bundles of short throwing spears, or the double-
curved Dornish bows they used so well from horseback.

There were three sorts of Dornishmen, the first King
Daeron had observed. There were the salty Dornishmen
who lived along the coasts, the sandy Dornishmen of the
deserts and long river valleys, and the stony Dornishmen
who made their fastnesses in the passes and heights of
the Red Mountains. The salty Dornishmen had the most
Rhoynish blood, the stony Dornishmen the least.

All three sorts seemed well represented in Doran's retinue. The salty Dornishmen were lithe and dark, with
smooth olive skin and long black hair streaming in the
wind. The sandy Dornishmen were even darker, their faces
burned brown by the hot Dornish sun. They wound long
bright scarfs around their helms to ward off sunstroke.
The stony Dornishmen were biggest and fairest, sons of
the Andals and the First Men, brown-haired or blond, with
faces that freckled or burned in the sun instead of
browning.

The lords wore silk and satin robes with jeweled belts
and flowing sleeves. Their armor was heavily enameled
and inlaid with burnished copper, shining silver, and soft
red gold. They came astride red horses and golden ones
and a few as pale as snow, all slim and swift, with long
necks and narrow beautiful heads. The fabled sand steeds
of Dorne were smaller than proper warhorses and could
not bear such weight of armor, but it was said that they
could run for a day and night and another day, and never
tire.

The Dornish leader forked a stallion black as sin with
a mane and tail the color of fire. He sat his saddle as if
he'd been born there, tall, slim, graceful. A cloak of pale
red silk fluttered from his shoulders, and his shirt was
armored with overlapping rows of copper disks that glittered like a thousand bright new pennies as he rode. His
high gilded helm displayed a copper sun on its brow, and

the round shield slung behind him bore the sun-and-spear of House Martell on its polished metal surface.

A Martell sun, but ten years too young, Tyrion thought as he reined up, *too fit as well, and far too fierce.* He knew what he must deal with by then. *How many Dornishmen does it take to start a war?* he asked himself. *Only one.* Yet he had no choice but to smile. "Well met, my lords. We had word of your approach, and His Grace King Joffrey bid me ride out to welcome you in his name. My lord father the King's Hand sends his greetings as well." He feigned an amiable confusion. "Which of you is Prince Doran?"

"My brother's health requires he remain at Sunspear." The princeling removed his helm. Beneath, his face was lined and saturnine, with thin arched brows above large eyes as black and shiny as pools of coal oil. Only a few streaks of silver marred the lustrous black hair that receded from his brow in a widow's peak as sharply pointed as his nose. *A salty Dornishmen for certain.* "Prince Doran has sent me to join King Joffrey's council in his stead, as it please His Grace."

"His Grace will be most honored to have the counsel of a warrior as renowned as Prince Oberyn of Dorne," said Tyrion, thinking, *This will mean blood in the gutters.* "And your noble companions are most welcome as well."

"Permit me to acquaint you with them, my lord of Lannister. Ser Deziel Dalt, of Lemonwood. Lord Tremond Gargalen. Lord Harmen Uller and his brother Ser Ulwyck. Ser Ryon Allyrion and his natural son Ser Daemon Sand, the Bastard of Godsgrace. Lord Dagos Manwoody, his brother Ser Myles, his sons Mors and Dickon. Ser Arron Qorgyle. And never let it be thought that I would neglect the ladies. Myria Jordayne, heir to the Tor. Lady Larra Blackmont, her daughter Jynessa, her son Perros." He raised a slender hand toward a black-haired woman to the rear, beckoning her forward. "And this is Ellaria Sand, mine own paramour."

Tyrion swallowed a groan. *His paramour, and bastard-born, Cersei will pitch a holy fit if he wants her at the wedding.* If she consigned the woman to some dark corner below the salt, his sister would risk the Red Viper's wrath. Seat her beside him at the high table, and every other lady on the dais was like to take offense. *Did Prince Doran mean to provoke a quarrel?*

Prince Oberyn wheeled his horse about to face his fellow Dornishmen. "Ellaria, lords and ladies, sers, see how well King Joffrey loves us. His Grace has been so kind as to send his own Uncle Imp to bring us to his court."

Bronn snorted back laughter, and Tyrion perforce must feign amusement as well. "Not alone, my lords. That would be too enormous a task for a little man like me." His own party had come up on them, so it was his turn to name the names. "Let me present Ser Flement Brax, heir to Hornvale. Lord Gyles of Rosby. Ser Addam Marbrand, Lord Commander of the City Watch. Jalabhar Xho, Prince of the Red Flower Vale. Ser Harys Swyft, my uncle Kevan's good father by marriage. Ser Merlon Crakehall. Ser Philip Foote and Ser Bronn of the Blackwater, two heroes of our recent battle against the rebel Stannis Baratheon. And mine own squire, young Podrick of House Payne." The names had a nice ringing sound as Tyrion reeled them off, but the bearers were nowise near as distinguished nor formidable a company as those who accompanied Prince Oberyn, as both of them knew full well.

"My lord of Lannister," said Lady Blackmont, "we have come a long dusty way, and rest and refreshment would be most welcome. Might we continue on to the city?"

"At once, my lady." Tyrion turned his horse's head, and called to Ser Addam Marbrand. The mounted gold cloaks who formed the greatest part of his honor guard turned their horses crisply at Ser Addam's command, and the column set off for the river and King's Landing beyond.

Oberyn Nymeros Martell, Tyrion muttered under his breath as he fell in beside the man. *The Red Viper of Dorne. And what in the seven hells am I supposed to do with him?*

He knew the man only by reputation, to be sure ... but the reputation was fearsome. When he was no more than sixteen, Prince Oberyn had been found abed with the paramour of old Lord Yronwood, a huge man of fierce

repute and short temper. A duel ensued, though in view
of the prince's youth and high birth, it was only to first
blood. Both men took cuts, and honor was satisfied. Yet
Prince Oberyn soon recovered, while Lord Yronwood's
wounds festered and killed him. Afterward men whispered
that Oberyn had fought with a poisoned sword, and ever
thereafter friends and foes alike called him the Red Viper.

That was many years ago, to be sure. The boy of sixteen
was a man past forty now, and his legend had grown a
deal darker. He had traveled in the Free Cities, learning
the poisoner's trade and perhaps arts darker still, if rumors
could be believed. He had studied at the Citadel, going so
far as to forge six links of a maester's chain before he grew
bored. He had soldiered in the Disputed Lands across the
narrow sea, riding with the Second Sons for a time before
forming his own company. His tourneys, his battles, his
duels, his horses, his carnality . . . it was said that he
bedded men and women both, and had begotten bastard
girls all over Dorne. The *sand snakes*, men called his
daughters. So far as Tyrion had heard, Prince Oberyn had
never fathered a son.

And of course, he had crippled the heir to Highgarden.

*There is no man in the Seven Kingdoms who will be
less welcome at a Tyrell wedding*, thought Tyrion. To
send Prince Oberyn to King's Landing while the city still
hosted Lord Mace Tyrell, two of his sons, and thousands
of their men-at-arms was a provocation as dangerous as
Prince Oberyn himself. *A wrong word, an ill-timed jest,
a look, that's all it will take, and our noble allies will be
at one another's throats.*

"We have met before," the Dornish prince said lightly
to Tyrion as they rode side by side along the kingsroad,
past ashen fields and the skeletons of trees. "I would not
expect you to remember, though. You were even smaller
than you are now."

There was a mocking edge to his voice that Tyrion
misliked, but he was not about to let the Dornishman
provoke him. "When was this, my lord?" he asked in tones
of polite interest.

"Oh, many and many a year ago, when my mother

ruled in Dorne and your lord father was Hand to a different king."

Not so different as you might think, reflected Tyrion.

"It was when I visited Casterly Rock with my mother, her consort, and my sister Elia. I was, oh, fourteen, fifteen, thereabouts, Elia a year older. Your brother and sister were eight or nine, as I recall, and you had just been born."

A queer time to come visiting. His mother had died giving him birth, so the Martells would have found the Rock deep in mourning. His father especially. Lord Tywin seldom spoke of his wife, but Tyrion had heard his uncles talk of the love between them. In those days, his father had been Aerys's Hand, and many people said that Lord Tywin Lannister ruled the Seven Kingdoms, but Lady Joanna ruled Lord Tywin. "He was not the same man after she died, Imp," his Uncle Gery told him once. "The best part of him died with her." Gerion had been the youngest of Lord Tytos Lannister's four sons, and the uncle Tyrion liked best.

But he was gone now, lost beyond the seas, and Tyrion himself had put Lady Joanna in her grave. "Did you find Casterly Rock to your liking, my lord?"

"Scarcely. Your father ignored us the whole time we were there, after commanding Ser Kevan to see to our entertainment. The cell they gave me had a featherbed to sleep in and Myrish carpets on the floor, but it was dark and windowless, much like a dungeon when you come down to it, as I told Elia at the time. Your skies were too grey, your wines too sweet, your women too chaste, your food too bland . . . and you yourself were the greatest disappointment of all."

"I had just been born. What did you expect of me?"

"*Enormity*," the black-haired prince replied. "You were small, but far-famed. We were in Oldtown at your birth, and all the city talked of was the monster that had been born to the King's Hand, and what such an omen might foretell for the realm."

"Famine, plague, and war, no doubt." Tyrion gave a sour smile. "It's always famine, plague, and war. Oh, and winter, and the long night that never ends."

"All that," said Prince Oberyn, "and your father's fall as well. Lord Tywin had made himself greater than King Aerys, I heard one begging brother preach, but only a god is meant to stand above a king. You were his curse, a punishment sent by the gods to teach him that he was no better than any other man."

"I try, but he refuses to learn." Tyrion gave a sigh. "But do go on, I pray you. I love a good tale."

"And well you might, since you were said to have one, a stiff curly tail like a swine's. Your head was monstrous huge, we heard, half again the size of your body, and you had been born with thick black hair and a beard besides, an evil eye, and lion's claws. Your teeth were so long you could not close your mouth, and between your legs were a girl's privates as well as a boy's."

"Life would be much simpler if men could fuck themselves, don't you agree? And I can think of a few times when claws and teeth might have proved useful. Even so, I begin to see the nature of your complaint."

Bronn gave out with a chuckle, but Oberyn only smiled. "We might never have seen you at all but for your sweet sister. You were never seen at table or hall, though sometimes at night we could hear a baby howling down in the depths of the Rock. You did have a monstrous great voice, I must grant you that. You would wail for hours, and nothing would quiet you but a woman's teat."

"Still true, as it happens."

This time Prince Oberyn did laugh. "A taste we share. Lord Gargalen once told me he hoped to die with a sword in his hand, to which I replied that I would sooner go with a breast in mine."

Tyrion had to grin. "You were speaking of my sister?"

"Cersei promised Elia to show you to us. The day before we were to sail, whilst my mother and your father were closeted together, she and Jaime took us down to your nursery. Your wet nurse tried to send us off, but your sister was having none of that. 'He's mine,' she said, 'and you're just a milk cow, you can't tell me what to do. Be quiet or I'll have my father cut your tongue out. A cow doesn't need a tongue, only udders.'"

"Her Grace learned charm at an early age," said Tyrion, amused by the notion of his sister claiming him as hers. *She's never been in any rush to claim me since, the gods know.*

"Cersei even undid your swaddling clothes to give us a better look," the Dornish prince continued. "You did have one evil eye, and some black fuzz on your scalp. Perhaps your head was larger than most . . . but there was no tail, no beard, neither teeth nor claws, and nothing between your legs but a tiny pink cock. After all the wonderful whispers, Lord Tywin's Doom turned out to be just a hideous red infant with stunted legs. Elia even made the noise that young girls make at the sight of infants, I'm sure you've heard it. The same noise they make over cute kittens and playful puppies. I believe she wanted to nurse you herself, ugly as you were. When I commented that you seemed a poor sort of monster, your sister said, 'He killed my mother,' and twisted your little cock so hard I thought she was like to pull it off. You shrieked, but it was only when your brother Jaime said, 'Leave him be, you're hurting him,' that Cersei let go of you. 'It doesn't matter,' she told us. 'Everyone says he's like to die soon. He shouldn't even have lived this long.'"

The sun was shining bright above them, and the day was pleasantly warm for autumn, but Tyrion Lannister went cold all over when he heard that. *My sweet sister.* He scratched at the scar of his nose and gave the Dornishman a taste of his "evil eye." *Now why would he tell such a tale? Is he testing me, or simply twisting my cock as Cersei did, so he can hear me scream?* "Be sure and tell that story to my father. It will delight him as much as it did me. The part about my tail, especially. I did have one, but he had it lopped off."

Prince Oberyn had a chuckle. "You've grown more amusing since last we met."

"Yes, but I *meant* to grow taller."

"While we are speaking of amusement, I heard a curious tale from Lord Buckler's steward. He claimed that you had put a tax on women's privy purses."

"It is a tax on whoring," said Tyrion, irritated all over

again. *And it was my bloody father's notion.* "Only a penny for each, ah . . . act. The King's Hand felt it might help improve the morals of the city." *And pay for Joffrey's wedding besides.* Needless to say, as master of coin, Tyrion had gotten all the blame for it. Bronn said they were calling it *the dwarf's penny* in the streets. "Spread your legs for the Halfman, now," they were shouting in the brothels and wine sinks, if the sellsword could be believed.

"I will make certain to keep my pouch full of pennies. Even a prince must pay his taxes."

"Why should you need to go whoring?" He glanced back to where Ellaria Sand rode among the other women. "Did you tire of your paramour on the road?"

"Never. We share too much." Prince Oberyn shrugged. "We have never shared a beautiful blonde woman, however, and Ellaria is curious. Do you know of such a creature?"

"I am a man wedded." *Though not yet bedded.* "I no longer frequent whores." *Unless I want to see them hanged.*

Oberyn abruptly changed the subject. "It's said there are to be seventy-seven dishes served at the king's wedding feast."

"Are you hungry, my prince?"

"I have hungered for a long time. Though not for food. Pray tell me, when will the *justice* be served?"

"Justice." *Yes, that is why he's here, I should have seen that at once.* "You were close to your sister?"

"As children Elia and I were inseparable, much like your own brother and sister."

Gods, I hope not. "Wars and weddings have kept us well occupied, Prince Oberyn. I fear no one has yet had the time to look into murders sixteen years stale, dreadful as they were. We shall, of course, just as soon as we may. Any help that Dorne might be able to provide to restore the king's peace would only hasten the beginning of my lord father's inquiry –"

"Dwarf," said the Red Viper, in a tone grown markedly less cordial, "spare me your Lannister lies. Is it sheep you take us for, or fools? My brother is not a bloodthirsty man, but neither has he been asleep for sixteen years. Jon Arryn came to Sunspear the year after Robert took the throne, and you can be sure that he was questioned closely. Him, and a hundred more. I did not come for some mummer's show of an *inquiry*. I came for justice for Elia and her children, and I will have it. Starting with this lummox Gregor Clegane ... but not, I think, ending there. Before he dies, the Enormity That Rides will tell me whence came his orders, please assure your lord father of that." He smiled. "An old septon once claimed I was living proof of the goodness of the gods. Do you know why that is, Imp?"

"No," Tyrion admitted warily.

"Why, if the gods were cruel, they would have made me my mother's firstborn, and Doran her third. I *am* a bloodthirsty man, you see. And it is me you must contend with now, not my patient, prudent, and gouty brother."

Tyrion could see the sun shining on the Blackwater Rush half a mile ahead, and on the walls and towers and hills of King's Landing beyond. He glanced over his shoulder, at the glittering column following them up the kingsroad. "You speak like a man with a great host at his back," he said, "yet all I see are three hundred. Do you spy that city there, north of the river?"

"The midden heap you call King's Landing?"

"That's the very one."

"Not only do I see it, I believe I smell it now."

"Then take a good sniff, my lord. Fill up your nose. Half a million people stink more than three hundred, you'll find. Do you smell the gold cloaks? There are near five thousand of them. My father's own sworn swords must account for another twenty thousand. And then there are the roses. Roses smell so sweet, don't they? Especially when there are so *many* of them. Fifty, sixty, seventy thousand roses, in the city or camped outside it, I can't really say how many are left, but there's more than I care to count, anyway."

Martell gave a shrug. "In Dorne of old before we married Daeron, it was said that all flowers bow before the sun.

Should the roses seek to hinder me I'll gladly trample them underfoot."

"As you trampled Willas Tyrell?"

The Dornishman did not react as expected. "I had a letter from Willas not half a year past. We share an interest in fine horseflesh. He has never borne me any ill will for what happened in the lists. I struck his breastplate clean, but his foot caught in a stirrup as he fell and his horse came down on top of him. I sent a maester to him afterward, but it was all he could do to save the boy's leg. The knee was far past mending. If any were to blame, it was his fool of a father. Willas Tyrell was green as his surcoat and had no business riding in such company. The Fat Flower thrust him into tourneys at too tender an age, just as he did with the other two. He wanted another Leo Longthorn, and made himself a cripple."

"There are those who say Ser Loras is better than Leo Longthorn ever was," said Tyrion.

"Renly's little rose? I doubt that."

"Doubt it all you wish," said Tyrion, "but Ser Loras has defeated many good knights, including my brother Jaime."

"By *defeated*, you mean *unhorsed*, in tourney. Tell me who he's slain in battle if you mean to frighten me."

"Ser Robar Royce and Ser Emmon Cuy, for two. And men say he performed prodigious feats of valor on the Blackwater, fighting beside Lord Renly's ghost."

"So these same men who saw the prodigious feats saw the ghost as well, yes?" The Dornishman laughed lightly.

Tyrion gave him a long look. "Chataya's on the Street of Silk has several girls who might suit your needs. Dancy has hair the color of honey. Marei's is pale white-gold. I would advise you to keep one or the other by your side at all times, my lord."

"At all times?" Prince Oberyn lifted a thin black eyebrow. "And why is that, my good Imp?"

"You want to die with a breast in hand, you said." Tyrion cantered on ahead to where the ferry barges waited on the south bank of the Blackwater. He had suffered all he meant to suffer of what passed for Dornish wit. *Father should have sent Joffrey after all. He could have asked Prince Oberyn if he knew how a Dornishman differed from a cowflop.* That made him grin despite himself. He would have to make a point of being on hand when the Red Viper was presented to the king.

ARYA

The man on the roof was the first to die. He was crouched down by the chimney two hundred yards away, no more than a vague shadow in the predawn gloom, but as the sky began to lighten he stirred, stretched, and stood. Anguy's arrow took him in the chest. He tumbled bonelessly down the steep slate pitch, and fell in front of the septry door.

The Mummers had posted two guards there, but their torch left them night blind, and the outlaws had crept in close. Kyle and Notch let fly together. One man went down with an arrow through his throat, the other through his belly. The second man dropped the torch, and the flames licked up at him. He screamed as his clothes took fire, and that was the end of stealth. Thoros gave a shout, and the outlaws attacked in earnest.

Arya watched from atop her horse, on the crest of the wooded ridge that overlooked the septry, mill, brewhouse, and stables and the desolation of weeds, burnt trees, and mud that surrounded them. The trees were mostly bare now, and the few withered brown leaves that still clung to the branches did little to obstruct her view. Lord Beric had left Beardless Dick and Mudge to guard them. Arya hated being left behind like she was some stupid *child*, but at least Gendry had been kept back as well. She knew better than to try and argue. This was battle, and in battle you had to obey.

The eastern horizon glowed gold and pink, and over-head a half moon peeked out through low scuttling clouds. The wind blew cold, and Arya could hear the rush of water and the creak of the mill's great wooden waterwheel. There was a smell of rain in the dawn air, but no drops were falling yet. Flaming arrows flew through the morning mists, trailing pale ribbons of fire, and thudded into the wooden walls of the septry. A few smashed through shut-tered windows, and soon enough thin tendrils of smoke were rising between the broken shutters.

Two Mummers came bursting from the septry side by side, axes in their hands. Anguy and the other archers were waiting. One axeman died at once. The other managed to duck, so the shaft ripped through his shoulder. He stag-gered on, till two more arrows found him, so quickly it was hard to say which had struck first. The long shafts punched through his breastplate as if it had been made of silk instead of steel. He fell heavily. Anguy had arrows tipped with bodkins as well as broadheads. A bodkin could pierce even heavy plate. *I'm going to learn to shoot a bow*, Arya thought. She loved swordfighting, but she could see how arrows were good too.

Flames were creeping up the west wall of the septry, and thick smoke poured through a broken window. A Myr-ish crossbowman poked his head out a different window, got off a bolt, and ducked down to rewind. She could hear fighting from the stables as well, shouts well mingled with the screams of horses and the clang of steel. *Kill them all*, she thought fiercely. She bit her lip so hard she tasted blood. *Kill every single one.*

The crossbowman appeared again, but no sooner had he loosed than three arrows hissed past his head. One rattled off his helm. He vanished, bow and all. Arya could see flames in several of the second-story windows. Between the smoke and the morning mists, the air was a haze of blowing black and white. Anguy and the other bowmen were creeping closer, the better to find targets.

Then the septry erupted, the Mummers boiling out like angry ants. Two Ibbenese rushed through the door with shaggy brown shields held high before them, and behind them came a Dothraki with a great curved *arakh* and bells in his braid, and behind him three Volantene sellswords covered with fierce tattoos. Others were climbing out windows and leaping to the ground. Arya saw a man take an arrow through the chest with one leg across a window-sill, and heard his scream as he fell. The smoke was thickening. Quarrels and arrows sped back and forth. Watty fell with a grunt, his bow slipping from his hand. Kyle was trying to nock another shaft to his string when a man in black mail flung a spear through his belly. She heard Lord Beric shout. From out of the ditches and trees the rest of his band came pouring, steel in hand. Arya saw Lem's bright yellow cloak flapping behind him as he rode down the man who'd killed Kyle. Thoros and Lord Beric were everywhere, their swords swirling fire. The red priest hacked at a hide shield until it flew to pieces, while his horse kicked the man in the face. A Dothraki screamed and charged the lightning lord, and the flaming sword leapt out to meet his *arakh*. The blades kissed and spun and kissed again. Then the Dothraki's hair was ablaze, and a moment later he was dead. She spied Ned too, fighting at the lightning lord's side. *It's not fair, he's only a little older than me, they should have let me fight.*

The battle did not last very long. The Brave Companions still on their feet soon died, or threw down their swords. Two of the Dothraki managed to regain their horses and flee, but only because Lord Beric let them go. "Let them carry the word back to Harrenhal," he said, with flaming sword in hand. "It will give the Leech Lord and his goat a few more sleepless nights."

Jack-Be-Lucky, Harwin, and Merrit o' Moontown braved the burning septry to search for captives. They emerged from the smoke and flames a few moments later with eight brown brothers, one so weak that Merrit had to carry him across a shoulder. There was a septon with them as well, round-shouldered and balding, but he wore black chainmail over his grey robes. "Found him hiding under the cellar steps," said Jack, coughing.

Thoros smiled to see him. "You are Utt."

"*Septon* Utt. A man of god."

"What god would want the likes o' you?" growled Lem.

"I have sinned," the septon wailed. "I know, I know. Forgive me, Father. Oh, grievously have I sinned."

Arya remembered Septon Utt from her time at Harrenhal. Shagwell the Fool said he always wept and prayed for forgiveness after he'd killed his latest boy. Sometimes he even made the other Mummers scourge him. They all thought that was very funny.

Lord Beric slammed his sword into its scabbard, quenching the flames. "Give the dying the gift of mercy and bind the others hand and foot for trial," he commanded, and it was done.

The trials went swiftly. Various of the outlaws came forward to tell of things the Brave Companions had done; towns and villages sacked, crops burned, women raped and murdered, men maimed and tortured. A few spoke of the boys that Septon Utt had carried off. The septon wept and prayed through it all. "I am a weak reed," he told Lord Beric. "I pray to the Warrior for strength, but the gods made me weak. Have mercy on my weakness. The boys, the sweet boys . . . I never mean to hurt them . . ."

Septon Utt soon dangled beneath a tall elm, swinging slowly by the neck, as naked as his name day. The other Brave Companions followed one by one. A few fought, kicking and struggling as the noose was tightened round their throats. One of the crossbowmen kept shouting, "I soldier, I soldier," in a thick Myrish accent. Another offered to lead his captors to gold; a third told them what a good outlaw he would make. Each was stripped and bound and hanged in turn. Tom Sevenstrings played a dirge for them on his woodharp, and Thoros implored the Lord of Light to roast their souls until the end of time.

A mummer tree, Arya thought as she watched them dangle, their pale skins painted a sullen red by the flames of the burning septry. Already the crows were coming, appearing out of nowhere. She heard them croaking and cackling at one another, and wondered what they were saying. Arya had not feared Septon Utt as much as she did Rorge and Biter and some of the others still at Harrenhal, but she was glad that he was dead all the same. *They should have hanged the Hound too, or chopped his head off*. Instead, to her disgust, the outlaws had treated Sandor Clegane's burned arm, restored his sword and horse and armor, and set him free a few miles from the hollow hill. All they'd taken was his gold.

The septry soon collapsed in a roar of smoke and flame, its walls no longer able to support the weight of its heavy slate roof. The eight brown brothers watched with resignation. They were all that remained, explained the eldest, who wore a small iron hammer on a thong about his neck to signify his devotion to the Smith. "Before the war we were four-and-forty, and this was a prosperous place. We had a dozen milk cows and a bull, a hundred beehives, a vineyard and an apple arbor. But when the lions came through they took all our wine and milk and honey, slaughtered the cows, and put our vineyard to the torch. After that . . . I have lost count of our visitors. This false septon was only the latest. There was one monster . . . we gave him all our silver, but he was certain we were hiding gold, so his men killed us one by one to make Elder Brother talk."

"How did the eight of you survive?" asked Anguy the Archer.

"I am ashamed," the old man said. "It was me. When it came my turn to die, I told them where our gold was hidden."

"Brother," said Thoros of Myr, "the only shame was not telling them at once."

The outlaws sheltered that night in the brewhouse beside the little river. Their hosts had a cache of food hidden beneath the floor of the stables, so they shared a simple supper; oaten bread, onions, and a watery cabbage soup tasting faintly of garlic. Arya found a slice of carrot floating in her bowl, and counted herself lucky. The brothers never asked the outlaws for names. *They know*, Arya thought. How could they not? Lord Beric wore the lightning bolt on breastplate, shield, and cloak, and Thoros his red robes, or what remained of them. One brother, a young novice, was bold enough to tell the red priest not to pray to his false god so long as he was under their roof.

"Bugger that," said Lem Lemoncloak. "He's our god too, and you owe us for your bloody lives. And what's false about him? Might be your Smith can mend a broken sword, but can he heal a broken man?"

"Enough, Lem," Lord Beric commanded. "Beneath their roof we will honor their rules."

"The sun will not cease to shine if we miss a prayer or two," Thoros agreed mildly. "I am one who would know."

Lord Beric himself did not eat. Arya had never seen him eat, though from time to time he took a cup of wine. He did not seem to sleep, either. His good eye would often close, as if from weariness, but when you spoke to him it would flick open again at once. The Marcher lord was still clad in his ratty black cloak and dented breastplate with its chipped enamel lightning. He even slept in that breastplate. The dull black steel hid the terrible wound the Hound had given him, the same way his thick woolen scarf concealed the dark ring about his throat. But nothing hid his broken head, all caved in at the temple, or the raw red pit that was his missing eye, or the shape of the skull beneath his face.

Arya looked at him warily, remembering all the tales told of him in Harrenhal. Lord Beric seemed to sense her fear. He turned his head, and beckoned her closer. "Do I frighten you, child?"

"No." She chewed her lip. "Only . . . well . . . I thought the Hound had killed you, but . . ."

"A wound," said Lem Lemoncloak. "A grievous wound, aye, but Thoros healed it. There's never been no better healer."

Lord Beric gazed at Lem with a queer look in his good eye and no look at all in the other, only scars and dried blood. "No better healer," he agreed wearily. "Lem, past time to change the watch, I'd think. See to it, if you'd be so good."

"Aye, m'lord." Lem's big yellow cloak swirled behind him as he strode out into the windy night.

"Even brave men blind themselves sometimes, when they are afraid to see," Lord Beric said when Lem was gone. "Thoros, how many times have you brought me back now?"

The red priest bowed his head. "It is R'hllor who brings you back, my lord. The Lord of Light. I am only his instrument."

"How many times?" Lord Beric insisted.

"Six," Thoros said reluctantly. "And each time is harder. You have grown reckless, my lord. Is death so very sweet?"

"Sweet? No, my friend. Not sweet."

"Then do not court it so. Lord Tywin leads from the rear. Lord Stannis as well. You would be wise to do the same. A seventh death might mean the end of both of us."

Lord Beric touched the spot above his left ear where his temple was caved in. "Here is where Ser Burton Crakehall broke helm and head with a blow of his mace." He unwound his scarf, exposing the black bruise that encircled his neck. "Here the mark the manticore made at Rushing Falls. He seized a poor beekeeper and his wife, thinking they were mine, and let it be known far and wide that he would hang them both unless I gave myself up to him. When I did he hanged them anyway, and me on the gibbet between them." He lifted a finger to the raw red pit of his eye. "Here is where the Mountain thrust his dirk through my visor." A weary smile brushed his lips. "That's thrice I have died at the hands of House Clegane. You would think that I might have learned . . ."

It was a jest, Arya knew, but Thoros did not laugh. He put a hand on Lord Beric's shoulder. "Best not to dwell on it."

"Can I dwell on what I scarce remember? I held a castle on the Marches once, and there was a woman I was pledged to marry, but I could not find that castle today, nor tell you the color of that woman's hair. Who knighted me, old friend? What were my favorite foods? It all fades. Sometimes I think I was born on the bloody grass in that grove of ash, with the taste of fire in my mouth and a hole in my chest. Are you my mother, Thoros?"

Arya stared at the Myrish priest, all shaggy hair and pink rags and bits of old armor. Grey stubble covered his cheeks and the sagging skin beneath his chin. He did not look much like the wizards in Old Nan's stories, but even so . . .

"Could you bring back a man without a head?" Arya asked. "Just the once, not six times. Could you?"

"I have no magic, child. Only prayers. That first time, his lordship had a hole right through him and blood in his mouth, I knew there was no hope. So when his poor torn chest stopped moving, I gave him the good god's own kiss to send him on his way. I filled my mouth with fire and breathed the flames inside him, down his throat to lungs and heart and soul. The *last kiss* it is called, and many a time I saw the old priests bestow it on the Lord's servants as they died. I had given it a time or two myself, as all priests must. But never before had I felt a dead man shudder as the fire filled him, nor seen his eyes come open. It was not me who raised him, my lady. It was the Lord. R'hllor is not done with him yet. Life is warmth, and warmth is fire, and fire is God's and God's alone."

Arya felt tears well in her eyes. Thoros used a lot of words, but all they meant was *no*, that much she understood.

"Your father was a good man," Lord Beric said. "Harwin has told me much of him. For his sake, I would gladly forgo your ransom, but we need the gold too desperately."

She chewed her lip. *That's true, I guess.* He had given the Hound's gold to Greenbeard and the Huntsman to buy provisions south of the Mander, she knew. "The last harvest burned, this one is drowning, and winter will soon be on us," she had heard him say when he sent them off. "The smallfolk need grain and seed, and we need blades and horses. Too many of my men ride rounseys, drays, and mules against foes mounted on coursers and destriers."

Arya didn't know how much Robb would pay for her, though. He was a king now, not the boy she'd left at Winterfell with snow melting in his hair. And if he knew the things she'd done, the stableboy and the guard at Harrenhal and all . . . "What if my brother doesn't want to ransom me?"

"Why would you think that?" asked Lord Beric.

"Well," Arya said, "my hair's messy and my nails are dirty and my feet are all hard." Robb wouldn't care about that, probably, but her mother would. Lady Catelyn always wanted her to be like Sansa, to sing and dance and sew and mind her courtesies. Just thinking of it made Arya try to comb her hair with her fingers, but it was all tangles and mats, and all she did was tear some out. "I ruined that gown that Lady Smallwood gave me, and I don't sew so good." She chewed her lip. "I don't sew *very well*, I mean. Septa Mordane used to say I had a blacksmith's hands."

Gendry hooted. "Those soft little things?" he called out. "You couldn't even hold a hammer."

"I could if I wanted!" she snapped at him.

Thoros chuckled. "Your brother will pay, child. Have no fear on that count."

"Yes, but what if he *won't*?" she insisted.

Lord Beric sighed. "Then I will send you to Lady Smallwood for a time, or perhaps to mine own castle of Blackhaven. But that will not be necessary, I'm certain. I do not have the power to give you back your father, no more than Thoros does, but I can at least see that you are returned safely to your mother's arms."

"Do you *swear*?" she asked him. Yoren had promised to take her home too, only he'd gotten killed instead.

"On my honor as a knight," the lightning lord said solemnly.

It was raining when Lem returned to the brewhouse, muttering curses as water ran off his yellow cloak to puddle on the floor. Anguy and Jack-Be-Lucky sat by the door rolling dice, but no matter which game they played one-eyed Jack had no luck at all. Tom Sevenstrings replaced a string on his woodharp, and sang "The Mother's Tears," "When Willum's Wife Was Wet," "Lord Harte Rode Out on a Rainy Day," and then "The Rains of Castamere."

> And who are you, the proud lord said,
> > that I must bow so low?
> Only a cat of a different coat,
> > that's all the truth I know.

In a coat of gold or a coat of red,
> *a lion still has claws,*
And mine are long and sharp, my lord,
> *as long and sharp as yours.*
And so he spoke, and so he spoke,
> *that lord of Castamere,*
But now the rains weep o'er his hall,
> *with no one there to hear.*
Yes now the rains weep o'er his hall,
> *and not a soul to hear.*

Finally Tom ran out of rain songs and put away his harp. Then there was only the sound of the rain itself beating down on the slate roof of the brewhouse. The dice game ended, and Arya stood on one leg and then the other listening to Merrit complain about his horse throwing a shoe.

"I could shoe him for you," said Gendry, all of a sudden. "I was only a 'prentice, but my master said my hand was made to hold a hammer. I can shoe horses, close up rents in mail, and beat the dents from plate. I bet I could make swords too."

"What are you saying, lad?" asked Harwin.

"I'll smith for you." Gendry went to one knee before Lord Beric. "If you'll have me, m'lord, I could be of use. I've made tools and knives and once I made a helmet that wasn't so bad. One of the Mountain's men stole it from me when we was taken."

Arya bit her lip. *He means to leave me too.*

"You would do better serving Lord Tully at Riverrun," said Lord Beric. "I cannot pay for your work."

"No one ever did. I want a forge, and food to eat, some place I can sleep. That's enough, m'lord."

"A smith can find a welcome most anywhere. A skilled armorer even more so. Why would you choose to stay with us?"

Arya watched Gendry screw up his stupid face, thinking. "At the hollow hill, what you said about being King Robert's men, and brothers, I liked that. I liked that you gave the Hound a trial. Lord Bolton just hanged folk or took off their heads, and Lord Tywin and Ser Amory were the same. I'd sooner smith for you."

"We got plenty of mail needs mending, m'lord," Jack reminded Lord Beric. "Most we took off the dead, and there's holes where the death came through."

"You must be a lackwit, boy," said Lem. "We're *outlaws*. Lowborn scum, most of us, excepting his lordship. Don't think it'll be like Tom's fool songs neither. You won't be stealing no kisses from a princess, nor riding in no tourneys in stolen armor. You join us, you'll end with your neck in a noose, or your head mounted up above some castle gate."

"It's no more than they'd do for you," said Gendry.

"Aye, that's so," said Jack-Be-Lucky cheerfully. "The crows await us all. M'lord, the boy seems brave enough, and we do have need of what he brings us. Take him, says Jack."

"And quick," suggested Harwin, chuckling, "before the fever passes and he comes back to his senses."

A wan smile crossed Lord Beric's lips. "Thoros, my sword."

This time the lightning lord did not set the blade afire, but merely laid it light on Gendry's shoulder. "Gendry, do you swear before the eyes of gods and men to defend those who cannot defend themselves, to protect all women and children, to obey your captains, your liege lord, and your king, to fight bravely when needed and do such other tasks as are laid upon you, however hard or humble or dangerous they may be?"

"I do, m'lord."

The marcher lord moved the sword from the right shoulder to the left, and said, "Arise Ser Gendry, knight of the hollow hill, and be welcome to our brotherhood."

From the door came rough, rasping laughter.

The rain was running off him. His burned arm was wrapped in leaves and linen and bound tight against his chest by a crude rope sling, but the older burns that marked his face glistened black and slick in the glow of their little fire. "Making more knights, Dondarrion?" the intruder said in a growl. "I ought to kill you all over again for that."

Lord Beric faced him coolly. "I'd hoped we'd seen the last of you, Clegane. How did you come to find us?"

"It wasn't hard. You made enough bloody smoke to be seen in Oldtown."

"What's become of the sentries I posted?"

Clegane's mouth twitched. "Those two blind men? Might be I killed them both. What would you do if I had?"

Anguy strung his bow. Notch was doing the same. "Do you wish to die so very much, Sandor?" asked Thoros. "You must be mad or drunk to follow us here."

"Drunk on rain? You didn't leave me enough gold to buy a cup of wine, you whoresons."

Anguy drew an arrow. "We're outlaws. Outlaws steal. It's in the songs, if you ask nice Tom may sing you one. Be thankful we didn't kill you."

"Come try it, Archer. I'll take that quiver off you and shove those arrows up your freckly little arse."

Anguy raised his longbow, but Lord Beric lifted a hand before he could loose. "Why did you come here, Clegane?"

"To get back what's mine."

"Your gold?"

"What else? It wasn't for the pleasure of looking at your face, Dondarrion, I'll tell you that. You're uglier than me now. And a robber knight besides, it seems."

"I gave you a note for your gold," Lord Beric said calmly. "A promise to pay, when the war's done."

"I wiped my arse with your paper. I want the gold."

"We don't have it. I sent it south with Greenbeard and the Huntsman, to buy grain and seed across the Mander."

"To feed all them whose crops you burned," said Gendry.

"Is that the tale, now?" Sandor Clegane laughed again. "As it happens, that's just what I meant to do with it. Feed a bunch of ugly peasants and their poxy whelps."

"You're lying," said Gendry.

"The boy has a mouth on him, I see. Why believe them and not me? Couldn't be my face, could it?" Clegane glanced at Arya. "You going to make her a knight too, Dondarrion? The first eight-year-old girl knight?"

"I'm *twelve*," Arya lied loudly, "and I could be a knight

if I wanted. I could have killed you too, only Lem took my knife." Remembering that still made her angry.

"Complain to Lem, not me. Then tuck your tail between your legs and run. Do you know what dogs do to wolves?"

"Next time I *will* kill you. I'll kill your brother too!"

"No." His dark eyes narrowed. "That you won't." He turned back to Lord Beric. "Say, make my horse a knight. He never shits in the hall and doesn't kick more than most, he deserves to be knighted. Unless you meant to steal him too."

"Best climb on that horse and go," warned Lem.

"I'll go with my gold. Your own god said I'm guiltless – "

"The Lord of Light gave you back your life," declared Thoros of Myr. "He did not proclaim you Baelor the Blessed come again." The red priest unsheathed his sword, and Arya saw that Jack and Merrit had drawn as well. Lord Beric still held the blade he'd used to dub Gendry. *Maybe this time they'll kill him.*

The Hound's mouth gave another twitch. "You're no more than common thieves."

Lem glowered. "Your lion friends ride into some village, take all the food and every coin they find, and call it *foraging*. The wolves as well, so why not us? No one robbed you, dog. You just been good and *foraged*."

Sandor Clegane looked at their faces, every one, as if he were trying to commit them all to memory. Then he walked back out into the darkness and the pouring rain from whence he'd come, with never another word. The outlaws waited, wondering . . .

"I best go see what he did to our sentries." Harwin took a wary look out the door before he left, to make certain the Hound was not lurking just outside.

"How'd that bloody bastard get all that gold anyhow?" Lem Lemoncloak said, to break the tension.

Anguy shrugged. "He won the Hand's tourney. In King's Landing." The bowman grinned. "I won a fair fortune myself, but then I met Dancy, Jayde, and Alayaya.

They taught me what roast swan tastes like, and how to bathe in Arbor wine."

"Pissed it all away, did you?" laughed Harwin.

"Not *all*. I bought these boots, and this excellent dagger."

"You ought t'have bought some land and made one o' them roast swan girls an honest woman," said Jack-Be-Lucky. "Raised yourself a crop o' turnips and a crop o' sons."

"Warrior defend me! What a waste that would have been, to turn my gold to turnips."

"I like turnips," said Jack, aggrieved. "I could do with some mashed turnips right now."

Thoros of Myr paid no heed to the banter. "The Hound has lost more than a few bags of coin," he mused. "He has lost his master and kennel as well. He cannot go back to the Lannisters, the Young Wolf would never have him, nor would his brother be like to welcome him. That gold was all he had left, it seems to me."

"Bloody hell," said Watty the Miller. "He'll come murder us in our sleep for sure, then."

"No." Lord Beric had sheathed his sword. "Sandor Clegane would kill us all gladly, but not in our sleep. Anguy, on the morrow, take the rear with Beardless Dick. If you see Clegane still sniffing after us, kill his horse."

"That's a good horse," Anguy protested.

"Aye," said Lem. "It's the bloody rider we should be killing. We could use that horse."

"I'm with Lem," Notch said. "Let me feather the dog a few times, discourage him some."

Lord Beric shook his head. "Clegane won his life beneath the hollow hill. I will not rob him of it."

"My lord is wise," Thoros told the others. "Brothers, a trial by battle is a holy thing. You heard me ask R'hllor to take a hand, and you saw his fiery finger snap Lord Beric's sword, just as he was about to make an end of it. The Lord of Light is not yet done with Joffrey's Hound, it would seem."

Harwin soon returned to the brewhouse. "Puddingfoot was sound asleep, but unharmed."

"Wait till I get hold of him," said Lem. "I'll cut him a new bunghole. He could have gotten every one of us killed."

No one rested very comfortably that night, knowing that Sandor Clegane was out there in the dark, somewhere close. Arya curled up near the fire, warm and snug, yet sleep would not come. She took out the coin that Jaqen H'ghar had given her and curled her fingers around it as she lay beneath her cloak. It made her feel strong to hold it, remembering how she'd been the ghost in Harrenhal. She could kill with a whisper then.

Jaqen was gone, though. He'd left her. *Hot Pie left me too, and now Gendry is leaving.* Lommy had died, Yoren had died, Syrio Forel had died, even her father had died, and Jaqen had given her a stupid iron penny and vanished. *"Valar morghulis,"* she whispered softly, tightening her fist so the hard edges of the coin dug into her palm. "Ser Gregor, Dunsen, Polliver, Raff the Sweetling. The Tickler and the Hound. Ser Ilyn, Ser Meryn, King Joffrey, Queen Cersei." Arya tried to imagine how they would look when they were dead, but it was hard to bring their faces to mind. The Hound she could see, and his brother the Mountain, and she would never forget Joffrey's face, or his mother's ... but Raff and Dunsen and Polliver were all fading, and even the Tickler, whose looks had been so commonplace.

Sleep took her at last, but in the black of night Arya woke again, tingling. The fire had burned down to embers. Mudge stood by the door, and another guard was pacing outside. The rain had stopped, and she could hear wolves howling. *So close,* she thought, *and so many.* They sounded as if they were all around the stable, dozens of them, maybe hundreds. *I hope they eat the Hound.* She remembered what he'd said, about wolves and dogs.

Come morning, Septon Utt still swung beneath the tree, but the brown brothers were out in the rain with spades, digging shallow graves for the other dead. Lord Beric thanked them for the night's lodging and the meal, and gave them a bag of silver stags to help rebuild. Harwin,

Likely Luke, and Watty the Miller went out scouting, but neither wolves nor hounds were found.

As Arya was cinching her saddle girth, Gendry came up to say that he was sorry. She put a foot in the stirrup and swung up into her saddle, so she could look down on him instead of up. *You could have made swords at Riverrun for my brother*, she thought, but what she said was, "If you want to be some stupid outlaw knight and get hanged, why should I care? I'll be at Riverrun, ransomed, with my brother."

There was no rain that day, thankfully, and for once they made good time.

BRAN

The tower stood upon an island, its twin reflected on the still blue waters. When the wind blew, ripples moved across the surface of the lake, chasing one another like boys at play. Oak trees grew thick along the lakeshore, a dense stand of them with a litter of fallen acorns on the ground beneath. Beyond them was the village, or what remained of it.

It was the first village they had seen since leaving the foothills. Meera had scouted ahead to make certain there was no one lurking amongst the ruins. Sliding in and amongst oaks and apple trees with her net and spear in hand, she startled three red deer and sent them bounding away through the brush. Summer saw the flash of motion and was after them at once. Bran watched the direwolf lope off, and for a moment wanted nothing so much as to slip his skin and run with him, but Meera was waving for them to come ahead. Reluctantly, he turned away from Summer and urged Hodor on, into the village. Jojen walked with them.

The ground from here to the Wall was grasslands, Bran knew; fallow fields and low rolling hills, high meadows and lowland bogs. It would be much easier going than the mountains behind, but so much open space made Meera uneasy. "I feel naked," she confessed. "There's no place to hide."

"Who holds this land?" Jojen asked Bran.

"The Night's Watch," he answered. "This is the Gift. The New Gift, and north of that Brandon's Gift." Maester Luwin had taught him the history. "Brandon the Builder gave all the land south of the Wall to the black brothers, to a distance of twenty-five leagues. For their . . . for their *sustenance and support.*" He was proud that he still remembered that part. "Some maesters say it was some other Brandon, not the Builder, but it's still Brandon's Gift. Thousands of years later, Good Queen Alysanne visited the Wall on her dragon Silverwing, and she thought the Night's Watch was so brave that she had the Old King double the size of their lands, to fifty leagues. So that was the New Gift." He waved a hand. "Here. All this."

No one had lived in the village for long years, Bran could see. All the houses were falling down. Even the inn. It had never been *much* of an inn, to look at it, but now all that remained was a stone chimney and two cracked walls, set amongst a dozen apple trees. One was growing up through the common room, where a layer of wet brown leaves and rotting apples carpeted the floor. The air was thick with the smell of them, a cloying cidery scent that was almost overwhelming. Meera stabbed a few apples with her frog spear, trying to find some still good enough to eat, but they were all too brown and wormy.

It was a peaceful spot, still and tranquil and lovely to behold, but Bran thought there was something sad about an empty inn, and Hodor seemed to feel it too. "Hodor?" he said in a confused sort of way. "Hodor? Hodor?"

"This is good land." Jojen picked up a handful of dirt, rubbing it between his fingers. "A village, an inn, a stout holdfast in the lake, all these apple trees . . . but where are the people, Bran? Why would they leave such a place?"

"They were afraid of the wildlings," said Bran. "Wildlings come over the Wall or through the mountains, to raid and steal and carry off women. If they catch you, they make your skull into a cup to drink blood, Old Nan used to say. The Night's Watch isn't so strong as it was in Brandon's day or Queen Alysanne's, so more get through. The places nearest the Wall got raided so much the smallfolk moved south, into the mountains or onto the Umber lands east of the kingsroad. The Greatjon's people get raided too, but not so much as the people who used to live in the Gift."

Jojen Reed turned his head slowly, listening to music only he could hear. "We need to shelter here. There's a storm coming. A bad one."

Bran looked up at the sky. It had been a beautiful crisp clear autumn day, sunny and almost warm, but there were dark clouds off to the west now, that was true, and the wind seemed to be picking up. "There's no roof on the inn and only the two walls," he pointed out. "We should go out to the holdfast."

"Hodor," said Hodor. Maybe he agreed.

"We have no boat, Bran." Meera poked through the leaves idly with her frog spear.

"There's a causeway. A stone causeway, hidden under the water. We could walk out." *They* could, anyway; he would have to ride on Hodor's back, but at least he'd stay dry that way.

The Reeds exchanged a look. "How do you know that?" asked Jojen. "Have you been here before, my prince?"

"No. Old Nan told me. The holdfast has a golden crown, see?" He pointed across the lake. You could see patches of flaking gold paint up around the crenellations. "Queen Alysanne slept there, so they painted the merlons gold in her honor."

"A causeway?" Jojen studied the lake. "You are certain?"

"Certain," said Bran.

Meera found the foot of it easily enough, once she knew to look; a stone pathway three feet wide, leading right out into the lake. She took them out step by careful step, probing ahead with her frog spear. They could see where the path emerged again, climbing from the water onto the island and turning into a short flight of stone steps that led to the holdfast door.

Path, steps, and door were in a straight line, which made you think the causeway ran straight, but that wasn't so. Under the lake it zigged and zagged, going a third of a way around the island before jagging back. The turns were treacherous, and the long path meant that anyone approaching would be exposed to arrow fire from the tower for a long time. The hidden stones were slimy and slippery too; twice Hodor almost lost his footing and shouted "*HODOR!*" in alarm before regaining his balance. The second time scared Bran badly. If Hodor fell into the lake with him in his basket, he could well drown, especially if the huge stableboy panicked and forgot that Bran was there, the way he did sometimes. *Maybe we should have stayed at the inn, under the apple tree*, he thought, but by then it was too late.

Thankfully there was no third time, and the water never got up past Hodor's waist, though the Reeds were in it up to their chests. And before long they were on the island, climbing the steps to the holdfast. The door was still stout, though its heavy oak planks had warped over the years and it could no longer be closed completely. Meera shoved it open all the way, the rusted iron hinges screaming. The lintel was low. "Duck down, Hodor," Bran said, and he did, but not enough to keep Bran from hitting his head. "That hurt," he complained.

"Hodor," said Hodor, straightening.

They found themselves in a gloomy strongroom, barely large enough to hold the four of them. Steps built into the inner wall of the tower curved away upward to their left, downward to their right, behind iron grates. Bran looked up and saw another grate just above his head. *A murder hole*. He was glad there was no one up there now to pour boiling oil down on them.

The grates were locked, but the iron bars were red with rust. Hodor grabbed hold of the lefthand door and gave it a pull, grunting with effort. Nothing happened. He tried pushing with no more success. He shook the bars, kicked, shoved against them and rattled them and punched the hinges with a huge hand until the air was filled with flakes of rust, but the iron door would not budge. The one down to the undervault was no more accommodating. "No way in," said Meera, shrugging.

The murder hole was just above Bran's head, as he sat

in his basket on Hodor's back. He reached up and grabbed the bars to give them a try. When he pulled down the grating came out of the ceiling in a cascade of rust and crumbling stone. *"HODOR!"* Hodor shouted. The heavy iron grate gave Bran another bang in the head, and crashed down near Jojen's feet when he shoved it off of him. Meera laughed. "Look at that, my prince," she said, "you're stronger than Hodor." Bran blushed.

With the grate gone, Hodor was able to boost Meera and Jojen up through the gaping murder hole. The crannogmen took Bran by the arms and drew him up after them. Getting Hodor inside was the hard part. He was too heavy for the Reeds to lift the way they'd lifted Bran. Finally Bran told him to go look for some big rocks. The island had no lack of those, and Hodor was able to pile them high enough to grab the crumbling edges of the hole and climb through. "Hodor," he panted happily, grinning at all of them.

They found themselves in a maze of small cells, dark and empty, but Meera explored until she found the way back to the steps. The higher they climbed, the better the light; on the third story the thick outer wall was pierced by arrow slits, the fourth had actual windows, and the fifth and highest was one big round chamber with arched doors on three sides opening onto small stone balconies. On the fourth side was a privy chamber perched above a sewer chute that dropped straight down into the lake.

By the time they reached the roof the sky was completely overcast, and the clouds to the west were black. The wind was blowing so strong it lifted up Bran's cloak and made it flap and snap. "Hodor," Hodor said at the noise.

Meera spun in a circle. "I feel almost a giant, standing high above the world."

"There are trees in the Neck that stand twice as tall as this," her brother reminded her.

"Aye, but they have other trees around them just as high," said Meera. "The world presses close in the Neck, and the sky is so much smaller. Here ... feel that wind, Brother? And look how large the world has grown."

It was true, you could see a long ways from up here.

To the south the foothills rose, with the mountains grey and green beyond them. The rolling plains of the New Gift stretched away to all the other directions, as far as the eye could see. "I was hoping we could see the Wall from here," said Bran, disappointed. "That was stupid, we must still be fifty leagues away." Just speaking of it made him feel tired, and cold as well. "Jojen, what will we do when we reach the Wall? My uncle always said how big it was. Seven hundred feet high, and so thick at the base that the gates are more like tunnels through the ice. How are we going to get past to find the three-eyed crow?"

"There are abandoned castles along the Wall, I've heard," Jojen answered. "Fortresses built by the Night's Watch but now left empty. One of them may give us our way through."

The ghost castles, Old Nan had called them. Maester Luwin had once made Bran learn the names of every one of the forts along the Wall. That had been hard; there were nineteen of them all told, though no more than seventeen had ever been manned at any one time. At the feast in honor of King Robert's visit to Winterfell, Bran had recited the names for his uncle Benjen, east to west and then west to east. Benjen Stark had laughed and said, "You know them better than I do, Bran. Perhaps you should be First Ranger. I'll stay here in your place." That was before Bran fell, though. Before he was broken. By the time he'd woken crippled from his sleep, his uncle had gone back to Castle Black.

"My uncle said the gates were sealed with ice and stone whenever a castle had to be abandoned," said Bran.

"Then we'll have to open them again," said Meera.

That made him uneasy. "We shouldn't do that. Bad things might come through from the other side. We should just go to Castle Black and tell the Lord Commander to let us pass."

"Your Grace," said Jojen, "we must avoid Castle Black, just as we avoided the kingsroad. There are hundreds of men there."

"Men of the Night's Watch," said Bran. "They say vows, to take no part in wars and stuff."

"Aye," said Jojen, "but one man willing to forswear himself would be enough to sell your secret to the ironmen or the Bastard of Bolton. And we cannot be certain that the Watch would agree to let us pass. They might decide to hold us or send us back."

"But my father was a friend of the Night's Watch, and my uncle is First Ranger. He might know where the three-eyed crow lives. And Jon's at Castle Black too." Bran had been hoping to see Jon again, and their uncle too. The last black brothers to visit Winterfell said that Benjen Stark had vanished on a ranging, but surely he would have made his way back by *now*. "I bet the Watch would even give us horses," he went on.

"Quiet." Jojen shaded his eyes with a hand and gazed off toward the setting sun. "Look. There's something . . . a rider, I think. Do you see him?"

Bran shaded his eyes as well, and even so he had to squint. He saw nothing at first, till some movement made him turn. At first he thought it might be Summer, but no. *A man on a horse.* He was too far away to see much else.

"Hodor?" Hodor had put a hand over his eyes as well, only he was looking the wrong way. "Hodor?"

"He is in no haste," said Meera, "but he's making for this village, it seems to me."

"We had best go inside, before we're seen," said Jojen.

"Summer's near the village," Bran objected.

"Summer will be fine," Meera promised. "It's only one man on a tired horse."

A few fat wet drops began to patter against the stone as they retreated to the floor below. That was well timed; the rain began to fall in earnest a short time later. Even through the thick walls they could hear it lashing against the surface of the lake. They sat on the floor in the round empty room, amidst gathering gloom. The north-facing balcony looked out toward the abandoned village. Meera crept out on her belly to peer across the lake and see what had become of the horseman. "He's taken shelter in the ruins of the inn," she told them when she came back. "It looks as though he's making a fire in the hearth."

"I wish we could have a fire," Bran said. "I'm cold. There's broken furniture down the stairs, I saw it. We could have Hodor chop it up and get warm."

Hodor liked that idea. "Hodor," he said hopefully.

Jojen shook his head. "Fire means smoke. Smoke from this tower could be seen a long way off."

"If there were anyone to see," his sister argued.

"There's a man in the village."

"One man."

"One man would be enough to betray Bran to his enemies, if he's the wrong man. We still have half a duck from yesterday. We should eat and rest. Come morning the man will go on his way, and we will do the same."

Jojen had his way, he always did. Meera divided the duck between the four of them. She'd caught it in her net the day before, as it tried to rise from the marsh where she'd surprised it. It wasn't as tasty cold as it had been hot and crisp from the spit, but at least they did not go hungry. Bran and Meera shared the breast while Jojen ate the thigh. Hodor devoured the wing and leg, muttering "Hodor" and licking the grease off his fingers after every bite. It was Bran's turn to tell a story, so he told them about another Brandon Stark, the one called Brandon the Shipwright, who had sailed off beyond the Sunset Sea.

Dusk was settling by the time duck and tale were done, and the rain still fell. Bran wondered how far Summer had roamed and whether he had caught one of the deer.

Grey gloom filled the tower, and slowly changed to darkness. Hodor grew restless and walked awhile, striding round and round the walls and stopping to peer into the privy on every circuit, as if he had forgotten what was in there. Jojen stood by the north balcony, hidden by the shadows, looking out at the night and the rain. Somewhere to the north a lightning bolt crackled across the sky, brightening the inside of the tower for an instant. Hodor jumped and made a frightened noise. Bran counted to eight, waiting for the thunder. When it came, Hodor shouted, *"Hodor!"*

I hope Summer isn't scared too, Bran thought. The dogs in Winterfell's kennels had always been spooked by thunderstorms, just like Hodor. *I should go see, to calm him . . .*

The lightning flashed again, and this time the thunder came at six. "Hodor!" Hodor yelled again. "HODOR! HODOR!" He snatched up his sword, as if to fight the storm.

Jojen said, "Be quiet, Hodor. Bran, tell him not to shout. Can you get the sword away from him, Meera?"

"I can try."

"Hodor, *hush*," said Bran. "Be quiet now. No more stupid hodoring. Sit down."

"Hodor?" He gave the longsword to Meera meekly enough, but his face was a mask of confusion.

Jojen turned back to the darkness, and they all heard him suck in his breath. "What is it?" Meera asked.

"Men in the village."

"The man we saw before?"

"Other men. Armed. I saw an axe, and spears as well." Jojen had never sounded so much like the boy he was. "I saw them when the lightning flashed, moving under the trees."

"How many?"

"Many and more. Too many to count."

"Mounted?"

"No."

"Hodor." Hodor sounded frightened. "Hodor. Hodor."

Bran felt a little scared himself, though he didn't want to say so in front of Meera. "What if they come out here?"

"They won't." She sat down beside him. "Why should they?"

"For shelter." Jojen's voice was grim. "Unless the storm lets up. Meera, could you go down and bar the door?"

"I couldn't even close it. The wood's too warped. They won't get past those iron gates, though."

"They might. They could break the lock, or the hinges. Or climb up through the murder hole as we did."

Lightning slashed the sky, and Hodor whimpered. Then a clap of thunder rolled across the lake. "HODOR!" he roared, clapping his hands over his ears and stumbling in a circle through the darkness. "HODOR! HODOR! HODOR!"

"*NO!*" Bran shouted back. "NO HODORING!"

It did no good. "HOOOODOR!" moaned Hodor. Meera tried to catch him and calm him, but he was too strong. He flung her aside with no more than a shrug. "HOOOOOODOOOOOOOR!" the stableboy screamed as lightning filled the sky again, and even Jojen was shouting now, shouting at Bran and Meera to shut him up.

"Be *quiet!*" Bran said in a shrill scared voice, reaching up uselessly for Hodor's leg as he crashed past, reaching, *reaching*.

Hodor staggered, and closed his mouth. He shook his head slowly from side to side, sank back to the floor, and sat crosslegged. When the thunder boomed, he scarcely seemed to hear it. The four of them sat in the dark tower, scarce daring to breathe.

"Bran, what did you do?" Meera whispered.

"Nothing." Bran shook his head. "I don't know." But he did. *I reached for him, the way I reach for Summer.* He had *been* Hodor for half a heartbeat. It scared him.

"Something is happening across the lake," said Jojen. "I thought I saw a man pointing at the tower."

I won't be afraid. He was the Prince of Winterfell, Eddard Stark's son, almost a man grown and a warg too, not some little baby boy like Rickon. *Summer would not be afraid.* "Most like they're just some Umbers," he said. "Or they could be Knotts or Norreys or Flints come down from the mountains, or even brothers from the Night's Watch. Were they wearing black cloaks, Jojen?"

"By night all cloaks are black, Your Grace. And the flash came and went too fast for me to tell what they were wearing."

Meera was wary. "If they were black brothers, they'd be mounted, wouldn't they?"

Bran had thought of something else. "It doesn't matter," he said confidently. "They couldn't get out to us even if they wanted. Not unless they had a boat, or knew about the causeway."

"The causeway!" Meera mussed Bran's hair and kissed

him on the forehead. "Our sweet prince! He's right, Jojen,
they won't know about the causeway. Even if they did
they could never find the way across at night in the rain."

"The night will end, though. If they stay till
morning..." Jojen left the rest unsaid. After a few
moments he said, "They are feeding the fire the first man
started." Lightning crashed through the sky, and light
filled the tower and etched them all in shadow. Hodor
rocked back and forth, humming.

Bran could feel Summer's fear in that bright instant.
He closed two eyes and opened a third, and his boy's skin
slipped off him like a cloak as he left the tower behind...

...and found himself out in the rain, his belly full of
deer, cringing in the brush as the sky broke and boomed
above him. The smell of rotten apples and wet leaves
almost drowned the scent of man, but it was there. He
heard the clink and slither of hardskin, saw men moving
under the trees. A man with a stick blundered by, a skin
pulled up over his head to make him blind and deaf. The
wolf went wide around him, behind a dripping thornbush
and beneath the bare branches of an apple tree. He could
hear them talking, and there beneath the scents of rain
and leaves and horse came the sharp red stench of fear...

JON

The ground was littered with pine needles and blown leaves, a carpet of green and brown still damp from the recent rains. It squished beneath their feet. Huge bare oaks, tall sentinels, and hosts of soldier pines stood all around them. On a hill above them was another roundtower, ancient and empty, thick green moss crawling up its side almost to the summit. "Who built that, all of stone like that?" Ygritte asked him. "Some king?"

"No. Just the men who used to live here."

"What happened to them?"

"They died or went away." Brandon's Gift had been farmed for thousands of years, but as the Watch dwindled there were fewer hands to plow the fields, tend the bees, and plant the orchards, so the wild had reclaimed many a field and hall. In the New Gift there had been villages and holdfasts whose taxes, rendered in goods and labor, helped feed and clothe the black brothers. But those were largely gone as well.

"They were fools to leave such a castle," said Ygritte.

"It's only a towerhouse. Some little lordling lived there once, with his family and a few sworn men. When raiders came he would light a beacon from the roof. Winterfell has towers three times the size of that."

She looked as if she thought he was making that up.

"How could men build so high, with no giants to lift the stones?"

In legend, Brandon the Builder *had* used giants to help raise Winterfell, but Jon did not want to confuse the issue. "Men can build a lot higher than this. In Oldtown there's a tower taller than the Wall." He could tell she did not believe him. *If I could show her Winterfell . . . give her a flower from the glass gardens, feast her in the Great Hall, and show her the stone kings on their thrones. We could bathe in the hot pools, and love beneath the heart tree while the old gods watched over us.*

The dream was sweet . . . but Winterfell would never be his to show. It belonged to his brother, the King in the North. He was a Snow, not a Stark. *Bastard, oathbreaker, and turncloak . . .*

"Might be after we could come back here, and live in that tower," she said. "Would you want that, Jon Snow? After?"

After. The word was a spear thrust. *After the war. After the conquest. After the wildlings break the Wall . . .*

His lord father had once talked about raising new lords and settling them in the abandoned holdfasts as a shield against wildlings. The plan would have required the Watch to yield back a large part of the Gift, but his uncle Benjen believed the Lord Commander could be won around, so long as the new lordlings paid taxes to Castle Black rather than Winterfell. "It is a dream for spring, though," Lord Eddard had said. "Even the promise of land will not lure men north with a winter coming on."

If winter had come and gone more quickly and spring had followed in its turn, I might have been chosen to hold one of these towers in my father's name. Lord Eddard was dead, however, his brother Benjen lost; the shield they dreamt together would never be forged. "This land belongs to the Watch," Jon said.

Her nostrils flared. "No one lives here."

"Your raiders drove them off."

"They were cowards, then. If they wanted the land they should have stayed and fought."

"Maybe they were tired of fighting. Tired of barring

their doors every night and wondering if Rattleshirt or someone like him would break them down to carry off their wives. Tired of having their harvests stolen, and any valuables they might have. It's easier to move beyond the reach of raiders." *But if the Wall should fail, all the north will lie within the reach of raiders.*

"You know nothing, Jon Snow. Daughters are taken, not wives. *You're* the ones who steal. You took the whole world, and built the Wall t' keep the free folk out."

"Did we?" Sometimes Jon forgot how wild she was, and then she would remind him. "How did that happen?"

"The gods made the earth for all men t' share. Only when the kings come with their crowns and steel swords, they claimed it was all theirs. *My trees,* they said, *you can't eat them apples. My stream, you can't fish here. My wood, you're not t' hunt. My earth, my water, my castle, my daughter, keep your hands away or I'll chop 'em off, but maybe if you kneel t' me I'll let you have a sniff.* You call us thieves, but at least a thief has t' be brave and clever and quick. A kneeler only has t' kneel."

"Harma and the Bag of Bones don't come raiding for fish and apples. They steal swords and axes. Spices, silks, and furs. They grab every coin and ring and jeweled cup they can find, casks of wine in summer and casks of beef in winter, and they take women in any season and carry them off beyond the Wall."

"And what if they do? I'd sooner be stolen by a strong man than be given t' some weakling by my father."

"You say that, but how can you know? What if you were stolen by someone you hated?"

"He'd have t' be quick and cunning and brave t' steal *me.* So his sons would be strong and smart as well. Why would I hate such a man as that?"

"Maybe he never washes, so he smells as rank as a bear."

"Then I'd push him in a stream or throw a bucket o' water on him. Anyhow, men shouldn't smell sweet like flowers."

"What's wrong with flowers?"

"Nothing, for a bee. For bed I want one o' these." Ygritte made to grab the front of his breeches.

Jon caught her wrist. "What if the man who stole you drank too much?" he insisted. "What if he was brutal or cruel?" He tightened his grip to make a point. "What if he was stronger than you, and liked to beat you bloody?"

"I'd cut his throat while he slept. You know nothing, Jon Snow." Ygritte twisted like an eel and wrenched away from him.

I know one thing. I know that you are wildling to the bone. It was easy to forget that sometimes, when they were laughing together, or kissing. But then one of them would say something, or do something, and he would suddenly be reminded of the wall between their worlds.

"A man can own a woman or a man can own a knife," Ygritte told him, "but no man can own both. Every little girl learns that from her mother." She raised her chin defiantly and gave her thick red hair a shake. "And men can't own the land no more'n they can own the sea or the sky. You kneelers think you do, but Mance is going t' show you different."

It was a fine brave boast, but it rang hollow. Jon glanced back to make certain the Magnar was not in earshot. Errok, Big Boil, and Hempen Dan were walking a few yards behind them, but paying no attention. Big Boil was complaining of his arse. "Ygritte," he said in a low voice, "Mance cannot win this war."

"He can!" she insisted. "You know nothing, Jon Snow. You have never seen the free folk fight!"

Wildlings fought like heroes or demons, depending on who you talked to, but it came down to the same thing in the end. *They fight with reckless courage, every man out for glory.* "I don't doubt that you're all very brave, but when it comes to battle, discipline beats valor every time. In the end Mance will fail as all the Kings-beyond-the-Wall have failed before him. And when he does, you'll die. All of you."

Ygritte had looked so angry he thought she was about to strike him. "All of *us*," she said. "You too. You're no crow now, Jon Snow. I swore you weren't, so you better not be." She pushed him back against the trunk of a tree and kissed him, full on the lips right there in the midst of the ragged column. Jon heard Grigg the Goat urging her on. Someone else laughed. He kissed her back despite all that. When they finally broke apart, Ygritte was flushed. "You're mine," she whispered. "Mine, as I'm yours. And if we die, we die. All men must die, Jon Snow. But first we'll live."

"Yes." His voice was thick. "First we'll live."

She grinned at that, showing Jon the crooked teeth that he had somehow come to love. *Wildling to the bone*, he thought again, with a sick sad feeling in the pit of his stomach. He flexed the fingers of his sword hand, and wondered what Ygritte would do if she knew his heart. Would she betray him if he sat her down and told her that he was still Ned Stark's son and a man of the Night's Watch? He hoped not, but he dare not take that risk. Too many lives depended on his somehow reaching Castle Black before the Magnar . . . assuming he found a chance to escape the wildlings.

They had descended the south face of the Wall at Greyguard, abandoned for two hundred years. A section of the huge stone steps had collapsed a century before, but even so the descent was a good deal easier than the climb. From there Styr marched them deep into the Gift, to avoid the Watch's customary patrols. Grigg the Goat led them past the few inhabited villages that remained in these lands. Aside from a few scattered roundtowers poking the sky like stone fingers, they saw no sign of man. Through cold wet hills and windy plains they marched, unwatched, unseen.

You must not balk, whatever is asked of you, the Halfhand had said. *Ride with them, eat with them, fight with them, for as long as it takes.* He'd ridden many leagues and walked for more, had shared their bread and salt, and Ygritte's blankets as well, but still they did not trust him. Day and night the Thenns watched him, alert for any signs of betrayal. He could not get away, and soon it would be too late.

Fight with them, Qhorin had said, before he surrendered his own life to Longclaw . . . but it had not come to that, till now. *Once I shed a brother's blood I am lost. I cross the Wall for good then, and there is no crossing back.*

After each day's march the Magnar summoned him to ask shrewd sharp questions about Castle Black, its garrison and defenses. Jon lied where he dared and feigned ignorance a few times, but Grigg the Goat and Errok listened as well, and they knew enough to make Jon careful. Too blatant a lie would betray him.

But the truth was terrible. Castle Black had no defenses, but for the Wall itself. It lacked even wooden palisades or earthen dikes. The "castle" was nothing more than a cluster of towers and keeps, two-thirds of them falling into ruin. As for the garrison, the Old Bear had taken two hundred on his ranging. Had any returned? Jon could not know. Perhaps four hundred remained at the castle, but most of those were builders or stewards, not rangers.

The Thenns were hardened warriors, and more disciplined than the common run of wildling; no doubt that was why Mance had chosen them. The defenders of Castle Black would include blind Maester Aemon and his half-blind steward Clydas, one-armed Donal Noye, drunken Septon Cellador, Deaf Dick Follard, Three-Finger Hobb the cook, old Ser Wynton Stout, as well as Halder and Toad and Pyp and Albett and the rest of the boys who'd trained with Jon. And commanding them would be red-faced Bowen Marsh, the plump Lord Steward who had been made castellan in Lord Mormont's absence. Dolorous Edd sometimes called Marsh "the Old Pomegranate," which fit him just as well as "the Old Bear" fit Mormont. "He's the man you want in front when the foes are in the field," Edd would say in his usual dour voice. "He'll count them right up for you. A regular demon for counting, that one."

If the Magnar takes Castle Black unawares, it will be red slaughter, boys butchered in their beds before they know they are under attack. Jon had to warn them, but how? He was never sent out to forage or hunt, nor allowed to stand a watch alone. And he feared for Ygritte as well. He could not take her, but if he left her, would the Magnar make her answer for his treachery? *Two hearts that beat as one . . .*

They shared the same sleeping skins every night, and he went to sleep with her head against his chest and her red hair tickling his chin. The smell of her had become a part of him. Her crooked teeth, the feel of her breast when he cupped it in his hand, the taste of her mouth . . . they were his joy and his despair. Many a night he lay with Ygritte warm beside him, wondering if his lord father had felt this confused about his mother, whoever she had been. *Ygritte set the trap and Mance Rayder pushed me into it.*

Every day he spent among the wildlings made what he had to do that much harder. He was going to have to find some way to betray these men, and when he did they would die. He did not want their friendship, any more than he wanted Ygritte's love. And yet . . . the Thenns spoke the Old Tongue and seldom talked to Jon at all, but it was different with Jarl's raiders, the men who'd climbed the Wall. Jon was coming to know them despite himself: gaunt, quiet Errok and gregarious Grigg the Goat, the boys Quort and Bodger, Hempen Dan the ropemaker. The worst of the lot was Del, a horsefaced youth near Jon's own age, who would talk dreamily of this wildling girl he meant to steal. "She's lucky, like your Ygritte. She's kissed by fire."

Jon had to bite his tongue. He didn't want to know about Del's girl or Bodger's mother, the place by the sea that Henk the Helm came from, how Grigg yearned to visit the green men on the Isle of Faces, or the time a moose had chased Toefinger up a tree. He didn't want to hear about the boil on Big Boil's arse, how much ale Stone Thumbs could drink, or how Quort's little brother had begged him not to go with Jarl. Quort could not have been older than fourteen, though he'd already stolen himself a wife and had a child on the way. "Might be he'll be born in some castle," the boy boasted. "Born in a castle like a lord!" He was very taken with the "castles" they'd seen, by which he meant watchtowers.

Jon wondered where Ghost was now. Had he gone to

Castle Black, or was he was running with some wolfpack in the woods? He had no sense of the direwolf, not even in his dreams. It made him feel as if part of himself had been cut off. Even with Ygritte sleeping beside him, he felt alone. He did not want to die alone.

By that afternoon the trees had begun to thin, and they marched east over gently rolling plains. Grass rose waist high around them, and stands of wild wheat swayed gently when the wind came gusting, but for the most part the day was warm and bright. Toward sunset, however, clouds began to threaten in the west. They soon engulfed the orange sun, and Lenn foretold a bad storm coming. His mother was a woods witch, so all the raiders agreed he had a gift for foretelling the weather. "There's a village close," Grigg the Goat told the Magnar. "Two miles, three. We could shelter there." Styr agreed at once.

It was well past dark and the storm was raging by the time they reached the place. The village sat beside a lake, and had been so long abandoned that most of the houses had collapsed. Even the small timber inn that must once have been a welcome sight for travelers stood half-fallen and roofless. *We will find scant shelter here*, Jon thought gloomily. Whenever the lightning flashed he could see a stone roundtower rising from an island out in the lake, but without boats they had no way to reach it.

Errok and Del had crept ahead to scout the ruins, but Del was back almost at once. Styr halted the column and sent a dozen of his Thenns trotting forward, spears in hand. By then Jon had seen it too: the glimmer of a fire, reddening the chimney of the inn. *We are not alone.* Dread coiled inside him like a snake. He heard a horse neigh, and then shouts. *Ride with them, eat with them, fight with them*, Qhorin had said.

But the fighting was done. "There's only one of them," Errok said when he came back. "An old man with a horse."

The Magnar shouted commands in the Old Tongue and a score of his Thenns spread out to establish a perimeter around the village, whilst others went prowling through the houses to make certain no one else was hiding amongst the weeds and tumbled stones. The rest crowded into the roofless inn, jostling each other to get closer to the hearth. The broken branches the old man had been burning seemed to generate more smoke than heat, but any warmth was welcome on such a wild rainy night. Two of the Thenns had thrown the man to the ground and were going through his things. Another held his horse, while three more looted his saddlebags.

Jon walked away. A rotten apple squished beneath his heel. *Styr will kill him.* The Magnar had said as much at Greyguard; any kneelers they met were to be put to death at once, to make certain they could not raise the alarm. *Ride with them, eat with them, fight with them.* Did that mean he must stand mute and helpless while they slit an old man's throat?

Near the edge of the village, Jon came face-to-face with one of the guards Styr had posted. The Thenn growled something in the Old Tongue and pointed his spear back toward the inn. *Get back where you belong,* Jon guessed. *But where is that?*

He walked toward the water, and discovered an almost dry spot beneath the leaning daub-and-wattle wall of a tumbledown cottage that had mostly tumbled down. That was where Ygritte found him sitting, staring off across the rain-whipped lake. "I know this place," he told her when she sat beside him. "That tower ... look at the top of it the next time the lightning flashes, and tell me what you see."

"Aye, if you like," she said, and then, "Some o' the Thenns are saying they heard noises out there. Shouting, they say."

"Thunder."

"They say shouting. Might be it's ghosts."

The holdfast did have a grim haunted look, standing there black against the storm on its rocky island with the rain lashing at the lake all around it. "We could go out and take a look," he suggested. "I doubt we could get much wetter than we are."

"Swimming? In the storm?" She laughed at the notion. "Is this a trick t' get the clothes off me, Jon Snow?"

"Do I need a trick for that now?" he teased. "Or is it

that you can't swim a stroke?" Jon was a strong swimmer himself, having learned the art as a boy in Winterfell's great moat.

Ygritte punched his arm. "You know nothing, Jon Snow. I'm half a fish, I'll have you know."

"Half fish, half goat, half horse . . . there's too many halves to you, Ygritte." He shook his head. "We wouldn't need to swim, if this is the place I think. We could walk."

She pulled back and gave him a look. "Walk on water? What southron sorcery is that?"

"No sorc –" he began, as a huge bolt of lightning stabbed down from the sky and touched the surface of the lake. For half a heartbeat the world was noonday bright. The clap of thunder was so loud that Ygritte gasped and covered her ears.

"Did you look?" Jon asked, as the sound rolled away and the night turned black again. "Did you see?"

"Yellow," she said. "Is that what you meant? Some o' them standing stones on top were yellow."

"We call them merlons. They were painted gold a long time ago. This is Queenscrown."

Across the lake, the tower was black again, a dim shape dimly seen. "A queen lived there?" asked Ygritte.

"A queen stayed there for a night." Old Nan had told him the story, but Maester Luwin had confirmed most of it. "Alysanne, the wife of King Jaehaerys the Conciliator. He's called the Old King because he reigned so long, but he was young when he first came to the Iron Throne. In those days, it was his wont to travel all over the realm. When he came to Winterfell, he brought his queen, six dragons, and half his court. The king had matters to discuss with his Warden of the North, and Alysanne grew bored, so she mounted her dragon Silverwing and flew north to see the Wall. This village was one of the places where she stopped. Afterward the smallfolk painted the top of their holdfast to look like the golden crown she'd worn when she spent the night among them."

"I have never seen a dragon."

"No one has. The last dragons died a hundred years ago or more. But this was before that."

"Queen Alysanne, you say?"

"Good Queen Alysanne, they called her later. One of the castles on the Wall was named for her as well. Queensgate. Before her visit they called it Snowgate."

"If she was so good, she should have torn that Wall down."

No, he thought. *The Wall protects the realm. From the Others . . . and from you and your kind as well, sweetling.* "I had another friend who dreamed of dragons. A dwarf. He told me – "

"*JON SNOW!*" One of the Thenns loomed above them, frowning. "Magnar wants." Jon thought it might have been the same man who'd found him outside the cave, the night before they climbed the Wall, but he could not be sure. He got to his feet. Ygritte came with him, which always made Styr frown, but whenever he tried to dismiss her she would remind him that she was a free woman, not a kneeler. She came and went as she pleased.

They found the Magnar standing beneath the tree that grew through the floor of the common room. His captive knelt before the hearth, encircled by wooden spears and bronze swords. He watched Jon approach, but did not speak. The rain was running down the walls and pattering against the last few leaves that still clung to the tree, while smoke swirled thick from the fire.

"He must die," Styr the Magnar said. "Do it, crow."

The old man said no word. He only looked at Jon, standing amongst the wildlings. Amidst the rain and smoke, lit only by the fire, he could not have seen that Jon was all in black, but for his sheepskin cloak. *Or could he?*

Jon drew Longclaw from its sheath. Rain washed the steel, and the firelight traced a sullen orange line along the edge. *Such a small fire, to cost a man his life.* He remembered what Qhorin Halfhand had said when they spied the fire in the Skirling Pass. *Fire is life up here*, he told them, *but it can be death as well.* That was high in the Frostfangs, though, in the lawless wild beyond the Wall. This was the Gift, protected by the Night's Watch and the power of Winterfell. A man should have been free to build a fire here, without dying for it.

"Why do you hesitate?" Styr said. "Kill him, and be done."

Even then the captive did not speak. "Mercy," he might have said, or "You have taken my horse, my coin, my food, let me keep my life," or "No, please, I have done you no harm." He might have said a thousand things, or wept, or called upon his gods. No words would save him now, though. Perhaps he knew that. So he held his tongue, and looked at Jon in accusation and appeal.

You must not balk, whatever is asked of you. Ride with them, eat with them, fight with them ... But this old man had offered no resistance. He had been unlucky, that was all. Who he was, where he came from, where he meant to go on his sorry sway-backed horse ... none of it mattered.

He is an old man, Jon told himself. *Fifty, maybe even sixty. He lived a longer life than most. The Thenns will kill him anyway, nothing I can say or do will save him.* Longclaw seemed heavier than lead in his hand, too heavy to lift. The man kept staring at him, with eyes as big and black as wells. *I will fall into those eyes and drown.* The Magnar was looking at him too, and he could almost taste the mistrust. *The man is dead. What matter if it is my hand that slays him?* One cut would do it, quick and clean. Longclaw was forged of Valyrian steel. *Like Ice.* Jon remembered another killing; the deserter on his knees, his head rolling, the brightness of blood on snow ... his father's sword, his father's words, his father's face ...

"Do it, Jon Snow," Ygritte urged. "You must. T' prove you are no crow, but one o' the free folk."

"An old man sitting by a fire?"

"Orell was sitting by a fire too. You killed him quick enough." The look she gave him then was hard. "You meant t' kill me too, till you saw I was a woman. And I was asleep."

"That was different. You were soldiers ... sentries."

"Aye, and you crows didn't want t' be seen. No more'n we do, now. It's just the same. Kill him."

He turned his back on the man. "No."

The Magnar moved closer, tall, cold, and dangerous. "I say yes. I command here."

"You command Thenns," Jon told him, "not free folk."

"I see no free folk. I see a crow and a crow wife."

"I'm no crow wife!" Ygritte snatched her knife from its sheath. Three quick strides, and she yanked the old man's head back by the hair and opened his throat from ear to ear. Even in death, the man did not cry out. "You know *nothing*, Jon Snow!" she shouted at him, and flung the bloody blade at his feet.

The Magnar said something in the Old Tongue. He might have been telling the Thenns to kill Jon where he stood, but he would never know the truth of that. Lightning crashed down from the sky, a searing blue-white bolt that touched the top of the tower in the lake. They could smell the fury of it, and when the thunder came it seemed to shake the night.

And death leapt down amongst them.

The lightning flash left Jon night-blind, but he glimpsed the hurtling shadow half a heartbeat before he heard the shriek. The first Thenn died as the old man had, blood gushing from his torn throat. Then the light was gone and the shape was spinning away, snarling, and another man went down in the dark. There were curses, shouts, howls of pain. Jon saw Big Boil stumble backward and knock down three men behind him. *Ghost*, he thought for one mad instant. *Ghost leapt the Wall.* Then the lightning turned the night to day, and he saw the wolf standing on Del's chest, blood running black from his jaws. *Grey. He's grey.*

Darkness descended with the thunderclap. The Thenns were jabbing with their spears as the wolf darted between them. The old man's mare reared, maddened by the smell of slaughter, and lashed out with her hooves. Longclaw was still in his hand. All at once Jon Snow knew he would never get a better chance.

He cut down the first man as he turned toward the wolf, shoved past a second, slashed at a third. Through the madness he heard someone call his name, but whether it was Ygritte or the Magnar he could not say. The Thenn fighting to control the horse never saw him. Longclaw was feather-light. He swung at the back of the man's calf, and felt the steel bite down to the bone. When the wildling fell the mare bolted, but somehow Jon managed to grab her mane with his off hand and vault himself onto her back. A hand closed round his ankle, and he hacked down and saw Bodger's face dissolve in a welter of blood. The horse reared, lashing out. One hoof caught a Thenn in the temple, with a *crunch*.

And then they were running. Jon made no effort to guide the horse. It was all he could do to stay on her as they plunged through mud and rain and thunder. Wet grass whipped at his face and a spear flew past his ear. *If the horse stumbles and breaks a leg, they will run me down and kill me*, he thought, but the old gods were with him and the horse did not stumble. Lightning shivered through the black dome of sky, and thunder rolled across the plains. The shouts dwindled and died behind him.

Long hours later, the rain stopped. Jon found himself alone in a sea of tall black grass. There was a deep throbbing ache in his right thigh. When he looked down, he was surprised to see an arrow jutting out the back of it. *When did that happen?* He grabbed hold of the shaft and gave it a tug, but the arrowhead was sunk deep in the meat of his leg, and the pain when he pulled on it was excruciating. He tried to think back on the madness at the inn, but all he could remember was the beast, gaunt and grey and terrible. *It was too large to be a common wolf. A direwolf, then. It had to be.* He had never seen an animal move so fast. *Like a grey wind . . .* Could Robb have returned to the north?

Jon shook his head. He had no answers. It was too hard to think . . . about the wolf, the old man, Ygritte, any of it . . .

Clumsily, he slid down off the mare's back. His wounded leg buckled under him, and he had to swallow a scream. *This is going to be agony.* The arrow had to come out, though, and nothing good could come of waiting. Jon curled his hand around the fletching, took a deep breath, and shoved the arrow forward. He grunted, then cursed.

It hurt so much he had to stop. *I am bleeding like a butchered pig*, he thought, but there was nothing to be done for it until the arrow was out. He grimaced and tried again . . . and soon stopped again, trembling. *Once more.* This time he screamed, but when he was done the arrowhead was poking through the front of his thigh. Jon pushed back his bloody breeches to get a better grip, grimaced, and slowly drew the shaft through his leg. How he got through that without fainting he never knew.

He lay on the ground afterward, clutching his prize and bleeding quietly, too weak to move. After a while, he realized that if he did not *make* himself move he was like to bleed to death. Jon crawled to the shallow stream where the mare was drinking, washed his thigh in the cold water, and bound it tight with a strip of cloth torn from his cloak. He washed the arrow too, turning it in his hands. Was the fletching grey, or white? Ygritte fletched her arrows with pale grey goose feathers. *Did she loose a shaft at me as I fled?* Jon could not blame her for that. He wondered if she'd been aiming for him or the horse. If the mare had gone down, he would have been doomed. "A lucky thing my leg got in the way," he muttered.

He rested for a while to let the horse graze. She did not wander far. That was good. Hobbled with a bad leg, he could never have caught her. It was all he could do to force himself back to his feet and climb onto her back. *How did I ever mount her before, without saddle or stirrups, and a sword in one hand?* That was another question he could not answer.

Thunder rumbled softly in the distance, but above him the clouds were breaking up. Jon searched the sky until he found the Ice Dragon, then turned the mare north for the Wall and Castle Black. The throb of pain in his thigh muscle made him wince as he put his heels into the old man's horse. *I am going home*, he told himself. But if that was true, why did he feel so hollow?

He rode till dawn, while the stars stared down like eyes.

APPENDIX
THE KINGS
AND THEIR COURTS

THE KING ON THE IRON THRONE

JOFFREY BARATHEON, the First of His Name, a boy
of thirteen years, the eldest son of King Robert I
Baratheon and Queen Cersei of House Lannister,
— his mother, QUEEN CERSEI, of House Lannister,
Queen Regent and Protector of the Realm,
— Cersei's sworn swords:
— SER OSFRYD KETTLEBLACK, younger
brother to Ser Osmund Kettleblack of the
Kingsguard,
— SER OSNEY KETTLEBLACK, youngest
brother of Ser Osmund and Ser Osfryd,
— his sister, PRINCESS MYRCELLA, a girl of nine,
a ward of Prince Doran Martell at Sunspear,
— his brother, PRINCE TOMMEN, a boy of eight,
next heir to the Iron Throne,
— his grandfather, TYWIN LANNISTER, Lord of
Casterly Rock, Warden of the West, and Hand of
the King,
— his uncles and cousins, paternal,
— his father's brother, STANNIS BARA-
THEON, rebel Lord of Dragonstone, styling
himself King Stannis the First,
— Stannis's daughter, SHIREEN, a girl of
eleven,
— his father's brother, {RENLY BARATHEON},

rebel Lord of Storm's End, murdered in the midst of his army,
— his grandmother's brother, SER ELDON ESTERMONT,
  — Ser Eldon's son, SER AEMON ESTERMONT,
    — Ser Aemon's son, SER ALYN ESTERMONT,
— his uncles and cousins, maternal,
  — his mother's brother, SER JAIME LANNISTER, called THE KINGSLAYER, a captive at Riverrun,
  — his mother's brother, TYRION LANNISTER, called THE IMP, a dwarf, wounded in the Battle of the Blackwater,
    — Tyrion's squire, PODRICK PAYNE,
    — Tyrion's captain of guards, SER BRONN OF THE BLACKWATER, a former sellsword,
    — Tyrion's concubine, SHAE, a camp follower now serving as bedmaid to Lollys Stokeworth,
  — his grandfather's brother, SER KEVAN LANNISTER,
    — Ser Kevan's son, SER LANCEL LANNISTER, formerly squire to King Robert, wounded in the Battle of the Blackwater, near death,
  — his grandfather's brother, {TYGETT LANNISTER}, died of a pox,
    — Tygett's son, TYREK LANNISTER, a squire, missing since the great riot,
      — Tyrek's infant wife, LADY ERMESANDE HAYFORD,
— his baseborn siblings, King Robert's bastards:
  — MYA STONE, a maid of nineteen, in the service of Lord Nestor Royce, of the Gates of the Moon,
  — GENDRY, an apprentice smith, a fugitive in the riverlands and ignorant of his heritage,

— EDRIC STORM, King Robert's only acknowledged bastard son, a ward of his uncle Stannis
on Dragonstone,

— his Kingsguard:
— SER JAIME LANNISTER, Lord Commander,
— SER MERYN TRANT,
— SER BALON SWANN,
— SER OSMUND KETTLEBLACK,
— SER LORAS TYRELL, the Knight of Flowers,
— SER ARYS OAKHEART,

— his small council:
— LORD TYWIN LANNISTER, Hand of the
King,
— SER KEVAN LANNISTER, master of laws,
— LORD PETYR BAELISH, called LITTLE-
FINGER, master of coin,
— VARYS, a eunuch, called THE SPIDER,
master of whisperers,
— LORD MACE TYRELL, master of ships,
— GRAND MAESTER PYCELLE,

— his court and retainers:
— SER ILYN PAYNE, the King's Justice, a
headsman,
— LORD HALLYNE THE PYROMANCER, a
Wisdom of the Guild of Alchemists,
— MOON BOY, a jester and fool,
— ORMOND OF OLDTOWN, the royal harper
and bard,
— DONTOS HOLLARD, a fool and a drunkard,
formerly a knight called SER DONTOS THE
RED,
— JALABHAR XHO, Prince of the Red Flower
Vale, an exile from the Summer Isles,
— LADY TANDA STOKEWORTH,
— her daughter, FALYSE, wed to Ser Balman
Byrch,
— her daughter, LOLLYS, thirty-four,

unwed, and soft of wits, with child after being raped,
— her healer and counselor, MAESTER FRENKEN,
— LORD GYLES ROSBY, a sickly old man,
— SER TALLAD, a promising young knight,
— LORD MORROS SLYNT, a squire, eldest son of the former Commander of the City Watch,
  — JOTHOS SLYNT, his younger brother, a squire,
  — DANOS SLYNT, younger still, a page,
— SER BOROS BLOUNT, a former knight of the Kingsguard, dismissed for cowardice by Queen Cersei,
— JOSMYN PECKLEDON, a squire, and a hero of the Battle of the Blackwater,
— SER PHILIP FOOTE, made Lord of the Marches for his valor during the Battle of the Blackwater,
— SER LOTHOR BRUNE, named LOTHOR APPLE-EATER for his deeds during the Battle of the Blackwater, a former freerider in service to Lord Baelish,
— other lords and knights at King's Landing:
  — MATHIS ROWAN, Lord of Goldengrove,
  — PAXTER REDWYNE, Lord of the Arbor,
    — Lord Paxter's twin sons, SER HORAS and SER HOBBER, mocked as HORROR and SLOBBER,
    — Lord Redwyne's healer, MAESTER BALLABAR,
  — ARDRIAN CELTIGAR, the Lord of Claw Isle,
  — LORD ALESANDER STAEDMON, called PENNYLOVER,
  — SER BONIFER HASTY, called THE GOOD, a famed knight,
  — SER DONNEL SWANN, heir to Stonehelm,
  — SER RONNET CONNINGTON, called RED RONNET, the Knight of Griffin's Roost,

— AURANE WATERS, the Bastard of Driftmark,
— SER DERMOT OF THE RAINWOOD, a
  famed knight,
— SER TIMON SCRAPESWORD, a famed
  knight,

— the people of King's Landing:
  — the City Watch (the "gold cloaks"),
    — {SER JACELYN BYWATER, called
      IRONHAND}, Commander of the City
      Watch, slain by his own men during the
      Battle of the Blackwater,
    — SER ADDAM MARBRAND, Com-
      mander of the City Watch, Ser Jacelyn's
      successor,
  — CHATAYA, owner of an expensive brothel,
    — ALAYAYA, her daughter,
    — DANCY, MAREI, JAYDE, Chataya's
      girls,
  — TOBHO MOTT, a master armorer,
  — IRONBELLY, a blacksmith,
  — HAMISH THE HARPER, a famed singer,
  — COLLIO QUAYNIS, a Tyroshi singer,
  — BETHANY FAIR-FINGERS, a woman singer,
  — ALARIC OF EYSEN, a singer, far-traveled,
  — GALYEON OF CUY, a singer notorious for
    the length of his songs,
  — SYMON SILVER TONGUE, a singer.

King Joffrey's banner shows the crowned stag of Baratheon,
black on gold, and the lion of Lannister, gold on crimson,
combatant.

THE KING IN THE NORTH
THE KING OF THE TRIDENT

ROBB STARK, Lord of Winterfell, King in the North, and King of the Trident, the eldest son of Eddard Stark, Lord of Winterfell, and Lady Catelyn of House Tully,

— his direwolf, GREY WIND,
— his mother, LADY CATELYN, of House Tully, widow of Lord Eddard Stark,
— his siblings:
  — his sister, PRINCESS SANSA, a maid of twelve, a captive in King's Landing,
    — Sansa's direwolf, {LADY}, killed at Castle Darry,
  — his sister, PRINCESS ARYA, a girl of ten, missing and presumed dead,
    — Arya's direwolf, NYMERIA, lost near the Trident,
  — his brother, PRINCE BRANDON, called BRAN, heir to the north, a boy of nine, believed dead,
    — Bran's direwolf, SUMMER,
    — Bran companions and protectors:
      — MEERA REED, a maid of sixteen, daughter of Lord Howland Reed of Greywater Watch,
      — JOJEN REED, her brother, thirteen,

— HODOR, a simpleminded stableboy, seven feet tall,
— his brother, PRINCE RICKON, a boy of four, believed dead,
  — Rickon's direwolf, SHAGGYDOG,
  — Rickon's companion and protector:
    — OSHA, a wildling captive who served as a scullion at Winterfell,
— his half-brother, JON SNOW, a Sworn Brother of the Night's Watch,
  — Jon's direwolf, GHOST,

— his uncles and aunts, paternal:
  — his father's elder brother, {BRANDON STARK}, slain at the command of King Aerys II Targaryen,
  — his father's sister, {LYANNA STARK}, died in the Mountains of Dorne during Robert's Rebellion,
  — his father's younger brother, BENJEN STARK, a man of the Night's Watch, lost beyond the Wall,
— his uncles, aunts, and cousins, maternal:
  — his mother's younger sister, LYSA ARRYN, Lady of the Eyrie and widow of Lord Jon Arryn,
    — their son, ROBERT ARRYN, Lord of the Eyrie,
  — his mother's younger brother, SER EDMURE TULLY, heir to Riverrun,
  — his grandfather's brother, SER BRYNDEN TULLY, called THE BLACKFISH,
— his sworn swords and companions:
  — his squire, OLYVAR FREY,
  — SER WENDEL MANDERLY, second son to the Lord of White Harbor,
  — PATREK MALLISTER, heir to Seagard,
  — DACEY MORMONT, eldest daughter of Lady Maege Mormont and heir to Bear Island,
  — JON UMBER, called THE SMALLJON, heir to Last Hearth,

— DONNEL LOCKE, OWEN NORREY, ROBIN FLINT, northmen,

— his lords bannermen, captains and commanders:
— (with Robb's army in the Westerlands)
   — SER BRYNDEN TULLY, the BLACKFISH, commanding the scouts and outriders,
   — JON UMBER, called THE GREATJON, commanding the van,
   — RICKARD KARSTARK, Lord of Karhold,
   — GALBART GLOVER, Master of Deepwood Motte,
   — MAEGE MORMONT, Lady of Bear Island,
   — {SER STEVRON FREY}, eldest son of Lord Walder Frey and heir to the Twins, died at Oxcross,
      — Ser Stevron's eldest son, SER RYMAN FREY,
         — Ser Ryman's son, BLACK WALDER FREY,
   — MARTYN RIVERS, a bastard son of Lord Walder Frey,

— (with Roose Bolton's host at Harrenhal),
   — ROOSE BOLTON, Lord of the Dreadfort,
   — SER AENYS FREY, SER JARED FREY, SER HOSTEEN FREY, SER DANWELL FREY
      — their bastard half-brother, RONEL RIVERS,
   — SER WYLIS MANDERLY, heir to White Harbor,
      — SER KYLE CONDON, a knight in his service,
   — RONNEL STOUT,
   — VARGO HOAT of the Free City of Qohor, captain of a sellsword company, the Brave Companions,
      — his lieutenant, URSWYCK called THE FAITHFUL,
      — his lieutenant, SEPTON UTT,

— TIMEON OF DORNE, RORGE, IGGO, FAT ZOLLO, BITER, TOGG JOTH of Ibben, PYG, THREE TOES, his men,
— QYBURN, a chainless maester and sometime necromancer, his healer,

— (with the northern army attacking Duskendale)
— ROBETT GLOVER, of Deepwood Motte,
— SER HELMAN TALLHART, of Torrhen's Square,
— HARRION KARSTARK, sole surviving son of Lord Rickard Karstark, and heir to Karhold,

— (traveling north with Lord Eddard's bones)
— HALLIS MOLLEN, captain of guards for Winterfell,
— JACKS, QUENT, SHADD, guardsmen,

— his lord bannermen and castellans, in the north:
— WYMAN MANDERLY, Lord of White Harbor,
— HOWLAND REED, Lord of Greywater Watch, a crannogman,
— MORS UMBER, called CROWFOOD, and HOTHER UMBER, called WHORESBANE, uncles to Greatjon Umber, joint castellans at the Last Hearth,
— LYESSA FLINT, Lady of Widow's Watch,
— ONDREW LOCKE, Lord of Oldcastle, an old man,
— {CLEY CERWYN}, Lord of Cerwyn, a boy of fourteen, killed in battle at Winterfell,
— his sister, JONELLE CERWYN, a maid of two-and-thirty, now the Lady of Cerwyn,
— {LEOBALD TALLHART}, younger brother to Ser Helman, castellan at Torrhen's Square, killed in battle at Winterfell,
— Leobald's wife, BERENA of House Hornwood,

— Leobald's son, BRANDON, a boy of fourteen,

— Leobald's son, BEREN, a boy of ten,

— Ser Helman's son, {BENFRED}, killed by ironmen on the Stony Shore,

— Ser Helman's daughter, EDDARA, a girl of nine, heir to Torrhen's Square,

— LADY SYBELLE, wife to Robett Glover, a captive of Asha Greyjoy at Deepwood Motte,

— Robett's son, GAWEN, three, rightful heir to Deepwood Motte, a captive of Asha Greyjoy,

— Robett's daughter, ERENA, a babe of one, a captive of Asha Greyjoy at Deepwood Motte,

— LARENCE SNOW, a bastard son of Lord Hornwood, and ward of Galbart Glover, thirteen, a captive of Asha Greyjoy at Deepwood Motte.

The banner of the King in the North remains as it has for thousands of years: the grey direwolf of the Starks of Winterfell, running across an ice-white field.

THE KING IN THE NARROW SEA

STANNIS BARATHEON, the First of His Name, second son of Lord Steffon Baratheon and Lady Cassana of House Estermont, formerly Lord of Dragonstone,
— his wife, QUEEN SELYSE of House Florent,
— PRINCESS SHIREEN, their daughter, a girl of eleven,
— PATCHFACE, her lackwit fool,
— his baseborn nephew, EDRIC STORM, a boy of twelve, bastard son of King Robert by Delena Florent,
— his squires, DEVAN SEAWORTH and BRYEN FARRING,
— his court and retainers:
— LORD ALESTER FLORENT, Lord of Brightwater Keep and Hand of the King, the queen's uncle,
— SER AXELL FLORENT, castellan of Dragonstone and leader of the queen's men, the queen's uncle,
— LADY MELISANDRE OF ASSHAI, called THE RED WOMAN, priestess of R'hllor, the Lord of Light and God of Flame and Shadow,
— MAESTER PYLOS, healer, tutor, counselor,
— SER DAVOS SEAWORTH, called THE

ONION KNIGHT and sometimes SHORT-
HAND, once a smuggler,
— Davos's wife, LADY MARYA, a carpen-
ter's daughter,
— their seven sons:
— {DALE}, lost on the Blackwater,
— {ALLARD}, lost on the Black-
water,
— {MATTHOS}, lost on the Black-
water,
— {MARIC}, lost on the Blackwater,
— DEVAN, squire to King Stannis,
— STANNIS, a boy of nine years,
— STEFFON, a boy of six years,
— SALLADHOR SAAN, of the Free City of Lys,
styling himself Prince of the Narrow Sea and
Lord of Blackwater Bay, master of the *Valyr-
ian* and a fleet of sister galleys,
— MEIZO MAHR, a eunuch in his hire,
— KHORANE SATHMANTES, captain of
his galley *Shayala's Dance*,
— "PORRIDGE" and "LAMPREY," two
gaolers,

— his lords bannermen,
— MONTERYS VELARYON, Lord of the Tides
and Master of Driftmark, a boy of six,
— DURAM BAR EMMON, Lord of Sharp Point,
a boy of fifteen years,
— SER GILBERT FARRING, castellan of
Storm's End,
— LORD ELWOOD MEADOWS, Ser Gil-
bert's second,
— MAESTER JURNE, Ser Gilbert's coun-
selor and healer,
— LORD LUCOS CHYTTERING, called
LITTLE LUCOS, a youth of sixteen,
— LESTER MORRIGEN, Lord of Crows Nest,

— his knights and sworn swords,

— SER LOMAS ESTERMONT, the king's maternal uncle,
  — his son, SER ANDREW ESTERMONT,
— SER ROLLAND STORM, called THE BASTARD OF NIGHTSONG, a baseborn son of the late Lord Bryen Caron,
— SER PARMEN CRANE, called PARMEN THE PURPLE, held captive at Highgarden,
— SER ERREN FLORENT, younger brother to Queen Selyse, held captive at Highgarden,
— SER GERALD GOWER,
— SER TRISTON OF TALLY HILL, formerly in service to Lord Guncer Sunglass,
— LEWYS, called THE FISHWIFE,
— OMER BLACKBERRY.

King Stannis has taken for his banner the fiery heart of the Lord of Light: a red heart surrounded by orange flames upon a yellow field. Within the heart is the crowned stag of House Baratheon, in black.

THE QUEEN ACROSS THE WATER

DAENERYS TARGARYEN, the First of Her Name, *Khaleesi* of the Dothraki, called DAENERYS STORMBORN, the UNBURNT, MOTHER OF DRAGONS, sole surviving heir of Aerys II Targaryen, widow of Khal Drogo of the Dothraki,
— her growing dragons, DROGON, VISERION, RHAEGAL,
— her Queensguard:
  — SER JORAH MORMONT, formerly Lord of Bear Island, exiled for slaving,
  — JHOGO, *ko* and bloodrider, the whip,
  — AGGO, *ko* and bloodrider, the bow,
  — RAKHARO, *ko* and bloodrider, the *arakh*,
  — STRONG BELWAS, a former eunuch slave from the fighting pits of Meereen,
    — his aged squire, ARSTAN called WHITE-BEARD, a man of Westeros,
— her handmaids:
  — IRRI, a Dothraki girl, fifteen,
  — JHIQUI, a Dothraki girl, fourteen,
— GROLEO, captain of the great cog *Balerion*, a Pentoshi seafarer in the hire of Illyrio Mopatis,

— her late kin:
  — {RHAEGAR}, her brother, Prince of Dragonstone and heir to the Iron Throne,

slain by Robert Baratheon on the Trident,
— {RHAENYS}, Rhaegar's daughter by Elia
  of Dorne, murdered during the Sack of
  King's Landing,
— {AEGON}, Rhaegar's son by Elia of
  Dorne, murdered during the Sack of
  King's Landing,
— {VISERYS}, her brother, styling himself King
  Viserys, the Third of His Name, called THE
  BEGGAR KING, slain in Vaes Dothrak by
  Khal Drogo,
— {DROGO}, her husband, a great *khal* of the
  Dothraki, never defeated in battle, died of a
  wound,
    — {RHAEGO}, her stillborn son by Khal
      Drogo, slain in the womb by Mirri Maz
      Duur,

— her known enemies:
  — KHAL PONO, once *ko* to Drogo,
  — KHAL JHAQO, once *ko* to Drogo,
    — MAGGO, his bloodrider,
  — THE UNDYING OF QARTH, a band of
    warlocks,
    — PYAT PREE, a Qartheen warlock,
  — THE SORROWFUL MEN, a guild of Qar-
    theen assassins,

— her uncertain allies, past and present:
  — XARO XHOAN DAXOS, a merchant prince
    of Qarth,
  — QUAITHE, a masked shadowbinder from
    Asshai,
  — ILLYRIO MOPATIS, a magister of the Free
    City of Pentos, who brokered her marriage to
    Khal Drogo,

— in Astapor:
  — KRAZNYS MO NAKLOZ, a wealthy slave
    trader,

— his slave, MISSANDEI, a girl of ten, of
the Peaceful People of Naath,
— GRAZDAN MO ULLHOR, an old slave
trader, very rich,
— his slave, CLEON, a butcher and cook,
— GREY WORM, a eunuch of the Unsullied,

— in Yunkai:
— GRAZDAN MO ERAZ, envoy and noble-
man,
— MERO OF BRAAVOS, called THE TITAN'S
BASTARD, captain of the Second Sons, a free
company,
— BROWN BEN PLUMM, a sergeant in the
Second Sons, a sellsword of dubious
descent,
— PRENDAHL NA GHEZN, a Ghiscari sell-
sword, captain of the Stormcrows, a free
company,
— SALLOR THE BALD, a Qartheen sellsword,
captain of the Stormcrows,
— DAARIO NAHARIS, a flamboyant Tyroshi
sellsword, captain of the Stormcrows,

— in Meereen:
— OZNAK ZO PAHL, a hero of the city.

The banner of Daenerys Targaryen is the banner of Aegon
the Conqueror and the dynasty he established: a three-
headed dragon, red on black.

KING OF THE ISLES
AND THE NORTH

BALON GREYJOY, the Ninth of His Name Since the Grey
    King, styling himself King of the Iron Islands and
    the North, King of Salt and Rock, Son of the Sea
    Wind, and Lord Reaper of Pyke,
    — his wife, QUEEN ALANNYS, of House Harlaw,
    — their children:
        — {RODRIK}, their eldest son, slain at Seagard
            during Greyjoy's Rebellion,
        — {MARON}, their second son, slain at Pyke
            during Greyjoy's Rebellion,
        — ASHA, their daughter, captain of the *Black
            Wind* and conqueror of Deepwood Motte,
        — THEON, their youngest son, captain of the
            Sea Bitch and briefly Prince of Winterfell,
            — Theon's squire, WEX PYKE, bastard son
                of Lord Botley's half-brother, a mute lad
                of twelve,
            — Theon's crew, the men of the *Sea Bitch*:
                — URZEN, MARON BOTLEY called
                    FISHWHISKERS, STYGG, GEVIN
                    HARLAW, CADWYLE,

    — his brothers:
        — EURON, called Crow's Eye, captain of the
            Silence, a notorious outlaw, pirate, and
            raider,

- VICTARION, Lord Captain of the Iron Fleet, master of the *Iron Victory*,
- AERON, called DAMPHAIR, a priest of the Drowned God,
- his household on Pyke:
  - MAESTER WENDAMYR, healer and counselor,
  - HELYA, keeper of the castle,
- his warriors and sworn swords:
  - DAGMER called CLEFTJAW, captain of *Foamdrinker*,
  - BLUETOOTH, a longship captain,
  - ULLER, SKYTE, oarsmen and warriors,
  - ANDRIK THE UNSMILING, a giant of a man,
  - QARL, called QARL THE MAID, beardless but deadly,

- people of Lordsport:
  - OTTER GIMPKNEE, innkeeper and whoremonger,
  - SIGRIN, a shipwright,

- his lords bannermen:
  - SAWANE BOTLEY, Lord of Lordsport, on Pyke,
  - LORD WYNCH, of Iron Holt, on Pyke,
  - STONEHOUSE, DRUMM, and GOODBROTHER of Old Wyk,
  - LORD GOODBROTHER, SPARR, LORD MERLYN, and LORD FARWYND of Great Wyk,
  - LORD HARLAW, of Harlaw,
  - VOLMARK, MYRE, STONETREE, and KENNING, of Harlaw,
  - ORKWOOD and TAWNEY of Orkmont,
  - LORD BLACKTYDE of Blacktyde,
  - LORD SALTCLIFFE and LORD SUNDERLY of Saltcliffe.

OTHER HOUSES GREAT
AND SMALL

HOUSE ARRYN

The Arryns are descended from the Kings of Mountain and Vale, one of the oldest and purest lines of Andal nobility. House Arryn has taken no part in the War of the Five Kings, holding back its strength to protect the Vale of Arryn. The Arryn sigil is the moon-and-falcon, white, upon a sky-blue field. The Arryn words are *As High As Honor*.

ROBERT ARRYN, Lord of the Eyrie, Defender of the Vale, Warden of the East, a sickly boy of eight years,
— his mother, LADY LYSA, of House Tully, third wife and widow of Lord Jon Arryn, and sister to Catelyn Stark,
— their household:
— MARILLION, a handsome young singer, much favored by Lady Lysa,
— MAESTER COLEMON, counselor, healer, and tutor,
— SER MARWYN BELMORE, captain of guards,
— MORD, a brutal gaoler,

— his lords bannermen, knights, and retainers:
— LORD NESTOR ROYCE, High Steward of the Vale and castellan of the Gates of the Moon, of the junior branch of House Royce,
— Lord Nestor's son, SER ALBAR,

— Lord Nestor's daughter, MYRANDA,
— MYA STONE, a bastard girl in his service, natural daughter of King Robert I Baratheon,
— LORD YOHN ROYCE, called BRONZE YOHN, Lord of Runestone, of the senior branch of House Royce, cousin to Lord Nestor,
  — Lord Yohn's eldest son, SER ANDAR,
  — Lord Yohn's second son, {SER ROBAR}, a knight of Renly Baratheon's Rainbow Guard, slain at Storm's End by Ser Loras Tyrell,
  — Lord Yohn's youngest son, {SER WAYMAR}, a man of the Night's Watch, lost beyond the Wall,
— SER LYN CORBRAY, a suitor to Lady Lysa,
  — MYCHEL REDFORT, his squire,
— LADY ANYA WAYNWOOD,
  — Lady Anya's eldest son and heir, SER MORTON, a suitor to Lady Lysa,
  — Lady Anya's second son, SER DONNEL, the Knight of the Gate,
— EON HUNTER, Lord of Longbow Hall, an old man, and a suitor to Lady Lysa,
— HORTON REDFORT, Lord of Redfort.

HOUSE FLORENT

The Florents of Brightwater Keep are Tyrell bannermen, despite a superior claim to Highgarden by virtue of a blood tie to House Gardener, the old Kings of the Reach. At the outbreak of the War of the Five Kings, Lord Alester Florent followed the Tyrells in declaring for King Renly, but his brother Ser Axell chose King Stannis, whom he had served for years as castellan of Dragonstone. Their niece Selyse was and is King Stannis's queen. When Renly died at Storm's End, the Florents went over to Stannis with all their strength, the first of Renly's bannermen to do so. The sigil of House Florent shows a fox head in a circle of flowers.

ALESTER FLORENT, Lord of Brightwater,
— his wife, LADY MELARA, of House Crane,
— their children:
— ALEKYNE, heir to Brightwater,
— MELESSA, wed to Lord Randyll Tarly,
— RHEA, wed to Lord Leyton Hightower,
— his siblings:
— SER AXELL, castellan of Dragonstone,
— {SER RYAM}, died in a fall from a horse,
— Ser Ryam's daughter, QUEEN SELYSE, wed to King Stannis Baratheon,
— Ser Ryam's son, {SER IMRY}, commanding Stannis Baratheon's fleet on the Blackwater, lost with the *Fury*,

— Ser Ryam's second son, SER ERREN, held
  captive at Highgarden,
— SER COLIN,
   — Ser Colin's daughter, DELENA, wed to
     SER HOSMAN NORCROSS,
      — Delena's son, EDRIC STORM, a
        bastard of King Robert I Baratheon,
        twelve years of age,
      — Delena's son, ALESTER NORCROSS,
        eight,
      — Delena's son, RENLY NORCROSS, a
        boy of two,
   — Ser Colin's son, MAESTER OMER, in ser-
     vice at Old Oak,
   — Ser Colin's son, MERRELL, a squire on
     the Arbor,
— his sister, RYLENE, wed to Ser Rycherd
  Crane.

HOUSE FREY

Powerful, wealthy, and numerous, the Freys are bannermen to House Tully, but they have not always been diligent in their duty. When Robert Baratheon met Rhaegar Targaryen on the Trident, the Freys did not arrive until the battle was done, and thereafter Lord Hoster Tully always called Lord Walder "the Late Lord Frey." It is also said of Walder Frey that he is the only lord in the Seven Kingdoms who could field an army out of his breeches.

At the onset of the War of the Five Kings, Robb Stark won Lord Walder's allegiance by pledging to wed one of his daughters or granddaughters. Two of Lord Walder's grandsons were sent to Winterfell to be fostered.

WALDER FREY, Lord of the Crossing,
— by his first wife, {LADY PERRA, of House Royce}:
— {SER STEVRON}, their eldest son, died after the Battle of Oxcross,
— m. {Corenna Swann, died of a wasting illness},
— Stevron's eldest son, SER RYMAN, heir to the Twins,
— Ryman's son, EDWYN, wed to Janyce Hunter,
— Edwyn's daughter, WALDA, a girl of eight,
— Ryman's son, WALDER, called BLACK WALDER,

— Ryman's son, PETYR, called PETYR PIMPLE,
   — m. Mylenda Caron,
   — Petyr's daughter, PERRA, a girl of five,
— m. {Jeyne Lydden, died in a fall from a horse},
— Stevron's son, AEGON, a halfwit called JINGLEBELL,
— Stevron's daughter, {MAEGELLE, died in childbed}, m. Ser Dafyn Vance,
   — Maegelle's daughter, MARIANNE, a maiden,
   — Maegelle's son, WALDER VANCE, a squire,
   — Maegelle's son, PATREK VANCE,
— m. {Marsella Waynwood, died in childbed},
— Stevron's son, WALTON, m. Deana Hardyng,
   — Walton's son, STEFFON, called THE SWEET,
   — Walton's daughter, WALDA, called FAIR WALDA,
   — Walton's son, BRYAN, a squire,
— SER EMMON, m. Genna of House Lannister,
   — Emmon's son, SER CLEOS, m. Jeyne Darry,
      — Cleos's son, TYWIN, a squire of eleven,
      — Cleos's son, WILLEM, a page at Ashemark, nine,
   — Emmon's son, SER LYONEL, m. Melesa Crakehall,
   — Emmon's son, TION, a captive at Riverrun,
   — Emmon's son, WALDER, called RED WALDER, fourteen, a squire at Casterly Rock,

— SER AENYS, m. {Tyana Wylde, died in childbed},
  — Aenys's son, AEGON BLOODBORN, an outlaw,
  — Aenys's son, RHAEGAR, m. Jeyne Beesbury,
    — Rhaegar's son, ROBERT, a boy of thirteen,
    — Rhaegar's daughter, WALDA, a girl of ten, called WHITE WALDA,
    — Rhaegar's son, JONOS, a boy of eight,
— PERRIANE, m. Ser Leslyn Haigh,
  — Perriane's son, SER HARYS HAIGH,
    — Harys's son, WALDER HAIGH, a boy of four,
  — Perriane's son, SER DONNEL HAIGH,
  — Perriane's son, ALYN HAIGH, a squire,

— by his second wife, {LADY CYRENNA, of House Swann}:
  — SER JARED, their eldest son, m. {Alys Frey},
    — Jared's son, SER TYTOS, m. Zhoe Blanetree,
      — Tytos's daughter, ZIA, a maid of fourteen,
      — Tytos's son, ZACHERY, a boy of twelve, training at the Sept of Old-town,
    — Jared's daughter, KYRA, m. Ser Garse Goodbrook,
      — Kyra's son, WALDER GOODBROOK, a boy of nine,
      — Kyra's daughter, JEYNE GOOD-BROOK, six,
  — SEPTON LUCEON, in service at the Great Sept of Baelor in King's Landing,

— by his third wife, {LADY AMAREI of House Crakehall}:

— SER HOSTEEN, their eldest son, m. Bellena Hawick,
  — Hosteen's son, SER ARWOOD, m. Ryella Royce,
    — Arwood's daughter, RYELLA, a girl of five,
    — Arwood's twin sons, ANDROW and ALYN, three,
— LADY LYTHENE, m. Lord Lucias Vypren,
  — Lythene's daughter, ELYANA, m. Ser Jon Wylde,
    — Elyana's son, RICKARD WYLDE, four,
  — Lythene's son, SER DAMON VYPREN,
— SYMOND, m. Betharios of Braavos,
  — Symond's son, ALESANDER, a singer,
  — Symond's daughter, ALYX, a maid of seventeen,
  — Symond's son, BRADAMAR, a boy of ten, fostered on Braavos as a ward of Oro Tendyris, a merchant of that city,
— SER DANWELL, m. Wynafrei Whent,
  — {many stillbirths and miscarriages},
— MERRETT, m. Mariya Darry,
  — Merrett's daughter, AMEREI, called AMI, a widow of sixteen, m. {Ser Pate of the Blue Fork},
  — Merrett's daughter, WALDA, called FAT WALDA, a wife of fifteen years, m. Lord Roose Bolton,
  — Merrett's daughter, MARISSA, a maid of thirteen,
  — Merrett's son, WALDER, called LITTLE WALDER, a boy of seven, taken captive at Winterfell while a ward of Lady Catelyn Stark,
— {SER GEREMY, drowned}, m. Carolei Waynwood,
  — Geremy's son, SANDOR, a boy of twelve, a squire to Ser Donnel Waynwood,

- — Geremy's daughter, CYNTHEA, a girl
  of nine, a ward of Lady Anya Wayn-
  wood,
- — SER RAYMUND, m. Beony Beesbury,
  - — Raymund's son, ROBERT, sixteen, in
    training at the Citadel in Oldtown,
  - — Raymund's son, MALWYN, fifteen,
    apprenticed to an alchemist in Lys,
  - — Raymund's twin daughters, SERRA and
    SARRA, maiden girls of fourteen,
  - — Raymund's daughter, CERSEI, six, called
    LITTLE BEE,

- — by his fourth wife, {LADY ALYSSA, of House
  Blackwood}:
  - — LOTHAR, their eldest son, called LAME
    LOTHAR, m. Leonella Lefford,
    - — Lothar's daughter, TYSANE, a girl of
      seven,
    - — Lothar's daughter, WALDA, a girl of four,
    - — Lothar's daughter, EMBERLEI, a girl of
      two,
  - — SER JAMMOS, m. Sallei Paege,
    - — Jammos's son, WALDER, called BIG
      WALDER, a boy of eight, taken captive at
      Winterfell while a ward of Lady Catelyn
      Stark,
    - — Jammos's twin sons, DICKON and
      MATHIS, five,
  - — SER WHALEN, m. Sylwa Paege,
    - — Whalen's son, HOSTER, a boy of twelve,
      a squire to Ser Damon Paege,
    - — Whalen's daughter, MERIANNE, called
      MERRY, a girl of eleven,
  - — LADY MORYA, m. Ser Flement Brax,
    - — Morya's son, ROBERT BRAX, nine, fos-
      tered at Casterly Rock as a page,
    - — Morya's son, WALDER BRAX, a boy of
      six,
    - — Morya's son, JON BRAX, a babe of three,

— TYTA, called TYTA THE MAID, a maid of twenty-nine,

— by his fifth wife, {LADY SARYA of House Whent}:
— no progeny,

— by his sixth wife, {LADY BETHANY of House Rosby}:
— SER PERWYN, their eldest son,
— SER BENFREY, m. Jyanna Frey, a cousin,
— Benfrey's daughter, DELLA, called DEAF DELLA, a girl of three,
— Benfrey's son, OSMUND, a boy of two,
— MAESTER WILLAMEN, in service at Longbow Hall,
— OLYVAR, squire to Robb Stark,
— ROSLIN, a maid of sixteen,

— by his seventh wife, {LADY ANNARA of House Farring}:
— ARWYN, a maid of fourteen,
— WENDEL, their eldest son, a boy of thirteen, fostered at Seagard as a page,
— COLMAR, promised to the Faith, eleven,
— WALTYR, called TYR, a boy of ten,
— ELMAR, formerly betrothed to Arya Stark, a boy of nine,
— SHIREI, a girl of six,

— his eighth wife, LADY JOYEUSE of House Erenford,
— no progeny as yet,

— Lord Walder's natural children, by sundry mothers,
— WALDER RIVERS, called BASTARD WALDER,
— Bastard Walder's son, SER AEMON RIVERS,

— Bastard Walder's daughter, WALDA RIVERS,

— MAESTER MELWYS, in service at Rosby,

— JEYNE RIVERS, MARTYN RIVERS, RYGER RIVERS, RONEL RIVERS, MELLARA RIVERS, others.

HOUSE LANNISTER

The Lannisters of Casterly Rock remain the principal support of King Joffrey's claim to the Iron Throne. They boast of descent from Lann the Clever, the legendary trickster of the Age of Heroes. The gold of Casterly Rock and the Golden Tooth have made them the wealthiest of the Great Houses. The Lannister sigil is a golden lion upon a crimson field. Their words are *Hear Me Roar!*

TYWIN LANNISTER, Lord of Casterly Rock, Warden of the West, Shield of Lannisport, and Hand of the King,
— his son, SER JAIME, called THE KINGSLAYER, a twin to Queen Cersei, Lord Commander of the Kingsguard, and Warden of the East, a captive at Riverrun,
— his daughter, QUEEN CERSEI, twin to Jaime, widow of King Robert I Baratheon, Queen Regent for her son Joffrey,
— her son, KING JOFFREY BARATHEON, a boy of thirteen,
— her daughter, PRINCESS MYRCELLA BARATHEON, a girl of nine, a ward of Prince Doran Martell in Dorne,
— her son, PRINCE TOMMEN BARATHEON, a boy of eight, heir to the Iron Throne,
— his dwarf son, TYRION, called THE IMP, called HALFMAN, wounded and scarred on the Blackwater,

— his siblings:
  — SER KEVAN, Lord Tywin's eldest brother,
      — Ser Kevan's wife, DORNA, of House
        Swyft,
      — their son, SER LANCEL, formerly a squire
        to King Robert, wounded and near death,
      — their son, WILLEM, twin to Martyn, a
        squire, captive at Riverrun,
      — their son, MARTYN, twin to Willem, a
        squire, a captive with Robb Stark,
      — their daughter, JANEI, a girl of two,
  — GENNA, his sister, wed to Ser Emmon Frey,
      — their son, SER CLEOS FREY, a captive at
        Riverrun,
      — their son, SER LYONEL,
      — their son, TION FREY, a squire, captive
        at Riverrun,
      — their son, WALDER, called RED WAL-
        DER, a squire at Casterly Rock,
  — {SER TYGETT}, his second brother, died of a
    pox,
      — Tygett's widow, DARLESSA, of House
        Marbrand,
      — their son, TYREK, squire to the king,
        missing,
  — {GERION}, his youngest brother, lost at sea,
      — Gerion's bastard daughter, JOY, eleven,

— his cousins:
  — {SER STAFFORD LANNISTER}, brother to
    the late Lady Joanna, slain at Oxcross,
      — Ser Stafford's daughters, CERENNA and
        MYRIELLE,
      — Ser Stafford's son, SER DAVEN,
  — SER DAMION LANNISTER, m. Lady Shiera
    Crakehall,
      — his son, SER LUCION,
      — his daughter, LANNA, m. Lord Antario
        Jast,

— MARGOT, m. Lord Titus Peake,

— his household:
  — MAESTER CREYLEN, healer, tutor, and counselor,
  — VYLARR, captain-of-guards,
    — LUM and RED LESTER, guardsmen,
  — WHITESMILE WAT, a singer,
  — SER BENEDICT BROOM, master-at-arms,

— his lords bannermen:
  — DAMON MARBRAND, Lord of Ashemark,
    — SER ADDAM MARBRAND, his son and heir,
  — ROLAND CRAKEHALL, Lord of Crakehall,
    — his brother, {SER BURTON CRAKEHALL}, killed by Lord Beric Dondarrion and his outlaws,
    — his son and heir, SER TYBOLT CRAKEHALL,
    — his second son, SER LYLE CRAKEHALL, called STRONGBOAR, a captive at Pinkmaiden Castle,
    — his youngest son, SER MERLON CRAKEHALL,
  — {ANDROS BRAX}, Lord of Hornvale, drowned during the Battle of the Camps,
    — his brother, {SER RUPERT BRAX}, slain at Oxcross,
    — his eldest son, SER TYTOS BRAX, now Lord of Hornvale, a captive at the Twins,
    — his second son, {SER ROBERT BRAX}, slain at the Battle of the Fords,
    — his third son, SER FLEMENT BRAX, now heir,
  — {LORD LEO LEFFORD}, drowned at the Stone Mill,
  — REGENARD ESTREN, Lord of Wyndhall, a captive at the Twins,

— GAWEN WESTERLING, Lord of the Crag, a captive at Seagard,
- — his wife, LADY SYBELL, of House Spicer,
  - — her brother, SER ROLPH SPICER,
  - — her cousin, SER SAMWELL SPICER,
- — their children:
  - — SER RAYNALD WESTERLING,
  - — JEYNE, a maid of sixteen years,
  - — ELEYNA, a girl of twelve,
  - — ROLLAM, a boy of nine,
— LEWYS LYDDEN, Lord of the Deep Den,
— LORD ANTARIO JAST, a captive at Pinkmaiden Castle,
— LORD PHILIP PLUMM,
- — his sons, SER DENNIS PLUMM, SER PETER PLUMM, and SER HARWYN PLUMM, called HARDSTONE,
— QUENTEN BANEFORT, Lord of Banefort, a captive of Lord Jonos Bracken,

— his knights and captains:
- — SER HARYS SWYFT, good-father to Ser Kevan Lannister,
  - — Ser Harys's son, SER STEFFON SWYFT,
    - — Ser Steffon's daughter, JOANNA,
  - — Ser Harys's daughter, SHIERLE, m. Ser Melwyn Sarsfield,
- — SER FORLEY PRESTER,
- — SER GARTH GREENFIELD, a captive at Raventree Hall,
- — SER LYMOND VIKARY, a captive at Wayfarer's Rest,
- — LORD SELMOND STACKSPEAR,
  - — his son, SER STEFFON STACKSPEAR,
  - — his younger son, SER ALYN STACKSPEAR,
- — TERRENCE KENNING, Lord of Kayce,
  - — SER KENNOS OF KAYCE, a knight in his service,
- — SER GREGOR CLEGANE, the Mountain That Rides,

— POLLIVER, CHISWYCK, RAFF THE SWEETLING, DUNSEN, and THE TICKLER, soldiers in his service,

— {SER AMORY LORCH}, fed to a bear by Vargo Hoat after the fall of Harrenhal.

HOUSE MARTELL

Dorne was the last of the Seven Kingdoms to swear fealty to the Iron Throne. Blood, custom, and history all set the Dornishmen apart from the other kingdoms. At the outbreak of the War of the Five Kings, Dorne took no part. With the betrothal of Myrcella Baratheon to Prince Trystane, Sunspear declared its support for King Joffrey and called its banners. The Martell banner is a red sun pierced by a golden spear. Their words are *Unbowed, Unbent, Unbroken*.

DORAN NYMEROS MARTELL, Lord of Sunspear, Prince of Dorne,
— his wife, MELLARIO, of the Free City of Norvos,
— their children:
    — PRINCESS ARIANNE, their eldest daughter, heir to Sunspear,
    — PRINCE QUENTYN, their elder son,
    — PRINCE TRYSTANE, their younger son, betrothed to Myrcella Baratheon,
— his siblings:
    — his sister, {PRINCESS ELIA}, wife of Prince Rhaegar Targaryen, slain during the Sack of King's Landing,
    — their children:
        — {PRINCESS RHAENYS}, a young girl, slain during the Sack of King's Landing,
        — {PRINCE AEGON}, a babe, slain during the Sack of King's Landing,

— his brother, PRINCE OBERYN, called THE RED VIPER,
- — Prince Oberyn's paramour, ELLARIA SAND,
- — Prince Oberyn's bastard daughters, OBARA, NYMERIA, TYENE, SARELLA, ELIA, OBELLA, DOREA, LOREZA, called THE SAND SNAKES,
- — Prince Oberyn's companions:
  - — HARMEN ULLER, Lord of Hellholt,
    - — Harmen's brother, SER ULWYCK ULLER,
  - — SER RYON ALLYRION,
    - — Ser Ryon's natural son, SER DAEMON SAND, the Bastard of Godsgrace,
  - — DAGOS MANWOODY, Lord of Kingsgrave,
    - — Dagos's sons, MORS and DICKON,
    - — Dagos's brother, SER MYLES MANWOODY,
  - — SER ARRON QORGYLE,
  - — SER DEZIEL DALT, the Knight of Lemonwood,
  - — MYRIA JORDAYNE, heir to the Tor,
  - — LARRA BLACKMONT, Lady of Blackmont,
    - — her daughter, JYNESSA BLACKMONT,
    - — her son, PERROS BLACKMONT, a squire,
— his household:
  - — AREO HOTAH, a Norvoshi sellsword, captain of guards,
  - — MAESTER CALEOTTE, counselor, healer, and tutor,
— his lords bannermen:
  - — HARMEN ULLER, Lord of Hellholt,
  - — EDRIC DAYNE, Lord of Starfall,

— DELONNE ALLYRION, Lady of Godsgrace,
— DAGOS MANWOODY, Lord of Kingsgrave,
— LARRA BLACKMONT, Lady of Blackmont,
— TREMOND GARGALEN, Lord of Salt Shore,
— ANDERS YRONWOOD, Lord of Yronwood,
— NYMELLA TOLAND.

HOUSE TULLY

Lord Edmyn Tully of Riverrun was one of the first of the
river lords to swear fealty to Aegon the Conqueror. The
victorious Aegon rewarded him by raising House Tully to
dominion over all the lands of the Trident. The Tully sigil
is a leaping trout, silver, on a field of rippling blue and
red. The Tully words are *Family, Duty, Honor*.

HOSTER TULLY, Lord of Riverrun,
— his wife, {LADY MINISA, of House Whent}, died
in childbed,
— their children:
— CATELYN, widow of Lord Eddard Stark of
Winterfell,
— her eldest son, ROBB STARK, Lord of
Winterfell, King in the North, and King
of the Trident,
— her daughter, SANSA STARK, a maid of
twelve, captive at King's Landing,
— her daughter, ARYA STARK, ten, missing for a year,
— her son, BRANDON STARK, eight,
believed dead,
— her son, RICKON STARK, four, believed
dead,
— LYSA, widow of Lord Jon Arryn of the
Eyrie,
— her son, ROBERT, Lord of the Eyrie and

Defender of the Vale, a sickly boy of seven years,
— SER EDMURE, his only son, heir to Riverrun,
— Ser Edmure's friends and companions:
— SER MARQ PIPER, heir to Pinkmaiden,
— LORD LYMOND GOODBROOK,
— SER RONALD VANCE, called THE BAD, and his brothers, SER HUGO, SER ELLERY, and KIRTH,
— PATREK MALLISTER, LUCAS BLACKWOOD, SER PERWYN FREY, TRISTAN RYGER, SER ROBERT PAEGE,
— his brother, SER BRYNDEN, called The Blackfish,
— his household:
— MAESTER VYMAN, counselor, healer, and tutor,
— SER DESMOND GRELL, master-at-arms,
— SER ROBIN RYGER, captain of the guard,
— LONG LEW, ELWOOD, DELP, guardsmen,
— UTHERYDES WAYN, steward of Riverrun,
— RYMUND THE RHYMER, a singer,
— his lords bannermen:
— JONOS BRACKEN, Lord of the Stone Hedge,
— JASON MALLISTER, Lord of Seagard,
— WALDER FREY, Lord of the Crossing,
— CLEMENT PIPER, Lord of Pinkmaiden Castle,
— KARYL VANCE, Lord of Wayfarer's Rest,
— NORBERT VANCE, Lord of Atranta,
— THEOMAR SMALLWOOD, Lord of Acorn Hall,
— his wife, LADY RAVELLA, of House Swann,
— their daughter, CARELLEN,
— WILLIAM MOOTON, Lord of Maidenpool,

— SHELLA WHENT, dispossessed Lady of Harrenhal,
— SER HALMON PAEGE,
— TYTOS BLACKWOOD, Lord of Raventree

HOUSE TYRELL

The Tyrells rose to power as stewards to the Kings of the Reach, whose domain included the fertile plains of the southwest from the Dornish marches and Blackwater Rush to the shores of the Sunset Sea. Through the female line, they claim descent from Garth Greenhand, gardener king of the First Men, who wore a crown of vines and flowers and made the land bloom. When Mern IX, last king of House Gardener, was slain on the Field of Fire, his steward Harlen Tyrell surrendered Highgarden to Aegon the Conqueror. Aegon granted him the castle and dominion over the Reach. The Tyrell sigil is a golden rose on a grass-green field. Their words are *Growing Strong*.

Lord Mace Tyrell declared his support for Renly Baratheon at the onset of the War of the Five Kings, and gave him the hand of his daughter Margaery. Upon Renly's death, Highgarden made alliance with House Lannister, and Margaery was betrothed to King Joffrey.

MACE TYRELL, Lord of Highgarden, Warden of the South, Defender of the Marches, and High Marshall of the Reach,
— his wife, LADY ALERIE, of House Hightower of Oldtown,
— their children:
— WILLAS, their eldest son, heir to Highgarden,
— SER GARLAN, called THE GALLANT, their second son,

        — his wife, LADY LEONETTE of House
           Fossoway,
     — SER LORAS, the Knight of Flowers, their
        youngest son, a Sworn Brother of the
        Kingsguard,
     — MARGAERY, their daughter, a widow of
        fifteen years, betrothed to King Joffrey I
        Baratheon,
        — Margaery's companions and ladies-in-
           waiting:
           — her cousins, MEGGA, ALLA, and
             ELINOR TYRELL,
             — Elinor's   betrothed,   ALYN
               AMBROSE, squire,
           — LADY ALYSANNE BULWER, a girl
             of eight,
           — MEREDYTH   CRANE,   called
             MERRY,
           — TAENA OF MYR, wife to LORD
             ORTON MERRYWEATHER,
           — LADY ALYCE GRACEFORD,
           — SEPTA NYSTERICA, a sister of the
             Faith,
  — his widowed mother, LADY OLENNA of House
  Redwyne, called the Queen of Thorns,
     — Lady Olenna's guardsmen, ARRYK and
        ERRYK, called LEFT and RIGHT,
  — his sisters:
     — LADY MINA, wed to Paxter Redwyne, Lord
        of the Arbor,
     — their children:
        — SER   HORAS   REDWYNE,   twin   to
           Hobber, mocked as HORROR,
        — SER HOBBER REDWYNE, twin to Horas,
           mocked as SLOBBER,
        — DESMERA REDWYNE, a maid of
           sixteen,
     — LADY JANNA, wed to Ser Jon Fossoway,
  — his uncles and cousins:

— his father's brother, GARTH, called THE GROSS, Lord Seneschal of Highgarden,
   — Garth's bastard sons, GARSE and GARRETT FLOWERS,
— his father's brother, SER MORYN, Lord Commander of the City Watch of Oldtown,
   — Moryn's son, {SER LUTHOR}, m. Lady Elyn Norridge,
      — Luthor's son, SER THEODORE, m. Lady Lia Serry,
         — Theodore's daughter, ELINOR,
         — Theodore's son, LUTHOR, a squire,
      — Luthor's son, MAESTER MEDWICK,
      — Luthor's daughter, OLENE, m. Ser Leo Blackbar,
   — Moryn's son, LEO, called LEO THE LAZY,
— his father's brother, MAESTER GORMON, a scholar of the Citadel,
— his cousin, {SER QUENTIN}, died at Ashford,
   — Quentin's son, SER OLYMER, m. Lady Lysa Meadows,
      — Olymer's sons, RAYMUND and RICKARD,
      — Olymer's daughter, MEGGA,
— his cousin, MAESTER NORMUND, in service at Blackcrown,
— his cousin, {SER VICTOR}, slain by the Smiling Knight of the Kingswood Brotherhood,
   — Victor's daughter, VICTARIA, m. {Lord Jon Bulwer}, died of a summer fever,
      — their daughter, LADY ALYSANNE BULWER, eight,
   — Victor's son, SER LEO, m. Lady Alys Beesbury,
      — Leo's daughters, ALLA and LEONA,
      — Leo's sons, LYONEL, LUCAS, and LORENT,

— his household at Highgarden:
  — MAESTER LOMYS, counselor, healer, and tutor,
  — IGON VYRWEL, captain of the guard,
  — SER VORTIMER CRANE, master-at-arms,
  — BUTTERBUMPS, fool and jester, hugely fat,

— his lords bannermen:
  — RANDYLL TARLY, Lord of Horn Hill,
  — PAXTER REDWYNE, Lord of the Arbor,
  — ARWYN OAKHEART, Lady of Old Oak,
  — MATHIS ROWAN, Lord of Goldengrove,
  — ALESTER FLORENT, Lord of Brightwater Keep, a rebel in support of Stannis Baratheon,
  — LEYTON HIGHTOWER, Voice of Oldtown, Lord of the Port,
  — ORTON MERRYWEATHER, Lord of Longtable,
  — LORD ARTHUR AMBROSE,
— his knights and sworn swords:
  — SER MARK MULLENDORE, crippled during the Battle of the Blackwater,
  — SER JON FOSSOWAY, of the green-apple Fossoways,
  — SER TANTON FOSSOWAY, of the red-apple Fossoways.

REBELS, ROGUES, AND SWORN BROTHERS

THE SWORN BROTHERS OF THE NIGHT'S WATCH

(ranging Beyond the Wall)
  JEOR MORMONT, called THE OLD BEAR, Lord Commander of the Night's Watch,
  — JON SNOW, the Bastard of Winterfell, his steward and squire, lost while scouting the Skirling Pass,
    — GHOST, his direwolf, white and silent,
  — EDDISON TOLLETT, called DOLOROUS EDD, his squire,
  — THOREN SMALLWOOD, commanding the rangers,
  — DYWEN, DIRK, SOFTFOOT, GRENN, BEDWYCK called GIANT, OLLO LOPHAND, GRUBBS, BERNARR called BROWN BERNARR, another BERNARR called BLACK BERNARR, TIM STONE, ULMER OF KINGSWOOD, GARTH called GREYFEATHER, GARTH OF GREENAWAY, GARTH OF OLDTOWN, ALAN OF ROSBY, RONNEL HARCLAY, AETHAN, RYLES, MAWNEY, rangers,
  — JARMEN BUCKWELL, commanding the scouts,
  — BANNEN, KEDGE WHITEYE, TUMBERJON, FORNIO, GOADY, rangers and scouts,
  — SER OTTYN WYTHERS, commanding the rearguard,

— SER MALADOR LOCKE, commanding the
baggage,
  — DONNEL HILL, called SWEET DONNEL,
  his squire and steward,
  — HAKE, a steward and cook,
  — CHETT, an ugly steward, keeper of hounds,
  — SAMWELL TARLY, a fat steward, keeper of
  ravens, mocked as SER PIGGY,
  — LARK called THE SISTERMAN, his cousin
  ROLLEY OF SISTERTON, CLUBFOOT
  KARL, MASLYN, SMALL PAUL, SAW-
  WOOD, LEFT HAND LEW, ORPHAN OSS,
  MUTTERING BILL, stewards,
— {QHORIN HALFHAND}, commanding the
rangers from the Shadow Tower, slain in the Skir-
ling Pass,
  — {SQUIRE DALBRIDGE, EGGEN}, rangers,
  slain in the Skirling Pass,
  — STONESNAKE, a ranger and mountaineer,
  lost afoot in Skirling Pass,
  — BLANE, Qhorin Halfhand's second, com-
  manding the Shadow Tower men on the Fist
  of the First Men,
  — SER BYAM FLINT,

(at Castle Black)
BOWEN MARSH, Lord Steward and castellan,
  — MAESTER AEMON {TARGARYEN}, healer
  and counselor, a blind man, one hundred
  years old,
    — his steward, CLYDAS,
  — BENJEN STARK, First Ranger, missing,
  feared dead,
    — SER WYNTON STOUT, eighty years a
    ranger,
    — SER ALADALE WYNCH, PYPAR, DEAF
    DICK FOLLARD, HAIRY HAL, BLACK
    JACK BULWER, ELRON, MATTHAR,
    rangers,
  — OTHELL YARWYCK, First Builder,

— SPARE BOOT, YOUNG HENLY, HALDER, ALBETT, KEGS, SPOTTED PATE OF MAIDENPOOL, builders,

— DONAL NOYE, armorer, smith, and steward, one-armed,

— THREE-FINGER HOBB, steward and chief cook,

— TIM TANGLETONGUE, EASY, MULLY, OLD HENLY, CUGEN, RED ALYN OF THE ROSEWOOD, JEREN, stewards,

— SEPTON CELLADOR, a drunken devout,

-- SER ENDREW TARTH, master-at-arms,

— RAST, ARRON, EMRICK, SATIN, HOP-ROBIN, recruits in training,

— CONWY, GUEREN, recruiters and collectors,

(at Eastwatch-by-the-Sea)
COTTER PYKE, Commander Eastwatch,

— MAESTER HARMUNE, healer and counselor,

— SER ALLISER THORNE, master-at-arms,

— JANOS SLYNT, former commander of the City Watch of King's Landing, briefly Lord of Harrenhal,

— SER GLENDON HEWETT,

— DAREON, steward and singer,

— IRON EMMETT, a ranger famed for his strength,

(at Shadow Tower)
SER DENYS MALLISTER, Commander, Shadow Tower

— his steward and squire, WALLACE MASSEY,

— MAESTER MULLIN, healer and counselor.

THE BROTHERHOOD WITHOUT BANNERS
AN OUTLAW FELLOWSHIP

BERIC DONDARRION, Lord of Blackhaven, called
THE LIGHTNING LORD, oft reported dead,
— his right hand, THOROS OF MYR, a red priest,
— his squire, EDRIC DAYNE, Lord of Starfall,
twelve,
— his followers:
— LEM, called LEM LEMONCLOAK, a one-
time soldier,
— HARWIN, son of Hullen, formerly in service
to Lord Eddard Stark at Winterfell,
— GREENBEARD, a Tyroshi sellsword,
— TOM OF SEVENSTREAMS, a singer of dubi-
ous report, called TOM SEVENSTRINGS and
TOM O' SEVENS,
— ANGUY THE ARCHER, a bowman from the
Dornish Marches,
— JACK-BE-LUCKY, a wanted man, short an
eye,
— THE MAD HUNTSMAN, of Stoney Sept,
— KYLE, NOTCH, DENNETT, longbowmen,
— MERRIT O' MOONTOWN, WATTY THE
MILLER, LIKELY LUKE, MUDGE, BEARD-
LESS DICK, outlaws in his band,

— at the Inn of the Kneeling Man:
— SHARNA, the innkeep, a cook and midwife,

  — her husband, called HUSBAND,
  — BOY, an orphan of the war,

— at the Peach, a brothel in Stoney Sept:
  — TANSY, the red-haired proprietor,
    — ALYCE, CASS, LANNA, JYZENE, HELLY, BELLA, some of her peaches,

— at Acorn Hall, the seat of House Smallwood:
  — LADY RAVELLA, formerly of House Swann, wife to Lord Theomar Smallwood,

— here and there and elsewhere:
  — LORD LYMOND LYCHESTER, an old man of wandering wit, who once held Ser Maynard at the bridge,
    — his young caretaker, MAESTER ROONE,
  — the ghost of High Heart,
  — the Lady of the Leaves,
  — the septon at Sallydance.

the WILDLINGS, or
the FREE FOLK

MANCE RAYDER, King-beyond-the-Wall,
— DALLA, his pregnant wife,
   — VAL, her younger sister,

— his chiefs and captains:
   — HARMA, called DOGSHEAD, commanding his van,
   — THE LORD OF BONES, mocked as RATTLE-SHIRT, leader of a war band,
      — YGRITTE, a young spearwife, a member of his band,
      — RYK, called LONGSPEAR, a member of his band,
      — RAGWYLE, LENYL, members of his band,
      — his captive, JON SNOW, the crow-come-over,
         — GHOST, Jon's direwolf, white and silent,
   — STYR, Magnar of Thenn,
   — JARL, a young raider, Val's lover,
      — GRIGG THE GOAT, ERROK, QUORT, BODGER, DEL, BIG BOIL, HEMPEN DAN, HENK THE HELM, LENN, TOE-FINGER, STONE THUMBS, raiders,
   — TORMUND, Mead-King of Ruddy Hall,

called GIANTSBANE, TALL-TALKER, HORN-BLOWER, and BREAKER OF ICE, also THUNDERFIST, HUSBAND TO BEARS, SPEAKER TO GODS, and FATHER OF HOSTS, leader of a war band,

- — his sons, TOREGG THE TALL, TORWYRD THE TAME, DORMUND, and DRYN, his daughter MUNDA,
- — {ORELL, called ORELL THE EAGLE}, a skinchanger slain by Jon Snow in the Skirling Pass,
- — MAG MAR TUN DOH WEG, called MAG THE MIGHTY, of the giants,
- — VARAMYR called SIXSKINS, a skinchanger, master of three wolves, a shadowcat, and a snow bear,
- — THE WEEPER, a raider and leader of a war band,
- — {ALFYN CROWKILLER}, a raider, slain by Qhorin Halfhand of the Night's Watch,

CRASTER, of Craster's Keep, who kneels to none,

- — GILLY, his daughter and wife, great with child,
- — DYAH, FERNY, NELLA, three of his nineteen wives.

ACKNOWLEDGMENTS

If the bricks aren't well made, the wall falls down.

This is an awfully big wall I'm building here, so I need a lot of bricks. Fortunately, I know a lot of brickmakers, and all sorts of other useful folks as well.

Thanks and appreciation, once more, to those good friends who so kindly lent me their expertise (and in some cases, even their *books*) so my bricks would be nice and solid – to my Archmaester Sage Walker, to First Builder Carl Keim, to Melinda Snodgrass my master of horse.

And as ever, to Parris.

Faerie Tale
Raymond E. Feist

An imaginative work of fiction from the master of modern fantasy. With *Faerie Tale* Raymond E. Feist turns his pen to the timeless worlds of ancient Celtic myth – and the unspeakable terror that lurks beneath the ordered surface of everyday life.

When successful screenwriter Phil Hastings decided to move his family from sunny California to a ramshackle farmhouse in New York State, the old Kessler place seemed like an ideal base from which to pick up the threads of his career as a novelist.

But the Kessler place was originally known as Elf King Hill – 'Hill of the Elf King'. Soon Phil's wife and daughter, and their two mischievous eight-year-old boys, began to sense that strange presences were moving in the centuries-old wood that tangled around their new home like the enchanted web of a huge, malignant spider . . .

'A tantalizing sense of foreboding . . . highly readable'
Library Journal

ISBN 0 586 07139 3

Assassin's Apprentice
Book One of The Farseer Trilogy
Robin Hobb

A glorious classic fantasy combining the magic of Le Guin with the epic mastery of Tolkien

Fitz is a royal bastard, cast out into the world with only his magical link with animals for solace and companionship.

But when Fitz is adopted into the royal household, he must give up his old ways and learn a new life: weaponry, scribing, courtly manners; and how to kill a man secretly. Meanwhile, raiders ravage the coasts, leaving the people Forged and soulless. As Fitz grows towards manhood, he will have to face his first terrifying mission, a task that poses as much risk to himself as it does to his target: for Fitz is a threat to the throne . . . but he may also be the key to the future of the kingdom.

'Refreshingly original'   JANNY WURTS

'I couldn't put this novel down'   *Starburst*

ISBN: 0-00-648009-8

Ship of Magic

Book One of The Liveship Traders

Robin Hobb

A superb new epic from the author of
the magical FARSEER TRILOGY.

Wizardwood - a sentient wood. The most precious commodity
in the world. Like many other legendary wares, it comes from
the Rain River Wilds.

A liveship is a difficult ship to come by. Rare and valuable, it
will quicken only when three family members, from successive
generations, have died on board. The liveship Vivacia is about
to undergo her quickening, as Althea Vestrit's father is carried
to her deck in his death- throes. Althea waits with awe and
anticipation for the ship that she loves more than anything in
the world to awaken. Only to find that her family has other
plans for her . . .

Praise for The Liveship Traders series:

'Promises to be a truly extraordinary saga . . . the characterisa-
tions are consistently superb, and [Hobb] animates everything
with love for and knowledge of the sea.   *Booklist*

'Robin Hobb writes achingly well'   *SFX*

'A wonderful book, by a writer at the height of her abilities'
                                                         J V JONES

ISBN: 0-00-649885-X

David Eddings

Domes of Fire

Book one of
The Tamuli

PRINCE SPARHAWK AND
THE TROLL-GODS

Queen Ehlana and the Pandion Knight Sir Sparhawk are
married, their kingdom peaceful at last, their union
blessed with a very special daughter named Danae. But
soon trouble sweeps westward from the Tamul Empire to
disrupt not only the living of Eosia but the dead: horrific
armies are being raised from the dust of the long-past Age
of Heroes, threatening the peace won at such cost in
Zemoch.

Prince Sparhawk is called upon to help the Tamuli nations
defeat these ancient horrors. Perhaps the Troll-Gods are
once more loose in the world! With Ehlana and a retinue
of Pandion Knights, Sparhawk will make the hazardous
journey to the Tamul Empire . . . only to discover in fire-
domed Matherion, the incandescent Tamul capital, that
the enemy is already within its gates.

Full of marvels and humour, romance and shrewdness,
above all full of magic, the resources of the epic form are
mined deep by the greatest of modern fantasy writers.

ISBN 0 00 721706 4

Daggerspell

Volume I of The Epic Deverry Series

Katharine Kerr

Enter a fantastical world where even death itself is cowed by the powers of passion and high magic.

In a world outside reality, the flickering spirit of a young girl hovers between the incarnations, knowing neither her past nor her future. But in the temporal world there is one who knows and waits: Nevyn, the wandering sorcerer. On a bloody day long ago he relinquished the maiden's hand in marriage – and so forged a terrible bond of destiny between three souls that would last through three generations. Now Nevyn is doomed to follow them across the plains of time, never resting until he atones for the tragic wrong of his youth . . .

Here in this newly revised edition comes the incredible novel that began one of the best-loved fantasy series of recent years. From long-standing fans to those who have yet to experience the series, *Daggerspell* is a rare and special treat.

0 00 648224 4

Curse of the Mistwraith
Janny Wurts

The first volume of Janny Wurts' new and
exciting epic fantasy

Two brothers worlds apart, their fates interlocked in
enmity by the curse of the Mistwraith . . .

The world of Athera lives in eternal fog, its skies obscured
by the malevolent Mistwraith. Only the combined powers
of two half-brothers can challenge the Mistwraith's strangle-
hold: Arithon - Master of Shadows and Lysaer - Lord of
Light.

Arithon and Lysaer will find that they are inescapably
bound inside a pattern of events dictated by their deepest
convictions. Yet there is much more at stake than one
battle with the Mistwraith - as the sorcerers of the
Fellowship of Seven know well. For between them the
half-brothers hold the balance of the world, its harmony
and its future in their hands.

'Astonishingly original and compelling'   *Raymond E. Feist*

ISBN 0 586 21069 5

Conqueror's Moon

The Boreal Moon Tale: Book One

Julian May

To forge a kingdom takes a will of iron . . .

Prince Conrig of Cathra has a vision: to unite all four provinces of the island of High Blenholme under Cathran sovereignty. One of the provinces is stubbornly refusing to bend to his will, but Conrig has a new secret weapon. He has formed an alliance with Ullanoth, princess of the remote northern province of Moss and a fearsome sorceress.

Meanwhile, Ullanoth is tending to her own schemes. Possessing the talent to call on the unearthly powers of the Beaconfolk, mysterious otherworldly beings who appear as lights in the sky, her power is undeniable. But the Lights are fickle, and their interference in human affairs unpredictable. If Ullanoth calls on them to help Conrig, they may extract a perilous price . . .

A powerful new fantasy adventure filled with dark magic and deadly intrigue from the celebrated author of the *Saga of the Pliocene Exile*.

0 00 712320 5

Red Mars
Kim Stanley Robinson

WINNER OF THE NEBULA AWARD

MARS. THE RED PLANET.
Closest to Earth in our solar system,
surely life must exist on it?

We dreamt about the builders of the canals we could see by telescope, about ruined cities, lost Martian civilisations, the possibilities of alien contact. Then the Viking and Mariner probes went up, and sent back - nothing. Mars was a barren planet: lifeless, sterile, uninhabited.

In 2019 the first man set foot on the surface of Mars: John Boone, American hero. In 2027 one hundred of the Earth's finest engineers and scientists made the first mass-landing. Their mission? To create a New World.

To terraform a planet with no atmosphere, an intensely cold climate and no magnetosphere into an Eden full of people, plants and animals. It is the greatest challange mankind has ever faced: the ultimate use of intelligence and ability: our finest dream.

'A staggering book . . . The best novel on the colonization of Mars that has ever been written'　　　　　*Arthur C. Clarke*

'First of a mighty trilogy, *Red Mars* is the ultimate in future history'　　　　　*Daily Mail*

'*Red Mars* may simply be the best novel ever written about Mars'
Interzone

ISBN 0 586 21389 9

Legends II

Edited by Robert Silverberg

From the most celebrated writers of modern fantasy fiction, the most fabulous worlds ever created. Eleven breathtaking new short novels, each set in the unique universe that brought its author world-wide acclaim, are here gathered together in one outstanding volume.

Robin Hobb
George R. R. Martin
Orson Scott Card
Diana Gabaldon
Robert Silverberg
Tad Williams
Anne McCaffrey
Raymond E. Feist
Elizabeth Haydon
Neil Gaiman
Terry Brooks

ISBN 0-00-715436-4